EXTRAORDINARY PRAISE FOR NELSON DeMILLE'S *CATHEDRAL*

"From the beginning...until the final chapters when you find yourself frantically turning pages, it's truly impossible to lay aside CATHEDRAL."

—*Dallas Times Herald*

"TOO TRUE TO LIFE FOR COMFORT... ENTERTAINS...The writing is crisp, terse, and highly realistic."

—*New York Daily News*

"There ought to be a law against Nelson DeMille. CATHEDRAL held me spellbound for three solid days...It's better than *By the Rivers of Babylon* by a long margin—and I can't think of higher praise than that. In short, it's a masterwork."

—Harrison E. Salisbury

"THOROUGHLY CREDIBLE AND ABSO-LUTELY ABSORBING...Motivation, characterization, and plotting are all exceptional...Will keep readers engrossed till the final page."

—United Press International

Novels by Nelson DeMille

Available from Grand Central Publishing

By the Rivers of Babylon
Cathedral
The Talbot Odyssey
Word of Honor
The Charm School
The Gold Coast
The General's Daughter
Spencerville
Plum Island
The Lion's Game
Up Country
Night Fall
Wild Fire
The Gate House
The Lion
The Panther
The Quest
Radiant Angel

WITH THOMAS BLOCK
Mayday

For more information please visit:
www.nelsondemille.net

Nelson DeMille

Cathedral

GCC

GRAND CENTRAL
PUBLISHING

New York Boston

Copyright © 1981 by Nelson DeMille
Introduction copyright © 2011 by Nelson DeMille
Excerpt from *Radiant Angel* copyright © 2015 by Nelson DeMille

This Hachette Book Group edition is published by arrangement with the author.

Grand Central Publishing
Hachette Book Group
1290 Avenue of the Americas
New York, NY 10104

www.HachetteBookGroup.com

Grand Central Publishing is a division of Hachette Book Group, Inc. The Grand Central Publishing name and logo are trademarks of Hachette Book Group, Inc.

The Hachette Speakers Bureau provides a wide range of authors for speaking events. To find out more, go to www.hachettespeakersbureau.com or call (866) 376-6591.

The publisher is not responsible for websites (or their content) that are not owned by the publisher.

Printed in the United States of America

First mass market edition: December 1990
First oversize mass market edition: October 2015

10 9 8 7 6 5 4 3 2

OPM

For my three wonder kids,
Lauren, Alex, and James

Acknowledgments

I wish to thank the following people for their editorial help, dedication, and above all, patience: Bernard and Darlene Geis, Joseph Elder, David Kleinman, Mary Crowley, Eleanor Hurka, and Rose Ann Ferrick. And very special thanks to Judith Shafran.

The following organizations have provided information for this book: the New York Police Department Public Information Office; the St. Patrick's Parade Committee; the 69th Infantry, NYARNG: Amnesty International; the Irish Consulate, the British Consulate, and the Irish Tourist Board.

Introduction

Cathedral was first published in 1981, and when I sat down to write this book, the Irish Troubles were front page news with bombings and murders in Belfast and London, and all over England and Northern Ireland. The Irish Republican Army prisoners in British jails were on hunger strikes, and each side was engaged in ever-worsening acts of violence against the other. I was actually in London on a day when an IRA bomb went off. I'd been standing on the steps of my hotel when the ground shook. I hadn't heard anything, but the doorman said, almost nonchalantly, "IRA bomb," which indeed it turned out to be. That, more than anything I'd seen on the TV news over the years, made this conflict real and frightening.

My first instinct as I contemplated writing this book was *not* to write it; it was a touchy and inflammatory subject at the time. Passions were running high in the Irish-American community, especially in New York where I live, and it seemed that half the cars in the metropolitan area had bumper stickers saying, "England out of Ireland." Additionally, there were a good number of Irish citizens in New York who were here "on business," meaning, they were raising money for the IRA, and also giving press interviews. A few of these men and women frequented the same Irish pubs that I did in those days, and when the word went out that I was writing a novel about the Irish Troubles—something I probably should not have mentioned, except that I needed some information—I was given not only information, but also unsolicited advice, some of which could be construed as a warning to be easy on the boys who were fighting to reunite Ireland. So, as I said, I thought about finding a safer subject. But in the end, I decided to press on and see if I, as a novelist, could find some middle ground, or at least some truth and understanding of both sides of this age-old conflict.

When *Cathedral* was published, it got a lot of attention. Most reviewers loved the book and thought it accurately reflected the ongoing conflict without taking sides or being a propaganda tool for either cause. A few reviewers and columnists, however—mostly in Irish-American publications—had a less positive view of *Cathedral*. Some of them suggested that I, an American with no Irish ancestry, should not be writing about something I could not possibly understand. My belief, however, is that the truth is the truth, and that you don't need to be emotionally or genetically involved to be a good reporter or a good writer. Just the opposite. In fact, as most of my Irish friends agree, one of the best novels ever written about the Irish struggle was written by an American Jew: *Trinity* by Leon Uris, published in 1976, about a year before I began writing *Cathedral*. *Trinity* was, in fact, what got me interested in the subject.

In the weeks after publication, I received a number of letters, mostly unsigned, that could be construed as veiled threats. Some of these letter writers thought I had not presented the Irish Catholic cause in a good light, and some thought I was taking the English or Protestant side. Also, during my cross-country publicity tour, I sometimes found myself on radio shows speaking to angry callers and on TV shows with other guests who'd apparently been invited to argue with me. Also, there were some unfriendly people at my book signings. Again, passions were running high then, though now it's hard to go back in time and memory to understand how divisive this conflict was. But to understand how a work of fiction about the Irish Troubles could inflame such passions, think about a similarly controversial novel today about Islam; *The Satanic Verses* comes to mind.

Ironically, as I said, I had gone out of my way to present both sides, but that only served to annoy each side.

When I returned to New York, which was then, along with Boston, the center of IRA sympathy in America, I decided to meet the beast, so to speak. So I gathered a group of Irish-American friends and two or three Irish nationals (who may have had IRA connections) and went pub hopping, or as we used to say, we did a pub crawl.

I'd asked the publisher to drop off or send multiple copies of *Cathedral* to a few dozen pubs right after

publication, and some of these copies were promi-
nently displayed on the bar shelves, and I autographed
them. Many of the bartenders, wait staff, and patrons I
ran into that night had read the book and were happy
to discuss it. The pub reviews were generally favorable,
though a few people said I treated the IRA unfairly,
while others thought I had glamorized it. I was reminded of an old adage that says one man's terrorist is
another man's freedom fighter.

One Irish pub, Ryan McFadden's on the corner
of Second Avenue and 42nd Street, was the favorite
watering hole of a number of British journalists who
had offices across the street in the Daily News building. I had become friendly with a number of them,
and I invited them to meet me at McFadden's one
night. They also had been sent copies of *Cathedral*,
and we discussed the book. Most of them felt that I
had not glamorized the Irish Republican Army, and
most of them thought I'd been fair in regard to the
British position on the issues of Northern Ireland. A
few, however, had the opposite opinion. My opinion,
for what it's worth, is that I'd done a good job of pleas-
ing or annoying everyone.

In a related story, when Prince Charles and Lady
Diana were married on July 29, 1981—two months
after *Cathedral* was published—the British journalists
who frequented Ryan McFadden's asked if they could
have a party in the pub to celebrate the marriage. The
owners agreed and the scheduled party made the news:
British royal wedding celebration in Irish pub.

The party started at 4 a.m. to coincide with live
television coverage coming from London, where it was

10 a.m. By dawn, the bar was full of revelers of all ancestry and religious beliefs, myself included. The two owners of the bar, both Irish-Americans, received no fewer than three telephoned IRA bomb threats during the party, which they announced, though no one left the premises. The quite logical belief was that these threats were hoaxes, and that the Irish Republican Army would not blow up an Irish pub in New York City and kill a lot of Americans just to blow up a dozen British journalists. The British journalists believed that, too, and we all watched the royal couple on TV and had beer and bangers for breakfast.

The point of this story is that the Irish conflict, while brutal, had a few rules, one of which was that the Troubles were not going to spill over into America. Our current war on terrorism has no such rules, obviously. *Cathedral*, however, is about just such a scenario: the Irish war spills over into America—specifically, New York City—and does so in a very dramatic way.

Without giving away the plot, a splinter group of the Irish Republican Army plans to seize St. Patrick's Cathedral on New York's Fifth Avenue. And they decide to do it on St. Patrick's Day during the Fifth Avenue parade when over a million marchers, spectators, and partiers are crammed into midtown Manhattan. All the ingredients for chaos are in place—the media are covering the parade, the Cardinal and church dignitaries are on the steps of the cathedral, the reviewing stands on Fifth Avenue are filled with politicians and VIPs, the police are overstretched, and the citizens are . . . well, not feeling any pain. The only people who have any clear idea of what is happening are the people who are about to seize the cathedral and take hostages.

Where do I get ideas like this? Well, it had been my privilege for many years to be included as a guest on the steps of St. Patrick's Cathedral during the annual parade, along with church dignitaries, city officials, police brass, and other worthy citizens. Maybe they should not have invited an action/adventure writer with an overactive imagination to be among those up-standing citizens.

In 1977, while I was putting the finishing touches on *By the Rivers of Babylon*, I took time out to go to the parade on March 17. It was a cold but clear day, and as I stood on the steps of St. Pat's and watched the tens of thousands of people parading up Fifth Avenue, I had a thought. A police captain I knew was standing next to me, and I said to him, "What if the IRA seized the cathedral now and took the Cardinal hostage?"

He didn't like that "what if" and replied, "Bite your tongue, son." Then he said, "Impossible."

Nothing is impossible—especially in fiction. I needed an idea for my next book and I'd just found it.

The next day, I began my research. First, I wrote to the Rector of St. Pat's, whom I knew, and without bothering him with the plot, I asked him if he'd help me with my research on a book about the cathedral, especially the physical layout. He referred me to a man named Knight Sturgis, the consulting architect of St. Patrick's, now deceased.

Mr. Sturgis took the time to give me several tours of the usually inaccessible parts of the cathe-dral, including the bell tower, the attic, crypt, and underground passages. He also provided me with detailed blueprints of the cathedral, some of which are reproduced in this book. Mr. Sturgis did not know exactly what my book was going to be about, and that was just as well. He did, however, see from a book reviewer an advance reading copy of *Cathedral*, in which I cited Mr. Sturgis's assistance in the Acknowledgments. He asked me to delete his name from the final copy, which I did, so you won't see him listed in the Acknowledgments here or in earlier editions, though through an oversight he is listed in the original book club edition. Similarly, St. Patricks' rector, whose name I won't mention, though he's also deceased, asked me to expunge his name from the credits. After *Cathedral* was published, I became persona non grata on the steps of St. Patrick's during the parade—but I was still welcome the other 364 days of the year, especially for Saturday Confession.

Also after *Cathedral* was published, there was some debate in the media about irresponsible authors giving ideas to potential terrorists. My position was and remains that "what if" fiction is a cautionary tale, a wake-up call to citizens and to the people who are entrusted with our security. Prior to *Cathedral* being published, there were no contingency plans in place if something like I describe in this book actually happened in real life. As a result of the Munich Olympics tragedy, New York City had just formed a Hostage Negotiation Unit headed by Captain Frank Bolz, whom I knew, and there was a relatively small NYPD SWAT team in place. But other than that, there was no clear plan of action in the event of a takeover of a public building or a historic landmark. One of the things that resulted, I've been told, from the publication of *Cathedral* was that the NYPD began acquiring blueprints of places like St. Patrick's, Grand Central Station, the Empire State Building, the U.N. Headquarters, foreign consulates, and other buildings that could be at risk for a takeover or attack by terrorist groups.

Anti-terrorism in those days was in its infancy, and writers of fiction and nonfiction were often far in advance of the security apparatus in terms of terrorist scenarios that could be played out in America. That has changed, of course, but the people who wish to do us harm only have to be half a step ahead of us to succeed. Books like this, then, can help, not hurt, the cause of national security. *Cathedral* didn't give the IRA any ideas; it gave the police some ideas.

We're much more sophisticated now than we were in the early 1980s, and we've seen things happen that not even a novelist with a good imagination could have conceived. But back then, we believed if we didn't write about it, or think about it, it wouldn't happen, (i.e., "bite your tongue"). We all wish that were true, but we know it's not.

I'm not suggesting that this book was published as a public service. It was controversial and I took some flak for it. But with the passage of time, most of the public, the media, and the people entrusted with our security view books like this as a reflection of reality, or as I said, a warning to be prepared.

The Irish Republican Army never did come to America to cause us harm—only to raise money and buy guns and explosives—but it goes without saying that America is now in the crosshairs of many other groups who have and will cause us harm.

Upon publication, *Cathedral* was an instant bestseller and a Main Selection of the Literary Guild. It's been translated into over twenty foreign languages and is still in print around the world. *Cathedral* is very cinematic, and it had the most movie interest of any of my novels, but if you think you've missed the movie, you haven't; it's never been made. In the end, most moviemakers thought it was too controversial or too inflammatory, which is similar to how Hollywood feels today about Islamic terrorist themes.

Cathedral was my second hardcover novel, following *By the Rivers of Babylon*, and because of its success, I felt I had overcome what is called in the business Second Book Syndrome, which is the inevitably bad and self-conscious book that follows an author's bestselling debut. I credit this success in part to the subject matter, i.e., it was the right book at the right time, as was *By the Rivers of Babylon*.

When I recently re-read *Cathedral*, I was concerned that I might find it almost quaint and unsophisticated by today's standards of terrorist novels, and terrorist reality. The reader, too, might find something that seems to belong in another era. But the book and the story have stood up very well to the passage of time, and it has remained one of my bestselling novels for over thirty years. The book's characters on both sides—inside and outside the cathedral—are as engaging and complex as when I first created them.

The passion is alive on the pages, and the double-crossing and deceit are all too familiar. Maybe some of what was high-tech then is not so high-tech now, but this story is more about the human mind and our capacity for good and evil, and our justifications and motivations for both.

When you read this story, keep in mind that it is about a conflict that we as Americans had trouble understanding, partly because we were not a target of that conflict for a change. We, or most of us, feel an affinity for the Irish and the English, and it made us unhappy that they were killing each other. This is what I try to capture in this story—the media's and the public's ambivalence as the Irish Republican Army perpetrates this attack on American soil, in a holy place that is also holy to the perpetrators. The issues were complex and the hate was not always comprehensible, not even to those directly involved. And maybe for that reason this conflict has apparently come to an end. In the final analysis, it was senseless and the modern world overtook the ancient hatreds.

But now, let's return to the early 1980s at the height of the Troubles. It is St. Patrick's Day in New York City, and on this day everyone is Irish and everyone is having a grand time. Until the first shot is fired.

Nelson DeMille
New York, 2011

Author's Note

Regarding places, people, and events: The author has learned that in any book dealing with the Irish, literary license and other liberties should not only be tolerated but expected.

St. Patrick's Cathedral in New York has been described with care and accuracy. However, as in any work of fiction, especially in one set in the future, dramatic liberties have been exercised in some instances.

The New York police officers represented in this novel are not based on real people. The fictional hostage negotiator, Captain Bert Schroeder, is not meant to represent the present New York Police Department Hostage Negotiator, Frank Bolz. The only similarity shared is the title of Hostage Negotiator. Captain Bolz is an exceptionally competent officer whom the author has had the pleasure of meeting on three occasions, and Captain Bolz's worldwide reputation as innovator of the New York Plan of hostage negotiating is well deserved. To the people of the city of New York, and especially to the people whose lives he's been instrumental in saving, he is a true hero in every sense of the word.

The Catholic clergy represented in this work are not based on actual persons. The Irish revolutionaries in this novel are based to some extent on a composite of real people, as are the politicians, intelligence people, and diplomats, though no individual character is meant to represent an actual man or woman.

The purpose of this work was not to write a roman à clef or to represent in any way, favorably or unfavorably, persons living or dead.

The story takes place not in the present or the past but in the future; the nature of the story, however, compels the author to use descriptive job titles and other factual designations that exist at this writing. Beyond these designations there is no identification meant or intended with the public figures who presently hold those descriptive job titles.

Historical characters and references are for the most part factual except where there is an obvious blend of fact and fiction woven into the story line.

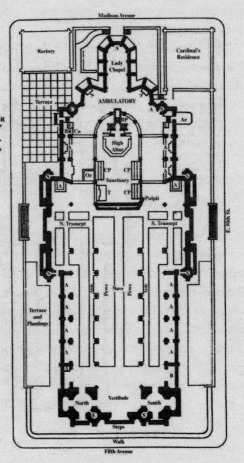

St. Patrick's Cathedral First Floor Plan

Key:

Altars–A
Archbishop's Sacristy–Ar
Archbishop's Throne–T
Bookstore–B
Bride's Room–BR
Bronze Plate–BP
Chimney–C
Clergy Pews–CP
Confessional–Co
Elevators–E
Organ Keyboard–Or
Spiral Staircases–S

← N

Madison Avenue

Rectory

Cardinal's Residence

Lady Chapel

A

Terrace

AMBULATORY

Ar

A

BP

BR Co

High Altar

Ar

A

A

S

CP CP

Or

T CP

Sanctuary

Pulpit

A

N. Transept

S. Transept

E. 50th St.

S

Terrace and Plantings

A
A
A
A
A
A

Aisle

Pews   Nave   Pews

Aisle

A
A
A
A
A
A

B

North

Vestibule

South

E

S

Steps

Walk

Fifth Avenue

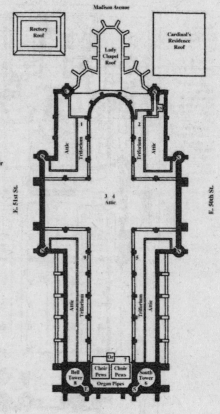

St. Patrick's
Cathedral
Triforium Plan
and Attics

Key (clockwise):

Eamon Farrell–1
Frank Gallagher–2
Jean Kearney–3
Arthur Nulty–4
George Sullivan–5
Rory Devane–6
Jack Leary–7
Donald Mullins–8
Abby Boland–9

Chimney–C
Elevator–E
Elevator Shaft–ES
Organ Keyboard–Or
Spiral Staircases–S

← N

Madison Avenue

Rectory Roof

Cardinal's Residence Roof

Lady Chapel Roof

1

2

Attic

Triforium

Triforium

Attic

3 4
Attic

9

5

Attic

Triforium

Triforium

Attic

Or 7

Bell Tower 8

Choir Pews

Choir Pews

South Tower 6

Organ Pipes

E. 51st St.

E. 50th St.

Fifth Avenue

BOOK I

Northern Ireland

Now that I've learned a great deal about Northern Ireland, there are things I can say about it: that it's an unhealthy and morbid place, where people learn to die from the time that they're children; where we've never been able to forget our history and our culture—which are only other forms of violence; where it's so easy to deride things and people; where people are capable of much love, affection, human warmth and generosity. But, my God! How much we know how to hate!

Every two or three hours, we resurrect the part, dust it off and throw it in someone's face.

Betty Williams,
Northern Irish peace
activist and winner of
the Nobel Peace Prize

CHAPTER 1

The tea has got cold." Sheila Malone set down her cup and waited for the two young men who sat opposite her, clad in khaki underwear, to do the same.

The younger man, Private Harding, cleared his throat. "We'd like to put on our uniforms."

Sheila Malone shook her head. "No need for that."

The other man, Sergeant Shelby, put down his cup. "Let's get done with it." His voice was steady, but his hand shook and the color had drained from under his eyes. He made no move to rise.

Sheila Malone said abruptly, "Why don't we take a walk?"

The sergeant stood. The other man, Harding, looked down at the table, staring at the scattered remains of the bridge game they'd all passed the morning with. He shook his head. "No."

Sergeant Shelby took the younger man's arm and tried to grip it, but there was no strength in his hand. "Come on, now. We could use some air."

Sheila Malone nodded to two men by the fire. They rose and came up behind the British soldiers. One of them, Liam Coogan, said roughly, "Let's go. We've not got all day."

Shelby looked at the men behind him. "Give the lad a second or two," he said, pulling at Harding's arm. "Stand up," he ordered. "That's the hardest part."

The young private rose slowly, then began to sink back into his chair, his body trembling.

Coogan grasped him under the arms and propelled him toward the door. The other man, George Sullivan, opened the door and pushed him out.

Everyone knew that speed was important now, that it had to be done quickly, before anyone's courage failed. The sod was wet and cold under the prisoners' feet, and a January wind shook water off the rowan trees. They passed the outdoor privy they had walked to every morning and every evening for two weeks and kept walking toward the ravine near the cottage.

Sheila Malone reached under her sweater and drew a small revolver from her waistband. During the weeks she had spent with these men she had grown to like them, and out of common decency someone else should have been sent to do it. Bloody insensitive bastards.

The two soldiers were at the edge of the ravine now, walking down into it.

Coogan poked her roughly. "Now, damn you! Now!"

She looked back toward the prisoners. "Stop!"

The two men halted with their backs to their executioners. Sheila Malone hesitated, then raised the pistol with both hands. She knew she would hit only their backs from that range, but she couldn't bring herself to move closer for a head shot. She took a deep breath and fired, shifted her aim, and fired again.

Shelby and Harding lurched forward and hit the ground before the echo of the two reports died away. They thrashed on the ground, moaning.

Coogan cursed. "Goddamn it!" He ran into the ravine, pointed his pistol at the back of Shelby's head, and fired. He looked at Harding, who was lying on his side. Frothy blood trickled from his mouth and his chest heaved. Coogan bent over, placed the pistol between Harding's wide-open eyes, and fired again. He put his revolver in his pocket and looked up at the edge of the ravine. "Bloody stupid woman. Give a woman a job to do and..."

Sheila Malone pointed her revolver down at him. Coogan stepped backward and tripped over Shelby's body. He lay between the two corpses with his hands still held high. "No! Please. I didn't mean anything by it. Don't shoot!"

Sheila lowered the pistol. "If you ever touch me again, or say anything to me again...I'll blow your fucking head off!"

Sullivan approached her cautiously. "It's all right now. Come on, Sheila. We've got to get away from here."

"He can find his own bloody way back. I'll not ride with him."

Sullivan turned and looked down at Coogan. "Head out through the wood, Liam. You'll pick up a bus on the highway. See you in Belfast."

Sheila Malone and George Sullivan walked quickly to the car waiting off the lane and climbed in behind the driver, Rory Devane, and the courier, Tommy Fitzgerald.

"Let's go," said Sullivan.

"Where's Liam?" asked Devane nervously.

"Move out," said Sheila.

The car pulled into the lane and headed south toward Belfast.

Sheila drew from her pocket the two letters the soldiers had given her to mail to their families. If she were stopped at a roadblock and the Royal Ulster Constabulary found the letters . . . She opened the window and threw her pistol out, then let the letters sail into the wind.

Sheila Malone jumped out of her bed. She could hear motors in the street and the sounds of boots against the cobbles. Residents of the block were shouting from windows, and trash-can lids were being beaten to sound the alarm. As she began pulling her slacks on under her nightdress her bedroom door crashed open, and two soldiers rushed in without a word. A shaft of light from the hall made her cover her eyes. The red-bereted paratroopers pushed her against the wall and ripped the slacks from around her legs. One of them raised her nightdress over her head, and then ran his hands over her body, searching for a weapon. She spun and swung her fists at him. "Get your filthy hands . . ."

One of the soldiers punched her in the stomach, and she doubled over and lay on the floor, her nightdress gathered up around her breasts.

The second soldier bent down, grabbed her long hair, and dragged her to her feet. He spoke for the first time. "Sheila Malone, all I'm required to tell you is that you are being arrested under the Special Powers Act. If you make one fucking sound when we take you out to the trucks, we'll beat you to a pulp."

The two soldiers pushed her into the hall, down the stairs, and into the street, which was filled with shouting people. Everything passed in a blur as she was half-carried to the intersection where the trucks were parked. Voices called insults at the British soldiers and the Royal Ulster Constabulary who were assisting them. A boy's voice shouted, "Fuck the Queen." Women and children were crying, and dogs were barking. She saw a young priest trying to calm a group of people. An unconscious man, his head bloodied, was dragged past her. The soldiers picked her up and threw her into the back of a small truck filled with a dozen other prisoners. An RUC guard stood at the front of the truck, fondling a large truncheon. "Lie down, bitch, and shut your mouth."

She lay down by the tailgate and listened to her own breathing in the totally silent truck. After a few minutes the gates of the truck closed and it pulled away.

The guard shouted above the noise of the convoy. "The Pope is a fucking queer."

Sheila Malone lay against the tailgate, trying to calm herself. In the dark truck some men slept or were unconscious; a few were weeping. The guard kept up an anti-Catholic tirade until the truck stopped and the tailgate swung open, revealing a large, floodlit enclosure surrounded by barbed wire and machine-gun towers. Long Kesh, known to the Catholics of Northern Ireland as Dachau.

A soldier shouted into the truck, "Clear out! Quick! Move it!"

A few men scrambled over and around Sheila, and she heard the sounds of blows, shouts, and cries as the men left the truck. A voice cried out, "Take it easy, I'm an old man." A young boy clad in pajamas crawled over her and tumbled to the ground. The RUC guard was kicking everyone toward the tailgate now, like a trash man sweeping the floor of his truck clean at the dump. Someone pulled her out by her legs, and she fell on the soft, wet earth. She tried to stand but was knocked down.

"Crawl! Crawl, you bastards!"

She picked up her head and saw two lines of paratrooper boots. She crawled as quickly as she could between the gauntlet as blows fell on her back and buttocks. A few of the men made obscene remarks as she passed by on her hands and knees, but the blows were light and the obscenities were shouted by boyish, embarrassed voices, which somehow made it all the more obscene.

At the end of the gauntlet two soldiers picked her up and pushed her into a long Nissen hut. An officer with a swagger stick pointed to an open door, and the soldiers pushed her onto the floor of a small room and shut the door as they left. She looked up from where she lay in the center of the tiny cubicle.

A matron stood behind a camp table. "Strip. Come on, you little tramp. Stand up and take them off."

Within minutes she was stripped and searched and was wearing a gray prison dress and prison underwear. She could hear blows being struck outside the small cubicle and cries and shouts as the harvest of the sweep was processed—transformed from sleeping civilians into gray, terrified internees.

Sheila Malone had no doubt that a good number of them were guilty of some kind of anti-British or antigovernment activity. A few were actually IRA. A smaller number might even be arsonists or bombers...or murderers like herself. There was a fifty-fifty chance of getting out of internment within ninety days if you didn't crack and confess to something. But if they had something on you—something as serious as murder...Before she could gather her thoughts and begin to formulate what she was going to say, someone placed a hood over her head and she was pushed through a door that closed behind her.

A voice shouted directly in her ear, and she jumped. "I said, spell your name, bitch!"

She tried to spell it but found to her surprise that she could not. Someone laughed.

Another voice shouted, "Stupid cunt!"

A third voice screamed in her other ear. "So, you shot two of our boys, did you?"

There it was. They knew. She felt her legs begin to shake.

"Answer me, you little murdering cunt!"

"N-n-no."

"*What*? Don't lie to us, you cowardly, murdering bitch. Like to shoot men in the back, do you? Now it's your turn!"

She felt something poke her in the back of the head and heard the sound of a pistol cocking. The hammer fell home and made a loud, metallic thud. She jumped and someone laughed again. "Next time it won't be empty, bitch."

She felt sweat gather on her brow and soak the black hood.

"All right. Pull up your dress. That's right. All the way!"

She pulled her skirt up and stood motionless as someone pulled her pants down to her ankles.

After an hour of pain, insults, humiliation, and leering laughter, the three interrogators seemed to get bored. She was certain now that they were just fishing, and she could almost picture being released at dawn.

"Fix yourself up."

She let her aching arms fall and bent over to pull up her pants. Before she straightened up she heard the three men leave the room as two other people entered. The hood was pulled from her head, and the bright lights half-blinded her. The man who had taken the hood moved to the side and sat in a chair just out of range of her vision. She focused her eyes straight ahead.

A young British army officer, a major, sat in a chair behind a small camp desk in the center of the windowless room. "Sit down, Miss Malone."

She walked stiffly toward a stool in front of the desk and sat slowly. Her buttocks hurt so much that she would almost rather have remained standing. She choked down a sob and steadied her breathing.

"Yes, you can have a bed as soon as we finish this." The major smiled. "My name is Martin. Bartholomew Martin."

"Yes . . . I've heard of you."

"Really? Good things, I trust."

She leaned forward and looked into his eyes. "Listen, Major Martin, I was beaten and sexually abused."

He shuffled some papers. "We'll discuss all of that as soon as we finish with this." He picked out one sheet of paper. "Here it is. A search of your room has uncovered a pistol and a satchel of gelignite. Enough to blow up the whole block." He looked at her. "That's a dreadful thing to keep in your aunt's house. I'm afraid she may be in trouble now as well."

"There was no gun or explosives in my room, and you know it."

He drummed his fingers impatiently on the desk. "Whether they were there or not is hardly the point, Miss Malone. The point is that my report *says* a gun and explosives were found, and in Ulster there is not a great deal of difference between the charges and the realities. In fact, they are the same. Do you follow me?"

She didn't answer.

"All right," said the major. "That's not important. What is important," he continued as he stared into her eyes, "are the murders of Sergeant Thomas Shelby and Private Alan Harding."

She stared back at his eyes and displayed no emotion, but her stomach heaved. They had her, and she was fairly certain she knew how they had gotten her.

"I believe you know a Liam Coogan, Miss Malone. An associate of yours. He's turned Queen's evidence." An odd half smile passed over his face. "I'm afraid we've got you now."

"If you know so goddamned much, why did your men—"

"Oh, they're not my men. They're paratroop lads. Served with Harding and Shelby. Brought them here for the occasion. I'm in Intelligence, of course." Major Martin's voice changed, became more intimate. "You're damned lucky they didn't kill you."

Sheila Malone considered her situation. Even under normal British law she would probably be convicted on Coogan's testimony. Then why had she been arrested under the Special Powers Act? Why had they bothered to plant a gun and explosives in her room? Major Martin was after something else.

Martin stared at her, then cleared his throat. "Unfortunately, there is no capital punishment for murder in our enlightened kingdom. However, we're going to try something new. We're going to try to get an indictment for treason—I think we can safely say that the Provisional Irish Republican Army, of which you are a member, has committed treason toward the Crown."

He looked down at an open book in front of him. "'Acts that constitute treason. Paragraph 811—Levies war against the Sovereign in her realm . . . .' I think you fill that bill nicely." He pulled the book closer and read, "'Paragraph 812—The essence of the offense of treason lies in the violation of the allegiance owed to the Sovereign . . . .' And Paragraph 813 is my favorite. It says simply"—he looked at her without reading from the book—"'The punishment for treason is death by hanging.'" He stressed the last words and looked for a reaction, but there was none. "It was Mr. Churchill, commenting on the Irish uprising of 1916, who said, 'The grass grows green on the battlefield, but never on the scaffold.' It's time we started hanging Irish traitors again. You first. And beside you on the scaffold will be your sister, Maureen."

She sat up. "My sister? Why . . . ?"

"Coogan says *she* was there as well. You, your sister, and her lover, Brian Flynn."

"That's a bloody lie."

"Why would a man turn Queen's evidence and then lie about who committed the murders?"

"Because *he* shot those soldiers—"

"There were two calibers of bullets. We can try two people for murder—any two. So why don't you let me work out who did what to whom?"

"You don't care who killed those soldiers. It's Flynn you want to hang."

"*Someone* must hang." But Major Martin had no intention of hanging any of them and making more Irish martyrs. He wanted to get Flynn into Long Kesh, where he could wring out every piece of information that he possessed about the Provisional IRA. Then he would cut Brian Flynn's throat with a piece of glass and call it suicide.

He said, "Let's assume that you escape the hangman's noose. Assume also that we pick up your sister, which is not unlikely. Consider if you will, Miss Malone, sharing a cell with your sister for the rest of your natural lives. How old are you? Not twenty yet? The months, the years pass slowly. *Slowly.* Young girls wasting their lives . . . and for what? A philosophy? The rest of the world will go on living and loving, free to come and go. And you . . . well, the real hell of it is that Maureen, at least, is innocent of murder. You are the reason she'd be there—because you wouldn't name her lover. And Flynn will have found another woman, of course. And Coogan, yes, Coogan will have gone to London or America to live and—"

"Shut up! For God's sake, shut up!" She buried her face in her hands and tried to think before he started again.

"Now there *is* a way out." He looked down at his papers, then looked up again. "There always is, isn't there? What you must do is dictate a confession naming Brian Flynn as an officer in the Provisional IRA—which he is—and naming him as the murderer of Sergeant Shelby and Private Harding. You will be charged as an accessory after the fact and be free within . . . let's say, seven years."

"And my sister?"

"We'll put out a warrant for her arrest only as an accessory. She should leave Ulster and never return. We will not look for her and will not press any country for extradition. But this arrangement is operative only if we find Brian Flynn." He leaned forward. "Where is Brian Flynn?"

"How the hell should I know?"

Martin leaned back in his chair. "Well, we must charge you with something within ninety days of internment. That's the law, you understand. If we don't find Flynn by the ninetieth day, we will charge you with double homicide—perhaps treason as well. So, if you can remember anything that will lead us to him, please don't hesitate to tell us." He paused. "Will you think about where Flynn might be?"

She didn't answer.

"Actually, if you really don't know, then you're useless to me...unless...You see, your sister will try to free you, and with her will be Flynn...so perhaps—"

"You won't use me for bait, you bastard."

"No? Well, we'll have to see about that, won't we?"

"May I have a bed?"

"Certainly. You may stand now."

She stood. "No more Gestapo tactics?"

"I'm sorry, I don't understand." He rose from his chair. "The matron will escort you to a cell. Good night."

She turned and opened the door. A hood came down over her head, but before it did she saw not the matron but two young Royal Ulster Constabulary men and three grinning paratroopers.

CHAPTER 2

Brian Flynn looked up at Queen's Bridge, shrouded in March mist and darkness. The Lagan River fog rolled down the partially lit street and hung between the red-brick buildings of Bank Road. The curfew was in effect, and there was no traffic.

Maureen Malone looked at him. His handsome, dark features always seemed sinister at night. She pulled back the sleeve of her trench coat and looked at her watch. "It's after four. Where the hell are—"

"Quiet! Listen."

She heard the rhythmic footsteps coming out of Oxford Street. In the mist a squad of Royal Ulster Constabulary appeared and turned toward them, and they crouched behind a stack of oil drums.

They waited in silence, their breathing coming ir-regularly in long plumes of fog. The patrol passed, and a few seconds later they heard the whining of a truck changing gears and saw the headlights in the mist. A Belfast Gas Works truck pulled up to the curbstone near them, and they jumped in the open side door. The driver, Rory Devane, moved the truck slowly north toward the bridge. The man in the passenger seat,

Tommy Fitzgerald, turned. "Road block on Cromac Street."

Maureen Malone sat on the floor. "Is everything set?"

Devane spoke as he steered slowly toward the bridge. "Yes. Sheila left Long Kesh in an RUC van a half hour ago. They took the A23 and were seen passing through Castlereagh not ten minutes ago. They'll be coming over the Queen's Bridge about now."

Flynn lit a cigarette. "Escort?"

"No," said Devane. "Just a driver and guard in the cab and two guards in the back, according to our sources."

"Other prisoners?"

"Maybe as many as ten. All going to Crumlin Road Jail, except for two women going up to Armagh." He paused. "Where do you want to hit them?"

Flynn looked out the rear window of the truck. A pair of headlights appeared on the bridge. "Collins's men are set up on Waring Street. That's the way they'll have to go to Crumlin Road." He wiped the fog from the window and stared. "Here's the RUC van." Devane cut off the engine and shut the lights.

The black, unmarked RUC van rolled off the bridge and headed into Ann Street. Devane waited, then restarted his truck and followed at a distance with his lights off. Flynn said to Devane, "Circle round to High Street."

No one spoke as the truck moved through the quiet streets. They approached Waring Street, and Tommy Fitzgerald reached under his seat and pulled out two weapons, an old American Thompson submachine gun and a modern Armalite automatic rifle. "The tommy gun is for you, Brian, and the light gun for my lady." He passed a short cardboard tube to Flynn. "And this...if, God forbid, we run into a Saracen." Flynn took the tube and stuck it under his trench coat.

They swung off Royal Avenue into Waring Street from the west at the same time the RUC van entered from the east at Victoria Street. The two vehicles approached each other slowly. A black sedan fell in behind the RUC van, and Fitzgerald pointed. "That'll be Collins and his boys."

Flynn saw that the RUC van was moving more slowly now, the driver realizing that he was being boxed in and looking for a way out.

"Now!" shouted Flynn. Devane swung the truck so that it blocked the road, and the RUC van screeched to a stop. The black sedan following the van came to a halt, and Collins with three of his men jumped out and ran toward the rear of the van with submachine guns.

Flynn and Maureen were out of the truck and moving toward the trapped van twenty-five yards up the road. The RUC guard and driver dropped below the windshield, and Flynn pointed his rifle. "Come out with your hands raised!" But the men didn't come out, and Flynn knew he couldn't shoot at the unarmored van filled with prisoners. He yelled to Collins, "I've got them covered! Go on!"

Collins stepped up to the van and struck the rear doors with his rifle butt. "Guards! You're surrounded! Open the doors and you won't be harmed!"

Maureen knelt in the road, her rifle across her knees. She felt her heart beating heavily in her chest. The idea of freeing her sister had become an obsession over the months and had, she realized, clouded her judgment. Suddenly all the things that were wrong with this operation crystallized in her mind—the van riding very low as though it were weighted, the lack of an escort, the predictable route. "Run! Collins—"

She saw Collins's surprised face under the glare of a streetlamp as the doors swung out from the RUC van.

Collins stood paralyzed in front of the open doors and stared at the British paratrooper berets over the top of a sandbag wall. The two barrels of the machine guns blazed in his face.

Flynn watched as his four men were cut down. One machine gun continued to pour bullets into the bodies while the other shifted its fire and riddled the sedan with incendiary rounds, hitting the gas tank and blowing it up. The street echoed with the explosion and the chattering sound of the machine guns, and the night was illuminated by the fire of the burning sedan.

Maureen grabbed Flynn's arm and pulled him toward their truck as pistol shots rang out from the doorway where the guard and driver had disappeared. She fired a full magazine into the doorway and the shooting stopped. The streets were alive with the sounds of whistles, shouting, and running men, and they could hear motor vehicles closing in.

Flynn turned and saw that the truck's windshield was shot out and the tires were flat. Fitzgerald and Devane were running up the street. Fitzgerald's body jerked, and he slid across the cobblestones. Devane kept running and disappeared into a bombed-out building.

Behind him Flynn could hear soldiers jumping from the RUC van and racing toward them. He pulled Maureen's arm, and they started to run as a light rain began to fall.

Donegall Street entered Waring Street from the north, and they turned into it, bullets kicking up chips of cobble behind them. Maureen slipped on the wet stone and fell, her rifle clattering on the pavement and skidding away in the darkness. Flynn lifted her, and they ran into a long alleyway, coming out into Hill Street.

A British Saracen armored car rolled into the street, its six huge rubber wheels skidding as it turned. The Saracen's spotlight came on and found them. The armored car turned and came directly at them, its loudspeaker blaring into the rainy night. "HALT! HANDS ON YOUR HEADS!"

Behind him Flynn could hear the paratroopers coming into the long alley. He pulled the cardboard tube from his trench coat and knelt. He broke the seal and extended the telescoped tubes of the American-made M-72 antitank weapon, raised the plastic sights, and aimed at the approaching Saracen.

The Saracen's two machine guns blazed, pulverizing the brick walls around him, and he felt shards of brick bite into his chest. He put his finger on the percussion ignition switch and tried to steady his aim as he wondered if the thing would work. A disposable cardboard rocket launcher. Like a disposable diaper. Who but the Americans could make a throwaway bazooka? *Steady, Brian. Steady.*

The Saracen fired again, and he heard Maureen give

a short yell behind him and felt her roll against his legs. "Bastards!" He squeezed the switch, and the 66mm HEAT rocket roared out of the tube and streaked down the dark, foggy street.

The turret of the Saracen erupted into orange flame, and the vehicle swerved wildly, smashing into a bombed-out travel agency. The surviving crew stumbled out holding their heads from the pain of the deafening rocket hit, and Flynn could see their clothes smoking. He turned and looked down at Maureen. She was moving, and he put his arm under her head. "Are you hit badly?"

She opened her eyes and began to sit up in his arms. "I don't know. Breast."

"Can you run?"

She nodded, and he helped her up. In the streets around them they could hear whistles, motors, shouts, tramping feet, and dogs. Flynn carefully wiped his fingerprints from the Thompson submachine gun and threw it into the alley.

They headed north toward the Catholic ghetto around New Lodge Road. As they entered the residential area they kept to the familiar maze of back alleys and yards between the row houses. They could hear a column of men double-timing on the street, rifle butts knocking on doors, windows opening, angry exchanges, babies wailing. The sounds of Belfast.

Maureen leaned against a brick garden wall. The running had made the blood flow faster through her wound, and she put her hand under her sweater. "Oh."

"Bad?"

"I don't know." She drew her hand away and looked at the blood, then said, "We were set up."

"Happens all the time," he said.

"Who?"

"Coogan, maybe. Could have been anyone, really." He was fairly certain he knew who it was. "I'm sorry about Sheila."

She shook her head. "I should have known they would use her as bait to get us....You don't think *she...*" She put her face in her hands. "We lost some good people tonight."

He peered over the garden wall, then helped her over, and they ran through a block of adjoining yards. They entered a Protestant neighborhood, noticing the better built and maintained homes. Flynn knew this neighborhood from his youth, and he remembered the schoolboy pranks—breaking windows and running like hell—like now—through these alleys and yards. He remembered the smells of decent food, the clotheslines of white gleaming linen, the rose gardens, and the lawn furniture.

They headed west and approached the Catholic enclave of the Ardoyne. Ulster Defense League civilian patrols blocked the roads leading into the Arodyne, and the Royal Ulster Constabulary and British soldiers were making house searches. Flynn crouched behind a row of trash bins and pulled Maureen down beside him. "We've gotten everyone out of their beds tonight."

Maureen Malone glanced at him and saw the half smile on his face. "You enjoy this."

"So do they. Breaks the monotony. They'll swap

brave tales at the Orange lodges and in the barracks. Men love the hunt."

She flexed her arm. A stiffness and dull pain were spreading outward from her breast into her side and shoulder. "I don't think we have much chance of getting out of Belfast."

"All the hunters are here in the forest. The hunters' village is therefore deserted."

"Which means?"

"Into the heart of the Protestant neighborhood. The Shankill Road is not far."

They turned, headed south, and within five minutes they entered Shankill Road. They walked up the deserted road casually and stopped on a corner. It was not as foggy here, and the streetlights were working. Flynn couldn't see any blood on Maureen's black trench coat, but the wound had drained the color from her face. His own wound had stopped bleeding, and the dried blood stuck to his chest and sweater. "We'll take the next outbound bus that comes by, sleep in a barn, and head for Derry in the morning."

"All we need is an outbound bus, not to mention an appearance of respectability." She leaned back against the bus-stop sign. "When do we get our discharge, Brian?"

He looked at her in the dim light. "Don't forget the IRA motto," he said softly. "Once in, never out. Do you understand?"

She didn't answer.

A Red Bus appeared from the east. Flynn pulled Maureen close to him and supported her as they mounted the steps. "Clady," said Flynn, and he smiled at the driver as he paid the fare. "The lady's had rather too much to drink, I'm afraid."

The driver, a heavy-set man with a face that looked more Scottish than Irish, nodded uncaringly. "Do you have your curfew card?"

Flynn glanced down the length of the bus. Less than a dozen people, mostly workers in essential services, and they looked mostly Protestant—as far as he could tell—like the driver. Perhaps everyone looked like Prods tonight. No sign of police, though. "Yes. Here it is." He held his wallet up close to the driver's face.

The driver glanced at it and moved the door lever closed, then put the bus in gear.

Flynn helped Maureen toward the rear of the bus, and a few of the passengers gave them looks ranging from disapproval to curiosity. In London or Dublin they would be dismissed for what they claimed to be— drunks. In Belfast people's minds worked in different directions. He knew they would have to get off the bus soon. They sat in the back seat.

The bus rolled up Shankill Road, through the Protestant working-class neighborhood, then headed northwest into the mixed neighborhoods around Old-park. Flynn turned to Maureen and spoke softly. "Feeling better?"

"Oh, quite. Let's do it again."

"Ah, Maureen..."

An old woman sitting alone in front of them turned around. "How's the lady? How are you, dear? Feelin' better, then?"

Maureen looked at her without answering. The citizens of Belfast were capable of anything from murder and treachery to Christian kindness.

The old woman showed a toothless smile and spoke quietly. "Between Squire's Hill and McIlwhan's Hill is a wee valley called the Flush. There's an abbey there—you know it—Whitehorn Abbey. The priest, Father Donnelly, will give you lodgings for the night."

Flynn fixed the woman with a cold stare. "What makes you think we need a place to stay? We're headed home."

The bus stopped, and the old woman stood without another word and trundled off to the front of the bus and stepped off.

The bus started again. Flynn was very uneasy now. "Next stop. Are you up to it?"

"I'm not up to one more second on this bus." She paused thoughtfully. "The old woman . . . ?"

Flynn shook his head.

"I think we can trust her."

"I don't trust anyone."

"What kind of country do we live in?"

He laughed derisively. "What a bloody stupid thing to say, Maureen. *We* are the ones who helped make it like it is."

She lowered her head. "You're right, of course . . . as usual."

"You must accept what you are. I accept it. I'm well adjusted."

She nodded. With that strange logic of his he had turned the world upside down. Brian was normal. She was not. "I'm going to Whitehorn Abbey."

He shrugged. "Better than a barn, I suppose. You'll

be needing bandaging...but if the good rector there turns us in..."

She didn't answer and turned away from him.

He put his arm around her shoulders. "I *do* love you, you know."

She looked down and nodded.

The bus stopped again about a half-mile up the road, and Flynn and Maureen moved toward the door.

"This isn't Clady," said the driver.

"That's all right," answered Flynn. They stepped off the bus and into the road. Flynn took Maureen's arm. "That bastard will report us at the next stop." They crossed the road and headed north up a country lane lined with rowan trees. Flynn looked at his watch, then at the eastern sky. "Almost dawn. We have to be there before the farmers start running about—they're almost all Prods up here."

"I know that." Maureen breathed deeply as they walked in the light rain. The filthy air and ugliness of Belfast were far behind, and she felt better. Belfast—a blot of ash on the green loveliness of County Antrim, a blot of ash on the soul of Ireland. Sometimes she wished that the city would sink back into the bog it grew out of.

They passed hedgerows, well-tended fields, and pastures dotted with cattle and bales of fodder. An exhilarating sodden scent filled the air, and the first birds of morning began to sing.

"I'm not going back to Belfast."

He put his arm around her and touched her face with his hand. She was becoming feverish. "I understand. See how you feel in a week or two."

"I'm going to live in the south. A village."

"Good. And what will you do there? Tend pigs? Or do you have independent means, Maureen? Will you buy a country estate?"

"Do you remember the cottage overlooking the sea? You said we'd go there some day to live our lives in peace."

"Someday maybe we will."

"I'll go to Dublin, then. Find a job."

"Yes. Good jobs in Dublin. After a year they'll give you the tables by the window where the American tourists sit. Or the sewing machine by the window where you can get a bit of air and sun. That's the secret. By the window."

After a while she said, "Perhaps Killeen..."

"No. You can never go back to your own village. It's never the same, you know. Better to go to any other pig village."

"Let's go to America."

"No!" The loudness of his own voice surprised him.

"No. I won't do what they all did." He thought of his family and friends, so many of them gone to America, Canada, or Australia. He had lost them as surely as he had lost his mother and father when he buried them. Everyone in Ireland, north and south, lost family, friends, neighbors, even husbands and wives and lovers, through emigration. Like some great plague sweeping the land, taking the firstborn, the brightest, and the most adventurous, leaving the old, the sick, the timid, the self-satisfied rich, the desperately poor. "This is my country. I won't leave here to become a laborer in America."

She nodded. Better to be a king of the dunghills of Belfast and Londonderry. "I may go alone."

"You probably should."

They walked quietly, their arms around each other's waists, both realizing that they had lost something more than a little blood this night.

CHAPTER 3

The lane led into a small, treeless valley between two hills. In the distance they saw the abbey. The moonlight lit the white stone and gave it a spectral appearance in the ground mist.

They approached the abbey cautiously and stood under a newly budded sycamore tree. A small oblong cemetery, hedged with short green plants, spread out beside the abbey wall. Flynn pushed through the hedge and led Maureen into the cemetery.

The churchyard was unkempt, and vines grew up the gravestones. Whitehorn plants—which gave the abbey its name and which were omens of good luck or bad luck, depending on which superstition you believed—clogged the narrow path. A small side gate in a high stone wall led into the abbey's cloister. Flynn pushed it open and looked around the quiet court. "Sit on this bench. I'll find the brothers' dormitory."

She sat without answering and let her head fall to her chest. When she opened her eyes again, Flynn was standing over her with a priest.

"Maureen, this is Father Donnelly."

She focused on the elderly priest, a frail-looking man with a pale face. "Hello, Father."

He took her hand and with his other hand held her forearm in that way they had of claiming instant intimacy. He was the pastor; she was now one of his flock. Presto. Everyone's role had been carved in stone two millennia ago.

"Follow me," he said. "Hold my arm."

The three of them walked across the cloister and entered the arched door of a polygon-shaped building. Maureen recognized the traditional configuration of the chapter house, the meeting place of the monks. For a moment she thought she was going to face an assemblage, but she saw by the light of a table lamp that the room was empty.

Father Donnelly stopped abruptly and turned. "We have an infirmary, but I'm afraid I'll have to put you in the hole until the police and soldiers have come round looking for you."

Flynn didn't answer.

"You can trust me."

Flynn didn't trust anyone, but if he was betrayed, at least the War Council wouldn't think him too foolish for having trusted a priest. "Where's this hole, then? We don't have much time, I think."

The priest led them down a corridor, then opened the door at the end of the passage. Gray dawn came through stained glass, emitting a light that was more sensed than seen. A single votive candle burned in a red jar, and Flynn could see he was in the abbey's small church.

The priest lit a candle on a wall sconce and took it down. "Follow me up the altar. Be careful."

Flynn helped Maureen up to the raised altar sanctuary and watched the priest fumble with some keys and then disappear behind the reredos wall in back of the altar.

Flynn glanced around the church but neither saw nor heard anything in the shadows to signal danger. He noticed that the oppressive smell of incense and tallow was missing, and the church smelled like the outside air. The priest had told him that the abbey was deserted. Father Donnelly was apparently not the abbot but served in something like a caretaker capacity, though he didn't seem the type of priest that a bishop would exile to such a place, thought Flynn. Nor did he seem the type to hide members of the provisional IRA just to get a thrill out of it.

The priest reappeared holding his candle in the darkness. "Come this way." He led them to a half-open door made of scrolled wrought iron in the rear of the altar. "This is the place we use." He looked at the two fugitives to see why they weren't moving toward it. "The crypt," he added as if to explain.

"I know what it is. Everyone knows there's a crypt beneath an altar's sanctuary."

"Yes," said Father Donnelly. "First place they always look. Come along."

Flynn peered down the stone steps. A candle in an amber glass, apparently always kept burning, illuminated a wall and floor of white limestone. "Why is it I've not heard of this abbey as a place of safety before tonight?"

The priest spoke softly, evenly. "You had no need of it before tonight."

Typical priests' talk, thought Flynn. He turned to Maureen. She looked down the stairway, then at the priest. Her instincts, too, rebelled against entering the crypt. Yet her conditioned response was to do what the priest urged. She stepped toward the stairway and descended. Flynn glanced at the priest, then stepped through the doorway.

Father Donnelly led them along the limestone wall past the tombs of the former abbots of Whitehorn Abbey. He stopped and opened the bronze door of one of the tombs, marked *Fr. Seamus Cahill*, held up his candle, and entered the tomb. A wooden casket lay on a stone plinth in the middle of the chamber.

Father Donnelly passed the candle to Flynn and raised the lid of the casket. Inside was a body wrapped in heavy winding sheets, the linen covered with fuzz of green mold. "Sticks and straw," he said. He reached into the casket and released a concealed catch, and the coffin bottom swung downward with the bogus mummy still affixed to it. "Yes, yes. Melodramatic for our age, but when it was conceived, it was necessary and quite common. Go on. Climb in. There's a staircase. See it? Follow the passageway at the bottom until you enter a chamber. Use your candle to light the way. There are more candles in the chamber."

Flynn mounted the plinth and swung his legs over the side. His feet found the top step, and he stood in the casket. A dank, almost putrid smell rose out of the dark hole. He stared at Father Donnelly questioningly.

"It's the entranceway to hell, my boy. Don't fear. You'll find friends down there."

Flynn tried to smile at the joke, but an involuntary shudder ran up his spine. "I suppose we should be thanking you."

"I suppose you should. But just hurry on now. I want to be in the refectory having breakfast when they arrive."

Flynn took a few steps down as Father Donnelly helped Maureen up the plinth and over the side of the casket onto the first step. Flynn held her arm with one hand and held the candle high with the other. She avoided the wrapped figure as she descended.

Father Donnelly pulled the casket floor up, then shut the lid and left the tomb, closing the bronze door behind him.

Flynn held the candle out and followed the narrow, shoulder-width passageway for a distance of about fifty feet, grasping Maureen's hand behind him. He entered an open area and followed the wall to his right. He found candles in sconces spaced irregularly around the unhewn and unmortared stone walls and lit them, completing the circuit around the room. The air in the chamber was chilly, and he saw his own breath. He looked around slowly at the half-lit room. "Odd sort of place."

Maureen wrapped herself in a gray blanket she had found and sat on a footstool. "What did you expect, Brian—a game room?"

"Ah, I see you're feeling better."

"I'm feeling terrible."

He walked around the perimeter of the six-sided room. On one wall was a large Celtic cross, and under the cross was a small chest on a wooden stand. Flynn placed his hand on the dusty lid but didn't open it. He turned back to Maureen. "You trust him?"

"He's a priest."

"Priests are no different from other men."

"Of course they are."

"We'll see." He now felt the fatigue that he had fought off for so long, and he sank down to the damp floor. He sat against the wall next to the chest, facing the stairway. "If we awake in Long Kesh..."

"My fault. All right? Go to sleep."

Flynn drifted off into fitful periods of sleep, opening his eyes once to see Maureen, wrapped in the blanket, lying on the floor beside him. He awoke again when he heard the casket bottom swing down and strike the wall of the passageway. He jumped up and stood at the entrance to the passage. In a shaft of light from the crypt he could see the coffin floor hanging, its grotesque mockery of a dead man stuck to it like a lizard on a wall.

The torso of a man appeared: black shoes, black trousers, the Roman collar, then the face of Father Donnelly. He held a tea tray high above his head as he made his way. "They were here and they're gone."

Flynn moved down the passageway and took the tray that the priest passed to him. Father Donnelly closed the coffin, and they walked into the chamber, Flynn placing the tray on a small wooden table.

Father Donnelly looked around the chamber the way a host examines a guest room. He stared at Maureen's sleeping figure, then turned to Flynn. "So, you blew up a sixer, did you? Rather daring, I'd say."

Flynn didn't answer.

"Well, anyway, they traced you as far as the McGloughlin farm up the lane. Good, loyal Ulstermen, the McGloughlins. Solid Presbyterians. Family came over from Scotland with Cromwell's army. Another three hundred years and they'll think this is their country. How's the lady?"

Flynn knelt beside her. "Sleeping." He touched her forehead. "Feverish."

"There's some penicillin tablets and an army aid kit along with the tea and bacon." He took a small bottle from his pocket. "And some Dunphy's, if you've the need of it."

Flynn took the bottle. "Rarely have I needed it more." He uncorked it and took a long drink.

Father Donnelly found two footstools, pulled them to the table, and sat. "Let her sleep. I'll take tea with you."

Flynn sat and watched the priest go through the fussy motions of a man who took food and drink seriously. "Who was here?" asked Flynn.

"The Brits and the RUCs. As usual the RUCs wanted to tear the place apart, but a British army officer restrained them. A Major Martin. Know him, do you? Yes, he's quite infamous. Anyway, they all played their roles wonderfully."

"I'm glad everyone had a good time. I'm only sorry I had to waken everyone so early."

"You know, lad, it's as if the participants in this war secretly appreciate each other. The excitement is not entirely unwelcome."

Flynn looked at the priest. Here was one man, at least, who didn't lie about it. "Can we get out of here?" he asked as he sipped the hot tea.

"You'll have to wait until they clear out of the hedgerows. Binoculars, you understand. Two days at least. Leave at night, of course."

"Doesn't everyone travel at night?"

The priest laughed. "Ah, Mister..."

"Cocharan."

"Whatever. When will this all stop?"

"When the British leave and the northern six counties are reunited with the southern twenty-six."

The priest put down his teacup. "Not true, my boy. The real desire of the IRA, the most secret dark desire of the Catholics, no matter what we all say about living in peace after the reunification, is to deport all the Protestants back to England, Scotland, and Wales. Send the McGloughlins back to a country they haven't seen in three hundred years."

"That's bloody rubbish."

The priest shrugged. "I don't care personally, you understand. I only want you to examine your own heart."

Flynn leaned across the table. "Why are you in this? The Catholic clergy has never supported any Irish rebellion against the British. So why are you risking internment?"

Father Donnelly stared down into his cup, then looked up at Flynn. "I don't involve myself with any of the things that mean so much to you. I don't care what your policy is or even what Church policy is. My only role here is to provide sanctuary. A haven in a country gone mad."

"To anyone? A murderer like me? Protestants? British troops?"

"Anyone who asks." He stood. "In this abbey was once an order of fifty monks. Now, only me." He paused and looked down at Flynn. "This abbey has a limited future, Mr. Cocharan, but a very rich past."

"Like you and me, Father. But I hope not like our country."

The priest seemed not to hear him and went on. "This chamber was once the storage cellar of an ancient Celtic Bruidean house. You know the term?"

"Yes, I think so."

"The House of the Hostages, it was called. A six-sided structure where six roads met. Coincidentally—or maybe not so—chapter houses are traditionally polygons, and the chapter house we passed through is built on these foundations." He gestured above. "Here in the Bruidean a traveler or a fugitive could shelter from the cold, dark road, protected by tradition and the king's law. The early Celts were not complete barbarians, after all." He looked at Flynn. "So you see, you've come to the right place."

"And you've taken it upon yourself to combine a bit of paganism with Christian charity."

The priest smiled. "Irish Catholicism has always been a blend of paganism and Christianity. The early Christians after Patrick specifically built their churches on Druid holy spots such as this. I suspect early Christians burnt this Bruidean down, then constructed a crude church on its foundations. You can still see the charred foundation stones. Then the Vikings destroyed the original monastery, and the next one was destroyed by the English army when Cromwell passed through. This is the last abbey to be built here. The

Protestant plantations took all the good land in Ireland, but the Catholics held on to most of the good church sites."

"What more could you want?"

The priest regarded Flynn for a long time, then spoke softly. "You'd better wake the lady before the tea gets cold."

Flynn rose and crossed the floor to where Maureen was lying, knelt beside her, and shook her. "Tea."

She opened her eyes.

He said, "Hold on to me." He stood her up and helped her to his stool. "How are you feeling?"

She looked around the candlelit room. "Better."

Flynn poured the tea, and Father Donnelly extracted a pill from a vial. "Take this."

She swallowed the pill and took some tea. "Did the British come?"

The priest felt her forehead. "Came and went. In a few days you'll be on your way."

She looked at him. He was so accepting of them, what they were and what they had done. She felt disreputable. Whenever her life was revealed to people not in the movement, she felt not proud but ashamed, and that was not the way it was supposed to be. "Can you help us?"

"I am, dear. Drink your tea."

"No, I mean can you help us … get out of this?"

The priest nodded. "I see. Yes, I can help you if you want. It's rather easy, you know."

Flynn seemed impatient. "Father, save souls on your own time. I need some sleep. Thank you for everything."

"You're quite welcome."

"Could you do one more favor for us? I'll give you a number to call. Tell the person who answers where we are. Tell them that Brian and Maureen need help. Let me know what they say."

"I'll use a phone in the village in case this one is tapped."

Flynn smiled appreciatively. "If I've seemed a bit abrupt—"

"Don't let it trouble you." He repeated the number Flynn gave him, turned, and disappeared into the narrow passageway.

Flynn took the bottle of Dunphy's from the table and poured some in Maureen's teacup. She shook her head impatiently. "Not with the penicillin, Brian."

He looked at her. "We're not getting along, are we?"

"I'm afraid not."

He nodded. "Well, let's have a look at the nick, then."

She stood slowly, pulled her wet sweater over her head, and dropped it on the stool. Flynn saw that she was in pain as she unhooked her bloodied bra, but he didn't offer to help. He took a candle from the table and examined the wound, a wide gash running along the outside of her right breast and passing under her armpit. An inch to the left and she would have been dead. "Just a graze, really."

"I know."

"The important thing is that you won't need a doctor." The wound was bleeding again from the movement of her undressing, and he could see that it had bled and coagulated several times already. "It's going to hurt a bit." He dressed the wound while she stood with her arm raised. "Lie down and wrap yourself in the blanket."

She lay down and stared at him in the flickering light. She was cold, wet, and feverish. Her whole side ached, and the food had made her nauseous, though she was very thirsty. "We live like animals, licking our wounds, cut off from humanity...from..."

"God? But don't settle for this second-class Popish nonsense, Maureen. Join the Church of England— then you'll have your God, your respectability, and you can sit over tea with the Ladies' Auxiliary and complain about the IRA's latest outrage."

She closed her eyes, and tears ran down her cheeks.

When he saw that she was sleeping, he took the cup of Dunphy's and drained it, then began walking around the cellar. He examined the walls again and saw the scorch marks. How many times had this place been put to the torch? What made this location holy to both the Druids and the Christians? What spirit lived here in the heart of the earth? He carried a candle to the wooden chest and studied it. After some time he reached out and lifted the lid.

Inside he saw fragments of limestone that bore ancient Celtic inscriptions and a few unidentifiable pieces of metal, bronze, rusted iron. He pushed some of the objects aside, revealing a huge oval ring crusted with verdigris. He slipped it on his ring finger. It was large, but it stayed on his finger well enough. He clenched his fist and studied the ring. It bore a crest, and through the tarnish he could make out Celtic writing around a crudely molded bearded face.

He rubbed his fingers over the ring and wiped away some of the encrustation. The crude face stared back at him like a child's rendering of a particularly fearsome man. He felt dizzy and sensed his legs buckling under him. He was aware of hitting the floor. Then he blacked out.

CHAPTER 4

B rian Flynn woke to find a face staring down at him.

"It's noon," said Father Donnelly. "I've brought you some lunch."

Flynn focused on the ruddy face of the old man. He saw that the priest was staring at the ring on his finger. He got to his feet and looked around. Maureen was sitting at the table wearing a new pullover and eating from a steaming bowl. The priest had been there for some time, and that annoyed him. He walked over and sat opposite her. "Feeling better?"

"Much."

Father Donnelly pulled up a stool. "Would you mind if I joined you?"

"It's your food and your table," said Flynn.

The priest smiled. "One never gets used to dining alone."

Flynn took a spoon. "Why don't they send you a...monk or something?" He took a spoonful of stew.

"There's a lay brother who does the caretaking, but he's on leave." He leaned forward. "I see you've found the treasure of Whitehorn Abbey."

Flynn continued to eat as he spoke. "Sorry. Couldn't resist the temptation."

"That's all right."

Maureen looked up. "What are we talking about, please?"

Flynn slipped off the ring, passed it to her, and motioned toward the opened chest.

She examined the ring, then passed it to Father Donnelly. "It's an extraordinary ring."

Father Donnelly toyed with the ring. "Extraordinarily large, in any case."

Flynn poured a bottle of Guinness into a glass. "Where did it come from?"

The priest shook his head. "The last abbot said it was always here with the other things in that box. It may have been excavated here during one of the rebuildings. Perhaps under this floor."

Flynn stared at the ring in the priest's hand. "Pre-Christian?"

"Yes. Pagan. If you want a romantic story, it is said that it was a warrior king's ring. More specifically, Fenian. It's certainly a man's ring, and no average man at that."

Flynn nodded. "Why not MacCumail's ring? Or Dermot's?"

"Why not, indeed? Who would dare wear a ring larger than this?"

Flynn smiled. "You've a pagan streak in you, Father. Didn't Saint Patrick consign the departed Fenians to hell? What was their crime, then, that they must spend eternity in hell?"

"No crime. Just born at the wrong time." He smiled. "Like many of us."

"Right." Flynn liked a priest who could laugh at his dogma.

The priest leaned across the table. "When Oisin, son of Finn MacCumail, returned from the Land of Perpetual Youth, he found Ireland Christian. The brave warrior was confused, sad. Oisin rejected the ordered Christian society and longed with nostalgia for the untamed lustiness of old Erin. If he or his father, Finn MacCumail, came into Ulster today, they would be overjoyed at this Christian warfare. And they would certainly recognize the new pagans among us."

"Meaning me?"

Maureen poured tea into three mugs. "He's talking to you, Brian, isn't he?"

Father Donnelly rose. "I'll take my tea in the refectory."

Maureen Malone rose, too. "Don't leave."

"I really must." His demeanor had changed from paternal to businesslike. He looked at Flynn. "Your friends want you to stay here for two more days. They'll contact me and let me know the plan. Any reply?"

Flynn shook his head. "No."

Maureen looked at Flynn, then at Father Donnelly. "I have a reply. Tell them I want safe passage to Dublin, a hundred pounds, and a work visa for the south."

The priest nodded. He turned to go, hesitated, and came back. He placed the ring on the small table. "Mister..."

"Cocharan."

"Yes. Take this ring."

"Why?"

"Because you want it and I don't."

"It's a valuable relic."

"So are you."

"I won't ask you what you mean by that." He stood and looked hard at the priest, then took the ring from the table and placed it on his finger. Several new thoughts were forming in his mind, but he had no one to share them with. "Thank you." He looked at the ring. "Any curse attached to it that I should know about?"

The priest replied, "You should assume there is."

He looked at the two people standing before him. "I can't approve of the way you live your lives, but I find it painful to see a love dying. Any love, anywhere in this unloving country." He turned and made his way out of the cellar.

Flynn knew that Maureen had been talking to the priest while he'd been sleeping. He was having difficulty dealing with all that had happened in so short a time. Belfast, the old lady and the abbey, a priest who used pagan legends to make Christian statements, Maureen's aloofness. He was clearly not in control. He stood motionless for a time, then turned toward her. "I'd like you to reconsider about Dublin."

She looked down and shook her head.

"I'm asking you to stay...not only because I...What I mean is..."

"I know what you mean. Once in, never out. I'm not afraid of them."

"You should be. I can't protect you—"

"I'm not asking you to." She looked at him. "We're both better off."

"You're probably right. You understand these things better than I."

She knew that tone of voice. Remote. Sarcastic. The air in the cellar felt dense, oppressive. Church or not, the place made her uneasy. She thought about the coffin through which they had entered this hole, and that had been a little like dying. When she came out again she wanted to leave behind every memory of the place, every thought of the war. She looked at the ring on his hand. "Leave the damned thing here."

"I'm not only taking the ring, Maureen, I'm taking the name as well."

"What name?"

"I need a new code name . . . Finn MacCumail."

She almost laughed. "In any other country they'd treat you for megalomania. In Northern Ireland they'll find you quite normal, Brian."

"But I am normal."

"Not bloody likely."

He looked at her in the dim candlelight. He thought he had never seen anyone so lovely, and he realized that he hadn't thought of her in that way for a long time. Now she was flushed with the expectation of new beginnings, not to mention the flush of fever that reddened her cheeks and caused her eyes to burn bright. "You may well be right."

"About your being a lunatic?"

"Well, that too." He smiled at the small shared joke. "But I meant about you going off to Dublin."

"I'm sorry."

"Don't be. I'm only sorry I can't go with you."

"Perhaps, Brian, some day you'll get tired of this."

"Not bloody likely."

"No."

"Well, I'll miss you."

"I hope so," she said.

He stayed silent for a moment, then said, "I still don't know if we can trust him."

"He's a saint, for God's sake, Brian. Take him for what he appears to be."

"He appears different to me. Something odd about him. Anyway, we're not home free yet."

"I know."

"If anything happens and I don't have time to make a proper parting . . . well . . ."

"You've had time enough over the years to say what you felt. Time wasn't the problem. Tea?"

"Yes, please."

They sat silently, drinking their tea.

Flynn put down his cup. "Your sister . . ."

She shook her head. "Sheila is beyond our help."

"Maybe not."

"I don't want to see anyone else killed . . . ."

"There are other ways . . . ." He lapsed into silence, then said, "The keys to the jails of Ulster are in America."

A month later, when spring was firmly planted in the countryside and three weeks after Maureen Malone left for Dublin, Brian Flynn hired a car and went out to the abbey to thank Father Donnelly and to ask him about possible help in the future.

He found all the gates to the abbey locked, and no one answered any of the pull bells. A farmer riding by on a cart told him that the abbey was looked after by villagers employed by the diocese. And that no one had lived there for many years.

BOOK II

New York

*English, Scotchmen, Jews, do well in Ireland—Irishmen, never;
even the patriot has to leave Ireland to get a hearing.*

George Moore,
Ave (Overture)

CHAPTER 5

Brian Flynn, dressed in the black clothing and white collar of a Roman Catholic priest, stood in the dim morning light near the south transept entrance to St. Patrick's Cathedral. He carried a small parcel wrapped in white paper decorated with green shamrocks. A few older women and two men stood at the base of the steps near him, huddled against the cold.

One of the two large transept doors swung open, and the head of a sexton appeared and nodded. The small crowd mounted the steps and passed through the side vestibule, then entered the Cathedral. Brian Flynn followed.

Inside the Cathedral, Flynn kneeled at the communion rail. The raised marble area, the altar sanctuary, was decked with fields of green carnations, and he studied the festive decorations. It had been four years since he had left Whitehorn Abbey; four years since he had seen her. Today he would see her again, for the last time.

He rose and turned toward the front of the Cathedral, slipping his right hand into his black overcoat pocket to feel the cold steel of the automatic pistol.

Father Timothy Murphy left his room in the rectory and made his way to the underground passage between the rectory and the Cathedral. At the end of a corridor he came to a large paneled door and opened it, then stepped into a dark room and turned on a wall switch. Soft lights glowed in the marble-vaulted sacristy.

He walked to the priests' chapel in the rear of the sacristy and knelt, directing his prayers to St. Patrick, whose feast day it was, and asking as he did every year for peace in Northern Ireland, his native land. He asked also for good weather for the parade and a peaceful and relatively sober day in his adopted city.

He rose, crossed the sacristy, mounted a short flight of marble stairs, and unlocked a pair of brass gates. He rolled the gates back on their tracks into the marble archway, then continued up the steps.

On the first landing he stopped and peered through a barred door into the crypt that contained the remains of the past archbishops of New York. A soft yellow light burned somewhere in the heart of the crypt.

The staircase split in two directions on the landing, and he took the flight to the left. He came around the altar and walked toward the high pulpit. He mounted the curving stone steps and stood beneath the bronze canopy high above the pews.

The Cathedral spread out before him, covering an entire city block. The lighter spots of the towering stained-glass windows—the flesh tones of faces and hands—picked up the early morning light, changing the focus of the scenes from the Scriptures depicted on them in a way that their artisans never intended. Disembodied heads and limbs stared out of the cobalt blues and fiery reds, looking more damned than saved.

Father Murphy turned away from the windows and peered down at the worshipers. A dozen people were widely scattered over the length and breadth of this massive-columned house, none of them with any companion but God. He lifted his eyes toward the great choir loft over the front portals. The large pipe organ rose up like a miniature cathedral, its thousands of brass pipes soaring like spires against the diffused light of the massive rose window above them.

From his pocket Father Murphy drew his typed sermon and laid it over the open pages of the lectionary, then adjusted the microphone upward. He checked his watch. Six-forty. Twenty minutes until Mass.

Satisfied with these small details, he looked up again and noticed a tall priest standing beside the altar of St. Brigid. He didn't recognize the man, but St. Patrick's would be filled with visiting priests on this day; in fact, the priest appeared to be sightseeing, taking in the wide expanses of the Cathedral. A country bumpkin, thought Murphy, just as he himself had been years before. Yet there was something self-assured about the man's bearing. He seemed to be not awed but critical, as though he were considering buying the place but was unhappy with some of the appointments.

Father Murphy came down from the pulpit. He studied the bouquets of green-dyed carnations, then snapped one off and stuck it in the lapel of his coat as he descended the steps of the altar sanctuary and walked down the center aisle. In the large vestibule under the bell tower he came within a dozen feet of the tall priest, that area of space within which greeting had to be made. He paused, then smiled, "Good morning, Father."

The tall priest stared. "Morning."

Father Murphy considered extending his hand, but the other priest had his right hand deep in his overcoat pocket and held a gift-wrapped box under his other arm. Murphy passed by the priest and crossed the cold stone vestibule to the front door. He drew the floor bolt, then pushed the door open and stepped out to the front steps of the Cathedral. His clear blue eyes drifted across Fifth Avenue and upward to the top of the International Building in Rockefeller Center. A glint of sunlight reflected from the bronze work of the building. It was going to be a sunny day for the Irish, a great day for the Irish.

He looked to his right. Approaching from the north was a vehicle with flashing yellow lights. Hissing noises emanated from it as it drew opposite the Cathedral. Murphy saw the stream of Kelly-green paint coming from the rear of the machine, drawing a line down the middle of Fifth Avenue and covering the white traffic line.

His eyes focused on the huge bronze statue of Atlas—facing him from across the street in front of the International Building—holding up the world in a classic pose, heroic but pagan. He had never liked that statue—it mocked his church. Rockefeller Center itself mocked his church, its gray masonry buildings a colossal monument to the ego of one man, soaring above the marble spires of the Cathedral.

He stared at the naked physique of the god opposite him and was reminded of the tall priest in the Cathedral.

Brian Flynn moved to an arched oak door in a wall of the vestibule below the bell tower, opened it, and stepped into a small elevator. He pushed the only button on the panel, and the elevator rose. Flynn stepped out into the choir practice room, walked through it into the choir loft, and stood at the parapet rail.

Flynn looked beyond the sea of wooden pews toward the raised altar, its bronze work bathed in soft illumination and its marble gleaming from unseen light sources. White statuary reflected the ambient lighting and seemed—as it was supposed to seem—ethereal and animated. The statue of St. Patrick opposite the pulpit appeared to be looking up at him. Behind the carnation-decked altar was the rounded apse that held the Lady Chapel, the tall, slender, stained-glass windows alight with the rising sun. The fifteen altars that stood on the periphery of the Cathedral were aglow with votive candles.

If the intention was to awe, to mystify, to diminish man in the face of God, then this Gothic structure accomplished its purpose very well. What masters of suspense and mystery these Catholics were, Flynn thought, what incredible manipulators of physical reality and, hence, inner reality. Bread and wine into flesh and blood, indeed. Yet inside this Cathedral the years of childhood programming had their effect, and his thinking was involved with too many forgotten emotions. Outside the Church was a world that didn't diminish him or play tricks with his mind and eyes. He gave the Cathedral a last look, then made his way to a small door off the choir loft and opened it.

A rush of cold air hit him, and he shivered as he stepped into the bell tower. When his eyes had adjusted to the darkness he moved forward and found a spiral staircase with handrails in the center of the tower and began to climb, steadying himself with one hand and holding the parcel with the other.

The tower was dark, but translucent glass let in a grayish light. Flynn could see his breath as he climbed. The stairs gave way to ladders, and the ladders became shakier at each succeeding landing. He wondered if anyone ever came up here; he couldn't imagine why they would. He stopped to catch his breath on a landing below what he believed to be the first bell room.

He saw some movement to his right and drew his pistol. He walked in a crouch toward the movement, but it was only the straps of the bells hanging down the wall in a sinister fashion, swaying in the drafts as they passed through a hole in the landing.

He looked around. The place was eerie. The diffused light added to the effect, and the sounds of the surrounding city were changed into odd noises that seemed to come from the tower itself. The draft was eerie also because he couldn't quite tell from which direction it came. It seemed to come from some hidden respiratory organ belonging to the Cathedral itself—in a way, the secret breath of St. Patrick's—or St. Patrick himself. Yet he felt somehow that this breath was not sanctified and that there was an evil about the place. He had felt that in Whitehorn Abbey, and afterward realized that what the faithful took to be the presence of the Holy Spirit was something quite different for the faithless.

He tried to light a cigarette, but the matches would not stay lit. The brief light illuminated the small, polygon-shaped chamber of the tower, and again his thoughts were drawn back to the subbasement of Whitehorn's chapter house. He rubbed his hand over the large ring that he still wore. He thought of Maureen and pictured her as he had last seen her in that basement: frightened, sick, saddened at their parting. He wondered what her first words to him would be after these four years.

He looked at his watch. In ten minutes the bells would ring the Angelus, and if he were near them he would be deafened. He mounted the ladder and ascended. He had an impulse to shout a blasphemy up into the dark tower to rouse those spirits in their aerie, to tell them that Finn MacCumail was approaching and to make way.

The ladder reached into the first bell room, which held three of the Cathedral's nineteen cast-bronze bells hanging from a crossbeam. Flynn checked his watch again. Eight minutes to seven. Setting a flashlight on a crossbeam, he worked swiftly to unwrap the package, exposing a black metal box. He found the electrical wire that led to the utility work light fixed on the beam and cut the wire, connecting each end to terminals in the metal box. He set an electrical timer on the box to 5:00 p.m., then pulled the chain of the utility light.

The bell room was partially illuminated, revealing the accumulated dust and cobwebs of a century, and the timer began ticking loudly in the still room.

He touched one of the bronze bells and felt its coldness, thinking that today might be the last day New York would hear it.

CHAPTER 6

Maureen Malone stood naked in front of the full-length door mirror, cold water clinging to her face and shoulders and glistening in the harsh bathroom light. Her hand moved to her right breast, and she felt the cold, jagged flesh along the side of it. She stared at the purple gash. God, the damage a tiny bullet could do. She had once considered plastic surgery, but the wound went down into her soul where no surgeon's hands could reach it.

She took a hotel bath towel, wrapped herself in it, and stepped into the bedroom. She walked slowly across the thick carpet, parted the heavy drapery, and looked out into the city from the forty-second floor of the Waldorf's north tower.

She tried to focus on the lights a few at a time. Strings of highway and bridge lamps cut across the waterways and flatlands around the island, and the island itself was jammed with incredibly huge buildings. She scanned the buildings closest to her and saw the Cathedral laid out in the shape of a cross, bathed in a cold blue light. The apse faced her, and the entrance was on a wide avenue. Its twin spires rose gracefully amid the rectangular hulks around it, and she could see traffic moving on many of the city's streets, an incredible thing at that hour, she thought.

The lights of the city blurred in her eyes, and her mind wandered back to the dinner in the Empire Room downstairs where she had been a speaker. What had she told those ladies and gentlemen of Amnesty International? That she was there for the living and dead of Ireland. *What was her mission?* they asked. To convince the British to release the men and women interned in Northern Ireland under the Special Powers Act. After that, and only after that, would her former comrades-in-arms talk peace.

The newspapers had said that her appearance on the steps of St. Patrick's Cathedral on the saint's feast day, with Sir Harold Baxter, the British Consul General in New York, would be a historical precedent. Never had a Cardinal allowed anyone remotely political to stand with him on the steps on this day. The political types mounted the steps, she was told, saluted the Prince of the Church and his entourage, then rejoined the parade and marched to the reviewing stands fourteen blocks farther north. But Maureen Malone, ex-IRA terrorist, had been invited. Hadn't Jesus forgiven Mary Magdalene? the Cardinal had asked her. Wasn't this what Christ's message was all about? She didn't know if she liked the comparison with that famous whore, but the Cardinal had seemed so sincere.

Sir Harold Baxter, she knew, was as uncomfortable with the arrangement as she was, but he could not have accepted without the approval of his Foreign Office, so that at least was a breakthrough. Peace initiatives, unlike war initiatives, always had such small, meek, tentative beginnings.

She felt a sudden chill by the window and shivered. Her eyes went back to the blue-lit Cathedral. She tried to envision how the day would end but couldn't, and this frightened her. Another chill, a different kind, ran down her spine. *Once in, never out.*

Somehow she knew Brian Flynn was close, and she knew he would not let her get away with this.

* * *

Terri O'Neal woke to the sound of early morning traffic coming through the second-story window. She sat up slowly in the bed. A streetlight outside the window partially illuminated the room. The man next to her—Dan, yes, Dan—turned his head and stared at her. She could see that his eyes were clear, unclouded by either drink or sleep. She suspected that he had been awake for some time, and this made her uneasy, but she didn't know why. "Maybe I should get going. Work today."

He sat up and held her arm. "No work today. You're going to the parade. Remember?"

His voice, a light brogue, was not husky with sleep. He *had* been awake—and how did he know she wasn't going to work today? She never told her pickups anything more than they had to know—in case it didn't go well. "Are *you* going to work today?"

"I am at work." He laughed as he took a cigarette from the night table.

She forced a smile, swung her legs out of bed, and stood. She felt his eyes taking in her figure as she walked to the big bay window and knelt in the window bench facing the street. She looked out. A lovely street. Sixty-something—off Fifth, a street of brownstone and granite town houses.

She looked westward. A big police van was parked on the corner of Fifth, and across the street from it was a television truck. On the far side of the Avenue were the reviewing stands that had been assembled in front of the park.

She looked directly below her. A long line of police scooters were angle-parked on the street. Dozens of helmeted police officers were milling about, blowing into their hands or drinking coffee. Their proximity made her feel better.

She turned and sat facing the bed. She noticed that he had put on his jeans, but he was still sitting on the bed. She became apprehensive again, and her voice came out low and tremulous. "Who—who are you?"

He got off the bed and walked to her. "I'm your lover of last evening, Mrs. O'Neal." He stood directly in front of her, and she had to crane her neck to look up into his face.

Terri O'Neal was frightened. This man did not act, look, or talk like a crazy—yet he was going to do something to her that she was not going to like. She was sure of that. She pulled free of his stare and turned her eyes slightly toward the side panel of the bay window. A loud scream would do it. She hoped to God it would do it.

Dan Morgan didn't follow her eyes, but he knew what was out there. "Not a peep, lass. Not a peep..."

Reluctantly she swung her head back toward him

and found herself staring into a big, black silencer at the end of a bigger black pistol. Her mouth went dry.

"...or I'll put a bullet through your pretty, dimpled kneecap."

It was several seconds before she could form a thought or a word, then she said softly, "What do you want?"

"Just your company for a while."

"Company?" Her brain wasn't taking in any of this.

"You're kidnapped, darlin'. Kidnapped."

CHAPTER 7

Detective Lieutenant Patrick Burke sat huddled against the cold dawn on the top riser of the reviewing stands and looked down into the Avenue. The freshly painted green line glistened in the thin sunlight, and policemen stepped carefully over it as they crossed the street.

A bomb squad ambled through the risers picking up paper bags and bottles, none of them containing anything more lethal than the dregs of cheap wine. A bum lay covered with newspaper on the riser below him, undisturbed by the indulgent cops.

Burke looked east into Sixty-fourth Street. Police motor scooters lined the street, and a WPIX television van had taken up position on the north corner. A police mobile headquarters van was parked on the south corner, and two policemen were connecting the van's cables to an access opening at the base of a streetlamp.

Burke lit a cigarette. In twenty years of intelligence work this scene had not changed nearly so much as everything else in his life had. He thought that even the bum might be the same.

Burke glanced at his watch—five minutes to kill. He

watched the uniformed patrolmen queue up to a PBA canteen truck for coffee. Someone at the back of the line was fortifying the cups of coffee with a dark liquid poured from a Coke bottle, like a priest, thought Burke, sprinkling holy water on the passing troops. It would be a long, hard day for the uniformed cops. Over a million people, Irish and otherwise, would crowd the sidewalks of Fifth Avenue and the bars and restaurants of midtown Manhattan. Surprisingly, for all the sound and fury of the day there had never been a serious political incident in over two centuries of St. Patrick's days in New York. But Burke felt every year that it would happen, that it must happen eventually.

The presence of the Malone woman in New York disturbed him. He had interviewed her briefly in the Empire Room of the Waldorf the previous evening. She seemed likable enough, pretty, too, and undaunted by his suggestion that someone might decide to murder her. She had probably become accustomed to threats on her life, he thought.

The Irish were Burke's specialty, and the Irish, he believed, were potentially the most dangerous group of all. But if they struck, would they pick *this* day? This day *belonged* to the Irish. The parade was their trooping of the colors, their showing of the green, necessary in those days when they were regarded as America's first unwanted foreigners. He remembered a joke his grandfather used to tell, popular at the turn of the century: What is St. Patrick's Day? It's the day the Protestants and Jews look out the windows of their town houses on Fifth Avenue to watch their employees march by.

What had begun as America's first civil rights demonstration was now a reminder to the city—to the nation—that the Irish still existed as a force. This was the day that the Irish got to fuck up New York City, the day they turned Manhattan on its ear.

Burke stood, stretched his big frame, then bounded down the rows of benches and jumped onto the sidewalk. He walked behind the stands until he came to an opening in the low stone wall that bordered Central Park, where he descended a flight of stone steps. In front of him rose the huge, castlelike Arsenal—actually a park administration building—flying, along with the American flag, the green, white, and orange tricolor of the Republic of Ireland. He circled around it to his right and came to a closed set of towering wrought-iron gates. Without much enthusiasm he climbed to the top of the gates, then dropped down into the zoo.

The zoo was deserted and much darker than the Avenue. Ornate lamps cast a weak light over the paths and brick buildings. He proceeded slowly down the straight lane, staying in the shadows. As he walked he unholstered his service revolver and slipped it into his coat pocket, more as a precaution against muggers than professional assassins.

The shadows of bare sycamores lay over the lane, and the smell of damp straw and animals hung oppressively in the cold, misty air. To his left seals were barking in their pool, and birds, captive and free, chirped and squawked in a blend of familiar and exotic sounds.

Burke passed the brick arches that supported the Delacorte clock and peered into the shadows of the colonnade, but no one was there. He checked his watch against the clock. Ferguson was late or dead. He leaned against one of the clock arches and lit another cigarette. Around him he saw, to the east, south, and west, towering skyscrapers silhouetted against the dawn, crowded close to the black treelines like sheer cliffs around a rain forest basin.

He heard the sound of soft footsteps behind him and turned, peering around the arch into the path that led to the Children's Zoo deeper into the park.

Jack Ferguson passed through a concrete tunnel and stepped into a pool of light, then stopped. "Burke?"

"Over here." Burke watched Ferguson approach. The man walked with a slight limp, his oversized vintage trench coat flapping with every step he took.

Ferguson offered his hand and smiled, showing a set of yellowed teeth. "Good to see you, Patrick."

Burke took his hand. "How's your wife, Jack?"

"Poorly. Poorly, I'm afraid."

"Sorry to hear that. You're looking a bit pale yourself."

Ferguson touched his face. "Am I? I should get out more."

"Take a walk in the park—when the sun's up. Why are we meeting here, Jack?"

"Oh God, the town's full of Micks today, isn't it? I mean we could be seen anywhere by anybody."

"I suppose." Old revolutionaries, thought Burke, would wither and die without their paranoia and conspiracies. Burke pulled a small thermal flask from his coat. "Tea and Irish?"

"Bless you." Ferguson took it and drank, then

handed it back as he looked around into the shadows. "Are you alone?"

"Me, you, and the monkeys." Burke took a drink and regarded Ferguson over the rim of the flask. Jack Ferguson was a genuine 1930s City College Marxist whose life had been spent in periods of either fomenting or waiting for the revolution of the working classes. The historical tides that had swept the rest of the world since the war had left Jack Ferguson untouched and unimpressed. In addition he was a pacifist, a gentle man, though these seemingly disparate ideals never appeared to cause him any inner conflict. Burke held out the flask. "Another rip?"

"No, not just yet."

Burke screwed the cap back on the Thermos as he studied Ferguson, who was nervously looking around him. Ferguson was a ranking officer in the Official Irish Republican Army, or whatever was left of it in New York, and he was as burnt out and moribund as the rest of that group of geriatrics. "What's coming down today, Jack?"

Ferguson took Burke's arm and looked up into his face. "The Fenians ride again, my boy."

"Really? Where'd they get the horses?"

"No joke, Patrick. A renegade group made up mostly from the Provos in Ulster. They call themselves the Fenians."

Burke nodded. He had heard of them. "They're here? In New York?"

"Afraid so."

"For what purpose?"

"I couldn't say, exactly. But they're up to mischief."

"Are your sources reliable?"

"Very."

"Are these people into violence?"

"In the vernacular of the day, yes, they're into violence. Into it up to their asses. They're murderers, arsonists, and bombers. The cream of the Provisional IRA. Between them they've leveled most of downtown Belfast, and they're responsible for hundreds of deaths. A bad lot."

"Sounds like it, doesn't it? What do they do on weekends?"

Ferguson lit a cigarette with unsteady hands. "Let's sit awhile."

Burke followed him toward a bench facing the ape house. As he walked he watched the man in front of him. If ever there was a man more anachronistic, more quixotic than Jack Ferguson, he had never met him. Yet Ferguson had somehow survived in that netherworld of leftist politics and had even survived a murder attempt—or an assassination attempt, as Ferguson would have corrected him. And he was unusually reliable in these matters. The Marxist-oriented Officials distrusted the breakaway Provisionals and vice versa. Each side still had people in the opposite camp, and they were the best sources of information about each other. The only common bond they shared was a deep hate for the English and a policy of hands-off-America. Burke sat next to Ferguson. "The IRA has not committed acts of violence in America since the Second World War," Burke recited the conventional wisdom, "and I don't think they're ready to now."

"That's true of the Officials, certainly, and even the Provisionals, but not of these Fenians."

Burke said nothing for a long time, then asked, "How many?"

Ferguson chain-lit a cigarette. "At least twenty, maybe more."

"Armed?"

"Not when they left Belfast, of course, but there are people here who would help them."

"Target?"

"Who knows? No end of targets today. Hundreds of politicians in the reviewing stands, in the parade. People on the steps of the Cathedral. Then, of course, there's the British Consulate, British Airways, the Irish Tourist Board, the Ulster Trade Delegation, the—"

"All right. I've got a list too." Burke watched a gorilla with red, burning eyes peering at them through the bars of the ape house. The animal seemed interested in them, turning its head whenever they spoke. "Who are the leaders of these Fenians?"

"A man who calls himself Finn MacCumail."

"What's his real name?"

"I may know this afternoon. MacCumail's lieutenant is John Hickey, code name Dermot."

"Hickey's dead."

"No, he's living right here in New Jersey. He must be close to eighty by now."

Burke had never met Hickey, but Hickey's career in the IRA was so long and so blood-splattered that he was mentioned in history books. "Anything else?"

"No, that's it for now."

"Where can we meet later?"

"Call me at home every hour starting at noon. If you don't reach me, meet me back here on the terrace of the restaurant at four thirty...unless, of course, whatever is to happen has already happened. In that case I'll be out of town for a while."

Burke nodded. "What can I do for you?"

Ferguson acted both surprised and indifferent, the way he always did at this point. "Do? Oh, well...let's see.... How's the special fund these days?"

"I can get a few hundred."

"Fine. Things are a bit tight with us."

Burke didn't know if he was referring to himself and his wife or his organization. Probably both. "I'll try for more."

"As you wish. The money isn't so important. What is important is that you avoid bloodshed, and that the department knows we're helping you. And that no one else knows it."

"That's the way we've always done it."

Ferguson stood and put out his hand. "Good-bye, Patrick. *Erin go bragh.*"

Burke stood and took Ferguson's hand. "Do what you can, Jack, but be careful."

Burke watched Ferguson limp away down the path and disappear under the clock. He felt very chilled and took a drink from his flask. *The Fenians ride again.* He had an idea that this St. Patrick's Day would be the most memorable of all.

CHAPTER 8

Maureen Malone put down her teacup and let her eyes wander around the hotel breakfast room.

"Would you like anything else?" Margaret Singer, Secretary of Amnesty International, smiled at her from across the table.

"No, thank you—" She almost added ma'am but caught herself. Three years as a revolutionary didn't transform a lifetime of inbred deference.

Next to Margaret Singer sat Malcolm Hull, also of Amnesty. And across the round table sat a man introduced only as Peter who had his back to the wall and faced the main entrance to the dining room. He neither ate nor smiled but drank black coffee. Maureen knew the type.

The fifth person at the table was recently arrived and quite unexpected: Sir Harold Baxter, British Consul General. He had come, he said frankly, to break the ice so there would be no awkwardness when they met on the steps of the Cathedral. The British, reflected Maureen, were so civilized, polite, and practical. It made one sick, really.

Sir Harold poured a cup of coffee and smiled at her. "Will you be staying on awhile?"

She forced herself to look into his clear gray eyes. He looked no more than forty, but his hair was graying at the temples. He was undeniably good-looking. "I think I'll go on to Belfast tonight."

His smile never faded. "Not a good idea, actually. London or even Dublin would be better."

She smiled back at his words. Translation: After today they'll surely murder you in Belfast. She didn't think he cared personally if the IRA murdered her, but his government must have decided she was useful. Her voice was cool. "When the Famine killed a million and a half Irish, it also scattered as many throughout the English-speaking world, and among these Irish are always a few IRA types. If I'm to die by their bullets, I'd rather it be in Belfast than anywhere else."

No one said anything for a few seconds, then Sir Harold spoke. "Certainly you overestimate the strength of these people outside of Ulster. Even in the south, the Dublin government has outlawed them—"

"The Dublin government, Sir Harold, are a bunch of British lackeys." There. She had really broken the ice now. "The only hope for the Catholics of the six counties—or Ulster, as you call it—has become the Irish Republican Army—not London or Dublin or Washington. Northern Ireland needs an alternative to the IRA, so Northern Ireland is where I must be."

Harold Baxter's eyes grew weary. He was sick to death of this problem but felt it his duty to respond. "And you are the alternative?"

"I'm searching for an alternative to the killing of innocent civilians."

Harold Baxter put on his best icy stare. "But

not British soldiers? Tell me, why would Ulster Catholics wish to unite with a nation governed by British lackeys?"

Her response was quick, as his had been. They both knew their catechism. "I think a people would rather be governed by their own incompetent politicians than by foreign incompetents."

Baxter sat back and pressed his palms together. "Please don't forget the two-thirds of the Ulster population who are Protestant and who consider Dublin, not London, to be a foreign capital."

Maureen Malone's face grew red. "That bunch of Bibletoting bigots does not recognize any allegiance except money. They'd throw you over in a second if they thought they could handle the Catholics themselves. Every time they sing 'God Save the Queen' in their silly Orange Lodges, they wink at each other. They think the English are decadent and the Irish Catholics are lazy drunks. They are certain *they* are the chosen people. And they've guiled you into thinking they're your loyal subjects." She realized that she had raised her voice and took a deep breath, then fixed Baxter with a cold stare to match his own. "English blood and the Crown's money keep Belfast's industry humming—don't you feel like fools, Sir Harold?"

Harold Baxter placed his napkin on the table. "Her Majesty's government would no more abandon one million subjects—loyal or disloyal—in Ulster than they would abandon Cornwall or Surrey, madam." He stood. "If this makes us fools, so be it. Excuse me." He turned and headed toward the door.

Maureen stared after him, then turned toward her

host and hostess. "I'm sorry. I shouldn't have picked an argument with him."

Margaret Singer smiled. "That's all right. But I'd advise you not to argue politics with the other side. If we tell the Russians what bullies they are and then try to get a Soviet Jew released from the camps, we don't have much luck, you know."

Hull nodded in assent. "You won't agree, but I can assure you that the British are among the fairest people in this troubled world. If you want to get them to end internment, you'll have to appeal to that sense of fairness. You broke with the IRA to travel this path."

Margaret Singer added, "We all must deal with our devils—and we do." She paused. "They hold the keys to the camps."

Maureen took the gentle rebuke without answering. The good people of the world were infinitely more difficult to deal with than the bad. "Thank you for breakfast. Excuse me." She stood.

A bellhop came toward the table. "Miss Malone?"

She nodded slowly.

"For you, miss." He held up a small bouquet of green carnations. "I'll put them in a nice vase in your room, ma'am. There's a card I can give you now, if you wish."

She stared at the small buff envelope, then took it. It was blank. She looked questioningly at Singer and Hull. They shook their heads. She broke the seal on the envelope.

Maureen's mind went back to London five years earlier. She and Sheila had been hiding in a safe house in an Irish neighborhood in the East End. Their mission had been secret, and only the Provisional IRA War Council knew of their whereabouts.

A florist had come to the door one morning and delivered a bouquet of English lavender and foxglove, and the Irishwoman who owned the house had gone up to their room and thrown the flowers on their bed. "Secret mission," she had said, and had spit on the floor. "What a bloody bunch of fools you all are."

She and Sheila had read the accompanying card: *Welcome to London. Her Majesty's government hope you enjoy your visit and trust you will avail yourself of the pleasures of our island and the hospitality of the English people.* Right out of a government travel brochure. Except that it wasn't signed by the Tourist Board but by Military Intelligence.

She had never been so humiliated and frightened in her life. She and Sheila had run out of the house with only the clothes on their backs, and spent days in the parks and the London Underground. They hadn't dared to go to any other contacts for fear they were being followed for that purpose. Eventually, after the worst fortnight she had ever passed in her life, they had made it to Dublin.

She pulled the card half out of its envelope to read the words. *Welcome to New York. We hope your stay will be pleasant and that you will take advantage of the pleasures of the island and the hospitality of the people.*

She didn't have to pull the rest of the card out to see the signature, but she did anyway, and read the name of Finn MacCumail.

Maureen closed the door of her room and bolted it. The flowers were already on the dresser. She pulled them from the vase and took them into the bathroom. She tore and ripped them and flushed them down the toilet. In the mirror she could see the reflection of the bedroom and the partly opened door to the adjoining sitting room. She spun around. The closet door was also ajar, and she hadn't left either of those doors open. She took several deep breaths to make sure her voice was steady. "Brian?"

She heard a movement in the sitting room. Her knees were beginning to feel shaky, and she pressed them together. "Damn you, Flynn!"

The connecting door to the sitting room swung open. "Ma'am?" The maid looked across the room at her.

Maureen took another long breath. "Is anyone else here?"

"No, ma'am."

"Has anyone been here?"

"Only the boy with the flowers, ma'am."

"Please leave."

"Yes, ma'am." The maid pushed her cart into the hall. Maureen followed her and bolted the door, then sat in the armchair and stared at the Paisley wallpaper.

She was surprised by her calmness. She almost wished he would roll out from under the bed and smile at her with that strange smile that was not a smile at all. She conjured up an image of him standing in front of her. He would say, "It's been a damned long time, Maureen." He always said that after they had been separated. Or "Where are my flowers, lass? Did you put them in a special place?"

"Yes, very special," she said aloud. "I flushed them down the goddamned john."

She sat there for several minutes carrying on her imaginary conversation with him. She realized how much she missed him and how she wanted to hear his voice again. She was both excited and frightened by the knowledge that he was close and that he would find her.

The phone next to her rang. She let it ring for a long time before she picked it up.

"Maureen? Is everything all right?" It was Margaret Singer. "Shall I come up and get you? We're expected at the Irish Pavilion—"

"I'll be right down." She hung up and rose slowly from the chair. The Irish Pavilion for a reception, then the steps of St. Patrick's, the parade, and the reviewing stands at the end of the day. Then the Irish Cultural Society Benefit Dinner for Ireland's Children. Then Kennedy Airport. What a lot of merrymaking in the name of helping soothe the ravages of war. Only in America. The Americans would turn the Apocalypse into a dinner dance.

She walked across the sitting room and into the bedroom. On the floor she saw a single green carnation, and she knelt to pick it up.

CHAPTER 9

Patrick Burke looked out of the telephone booth into the dim interior of the Blarney Stone on Third Avenue. Cardboard shamrocks were pasted on the bar mirror, and a plastic leprechaun hat hung from the ceiling. Burke dialed a direct number in Police Plaza. "Langley?"

Inspector Philip Langley, head of the New York Police Department's Intelligence Division, sipped his coffee. "I got your report on Ferguson." Langley looked down from his thirteenth-story window toward the Brooklyn Bridge. The sea fog was burning off. "It's like this, Pat. We're getting some pieces to a puzzle here, and the picture that's taking shape doesn't look good. The FBI has received information from IRA informers that a renegade group from Ireland has been poking around the New York and Boston IRA—testing the waters to see if they can have a free hand in something that they're planning in this country."

Burke wiped his neck with a handkerchief. "In the words of the old cavalry scout, I see many hoofprints going in and none coming out."

Langley said, "Of course, nothing points directly to New York on Saint Patrick's Day—"

"There is a law that says that if you imagine the worst possible thing happening at the worst possible moment, it will usually happen, and Saint Patrick's Day is a nightmare under the best of circumstances. It's Mardi Gras, Bastille Day, Carnivale, all in one. So if I were the head of a renegade Irish group and I wanted to make a big splash in America, I would do it in New York City on March seventeenth."

"I hear you. How do you want to approach this?"

"I'll start by digging up my contacts. Barhop. Listen to the barroom patriots talk. Buy drinks. Buy people."

"Be careful."

Burke hung up, then walked over to the bar.

"What'll you be having?"

"Cutty." Burke placed a twenty-dollar bill on the bar. He recognized the bartender, a giant of a man named Mike. Burke took his drink and left the change on the bar. "Buy you one?"

"It's a little early yet." The bartender waited. He knew a man who wanted something.

Burke slipped into a light brogue. "I'm looking for friends."

"Go to church."

"I won't be finding them there. The brothers Flannagan. Eddie and Bob. Also John Hickey."

"You're a friend?"

"Meet them every March seventeenth."

"Then you should know that John Hickey is dead— may his soul rest in peace. The Flannagans are gone back to the old country. A year it's been. Drink up now and move along. You'll not be finding any friends here."

"Is this the bar where they throw a drunk through the window every Saint Patrick's Day?"

"It will be if you don't move along." He stared at Burke.

A medium-built man in an expensive topcoat suddenly emerged from a booth and stood beside Burke. The man spoke softly, in a British accent. "Could I have a word with you?"

Burke stared at the man, who inclined his head toward the door. Both men walked out of the bar. The man led Burke across the street, stopping on the far corner. "My name is Major Bartholomew Martin of British Military Intelligence." Martin produced his diplomatic passport and military I.D. card.

Burke hardly glanced at them. "Means nothing."

Martin motioned to a skyscraper in the center of the block. "Then perhaps we'd better go in there."

Burke knew the building without looking at it. He saw two big Tactical Policemen standing a few yards from the entrance with their hands behind their backs. Martin walked past the policemen and held open the door. Burke entered the big marble lobby and picked out four Special Services men standing at strategic locations. Martin moved swiftly to the rear of the lobby, behind a stone façade that camouflaged the building's elevators. The elevator doors opened, and both men moved inside. Burke reached out and pushed floor nine.

Martin smiled. "Thank you."

Burke looked at the man standing in a classical elevator pose, feet separated, hands behind his back, head tilted upward, engrossed in the progression of illuminated numbers. Despite his rank there was nothing military about Bartholomew Martin, thought Burke. If anything he looked like an actor who was trying to get into character for a difficult role. He hadn't mastered control of the mouth, however, which was hard and unyielding, despite the smile. A glimpse of the real man, perhaps.

The elevator stopped, and Burke followed the major into the corridor. Martin nodded to a man who stood to the left, dressed in a blue blazer with polished brass buttons.

On the wall of the corridor, opposite Burke, was the royal coat of arms and a highly polished bronze plaque that read: BRITISH INFORMATION SERVICES. There was no sign to indicate that this was where the spies usually hung out, but as far as Burke knew, nobody's consulate or embassy information office made that too clear.

Burke followed Martin through a door into a large room. A blond receptionist, dressed in a blue tweed suit that matched the Concorde poster above her desk, stood as they approached and said in a crisp British accent, "Good morning, Major."

Martin led Burke through a door just beyond the desk, through a microfilm reading room, and into a small sitting room furnished in a more traditional style than the rest of the place. The only detail that suggested a government office was a large travel poster that showed a black and white cow standing in a sunny meadow, captioned: "Find peace and tranquility in an English village."

Martin drew the door shut, locked it, and hung his topcoat on a clothes tree. "Have a seat, Lieutenant."

Burke left his coat on, walked to the sideboard and took the stopper out of a decanter, smelled it, then poured a drink. He looked around the well-furnished room. The last time he'd been in the consulate was a week before last St. Patrick's Day. A Colonel Hayes that time. Burke leaned back against the sideboard. "Well, what can you do for me?"

Major Martin smiled. "A great deal, I think."

"Good."

"I've already given Inspector Langley a report on a group of Irish terrorists called the Fenians, led by a Finn MacCumail. You've seen the report?"

"I've been apprised of the details."

"Fine. Then you know something may happen here today." Major Martin leaned forward. "I'm working closely with the FBI and CIA, but I'd like to work more closely with your people—pool our information. The FBI and CIA tell us things they don't tell you, but I'd keep you informed of their progress as well as ours. I've already helped your military intelligence branches set up files on the IRA, and I've briefed your State Department intelligence service on the problem."

"You've been busy."

"Yes. You see, I'm a sort of clearinghouse in this affair. British Intelligence knows more about the Irish revolutionaries than anyone, of course, and now you seem to need that information, and we have a chance to do you a good turn."

"What's the price?"

Major Martin played with a lighter on the coffee

table. "Yes, price. Well, better information from you in future on the transatlantic IRA types in New York. Gunrunning. Fund raising. IRA people here on R and R. That sort of thing."

"Sounds fair."

"It *is* fair."

"So what do you want of me particularly?"

Major Martin looked at Burke. "Just wanted to tell you directly about all of this. To meet you." Martin stood. "Look here, if you want to get a bit of information to me directly, call here and ask for Mr. James. Someone will take the message and pass it on to me. And I'll leave messages for you here as well. Perhaps a little something you can give to Langley as your own. You'll make a few points that way. Makes everyone look good."

Burke moved toward the door, then turned. "They're probably going after the Malone woman. Maybe even after the consul general."

Major Martin shook his head. "I don't think so. Sir Harold has no involvement whatsoever in Irish affairs. And the Malone woman—I knew her sister, Sheila, in Belfast, incidentally. She's in jail. An IRA martyr. They should only know—but that's another story. Where was I?—Maureen Malone. She's quite the other thing to the IRA. A Provisional IRA tribunal has condemned her to death in absentia, you know. She's on borrowed time now. But they won't shoot her down in the street. They'll grab her someday in Ireland, north or south, have a trial with her present this time, kneecap her, then a day or so later shoot her in the head and leave her on a street in Belfast. And the Fenians, whoever they are, won't do anything that would preempt the Provos' death sentence. And don't forget, Malone and Sir Harold will be on the steps of Saint Patrick's most of the day, and the Irish respect the sanctuary of the church no matter what their religious or political beliefs. No, I wouldn't worry about those two. Look for a more obvious target. British property. The Ulster Trade Delegation. The Irish always perform in a predictable manner."

"Really? Maybe that's why my wife left me."

"Oh, you're Irish, of course . . . sorry . . . ."

Burke unbolted the door and walked out of the room.

Major Martin threw back his head and laughed softly, then went to the sideboard and made himself a martini. He evaluated his conversation with Burke and decided that Burke was more clever than he had been led to believe. Not that it would do him any good this late in the game.

BOOK III

The Parade

Saint Patrick's Day in New York is the most fantastic affair, and in past years on Fifth Avenue, from Forty-fourth Street to Ninety-sixth Street, the white traffic lines were repainted green for the occasion. All the would-be Irish, has-been Irish and never-been Irish, seem to appear true-blue Irish overnight. Everyone is in on the act, but it is a very jolly occasion and I have never experienced anything like it anywhere else in the world.

Brendan Behan,
Brendan Behan's New York

CHAPTER 10

In the middle of Fifth Avenue, at Forty-fourth Street, Pat and Mike, the two Irish wolfhounds that were the mascots of the Fighting 69th Infantry Regiment, strained at their leashes. Colonel Dennis Logan, Commander of the 69th, tapped his Irish blackthorn swagger stick impatiently against his leg. He glanced at the sky and sniffed the air, then turned to Major Matthew Cole. "What's the weather for this afternoon, Major?"

Major Cole, like all good adjutants, had the answer to everything. "Cold front moving through later, sir. Snow or freezing rain by nightfall."

Logan nodded and thrust his prominent jaw out in a gesture of defiance, as though he were going to say, "Damn the weather—full speed ahead."

The young major struck a similar pose, although his jaw was not so grand. "Parade'll be finished before then, I suspect, Colonel." He glanced at Logan to see if he was listening. The colonel's marvelously angular face had served him well at staff meetings, but the rocklike quality of that visage was softened by misty green eyes like a woman's. Too bad.

Logan looked at his watch, then at the big iron stanchion clock in front of the Morgan Guaranty Trust Building on Fifth Avenue. The clock was three minutes fast, but they would go when that clock struck noon. Logan would never forget the newspaper picture that showed his unit at parade rest and the clock at three minutes after. The caption had read: THE IRISH START LATE. Never again.

The regiment's staff, back from their inspection of the unit, was assembled in front of the color guard. The national and regimental colors snapped in a five-mile-an-hour wind that came down the Avenue from the north, and the multicolored battle streamers, some going back to the Civil War and the Indian wars, fluttered nicely. Logan turned to Major Cole. "What's your feel?"

The major searched his mind for a response, but the question threw him. "Feel . . . sir?"

"Feel, man. *Feel.*" He accentuated the words.

"Fine. Fine."

Logan looked at the battle ribbons on the major's chest. A splash of purple stood out like the wound it represented. "In 'Nam, did you ever get a feeling that everything was not fine?"

The major nodded thoughtfully.

Logan waited for a response that would reinforce his own feelings of unease, but Cole was too young to have fully developed that other sense to the extent that he could identify what he felt in the jungle and recognize it in the canyons of Manhattan Island. "Keep a sharp eye out today. This is not a parade—it's an operation. Don't let your head slide up your ass."

"Yes, sir."

Logan looked at his regiment. They stood at parade rest, their polished helmets with the regimental crest reflecting the overhead sunlight. Slung across their shoulders were M-16 rifles.

The crowd at Forty-fourth Street, swelled by office workers on their lunch hour, was jostling for a better view. People had climbed atop the WALK–DON'T WALK signs, the mailboxes, and the cement pots that held the newly budded trees along the Avenue.

In the intersection around Colonel Logan newsmen mixed with politicians and parade officials. The parade chairman, old Judge Driscoll, was patting everyone on the back as he had done for over forty years. The formation marshals, resplendent in black morning coats, straightened their tricolor sashes and top hats. The Governor was shaking every hand that looked as if it could pull a voting lever, and Mayor Kline was wearing the silliest green derby that Logan had ever seen.

Logan looked up Fifth Avenue. The broad thoroughfare was clear of traffic and people, an odd sight reminiscent of a B-grade science-fiction movie. The pavement stretched unobstructed to the horizon, and Colonel Logan was more impressed with this sight than anything else he had seen that day. He couldn't see the Cathedral, recessed between Fiftieth and Fifty-first Streets, but he could see the police barriers around it and the guests on the lower steps.

A stillness began to descend on the crossroads as the hands of the clock moved another notch toward the twelve. The army band accompanying the 69th ceased their tuning of instruments, and the bagpipes of the

Emerald Society on the side street stopped practicing. The dignitaries, whom the 69th Regiment was charged with escorting to the reviewing stands, began to fall into their designated places as Judge Driscoll looked on approvingly.

Logan felt his heart beat faster as he waited out the final minutes. He was aware of, but did not see, the mass of humanity huddled around him, the hundreds of thousands of spectators along the parade route to his front, the police, the reviewing stands in the park, the cameras and the newspeople. It was to be a day of dedication and celebration, sentimentality and even sorrow. In New York this day had been crowned by the parade, which had gone on uninterrupted by war, depression, or civil strife since 1762. It was, in fact, a mainstay of Irish culture in the New World, and it was not about to change, even if every last man, woman, and child in old Ireland did away with themselves and the British to boot. Logan turned to Major Cole. "Are we ready, Major?"

"The Fighting Irish are always ready, Colonel."

Logan nodded. The Irish were always ready for anything, he thought, and prepared for nothing.

Father Murphy looked around him as a thousand guests crowded the steps of the Cathedral. He edged over and stood on the long green carpet that had been unrolled from the main portal between the brass handrail and down into the street. In front of him, between the handrails, stood the Cardinal and the Monsignor, shoulder to shoulder. Flanking them were the British consul, Baxter, next to the Cardinal, and the Malone woman next to the Monsignor. Murphy smiled. The arrangement wasn't strictly protocol, but they couldn't get at each other's throats so easily now.

Standing in loose formation around the Cardinal's group were priests, nuns, and church benefactors. Murphy noticed at least two men who were probably undercover police. He looked up over the heads of the people in front of him toward the crowd across the Avenue. Boys and girls had climbed to the top of the pedestal of the Atlas and were passing bottles back and forth. His eyes were drawn to a familiar face: Standing in front of the pedestal, with his hands resting on a police barricade, was Patrick Burke. The man towered above the crowd around him and seemed strangely unaffected by the animated throng pressing against him on the sidewalk. Murphy realized that Burke's presence reassured him, though he didn't know why he felt he needed that assurance.

The Cardinal turned his head toward Harold Baxter and spoke in a voice that had that neutral tone of diplomacy so like his own. "Will you be staying with us for the entire day, Mr. Baxter?"

Baxter was no longer used to being called mister, but he didn't think the Cardinal meant anything by it. He turned his head to meet the Cardinal's eyes. "If I may, Your Eminence."

"We would be delighted."

"Thank you." He continued to look at the Cardinal, who had now turned away. The man was old, but his eyes were bright. Baxter cleared his throat. "Excuse me, Your Eminence, but I was thinking that perhaps I should stand away from the center of things a bit."

The Cardinal waved to well-wishers in the crowd as he spoke. "Mr. Baxter, you *are* the center of things today. You and Miss Malone. This little display of ours has captured the imagination of political commentators. It is, as they say, newsworthy. Everyone loves these precedents, this breaking with the past." He turned and smiled at Baxter, a wide Irish smile. "If you move an inch, they will be pulling their hair in Belfast, Dublin, London, and Washington." He turned back to the crowds and continued moving his arm in a blending of cheery waving and holy blessing.

"Yes, of course. I wasn't taking into account the political aspect—only the security aspect. I wouldn't want to be the cause of anyone being injured or—"

"God is watching over us, Mr. Baxter, and Commissioner Dwyer assures me that the Police Department is doing the same."

"That's reassuring on both counts. You've spoken to him recently? The Police Commissioner, I mean."

The Cardinal turned and fixed Baxter with a smile that showed he understood the little joke but did not find it amusing.

Baxter stared back for a moment, then turned away. It was going to be a long day.

Patrick Burke regarded the steps. He noticed his friend Father Murphy near the Cardinal. It must be a strange life for a man, he reflected. The celibacy. The paternal and maternal concern of monsignors and mother superiors. Like being an eternal boy. His mother had wanted that for him. A priest in the family was the ultimate status for those old Irish, but he had become a cop instead, which was almost as good in the old neighborhoods, and no one was disappointed, least of all himself.

He saw that the Monsignor was smiling and talking with the ex-IRA woman. Burke focused on her. She looked pretty, even from this distance. Angelic, almost. Her blond hair moved nicely in the breeze, and she kept brushing wisps of hair from her face.

Burke thought that if he were Harold Baxter or Maureen Malone he would not be on those steps at all, and certainly not together. And if he were the Cardinal, he would have invited them for yesterday, when they could have shared the steps with indifferent pigeons, bag ladies, and winos. He didn't know whose idea it had been to wave this red flag in the face of the Irish rebels, but if it was supposed to bring peace, someone had badly miscalculated.

He looked up and down the Avenue. Workers and high school kids, all playing hooky to get in on the big bash, mingled with street vendors, who were making out very well. Some young girls had painted green shamrocks and harps on their faces and wore *Kiss Me, I'm Irish* buttons, and they were being taken up on it by young men, most of whom wore plastic leprechaun bowlers. The older crowd settled for green carnations and *Erin Go Bragh* buttons.

Maureen Malone had never seen so many people. All along the Avenue, American and Irish flags hung from staffs jutting out of the gray masonry buildings. A group in front of the British Empire Building was hoisting a huge green banner, and Maureen read the familiar words: ENGLAND GET OUT OF IRELAND. Margaret Singer had told her that this was the only political slogan she would see, the only one sanctioned by the Grand Marshal, who had also specified that the banners be neatly made with white lettering on green background. The police had permission to seize any other banner. She hoped Baxter saw it; she didn't see how he could miss it. She turned to Monsignor Downes. "All these people are certainly not Irish."

Monsignor Downes smiled. "We have a saying in New York. 'On Saint Patrick's Day, everyone is Irish!'"

She looked around again, as though she still didn't believe what she was seeing. Little Ireland, poor and underpopulated, with its humble patron saint, almost unknown in the rest of the Christian world, causing all this fuss. It gave her goose bumps, and she felt a choking in her throat. Ireland's best exports, it was said bitterly, were her sons and daughters. But there was nothing to be bitter about, she realized. They had kept the faith, although in an Americanized version.

Suddenly she heard a great noise coming from the crowd and turned her head toward the commotion. A group of men and women, about fifteen of them, had unfurled a green banner reading: VICTIMS OF BRITISH INTERNMENT AND TORTURE. She recognized a friend of her sister's.

A police mounted unit galloped south down the Avenue, Plexiglas helmet-visors down, long batons raised above their heads. From the north side of the Cathedral on Fifty-first Street, scooter police roared past the mobile headquarters truck and onto Fifth Avenue.

A man with a bullhorn shouted, "LONG KESH! ARMAGH PRISON! CRUMLIN ROAD JAIL! CONCENTRATION CAMPS, BAXTER, YOU BASTARD! MAUREEN MALONE—TRAITOR!"

She turned and looked at Harold Baxter across the empty space left by the Cardinal and Monsignor who had been moved up the steps by the security police. He remained in a rigid position of attention, staring straight ahead. She knew there were news cameras trained on him to record his every movement, every betrayal of emotion, whether anger or fear. But they were wasting their time. The man was British.

She realized that cameras were on her as well, and she turned away from him and looked down into the street. The banner was down now, and half the demonstrators were in the hands of the police, but the other half had broken through the police barricades and were coming toward the steps, where a line of mounted police waited almost nonchalantly.

Maureen shook her head. The history of her people: forever attempting the insurmountable and, in the end, finding it indeed insurmountable.

Maureen watched, transfixed, as one of the last standing men cocked his arm and threw something toward the steps. Her heart skipped a beat as she saw it sailing through the air. It seemed to hang for a second before drifting downward slowly; the sunlight sparkled from it, making it difficult to identify. "Oh God." She began to drop to the ground but caught a glimpse of Baxter out of the corner of her eye. He hadn't moved a muscle and, whether it was a bomb or a carnation heading his way, he acted as if he could not care less. Reluctantly she straightened up. She heard a bottle crash on the granite steps directly behind her and waited for the sound of exploding petrol or nitro, but there was only a choked-off exclamation from the crowd, then a stillness around her. Green paint from the shattered bottle flecked the clothing of the people standing closest to where it hit. Her legs began to shake in relief, and her mouth became dry.

Sir Harold Baxter turned his head and looked at her. "Is this traditional?"

She could not control her voice sufficiently to speak, and she stared at him.

Baxter moved beside her. Their shoulders touched. Her reaction was to move away, but she didn't. He turned his head slightly. "Will you stand next to me for the rest of this thing?"

She moved her eyes toward him. Camera shutters clicked around them. She spoke softly. "I believe there's an assassin out there who intends to kill me today."

He didn't appear to react to this information. "Well, there are probably several out there who intend to kill me.... I promise I won't throw myself in front of you if you promise the same."

She let herself smile. "I think we can agree on that."

Burke stood firm as the crowd pushed and shoved around him. He looked at his watch. The episode had taken just two minutes. For a moment he had thought this was it, but within fifteen seconds he knew these were not the Fenians.

The security police on the steps had acted quickly but not really decisively in front of the partisan crowd. If that bottle had been a bomb, there would have been more than green paint to mop up. Burke took a long drink from his flask. He knew the whole day was a security problem of such magnitude that it had ceased to be a problem.

Burke considered the little he knew of the Fenians. They were veterans, said Ferguson, survivors, not suicidal fanatics. Whatever their mission they most probably intended to get away afterward, and that, thought Burke, would make their mission more difficult and make his job just a little easier. He hoped.

Colonel Dennis Logan was calming Pat and Mike, who had been aroused by shouts from the crowd.

Logan straightened up and looked at the stanchion clock. One minute past noon. "Oh, shit!" He turned to his adjutant, Major Cole. "Start this fucking parade."

"Yes, sir!" The adjutant turned to Barry Dugan, the police officer who for twenty-five years had blown the green whistle to begin the parade. "Officer Dugan! Do it!"

Dugan put the whistle to his lips, filled his lungs, and let out the longest, loudest whistle in all his quarter century of doing it.

Colonel Logan placed himself in front of the formation and raised his arm. Logan looked up the six blocks and saw the mass of newsmen and blue uniforms milling around a paddy wagon. They'd take their time if left to their own devices. He remembered his regiment's motto: Clear the way! He lowered his arm and turned his head over his right shoulder. "Foowaard—MARCH!" The regiment stepped off.

The army band struck up the "Garryowen," and the two hundred and twenty-third St. Patrick's Day Parade began.

CHAPTER 11

Patrick Burke walked across the Avenue to the curb in front of the Cathedral and stood by the barricades. The 69th Regiment came abreast of the Cathedral, and Colonel Logan called the regiment to a halt.

The barriers behind Burke were parted where the green carpet came into the street, and a group of men in morning dress left the parade line and approached the Cathedral.

Burke remembered that the Cardinal had mentioned, casually, to the newspapers the day before that his favorite song was "Danny Boy," and the army bandleader apparently had taken this as a command and ordered the band to play the sweet, lilting air. Some of the people on the steps and many in the crowd around the Cathedral broke into spontaneous song. It was difficult for an Irishman, thought Burke, not to respond to that music, especially if he had had a few already.

"O Danny Boy, the pipes, the pipes are calling
From glen to glen, and down the mountain side,

The summer's gone, and all the roses falling,
'Tis you, 'tis you, must go and I must bide."

Burke watched the entourage of dignitaries as they
mounted the steps: the marshals, Mayor Kline, Governor Doyle, senators, congressmen, all the secular
power in the city and state, and many from the national
level. They all passed through the space in those barriers, walked across the narrow carpet, and presented
themselves to the Cardinal, then left quickly, as protocol demanded. The faithful knelt and kissed the green-
jeweled ring; others bowed or shook hands.

"But come ye back when summer's in the meadow,
Or when the valley's hushed and white with
snow,
For I'll be here in sunshine or in shadow,
O Danny Boy, O Danny Boy, I love you so."

Maureen felt the excitement, the heightening of
perceptions that led to fear, to apprehension. Everyone
was smiling and bowing, kissing the Cardinal's ring,
shaking her hand, the Monsignor's hand, Baxter's
hand. Hands and wide smiles. The Americans had su-
per teeth. Not a bad one in the lot.

She noticed a few steely-eyed men near her who
wore the same expression of suppressed anxiety that
she knew was on her face. Down by the space in
the barriers she recognized Lieutenant Burke from the
Waldorf. He was eyeing everyone who approached, as
though they were all ax murderers instead of important
citizens, and she felt a little comforted.

Around her the crowd was still singing, trying to re-member the words and humming where they couldn't, as the flutes and horns of the army band played.

> "But when ye leave, and all the flowers are dying,
> And I am dead, as dead I may well be,
> Then will ye come and find the place where I am lying,
> And kneel and say an Ave there for me?"

Maureen shook her head. What a typically morbid Irish song. She tried to turn her thoughts to other things, but the intrusive words of the ballad reminded her of her own life—her own tragic love. Danny Boy was Brian, as Danny Boy was every Irish girl's lover. She could not escape its message and meaning for her as an Irishwoman; she found her eyes had gone misty, and there was a lump in her throat.

> "And I shall hear tho soft ye tread above me,
> And tho my grave will warmer, sweeter be,
> And you shall bend and tell me that you love me,
> And I shall sleep in peace until you come to me."

Burke watched the 69th move out. When the last unit was clear of the Cathedral, he breathed easier. The potential targets were no longer clustered around the Cathedral, they were scattered again—on the steps, moving around the regiment in small groups, some riding now in limousines up Park Avenue to the re-viewing stands, some on their way home or to the airports.

At the end of the 69th Regiment Burke saw the regimental veterans in civilian clothes marching in a unit. Behind them was the Police Emerald Society Pipes and Drums, kilts swirling and their bagpipes wailing as their drums beat out a warlike cadence. At the head of the unit their longtime commander, Finbar Devine, raised his huge mace and ordered the pipers to play "Danny Boy" as they passed the Cathedral. Burke smiled. One hundred and ninety-six marching bands would play "Danny Boy" for the Cardinal today, such was the combined power of the press and the Cardinal's casual remark. Before the day was out His Eminence would wish he had never heard the song and pray to God that he would never hear it again as long as he lived.

Burke joined the last rank of the old veterans at the end of the 69th Regiment. The next likely point of trouble was the reviewing stands at Sixty-fourth Street, where the targets would again be bunched up like irresistibly plump fruit, and on St. Patrick's Day the fastest way to get uptown was to be in the parade.

Central Park was covered with people on hillocks and stone outcroppings, and several people were sitting in trees.

Colonel Logan knew that thousands of marchers had fallen in behind him now. He could feel the electricity that was passing through his regiment into the crowd around him and down the line of marchers, until the last units—the old IRA vets—had caught the tempo and the spirit. Cold and tired in the fading light, the old soldiers would hold their heads high as they passed the spectators, who by this time were jaded, weary, and drunk.

Logan watched the politicians as they left the march and headed toward the reviewing stands to take their seats. He gave the customary order of "eyes left" as they passed the stands and saluted, breathing more easily now that his escort mission had been accomplished.

Patrick Burke left the parade formation at Sixty-fourth Street, made his way through the crowd, and entered the rear door of the police mobile headquarters van. A television set was tuned to the WPIX news program that was covering the parade. Lights flashed on the consoles, and three radios, each tuned to a different command channel, crackled in the semidarkness. A few men occupied with paperwork or electronics sat on small stools.

Burke recognized Sergeant George Byrd from the Bureau of Special Services. "Big Byrd."

Byrd looked up from a radio and smiled. "Patrick Burke, the scourge of Irish revolutionaries, defender of the faith."

"Eat it, George." He lit a cigarette.

"I read the report you filed this morning. Who are the Finnigans? What do they want?"

Burke sat on a small jump seat. "Fenians."

"Fenians. Finnigans. Micks. Who are they?"

"The Fenians were a group of Irish warriors and poets. About 200 A.D. There was also an Irish anti-British guerrilla army in the nineteenth century who called themselves Fenians—"

Byrd laughed. "That's kind of old intelligence, Burke. Must have been held up in Police Plaza."

"Filed with your promotion papers, no doubt."

Byrd grunted and leaned back against the wall. "And who's Finn Mac—something?"

"Head of the original Fenians. Been dead seventeen hundred years now."

"A code name?"

"I hope so. Wouldn't want to meet the real one."

Byrd listened to the radios. The command posts up and down the Avenue were reporting: The post at the Presbyterian church at Fifty-fourth Street reported all quiet. The post on the twentieth floor of the General Motors Building reported all quiet. The mobile headquarters at the Cathedral reported all quiet. Byrd picked up the radiophone and hesitated, then spoke softly. "Mobile at Sixty-fourth. All quiet at the reviewing stands. Out." He replaced the phone and looked at Burke. "Too quiet?"

"Don't start that shit." Burke picked up a telephone and dialed. "Jack?"

Jack Ferguson glanced at the closed bedroom door where his wife slept fitfully, then spoke in a low voice. "Patrick"—he looked at a wall clock in the kitchen— "it's twelve-thirty. You're supposed to call me on the hour."

"I was in the parade. What do you have?"

Ferguson looked at some notes scribbled on a pad near the telephone. "It's hard to find anyone today."

"I know, Jack. That's why today is the day."

"Exactly. But I did learn that the man called MacCumail has recruited some of the more wild-eyed members of the Boston Provisional IRA."

"Interesting. Any line on weapons? Explosives?"

"No," answered Ferguson, "but you can buy anything you want in this country, from pistols to tanks."

"Anything else?"

"A partial description of the man called MacCumail—tall, lean, dark—"

"That could be my mother."

"He wears a distinctive ring. Always has it."

"Not very smart."

"No. He may believe it's a charm of some sort. The Irish are a superstitious lot. The ring is oversized, probably an antique or a family heirloom. Also, I did find out something interesting about this MacCumail. It's only hearsay...but apparently he was captured once and possibly compromised by British Intelligence."

"Hold on." Burke tried to arrange his thoughts. It occurred to him, not for the first time, that there was more than one game in town today. Where there was an Irish conspiracy, there was sure to be an English conspiracy. After eight hundred years of almost continuous strife, it was as though the two adversaries were inseparably bonded in a bizarre embrace destined to last eternally. If the Irish war was coming to America, then the English would be here to fight it. It was Major Bartholomew Martin's presence in New York, more than anything Ferguson said, that signaled an approaching battle. And Major Martin knew more than he was telling. Burke spoke into the mouthpiece. "Do you have anything else?"

"No...I'm going to have to do some legwork now. I'll leave messages with Langley at Police Plaza if anything turns up. I'll meet you at the zoo at four-thirty if nothing has happened by then."

"Time is short, Jack," Burke said.

"I'll do what I can to avoid violence. But you must try to go easy on the lads if you find them. They're brothers."

"Yeah...brothers...." Burke hung up and turned to Byrd. "That was one of my informers. A funny little guy who's caught between his own basic decency and his wild politics."

Burke left the van and stood in the crowd at the corner of Sixty-fourth Street. He looked at the reviewing stands across Fifth Avenue, thick with people. If there was going to be trouble, it would probably happen at the reviewing stands. The other possible objectives that Major Martin suggested—the banks, the consulates, the airline offices, symbols of the London, Dublin, or Belfast governments—were small potatoes compared to the reviewing stands crowded with American, British, Irish, and other foreign VIPs.

The Cathedral, Burke understood, was also a big potato. But no Irish group would attack the Cathedral. Even Ferguson's Official IRA—mostly nonviolent Marxists and atheists—wouldn't consider it. The Provisionals were violent but mostly Catholic. Who but the Irish could have peaceful Reds and bomb-throwing Catholics?

Burke rubbed his tired eyes. Yes, if there was an action today, it had to be the reviewing stands.

Terri O'Neal was lying on the bed. The television set was tuned to the parade. Dan Morgan sat on the window seat and looked down Sixty-fourth Street. He noticed a tall man in civilian clothes step down from the police van, and he watched him as he lit a cigarette and stared into the street, scanning the buildings. Eventually the police, the FBI, maybe even the CIA and British Intelligence, would start to get onto them. That was expected. The Irish had a tradition called Inform and Betray. Without that weakness in the national character they would have been rid of the English centuries ago. But this time was going to be different. MacCumail was a man you didn't want to betray. The Fenians were a group more closely knit than an ancient clan, bound by one great sorrow and one great hate.

The telephone rang. Morgan walked into the living room, closed the door behind him, then picked up the receiver. "Yes?" He listened to the voice of Finn MacCumail, then hung up and pushed open the door. He stared at Terri O'Neal. It wasn't easy to kill a woman, yet MacCumail wasn't asking him to do something he himself wouldn't do. Maureen Malone and Terri O'Neal. They had nothing in common except their ancestry and the fact that both of them had only a fifty-fifty chance of seeing another dawn.

CHAPTER 12

Patrick Burke walked down Third Avenue, stopping at Irish pubs along the way. The sidewalks were crowded with revelers engaged in the traditional barhopping. Paper shamrocks and harps were plastered against the windows of most shops and restaurants. There was an old saying that St. Patrick's Day was the day the Irish marched up Fifth Avenue and staggered down Third, and Burke noticed that ladies and gentlemen were beginning to wobble a bit. There was a great deal of handshaking, a tradition of sorts, as though everyone were congratulating each other on being Irish or on being sober enough to find his hand.

Burke approached P. J. Clarke's at Fifty-fifth Street, an old nineteenth-century brick relic, spared by the wrecker's ball but left encapsulated in the towering hulk around it—the Marine Midland Bank Building, which resembled a black Sony calculator with too many buttons.

Burke walked in through the frosted glass doors, made his way to the crowded bar, and ordered a beer. He looked around for familiar faces, an informant, an old friend, someone who owed him, but there was no one. Too many familiar faces missing this afternoon.

He made his way back into the street and breathed the cold north wind until his head cleared. He continued to walk, stopping at a half-remembered bar, an Irish-owned shop, or wherever a group of people huddled and spoke on the sidewalk. His thoughts raced rapidly and, unconsciously, he picked up his pace to keep abreast of the moving streams of people.

This day had begun strangely, and every incident, every conversation, added to his sense of unreality. He took a cigarette from his pocket, lit it, and headed south again.

Burke stared up at the gilt lettering on the window of J. P. Donleavy's, a small, inconspicuous pub on Forty-seventh Street. Donleavy's was another haunt of the quasi-IRA men and barroom patriots. Occasionally there would be a real IRA man there from the other side, and you could tell who he was because he rarely stood at the bar but usually sat alone in a booth. They were always pale, the result of Ireland's perpetual mist or as a result of some time in internment. New York and Boston were their sanctuaries, places of Irish culture, Irish pubs, Irish people without gelignite.

Burke walked in and pushed his way between two men who were talking to each other at the bar. He slipped into his light brogue for the occasion. "Buy you a drink, gentlemen. A round here, barkeeper!" He turned to the man on his left, a young laborer. The man looked annoyed. Burke smiled. "I'm to meet some friends in P.J.'s, but I can't remember if they said P.J. Clarke's, P.J. O'Hara's, P.J. Moriarty's, P.J. O'Rourke's or here. Bloody stupid of me—or of them." The beer came and Burke paid for it. "Would you know Kevin Michaels or Jim Malloy or Liam Connelly? Have you seen them today?"

The man to Burke's right spoke. "That's an interesting list of names. If you're looking for them, you can be sure they'll find *you*."

Burke looked into the man's eyes. "That's what I'm counting on."

The man stared back but said nothing.

Burke smelled the sour beer on the man's breath, on his clothes. "I'm looking, too, for John Hickey."

Neither man spoke.

Burke took a long drink and put his glass down. "Thank you, gentlemen. I'm off to the Green Derby. Good day." He turned and walked down the length of the bar. An angled mirror reflected the two men huddled with the bartender, looking at him as he left.

He repeated his story, or one like it, in every bar that he thought might be promising. He switched from whiskey to stout to hot coffee and had a sandwich at a pub, which made him feel better. He crossed and recrossed Third Avenue, making his way southward. In every bar he left a forwarding address, and at every street corner he stopped and waited for the sound of shoes against the cold concrete to hesitate, to stop behind him. He was trolling, using himself as bait, but no one was rising to it today.

Burke picked up his pace. Time was running out. He looked at his watch; it was past four, and he had to be at the zoo at four-thirty. He stopped at a phone booth. "Langley? I need five hundred for Ferguson."

"Later. You didn't call for that."

Burke lit a cigarette. "What do you know about a Major Bartholomew Martin?"

There was a long silence on the phone, then Langley said, "Oh, you mean the British Intelligence guy. Don't worry about him."

"Why not?"

"Because I said so." Langley paused. "It's very complicated . . . CIA . . ."

"Tell me about it someday. Anything else I should know?"

"The FBI has finally decided to talk to us," Langley said. "They've uncovered an arms buy in New Jersey. A dozen M-16 rifles, a few sniper rifles, pistols, and plastic explosives. Also, a half dozen of those disposable rocket launchers. U.S. Army issue."

"Any other particulars?"

"Only that the buyers had Irish accents, and they didn't arrange for shipping to Ireland the way they usually do."

"Sounds ominous."

"I'll say—what are they *waiting* for?"

Burke shook his head. "I don't know. The parade has less than an hour to run. The weapons should be a clue to the type of operation."

"Martin thinks they're going to knock over a British bank down in the Wall Street area. The Police Commissioner has diverted detectives and patrolmen down there," said Langley.

"Why should they come all the way here to knock over a British bank? They want something . . . something they can only get *here*."

"Maybe." Langley paused. "We're really not getting any closer, are we?"

"Too many targets. Too much beach to guard. The attackers always have the initiative."

"I'll remember that line when I stand in front of the Commissioner."

Burke looked at his watch. "I have to meet Ferguson. He's my last play." He hung up, stepped into Third Avenue, and hailed a cab.

Burke passed through the open gate beside the armory. The zoo looked less sinister in the light of day. Children with parents or governesses walked on the paths, holding candy or balloons, or some other object that was appropriate to their mission and the setting.

The Delacorte clock showed four thirty. Brass monkeys in the clock tower suddenly came to life, circled the bell with hammers raised, and struck it. As the mast gong sounded a recording played "MacNamara's Band."

Burke found Ferguson in the Terrace Restaurant at a small table, his face buried in *The New York Times*. Two containers of tea steamed on the table. Burke pulled up a chair opposite him and took a container.

Ferguson lowered the newspaper. "Well, the word on the street is that there is to be a robbery of a major British bank in the Wall Street area."

"Who told you that?"

Ferguson didn't answer.

Burke looked over the zoo, scanning the men on the benches, then turned back to Ferguson and fixed him with a sharp look.

Ferguson said nothing. "Major Martin," Burke said, "is what is known as an agent provocateur. What his game is, I don't know yet. But I think he knows more than he's telling any of us." Burke ground out his cigarette. "All right, forget what Martin told you. Tell me what *you* think. Time is—"

Ferguson turned up the collar of his trench coat against the rising wind. "I know all about time. It's very relative, you know. When they're kneecapping you in that new way with an electric drill instead of a bullet, then time moves very slowly. If you're trying to discover something by dusk, it goes quickly. If you were ten minutes early instead of late, you might have had the time to do something."

"About what?"

Ferguson leaned across the table. "I just came from the Cathedral. John Hickey, who hasn't been inside a church since he robbed Saint Patrick's in Dublin, was sleeping in the first pew. The old man wears a beard now, but I'd know him anywhere."

"Go on."

"The four o'clock Mass is ending soon, and there'll be thousands of people coming out of the Cathedral. Quitting time for most citizens is also at five."

"Right. It's called rush hour—"

"The counties and the IRA vets are marching now. Both groups are composed of people in civilian dress, and there are people who don't know each other in each unit. Anyone could be infiltrated among them."

"I'm listening, but hurry it up."

"I have to give you my thoughts so you can deduce—"

"Go on."

"All right. The police are tired. Some units are going off duty, the crowd is restless, drunk."

"I hear you."

"Events are moving inexorably toward their end. The gathering storm is about to break."

"No poetry, please."

"Finn MacCumail is Brian Flynn. Before Maureen Malone's desertion from the IRA, she and Brian Flynn were lovers."

Burke stood. "He's going after her."

"It's the kind of insane thing a man who calls himself Finn MacCumail, Chief of the Fenians, would do."

"At the Cathedral?"

"What better place? The Irish have a love of spectacle, grand gestures. Whether they win or not is unimportant. Ireland will always remember her martyrs and heroes for their style, not their success or lack of it. So, who will soon forget the resurrected Finn MacCumail and his Fenians when they kidnap or kill his faithless lover at Saint Patrick's Cathedral in New York on Saint Patrick's Day? No, it won't be soon forgotten."

Burke's mind raced. "I didn't believe they'd hit the Cathedral . . . but it fits the facts—"

"To hell with the facts. It fits their characters. It fits with history, with destiny, with—"

"Fuck history." Burke ran toward the terrace steps. "Fuck destiny, Jack." He tore down the path toward Fifth Avenue.

Ferguson called out after him. "Too late! Too late!"

Terri O'Neal watched the IRA veterans pass on the television screen. The scene shifted from Sixty-fourth

Street to a view from the roof of Rockefeller Center. The County Tyrone unit passed in front of the Cathedral, and the camera zoomed in. She sat up and leaned closer to the television set. Her father's face suddenly filled the screen, and the announcer, who had recognized him, made a passing comment. She put her hand over her face as the enormity of what was going to happen—to her, to him, to everyone—at last dawned on her. "Oh, no.... Dad! Don't let them get away with this...."

Dan Morgan looked at her. "Even if he could hear you, there's not a thing he can do now."

The telephone rang, and Morgan answered it. He listened. "Yes, as ready as I'll ever be." He hung up, then looked at his watch and began counting off sixty seconds as he walked into the bedroom.

Terri O'Neal looked up from the television and watched him. "Is this it?"

He glanced at the parade passing by on the screen, then at her. "Yes. And God help us if we've misjudged...."

"God help you, anyway."

Morgan went into the bedroom, opened the side panel of the bay window, and waved a green shamrock flag.

CHAPTER 13

Brendan O'Connor stood with the crowd on Fifth Avenue. He looked up and saw the shamrock flag waving from the window on Sixty-fourth Street. He took a deep breath and moved behind the reviewing stands where pedestrian traffic was allowed to pass under the scrutiny of patrolmen. He lit a cigarette and watched the smoke blow southward, over his shoulder.

O'Connor reached his right hand into the pocket of his overcoat, slid the elastic off the handle of a grenade that had the pin removed, and held the handle down with his thumb. As he moved through the closely pressed crowd he pushed the grenade through a slit in his pocket and let it fall to the sidewalk. He felt the detonator handle hit his ankle as it flew off. He repeated the procedure with a grenade in his left pocket, pushing quickly through the tight crowd as it fell.

Both seven-second fuses popped in sequence. The first grenade, a CS gas canister, hissed quietly. The second grenade, a smoke signaling device, billowed huge green clouds that floated south into the stands. Brendan O'Connor kept walking. Behind him he could hear the sounds of surprise as the CS gas rose to face level, followed by the sounds of fear and panic as the smoke and choking gas swept over the crowd on the sidewalk and up to the reviewing stands. O'Connor released four more canisters through his pockets, then walked through an opening in the stone wall and disappeared into the park.

* * *

Patrick Burke vaulted the low stone wall of Central Park and barreled into the crowd on the sidewalk near the reviewing stands. Billowing green smoke rolled over the stands toward him, and even before it reached him his eyes began to tear. "Shit." He put a handkerchief to his face and ran into the Avenue, but panic had seized the marchers, and Burke was caught in the middle of the confusion. The banner of the unit had fallen to the pavement, and Burke glimpsed it under the feet of the running men—BELFAST IRISH REPUBLICAN ARMY VETERANS. As he fought his way across the Avenue, Burke could see that their ranks were laced with agitators and professional shriekers, as he called them. *Well planned*, he thought. *Well executed.*

* * *

James Sweeney put his back to the streetlight pole at Sixty-fourth Street and held his ground against the press of people around him. His hands reached through the pockets of his long trench coat and grabbed a long-handled bolt cutter hanging from his belt. He let the skirts of his coat fall over the cable connections from the mobile headquarters van as he clipped the telephone lines and then the electric power lines at the base of the pole.

Sweeney took three steps into the shoving crowd and let the bolt cutter slide into the storm drain at the curb. He allowed himself to be carried along with the flow of the moving mass of marchers and spectators up Sixty-fourth Street, away from the Avenue and the choking gas.

* * *

Inside the mobile headquarters van the telephone operators heard an odd noise, and the four telephones went dead. All the lights in the van went out a second later. One of the operators looked up at George Byrd silhouetted against a small side window. "Phones out!"

Byrd pressed his face to the small window and looked down at the base of the streetlight. "Oh Christ! Sons of bitches." He turned back and grabbed at a radio as the van driver started the engine and switched to internal power. Byrd transmitted: "All stations! Mobile at Sixty-fourth. Power line cut. We're operating radios on generator. Telephone lines cut. Situation unclear—"

Burke burst through the door and grabbed the radiophone from Byrd's hand. "Mobile at Fifty-first—do you read?"

The second mobile van beside the Cathedral answered. "Roger. All quiet here. Mounted and scooter units headed your way—"

"No! Listen—"

As the nineteen bronze bells in the north spire of St. Patrick's Cathedral chimed five o'clock, the timer on the box resting on the crossbeam above the bells completed the electrical circuit. The box, a broadband transmitter, began sending out static over the entire spectrum of the radio band. From its transmitting point, high above the street, the transmitter jammed all two-way radios in the midtown area.

A high, piercing sound filled Burke's earphone. "Mobile at Fifty-first—do you read? Action will take place at *Cathedral...*." The sound grew louder and settled into a pattern of continuous high-pitched static. "Mobile at Fifty-first..." He let the radiophone fall from his hand and turned to Byrd. "Jammed."

"I hear it—shit!" Byrd grabbed at the radio and switched to alternate command channels, but they were all filled with static. "Bastards!"

Burke grabbed his arm. "Listen, get some men to the public telephones. Call Police Plaza and the rectory. Have them try to get a message to the police around the Cathedral. The mobile van there may still have telephone communication."

"I doubt it."

"Tell them—"

"I know, I know. I heard you." Byrd sent four men out of the van. He looked out the side window at the crowd streaming by and watched his men pushing through it. He turned around to speak to Burke, but he was gone.

On the steps of the Cathedral, Maureen watched the plainclothesman standing in front of her trying to get his hand radio to work. Several policemen were running around, passing on messages and receiving orders, and she could tell by their manner that there was some confusion among them. Police were moving in and out of the van on the corner to her right. She noticed the spectators on the sidewalks; they seemed to have received some message that those on the steps had not. There was a murmur running through the crowd, and heads craned north, up the Avenue, as though the message had come from that direction as in a child's game of Pass-It-On. She looked north but could see nothing unusual except the unsettled crowd. Then she noticed that the pace of the marchers had slowed. She turned to Harold Baxter and said quietly, "Something is wrong."

The bells struck the last of the five chimes, then began their traditional five o'clock hymns with "Autumn."

Baxter nodded. "Keep alert."

The County Cork unit passed slowly in front of the Cathedral, and behind them the County Mayo unit marked time as the parade became inexplicably stalled. Parade marshals and formation marshals spoke to policemen. Maureen noticed that the Cardinal looked annoyed but not visibly concerned about the rising swell of commotion around him.

Office workers and store clerks began streaming

out of the lobbies of Rockefeller Center, the Olympic Tower, and the surrounding skyscrapers onto the already crowded sidewalks. They jostled to get away from the area, or to get a better view of the parade.

Suddenly there was a loud cry from the crowd. Maureen turned to her left. From the front doors of Saks Fifth Avenue burst a dozen men dressed in black suits and derbies. They wore white gloves and bright orange sashes across their chests, and most of them carried walking sticks. They pushed aside a police barricade and unfurled a long banner that read: GOD SAVE THE QUEEN. ULSTER WILL BE BRITISH FOREVER.

Maureen's pulse quickened, and her mind flashed back to Ulster, to the long summer marching season when the Orangemen paraded through the cities and villages, proclaiming their loyalty to God and Queen and their hate of their Catholic neighbors.

The crowd began to howl and hiss. An old IRA veteran fortified with spirits crashed through the police barrier and ran into the street, racing at the Orangemen, screaming as he ran, "Fucking bloody murdering bastards! I'll kill you!"

A half dozen of the Orangemen hoisted bullhorns and broke into song:

"A rope, a rope, to hang the Pope!
A pennyworth o' cheese to choke him!
A pint o' lamp oil to wrench it down,
And a big hot fire to roast him!"

Several of the enraged crowd broke from the sidewalks and ran into the street, spurred on by a few men who seemed to have materialized suddenly as their leaders. This vanguard was soon joined by streams of men, women, and teen-agers as the barriers began falling up and down the Avenue.

The few mounted police who had not headed to the reviewing stands formed a protective phalanx around the Orangemen, and a paddy wagon escorted by patrol cars began moving up Fiftieth Street to rescue the Orangemen from the crowd that had suddenly turned into a mob. The police swung clubs to keep the surging mob away from the still singing Orangemen. All the techniques of crowd control, learned in the Police Academy and learned on the streets, were employed in an effort to save the dozen Orangemen from being lynched, and the Orangemen themselves seemed finally to recognize their perilous position as hundreds of people ran out of control. They laid down their bullhorns and banner and joined the police in fighting their way to the safety of the approaching paddy wagon.

Patrick Burke ran south on Fifth Avenue, weaving in and out of the spectators and marchers who filled the street. He drew up in front of a parked patrol car, out of breath, and held up his badge. "Can you call mobile at the Cathedral?"

The patrolman shook his head and pointed to the static-filled radio.

"Take me to the Cathedral. Quick!" He grabbed the reardoor handle.

The uniformed sergeant sitting beside the driver called out. "No way! We can't move through this mob. If we hit someone, they'll tear us apart."

"Shit." Burke slammed the door and recrossed the Avenue. He vaulted the wall into Central Park and ran south along a path paralleling the Avenue. He came out of the park at Grand Army Plaza and began moving south through the increasingly disorderly mob. He knew it could take him half an hour to move the remaining nine blocks to the Cathedral, and he knew that the parallel avenues were probably not much better, even if he could get to them through a side street. He was not going to make it.

Suddenly a black horse appeared in front of him. A young policewoman, with blond hair tucked under her helmet, was sitting impassively atop the horse. He pushed alongside the woman and showed his badge. "Burke, Intelligence Division. I have to get to the Cathedral. Can you push this nag through this mob with me on the back?"

She regarded Burke, taking in his disheveled appearance. "This is not a nag, Lieutenant, but if you're in so much of a hurry, jump on." She reached down. Burke took her hand, put his foot in the stirrup, and swung heavily onto the rear of the horse.

The policewoman spurred the horse forward. "Giddyap! Come on, Commissioner!"

"I'm only a lieutenant."

The policewoman glanced over her shoulder as the horse began to move forward. "That's the horse's name—Commissioner."

"Oh. What's your...?"

"Police Officer Foster...Betty."

"Nice. Good names. Let's move it."

The trained police horse and the rider were in their

element, darting, weaving, cutting into every brief opening, and scattering knots of people in their path without seriously injuring anyone.

Burke held tightly to the woman's waist. He looked up and saw that they were approaching the intersection at Fifty-seventh Street. He shouted into her ear, "You dance good, Betty. Come here often?"

The policewoman turned her head and looked at him. "This run had damned well better be important, Lieutenant."

"It's the most important horse ride since Paul Revere's."

Major Bartholomew Martin stood at the window of a small room on the tenth floor of the British Empire Building in Rockefeller Center. He watched the riot that swirled around the Cathedral, then turned to the man standing beside him. "Well, Kruger, it appears that the Fenians have arrived."

The other man, an American, said, "Yes, for better or for worse." He paused, then asked, "Did you know this was going to happen?"

"Not exactly. Brian Flynn does not confide in me. I gave him some ideas, some options. His only prohibition was not to attack British property or personnel—like blowing up this building, for instance. But you never quite know with these people." Major Martin stared off into space for a few seconds, then spoke in a faraway voice. "You know, Kruger, when I finally caught up with the bastard in Belfast last winter, he was a beaten man—physically as well as mentally. All he wanted was for me to kill him quickly. And I wanted very much to accommodate him, I assure you, but then I thought better of it. I turned him around, as we say, then pointed him at America and set him loose. A dangerous business, I know, like grabbing that tiger by the tail. But it's paid off, I think."

Kruger stared at him for a long time, then said, "I hope we've calculated American public reaction correctly."

Martin smiled as he took some brandy from a flask. "If the American public was ambivalent about the Irish problem yesterday, they are not so ambivalent today." He looked at Kruger. "I'm sure this will help your service a bit."

Kruger replied, "And if it doesn't help, then you owe us a favor. In fact, I wanted to speak to you about something we have planned in Hong Kong."

"Ah, intrigue. Yes, yes, I want to hear all about it. But later. Enjoy the parade." He opened the window, and the sound of crashing windows, police sirens, and thousands of people filled the small room. "*Erin go bragh*, as they say."

CHAPTER 14

Maureen Malone felt someone tap her on the shoulder. She turned to see a man holding a badge in front of her face. "Bureau of Special Services, Miss Malone. Some of the crowd is turning their attention up here. We have to get you into the Cathedral. Mr. Baxter, you too. Please follow us."

Baxter looked down at the crowd in the street and at the police line, arms locked, at the curb. "I think we're perfectly safe here for now."

The man answered, "Sir, you have to get out of here for the safety of the other people on the steps— please—"

"Yes, yes, I see. All right. Miss Malone, he's quite right."

Maureen and Baxter turned and mounted the steps. Maureen saw the red vestments of the Cardinal as he moved through the crowded steps in front of them, flanked by two men.

Other BSS men on the steps had moved around the Monsignor and the other priests and church people, eyeing the crowd closely. Two BSS men noticed that the Cardinal, Malone, and Baxter were being led away by unknown men and began to follow, pushing their way toward the portals. Two priests on the top step fell in behind them, and the two BSS men felt the press of something hard on their backs. "Freeze," said one of the priests softly, "or we'll blow your spines open."

The police in the mobile headquarters van beside the Cathedral had lost radio communication as static filled the frequencies, but they were still reporting by telephone. Without warning an ambulance coming down Fifty-first Street swerved and sideswiped the headquarters van. The van shot forward, and the lines connecting it to the streetlamp snapped. The ambulance drivers abandoned their vehicle and disappeared quickly into the crowded lobby of the Olympic Tower.

Maureen Malone, Harold Baxter, and the Cardinal walked abreast down the main aisle of the crowded Cathedral. Two men walked behind them, and two men set the pace in front. Maureen could see that the priest in the pulpit was Father Murphy, and another priest was kneeling at the communion rail. As she moved closer to the kneeling priest she was aware that there was something familiar about him.

The Cardinal turned and looked back up the aisle, then asked his escort, "Where is Monsignor Downes? Why aren't the others with us?"

One of the men answered, "They'll be along. Please keep moving, Your Eminence."

Father Murphy tried to continue the Mass, but he was distracted again by the shouts and sirens outside. He looked out over the two thousand worshipers in the pews and in the aisles, and his eye caught a movement of brilliant red in the main aisle. He stared at the disturbing sight of the Cardinal walking toward the altar, flanked by Malone and Baxter and escorted by security men. The thought that something was happening outside to mar this great day upset him. He forgot where he was in the Mass and said abruptly, "The Mass is ended. Go in peace." He added hurriedly, "No. Wait. Stay until we know what is happening. Stay in your seats, please."

Father Murphy turned and saw the priest who had been kneeling at the communion rail now standing on the top step of the pulpit. He recognized the tall priest with the deep green eyes and was, oddly, not surprised to see him again. He cleared his throat. "Yes?"

Brian Flynn slipped a pistol from under his black coat and kept it near his side. "Stand back."

Murphy took a deep breath. "Who the hell are you?"

"I'm the new archbishop." Flynn pushed Murphy into the rear of the pulpit and took the microphone. He watched the Cardinal approaching the altar, then began to address the worshipers who were still standing in the pews. "Ladies and gentlemen," he began in a carefully measured cadence, "may I have your attention...."

Maureen Malone stopped abruptly in the open area a few feet from the altar rail. She stared up at the pulpit, transfixed by the tall, dark figure standing there in the dim light. The man behind her nudged her forward. She turned slowly. "Who are you?"

The man revealed a pistol stuck in his waistband. "Not the police, I assure you." The New York accent had disappeared, replaced by a light brogue. "Keep walking. You, too, Baxter, Your Eminence."

One of the men in front opened the gate in the marble altar railing and turned. "Come in, won't you?"

Patrick Burke, seated uneasily on the horse, looked over the heads of the crowd. Two blocks beyond he could see mass confusion, worse than that which swirled around him. The shop windows of Cartier and Gucci were broken, as were most of the other windows along the Avenue. Uniformed police stood in front of the displays of many of the shops, but there was no apparent looting, only that strange mixture of fighting and reveling that the Irish affectionately called a donnybrook. Burke could see the Cathedral now, and it was obvious that whatever had sparked this turmoil had begun there.

The crowd immediately around him was made up of marching units that were staying together, passing bottles, and singing. A brass band was playing "East Side, West Side," backed by an enthusiastic chorus. The policewoman spurred the horse on.

Midway down the block before the Cathedral the crowd became tighter, and the horse was straining to sidestep through. Bodies crushed against the riders' legs, then fell away as the horse made another lunge. "Keep pushing! Keep going!" called Burke.

The policewoman shouted, "God, they're packed so

tight...." She pulled back on the reins, and the horse reared up. The crowd scattered, and she drove into the opening, then repeated the maneuver.

Burke felt his stomach heave and caught his breath. "Nice! Nice! Good work!"

"How far do I have to get?"

"When Commissioner is kneeling at the communion rail, I'll tell you!"

Brian Flynn waited until the Cardinal and the others were safely inside the railing of the high altar, then said into the microphone, "Ladies and gentlemen, there is a small fire in the basement. Please stay calm. Leave quickly through the doors, including the front doors."

A cry went up from the congregation, and a few men interspersed throughout the Cathedral shouted, "Fire! Fire! Run!"

The pews emptied rapidly, and the aisles streamed with people pushing toward the exits. Racks of votive candles went down, spilling and cracking on the floor. The bookshop near the south spire emptied, and the first wave of people filled the vestibules and surged through the three sets of front doors, pouring out onto the steps.

The spectators on the steps suddenly found themselves pushed by a sea of people coming through the portals, and were swept down across the sidewalk, into the police barricades, through the line of policemen, and into the riot on Fifth Avenue.

Monsignor Downes tried to fight against the tide and get into the Cathedral, but found himself in the street squeezed between a heavy woman and a burly police officer.

The two bogus priests who had been pressing guns into the backs of the Bureau of Special Services men blended into the moving throng and disappeared. The two BSS men turned and tried to remount the steps but were carried down into the Avenue by the crowd.

Police scooters toppled, and patrol cars were covered with people trying to escape the crush of the crowd. Marching units broke ranks and became engulfed in the mob. Police tried to set up perimeters to keep the area of the disturbance contained, but without radio communication their actions were uncoordinated and ineffective.

Television news crews filmed the scene until they were overwhelmed by the surging mob.

Inspector Philip Langley peered down from the New York Police Department command helicopter into the darkening canyons below. He turned to Deputy Police Commissioner Rourke and shouted above the beat of the rotor blades. "I think the Saint Patrick's Day Parade is over."

The Deputy Commissioner eyed him for a long second, then looked down at the incredible scene. Rush hour traffic was stalled for miles, and a sea of people completely covered the streets and sidewalks as far south as Thirty-fourth Street and as far north as Seventy-second Street. Close to a million people were in the small midtown area at this hour, and not one of them was going to get home in time for dinner. "Lot of unhappy citizens down there, Philip."

Langley lit a cigarette. "I'll hand in my resignation tonight."

The Deputy Commissioner looked up at him. "I hope there's somebody around to accept it." He looked back at the streets. "Almost every ranking officer in the New York Police Department is down there somewhere, cut off from communication, cut off from their command." He turned to Langley. "This is the worst yet."

Langley shook his head. "I think the worst is yet to come."

In the intersection at Fiftieth Street, Burke could see the bright orange sashes of men being led into a paddy wagon. Burke remembered the Irish saying: "If you want an audience, start a fight." These Orangemen had wanted an audience, and he knew why; he knew, too, that they were not Orangemen at all but Boston Provos recruited to cause a diversion—dumb Micks with more courage than brains.

The policewoman turned to him as she urged the horse on. "Who are those people with orange sashes?"

"It's a long story. Go on. Almost there—"

Brian Flynn came down from the pulpit and faced Maureen Malone. "It's been a damned long time, Maureen."

She looked at him and replied in an even voice, "Not long enough."

He smiled. "Did you get my flowers?"

"I flushed them."

"You have one in your lapel."

Her face reddened. "So you've come to America after all, Brian."

"Yes. But as you can see, on my terms." He looked out over the Cathedral. The last of the worshipers were jamming the center vestibule, trying to squeeze through the great bronze doors. Two Fenians, Arthur Nulty dressed as a priest and Frank Gallagher dressed as a parade marshal, stood behind them and urged them on through the doors, onto the packed steps, but the crowd began to back up into the vestibule. All the other doors had been swung closed and bolted. Flynn looked at his watch. This was taking longer than he expected. He turned to Maureen. "Yes, on my terms. Do you see what I've *done*? Within half an hour all of America will see and hear this. We'll provide some good Irish theater for them. Better than the Abbey ever did."

Maureen saw in his eyes a familiar look of triumph, but mixed with that look was one of fear that she had never seen before. Like a little boy, she thought, who had stolen something from a shop and knows he might have to answer for his transgression very shortly. "You won't get away with this, you know."

He smiled, and the fear left his eyes. "Yes, I will."

Two of the Fenians who had posed as police walked around the altar and descended the stairs that led down to the sacristy. From the open archway on the left-hand wall of the sacristy, they heard footsteps approaching in the corridor that led from the rectory. Excited voices came from a similar opening on the opposite wall that led to the Cardinal's residence. All at once priests and uniformed policemen burst into the sacristy from both doors.

The two Fenians drew the sliding gates out of the wall until they met with a loud metallic ring, and the people in the sacristy looked up the stairs. A uniformed sergeant called out, "Hey! Open those gates!" He advanced toward the stairs.

The Fenians tied a chain through the scrolled brasswork and produced a padlock.

The sergeant drew his pistol. Another policeman came up behind him and did the same.

The Fenians seemed to pay no attention to the officers and snapped the heavy lock on the ends of the wrapped chain. One of them looked up, smiled, and gave a brief salute. "Sorry, lads, you'll have to go round." Both Fenians disappeared up the stairs. One of them, Pedar Fitzgerald, sat near the crypt door where he could see the gate. The other, Eamon Farrell, came around the altar and nodded to Flynn.

Flynn turned to Baxter for the first time. "Sir Harold Baxter?"

"That's correct."

He stared at Baxter. "Yes, I'd enjoy killing you."

Baxter replied without inflection, "Your kind would enjoy killing anyone."

Flynn turned away and looked at the Cardinal. "Your Eminence." He bowed his head, and it wasn't clear if he was mocking or sincere. "My name is Finn MacCumail, Chief of the new Fenian Army. This church is now mine. This is my Bruidean. You know the term? My place of sanctuary."

The Cardinal seemed not to hear him. He asked abruptly, "Is this Cathedral on fire?"

"That depends to a large extent on what happens in the next few minutes."

The Cardinal stared at him, and neither man flinched. The Cardinal finally spoke. "Get out of here. Get out while you can."

"I can't, and I don't want to." He looked up at the choir loft over the main doors where Jack Leary, dressed as a colonial soldier, stood with a rifle. Flynn's eyes dropped to the main doors nearly a block away. People still jammed the vestibule, and noise and light passed in through the open doors. He turned to Father Murphy, who stood next to him. "Father, you may leave. Hurry down the aisle before the doors close."

Murphy strode deliberately to a spot beside the Cardinal. "We are both leaving."

"No. No, on second thought, we may find a use for you later." Flynn turned to Maureen again and moved closer to her. He spoke softly. "You knew, didn't you? Even before you got the flowers?"

"I knew."

"Good. We still know each other, don't we? We've spoken over the years and across the miles, haven't we, Maureen?"

She nodded.

A young woman dressed as a nun appeared at the altar rail holding a large pistol. In the front pew a bearded old man, apparently sleeping on the bench, rose, stretched, and came up behind her. Everyone watched as the two people ascended the steps of the altar sanctuary.

The old man nodded to the hostages and spoke in a clear, vibrant voice. "Your Eminence, Father Murphy, Miss Malone, Sir Harold. I am John Hickey, fancifully code-named Dermot, in keeping with the pagan motif suggested by our leader, Finn MacCumail." He made an exaggerated bow to Flynn. "I am a poet, scholar, soldier, and patriot, much like the original Fenians. You may have heard of me." He looked around and saw the signs of recognition in the eyes of the four hostages. "No, not dead, as you can plainly see. But dead before the sun rises again, I'll wager. Dead in the ruins of this smoldering Cathedral. A magnificent funeral pyre it'll be, befitting a man of my rank. Oh, don't look so glum, Cardinal, there's a way out—if we all keep our senses about us." He turned to the young woman beside him. "May I present our Grania—or, as she prefers her real name, Megan Fitzgerald."

Megan Fitzgerald said nothing but looked into the face of each hostage. Her eyes came to rest on Maureen Malone, and she looked her up and down.

Maureen stared back at the young woman. She knew there would be a woman. There always was with Flynn. Flynn was that type of man who needed a woman watching in order to stiffen his courage, the way other men needed a drink. Maureen looked into the face of Megan Fitzgerald: high cheekboned, freckled, with a mouth that seemed set in a perpetual sneer, and eyes that should have been lovely but were something quite different. Too young, and not likely to get much older in the company of Brian Flynn. Maureen saw herself ten years before.

Megan Fitzgerald stepped up to her, the big pistol swinging nonchalantly from her left hand, and put her mouth close to Maureen's ear. "You understand that I'm looking for an excuse to kill you."

"I hope I find the courage to do something to give you one. Then we'll see how *your* courage stands up."

Megan Fitzgerald's body tensed visibly. After a few seconds she stepped back and looked around the altar, sweeping each person standing there with a cold stare and meeting Flynn's look of disapproval. She turned, walked down from the altar, and then strode down the main aisle toward the center doors.

Flynn watched her, then looked past her into the vestibule. The doors were still open. He hadn't counted on the crowd being so large. If they couldn't get the doors closed and bolted soon, the police would force their way in and there would be a fire fight. As he watched, Megan passed into the vestibule and raised her pistol. He saw the smoke flash from the upturned muzzle of her gun, then heard the report roll through the massive church and echo in and out of the vaults and side altars. A scream went up from the crowd in the vestibule, and their backs receded as they found a new strength and a more immediate reason to push through the crowd blocking the steps.

Flynn watched Megan bring the gun down into a horizontal position and aim it at the opening. Nulty and Gallagher maneuvered around, and each took up a position behind the doors, pushing them against the last of the fleeing worshipers.

Megan dropped to one knee and steadied her aim with both hands.

Patrick Burke shouted to the policewoman, "Up the steps! Up to the front door!"

Betty Foster spurred the horse up the steps where they curved around to Fifty-first Street, and moved diagonally through the crowd toward the center doors.

Burke saw the last of the worshipers flee through the doors, and the horse broke into the open space between them and the portals. The policewoman reined the horse around and kicked its flanks. "Come on, Commissioner! Up! Up!"

Burke drew his service revolver and shouted, "Draw your piece! Through the doors!"

Betty Foster held the reins with her left hand and drew her revolver.

A few yards from the portals the big bronze ceremonial doors—sixteen feet across, nearly two stories high, and weighing ten thousand pounds apiece—began closing. Burke knew they were pushed by unseen persons standing behind them. The dimly lit vestibule came into sight, and he saw a nun kneeling there. Behind her, the vast, deserted Cathedral stretched back a hundred yards, through a forest of stone columns, to the raised altar sanctuary where Burke could see people standing. A figure in bright red stood out against the white marble.

The doors were half closed now, and the horse's head was a yard from the opening. Burke knew they were going to make it. And then...what?

Suddenly the image of the kneeling nun filled his

brain, and his eyes focused on her again. From her extended arm Burke saw a flash of light, then heard a loud, echoing sound followed by a sharp crack.

The horse's front legs buckled, and the animal pitched forward. Burke was aware of Betty Foster flying into the air, then felt himself falling forward. His face struck the granite step a foot from the doors. He crawled toward the small opening, but the bronze doors came together and shut in his face. He heard, above all the noise around him, the sound of the floor bolts sliding home.

Burke rolled onto his back and sat up. He turned to the policewoman, who was lying on the steps, blood running from her forehead. As he watched, she sat up slowly.

Burke stood and offered her his hand, but she got to her feet without his aid and looked down at her mount. A small wound on Commissioner's chest ran with blood; frothy blood trickled from the horse's open mouth and steamed in a puddle as it collected on the cold stone. The horse tried to stand but fell clumsily back onto its side. Betty Foster fired into his head. After putting her hand to the horse's nostrils to make certain he was dead, she holstered her revolver. She looked up at Burke, then back at her horse. Walking slowly down the steps, she disappeared into the staring crowd.

Burke looked out into the Avenue. Rotating beacons from the police cars cast swirling red and white light on the chaotic scene and across the façades of the surrounding buildings. Occasionally, above the general bedlam, Burke could hear a window smash, a whistle blow, a scream ring out.

He turned around and stared at the Cathedral. Taped to one of the bronze ceremonial doors, over the face of St. Elizabeth Seton, was a piece of cardboard with handlettering on it. He stepped closer to read it in the fading light.

THIS CATHEDRAL IS UNDER THE CONTROL OF
THE IRISH
FENIAN ARMY

It was signed, FINN MACCUMAIL.

BOOK IV

The Cathedral: Siege

Friendship, joy and peace! If the outside world only realized the wonders of this Cathedral, there would never be a vacant pew.
—Parishioner

CHAPTER 15

Patrick Burke stood at the front doors of St. Patrick's Cathedral, his hands in his pockets and a cigarette in his mouth. Lightly falling sleet melted on the flanks of the dead horse and ran in rivulets onto the icy stone steps.

The crowds in the surrounding streets were not completely under control, but the police had rerouted the remainder of the marching units west to Sixth Avenue. Burke could hear drums and bagpipes above the roar of the mob. The two hundred and twenty-third St. Patrick's Day Parade would go on until the last marcher arrived at Eighty-fourth Street, even if it meant marching through Central Park to get there.

Automobile horns were blaring incessantly, and police whistles and sirens cut through the windy March dusk. *What a fucking mess.* Burke wondered if anyone out there knew that the Cathedral was under the control of gunmen. He looked at his watch—not yet five thirty. The six o'clock news would begin early and not end until this ended.

Burke turned and examined the bronze ceremonial

doors, then put his shoulder to one of them and pushed. The door moved slightly, then sprang back, closing. From behind the doors Burke heard a shrill alarm. "Smart sons of bitches." It wasn't going to be easy to get the Cathedral away from Finn MacCumail. He heard a muffled voice call out from behind the door. "Get away! We're putting mines on the doors!"

Burke moved back and stared up at the massive doors, noticing them for the first time in twenty years. On a righthand panel a bronze relief of St. Patrick stared down at him, a crooked staff in one hand, a serpent in the other. To the saint's right was a Celtic harp, to his left the mythical phoenix, appropriated from the pagans, rising to renewed life from its own ashes. Burke turned slowly and started walking down the steps. "Okay, Finn or Flynn, or whatever you call yourself—you may have gotten in standing tall, but you won't be leaving that way."

Brian Flynn stood at the railing of the choir loft and looked out over the vast Cathedral spread out over an area larger than a football field. Seventy towering stained-glass windows glowed with the outside lights of the city like dripping jewels, and dozens of hanging chandeliers cast a soft luminescence over the dark wooden pews. Rows of gray granite pillars reached up to the vaulted ceiling like the upraised arms of the faithful supporting the house of God. Flynn turned to John Hickey. "It would take some doing to level this place."

"Leave it to me, Brian."

Flynn said, "The first priority of the police is that

mob out there. We've bought some time to set up our defense." Flynn raised a pair of field glasses and looked at Maureen. Even at this distance he saw that her face was red, and her jaw was set in a hard line. He focused on Megan who had assembled three men and two women and was making an inspection of the perimeter walls. She had taken off the nun's wimple, revealing long red hair that fell to her shoulders. She walked quickly, now peeling off her nun's habit and throwing the black and white garments carelessly onto the floor until she was clad in only jeans and a T-shirt, which had a big red apple on it and the words *I Love New York*. She stopped by the north transept doors and looked up at the southeast triforium as she called out, "Gallagher!"

Frank Gallagher, dressed in the morning coat and striped pants of a parade marshal, leaned over the balcony parapet and pointed his sniper rifle at her, taking aim through the scope. He shouted back, "Check!"

Megan moved on.

Flynn unrolled a set of blueprints and rested them on the rail of the choir loft. He tapped the plans of the Cathedral with his open hand and said, as though the realization had just come to him, "We took it."

Hickey nodded and stroked his wispy beard. "Aye, but can we keep it? Can we hold it with a dozen people against twenty thousand policemen?"

Flynn turned to Jack Leary standing near the organ keyboard beside him. "Can we hold it, Jack?"

Leary nodded slowly. "Twenty thousand, or twenty, they can only come in a few at a time." He patted his modified M-14 rifle with attached scope. "Anyone who survives the mines on the doors will be dead before he gets three paces."

Flynn looked closely at Leary in the subdued light. Leary looked comical in his colonial marching uniform and with his green-painted rifle. But there was nothing funny about his eyes or his expressionless voice.

Flynn looked back over the Cathedral and glanced at the blueprints. This building was shaped like a cross. The long stem of the cross was the nave, holding the main pews and five aisles; the cross-arms were the transepts, containing more pews and an exit from the end of each arm. Two arcaded triforia, long, dark galleries supported by columns, overhung the nave, running as far as the transepts. Two shorter triforia began at the far side of the transepts and overlooked the altar. This was the basic layout of the structure to be defended.

Flynn looked at the top of the blueprints. They showed the five-story rectory nestled in the northeast quadrant of the cross outside the Cathedral. The rectory was connected to the Cathedral by basement areas under the terraces, which did not appear on the blueprints. In the southeast quadrant was the Cardinal's residence, also separated by terraces and gardens and connected underground. These uncharted connections, Flynn understood, were a weak point in the defense. "I wish we could have held the two outside buildings."

Hickey smiled. "Next time."

Flynn smiled in return. The old man had remained an enigma, swinging precipitantly between clownishness and decisiveness. Flynn looked back at the blueprints.

The top of the cross was the rounded area called the apse. In the apse was the Lady Chapel, a quiet, serene area of long, narrow stained-glass windows. Flynn pointed to the blueprint. "The Lady Chapel has no outside connections, and I've decided not to post a man there—can't spare anyone."

Hickey leaned over the blueprints. "I'll examine it for hidden passages. Church architecture wouldn't be church architecture, Brian, without hollow walls and secret doors. Places for the Holy Ghost to run about— places where priests can pop up on you unawares and scare the hell out of you by whispering your name."

"Have you heard of Whitehorn Abbey outside of Belfast?"

"I spent a night there once. Did you get a scare there, lad?" Hickey laughed.

Flynn looked out over the Cathedral again, concentrating on the raised area of black and white marble called the altar sanctuary. In the middle of the sanctuary sat the altar, raised still higher on a broad marble plinth. The cold marble and bronze of the area was softened by fields of fresh green carnations, symbolizing, Flynn imagined, the green sod of Ireland, which would not have looked or smelled as nice on the altar.

On both sides of the sanctuary were rows of wooden pews reserved for clergy. In the pews to the right sat Maureen, Baxter, and Father Murphy, all looking very still from this distance. Flynn placed his field glasses to his eyes and focused on Maureen again. She didn't appear at all frightened, and he liked that. He noticed that her lips were moving as she stared straight ahead. Praying? No, not Maureen. Baxter's lips were moving also. And Father Murphy's. "They're plotting dark things against us, John."

"Good," said Hickey. "Maybe they'll keep us entertained."

Flynn swung the field glasses to the left. Facing the hostages across the checkered marble floor sat the Cardinal on his elevated throne of red velvet, absolutely motionless. "No sanctuary in the sanctuary," commented Flynn under his breath.

Leary heard him and called out, "A sanctuary of sorts. If they leave that area, I'll kill them."

Flynn leaned farther over the rail. Directly behind the altar were the sacristy stairs, not visible from the loft, where Pedar Fitzgerald, Megan's brother, sat on the landing holding a submachine gun. Fitzgerald was a good man, a man who knew that those chained gates had to be protected at any cost. He had his sister's courage without her savagery. "We still don't know if there's a way they can enter the crypt from an underground route and come up behind Pedar."

Hickey glanced again at the blueprints. "We'll get the crypt keys and the keys to this whole place later and have a proper look around the real estate. We need time, Brian. Time to tighten our defense. Damn these blueprints, they're not very detailed. And damn this church. It's like a marble sieve with more holes in it than the story of the Resurrection."

"I hope the police don't get hold of the architect."

"You should have kidnapped him last night along with Terri O'Neal," Hickey said.

"Too obvious. That would have put Intelligence onto something."

"Then you should have killed him and made it look like an accident."

Flynn shook his head. "One has to draw a line somewhere. Don't you think so?"

"You're a lousy revolutionary. It's a wonder you've come as far as you have."

"I've come farther than most. I'm here."

CHAPTER 16

Major Bartholomew Martin put down his field glasses and let out a long breath. "Well, they've done it. No apparent casualties...except that fine horse." He closed the window against the cold wind and sleet. "Burke almost got himself killed, however."

Kruger shrugged. It never paid to examine these things too closely.

Major Martin put on his topcoat. "Sir Harold was a good sort. Played a good game of bridge. Anyway, you see, Flynn went back on his word. Now they'll want to kill poor Harry as soon as things don't go their way."

Kruger glanced out the window. "I think you planned on Baxter getting kidnapped."

Major Martin moved toward the door. "I planned *nothing*, Kruger. I only provided the opportunity and the wherewithal. Most of this is as much a surprise to me as it is to you and the police." Martin looked at his watch. "My consulate will be looking for me, and your people will be looking for you. Remember, Kruger, the first requirement of a successful liar is a good memory. Don't forget what you're not supposed to know, and please remember the things you *are* supposed to know." He pulled on his gloves as he left.

* * *

Megan Fitzgerald motioned to the three men and two women with her and moved quickly toward the front of the Cathedral. The five of them followed her, burdened with suitcases, slung rifles, and rocket tubes. They entered the vestibule of the north tower, rode up the small elevator, and stepped off into the choir practice room in the tower. Megan moved into the choir loft.

Jack Leary was standing at the end of the loft, some distance from Flynn and Hickey, establishing his fields of fire. Megan said curtly, "Leary, you understand your orders?"

The sniper turned and stared at her.

Megan stared back into his pale, watery eyes. Soft eyes, she thought, but she knew how they hardened as the rifle traveled up to his shoulder. Eyes that saw things not in fluid motion but in a series of still pictures, like a camera lens. She had watched him in practice many times. Perfect eye-hand coordination—"muscle memory" he had called it on the one occasion he had spoken to her. Muscle memory—a step below instinct, as though the brain wasn't even involved in the process— optic nerves and motor nerves, bypassing the brain, controlled by some primitive bundle of fibers found only in the lower forms of life. The others stayed away from Leary, but Megan was fascinated by him. "Answer me, Leary. Do you know your orders, man?"

He nodded almost imperceptibly as his eyes took in the young woman standing in front of him.

Megan walked along the rail and came up beside Flynn and Hickey. She placed the field phone on the railing and looked at the outside telephone on the organ. "Call the police."

Flynn didn't look up from the blueprints. "They'll call us."

Hickey said to her, "I'd advise you not to upset Mr. Leary. He seems incapable of witty bantering, and he'd probably shoot you if he couldn't think of anything to say."

Megan looked back at Leary, then said to Hickey, "We understand each other."

Hickey smiled. "Yes, I've noticed a silent communication between you—but what other type could there be with a man who has a vocabulary of fourteen words, eight of which have to do with rifles?"

Megan turned and walked back to the entrance of the choir practice room where the others were waiting, and she led them up a spiral iron staircase. At a level above the choir practice room she found a door and kicked it open, motioning to Abby Boland. "Come with me," she said.

The long triforium stretched out along the north side of the Cathedral, an unlit gallery of dusty stone and air-conditioning ducts. A flagpole of about twenty feet in length jutted out from the parapet over the nave, flying the white and yellow Papal flag.

Megan turned to Abby Boland, who was dressed in the short skirt and blue blouse of a twirler from Mother Cabrini High School, a place neither of them had heard of until a week before. "This is your post," said Megan. "Remember, the rocket is to use if you see a Saracen—or whatever they call them here—coming through your assigned door. The sniper rifle is for close-in defense, if they come through the tower door there—and for blowing your own brains out if you've a mind to. Any questions? No?" She looked the girl up and down. "You should have thought to bring some clothes with you. It'll be cold up here tonight." Megan returned to the tower.

Abby Boland unslung her rifles and put them down beside the rocket. She slipped off her tight-fitting shoes, unbuttoned her constricting blouse, and sighted through the scope of the sniper rifle, then lowered it and looked around. It occurred to her that rather than freeing her husband, Jonathan, she might very well end up in jail herself, on this side of the Atlantic, too long a distance to intertwine their fingers through the mesh wire of Long Kesh. She might also end up dead, of course, which might be better for both of them.

Megan Fitzgerald continued up the stairs of the bell tower and turned into a side passage. She found a pull chain and lit a small bulb revealing a section of the huge attic. Wooden catwalks ran over the plaster lathing of the vaulted ceiling below and stretched back into the darkness. The four people with her walked quickly over the catwalks, turning on lights in the cold, musty attic.

Megan could see the ten dormered hatches overhead that led to the slate roof above. On the floor, at intervals, were small winches that lowered the chandeliers to the floors below for maintenance. She turned and moved to the big arched window at the front peak of the attic. Stone tracery on the outside of the Cathedral partially blocked the view, and grime covered the small panes in front of her. She wiped a section with her hand and stared down into Fifth Avenue. The block in front of the Cathedral was nearly deserted, but the police had not yet cleared the crowds out of the intersections on either side. Falling sleet was visible against the streetlights, and ice covered the streets and sidewalks and collected on the shoulders of Atlas.

Megan looked up at the International Building in Rockefeller Center directly across from her. The two side wings of the building were lower than the attic, and she could see people moving through the ice, people sitting huddled on the big concrete tubs that held bare plants and trees. The uniformed police had no rifles, and she knew that the Cathedral was not yet surrounded by the SWAT teams euphemistically called the Emergency Services Division in New York. She saw no soldiers, either, and remembered that Americans rarely called on them.

She turned back to the attic. The four people had opened the suitcases and deposited piles of votive candles at intervals along the catwalks. Megan called out to Jean Kearney and Arthur Nulty. "Find the fire axes, chop wood from the catwalks, and build pyres around the candles. Cut the fire hoses up here and string the wire for the field telephone. Be quick about it. Mullins and Devane, grab an ax and come with me."

Megan Fitzgerald retraced her steps out of the attic, followed by the two men who had posed as BSS Security, Donald Mullins and Rory Devane. She continued her climb up to the bell tower. Mullins carried a roll of communication wire, which he played out behind him. Devane carried the weapons and axes.

Arthur Nulty offered Jean Kearney a cigarette. He looked over her Kelly-green Aer Lingus stewardess uniform. "You look very sexy, lass. Would it be a sacrilege to do it up here, do you think?"

"We'll not have time for that."

"Time is all we've got up here. God, but it's cold. We'll need some warming and there's no spirits allowed, so that leaves..."

"We'll see. Jesus, Arthur, if your wife—what happens to us if we get her out of Armagh?"

Arthur Nulty let go of her arm and looked away. "Well...now...let's take things one a time." He picked up an ax and swung it, shattering a wooden railing, then ripped the railing from its post and threw it atop a pile of votive candles. "Whole place is wood up here. Never thought I'd be burning a church. If Father Flannery could see me now." He took another swing with the ax. "Jesus, I hope it doesn't come to that. They'll give in before they see this Cathedral burned. In twenty-four hours your brothers will be in Dublin. Your old dad will be pleased, Jean. He thought he'd never see the boys again." He threw a post on the woodpile. "She called them pyres, Megan did. Doesn't she know that pyres refer only to places to burn corpses?"

CHAPTER 17

Patrick Burke posted patrolmen at each of the Cathedral's portals with the warning that the doors were mined, then came back to the front of the Cathedral and approached a parked patrol car. "Any commo yet?"

The patrolman shook his head. "No, sir. What's going on in there?"

"There are armed gunmen inside, so keep pushing the crowd back. Tell the officer in charge to begin a cordon operation."

"Yes, sir." The patrol car moved away through the nearly deserted Avenue.

Burke remounted the steps and saw Police Officer Betty Foster kneeling in the ice beside her horse.

She looked up at him. "You still here?" She looked back at the horse. "I have to get the saddle." She unhooked the girth. "What the hell's going on in there?" She tugged at the saddle. "You almost got me killed."

He helped her pull at the saddle, but it wouldn't come loose. "Leave this here."

"I can't. It's police property."

"There's police property strewn up and down Fifth

Avenue." He let go of the saddle and looked at the bell tower. "There'll be people in these towers soon, if they're not there already. Get this later when they recover the horse."

She straightened up. "Poor Commissioner. Both of them."

"What do you mean?"

"Police Commissioner Dwyer died of a heart attack—at the reviewing stands."

"Jesus Christ." Burke heard a noise from the bell tower overhead and pulled Betty Foster under the alcove of the front door. "Somebody's up there."

"Are you staying here?"

"Until things get straightened out."

She looked at him and said, "Are you brave, Lieutenant Burke?"

"No. Just stupid."

"That's what I thought." She laughed. "God, I thought I was going to pass out when I saw that nun—I guess it wasn't a nun—"

"Not likely."

"That woman, pointing a gun at us."

"You did fine."

"Did I? I guess I did." She paused and looked around. "I'm going to be on duty for a long time. I have to go back to Varick Street and get remounted."

"Remounted?" A bizarre sexual image flashed through his mind. "Oh. Right. Keep close to the wall. I don't know if those people up in the tower are looking for blue targets, but it's better to assume they are."

She hesitated. "See you later." She moved out of the alcove, keeping close to the wall. She called back, "I didn't just come back for the saddle. I wanted to see if you were all right."

Burke watched her round the corner of the tower. This morning neither he nor Betty Foster would have given each other a second glance. Now, however, they had things going for them—riots, gunpowder, horses—great stimulants, powerful aphrodisiacs. He looked at his watch. This lull would not last much longer.

Megan Fitzgerald climbed into the bell room and stood catching her breath as she looked around the cold room, peering into the weak light cast by the single bulb. She saw Flynn's radio jamming device on a crossbeam from which hung three huge bells, each with a turning wheel and a pull strap. Gusts of cold March wind blew in from the eight sets of copper louvers in the octagon-shaped tower room. The sound of police bullhorns and sirens was carried up into the eighteen-story-high room.

Megan grabbed a steel-cut fire ax from Rory Devane, turned suddenly, and swung it at one of the sets of louvers, ripping them open and letting in the lights of the city. Mullins set to work on the other seven louvers, cutting them out of their stone casements as Devane knelt on the floor and connected a field telephone.

Megan turned to Mullins, who had moved to the window overlooking Fifth Avenue. "Remember, Mullins, report *anything* unusual. Keep a sharp eye for helicopters. No shooting without orders."

Mullins looked out at Rockefeller Center. People

were pressed to the windows opposite him, and, on the roofs below, people were pointing up at the ripped louvers. A police spotlight in the street came on, and its white beam circled and came to rest on the opening where Mullins stood. He moved back and blinked his eyes. "I'd like to put that spot out."

Megan nodded. "Might as well set them straight now."

Mullins leaned out of the opening and squinted into his sniper scope. He saw figures moving around at the periphery of the spotlight. He took a long breath, steadied his aim, then squeezed the trigger. The sound of the rifle exploded in the bell room, and Mullins saw the red tracer round streak down into the intersection. The spotlight suddenly lost its beam, fading from white to red to black. A hollow popping sound drifted into the bell room, followed by sounds of shouting. Mullins stepped back behind the stonework and blew his nose into a handkerchief. "Cold up here."

Devane sat on the floor and cranked the field phone. "Attic, this is bell tower. Can you hear me?"

The voice of Jean Kearney came back clearly. "Hear you, bell tower. What was that noise?"

Devane answered. "Mullins put out a spot. No problem."

"Roger. Stand by for commo check with choir loft. Choir loft, can you hear bell tower and attic?"

John Hickey's voice came over the line. "Hear you both. Commo established. Who the hell authorized you to shoot at a spotlight?"

Megan grabbed the field phone from Devane. "I did."

Hickey's voice had an edge of sarcasm and annoyance. "Ah, Megan, that was a rhetorical question, lass. I knew the answer to that. Watch yourself today."

Megan dropped the field phone on the floor and looked down at Devane. "Go on down and string the wire from the choir loft to the south tower, then knock out the louvers and take your post there."

Devane picked up a roll of communication wire and the fire ax and climbed down out of the bell room.

Megan moved from opening to opening. The walls of the Cathedral were bathed in blue luminescence from the Cathedral's floodlights in the gardens. To the north the massive fifty-one-story Olympic Tower reflected the Cathedral from its glass sides. To the east the Waldorf-Astoria's windows were lit against the black sky, and to the south the Cathedral's twin tower rose up, partially blocking the view of Saks Fifth Avenue. Police stood on the Saks roof, milling around, flapping their arms against the cold. In all the surrounding streets the crowd was being forced back block by block, and the deserted area around the Cathedral grew in size.

Megan looked back at Mullins, who was blowing into his hands. His young face was red with cold, and tinges of blue showed on his lips. She moved to the ladder in the middle of the floor. "Keep alert."

He watched Megan disappear down the ladder and suddenly felt lonely. "Bitch." She was not much older than he, but her movements, her voice, were those of an older woman. She had lost her youth in everything but her face and body.

Mullins looked around his solitary observation post,

then peered back into Fifth Avenue. He unfastened a rolled flag around his waist and tied the corners to the louvers, then let it unfurl over the side of the tower. A wind made it snap against the gray marble, and the Cathedral's floodlights illuminated it nicely.

From the street and the rooftops an exclamation rose from the reporters and civilians still in the area. A few people cheered, and a few applauded. There were a few jeers as well.

Mullins listened to the mixed reaction, then pulled his head back into the tower and wiped the cold sleet from his face. He wondered with a sense of awe how he came to be standing in the bell tower of St. Patrick's Cathedral with a rifle. Then he remembered his older sister, Peg, widowed with three children, pacing the prison yard of Armagh. He remembered the night her husband, Barry Collins, was killed trying to take a prison van that was supposed to contain Maureen Malone's sister, Sheila. He remembered his mother looking after Peg's three children for days at a time while Peg went off with hard-looking men in dark coats. Mullins remembered the night he went into the streets of Belfast to find Brian Flynn and his Fenians, and how his mother wept and cursed after him. But most of all he remembered the bombs and gunfire that had rocked and split the Belfast nights ever since he was a child. Thinking back, he didn't see how he could have traveled any road that didn't lead here, or someplace like it.

Patrick Burke looked up. A green flag, emblazoned with the gold Irish harp, hung from the ripped louvers, and Burke could make out a man with a rifle standing in the opening. Burke turned and watched the police in the intersection wheeling away the smashed spotlight. The crowd was becoming more cooperative, concluding that anyone who could put out a spotlight at two hundred yards could put them out just as easily. Burke moved into the alcove of the tower door and spoke to the policeman he had posted there. "We'll just stand here awhile. That guy up there is still manufacturing adrenaline."

"I know the feeling."

Burke looked out over the steps. The green carpet was white with sleet now, and green carnations, plastic leprechaun hats, and paper pompoms littered the steps, sidewalks, and street. In the intersection of Fiftieth Street a huge Lambeg drum left by the Orangemen lay on its side. Black bowlers and bright orange sashes moved slowly southward in the wind. From the buildings of Rockefeller Center news cameramen were cautiously getting it all on film. Burke pictured it as it would appear on television. Zoom-in shots of the debris, a bowler tumbling end over end across the icy street. The voice-over, deep, resonant—"Today the ancient war between the English and the Irish came to Fifth Avenue...." The Irish always gave you good theater.

* * *

Brian Flynn leaned out over the parapet rail of the choir loft and pointed to a small sacristy off the ambulatory as he said to Hickey, "Since we can't see the outside door of the bishop's sacristy or the elevator door, the police could theoretically beat the alarms and mines. Then we'd have policemen massed in that small sacristy."

Leary, who seemed to be able to hear things at great distances, called out from the far end of the choir loft. "And if they stick their heads into the ambulatory, I'll blow—"

Hickey shouted back, "Thank you, Mr. Leary. We know you will." He said softly to Flynn, "God Almighty, where'd you get that monster? I'll be afraid to scratch my ass down there."

Flynn answered quietly, "Yes, he has good eyes and ears."

"An American, isn't he?"

"Irish-American. Marine sniper in Vietnam."

"Does he know why he's here? Does he even know where the hell he *is*?"

"He's in a perch overlooking a free-fire zone. That's all he knows and all he cares about. He's being paid handsomely for his services. He's the only one of us besides you and me who has no relatives in British jails. I don't want a man up here with emotional ties to us. He'll kill according to standing orders, he'll kill any one of us I tell him to kill, and if we're attacked and overcome, he'll kill any of us who survives, if he's still able. He's the Angel of Death, the Grim Reaper, and the court of last resort."

"Does everyone know all of this?"

"No."

Hickey smiled, a half-toothless grin. "I underestimated you, Brian."

"Yes. You've been doing that. Let's go on with this.

The Archbishop's sacristy—a problem, but only one of many—"

"I wish you'd brought more people."

Flynn spoke impatiently. "I have a great deal of help on the outside, but how many people do you think I could find to come in here to die?"

A distant look came over the old man's face. "There were plenty of good men and women in Dublin on Easter Monday, 1916. More than the besieged buildings could hold." Hickey's eyes took in the quiet Cathedral below. "No lack of volunteers then. And faith! What faith we all had. In the early days of the First War, sometime before the Easter Rising, my brother was in the British Army. Lot of Irish lads were then. Still are. You've heard of the Angels of Mons? No? Well, my brother Bob was with the British Expeditionary Force in France, and they were about to be annihilated by an overwhelming German force. Then, at a place called Mons, a host of heavenly angels appeared and stood between them and the Germans. Understandably the Germans fell back in confusion. It was in all the papers at the time. And people *believed* it, Brian. They believed the British Army was so blessed by God that He sent His angels to intervene on their behalf against their enemy."

Flynn looked at him. "Sounds like a mass hallucination of desperate men. When we start seeing angels here, we'll know we've had it, and—" He broke off abruptly and looked at Hickey closely in the dim light. For a brief second he imagined he was back in Whitehorn Abbey, listening to the stories of the old priest.

"What is it, lad?"

"Nothing. I suppose one shouldn't doubt the intervention of the supernatural. I'll tell you about it tomorrow."

Hickey laughed. "If you can tell it tomorrow, I'll believe it."

Flynn forced a smile in return. "I may be telling it to you in another place."

"Then I'll surely believe it."

Megan Fitzgerald came up behind George Sullivan setting the last of the mines on the south transept door. "Finished?"

Sullivan turned abruptly. "Jesus, don't do that, Megan, when I'm working with explosives."

She looked at Sullivan, dressed splendidly in the kilts of a bagpiper of the New York Police Emerald Society. "Grab your gear and follow me. Bring your bagpipes." She led him to a small door at the corner of the transept, and they walked up a spiral stone staircase, coming out onto the long south triforium. A flagpole with a huge American flag hanging from it pointed across the nave toward the Papal flag on the opposite triforium. Megan looked to the left, at the choir loft below, and watched Flynn and Hickey poring over their blueprints like two generals on the eve of battle. She found it odd that such different men seemed to be getting on well. She hadn't liked the idea of bringing John Hickey in at the last moment. But the others felt they needed the old hero to legitimize themselves, a bona fide link with 1916, as though Hickey's presence could make them something other than the outcasts they all were.

She saw no need to draw on the past. The world had taken form for her in 1973 when she had seen her first bomb casualties in downtown Belfast on the way home from school, and had taken meaning and purpose when her older brother Tommy had been wounded and captured trying to free Sheila Malone. The distant past didn't exist, any more than the near future did. Her own personal memories were all the history she was concerned with.

She watched Flynn pointing and gesturing. He seemed not much different from the old man beside him. Yet he had been different once. To Tommy Fitzgerald, Brian Flynn was everything a man should be, and she had grown up seeing Brian Flynn, the legend in the making, through her older brother's eyes. Then came Brian's arrest and his release, suspicious at best. Then the break with the IRA, the forming of the new Fenian Army, his recruiting of her and her younger brother Pedar, and, finally, her inevitable involvement with him. She had not been disappointed in him as a lover, but as a revolutionary he had flaws. He would hesitate before destroying the Cathedral, but she would see to it that this decision was out of his hands.

Sullivan called out from the far end of the triforium, "The view is marvelous. How's the food?"

Megan turned to him. "If you've no qualms about feasting on blood, it's good and ample."

Sullivan sighted through his rifle. "Don't be a beast, Megan." He raised the rifle and focused the scope on Abby Boland, noticing her open blouse. She saw him and waved. He waved back. "So near, yet so far."

"Give it a rest, George," said Megan impatiently. "You'll not be using it for much but peeing for yet a while." She looked at him closely. George Sullivan was not easily intimidated by her. He had that combination of smugness and devil-may-care personality that came with handling high explosives, a special gift of the gods, he had called it. Maybe. "Are you certain Hickey knows how to rig the bombs?"

Sullivan picked up his bagpipe and began blowing into it. He looked up. "Oh, yes. He's very good. World War Two techniques, but that's all right, and he's got the nerve for it."

"I'm interested in his skill, not his nerve. I'm to be his assistant."

"Good for you. Best to be close by if it goes wrong. Never feel a thing. It'll be us poor bastards up here who'll be slowly crushed by falling stone. Picture it, Megan. Like Samson and Delilah, the temple falling about our heads, tons of stone quivering, falling.... Someone should have brought a movie camera."

"Next time. All right, George, the north transept is your sector of fire if they break in. But if they use armor through that door, Boland will lean over the north triforium and launch a rocket directly down at it. Your responsibility for armor is the south transept door below you. She'll cover you and you'll cover her with rifle fire."

"What if one of us is dead?"

"Then the other two, Gallagher and Farrell, will divide up the sector of the dead party."

"What if we're all dead?"

"Then it doesn't matter, does it, George? Besides, there's always Leary. Leary is immortal, you know."

"I've heard." He put the blowpipe to his mouth.

"Can you play 'Come Back to Erin'?"

He nodded as he puffed.

"Then play it for us, George."

He took a long breath and said, "To use an expression, Megan, you've not paid the piper, and you'll not call the tune. I'll play 'The Minstrel Boy' and you'll damn well like it. Go on, now, and leave me alone."

Megan looked at him, turned abruptly, and entered the small door that led down to the spiral stairs.

Sullivan finished inflating the bagpipe, bounced a few notes off the wall behind him, made the necessary tuning, then turned, bellied up to the stone parapet, and began to play. The haunting melody carried into every corner of the Cathedral and echoed off the stone. Acoustically bad for an organ or choir, Sullivan thought, but for a bagpipe it was lovely, sounding like the old Celtic warpipes echoing through the rocky glens of Antrim. The pipes were designed to echo from stone, he thought, and now that he heard his pipes in here, he would recommend their use in place of organs in Ireland. He had never sounded better.

He saw Abby Boland leaning across the parapet, looking at him, and he played to her, then turned east and played to his wife in Armagh prison, then turned to the wall behind him and played softly for himself.

CHAPTER 18

Brian Flynn listened to Sullivan for a few seconds. "The lad's not bad."

Hickey found his briar pipe and began filling it. "Reminds me of those Scottish and Irish regiments in the First War. Used to go into battle with pipes skirling. Jerry's machine guns ripped them up. Never missed a note, though—good morale-builder." He looked down at the blueprints. "I'm beginning to think whoever designed this place designed Tut's tomb."

"Same mentality. Tricks with stone. Fellow named Renwick in this case. There's a likeness of him on one of those stainedglass windows. Over there. Looks shifty."

"Even God looks shifty in stained glass, Brian."

Flynn consulted the blueprints. "Look, there are six large supporting piers—they're towers, actually. They all have doors either on the inside or outside of the Cathedral, and they all have spiral staircases that go into the triforia....All except this one, which passes through Farrell's triforium. It has no doors, either on the blueprints or in actuality."

"How did he get up there?"

"From the next tower which has an outside door." Flynn looked up at Eamon Farrell. "I told him to look for the way into this tower, but he hasn't found it."

"Aye, and probably never will. Maybe that's where they burn heretics. Or hide the gold."

"Well, you may joke about it, but it bothers me. Not even a church architect wastes time and money building a tower from basement to roof without putting it to some use. I'm certain there's a staircase in there, and entrances as well. We'll have to find out where."

"We may find out quite unexpectedly," said Hickey.

"That we may."

"Later," said Hickey, "perhaps I'll call on Renwick's ghost for help."

"I'd settle for the present architect. Stillway." Flynn tapped his finger on the blueprints. "I think there are more hollow spaces here than even Renwick knew. Passages made by masons and workmen—not unusual in a cathedral of this size and style."

"Anyway, you've done a superb job, Brian. It will take the police some time to formulate an attack."

"Unless *they* get hold of Stillway and his set of blueprints before our people on the outside find him." He turned and looked at the telephone mounted on the organ. "What's taking the police so long to call?"

Hickey picked up the telephone. "It's working." He came back to the rail. "They're still confused. You've disrupted their chain of command. They'll be more angry with you for that than for this."

"Aye. It's like a huge machine that has malfunctioned. But when they get it going again, they'll start to grind away at us. And there's no way to shut it down again once it starts."

Eamon Farrell, a middle-aged man and the oldest of the Fenians, except for Hickey, looked down from the six-story-high northeast triforium, watching Flynn and Hickey as they came out of the bell-tower lobby. Flynn wore the black suit of a priest, Hickey an old tweed jacket. They looked for all the world like a priest and an architect talking over renovations. Farrell shifted his gaze to the four hostages sitting in the sanctuary, waiting for some indication as to their fate. He felt sorry for them. But he also felt sorry for his only son, Eamon, Jr., in Long Kesh. The boy was in the second week of a hunger strike and wouldn't last much longer.

Farrell slipped his police tunic off and hung it over the parapet, then turned and walked back to the wooden kneewall behind him. In the wall was a small door, and he opened it, knelt, and shone his flashlight at the plaster lathing of the ceiling of the bride's room below him. He walked carefully in a crouch onto a rafter, and played the light around the dark recess, moving farther out onto the wooden beam. There was a fairly large space around him, a sort of lower attic below the main attic, formed by the downward pitch of the triforium roof before it met the outside wall of stone buttresses.

He stepped to the beam on his right and raised his light to the corner where the two walls came together. In the corner was part of a rounded tower made of brick and mortar. He made his way toward it and knelt precariously on a beam over the plaster. He reached out and ran his hand over a very small black iron door, almost the color of the dusty brick.

Eamon Farrell unhooked the rusty latch and pulled the door open. A familiar smell came out of the dark opening, and he reached his hand in and touched the inside of the brick, then brought his hand away and looked at it. Soot.

Farrell directed the light through the door and saw that the round hollow space was at least six feet across. He angled the light down but could see nothing. Carefully he eased his head and shoulders through the door and looked up. He sensed rather than saw the lights of the towering city above him. A cold downdraft confirmed that the hollow tower was a chimney.

Something caught his eye, and he pointed the light at it. A rung set into the brick. He played the light up and down the chimney and saw a series of iron rungs that ran up the chimney to the top. He withdrew from the opening and closed the thick steel door, then latched it firmly shut. He remained crouched on the beam for a long time, then came out of the small attic and moved to the parapet, calling down to Flynn.

Flynn quickly moved under the triforium. "Did you find something, Eamon?"

Farrell hesitated, then made a decision. "I see the tower as it comes through behind the triforium. There's no doorway."

Flynn looked impatient. "Throw me the rope ladder, and I'll have a look."

"No. No, don't bother. I'll keep looking."

Flynn considered, then said, "That tower has a function—find out what it is."

Farrell nodded. "I will." But he had already found it, and found an escape route for himself, a way to get out of this mess alive if the coming negotiations failed.

Frank Gallagher looked out from the southeast triforium. Everyone seemed to be in place. Directly across from him was Farrell. Sullivan, he noticed, was making eyes at Boland across the nave. Jean Kearney and Arthur Nulty were in the attic building bonfires and discussing, no doubt, the possibility of getting in a quick one before they died. Megan's brother, Pedar, was on the crypt landing watching the sacristy gates. He was young, not eighteen, but steady as a rock. *For thou art Peter, and upon this Rock*, thought Gallagher, who was devoutly Catholic, *upon this Rock, I will build my church; and the gates of hell shall not prevail against it*. The Thompson submachine gun helped, too.

Devane and Mullins had the nicest views, Gallagher thought, but it was probably cold up there. Megan, Hickey, and Flynn floated around like nervous hosts and hostess before a party, checking on the seating and ambience.

Frank Gallagher removed the silk parade marshal's sash and dropped it on the floor. He sighted his rifle at the choir loft, and Leary came into focus. He quickly put the rifle down. You didn't point a rifle at Leary. You didn't do anything to, with, or for Leary. You just avoided Leary like you avoided dark alleys and contagion wards.

Gallagher looked down at the hostages. His orders

were simple. *If they leave the sanctuary, unescorted, shoot them.* He stared at the Cardinal. Somehow Frank Gallagher had to square this thing he was doing, square it with the Cardinal or his own priest later— later, when it was over, and people saw what a fine thing they had done.

CHAPTER 19

Maureen watched Flynn as he moved about the Cathedral. He moved with a sense of purpose and animation that she recognized, and she knew he was feeling very alive and very good about himself. She watched the Cardinal sitting directly across from her. She envied him for what she knew was his absolute confidence in his position, his unerring belief that he was a blameless victim, a potential martyr. But for herself, and perhaps for Baxter, there was some guilt, and some misgivings, about their roles. And those feelings could work to undermine their ability to resist the pressures that the coming hours or days would bring.

She glanced quickly around at the triforia and choir loft. *Well done, Brian, but you're short of troops.* She tried to remember the faces of the people she had seen close in, and was fairly certain that she didn't know any of them except Gallagher and Devane. Megan and Pedar Fitzgerald she knew of through their brother, Tommy. What had become of all the people she once called sisters and brothers? The camps or the grave. These were their relatives, recruited in that endless cycle of blood vengeance that characterized the Irish war.

With that kind of perpetual vendetta she couldn't see how it would end until they were all dead.

She spoke to Baxter. "If we run quickly to the south transept doors, we could be in the vestibule, hidden from the snipers, before they reacted. I can disarm almost any mine in a few seconds. We'd be through the outer door and into the street before anyone reached the vestibule."

Baxter looked at her. "What in the world are you talking about?"

"I'm talking about getting out of here alive."

"Look up there. Five snipers. And how can we run off and leave the Cardinal and Father Murphy?"

"They can come with us."

"Are you mad? I won't hear of it."

"I'll do what I damned well please."

He saw her body tense and reached out and held her arm.

"No, you don't. Listen here, we have a chance to be released if—"

"No chance at all. From what I picked up of their conversation, they are going to demand the release of prisoners in internment. Do you think your government will agree to *that*?"

"I'm . . . I'm sure something will be worked out . . ."

"Bloody stupid diplomat. I know these people better than you do, and I know your government's position on Irish terrorists. No negotiation. End of discussion."

" . . . but we have to wait for the right moment. We need a plan."

She tried to pull her arm away, but he held it tightly.

She said, "I wish I had a shilling for every prisoner who stood in front of a firing squad because he waited for the right moment to make a break. The right moment, according to your own soldier's manual, is as soon after capture as possible. Before the enemy settles down, before they get their bearings. We've already waited too long. Let go of me."

"No. Let me think of something—something less suicidal."

"Listen to me, Baxter—we're not physically bound in any way yet. We must act now. You and I are as good as dead. The Cardinal and the priest may be spared. We won't be."

Baxter took a long breath, then said, "Well . . . it may be that I'm as good as dead . . . but don't you know this fellow, Flynn? Weren't you in the IRA together . . . ?"

"We were lovers. That's another reason I won't stay here at his mercy for one more second."

"I see. Well, if you want to commit suicide, that's one thing. But don't tell me you're trying to escape. And don't expect me to get myself killed with you."

"You'll wish later you'd taken a quick bullet."

He spoke evenly. "If an opportunity presents itself, I *will* try to escape." He paused. "If not, then when the time comes I'll die with some dignity, I hope."

"I hope so, too. You can let go of my arm now. I'll wait. But if we're bound or thrown into the crypt or something like that—then, as you're thrashing about with two shattered kneecaps, you can think about how we could have run. That's how they do it, you know. They kneecap you hours before they shoot you in the heart."

Baxter drew a deep breath. "I suppose I lack a sufficiently vivid imagination to be frightened enough to try anything . . . But you're supplying me with the necessary picture." He took his hand away from hers and sat watching her out of the corner of his eyes, but she seemed content to sit there. "Steady."

"Oh, take your bloody British steady and shove it."

Baxter remembered her bravery on the steps and realized that part of that, consciously or unconsciously, was for him, or more accurately, what he represented. He realized also that her survival was to some extent in his hands. As for himself, he felt indignant over his present position but felt no loss of dignity. The distinction was not a small one and would determine how each of them would react to their captivity, and if they were to die, how they would die. He said, "Whenever you're ready . . . I'm with you."

Pedar Fitzgerald looked up the right-hand stairs as his sister came down toward him. He stood and cradled the Thompson submachine gun under his arm. "How's it going, Megan?"

"Everything's set but the bombs." She looked down the stairs through the gate into the empty sacristy. "Any movement?"

"No. Things are quiet." He forced a smile. "Maybe they don't know we're here."

She smiled back. "Oh, they know. They know, Pedar." She drew her pistol and descended the stairs, then examined the lock and chain on the gates. She listened, trying to hear a sound from the four side corridors that led into the sacristy. Something moved, someone coughed quietly. She turned and said to her brother in a loud voice, "When you shoot, boys, shoot between the bars. Don't damage the lock and chain. Those Thompsons can get away from you."

Pedar smiled. "We've handled them enough times."

She winked at him and climbed back up the stairs, sticking the pistol in the waistband of her jeans. She moved close to him and touched his cheek lightly. "We're putting all we've got on this, Pedar. Tommy is in for life. We could be dead or in an American prison for life. Mum is near dead for worry. None of us will see each other again if this goes badly."

Pedar Fitzgerald felt tears forming in his eyes but fought them back. He found his voice and said, "We've all put everything on Brian, Megan. Do you ... do you trust him ...? Can he do it, then?"

Megan Fitzgerald looked into her brother's eyes. "If he can't and we see he can't, then ... you and I, Pedar ... we'll take over. The family comes first." She turned and climbed up to the sanctuary, came around the altar, and looked at Maureen sitting in the pew. Their eyes met and neither looked away.

Flynn watched from the ambulatory, then called out, "Megan. Come take a walk with us."

Megan Fitzgerald turned away from Maureen and joined Flynn and Hickey as they began walking up the center aisle. "There are people in the sacristy corridors," she said.

Flynn nodded as he walked. "They won't do anything until they've established who we are and what we want. We've a little time yet."

When they reached the front door, Flynn ran his

hands over the cold bronze ceremonial doors. "Magnificent. I'd like to take one with me." He examined the mines, then turned back and motioned around the Cathedral. "We've set up a perfect and very deadly cross fire from five long, concealed perches protected by stone parapets. As long as we hold the high spots we can dominate the Cathedral. But if we lose the high ground and the fight takes place on the floor, it will be very difficult."

Hickey relit his pipe. "As long as there's no fighting in the bookstore."

Megan looked at him. "I hope you keep your sense of humor when the bullets start ripping through the smoke around your face."

He blew smoke toward her. "Lass, I've been shot at more times than you've had your period."

Flynn interrupted. "If you were a police commander, John, what would you do?"

Hickey thought a moment, then said, "I'd do what the British Army did in downtown Dublin in 1916. I'd call in the artillery and level the fucking place. Then I'd offer surrender terms."

"But this is not Dublin, 1916," said Flynn. "I think the people out there have to act with great restraint."

"You may call it restraint, I'd call it cunning. They'll eventually have to attack when they see we won't be talked out. But they'll do it without the big guns. More tactics, less gunpowder—gas, helicopters, concussion grenades that don't damage property. There's a lot available to them today." He looked around. "But we may be able to hold on."

Megan said, "We *will* hold on."

Flynn added, "We have gas masks, incidentally."

"Do you, now? You're a very thorough man, Brian. The old IRA was always going off half-cocked to try to grab the British lion's balls. And the lion loved it— loved feasting on IRA." He looked up at the triforia, then down at the deserted main floor. "Too bad, though, you couldn't find more men—"

Flynn interrupted. "They're a good lot. Each of them is worth twenty of the old-type ruffians."

"Are they, then? Even the women?"

Megan stiffened and started to speak.

Flynn interjected, "Nothing wrong with women, you old bastard. I've learned that over the years. They're steady. Loyal."

Hickey glanced at the sanctuary where Maureen sat, then made an exaggerated pretense of looking away quickly. "I suppose many of them are." He sat at the edge of a pew and yawned. "Tiring business. Megan, lass, I hope you didn't think I included you when I spoke about women."

"Oh, go to hell." She turned and walked away.

Flynn let out a long breath of annoyance. "Why are you provoking her?"

Hickey watched her walk toward the altar. "Cold, cold. Must be like fucking a wooden icebox."

"Look, John—"

The telephone on the chancel organ beside the altar rang loudly, and everyone turned toward it.

CHAPTER 20

Brian Flynn put his hand on the ringing phone and looked at Hickey. "I was beginning to believe no one cared—one hears such stories about New York indifference."

Hickey laughed. "I can't think of a worse nightmare for an Irish revolutionary than to be ignored. Answer it, and if it's someone wanting to sell aluminum siding for the rectory, I suggest we just go home."

Flynn drew a deep breath and picked up the receiver. "MacCumail here."

There was a short silence, then a man's voice said, "Who?"

"This is Finn MacCumail, Chief of the Fenians. Who is this?"

The voice hesitated for a moment, then the man said, "This is Police Sergeant Tezik. Tactical Patrol Unit. I'm calling from the rectory. What the hell is going on in there?"

"Not much of anything at the moment."

"Why are the doors locked?"

"Because there are mines attached to each one. It's for your own protection, actually."

"Why . . . ?"

"Listen, Sergeant Tezik, and listen very closely. We have four hostages in here—Father Timothy Murphy, Maureen Malone, Sir Harold Baxter, and the Cardinal himself. If the police try to force their way in, the mines will explode, and if they keep coming, the hostages will be shot and the Cathedral will be set afire. Do you understand?"

"Jesus Christ . . ."

"Get this message to your superiors quickly, and get a ranking man on the phone. Be quick about it, Sergeant Tezik."

"Yeah . . . all right . . . . Listen, everything's pretty screwed up here, so just take it easy. As soon as we get things sorted out, we'll have a police official on the phone with you. Okay?"

"Make it quick. And no nonsense or there will be a great number of dead people you'll have to answer for. No helicopters in the area. No armored vehicles on the streets. I have men in the towers with rockets and rifles. I've got a gun pointed at the Cardinal's head right now."

"Okay—take it easy. Don't—"

Flynn hung up and turned to Hickey and Megan, who had joined them. "A TPU sergeant—spiritual kin to the RUCs and the Gestapo. I didn't like the tone of his voice."

Hickey nodded. "It's their height. Gives them a sense of superiority." He smiled. "Easier targets, though."

Flynn looked at the doors. "We caused a bit *too* much confusion. I hope they reestablish some chain of command before the hotheaded types start acting. The next few minutes are going to be critical."

Megan turned to Hickey and spoke quickly. "Do you want Sullivan to help you place the bombs?"

"Megan, love, I want *you* to help me. Run along and get what we need." He waited until Megan left, then turned to Flynn. "We have to make a decision now about the hostages—a decision about who kills which one."

Flynn looked at the Cardinal sitting straight on his throne, looking every inch a Prince of the Church. He knew it wasn't vanity or affectation he was observing but a product of two thousand years of history, ceremony, and training. The Cardinal would be not only a difficult hostage but a difficult man to make a corpse of. He said to Hickey, "It would be a hard man who could put a bullet into him."

Hickey's eyes, which normally twinkled with an old man's mischief, turned narrow and malevolent. "Well, I'll do him, if"—Hickey inclined his head toward Maureen— "if you'll do her."

Flynn glanced at Maureen sitting in the clergy pews between Baxter and Father Murphy. He hesitated, then said, "Yes, all right. Go on and plant the bombs."

Hickey ignored him. "As for Baxter, anyone will kill him. You tell Megan to do the priest. The little bitch should draw her first blood the hard way—not with Maureen."

Flynn looked at Hickey closely. It was becoming apparent that Hickey was obsessed with taking as many people with him as possible. "Yes," he said, "that seems the way to handle it." He looked out over the vast expanse around him and said, more to himself than to

Hickey, "God, how did we get in this place, and how can we get out?"

Hickey took Flynn's arm and pressed it tightly. "Funny, that's almost exactly what Padraic Pearse said when his men seized the General Post Office in Dublin, Easter Monday. I remember it very clearly. The answer then, as it is now, is that you got in with luck and blarney, but you'll not get out alive...." He released Flynn's arm and slapped him on the back. "Cheer up, lad, we'll take a good number of them with us, like we did in 1916. Burn this place down while we're about it. Blow it up, too, if we get those bombs in place."

Flynn stared at Hickey. He might have to kill Hickey before Hickey got them all killed.

* * *

Megan Fitzgerald mounted the sanctuary, carrying two suitcases. She walked rapidly to the right side of the high altar, and placed them beside a bronze plate set into the marble floor, then lifted the plate. John Hickey came up beside her and picked up the suitcases. "Go on."

Megan descended a shaky metal ladder, found a light chain, and pulled it. Hickey climbed down and handed the suitcases to Megan, who placed them gently on the floor. They examined the unevenly excavated crawl space. Building rubble, pipes, and ducts nearly filled the space around them, and it was difficult to move or to see clearly. Megan called out, "Here's the outer wall of the crypt."

Hickey called back, "Yes, and here's the wall of the staircase that continues down into the sacristy. Come along." Hickey turned on a flashlight and probed the area to his front as he moved, dragging one of the suitcases behind him.

They followed a parallel course to the descending staircase wall, hunching lower as they progressed. The dirt floor turned to Manhattan bedrock, and Hickey called out, "I see it up ahead." He crawled to a protruding mound from which rose the footing of a massive column. "Here it is. Come closer." He played the light around the dark spaces. "See? Here's where they cut through the old foundation and footing to let the sacristy stairs pass through. If we dug down farther, we'd find the sacristy's subbasement. It's somewhat like the layout of a modern splitlevel home."

Megan was skeptical. "Damned confusing sort of place. The fire in the attic is much surer."

"Don't be getting cold feet, now, Megan. I'll not blow you up."

"I'm only concerned with placing them properly."

"Of course." Hickey ran his hand over the column. "Now the story is that when they blasted the new stairs through the foundation in 1904 they weakened these flanking columns. In architectural terms, they're under stress. The old boy whose father worked on the blasting told me that the Irish laborers believed only God Almighty kept the whole place from collapsing when they set the dynamite. But God Almighty doesn't live here anymore, so when we plant this plastic and it blows, nothing will hold up the roof."

"And if it does hold up, will you be a believer then?"

"No. I'll think we didn't place the explosives properly." Hickey opened the suitcase and pulled out twenty white bricks wrapped in cellophane. He tore the cellophane from the white, putty-like substance and molded a brick into the place where the bedrock met the hewn and mortared stone of the column footing. Megan joined him, and they sculpted the bricks around the footing. He handed her the flashlight. "Hold this steady."

Hickey implanted four detonators, connected by wires to a battery pack, into the plastic. He picked up an alarm clock and looked at his watch. "It's four minutes after six now. The clock doesn't know a.m. from p.m., so the most time I can give it is eleven hours and fifty-nine minutes." He began turning the clock's alarm dial slowly counter-clockwise, talking as he did. "So I'll set the alarm for five minutes after six—no, I mean three minutes after six." He laughed as he kept turning the dial. "I remember once, a lad in Galway who didn't understand that. At midnight he set the timer to go off at one minute after twelve, in what he thought would be the afternoon. British officer's club, I think it was. Yes, lunchtime, he thought. Anyway, at one minute past midnight...he was standing before his Maker, who must have wondered how he became so unmade." He laughed again as he joined the clock wire to the batteries.

"At least don't get us killed until we've set the one on the other side."

"Good point. Did I do that right? Well, I hope so." He pulled the clock switch, and the loud ticking filled the damp space. He looked at her. "And don't forget, my sharp little lass, only you and I know exactly where these are planted, which gives us some advantages and a bit of power with your friend, Mr. Flynn. Only you and I can decide if we want to give an extension of the deadline to meet our demands." He laughed as he pushed the clock into the explosives and molded the plastic around it. "But if the police have killed us before then, well, at three minutes after six—which incidentally happens to be the exact time of sunrise— they'll get a message from us, directly from hell." He took some earth from the floor and pressed it into the white plastic. "There. That looks innocent, doesn't it? Give me a hand here." He spoke as he continued to camouflage the plastic explosives. "You're young. You don't want it to end so soon, I know, but you must have some sort of death wish to get mixed up in this. Nobody dropped you in through the roof. You people planned this for over a year. Wish I'd had a year to think about it. I'd be home now where I belong."

He picked up the flashlight and turned it onto her face. Her bright green eyes glowed back at him. "I hope you had a good look at this morning's sunrise, lass, because the chances are you'll not see another one."

Patrick Burke moved carefully from under the portal of the bronze ceremonial doors and looked up at the north tower. The Cathedral's floodlights cast a blue-white brilliance over the recently cleaned stonework and onto the fluttering harp flag of green and gold, reminding Burke irreverently of a Disney World castle. Burke looked over the south tower. The louvers were torn open, and a man was looking down at him through a rifle scope. Burke turned his back on the sniper and saw a tall uniformed patrolman of the Tactical Patrol Unit hurrying toward him through the sleet.

The young patrolman hesitated, then said, "Are you a sergeant or better?"

"Can't you tell?"

"I..."

"Lieutenant, Intelligence."

The patrolman began speaking rapidly. "Christ, Lieutenant, my sergeant, Tezik, is in the rectory. He's got a platoon of TPU ready to move. He wants to hit the doors with trucks—I don't think we should do anything until we get orders—"

Burke moved quickly across the steps and followed the north wall of the Cathedral through the gardens and terraces until he came to the rear of the rectory. He entered a door that led to a large vestibule. Scattered throughout the halls and offices and sitting on the stairs were about thirty men of the Tactical Patrol Unit, an elite reaction force, looking fresh, young, big, and eager. Burke turned to the patrolman who had followed him. "Where's Tezik?"

"In the Rector's office." He leaned toward Burke and said quietly, "He's a little...high-strung. You know?"

Burke left the patrolman in the vestibule and moved quickly up the stairs between the sitting TPU men. On the next landing he opened a door marked RECTOR.

Monsignor Downes sat at his desk in the center of the large, old-fashioned office, still wearing his topcoat and smoking a cigarette. Burke stood in the doorway. "Monsignor, where's the police sergeant?"

Monsignor Downes looked up blankly. "Who are you?"

"Burke. Police. Where is—?"

Monsignor Downes spoke distractedly. "Oh, yes. I know you. Friend of Father Murphy…saw you last night at the Waldorf…Maureen Malone…you were—"

"Yes, sir. Where is Sergeant Tezik?"

A deep voice called out from behind a set of double doors to Burke's right. "I'm in here!"

Burke moved through the doors into a larger inner office with a fireplace and bookshelves. Sergeant Tezik sat at an oversized desk in the rear room. "Burke. ID. Get your men out of the rectory and on the street where they belong. Help with crowd control."

Sergeant Tezik stood slowly, revealing a frame six-and-a-half feet tall, weighing, Burke guessed, about two seventy-five. Tezik said, "Who died and left you in charge?"

Burke closed the door behind him. "Actually, Commissioner Dwyer *is* dead. Heart attack."

"I heard. That don't make *you* the PC."

"No, but I'll do for now." Burke moved farther into the room. "Don't try to take advantage of this mess, Tezik. Don't play macho man with other people's lives. You know the saying, Tezik: When a citizen is in trouble he calls a cop; when a cop is in trouble he calls Emergency Service."

"I'm using what they call personal initiative, Lieutenant. I figure that before those bastards get themselves dug in—"

"Who have you called? Where are your orders coming from?"

"They're coming from my brains."

"That's too bad."

Tezik continued, unperturbed, "I can't get an open line no place."

"Did you try Police Plaza?"

"I *told* you, I can't get through. This is a revolution, for Christ's sake. You know?" He hesitated, then added, "Only the interphone in the Cathedral complex is working.... I spoke to somebody..."

Burke moved to the desk. "Who did you speak to?"

"Some guy—Finn?—something. Name's on the Cathedral doors."

"What did he say?"

"Nothing." He thought a moment. "Said he had four hostages."

"Who?"

"The Cardinal—"

"Shit!"

"Yeah. And they got a priest, too—Murphy. And some broad whose name I don't remember—that peace woman, I think. Name was in the papers. And some English royalty guy, Baker."

"Jesus Christ. What else did he say, Tezik? Think."

Tezik seemed to be thinking. "Let me see.... He said he'd kill them—they always say that. Right? And burn the Cathedral—how do you burn a Cathedral—?"

"With matches."

"Not possible. Stone don't burn. Anyway, the doors are supposed to be rigged with explosives, but, shit,

I have thirty-five TPU in the rectory, ready to go. I got a dozen more standing in the halls that lead to the sacristy. I got four-wheel-drive equipment from the Sanitation Department, with my men driving, ready to hit the doors, and—"

"Forget it."

"Like hell. Look, the longer you wait, the deeper the other guy digs in. That's a fact."

"Where did you learn that fact?"

"In the Marines. 'Nam."

"Sure. Listen, Tezik, this is midtown Manhattan, not Fuck Luck Province. A great cathedral full of art treasures has been seized, Tezik. And *hostages*, Tezik. The dinks never held hostages, did they? Police policy is containment, not cavalry charges. Right?"

"This is different. The command structure's broken down. One time, near Quangtri, I was on patrol—"

"Who cares?"

Tezik stiffened. "Let me see your shield."

Burke held out his badge case, then put it away. "Look, Tezik, these people who've taken the Cathedral do not present a clear or immediate danger to anyone outside the Cathedral—"

"They shot out a spotlight. They hung a flag from the steeple. They could be Reds, Burke—revolutionaries.... Fenians... what the hell *are* Fenians?"

"Listen to me—leave this to Emergency Services and the Hostage Negotiator. Okay?"

"I'm going in now, Burke. Now, before they start shooting into the city—before they start shooting the hostages... or burning the Cathedral—"

"It's stone."

"Back off, Lieutenant. I'm the man on the spot, and I have to do what I have to do."

Burke unbuttoned his topcoat and hooked his thumbs into his belt. "No way."

Neither man spoke for several seconds, then Tezik said, "I'm walking to that door."

Burke said, "Try it."

The office was very still except for the ticking of a mantel clock.

They both sidestepped clear of the desk, then faced off, each man knowing that he had unwittingly backed the other against a wall, and neither knowing what to do about it.

CHAPTER 21

Father Murphy addressed Maureen and Baxter sitting beside him on the pew. "I'm going to speak to His Eminence. Will you come with me?"

Maureen shook her head.

Baxter said, "I'll be along shortly."

Father Murphy crossed the marble floor, knelt at the throne and kissed the episcopal ring, then rose and began speaking to the Cardinal in a low voice. Maureen watched them, then said to Baxter, "I can't stay here another moment."

He studied her closely. Her eyes were darting around wildly, and he saw that her body was shaking again.

He put his hand on her arm. "You really must get a grip on yourself."

"Oh, go to hell! How could you understand? For me this is like sitting in a room full of nightmares come to life."

"Let me see if I can get you a drink. Perhaps they have tranquilizers—"

"No! Listen, I'm not afraid of..."

"Talk about it if it will help."

Maureen tried to steady her shaking legs. "It's lots of things.... It's *him*. Flynn. He can...he has a power...no, not a power...a way of making you do things, and afterward you wished you hadn't done them, and you feel awful. Do you understand?"

"I think—"

"And...these people...They're my people, you see, yet they're not. Not anymore. I don't know how to react to them.... It's like a family meeting, and I've been called in because I've done something terrible. They're not saying anything, just watching me...." She shook her head. *Once in, never out.* She was beginning to understand what that really meant, and it had nothing to do with them but with oneself. She looked at Baxter. "Even if they don't kill us...There are worse things...."

Baxter pressed her arm. "Yes...I think I understand—"

"I'm not explaining myself very well."

She knew of that total suppression of ego that made hostages zombies, willing participants in the drama. And afterward the mixed feelings, confusion, guilt. She remembered what one psychologist had said, *Once you're a hostage, you're a hostage for the rest of your life.* She shook her head. No. She wouldn't let that happen to her. No. "No!"

Baxter squeezed her hand. "Look here, we may have to die, but I promise you, I won't let them abuse you...us. There'll be no mock trial, no public recanting, no..." He found it difficult to say what he knew her fears were. "No sadistic games, no psychological torture..."

She studied his face closely. He had more insight into these things than she would have thought of a prim career diplomat.

He cleared his throat and said, "You're a very proud woman.... It's easier for me, actually. I hate them, and anything they do to me just diminishes *them*—not *me*. It would help if you established the proper relationship between yourself and them."

She shook her head. "Yes. I feel like a traitor, and I'm a patriot. I feel guilty, and I'm the victim. How can that be?"

"When we know the answers to that, we'll know how to deal with people like Brian Flynn."

She forced a smile. "I'm sorry I bothered you with all of this." Baxter started to interrupt, but she went on. "I thought you had a right to know, before I—"

Baxter grabbed at her arm, but she vaulted into the pew behind her, then jumped into the last row and grabbed at the two wooden columns of the carved screen, swinging her legs up to the balustrade before jumping down to the ambulatory six feet below.

Frank Gallagher leaned over the edge of the triforium. He pointed his rifle straight down at the top of her head, but the rifle was shaking so badly he didn't fire.

Eamon Farrell sighted across the sanctuary at her back but shifted his aim to her left and squeezed off a single round, which exploded into the stillness of the Cathedral.

George Sullivan and Abby Boland in the long triforium at the front of the Cathedral looked quickly at the source of the shot, then down at the aim of Farrell's rifle, but neither moved.

Leary had read the signs before Maureen even made her first move. As she came out of the pew he leaned farther over the parapet of the choir loft and followed her through his rifle scope. As she swung up to the balustrade he fired.

Maureen heard the sharp crack of Farrell's fire ring out behind her, then almost simultaneously heard the report roll down from the choir loft. Farrell's shot passed to her left. Leary's shot passed so close over her head she felt it touch her hair, and the wooden column near her left ear splintered in her face. Suddenly a pair of strong hands grabbed her shoulders and yanked her backward into the pew behind her. She looked up into the face of Harold Baxter. "Let go of me! Let go!"

Baxter was agitated and kept repeating, "Don't move! For God's sake, don't move!"

A sound of running footsteps came to the sanctuary, and Maureen saw Megan leaning into the pew, pointing a pistol at her face. Megan spoke softly. "Thank you." She cocked the pistol.

Baxter found himself sprawled over Maureen's body. "No! For God's sake, don't."

Megan screamed. "Move, you stupid bastard! Move!" She struck Baxter on the back of the head with her pistol, then pushed the muzzle into Maureen's throat.

The Cardinal was halfway across the sanctuary, shouting, "Stop that! Let them alone!" Father Murphy moved quickly behind Megan and grabbed her forearms. He picked her up high into the air, spun around, and dropped her on the floor. Megan slid on the polished marble, then shot up quickly into a kneeling position, and pointed the gun at the priest.

Brian Flynn's voice came clearly from the communion rail. "No!"

Megan pivoted around and stared at him, her pistol still leveled in front of her.

Flynn jumped over the gate and mounted the steps. "Go into the choir loft and stay there!"

Megan knelt on the floor, the pistol shaking in her hand. Everyone stood around her, motionless.

John Hickey quickly mounted the sanctuary steps. "Come with me, Megan." He walked to her, bent over at the waist, and took her arms in his hands. "Come on, then. That's it." He pulled her to her feet, and pushed her gunhand down to her side. He led her down the steps into the center aisle.

Flynn walked to the side of the pews and looked down. "Baxter, that was very gallant—very knightly. Stupid, too."

Harold Baxter picked himself up, then pulled Maureen up beside him.

Flynn looked at Maureen. "You won't get off that easy. And you almost got Sir Harry killed, too."

She didn't answer.

Baxter pressed a handkerchief to Maureen's cheek, where she had been hit by the wooden splinters.

Flynn's arm shot out and knocked Baxter's hand away. He went on calmly, "And don't think Mr. Leary is a bad shot. Had you gotten to the door he would have blown both your ankles away." Flynn turned. "And that goes as well for His Eminence and the good Father. And if by some miracle someone does get out of here, someone else dies for it." He looked at each of them. "Or should I just bind you all together? I'd rather not have to do that." He fixed each of the silent hostages with a cold stare. "Do not leave this sanctuary. Do we all understand the rules? Good. Everyone sit down." Flynn walked behind the altar and descended the steps to the crypt door landing. He spoke quietly to Pedar Fitzgerald. "Any movement down there?"

Fitzgerald answered softly. "Lot of commotion in the corridors, but it's quiet now. Is anyone hurt? Is my sister all right?"

"No one is hurt. Don't leave this post, no matter what you hear up there."

"I know. Look out for Megan, will you?"

"We're all watching out for Megan, Pedar."

A TPU man burst into the Monsignor's suite and ran to the inner office, out of breath. "Sergeant!"

Tezik and Burke both looked up.

The patrolman said excitedly, "The men in the corridors heard two shots fired—"

Tezik looked at Burke. "That's it. We're going in." Tezik moved quickly past Burke toward the door. Burke grabbed his shoulders and threw him back against the fireplace.

Tezik recovered his balance and shouted to the patrolman, "Arrest this man!"

The patrolman hesitated, then drew his service revolver.

The telephone rang.

Burke reached for it, but Tezik snatched the phone away and picked up the receiver. "Sergeant Tezik, NYPD."

Flynn sat at the chancel organ bench and said, "This is Finn MacCumail."

Tezik's voice was excited. "What happened in there? What's all that shooting?"

Flynn lit a cigarette. "Two shots hardly constitute 'all that shooting,' Sergeant. You ought to spend your next holiday in Belfast. Mothers fire two shots into the nursery just to wake the children."

"What—"

"No one is hurt," interrupted Flynn. "An automatic rifle discharged by accident." He said abruptly, "We're getting impatient, Sergeant."

"Just stay calm."

"The deadline for the demands I'm going to make is sunrise, and sunrise won't come any later because you're fucking around to find your chiefs." He hung up and drew on his cigarette. He thought about Maureen. He ought to tie her up for her own good, and for the good of them all, but perhaps he owed it to her to leave her options open and let her arrive at her own destiny without his interference. Sometime before sunrise they would be free of each other, or if not free, then together again, one way or the other.

CHAPTER 22

Sergeant Tezik replaced the receiver and glanced at Burke. "An automatic rifle went off by accident—that's what he said.... I don't know." Tezik seemed to have calmed down somewhat. "What do you think?"

Burke let out a long breath, then moved to the window overlooking the Cathedral and pulled back the drapes. "Take a look out there."

Sergeant Tezik looked at the floodlit Cathedral.

"Have you ever seen the inside of that place, Tezik?"

He nodded. "Holy Name Society communions. Couple of...funerals."

"Yeah. Well, remember the triforia—the balconies? The choir loft? The acre or so of pews? It's a deathtrap in there, Sergeant, a fucking shooting gallery, and the TPU will be ducks." Burke let the drape fall and faced Tezik. "My intelligence sources say that those people have automatic weapons and sniper rifles. Maybe rockets. What do you have, Tezik? Six-shooters? Go back to your post. Tell your men to stand fast."

Tezik walked to a sideboard, poured a glass of brandy, drank it, then stared off at a point in space for a full minute. He looked at Burke and said, "Okay, I'm no hero." He forced a smile. "Thought it might be a piece of cake. Couple of medals. Mayor's commendation . . . media stuff. You know?"

"Yeah, I've been to a lot of funerals like that."

The other TPU man holstered his revolver and left as Tezik moved sullenly toward the door.

"And no funny stuff, Sergeant."

Tezik walked into the outer office, then called back. "They want to speak to a high-ranking police official. Hope you can find one."

Burke moved to the desk and dialed a special number to his office in Police Plaza. After a long delay the phone rang and a woman answered. "Jackson."

"Louise, Burke here."

Duty Sergeant Louise Jackson, a middle-aged black woman, sounded tired. "Lieutenant! Where are you?"

"In the rectory of Saint Patrick's Cathedral. Put Langley on."

"The Inspector's in a helicopter with Deputy PC Rourke. They're trying to establish a command structure, but we lost radio contact with them when they got close to the Cathedral. Jamming device there. Every telephone line in the city is overloaded except these special ones, and they're not so good either. Everything's pretty crazy here."

"It's a little messy here, too. Listen, you call the Hostage Negotiator's office upstairs. Have them get hold of Bert Schroeder, quick. We have a hostage situation here."

"Damn it. That's what we thought. The BSS guarding the VIPs on the steps just called in. They lost some people in the shuffle, but they were a little vague about who and how."

"I'll tell you who and how in a second. Okay, call the Emergency Service office—Captain Bellini, if he's available. Explain that the Cathedral is held by gunmen and tell them to assemble siege equipment, snipers, and whatever other personnel and equipment is necessary, in the Cardinal's residence. Got that?"

"This one's going to be a bitch."

"For sure. Okay, I have a situation report and a message from the gunmen, Louise. I'll give it to you, and you call the Commissioner's office. They'll call everyone on the Situation A list. Ready to copy?"

"Shoot."

"At approximately 5:20 p.m. Saint Patrick's Cathedral was seized by an unknown number of gunmen—" Burke finished his report. "I'm designating the rectory as the command post. Get Ma Bell on the horn and have them put extra phone lines into the rectory according to existing emergency procedures. Got that?"

"Yes.... Pat, are you authorized—?"

Burke felt the sweat collecting around his collar and loosened it. "Louise, don't ask those kinds of questions. We've got to wing this one. Okay?"

"Okay."

"Do your best to contact those people. Stay cool."

"I'm cool. But you ought to see the people here. Everybody thinks it's some kind of *insurrection* or something. Albany and Washington called the PC's office—couldn't get a straight answer from City Hall or Gracie Mansion—PC's office called here. Want to know if it's an insurrection—or a race riot. Can you tell if it's an insurrection? Just for the record."

"Tell Albany and Washington that nobody in New York cares enough to start an insurrection. As far as I can make out, the Fenians provoked a disturbance to cover their seizing of the Cathedral. It got out of hand—a lot of happy citizens cutting loose. Do you have any reports from our people in the field?"

"Not a one. You're the first."

"One more thing. Get John Hickey's file sent here as soon as possible. And see what we have on a Northern Irishman named Brian Flynn." He hung up.

Burke walked into the outer office. "Monsignor?"

Monsignor Downes put down his telephone. "I can't get through to *anyone*. I have to speak to the Vicar General. I have to call the Apostolic Delegate in Washington. What's happening? What is going on here?"

Burke looked into Downes's ashen face, moved to the coffee table, and picked up a bottle of wine and a glass.

"Have some of this. The phones will be clear later. Couple of million people are trying to call home at the same time, that's all. We're going to have to use this rectory as a command post."

Monsignor Downes ignored the wine. "Command post?"

"Please clear the rectory and evacuate all the office personnel and priests. Leave a switchboard operator on until I can get a police operator here." Burke looked at his watch and considered a moment, then said, "How do I get into the corridor that connects with the sacristy?"

Monsignor Downes gave him a set of involved and disjointed instructions.

The door swung open and a tall man in a black topcoat burst in. He held up his badge case. "Lieutenant Young. Bureau of Special Services." He looked at the Monsignor, then at Burke, and said, "Who are you?"

"Burke. ID."

The man went directly to the coffee table and poured a glass of wine. "Christ—excuse me, Father—damn it, we've accounted for every VIP on the steps except three."

Burke watched him drink. "Let me guess—ID guys are good at guessing. You lost the Cardinal, Baxter, and the Malone woman."

Lieutenant Young looked at him quickly. "Where are they? They're not in the Cathedral, are they?"

"I'm afraid they are."

"Oh, Christ—sorry—shit. That's it. That's my job. Forget it. Forget it."

"Three out of about a hundred VIPs isn't bad."

"Don't joke! This is bad. Very bad."

"They're unharmed as far as I know," added Burke. "They also have a parish priest—Murphy. Not a VIP, so don't worry about that."

"Damn it. I lost three VIPs." He rambled on as he poured himself another glass. "Damn it, they should have sent the Secret Service. When the Pope came, the President sent the Secret Service to help us." He looked at Burke and the Monsignor and went on. "Most of the BSS was up by the reviewing stands. Byrd had all the good men. I got stuck with a handful of incompetents."

"Right." Burke moved to the door. "Get some competent men to stay with Monsignor Downes here. He's a VIP. I'm going to try to speak with the gunmen. They're VIPs, too."

Young glanced at Burke and said fiercely, "Why didn't you tell us something like this was going to happen, Burke?"

"You didn't ask." Burke left the office, descended the stairs, and found an elevator that took him into the basement. He came upon a worried-looking Hispanic custodian. "Sacristy," said Burke without preamble.

The man led him to a passage and pointed. Burke saw six TPU men standing along the walls with guns drawn. He held up his badge case and motioned the men to draw back from the sacristy. He unholstered his revolver, put it in his topcoat pocket, then walked down the short staircase to the opening of the passage. Burke put his head slowly around the corner and looked into the marble vaulted sacristy.

A TPU man behind him whispered, "Guy's got a Thompson at the top of those stairs."

Burke moved carefully into the sacristy, down the length of a row of vestment tables that ran along the wall to the right. At the end of the tables was another arched opening, and through it he could see a dimly lit polygon-shaped room of stone and brick.

Burke moved slowly toward the gates, keeping out of sight of the staircase opening. He heard muffled voices echoing down the staircase. Burke knew he had to speak with Finn MacCumail, and he had to have it together when he did. He leaned back against the marble wall to the side of the stairs and listened to his heart beat. He filled his lungs several times but couldn't find his voice. His hands clutched around the revolver in his pocket, and he pulled his hand free and steadied it against the wall. He looked at his watch. One minute. In one minute he would call for Finn MacCumail.

Maureen sat in the pew, her face in her hands, and Father Murphy and the Cardinal sat flanking her, keeping up a steady flow of soothing words. Baxter returned from the credence table, where a canteen of water had been placed. "Here."

She shook her head, then rose abruptly. "Let me alone. All of you. What do you know? You don't know the half of it. But you *will*."

The Cardinal motioned to the other two, and they followed him across the sanctuary and stood beside the throne. The Cardinal said quietly, "She has to make peace with herself. She's a troubled woman. If she wants us, she'll come to us." He looked up at the altar rising from the sanctuary. "God has brought us together in His house, and we are in His hands now—us, as well as them. His will be done, not ours. We must not provoke these people and give them cause to harm us or this church."

Baxter cleared his throat. "We have an obligation to escape if a clear opportunity presents itself."

The Cardinal gave him a look of slight annoyance. "We are operating from different sets of standards, I'm afraid. However, Mr. Baxter, I'm going to have to insist that in my church you do as I say."

Baxter replied evenly, "There's some question, I

think, concerning whose church this is at the moment, Your Eminence." He turned to Father Murphy. "What are your thoughts?"

Father Murphy seemed to vacillate, then said, "There's no use arguing about it. His Eminence is correct."

Baxter looked exasperated. "See here, I don't like being pushed about. We *must* offer some resistance, even if it's only psychological, and we must at least *plan* to escape if we're going to keep our sanity and self-respect. This may go on for days—weeks—and if I leave here alive, I want to be able to live with myself."

The Cardinal spoke. "Mr. Baxter, these people have treated us reasonably well, and your course of action would provoke retaliation and—"

"Treated us *well*? I don't give a damn *how* they treat us. They have no right to keep us here."

The Cardinal nodded. "You're right, of course. But let me make my final point, which is that I understand that much of the brashness of young men is a result of the proximity of young women—"

"I don't have to listen to this."

The Cardinal smiled thinly. "I seem to be annoying you. I'm sorry. Well, anyway, don't think for a moment that I doubt these people will kill me and Father Murphy as surely as they would you and Miss Malone. That's not important. What is important is that we not provoke them into the mortal sin of murder. And also important to me is my obligation as guardian of this church. This is the greatest Catholic Cathedral in America, Mr. Baxter, Domus Ecclesiae, the Mother Church, the spiritual center of Catholicism in North America. Try to think of it as Westminster Abbey."

Baxter's face reddened. He drew a breath. "I have a duty to resist, and I will."

The Cardinal shook his head. "Well, we have no such duty to wage war." He moved closer to Baxter. "Can't you leave this in God's hands? Or, if you're not so inclined, in the hands of the authorities outside?"

Baxter looked the Cardinal in the eye. "I've made my position clear."

The Cardinal seemed lost in thought, then said, "Perhaps I *am* overly concerned about this church. It's in my trust, you see, and as with anyone else, material values figure into my calculations. But we *are* agreed that lives are not to be needlessly sacrificed?"

"Of course."

"Neither our lives"—he motioned around the Cathedral—"nor theirs."

"I'm not so certain about theirs," said Harold Baxter.

"All God's children, Mr. Baxter."

"I wonder."

"Come now."

There was a long silence, broken by Maureen Malone's voice as she crossed the sanctuary. "Let me assure you, Cardinal, that each one of these people was spawned in hell. I know. Some of them may seem like rational men and women to you—jolly good Irishmen, sweet talk, lilting brogues, and all that. Perhaps a song or poem later. But they're quite capable of murdering us all and burning your church."

The three men looked silently at her.

She pointed to the two clerics. "It may be that you don't understand real evil, only abstract evil, but you've got Satan in the sanctuary right now." She moved her outstretched hand and pointed to Brian Flynn, who was mounting the steps into the sanctuary.

Flynn looked at them and smiled. "Did someone mention my name?"

CHAPTER 23

Burke moved closer to the stairway opening, drew a deep breath, and called out, "This is the police! I want to speak with Finn MacCumail!" He heard his words echo up the marble stairway.

A voice with a heavy Irish accent called back, "Stand at the gate—hands on the bars! No tricks. I've got a Thompson."

Burke moved into view of the stairway and saw a young man, a boy really, kneeling on the landing in front of the crypt door. Burke mounted the steps slowly and put his hands on the brass gate.

Pedar Fitzgerald pointed the submachine gun down the stairs. "Stand fast!" he called back up the stairs. "Get Finn! There's a fellow here wants a word with him!"

Burke studied the young man for a moment, then shifted his attention to the layout. The stairs split to the left and right at the crypt door landing. Above the crypt door was the rear of the altar, from which rose a huge cross of gold silhouetted against the towering ceiling of the Cathedral. It didn't look to him as if anyone could get through the gates and up those stairs without being cut to pieces by overhead fire.

He heard footsteps on the left-hand stairs, and a tall figure emerged and stood outlined against the eerie yellow light coming from the glass-paneled crypt doors. The figure passed beside the kneeling man and moved deliberately down the dimly lit marble stairs. Burke could not clearly see his features, but saw now that the man was wearing a white collarless shirt and black pants, the remains of a priest's suit. Burke said evenly, "Finn MacCumail?" To an Irishman familiar with Gaelic history, as he was, it sounded as preposterous as calling someone Robin Hood.

"That's right." The tall man kept coming. "Chief of the Fenians."

Burke almost smiled at this pomposity, but something in the man's eyes held him riveted.

Flynn stopped close to the gates and stared at Burke. "And to whom do I have the pleasure of speaking?"

"Chief Inspector Burke, NYPD, Commissioner's office." He met the stare of the man's deep, dark eyes, then looked down at his right hand and saw the large bronze ring.

Brian Flynn said, "I know who you are... *Lieutenant*. I have an Intelligence section too. That's a bit galling, isn't it? Well," he smiled, "if I can be Chief of the Fenians, you can be a Chief Inspector, I suppose."

Burke remembered with some chagrin the first rule of hostage negotiating—never get caught in a lie. He spoke in a slow, measured cadence. "I said that only to expedite matters."

"Admirable reason to lie."

The two men were only inches apart, but the gates

had the effect of lessening the intrusion into their zones of protected territory. Still, Burke felt uncomfortable but kept his hands on the brass bars. "Are the hostages all right?"

"For the time being."

"Let me speak with them."

Flynn shook his head.

"There were shots fired. Who's dead?"

"No one."

"What is it you want?" Burke asked, though it didn't matter what the Fenians wanted, he thought, since they were not going to get it.

Flynn ignored the question. "Are you armed?"

"Of course. But I won't go against that Thompson."

"Some people would. Like Sergeant Tezik."

"He's been taken care of." Burke wondered how Flynn knew Tezik was crazy. He imagined that kindred spirits could recognize each other by the tone of their voices.

Flynn looked over Burke's shoulder at the sacristy corridors.

Burke said, "I've pulled them back."

Flynn nodded.

Burke said, "If you'll tell me what you want, I will see that your demands are passed directly to the top." He knew he was operating off his beat, but he knew also that he had to stabilize the situation until the Hostage Negotiator, Bert Schroeder, took over.

Flynn tapped his fingers on the bars, his bronze ring clanging against the brass in a nervous and, at the same time, unnerving way. "Why can't I speak directly to someone of higher rank?"

Burke thought he heard a mocking tone in his voice. "They are all out of communication. If you turn off the jamming device—"

Flynn laughed, then said abruptly, "Has anyone been killed?"

Burke felt his hands getting sticky on the bars. "Maybe in the riot...Police Commissioner Dwyer...died of a heart attack." He added, "You won't be implicated in that—if you surrender now. You've made your point."

"I haven't even begun to make my point. Were those people on the horse injured?"

"No. Your men saw the policewoman from the towers. The man was me."

Flynn laughed. "Was it, now?" He thought a moment. "Well, that makes a difference."

"Why?"

"Let's just say that it makes it less likely that you are working for a certain English gentleman of my acquaintance." Flynn considered, then said, "Are you wearing a transmitter? Are there listening devices in the corridors?"

"I'm not wearing a wire. I don't know about the corridors."

Flynn took a pencil-shaped microphone detector from his pocket and passed it over Burke's body. "I think I can trust you, even if you are an intelligence officer specializing in hunting Irish patriots like myself."

"I do my job."

"Yes. Too well." He looked at Burke with some interest. "The universal bloodhound. Dogged, nosy, sniffing about. Always wanting to know things. I've known the likes of you in London, Belfast, and Dublin." He stared at Burke, then reached into his pocket and pushed a piece of paper through the gate. "You're as good as anyone, I suppose. Here is a list of one hundred and thirty-seven men and women held by the British in internment camps in Northern Ireland and England. I want these people released by sunrise. That's 6:03 a.m.—New York time. I want them flown to Dublin and granted amnesty by the British and Irish governments plus asylum in the south if they want it. The transfer will be supervised by the International Red Cross and Amnesty International. When I receive word from these two organizations that this is accomplished, we will give you back your Cathedral and release the hostages. If this is not done by sunrise, I will throw Sir Harold Baxter from the bell tower, followed by, in random order, the Cardinal, Father Murphy, and Maureen Malone. Then I will burn the Cathedral. Do you believe me, Lieutenant Burke?"

"I believe you."

"Good. It's important that you know that each of my Fenians has at least one relative in internment. It's also important you know that nothing is sacred to us, not church or priests, not human life or humanity in general."

"I believe you will do what you say you will do."

"Good. And you'll deliver not only the message but also the essence and spirit of what I'm saying. Do you understand that?"

"I understand."

"Yes, I think you do. Now, for ourselves, our purpose is to be reunited with our kin, so we'll not trade their imprisonment for ours. We want immunity from prosecution. We will walk out of here, motor to Kennedy Airport by means of our own conveyances, and leave New York for various destinations. We have passports and money and want nothing from you or your government except a laissez-passer. Understood?"

"Yes."

Flynn leaned nearer the bars so that his face was very close to Burke's. "I know what's going through your mind, Lieutenant Burke—can we talk them out, or do we have to blow them out? I know that your government—and the NYPD—has a shining history of never having given in to demands made at gunpoint. That history will be rewritten before sunrise. You see, we hold all the cards, as you say—Jack, Queen, King, Ace, and Cathedral."

Burke said, "I was thinking of the British government—"

"That, for a change, is Washington's problem, not mine."

"So it is."

"From now on, communicate with me only through the telephone extension on the chancel organ. I don't want to see anyone moving down here."

Burke nodded.

"And you'd better get your command structure established before some of your cowboys try something."

Burke said, "I'll see that they don't."

Flynn nodded. "Stay close, Lieutenant, I'll be wanting you later." He turned and mounted the steps slowly, then disappeared around the corner of the right-hand staircase.

Burke stared up at the kneeling man with the Thompson, and the man jerked the barrel in a motion of dismissal. Burke took his hands off the brass gate and stepped down the stairs and out of the line of sight of the staircase. He wiped his sweaty palms across his topcoat and lit a cigarette as he walked to the corridor opening.

He was glad he wouldn't have to deal again with the man named Brian Flynn, or with the personality of Finn MacCumail, and he felt sorry for Bert Schroeder, who did.

Captain Bert Schroeder stood with his foot on the rim of the fountain in Grand Army Plaza, smoking a short, fat cigar. A light sleet fell on his broad shoulders and soaked into his expensive topcoat. Schroeder watched the crowd slowly trailing away through the lamplit streets around him. Some semblance of order had been restored, but he doubted if he would be able to pick up his daughter and make it to his family party.

The unit he had been marching with, County Tyrone, his mother's ancestral county, had dispersed and drifted off, and he stood alone now, waiting, fairly certain of the instinct that told him he would be called. He looked at his watch, then made his way to a patrol car parked on Fifth Avenue and looked in the window. "Any news yet?"

The patrolman looked up. "No, sir. Radio's still out."

Bert Schroeder felt a sense of anger at the undignified

way the parade had ended but wasn't sure yet toward whom to direct it.

The patrolman added, "I think the crowd is thin enough for me to drive you someplace if you want."

Schroeder considered, then said, "No." He tapped a paging device on his belt. "This thing should still be able to receive a signal. But hang around in case I want you."

Schroeder's pager sounded, and he felt his heart pound in a conditioned response. He threw down his cigar and shut off the device.

The driver in the patrol car called out, "Somebody grabbed somebody, Captain. You're on."

Schroeder started to speak and found that his mouth was dry. "Yeah, I'm on."

"Give you a lift?"

"What! No...I have to...to call..." He tried to steady the pounding in his chest. He turned and looked up at the brightly lit Plaza Hotel on the far side of the square, then ran toward it. As he ran, a dozen possible scenarios flashed through his mind the way they always did when the call came—*hostages*—who? The Governor? The Mayor? Congressmen? Embassy people? But he pushed these speculations aside, because no matter what he imagined when the beeper sounded or the phone rang or the radio called his name, it always turned out to be something very different. All he knew for certain was that very shortly he would be bargaining hard for someone's life, or many lives, and he would do it under the critical eyes of every politician and police official in the city.

He bounded up the steps of the Plaza, ran through

the crowded lobby, then down a staircase to the line of wall phones outside Trader Vic's. A large crowd was massed around the phones, and Schroeder pushed through and grabbed a receiver from a man's hand. "Police business! Move back!"

He dialed a special operator number and gave her a number in Police Plaza. He waited a long time for a ring, and while he waited he lit another cigar and paced around to the extent of the phone cord.

He felt like an actor waiting for the curtain, apprehensive over his rehearsed lines, panicky that the ad libs would be disastrous. His heart was beating out of control now, and his mouth went dry as his palms became wet. He hated this. He wanted to be somewhere else. He loved it. He felt alive.

The phone rang at the other end, and the duty sergeant answered. Schroeder said calmly, "What's up, Dennis?"

Schroeder listened in silence for a full minute, then said in a barely audible voice, "I'll be at the rectory in ten minutes."

He hung up and, after steadying himself against the wall, pushed away from the phones and mounted the steps to the lobby, his body sagging, his face blank. Then his body straightened, his eyes came alive, and his breathing returned to normal. He walked confidently out the front doors and stepped into the police car that had followed him.

The driver said, "Bad, Captain?"

"They're all bad. Saint Pat's rectory on Madison. Step on it."

CHAPTER 24

Monsignor Downes's adjoining offices were filling rapidly with people. Burke stood by the window of the outer office sipping a cup of coffee. Mayor Kline and Governor Doyle came in looking very pale, followed by their aides. Burke recognized other faces as they appeared at the door, somewhat hesitantly, as though they were entering a funeral parlor. In fact, he thought, as people streamed in and exchanged subdued greetings the atmosphere became more wakelike, except that everyone still wore topcoats and green carnations— and there were no bereaved to pay condolences to, though he noticed that Monsignor Downes came close to filling that role.

Burke looked down into Madison Avenue. Streetlights illuminated the hundreds of police who, in the falling sleet, were clearing an area around the rectory. Police cars and limousines pulled up to the curb discharging police commanders and civilian officials. Lines were being brought in by the telephone company, and field phone wire was being strung by police to compensate for the lost radio communication. The machine was moving slowly, deliberately. Traffic was rolling; civilization, such as it was in New York, had survived another day.

"Hello, Pat."

Burke spun around. "Langley. Jesus, it's good to see someone who doesn't have much more rank than I do."

Langley smiled. "You making the coffee and emptying the ashtrays?"

"Have you been filled in?"

"Briefly. What a fucking mess." He looked around the Monsignor's office. "It looks like *Who's Who in the East* here. Has Commissioner Dwyer arrived yet?"

"That's not likely. He died of a heart attack."

"Christ. Nobody told me that. You mean that dipshit Rourke is in charge?"

"As soon as he gets here."

"He's right behind me. We put the chopper down in the courtyard of the Palace Hotel. Christ, you should have seen what it looked like from the air."

"Yeah. I think I would rather have seen it from the air." Burke lit a cigarette. "Are we in trouble?"

"We won't be invited to the Medal Day ceremonies this June."

"For sure." Burke tapped his ash on the windowsill. "But we're still in the game."

"You, maybe. You got a horse shot out from under you. I didn't have a horse shot out from under me. Any horses around?"

"I have some information from Jack Ferguson we can use when we're on the carpet." He took Langley's arm and drew him closer. "Finn MacCumail's real name is Brian Flynn. He's Maureen Malone's ex-lover."

"Ah," said Langley, "ex-lover. This is getting interesting."

Burke went on. "Flynn's lieutenant is John Hickey."

"Hickey's dead," said Langley. "Died a few years ago.... There was a funeral...in Jersey."

"Some men find it more convenient to hold their funeral before their demise."

"Maybe Ferguson was wrong."

"He saw John Hickey in Saint Pat's today. He doesn't make mistakes."

"We'll have the grave dug up." Langley felt chilled and moved away from the window. "I'll get a court order."

Burke shrugged. "You find a sober judge in Jersey tonight, and I'll dig it up myself. Anyway, Hickey's file is on the way, and Louise is checking out Brian Flynn."

Langley nodded. "Good work. The British can help us on Flynn."

"Right...Major Martin."

"Have you seen him?"

Burke inclined his head toward the double doors.

Langley said, "Who else is in there?"

"Schroeder and some police commanders, federal types, and people from the British and Irish consulates." As he spoke, Mayor Kline, Governor Doyle, and their aides went into the inner office.

Langley watched them, then said, "Has Schroeder begun his dialogue yet?"

"I don't think so. I passed on MacCumail's—

Flynn's—demands to him. He smiled and told me to wait outside. Here I am."

Deputy Police Commissioner Rourke hurried across the room and into the inner office, motioning to Langley to follow.

Langley turned to Burke. "Listen for the sounds of heads rolling across the floor. You may be the next Chief of Intelligence—I have this vision of Patrick Burke captured for eternity in a bronze statue, on the steps of Saint Patrick's, astride a horse with flaring nostrils, charging up—"

"Fuck off."

Langley smiled and hurried off.

Burke looked at the people milling about the room. The Speaker of the House of Representatives, past and present governors, senators, mayors, congressmen. It *was* a veritable *Who's Who in the East*, but they looked, he thought, rather common and frightened at the moment. He noticed that all the decanters on the coffee table were empty, then fixed his attention on Monsignor Downes, still sitting behind his desk. Burke approached him. "Monsignor—"

The Rector of St. Patrick's Cathedral looked up.

"Feeling better?"

"Why didn't the police know this was going to happen?"

Burke resisted several replies, then said, "We *should* have known. It was all there if we had only..."

Langley appeared at the double doors and motioned to Burke.

Burke looked at the Rector. "Come with me."

"Why?"

"It's your church, and you have a right to know what's going to happen to it. Your Cardinal and your priest are in there—"

"Priests make people uncomfortable sometimes. They get in the way . . . unintentionally."

"Good. That may be what this group needs."

Monsignor Downes rose reluctantly and followed Burke into the inner office.

In the big room about forty men and women stood or sat, their attention focused around the desk where Captain Bert Schroeder sat. Heads turned as Burke and Monsignor Downes came into the room.

Mayor Kline rose from his chair and offered it to Downes, who flushed and sat quickly. The Mayor smiled at his own beneficence and good manners, then held his hands up for silence. He began speaking in his adenoidal voice that made everyone wince. "Are we all here? Okay, let's begin." He cleared his throat. "All right, now, we have all agreed that the City of New York is, under law, primarily responsible for any action taken in this matter." He looked at his aide, Roberta Spiegel. She nodded, and he went on. "So, to avoid confusion, we will all speak to the perpetrators with one voice, through one man . . . ." He paused and raised his voice as though introducing a speaker. "The NYPD Hostage Negotiator . . . Captain Bert Schroeder."

The effect of the Mayor's delivery elicited some applause, which died away as it became apparent that it wasn't appropriate. Roberta Spiegel shot the Mayor a look of disapproval, and he turned red. Captain Schroeder rose and half acknowledged the applause.

Burke said softly to Langley, "I feel like a proctologist trapped in a room full of assholes."

Schroeder looked at the faces turned toward him and drew a deep breath. "Thank you, Your Honor." His eyes darted around the room. "I am about to open negotiations with the man who calls himself Finn MacCumail, Chief of the Fenian Army. As you may know, my unit, since it was started by Captain Frank Bolz, has concluded successfully every hostage situation that has gone down in this city, without the loss of a single hostage." He saw people nodding, and the terror of what he was about to undertake suddenly evaporated as he pictured himself concluding another successful case. He put an aggressive tone in his voice. "And since there's no reason to change tactics that have been so successful in criminal as well as political hostage situations, I will treat this as any other hostage situation. It will not be influenced by outside political considerations...but I do solicit your help and suggestions." He looked into the crowd and read expressions ranging from open hostility to agreement.

Burke said to Langley, "Not bad."

Langley replied, "He's full of shit. That man is the most political animal I know."

Schroeder went on. "In order to facilitate my job I'd like this room cleared of everyone except the following." He picked up a list written on Monsignor Downes's stationary and read from it, then looked up. "It's also been agreed that commanders of the field operations will headquarter themselves in the lower offices of the rectory. People connected with the negotiations who are not in this office with me will be in the Monsignor's outer office. I've spoken to the Vicar General by phone, and he's agreed that everyone else may use the Cardinal's residence."

Schroeder glanced at Monsignor Downes, then went on. "Telephones are being installed in the residence and...refreshments will be served in His Eminence's dining room. Voice speakers will be installed throughout both residences for paging and so that you may monitor my phone conversations with the perpetrators."

The room filled with noise as Schroeder sat down. The Mayor raised his hands for silence the way he had done so many times in the classroom. "All right. Let's leave the Captain to do his job. Everyone, Governor, ladies and gentlemen—please clear the room. That's right. Very good." The Mayor went to the door and opened it.

Schroeder mopped his brow and waited as the remaining people seated themselves. "All right. You know who I am. Everyone introduce themselves in turn." He pointed to the sole woman present.

Roberta Spiegel, a good-looking woman in her early forties, sat back in a rocking chair and crossed her legs, looking bored, sensual, and businesslike at the same time. "Spiegel. Mayor's aide."

A small man with flaming red hair, dressed in tweeds, said, "Tomas Donahue, Consul General, Irish Republic."

"Major Bartholomew Martin, representing Her Majesty's government in the...absence of Sir Harold Baxter."

"James Kruger, CIA."

A muscular man with a pockmarked face said, "Douglas Hogan, FBI."

A rotund young man with glasses said, "Bill Voight, Governor's office."

"Deputy Commissioner Rourke...Acting Police Commissioner."

A well-dressed man with a nasal voice said, "Arnold Sheridan, agent-in-charge, State Department Security Office, representing State."

"Captain Bellini, NYPD, Emergency Services Division."

"Inspector Philip Langley, NYPD, Intelligence Division."

"Burke, Intelligence."

Schroeder looked at Monsignor Downes, who, he realized, had not left. Schroeder considered for a moment as he sat at the man's desk with his gold-crossed stationery stacked neatly in a corner, then smiled. "And our host, you might say, Monsignor Downes, Rector of Saint Patrick's. Good of you to...come...and to let us use...Will you be staying?"

Monsignor Downes nodded hesitantly.

"Good," said Schroeder. "Good. Okay, let's start at the beginning. Burke, why the hell did you open negotiations? You know better than that."

Burke loosened his tie and sat back.

Schroeder thought the question may have sounded rhetorical, so he pressed on. "You didn't make any promises, did you? You didn't say anything that might compromise—"

"I told you what I said," interrupted Burke.

Schroeder stiffened. He glared at Burke and said,

"Please repeat the exchange, and also tell us how he seemed—his state of mind. That sort of thing."

Burke repeated what he had said earlier, and added, "He seemed very self-assured. And it wasn't bravado. He seemed intelligent, too."

"He didn't seem unbalanced?" asked Schroeder.

"His whole manner seemed normal—except for what he was saying, of course."

"Drugs—alcohol?" asked Schroeder.

"Probably had less to drink today than anyone here."

Someone laughed.

Schroeder turned to Langley. "We can't get an angle on this guy unless we know his real name. Right?"

Langley glanced at Burke, then at the Acting Commissioner. "Actually, I know who he is."

The room became quiet.

Burke stole a look at Major Martin, who seemed impassive.

Langley continued. "His name is Brian Flynn. The British will certainly have a file on him—psy-profile, that sort of thing. Maybe the CIA has something, too. His lieutenant is a man named John Hickey, thought to have died some years ago. You may have heard of him. He's a naturalized American citizen. We and the FBI have an extensive file on Hickey."

The FBI man, Hogan, said, "I'll check."

Kruger said, "I'll check on Flynn."

Major Martin added, "Both names seem familiar. I'll wire London."

Schroeder looked a bit happier. "Good. Good work. That makes my job—our jobs—a lot easier. Right?"

He turned to Burke. "One more thing—did you get the impression that the woman who fired at you was shooting to kill?"

Burke said, "I had the impression she was aiming for the horse. They probably have some discipline of fire-power, if that's what you're getting at."

The policemen in the room nodded. Commissioner Rourke said, "Does anybody know anything about this group—the Fenians?" He looked at Kruger and Hogan.

Kruger glanced at Major Martin, then replied, "We have almost no funds to maintain a liaison section on Northern Irish affairs. It has been determined, you see, that the IRA poses no immediate threat to the United States, and preventive measures were not thought to be justified. Unfortunately, we are paying for that frugality now."

Douglas Hogan added, "The FBI thought it was the Provisional IRA until Major Martin suggested otherwise. My section, which specializes in Irish organizations in America, is understaffed and partly dependent on British Intelligence for information."

Burke nodded to himself. He was beginning to catch the drift. Kruger and Hogan were being petulant, taking an I-told-you-so line. They were also covering themselves, rehearsing for later testimony, and laying the groundwork for the future. Nicely done, too.

Commissioner Rourke looked at Major Martin. "Then you are...I mean...you are not..."

Major Martin smiled and stood. "Yes, I'm not actually *with* the consulate. I'm with British Military

Intelligence. No use letting that get about, though."
He looked around the room, then turned to Langley.
"I told Inspector Langley that something was—what is
the term?—coming down. But unfortunately—"

Langley said dryly, "Yes, the Major has been very
helpful, as have the CIA and FBI. My own division
did admirably too; and actually missed averting this
act by only minutes. Lieutenant Burke should be com-
mended for his resourcefulness and bravery."

There was a silence during which, Burke noticed,
no one yelled "Hooray for Burke." It occurred to
him that each of them was identifying his own objectives, his own exposure, looking for allies, scape-
goats, enemies, and trying to figure how to use this
crisis to his advantage. "I told Flynn we wouldn't
keep him waiting."

Schroeder said, "I won't begin a dialogue until I
clarify our position." He looked at Bill Voight, the
Governor's aide. "Has the Governor indicated that he
is willing to grant immunity from prosecution?"

Voight shook his head. "Not at this time."

Schroeder looked at Roberta Spiegel. "What is the
Mayor's position regarding the use of police?"

Roberta Spiegel lit a cigarette. "No matter what
kind of deal is concluded with London or Washington
or anyone, the Mayor will enforce the law and order
the arrest of anyone coming out of that Cathedral. If
they don't come out, the Mayor reserves the right to
send the police in to get them."

Schroeder nodded thoughtfully, then looked at
Arnold Sheridan.

The State Department man said, "I can't speak for

the administration or State at this time, and I don't know what the Attorney General's position will be regarding immunity from federal prosecution. But you can assume nobody in Washington is going along with any of those demands."

Schroeder looked at Tomas Donahue.

The Irish Consul General glanced at Major Martin, then said, "The Irish Republican Army is outlawed in the Irish Republic, and my government will not accept members of the IRA or offer them sanctuary in the unlikely event the British government decides to release these people."

Major Martin added, "Although I do not represent Her Majesty's government, I can assure you the government's position is as always regarding the IRA or whatever they're calling themselves today: Never negotiate, and if you do negotiate, never concede a single point, and if you do concede a point, never tell them you've conceded it."

Roberta Spiegel said, "Now that we know what uncompromising bastards we are, let's negotiate."

Commissioner Rourke said to Schroeder, "Yes, now all you have to do is talk them out, Bert. They've involved the Red Cross and Amnesty, so we can't easily lie to them. You've got to be very...very..." He couldn't come up with the word he wanted and turned to Captain Bellini, who had said nothing so far. "Captain, in the unlikely event Bert can't do it, is the Emergency Services Division ready to mount an...assault?"

Bellini shifted his massive frame in his small chair. The blueblack stubble on his face gave him a hard appearance, but the area under his eyes had gone very pale. "Yeah...yes, sir. When the time comes, we'll be ready."

Schroeder reached for the telephone. "Okay. I know where everyone's coming from. Right?"

Monsignor Downes spoke. "May I say something?"

Everyone looked at him. Schroeder took his hand off the receiver, smiled, and nodded.

Downes said softly, "No one has said anything about the hostages yet. Or about the Cathedral." There was a silence in the room and Monsignor Downes went on. "If, as I assume, your first responsibility is to the hostages, and if you make this clear to your superiors and to the people inside the Cathedral, then I don't see why a compromise can't be worked out." He looked around the room.

No one took it upon himself to explain the realities of international diplomacy to the Monsignor.

Schroeder said, "I haven't lost a hostage—or for that matter a building—yet, Monsignor. It's often possible to get what you want without giving anything in return."

"Oh...I didn't know that," said Monsignor Downes quietly.

"In fact," continued Schroeder assuringly, "the tack I am going to take is pretty much as you suggested. Stick around, you'll see how it's done." He picked up the telephone and waited for the police operator at the switchboard. He looked around the room and said, "Don't be disturbed if he seems to be winning a few rounds. You have to give them the impression they're scoring. By sunrise he'll tire—you ever go shark fishing? You let them run out the line until you're ready to reel them in." He said to the police operator, "Yes, get me the extension at the chancel organ." He put his elbows on the desk and waited. No one in the room moved.

CHAPTER 25

Governor Doyle put down the telephone and looked around the crowded outer office. People were jockeying for the newly installed phones, and a cloud of blue smoke hung over the elegant furnishings, reminding him of a hotel suite on election night, and that reminded him of the next election. He spotted Mayor Kline talking to a group of city and police officials and came up behind the Mayor, taking his arm in a firm grip. "Murray, I have to speak to you."

The Mayor let himself be propelled by the bigger man into the hallway and up to a landing on the staircase that led to the priests' rooms. The Mayor escaped the Governor's grasp and said, "What is it, Bob? I have things to do."

"I just spoke to Albany. The main concern up there is civil disobedience."

"I didn't think enough people lived in Albany to have a riot."

"No, *here*. In *Manhattan*. That mob outside could explode again . . . with all the drinking . . . ."

The Mayor smiled. "What makes this Saint Patrick's night different from all other Saint Patrick's nights?"

"Look, Murray, this is not the time for your wise-cracking. The seizure of this Cathedral may be just a prelude to a larger civil insurrection. I think you should call a curfew."

"*Curfew*? Are you crazy? Rush hour traffic is still trying to get out of Manhattan."

"Call it later, then." The Governor lowered his voice. "My analysts in Albany say that the only thing keeping this situation cooled down is the sleet. When the sleet stops, the bars will empty and there could be trouble—"

The Mayor looked incredulous. "I don't care *what* your analysts in Albany say. This is *Saint Patrick's Day* in New York, for God's sake. The biggest parade in the world, outside of the May Day Parade in Moscow, has just ended. The largest single party in New York—maybe in America—is just beginning. People plan this day all year. There are over a million people in midtown alone, jammed into bars, restaurants, and house parties. More liquor and food is consumed tonight than any other night of the year. If I called a curfew...the Restaurant Owners' Association would have me *assassinated*. They'd pour all the unconsumed beer into the Rockefeller Center skating rink and drown me in it. Shit, you try to enforce a curfew tonight."

"But—"

"And it's *religious*. What kind of an Irishman are you? That's all we need—a Jewish Mayor calling off Saint Patrick's Day. It'd be easier to call off *Christmas*. What kind of yo-yos are giving you advice in Albany? Fucking farmers?"

The Governor began pacing around the small landing. "Okay, Murray. Take it easy." He stopped pacing and thought a moment. "Okay, forget the curfew. But I *do* think you need the State Police and the National Guard to help keep order."

"No. No soldiers, no State Police. I have twenty thousand police—more than a full army division. Little by little we'll get them out on the street."

"The Sixty-ninth Regiment is mustered and in a position to lend a hand."

"Mustered?" Kline laughed. "Plastered is more like it. Christ, the enlisted men got off duty from the armory at two o'clock. They're so shitfaced by now they wouldn't know a rifle from their bootlaces."

"I happen to know that the officers and most of the noncoms are at a cocktail party in the armory right now, and—"

"What are you trying to pull?"

"Pull?"

"*Pull.*"

The Governor coughed into his hand, then smiled good-naturedly. "All right, it's like this—you know damned well that this is the biggest disturbance to hit New York since the blackout of '77, and I have to show that I'm doing *something.*"

"Fly to Albany. Let me run my city."

"*Your* city. It's my *state*! I'm responsible to *all* the people."

"Right. Where were you when we needed money?"

"Look...look, I don't need your permission to call out the National Guard or the State Police."

"Call your Attorney General and check on

that." Mayor Kline turned and took a step toward the stairs.

"Hold on, Murray. Listen...suppose Albany foots the bill for this operation? I mean, God, this will cost the city *millions*. I'll take care of it, and I'll get Washington to kick in a little extra. I'll say it was an international thing, which it is—like the consulate protection money. Okay?"

The Mayor arrested his descent down the stairs and turned back toward the Governor. He smiled encouragingly.

The Governor went on. "I'll pay for it all if you let me send in my people—I need to show a state presence here—you understand. Okay? Whaddaya say, Murray?"

The Mayor said, "The money to be paid to the city within thirty days of billing."

"You got it."

"Including all overtime and regular time of all the city departments involved, including police, fire, sanitation, and other municipal departments for as long as the siege lasts, and all expenses incurred in the aftermath."

"All right...."

"Including costs of repair to municipal property, and aid to private individuals and businesses who sustain a loss."

The Governor swallowed. "Sure."

"But only the Sixty-ninth Regiment. No other guard units and no State Police—my boys don't get along with them."

"Let me send the State Police into the boroughs to fill the vacuum left by the reassignment to Manhattan."

The Mayor considered, then nodded and smiled. He stuck out his hand, and they shook on it. Mayor Kline said loudly, so that the people in the hallway below could hear, "Governor, I'd like you to call out the Sixty-ninth Regiment and the State Police."

Colonel Dennis Logan sat at the head table in the 69th Regiment Armory hall on Lexington Avenue. Over a hundred officers, noncommissioned officers, and civilian guests sat or stood around the big hall. The degree of intoxication ranged from almost to very. Logan himself felt a bit unsteady. The mood this year was not boisterous, Logan noticed, and there was a subdued atmosphere in the hall, a result of reports of the disturbance in midtown.

A sergeant came toward Logan with a telephone and plugged the phone into a jack. "Colonel, the Governor is on the line."

Logan nodded and sat up straight. He took the receiver, glanced at Major Cole, then said, "Colonel Logan speaking, sir. Happy Saint Patrick's Day to you, Governor."

"I'm afraid not, Colonel. A group of Irish revolutionaries has seized Saint Patrick's Cathedral."

The Colonel felt a heaviness in his chest, and every part of his body went damp, except his throat. "Yes, sir."

"I'm calling the Sixty-ninth Regiment to duty."

Colonel Logan looked around the hall at the scene spread out before him. Most of the officers and NCOs were wobbling, a few were slumped over tables. The enlisted men were home by now or scattered throughout every bar in the metropolitan area.

"Colonel?"

"Yes, sir."

"Full gear, riot-control equipment, weapons with live ammunition."

"Yes, sir."

"Assemble outside the Cardinal's residence on Madison for further orders. Don't delay."

"Yes, sir."

"Is the Sixty-ninth ready, Colonel?"

Logan started to say something rational, then cleared his throat and said, "The Fighting Irish are always ready, Governor."

"This is Captain Bert Schroeder of the New York Police Department." Schroeder reached out and turned on the switches that activated the speakers in both residences.

A voice with an Irish accent came into the room and echoed from the outer office, which quickly became still. "What took you so long?"

Burke nodded. "That's him."

Schroeder spoke softly, pleasantly, a tone designed to be soothing. "Things were a bit confused, sir. Is this—?"

"Finn MacCumail, Chief of the Fenians. I told Sergeant Tezik and Lieutenant Burke I wanted to speak with a high ranking man. I'm only up to a captain now."

Schroeder gave his standard reply. "Everyone that you would want to speak to is present. They are listening to us from speakers. Can you hear the echo? We've all agreed that to avoid confusion I will do the speaking for everyone. They'll relay messages through me."

"Who are *you*?"

"I have some experience in this."

"Well, that's interesting. Are there representatives of the Irish, British, and American governments present?"

"Yes, sir. The Police Commissioner, the Mayor, and the Governor, too."

"I picked a good day for this, didn't I?"

Burke said to Schroeder, "I forgot to tell you, he has a sense of humor."

Schroeder said into the telephone, "Yes, sir. So let's get right down to business."

"Let's back up and establish the rules, Captain. Is everyone in contact with their capitals?"

"Yes, sir."

"Have Amnesty International and the Red Cross been contacted?"

"It's being done, sir."

"And you are the mouthpiece?"

"Yes, sir. It's less confusing. I think you'll find the arrangement acceptable." Schroeder sat at the edge of his chair. This was the most difficult part, persuading wild-eyed lunatics that it was better to speak to him than to the President of the United States or the Queen of England. "So, if we can proceed . . ."

"All right. We'll see."

Schroeder exhaled softly. "We have your demands in front of us, and the list of people you want released from Northern Ireland. We want you to know that our primary concern is the safety of the hostages—"

"Don't forget the Cathedral. It's ready to be burned down."

"Yes. But our *primary* concern is human life."

"Sorry about the horse."

"What? Oh, yes. We are too. But no one—no human—has been killed, so let's all work to keep it that way."

"Commissioner Dwyer is feeling better, then?"

Schroeder shot a look at Burke and covered the mouthpiece. "What the hell did you tell him about Dwyer?"

"Rule number one. The truth."

"Shit!" Schroeder uncovered the mouthpiece. "The Commissioner's death was from natural causes, sir. You have not killed anyone." He stressed again, "Our goal is to protect lives—"

"Then I can burn down the Cathedral after I get what I want?"

Schroeder looked around the room again. Everyone was bent forward in their chairs, cigars and cigarettes discharging smoke into the quiet atmosphere. "No, sir. That would be arson, a felony. Let's not compound the problem."

"No problem here. Just do what you're told."

"Are the hostages safe?"

"I told Burke they were. If I say something, that's what I mean."

"I was just reassuring everyone here. There are a lot of people here . . . Mr. MacCumail, to hear what you have to say to them. The Rector of the Cathedral is here. He's very concerned about the Cardinal and the others. They're all counting on you to come through. Listen, is it possible to speak with the hostages? I'd like to—"

"Perhaps later."

"All right. Fine. Okay. Listen, I'd like to speak to you about that spotlight. That was a potentially dangerous act—"

"Not if you have the County Antrim shooting champion in the bell tower. Keep the spotlights off."

"Yes, sir. In the future, if you want something, just ask me. Try not to take things into your own hands. It's easier, sometimes, to ask."

"I'll try to remember that. Where exactly are you calling from?"

"I'm in the Rector's office."

"Good. Best not to get too far from the center of things."

"We're right here."

"So are we. All right, I have other things to see to. Don't be calling me every minute on some pretext. The next call I receive from you will inform me that the three governments and the two agencies involved are ready to begin working out the details of the transfer of prisoners."

"That may be some time. I'd like to be able to call you and give you progress reports."

"Don't make a nuisance of yourself."

"I'm here to help."

"Good. You can start by sending the keys to me."

"The keys?" He looked at Monsignor Downes, who nodded.

Flynn said, "All the keys to the Cathedral—not the city. Send them now, with Lieutenant Burke."

Schroeder said, "I'm not sure I can locate any keys—"

"Don't be starting that bullshit, Captain. I want them within ten minutes or I raze the Altar of the Blessed Sacrament. Tell that to Downes and he'll produce all the keys he's got, and about a hundred he hasn't got."

Monsignor Downes came toward the desk, looking very agitated.

Schroeder said quickly into the phone, "All right. There was a misunderstanding. The Monsignor informs me he has a complete set of keys."

"I thought you'd find them. Also, send in corned beef and cabbage dinners for forty-five people. I want it catered by...hold on, let me check with my American friend here." There was a short silence, then Flynn said, "John Barleycorn's on East Forty-fifth Street. Soda bread, coffee and tea as well. And a sweet, if you don't mind. I'll pay the bill."

"We'll take care of that...and the bill, too."

"Captain, before this night is through there won't be enough money in the city treasury to buy you a glass of beer. I'll pay for the food."

"Yes, sir. One more thing. About the time limit...you've presented us with some complicated problems and we may need more time to—"

Flynn's voice became belligerent. "No extensions! The prisoners named had better be free in Dublin when the first light breaks through the windows of the Lady Chapel. Dawn or dead, Schaeffer."

"Schroeder. Look—"

"Whatever. Happy Saint Paddy's Day to you. *Erin*

go bragh." There was a click, and the sound of the phone hummed in the room. Captain Schroeder put down his telephone, shut off the speakers, and relit his cigar. He tapped his fingers on the desk. It had not gone well. Yet he felt he'd dealt with harder men than Finn MacCumail. Never as well spoken, perhaps, but crazier, certainly.

He kept reminding himself of two facts. One was that he'd never had a failure. The other was that he'd never failed to get an extension of a deadline. And much of his success in the first fact was a result of his success in the second. He looked up at the silent assembly. "This one is going to be rough. I like them rough."

Captain Joe Bellini stood at the window with his tunic open, his thumbs hooked into his gun belt. His fingers ran over his cartridge loops. He had a mental picture of his Emergency Services Division assaulting the big gray lady out there. He didn't like them rough; he didn't like them easy. He didn't like them at all.

Brian Flynn sat at the chancel organ beside the sanctuary and looked at the book resting on the keycover. "Schaeffer." He laughed.

John Hickey picked up the book, titled *My Years as a Hostage Negotiator*, by Bert Schroeder. "Schaeffer. Very good, Brian. But he'll be on to you eventually."

Flynn nodded. "Probably." He pushed back the rolltop cover of the keyboard and pressed on a key, but no sound came from the pipes across the ambulatory. "We need the key to turn this on," he said absently. He looked up at Hickey. "We don't want to hurt him too badly professionally. We want him in there. And toward the end, if we have to, we'll play our trump card against him—Terri O'Neal." He laughed. "Did ever a poor bastard have so many cards stacked against him without knowing it?"

CHAPTER 26

Flynn said, "Hello, Burke."

Burke stopped at the bottom of the sacristy stairs.

Flynn said, "I asked for you so you'd gain stature with your superiors."

"Thanks." Burke held up a large key-ring. "You want these?"

"Hand them through."

Burke climbed the steps and handed the keys through the bars.

Flynn produced the microphone sensor and passed it over Burke's body. "They say that technology is dehumanizing, but this piece of technology makes it unnecessary to search you, which always causes strained feelings. This way it's almost like trusting one another." He put the device away.

Burke said, "What difference would it make if I *was* wired? We're not going to discuss anything that I won't report."

"That remains to be seen." He turned and called out to Pedar Fitzgerald on the landing. "Take a break." Fitzgerald cradled his submachine gun and left. Flynn and Burke stared at each other, then Flynn spoke. "How did you get on to us, Lieutenant?"

"That's no concern of yours."

"Of course it is. Major Martin?"

Burke realized that he felt much freer to talk without a transmitter sending his voice back to the rectory. He nodded and saw a strange expression pass briefly over Flynn's face. "Friend of yours?"

"Professional acquaintance," answered Flynn. "Did the good Major tell you my real name?"

Burke didn't answer.

Flynn moved closer to the gate. "There is an old saying in intelligence work—'It's not important to know who fired the bullet, but who paid for it.'" He looked at Burke closely. "Who paid for the bullets?"

"You tell me."

"British Military Intelligence provided the logistics for the Fenian Army."

"The British government would not take such a risk because of your petty war—"

"I'm talking about people who pursue their own goals, which may or may not coincide with those of their government. These people talk of historical considerations to justify themselves—"

"So do you."

Flynn ignored the interruption. "These people are monumental egotists. Their lives are meaningful only as long as they can manipulate, deceive, intrigue, and eliminate their enemies, real or imagined, on the other side or on their own side. They find self-expression only in situations of crisis and turmoil, which they often manufacture themselves. That's your basic intelligence man, or secret policeman, or whatever they call themselves. That's Major Bartholomew Martin."

"I thought you were describing yourself."

Flynn smiled coldly. "I'm a revolutionary. Counter-revolutionaries are far more despicable."

"Maybe I should get into auto theft."

Flynn laughed. "Ah, Lieutenant, you're an honest city cop. I trust you." Burke didn't answer, and Flynn said, "I'll tell you something else—I think Martin had help in America. He had to. Be careful of the CIA and FBI." Again Burke didn't respond, and Flynn said, "Who gains the most from what's happened today?"

Burke looked up. "Not you. You'll be dead shortly, and if what you say is true, then what does that make *you*? A pawn. A lowly pawn who's been played off by British Intelligence and maybe by the CIA and FBI, for their own game."

Flynn smiled. "Aye, I know that. But the pawn has captured the archbishop, you see, and occupies his square as well. Pawns should never be underestimated; when they reach the end of the board, they turn and may become knights."

Burke understood Brian Flynn. He said, "Assuming Major Martin is what you say he is, why are you telling me? Am I supposed to expose him?"

"No. That would badly compromise me, you understand. Just keep an eye on him. He wants me dead now that I've served his purpose. He wants the hostages dead and the Cathedral destroyed—to show the world what savages the Irish are. Be wary of his advice to your superiors. Do you understand?"

"I understand that you've gotten yourself in a

no-win situation. You've been sucked into a bad deal thinking you could turn it around, but now you're not so sure."

"My goal is uncompromised. It's up to the British government to release my people. It will be their fault if—"

"For God's sake, man, give it up," Burke said, his voice giving way to impatience and anger. "Take a few years for aggravated assault, false imprisonment, whatever the hell you can work out with the DA."

Flynn gripped the bars in front of him. "Stop talking like a fucking cop! I'm a soldier, Burke, not a bloody criminal who makes deals with DAs."

Burke let out a long breath and said softly, "I can't save you."

"I didn't ask you to—but the fact that you mentioned it tells me more about Patrick Burke, Irishman, than Patrick Burke, policeman, is willing to admit."

"Bullshit."

Flynn relaxed his grip on the bars. "Just take care of Major Martin and you'll save the hostages and the Cathedral. I'll save the Fenians. Now run along and bring the corned beef like a good fellow, won't you? We may chat again."

Burke put a businesslike tone in his voice. "They want to haul the horse away."

"Of course. An armistice to pick up the dead." He seemed to be trying to regain control of himself and smiled. "As long as they don't make corned beef out of it. One man with a rope and an open vehicle. No tricks."

"No tricks."

"No, there have been enough tricks for one day." Flynn turned and moved up the stairs, then stopped abruptly and said over his shoulder, "I'll show you what a decent fellow I am, Burke—everyone knows that Jack Ferguson is a police informer. Tell him to get out of town if he values his life." He turned again and ran up the stairs.

Burke watched him disappear around the corner on the landing. *I'm a soldier, not a bloody criminal.* It had been said without a trace of anguish in his voice, but the anguish was there.

Brian Flynn stood before the Cardinal seated on his throne. "Your Eminence, I'm going to ask you an important question."

The Cardinal inclined his head.

Flynn asked, "Are there any hidden ways—any secret passages into this Cathedral?"

The Cardinal answered immediately. "If there were, I wouldn't tell you."

Flynn stepped back and pointed to the towering ceiling at a point above the crypt where the red hats of the deceased archbishops of New York hung suspended by wire. "Would you like to have your hat hung there?"

The Cardinal looked at him coldly. "I am a Christian who believes in life everlasting, and I'm not intimidated by threats of death."

"Ah, Cardinal, you took it wrong. I meant I'd tell my people in the attic to take an ax to the plaster lathing until that beautiful ceiling is lying in the pews."

The Cardinal drew a short breath, then said softly,

"To the best of my knowledge, there are no secret passages. But that doesn't mean there aren't any."

"No, it doesn't. Because I suspect that there are. Now, think of when you were first shown your new cathedral by the Vicar General. Surely there must be an escape route in the event of insurrection. A priest's hole such as we have in Ireland and England."

"I don't believe the architect considered such a thing. This is America."

"That has less meaning with each passing year. Think, Your Eminence. Lives will be saved if you can remember."

The Cardinal sat back and looked over the vast church. Yes, there were hollow walls with staircases that went somewhere, passages that were never used, but he could not honestly say that he remembered them or knew if they led from or to an area not controlled by these people. He looked out over the marble floor in front of him. The crypt lay below and, around the crypt, a low-ceilinged basement. But they knew that. He'd seen Hickey and Megan Fitzgerald descend through the bronze plate beside the altar.

Two thirds of the basement was little more than crawl space, a darkness where rats could scurry beneath the marble floor above. And above that darkness six million people passed every year to worship God, to meditate, or just to look. But the darkness below their feet stayed the same, until now—now it was seeping into the Cathedral and into the consciousness and souls of the people in the Cathedral. The dark places became important, not the sanctified places of light.

The Cardinal looked up at the figures standing tensely in the triforia and the choir loft, like sentinels on dark, craggy cliffs, guards on city walls. The eternal watchman, frightened, isolated, whispering, "*Watchman, what of the night?*"

The Cardinal turned to Flynn. "I can think of no way in and, by the same token, no way out for you."

"The way out for me will be through the front doors." He questioned the Cardinal closely about the suspected basement beneath the nave, passages between the basements outside the Cathedral, and the crawl space below.

The Cardinal kept shaking his head. "Nonsense. Typical nonsense about the church. This is a house of God, not a pyramid. There are no secrets here, only the mysteries of the faith."

Flynn smiled. "And no hoards of gold, Cardinal?"

"Yes, there is a hoard of gold. The body and blood of Christ that rests in the Tabernacle, the joy and goodwill and the peace and love that resides with us here—that is our hoard of gold. You're welcome to take some of that with you."

"And perhaps a few odd chalices and the gold on the altars."

"You're welcome to all of that."

Flynn shook his head. "No, I'll take nothing out of here but ourselves. Keep your gold and your love." He looked around the Cathedral and said, "I hope it survives." He looked at the Cardinal. "Well, perhaps a tour will refresh your memory. Come with me, please."

The Cardinal rose, and both men descended the

steps of the sanctuary and walked toward the front of the Cathedral.

Father Murphy watched the Cardinal walk off with Flynn. Megan wasn't in sight, Baxter was sitting at the end of the pew, and John Hickey was at the chancel organ, speaking on the field phone. Murphy turned to Maureen. "You want desperately to do something, don't you?"

She looked at him. The catharsis of an escape from death made her feel strangely relaxed, almost serene, but the impulse for action still lay within her. She nodded slowly.

Father Murphy seemed to consider for a long time, then said, "Do you know any code—such as Morse code?"

"Yes. Morse code. Why?"

"You're in mortal danger, and I think you should make a confession, in the event something happens...suddenly...."

Maureen looked at the priest but didn't answer.

"Trust me."

"All right."

Murphy waited until Hickey put down the field phone and called out, "Mr. Hickey, could I have a word with you?"

Hickey looked over the sanctuary rail. "Use the one in the bride's room—wipe the seat."

"Miss Malone would like to make a confession."

"Oh," Hickey laughed. "That would take a week."

"This is not a joking matter. She feels her life is in mortal danger, and—"

"That it is. All right. No one's stopping you."

Father Murphy rose, followed by Maureen.

Hickey watched them move toward the side in the rail. "Can't you do it there?"

Murphy answered. "Not in front of everyone. In the confessional."

Hickey looked annoyed. "Be quick about it."

They descended the side steps and walked across the ambulatory to the confessional booth beside the bride's room. Hickey raised his hand to the snipers in the perches and called out to the two retreating figures. "No funny business. You're in the cross hairs."

Father Murphy showed Maureen into a curtained booth, then entered the archway beside it. He went through the priest's entrance to the confessional and sat in the small, dark enclosure, then pulled the cord to open the black screen.

Maureen Malone knelt and stared through the curtain at the dim shadow of the priest's profile. "It's been so long, I don't know how to begin."

Father Murphy said in the low, intimate whisper cultivated for the confessional, "You can begin by locating the button on the door frame."

"Excuse me?"

"There's a button there. If you press it, it buzzes in the upstairs hall of the rectory. It's to call a priest when confessions are not normally held, in case you have a need for instant forgiveness." He laughed softly at what Maureen thought must be an occupational joke in the rectory.

She said excitedly, "Do you mean we can communicate—"

"We can't get any signal back, and in any case we wouldn't want one. And I don't know if anyone will hear us. Quickly, now, signal a message—something useful to the people outside."

Maureen drew the curtain farther to cover her hand, then ran her fingers over the oak frame and found the button. She pressed it several times to attract someone's attention, then began in halting Morse code.

THIS IS MALONE. WITH FR. MURPHY.

What should she say? She thought back to her training—*Who, what, where, when, how many?*

OBSERVED 13-15 GUNMEN IN CATHEDRAL. SNIPER IN EACH TRIFORIUM. ONE IN CHOIR LOFT. MAN AT SACRISTY STAIRS WITH THOMPSON SUB. ONE OR TWO MEN/WOMEN IN EACH TOWER. TWO OR MORE IN ATTIC. POSTS CONNECTED BY FIELD PHONES. HOSTAGES ON SANCTUARY.

She stopped and thought of the snatches of conversation she'd overheard, then continued in a faster, more confident signal.

VOTIVE CANDLES PILED IN ATTIC. BOMB? UNDER SANCTUARY.

She stopped again and tried desperately to think— *Who, what, where...?* She went on.

MACCUMAIL IS BRIAN FLYNN. JOHN HICKEY,
LIEUTENANT. MEGAN FITZGERALD THIRD IN
COMMAND. OBSERVED MINES ON DOORS, SNIPER
RIFLES, AUTOMATIC RIFLES, PISTOLS, M-72
ROCKETS, GAS MAS—

"Stop!" Murphy's voice came urgently through the screen.

She pulled her hand away from the buzzer.

Murphy said somewhat loudly, "Do you repent all your sins?"

"I do."

The priest replied, "Say the rosary once."

Hickey's voice cut into the confessional. "*Once*? By God, I'd have her on her knees until Easter if we had that long. Come on out."

Maureen came out of the confessional as Father Murphy came through the archway. Murphy nodded to Hickey. "Thank you. Later I'd like the Cardinal to hear my confession."

Hickey's wrinkled face broke into a mocking smile. "Now, what have you done, Father?"

He stepped very close to Hickey. "I'll hear the confessions of your people, too, before this night is over."

Hickey made a contemptuous sound. "No atheists in cathedrals, eh, Padre?" He stepped back from the priest and nodded. "Someone once said, 'By night an atheist half believes in God.' Maybe you're right. By dawn they'll all turn to you as they see the face of death, with his obscene gaping grin, pressed against the pretty windows. But I'll not make a confession to any mortal man, and neither will Flynn nor that she-devil he sleeps with."

Father Murphy's face reddened. He went on, "I think Harold Baxter will want to make his peace as well."

"That heathen? In a Catholic church? Don't bet the poor-box money on it." Hickey turned and looked up at the solitary figure sitting in the pew on the sanctuary. "This whole operation may have been worth the while just to see that Protestant bastard on his knees in front of a Catholic priest. All right, let's get back to the corral."

Maureen said to Hickey, "I hope I live long enough to see how *you* face death." She turned and walked with the priest in silence to the communion rail. She said, "That man . . . There's something . . . wicked . . ."

The priest nodded. As they came up to the communion rail she said, "Do you think we got through?"

"I don't know."

"Do you know Morse code?"

He reached out and opened the gate in the rail. "No, but you'll write out those dots and dashes for me before I make my confession." He waved her through the rail absently. As she passed him she reached out and squeezed his hand. He suddenly came alert. "Wait!"

She turned on the steps. "What is it?"

He looked at Hickey, who was standing near the confessional watching them. He reached into his vestment and handed her a set of rosary beads. "Get back here and kneel at the rail."

She took the beads and glanced at Hickey. "Stupid of me—"

"My fault. Just pray he doesn't suspect." The priest walked into the sanctuary.

Maureen knelt at the rail and let the string of beads hang loosely from her hands. She turned. Her eyes rose over the Cathedral, and she peered into the dimly appreciated places. Dark figures like ravens stared down at her from the murky balconies. Megan was moving near the front doors like a shadow, and an unearthly stillness hung over the cold, gray towering stonework. She focused on John Hickey. He was staring at the confessional and smiling.

CHAPTER 27

Brian Flynn helped the Cardinal up into the bell room. The Cardinal looked at the torn copper louvers. Flynn said to Donald Mullins, "Have you formally met the Archbishop of New York?"

Mullins knelt and kissed the episcopal ring, then rose.

Flynn said, "Take a break, Donald. There's coffee in the bookstore."

Mullins went quickly down the ladder.

Flynn moved to the opening in the tower and looked out into the city. There was a long silence in the cold, drafty room. "That's incredible, you know...an armed revolutionary kneels in the dust and kisses your ring."

The Cardinal looked impatient. "Why are we up here? There can be no hidden passages up here."

Flynn said, "Have you had many dealings with Gordon Stillway?"

The Cardinal answered, "We planned the latest renovations together."

"And he never pointed out any curiosities to you? No secret—"

"I'm not in the habit of entertaining the same question more than once."

Flynn made an exaggerated bow. "Pardon me. I was only trying to refresh your memory, Your Eminence."

"What exactly do you want with me, Mr. Flynn?"

"I want you to speak with the negotiator, and I want you to talk to the world. I'm going to set up a conference in that press room so conveniently located in the subbasement below the sacristy. You will go on television and radio—"

"I'll do no such thing."

"Damn it, you've done enough talking on television and radio to damage our cause. You've used your pulpit long enough to speak out *against* the IRA. Now you'll undo that damage."

"I spoke out against murder and mayhem. If that equals speaking out against the IRA, then—"

Flynn's voice rose. "Have you seen a British internment camp? Do you know what they do to those poor bastards in there?"

"I've seen and heard reports, and I've condemned the British methods in Ulster along with the IRA methods."

"No one remembers that." He put his face close to the Cardinal's. "You'll announce to the world that as an Irish-American, and as a Catholic prelate, you are going to Northern Ireland to visit the camps."

"But if you clear them out, who is there left to visit, Mr. Flynn?"

"There are hundreds in those camps."

"And the ones to be released are the relatives of the men and women with you. Plus, I'm sure, a good number of important leaders. The rest can stay so you can still claim some moral justification for your bloody methods. I'm not as naïve as you believe, and I won't be used by you."

Flynn let out a deep breath. "Then I won't guarantee the safety of this church. I'll see that it's destroyed no matter what the outcome of the negotiations!"

The Cardinal moved near Flynn and said, "There is a price, Mr. Flynn, that each man must pay for each sin. This is not a perfect world, and the evildoers in it often escape punishment and die peacefully in their beds. But there is a higher court..."

"Don't try to frighten me with that. And don't be so certain that court would damn *me* and issue *you* wings. My concept of heaven and heavenly justice is a bit more pagan than yours. I picture Tirna-n'Og, where warriors are given the respect they no longer receive on earth. Your heaven has always sounded very effeminate to me."

The Cardinal didn't reply but shook his head.

Flynn turned away from him and looked into the blue city lights. After a time he said, "Cardinal, I'm a chosen man. I know I am. Chosen to lead the people of Northern Ireland out of British bondage."

He turned back to the Cardinal and thrust his right hand toward him. "Do you see this ring? This is the ring of Finn MacCumail. It was given me by a priest who wasn't a priest. A man who never was, in a place that never was what it seemed to be. A place sanctified by Druids a thousand years or more before the name Jesus Christ was ever heard in Erin. Oh, don't look so skeptical—you're supposed to believe in miracles, damn it."

The Cardinal looked at him sadly. "You've shut God's love out of your heart and taken into your soul dark things that should never be spoken of by a Christian." He held out his hand. "Give me the ring."

Flynn took an involuntary step back. "No."

"Give it to me, and we'll see if the Christian God, your true God, is effeminate."

Flynn shook his head and held up his hand balled into a fist.

The Cardinal dropped his outstretched arm and said, "I see my duty clearly now. I may not be able to save this church or save the lives of anyone in here. But before this night is over I'll try to save your soul, Brian Flynn, and the souls of the people with you."

Flynn looked down at the bronze ring, then at the Cardinal, and focused on the large cross hanging from his neck. "I wish sometimes that I'd gotten a sign from that God you believe in. But I never did. By morning one of us will know who's won this battle."

CHAPTER 28

Monsignor Downes stood at the window of his inner office, chain-smoking unfiltered cigarettes and staring out at the floodlit Cathedral through a haze of blue smoke. In his mind's eye he saw not only smoke but fire licking at the gray stone, reaching from the stained-glass windows and twining around the twin spires. He blinked his eyes and turned toward the people in the room.

Present now besides himself was Captain Schroeder, who probably wouldn't leave until the end, and sitting in his chairs were Lieutenant Burke, Major Martin, and Inspector Langley. Captain Bellini was standing. On the couch were the FBI man, Hogan, and the CIA man, Kruger—or was it the other way around? No, that was it. All six men were rereading a decoded message brought in by a detective.

Patrick Burke looked at his copy of the message.

—DER SANCTUARY.

MACCUMAIL IS BRIAN FLYNN. JOHN HICKEY, LIEUTENANT. MEGAN FITZGERALD THIRD IN COMMAND. OBSERVED MINES ON DOORS, SNIPER

RIFLES, AUTOMATIC RIFLES, PISTOLS, M-72 ROCKETS, GAS MAS—

Burke looked up. "D-E-R Sanctuary. Murder? Ladder? Under?"

Langley shrugged. "I hope whoever that was can send again. I have two men in the upstairs hall waiting to copy." He looked at the message again. "I don't like the way it ended so abruptly."

Bellini said, "I didn't like that inventory of weapons."

Burke said, "Malone or Baxter sent it. Either of them would know Morse code and know that this is the stuff we're looking for. Right? And if, as the Monsignor says, the buzzer is in the confessional, then we might rule out Baxter if he's, as I assume, of the Protestant persuasion."

Major Martin said, "You can assume he is."

The Monsignor interjected hesitantly. "I've been thinking...perhaps Mr. Baxter *will* make a confession...so they can send again. Father Murphy will hear His Eminence's confession and vice versa—so we can expect, perhaps, three more messages...."

"Then," said Martin, "we're out of sinners. They can't go twice, can they?"

Monsignor Downes regarded him coolly.

Bellini said, "Is that okay, Monsignor? I mean, to use the confessional to do that?"

Downes smiled for the first time. "It's okay."

Major Martin cleared his throat. "Look here, we haven't considered that this message might be a ruse, sent by Flynn to make us believe he's well armed.... A bit subtle and sophisticated for the Irish . . . but it's possible."

Langley replied, "If we had the complete message, we might have a better idea of its authenticity."

Schroeder said to Langley, "I need information on the personalities in there. Megan Fitzgerald. Third in command."

Langley shook his head. "I'll check the files, but I've never heard of her."

There was a period of silence in the room, while in the outer office men and women arrived and departed, telephones rang constantly, and people huddled in conversation. In the lower floors of the rectory police commanders coordinated crowd control and cordon operations. In the Cardinal's residence Governor Doyle and Mayor Kline met with government representatives and discussed larger issues around a buffet set up in the dining room. Phones were kept open to Washington, London, Dublin, and Albany.

One of the half-dozen newly installed telephones rang, and Schroeder picked it up, then handed it to the CIA man. Kruger spoke for a minute, then hung up, "Nothing on Brian Flynn or Megan Fitzgerald. Nothing on the Fenians. Old file on John Hickey. Not as good as yours." Two phones rang simultaneously, and Schroeder answered both, passing one to Hogan and one to Martin.

The FBI man spoke for a few seconds, then hung up and said, "Nothing on Flynn, Fitzgerald, or the Fenians. You have our file on Hickey. The FBI, incidentally, had an agent at his funeral checking out the mourners.

That's the last entry. Guess we'll have to add a postscript."

Major Martin was still on the telephone, writing as he listened. He put the receiver down. "A bit of good news. Our dossier on Flynn will be Telexed to the consulate shortly. There's a capability paper on the Fenian Army as well. Your files on Hickey are more extensive than ours, and you can send a copy to London, if you will." He lit a cigarette and said in a satisfied tone, "Also on the way is the file on Megan Fitzgerald. Here's a few pertinent details: Born in Belfast, age twenty-one. Father deserted family—brother Thomas in Long Kesh for attacking a prison van. Brother Pedar is a member of the IRA. Mother hospitalized for a nervous breakdown." He added caustically, "Your typical Belfast family of five." Martin looked at Burke. "Her description—red hair, blue eyes, freckles, five feet seven inches, slender—quite good-looking according to the chap I just spoke to. Sound like the young lady who pegged a shot at you?"

Burke nodded.

Martin went on. "She's Flynn's present girl friend." He smiled. "I wonder how she's getting on with Miss Malone. I think I'm starting to feel sorry for old Flynn."

A uniformed officer stuck his head in the door. "Chow's here from John Barleycorn's."

Schroeder reached for the telephone. "All right. I'll tell Flynn that Burke is ready with his fucking corned beef." He dialed the operator. "Chancel organ." He waited. "Hello, this is Captain Schroeder. Finn

MacCumail? . . ." He pushed the switches to activate all the speakers, and the next room became quiet.

"This is Dermot. MacCumail is praying with the Cardinal."

Schroeder hesitated. "Mr . . . . Dermot—"

"Just call me Hickey. John Hickey. Never liked these *noms de guerre!* Confuses everyone. Did you know I was in here? Have you got my file in front of you, Snider?"

"Schroeder." He looked down at the thick police file. Each man had to be played differently. Each man had his own requirements. Schroeder rarely admitted to having anyone's file in front of him as he negotiated, but it was equally important not to get caught lying to a direct question, and it was often convenient to play on a man's ego.

"Schroeder? You awake?"

Schroeder sat up. "Yes, sir. Yes, we knew you were in there. I have your file, Mr. Hickey."

Hickey cackled happily. "Did you read the part where I was caught trying to blow up Parliament in 1921?"

Schroeder found the dated entry. "Yes, sir. Quite"— he looked at Major Martin, who was staring tight-lipped—"quite daring. Daring escape too—"

"You bet your ass, sonny. Now look at 1941. I worked with the Germans then to blow up British shipping in New York harbor. Not proud of that, you understand; but a lot of us did that in the Second War. Shows how much we hated the Brits, doesn't it, to throw in with the bloody Nazis."

"Yes, it does. Listen—"

"The Dublin government and the British government both sentenced me to death in absentia on five different occasions. Well, as Brendan Behan once said, they can hang me five times in absentia, too." He laughed.

There was some laughter from the adjoining office. No one in the inner office laughed. Schroeder bit his cigar. "Mr. Hickey—"

"What do you have for February 12, 1979? Read it to me, Schaeffer."

Schroeder turned to the last page and read. "Died of natural causes, at home, Newark, New Jersey. Buried... buried in Jersey City Cemetery...."

Hickey laughed again, a high, piercing laugh. Neither man spoke for a few seconds, then Schroeder said, "Mr. Hickey, first I want to ask you if the hostages are all right."

"That's a stupid question. If they weren't, would I tell *you*?"

"But they *are* all right?"

"There you go again. Same stupid question," Hickey said impatiently. "They're fine. What did you call for?"

Schroeder said, "Lieutenant Burke is ready to bring the food you ordered. Where—?"

"Through the sacristy."

"He'll be alone, unarmed—"

Hickey's voice was suddenly ill-tempered. "You don't have to reassure me. For my part I'd like you to try something, because quicker than you can make it up those stairs with a chaincutter or ram, the Cardinal's brains would be running over the altar, followed by a great fucking explosion that they'd hear in the Vatican, and a fire so hot it'd melt the brass balls off Atlas. Do you understand, Schroeder?"

"Yes, sir."

"And stop calling me sir, you candy-assed flatfoot. When I was a lad, if you looked at a constable cross-eyed he'd knock you into next week. Now you're all going round calling murderers sir. No wonder they picked New York for this. Fucking cops would rather bat softballs with a bunch of slum brats than bat heads. Also, while I'm on the subject, I don't like your voice, Schroeder. You sound mealy-mouthed. How the hell did you get picked for this job? Your voice is all wrong."

"Yes, sir . . . Mr. Hickey . . . . What would you like me to call you . . . ?"

"Call me a son of a bitch, Schroeder, because that's what I am. Go on, you'll feel better."

Schroeder cleared his throat. "Okay . . . you're a son of a bitch."

"Oh, yeah? Well, I'd rather be a son of a bitch than an asshole like you." He laughed and hung up.

Schroeder put down the receiver, took a long breath, and turned off the speakers. "Well . . . I think . . ." He looked down at Hickey's file. "Very unstable. Maybe a little senile." He looked at Burke. "You don't have to go if you . . ."

"Yeah. I have to go. I damn well have to go. Where's the fucking food?" He stood.

Langley spoke. "I didn't like that part about the explosion."

Major Martin said, "I'd have been surprised if they hadn't set it up with explosives. That's their specialty."

Burke moved toward the door. "The Irish specialty is bullshit." He looked at Martin. "Not subtle or sophisticated bullshit, of course, Major. Just bullshit. And if they had as much gelignite and plastic as they have bullshit, they could have blown up the solar system." He opened the door and looked back over his shoulder. "Forty-five meals. Shit, I wouldn't want to have to eat every meal over the number of people they have in there."

Bellini called out at Burke's retreating figure. "I hope you're right, Burke. I hope to Christ you're right." He turned back to the people in the room. "*He* doesn't have to shoot his way in there."

Schroeder looked at Monsignor Downes, who appeared pale, then turned to Bellini and said irritably, "Damn it, Joe, stop that. No one is going to have to shoot his way into that Cathedral."

Major Martin was examining some curios on the mantelpiece. He said, as though to himself but loud enough for everyone to hear him, "I wonder."

CHAPTER 29

Flynn stood with Maureen on the landing in front of the crypt entrance. He found a key on the ring and opened the green, glass-paneled door. Inside, a set of stairs descended into the white-marbled burial chamber. He turned to Pedar Fitzgerald. "Somewhere in there may be a hidden passage. I'll be along shortly."

Fitzgerald cradled his submachine gun under his arm and moved down the stairs. Flynn shut the door and looked at the inscription in the bronze. *Requiescant In Pace.* "May they rest in peace," he said. Below the inscriptions were plaques bearing the names of the former archbishops of New York who were buried in the crypt. He turned to Maureen. "You remember how frightened we were to go down into Whitehorn Abbey's crypt?"

She nodded. "There have been too many graves in our lives, Brian, and too much running. God, look at you. You look ten years older than your age."

"Do I? Well...that's not just from the running. That's partly from not running fast enough." He paused, then added, "I was caught."

She turned her head toward him. "Oh...I didn't know."

"It was kept quiet. Major Martin. Remember the name?"

"Of course. He contacted me once, right after I'd gone to Dublin. He wanted to know where you were. He said it would go easier on Sheila...and he said they would cancel the warrant for my arrest...Pleasant sort of chap, actually, but you knew he'd pull your finger-nails out if he had you in Belfast."

Flynn smiled. "And what did you tell this pleasant chap?"

"I would have told him to go to hell except I thought he might actually go and find you there. So I told him to fuck off."

Flynn smiled again, but his eyes were appraising her thoughtfully.

She read the expression in his face. "I want you to understand that I never turned informer. Traitor, if you like, but never informer."

He nodded. "I believe you. If I didn't, I'd have killed you long ago."

"Would you?"

He changed the subject. "You're going to get people hurt if you try to escape again."

She didn't respond.

Flynn took a key from his pocket and held it out. "This is the key to the padlock on that chain. I'll open it now, and you can go."

"Not without the others."

"But you'd try to escape without the others."

"That's different."

He smiled and kept the key in front of her. "Ah, you're still a street fighter, Maureen. You understand that there's a price to pay—in advance—for a bit of freedom. Most men and women in this world would leave here quickly through the offered gate, and they wouldn't even entertain the thought of escaping with bullets whistling about their ears. You see, your values and requirements are reversed from ordinary people's. We changed you forever in those years we had you."

She remembered the way he had of interpreting for her all of her motives and actions, and how he had once had her so confused about who and what she was that she'd fallen into his power, willingly and gladly. She looked at him. "Shut up."

Flynn hesitated, then pocketed the key and shifted to another topic. "I chatted with the Cardinal. He believes in the ring, you know. You didn't believe because you thought that as a halfhearted Christian you shouldn't. But His Eminence is about as good a Christian as they make, you'll agree, and for that reason he believes."

She looked at the crypt door. "I never said I didn't believe in such things. I told you in Whitehorn Abbey on the evening I left that I couldn't understand why any power—good or evil—would pick *you* as their mortal emissary."

He laughed. "That's a terrible thing to say. You're a master of the low blow, Maureen. You'd be a bitch except you've got a good heart." He moved closer to her. "How do you explain the fact of Father Donnelly's disappearance? I've searched for that man—if man he was—over these past years, and no one has even heard of him."

She stared through a glass pane into the white, luminescent crypt and shook her head.

Flynn watched her, then put a different tone in his voice and took her arm in a firm grip. "Before I forget, let me give you one good piece of advice—don't provoke Megan."

She turned toward him. "The fact that I'm still breathing provokes her. Let me give *you* a piece of advice. If you get out of here alive, get as far from her as you can. She draws destruction like a lightning rod, Brian."

Flynn made no response and let go of her arm.

She went on. "And Hickey...that man is..." She shook her head. "Never mind. I see you've fallen in with a bad lot. We hardly know each other anymore, Brian. How can we give each other advice?"

He reached out and touched her cheek. There was a long silence on the crypt landing. Then from the sacristy corridor came the sound of footsteps and the squeaking of wheels on the marble floor. Maureen said suddenly, "If Major Martin caught you, how is it that you're alive?"

Flynn walked down the stairs and stood at the gate.

She followed. "Did you make a deal with him?"

He didn't answer.

"And you call yourself a patriot?"

He looked at her sharply. "So does Major Martin. So do you."

"I would never—"

"Oh, you'd make a deal. Popes, prime ministers, and

presidents make deals like that, and it's called diplomacy and strategy. That's what this life is all about, Maureen—illusion and semantics. Well, I'm making no deals today, no accommodations, no matter what names the negotiator gives me for it to make it more palatable. That should make you happy, since you don't like deals."

She didn't reply.

He went on. "If you agree that the deal I made with Major Martin wasn't so awful, I'll put Sheila's name on the list of people to be released."

She looked at him quickly. "You mean, it's not—"

"Changes things a bit, doesn't it? Looking ahead, were you, to a tearful reunion with little Sheila? Now you've nothing whatsoever to gain from this. Unless, of course, you see my point in trafficking with the enemy."

"Why is it so important to you that I tell you that?"

A voice called out, "This is Burke. Coming in."

Flynn said to Maureen, "We'll talk again later." He shouted into the sacristy, "Come on, then." He drew back his jacket and adjusted the pistol in his waistband, then said to her, "I respect your abilities as a fighter enough to treat you like a man. Don't try anything, don't make any sudden moves, don't stand behind me, and keep silent until you're spoken to."

She answered, "If that was a compliment, I'm not flattered. I've put that behind me."

"Aye, like a reformed whore puts the streets behind her, but the urge is still there, I'll wager."

She looked at him. "It is now."

He smiled.

Burke appeared from the sacristy corridor, pushing a serving cart. He rolled the cart over the marble floor and stopped at the bottom stair below the gate.

"Do you know Miss Malone?" Flynn asked.

Burke nodded to her. "We've met."

"That's right," said Flynn. "Last evening at the Waldorf. I have a report on it. Seems so long ago, doesn't it?" He smiled. "I've brought her here to assure you we haven't butchered the hostages." He said to her, "Tell him how well you've been treated, Maureen."

She said, "No one is dead yet."

Burke replied, "Please tell the others that we are doing all we can to see that you're safely released." He put a light note in his voice. "Tell Father Murphy he can hear my confession when this is over."

She nodded and gave him a look of understanding.

Flynn was silent a moment, then asked, "Is the priest a friend of yours?"

Burke replied, "They're all friends of mine."

"Really?" He came closer to the gate. "Are you wired, Burke? Do I have to go through the debugging routine?"

"I'm clean. The cart is clean. I don't want to be overheard either." Burke came up the seven steps and was acutely aware of the psychological disadvantage of standing on a step eight inches below Flynn. "And the food's not drugged."

Flynn nodded. "No, not with hostages. Makes all the difference in the world, doesn't it?"

Maureen suddenly grabbed the bars and spoke hurriedly. "His real name is Brian Flynn. He has only about twelve gunmen—"

Flynn pulled the pistol from his waistband and pressed it hard against her neck. "Don't be a hero, Maureen. It isn't required. Is it, Lieutenant?"

Burke kept his hands in full view. "Easy now. Nice and easy. Miss Malone, don't say anything else. That's right."

Flynn spoke to her through clenched teeth. "That's good advice, lass. You don't want to jeopardize others, such as Lieutenant Burke, who's already heard too much." He looked at Burke. "She's impulsive and hasn't learned the difference between bravery and recklessness. That's my fault, I'm afraid." He grabbed her arm with his free hand and pulled her away from the gate. "Leave."

Maureen looked at Burke and said, "I've made a confession to Father Murphy, and I'm not afraid to die. We'll *all* make our confessions soon. Don't give in to these bastards."

Burke looked at her and nodded. "I understand."

She smiled, turned, and mounted the steps to the altar.

Flynn held the pistol at his side and watched her go. He seemed to be thinking, then said, "All right, how much do I owe you?"

Burke slowly handed a bill to Flynn.

Flynn looked at it. "Five hundred sixty-one dollars and twelve cents. Not cheap to feed an army in New York, is it?" Flynn slipped the pistol into his waistband and counted out the money. "Here. Come closer."

Burke moved nearer the gate and took the bills and change.

Flynn said, "I deducted the sales tax on principle."

He laughed. "Make certain you report that to the press, Lieutenant. They love that sort of nonsense."

Burke nodded. Brian Flynn, he decided, was not a complete lunatic. He had the uneasy feeling that Flynn was sharper than Schroeder, and a better performer.

Flynn looked down at the cart laden with covered metal dishes. "It wouldn't be Saint Paddy's Day without the corned beef, would it, Burke? Had yours?"

"No. Been busy."

"Well, come in and join us, then. Everyone would enjoy your company."

"I can't."

"Can't?" Flynn made a pretense of remembering something. "Ah, yes. Hostages will neither be given nor exchanged under any circumstances. Police will not take the place of hostages. But I'll not keep you prisoner."

"You seem to know a lot about this."

Flynn thrust his face between the bars, close to Burke's. "I know enough not to do anything stupid. I hope you know as much."

"I'm sure we've had more experience with hostage situations than you—see that *you* don't make any mistakes."

Flynn lit a cigarette and said abruptly, "So, I should formally introduce myself now that Miss Malone was thoughtful enough to tell you my name. I am as the lady said—as you might have known from other sources—Brian Flynn. Ring any bells?"

"A few. Back in the late seventies. Over there."

"Yes, over there. Over here now. Unlike John Hickey, I'm not officially dead, only unofficially missing. All right, let's talk about our favorite subject. Is Major Martin present at your war councils?"

"Yes."

"Get him out of there."

"He's representing the British consulate for now."

Flynn forced a laugh. "Sir Harry will be distressed to hear that. Let me tell you that Martin will double-cross his own Foreign Office, too. His only loyalty is to his sick obsession with the Irish. Get him the hell away from the decision-making process."

"Maybe I'd rather have him close where I can see him."

Flynn shook his head. "You never see a man like that no matter how close he is. Get him out of the rectory, away from your commanders."

Burke said softly, "So your people on the outside can kill him?"

A slow smile passed over Flynn's face. "Oh, Lieutenant, you are the sharp one. Yes, indeed."

"Please don't do anything without talking to me first."

Flynn nodded. "Yes, I'll have to be straight with you. We may still be able to work together."

"Maybe."

Flynn said, "Look here, there's a lot of double-dealing going on, Burke. Only the New York police, as far as I can tell, have no ulterior motives. I'll count on you, Lieutenant, to do your job. You must play the honest broker and avert a bloodbath. Dawn tomorrow or—I promise you—this Cathedral will burn. That's as inevitable as the sunrise itself."

"You mean you have no control over that?"

Flynn nodded. "Very quick-witted of you. I control my people up to a point. But at dawn each man and woman in here will act on standing orders unless our demands have been met. Without a word from me the prisoners will be shot or thrown from the bell tower, fires will be set, and other destructive devices will automatically engage."

Burke said, "You did a damned stupid thing to relinquish that kind of control. Stupid and dangerous."

Flynn pressed his face to the bars. "But you could do worse than dealing with me. If anything happened to me, you would have to deal with Hickey and the woman we call Grania, so don't you or Schroeder or anyone out there try to undermine me. Work with me and no one will die."

"Better the devil you know than the devils you don't know."

"Quite right, Lieutenant. Quite right. You may go."

Burke moved backward down a step, away from the gate. He and Flynn looked at each other. Flynn made no move to turn away this time, and Burke remembered the hostage unit's injunction against turning your back on hostage takers. "Treat them like royalty," Schroeder liked to say on television talk shows. "Never show them your back. Never use negative words. Never use words like death, kill, die, dead. Always address them respectfully." Schroeder would have had a stroke if he had heard this exchange.

Burke took another step backward. Schroeder had his methods, yet Burke was becoming convinced that this situation called for flexibility, originality, and even compromise. He hoped Schroeder and everyone else out there recognized that before it was too late.

He turned his back to Flynn, went down the steps past the serving cart, and moved toward the corridor opening, all the while aware of the deep, dark eyes that followed him.

CHAPTER 30

Patrick Burke made the long underground walk from the sacristy past the silent policemen in the corridors. He noticed that the Tactical Patrol Unit had been replaced by the Emergency Services Division. They wore black uniforms and black flak jackets, they carried shotguns, sniper rifles, automatic weapons, and silenced pistols, and they looked very unlike the public image of a cop, he thought. Their eyes had that unfocused look, their bodies were exaggeratedly relaxed, and cigarettes dangled from tight lips.

Burke entered the rectory's basement and made his way upstairs to the Monsignor's office suite, through the crowded outer office, and into the next room, shutting the door firmly behind him. Burke met the stares of the twelve people whom he had labeled in his mind the Desperate Dozen. He remained standing in the center of the room.

Schroeder finally spoke. "What took you so long?"

Burke found a chair and sat. "You told me to get the measure of the man."

"No negotiating, Burke. That's my job. You don't know the procedure—"

"Anytime you want me to leave, I'm gone. I'm not looking to get on the cover of *Time*."

Schroeder stood. "I'm a little tired of getting ribbed about that goddamned *Time* story—"

Deputy Commissioner Rourke cut in. "All right, men. It's going to be a long night." He turned to Schroeder. "You want Burke to leave after he briefs us?"

Schroeder shook his head. "Flynn has made him his errand boy, and we can't upset Mr. Flynn."

Langley broke in. "What did Flynn say, Pat?"

Burke lit a cigarette and listened to the silence for a longer time than was considered polite. "He said the Cathedral will more or less self-destruct at sunrise."

No one spoke until Bellini said, "If I have to take that place by force, you better leave enough time for the Bomb Squad to comb every inch of it. They've only got two mutts now—Sally and Brandy...." He shook his head. "What a mess...damn it."

Schroeder said, "No matter what type of devices they have rigged, they can delay them. I'll get an extension."

Burke looked at him. "I don't think you understood what I said."

Langley interjected. "What else did he say, Pat?"

Burke sat back and gave them an edited briefing, glancing at Major Martin, who stood against the fireplace in a classic pose. Burke had the impression that Martin was filling in the missing sentences.

Burke focused on Arnold Sheridan, the quintessential Wasp from State, tight smile, correct manners, cultivated voice that said nothing. He was assigned to the security section but probably found it distasteful to be even a quasi-cop. Burke realized that, as the man on the scene, Sheridan might sway the administration either way. Hard line, soft line, or line straddling. Washington could push London into an accommodation, and then, like dominoes, Dublin, Albany, and the City of New York would tumble into line. But as he looked at Sheridan he had no idea of what was going on behind those polite, vacant eyes.

Burke looked back at Schroeder as he spoke. This was a man who was an accomplished listener as well as a talker. He heard every word, remembered every word, even interpreted nuances and made analyses and conclusions but ultimately, through some incredible process in his brain, never really *understood* a thing that was said. Burke flipped a cigarette ash into a coffee cup. "I don't think this guy is a textbook case. I don't think he's going to bend in his demands or give extensions, Schroeder."

Schroeder said, "They all give extensions, Burke. They want to play out the drama, and they always think a concession will come in the next minute, the next hour, the next day. It's human nature."

Burke shook his head. "Don't operate on the premise that you'll get more time."

Major Martin interrupted. "If I may say something—Lieutenant Burke's analysis is not correct. I've dealt with the Irish for ten years, and they are dreadful liars, fakes, and bluffers. Flynn will give you extensions if you keep him hopeful that—"

Burke stood. "Bullshit."

The Irish Consul General stood also and said

hesitantly, "Look here, Major, I . . . I think it's unfair to characterize the Irish . . ."

Martin forced an amiable tone into his voice. "Oh, sorry, Tomas. I was speaking only of the IRA, of course." He looked around the room. "I didn't mean to offend Irish Americans either. Commissioner Rourke, Mr. Hogan, Lieutenant Burke"—he looked at Schroeder and smiled—"or your better half."

Commissioner Rourke nodded to show there were no hard feelings, and spoke. "Everyone is a little tense. Let's take it easy. Okay?" He looked at Burke. "Lieutenant, the Major has a lot of experience in these things. He's providing us with valuable information, not to mention insight. I know Irish affairs are your specialty, but this is not an Irish-American affair. This is different."

Burke looked around the room. "I'd like to make it an American affair for a few minutes. Specifically, I'd like to speak to the Commissioner, Captain Schroeder, Inspector Langley, Mr. Kruger, and Mr. Hogan— alone."

Commissioner Rourke looked around the room, unsure of what to say. Major Martin moved to the door. "I've got to get to the consulate." Tomas Donahue made an excuse and followed. Monsignor Downes nodded and left. Arnold Sheridan rose and looked at his watch. "I have to call State."

Bellini said, "You want me here, Burke?"

"It doesn't concern you, Joe."

Bellini said, "It better not." He left.

The Governor's aide suddenly looked alert. "Oh . . ." He stood. "I have to go . . . ." He left.

Roberta Spiegel sat back in her rocker and lit another cigarette. "You can either go talk in the men's room—though that's no guarantee I won't follow—or you can talk here."

Burke decided he didn't mind her presence. He took Langley to the far end of the room and said quietly, "Did we hear from Jack Ferguson yet?"

Langley said, "We got through to his wife. She's sick in bed. She hasn't heard from him either."

Burke shook his head. He usually felt his first responsibility was to an informant who was in danger, but now he had no time for Jack Ferguson. Ferguson understood that—and understood, he hoped, that he was in danger. Burke moved to the center of the room and addressed the remaining people. "I've dealt a few cards from the bottom of the deck myself over the years, but never have I seen a card game as stacked as this one. And since I'm the one who almost got his head blown off this afternoon, I think you'll understand why I'm a little pissed off." He looked at Kruger and Hogan. "You two have some explaining to do." Burke took a long pull on his cigarette and continued. "Consider this—we have here a well-planned, well-financed operation. Too much so, from what we know of the IRA, domestic and foreign. I see here the hand of not so much the revolutionary but the counterrevolutionary—the government man." He looked at Kruger and Hogan.

No one spoke.

"Brian Flynn has told me that Major Batholomew Martin suggested an American operation to him and provided the necessary resources to carry it out. And if *that* is true, then I don't think Martin could have pulled it off without the help of some of your people—or at least without your well-known talent for looking the other way when it suits you."

Langley stood. "Careful."

Burke turned. "Come off it, Langley. You had your suspicions, too." He turned back to the people in front of him. "This whole thing has been a staged performance, but I think it got out of control because Brian Flynn wasn't playing his part as written. Maybe he was supposed to knock over an armory or blow a bank. But he got a better idea, and now we're all up to our asses in the consequences."

Kruger stood. "I've never heard such paranoid nonsense—"

Hogan reached out and put his hand on Kruger's arm, then sat forward. "Listen, Burke, what you say is not altogether untrue." He paused, then went on. "The FBI *did* stand to gain from this incident. Sure, when this is over they'll fire some people at the top, but then the analysis will show how powerless we were to stop it. And maybe we'll become the beneficiaries of a little power and money." He leaned farther forward and put an aggrieved tone in his voice. "But to even *hint* that *we*—"

Burke waved his arm to cut off the disclaimers. "I have no real evidence, and I don't want any. All I want you to know is that Patrick Burke knows. And I almost got my fucking head blown off finding out. And if Flynn starts making public statements, people will tend to believe him, and your two outfits will be in trouble—again."

Hogan shook his head. "He won't make any public charges about outside help, because he's not going to admit to the Irish people that he worked with British Intelligence—"

Kruger looked at him sharply. "Shut up, Hogan."

Douglas Hogan waved his hand in dismissal. "Oh, for Christ's sake, Kruger, there's no use trying to play it coy." He looked at the four policemen in the room. "We had some knowledge of this, but, as you say, it got out of control. I can promise you, though, that no matter what happens, we will cover you...so long as you do the same. What's happened is past. Now we have to work at making sure we come out of this not only blameless but looking good." Douglas Hogan spread his hands out in front of him and said coaxingly, "We have been handed a unique opportunity to make some important changes in intelligence procedures in this country. A chance to improve our image."

Commissioner Rourke stood. "You people are...crazy."

Langley turned to the Commissioner. "Sir, I think we have no choice but to keep to the problem at hand. We can't change the series of events that brought us here, but we can try to ensure that the outcome won't be disastrous...as long as we work together."

The Commissioner looked at the FBI man, the CIA man, then at his two intelligence officers. He understood very clearly that their logic was not his logic, their world not his world. He understood, also, that anyone who could do what Kruger and Hogan had apparently done were dangerous and desperate men. He looked at Roberta Spiegel. She nodded to him, and he sat down.

Burke glanced around the room and said, "It's important that you all understand that Bartholomew Martin is a danger to any negotiated settlement. He means to see that the Cathedral is destroyed and that blood is shed." He looked at Rourke and Schroeder. "He is not your good friend." He stared at Kruger and Hogan. "The most Martin hoped for was an arms steal or a bank heist, but *Flynn* presented him with a unique opportunity to influence public opinion in America the way the IRA murder of Lord Mountbatten did in the British Isles. However, if Flynn walks out of the Cathedral with no blood shed and the IRA prisoners are released, he'll be a hero to a large segment of the Irish population, and no one will ever believe he meant to harm anyone or destroy the Cathedral—and Major Martin cannot allow that to happen." Burke turned again to Kruger and Hogan. "I want him neutralized—no, that's not like one of your famous euphemisms for murder. Don't look so uncomfortable. Neutralized—inoperative. Watched. I want a regular Foreign Office man representing the British government in New York, not Martin. I've given *you* a unique opportunity to save your own asses."

Kruger stared at Burke, unconcealed hostility in his eyes.

Hogan nodded. "I'll do what I can."

Roberta Spiegel said, "End of discussion." She looked at Schroeder. "Captain, you're on."

Schroeder nodded and turned on the speakers in the rectory offices and in the Cardinal's residence. He placed the call through the switchboard and looked around the room while he waited. *New ball game for them*, he thought. But his ball game hadn't changed substantially. His only concern was the personality of Brian Flynn. His whole world was reduced to the electronic impulses between himself and Flynn. Washington, London, and Dublin could make it easier for him by capitulating, but they couldn't make it any more difficult than it already was. A voice in the earphone made him sit up. "Hello, Mr. Flynn? This is Captain Schroeder."

CHAPTER 31

Brian Flynn stood at the chancel organ and lit a cigarette as he cradled the receiver on his shoulder. "Schroeder, the corned beef was stringy. You didn't butcher the horse now, did you?"

The negotiator's voice came back with a contrived laugh in it. "No, sir. If there's anything else you want, please let us know."

"I'm about to do that. First of all, I'm glad you know my name. Now you know you're dealing with Ireland's greatest living patriot. Right?"

"Yes, sir...."

"There'll be a monument erected to me someday in Dublin and in a free Belfast. No one will remember you."

"Yes, sir."

Flynn laughed suddenly. "I hear you writing, Schroeder. What are you writing? 'Megalomania'?"

"No, sir. Just keeping notes."

"Good. Now just listen and take notes on this. First..." Flynn leafed through Schroeder's autobiography as he spoke. ".... make certain you leave the Cathedral's floodlights on. It looks so grand bathed in blue light. Also, that will make it difficult for your ESD men to climb up the sides. I've people in skyscrapers with field glasses. If they see anything moving outside, they'll signal the towers or call me directly. Which brings me to point two. Don't interfere with my outside telephone lines. Point three, if the lights in here so much as flicker, I'll shoot everyone. Point four, no psy-warfare, such as your usual prank of running that silly armored car you own around the Cathedral. My men in the towers have M-72 rockets. Anyway, we've seen more armored cars than you've seen taxis, Schroeder, and they don't frighten us. Point five, no helicopters. If my men in the towers see one, they'll fire on it. Point six, tell your ESD people that we've planned this for a long time, and an attack would cost them dearly. Don't waste them. You'll need them next time." Flynn wiped a line of sweat from his forehead. "Point seven, I say again, no extensions. Plan to wrap it up by dawn, Schroeder. Point eight, I want a nice twenty-one-inch color television set. I'll tell you when I want Burke to bring it. Point nine, I want to see continuous news coverage until dawn. Point ten, I want to hold a news conference in the press room below the sacristy. Prime time, 10:00 p.m., live. Got all that?"

After a long silence Schroeder's voice came through, sounding strained. "Yes, sir. We'll try to accommodate you on all those points."

"You *will* accommodate me. What have you heard from Dublin, London, and Washington?"

"They're tied into their representatives, who are here in the Cardinal's residence. They're making progress."

"It's good to see allies working so well together. I hope they're all keeping their tempers as we are doing, Captain. What have you heard from Amnesty and the Red Cross?"

"They are willing to cooperate in any way possible."

"Good for them. Good people. Always there to lend a hand. How about immunity from prosecution for my people in here?"

Schroeder cleared his throat. "The U.S. Attorney General and the State Attorney General are discussing it. So far, all I can promise you is—"

"A fair trial," interrupted Flynn. "Wonderful country. But I don't want *any* trial at all, Schroeder."

"I can't make that promise at this time."

"Let me make something clear—at the same time you tell me those prisoners are being released, you'd better have a guarantee of immunity for us or it's no deal. I'll shoot the hostages and blow this place apart." Flynn could hear Schroeder's breathing in the earpiece.

Schroeder said softly, "Everything you ask for is being considered very carefully, but these things take time. All I'm concerned with at the moment is the safety—"

"Schroeder, stop talking to me as though I were some sort of criminal lunatic. Save that for your next case, if you have one. I'm a soldier, and I want to be spoken to as a soldier. The prisoners in here are being treated correctly. And your tone is very patronizing."

"I'm sorry. I didn't mean to offend you. I'm only trying to assure you of our good intentions. My job is to negotiate a settlement we can all live with, and—"

Flynn suddenly stood and said, "How do you call it negotiation if you don't intend to *give* anything?"

Schroeder didn't reply.

"Have you *ever* made any real concessions in all of your career as a hostage negotiator, Schroeder? Never. You're not even *listening* to me, for Christ's sake. Well, you'd damn well *better* listen, because when this Cathedral is in ruins and the dead are lying everywhere, you'll wish to God you paid more attention, and that you'd acted in better faith."

"I *am* listening. I *am* acting—"

"You'll be known, Captain Bert Schroeder, as the man who failed to save Saint Patrick's Cathedral and who has innocent blood on his hands. You'll never hold your head up again, and you'll not accept many talk-show invitations, I think."

Schroeder's voice came back, agitated for the first time that anyone who was listening could remember. "I haven't lied to you, have I? We haven't tried to use force, have we? You asked for food, we gave you food. You asked—"

"I paid for the fucking food! Now listen to me closely. I know you're only a middleman for a lot of bastards, but..." Flynn looked at Schroeder's picture on the cover of his book. It was an action shot, taken during a bank robbery that had turned into a hostage situation. Schroeder, unlike his predecessor, who always wore a baseball cap and Windbreaker, was dressed nattily in a three-piece pinstripe. The face and massive body suggested he was more the baseball-cap type, but Schroeder was reaching for his own style. Flynn studied the face on the cover. Good profile, firm jaw, erect carriage. But the eyes were unmistakably fright-ened. A bad picture. Flynn continued, "But I trust you, Schroeder—trust you to use your influence and your good offices. I want you to keep talking to me all night, Captain. I want you to carry my message to the people around you."

Schroeder's voice sounded surprised at the sudden expression of confidence. "Yes, sir. I'll do that. You can talk to me." Both men remained silent for a time, then Schroeder said, "Now I'd like to ask two favors of you."

Flynn smiled and flipped absently through the auto-biography in front of him. "Go on."

"Well, for one thing, the jamming device is caus-ing confusion in command and control, and we don't want an incident to occur because of a lack of communication. Also, it's causing interference with commercial radio and the sound portions of televi-sion broadcasts."

Flynn threw aside the book. "Can't have that. I'll think about it. What else?"

"I'd like to say a few words to each of the hostages."

"Maybe after the press conference."

"All right. That's fair. There is one other thing."

"There always is."

"Yes, well, since you and I are building a rapport—building confidence in each other—and I'm the only one talking to you, I wonder if you'd do the same for me. I mean, I spoke to Mr. Hickey before, and—"

Flynn laughed and looked around, but Hickey wasn't in sight. "John gave you a bit of a rough time, did he, Captain? He enjoys making unpleasant jokes.

Well, just play along with him. He loves to talk—Irish, you know."

"Yes, but there could be a misunderstanding. You are the boss, and I want to keep my lines of communication open to *you*, and—"

Flynn dropped the receiver into its cradle and looked through a book of sheet music. He wanted to find something unchurchly that would take his mind away from the Cathedral. Of all the godforsaken places he'd ever found himself in, no place seemed more oddly forsaken than the Cathedral at this moment. Yet others, he knew, felt the presence of a divine spirit here, and he understood that the emptiness he felt was totally within himself. He found "The Rose of Tralee," turned the key into the organ, and played as he sang very softly.

> "The pale moon was rising above
> The green mountains,
> The sun was declining beneath
> The blue sea,
> As I strayed with my love to the
> Pure crystal fountain,
> That stands in the beauitful vale
> of Tralee . . . ."

Bert Schroeder looked for a long time at the dead speaker, folded his hands on the desk, and thought. Flynn talked about immunity, which showed he thought of a future, and by implication his desire to keep his crime from being compounded was strong. He had no intention of killing anyone, least of all himself. More importantly, Flynn was beginning to depend on him. That always happened. It was inevitable as he came to realize that Schroeder's voice was the only one that mattered. Schroeder looked up. "I think I'm getting an angle on this guy."

Burke said, "It sounds like he has an angle on *you*."

Schroeder's eyes narrowed, and he nodded reluctantly. "Yes, he seems to know something of my methods. I'm afraid the media has given my bureau too much coverage." He added, "I never sought publicity."

"You mean your autobiography was unauthorized? Christ, you should have at least waited until you retired before you released it." Burke smiled. "And now you've missed the big chapter. Catch it on the second printing. Talk to your agent about it." Burke put a conciliatory tone in his voice. "Look, Bert, I don't have all the answers, but—"

Schroeder stood. "No, you don't. And I'm tired of your sideline quarterbacking!"

No one spoke. Burke stood and moved toward the door.

Schroeder said, "Don't go far. Flynn may want coffee later."

Burke turned and said, "Up to this point we've had doublecrosses, incompetence, and some ordinary stupidity. And we've been damned lucky in spite of it. But if we don't get our act together by dawn, we're going to have a massacre, a desecration, and a lot of explaining to do."

Schroeder stared ahead and spoke placidly. "Just leave it to me."

CHAPTER 32

Father Murphy walked across the sanctuary and stood before the Cardinal's throne. "Your Eminence, I would like to make my confession."

The Cardinal nodded. "Take my hands."

Murphy felt the scrap of paper sticking to his palm. "No...I would like to go into the confessional."

The Cardinal stood. "We'll go into the Archbishop's sacristy."

"No..." Murphy felt a line of sweat collect on his brow. "They won't let us. We can go into the confessional where I heard Miss Malone's confession."

The Cardinal stared at him curiously, then nodded. "As you wish." He came down from the throne and walked toward the rear of the sanctuary, then descended the side steps that led into the ambulatory. Father Murphy glanced back at Maureen and Baxter. They nodded encouragingly, and he followed the Cardinal.

Leary leaned over the choir loft parapet, placed the cross hairs in front of the Cardinal's face, and led him as he walked from right to left across his magnified picture. Everyone in the triforia began shouting warnings to the two priests, shouting at Leary who they knew was about to fire, shouting for Flynn or Hickey.

The Cardinal seemed oblivious to the warnings. He stopped at the archway that led to the priests' entrance to the confessional and waited for Father Murphy, who walked hesitantly across the ambulatory.

Leary centered his cross hairs on the gold cross that hung over the Cardinal's heart and took up the slack in the trigger.

Flynn suddenly appeared in front of the two priests with his arms raised and looked into the balconies. The shouting stopped. Leary straightened his body and stood with his rifle resting in the crook of his arm. Even from this distance Flynn could see that Leary had that distinctive posture of a hunter who had just been denied his quarry, motionless, listening, watching. Flynn saw Megan appear in the loft and move beside Leary, speaking to him as though she were soothing his disappointment. Flynn turned to the two priests. "What the hell do you think you're doing?"

The Cardinal answered evenly, "I'm going to hear a confession."

Flynn spoke between clenched teeth. "Are you *mad*? You can't come down from there without permission."

The Cardinal answered, "I don't need your permission to go anywhere in this church. Please stand aside."

Flynn fought down the anger inside him. "Let me tell you two something. Those people up there have standing orders to shoot.... All right, four of them may not be priest killers, but the fifth man would kill you. He would shoot his mother if that's what he's contracted to do. Just as you took your vows, he has taken his."

The Cardinal's face turned crimson; he began to speak, but Flynn cut him off. "That man has spent fourteen years as a sniper for a dozen different armies. By now he sees the world through cross hairs. His whole being is compressed into that solitary act. And he loves it—the sound of the gun, the recoil of the stock against his shoulder, the flash of the muzzle, the smell of burnt powder in his nostrils. It's like a sexual act to him—can you two understand *that*?"

Neither the Cardinal nor the priest answered. The Cardinal turned his head and looked up into the shadows of the choir loft, then turned back to Flynn. "It's hard to believe such a man exists. You should be careful he doesn't shoot *you*." He stepped around Flynn and entered the wooden archway, then turned into the door of the confessional.

Father Murphy glanced at Flynn, then pushed aside the curtain and entered the confessional.

John Hickey stood some distance off near the Lady Chapel and watched silently.

Murphy knelt in the dark enclosure and began, "Bless me, Father..." He peered through a space in the curtain and saw Flynn walking away. He spoke in whispered tones to the Cardinal, making a hasty confession, then broke off abruptly and said, "Your Eminence, I'm going to use the call buzzer to send a coded message."

The dark outline of the Cardinal's profile behind the black screen stayed motionless as though he hadn't heard, then slowly the head nodded.

Murphy drew the curtain gently over the doorjamb and pressed the button in a series of alerting signals. He looked closely at the paper in his hand and squinted in the darkness. He began:

THIS IS FR. MURPHY.

Suddenly a hand flew through the curtain and grabbed his wrist. Hickey's voice filled the confessional. "While you're in there, Padre, confess to using the confessional for treachery." He flung the curtain aside, and Murphy blinked in the sudden light. Hickey snatched the paper out of the priest's hand and pulled the curtain closed. "Go on, finish your damned confession. I'll finish the message."

Murphy slumped against the screen and spoke softly to the Cardinal. "I'm sorry...."

Hickey stood outside the booth and looked around. Flynn was gone. No one was paying any attention to him except Malone and Baxter on the sanctuary, who looked both angry and disheartened. Hickey smiled at them, then read the coded message, put his finger on the buzzer, and began to send. He repeated the salutation—.

THIS IS FR. MURPHY IN CONFESSIONAL WITH CARDINAL.

He continued, reproducing the halting wrist of a man who was sending for the first time. He modified the written message as he sent.

ESTIMATE OF FENIAN STRENGTH: NO MORE
THAN EIGHT GUNMEN. ONE IN EACH OF EAST
TRIFORIA. NONE IN WEST TRIFORIA. NONE IN
CHOIR LOFT. ONE MAN AT SACRISTY STAIRS WITH
THOMPSON—ONLY AUTO WEAPON SEEN. ONE
MAN IN EACH TOWER. FIELD PHONES MALFUNC-
TIONING. HOSTAGES MOVED TO CRYPT. SAFE
FROM FIRE.

He stopped and picked up the text of the message.

MACCUMAIL IS BRIAN FLYNN. JOHN HICKEY,
LIEUTENANT. MEGAN THIRD IN COMMAND.

He improvised again.

NO MINES ON DOORS. GAS MASKS ARE OLD TYPE,
INEFFECTIVE FILTERS.

He stopped and thought a moment. Then went on.

FENIANS LOYAL TO HICKEY. WILL NOT NEGOTI-
ATE IN GOOD FAITH. SUICIDAL TALK. BAXTER
TO BE HANGED BEFORE DAWN DEADLINE AS AN
EXAMPLE. DO WHAT YOU MUST. WE ARE NOT
AFRAID. GOD BLESS YOU—FATHER MURPHY.

Hickey took his finger off the buzzer and smiled.
The people out there were a bit confused now...and
frightened. Fright led to desperation. Desperation led
to reckless acts. Hickey put himself in their place—dis-
counting the possibility of negotiation, concerned over

the hostages, underestimating the force holding the Cathedral. The police would submit a plan to take the Cathedral, and it would be accepted. And the politicians would have the message to justify that use of force. The police would burst through the doors, and they'd be met by explosions and an unexpected volume of killing fire.

Hickey pictured it in his mind as he looked around the Cathedral. Shattered marble, crumbling statues, dark red blood running over the altars and floors, the dead lying draped over the pews. The attic would be set aflame, and the ceiling would fall into the nave, blowing their precious stained glass into the streets. He saw dying bodies writhing among the rubble and the flames. And when they thought it was over, long after the last shot had been fired, as the dawn streaked in through dusty shafts revealing the rescuers and medics moving through the ruins, then the time bombs would detonate, and the two main columns would tremble and shudder and collapse in a deafening roar of granite and marble, plaster and bronze, wood and concrete. The Cathedral would die, brick by brick, stone by stone, column by column, wall by wall.... And in years to come when people looked on the most magnificent ruin in America they would remember John Hickey's last mission on earth.

Maureen Malone sat very still in the pew and watched as Hickey sent his message. She turned to Harold Baxter. "Bastard!"

Baxter looked away from Hickey. "Yes, well, that's

his prerogative, isn't it? But, no harm done. Especially if the first message was received."

"I don't think you understand," she said. "The people outside still believe we control that signal. Hickey is not sending them a rude message or something of that sort. He's reading from our message and sending a misleading intelligence report over our signatures."

Baxter looked at Hickey, and the comprehension of what she was saying came to him.

"And God only knows what he's telling them. He's mad, you know. Flynn is a paragon of rationality compared to Hickey."

"Hickey is not mad," said Baxter. "He's something far more dangerous than mad."

She looked down at the floor. "Anyway, I'll not apologize for trying."

"I'm not asking you to. But I think the next plan should be mine."

"Really?" She spoke with a frigid tone in her voice. "I don't think we have the time to wait for either your plan or your much discussed right moment."

He answered without anger. "Just give me a few more minutes. I think I know a way out of here."

Burke walked into the Monsignor's inner office, followed by Inspector Langley. A uniformed officer handed them each a copy of the decoded message. Burke sat on Schroeder's desk and read the message. He looked around at the people present—Schroeder, Commissioner Rourke, Roberta Spiegel, and Bellini— the hard core of the Desperate Dozen, with Langley and himself added or subtracted as the situation changed.

Captain Bellini looked up from his copy and spoke to Commissioner Rourke. "If this is accurate, I can take the Cathedral with an acceptable risk to my people. If the hostages are in the crypt, they have a fair chance of surviving...though I can't guarantee that." He looked at the message again. "They don't seem to stand much chance with the Fenians anyway." He stood. "I'll need a few more hours to plan."

Burke thought of Maureen's statement at the sacristy gate. *Twelve gunmen.* Now Murphy said eight. He looked across the room at Bellini. "And if it's not accurate?"

Bellini said, "How far off can they be? They're heads-up people. Right? They can count. Look, I'm not real anxious to do this, but I feel a little better about it now."

Langley said, "We can't discount the possibility that one or both of these messages are from the Fenians." He looked at his copy and compared it to the earlier message, which he held in his hand. "I'm a little confused. Something is wrong here." He looked up. "Bellini, as an intelligence officer, I'd advise you not to believe either of these."

Bellini looked distraught. "Well, where the hell does that put me? Square fucking one, that's where."

Roberta Spiegel said, "Whether or not we believe either of these messages, everybody in the Cardinal's residence and in the next room is reading this last message, and they will come to their own conclusions." She looked at Rourke. "This justifies a preemptive attack, Commissioner. That's what's going through their minds out there." She turned to Bellini. "Captain, be prepared to mount an attack at very short notice."

Bellini nodded distractedly.

The door opened, and Monsignor Downes came into the office. "Did someone want to see me?"

The five men looked at each other questioningly, then Roberta Spiegel said, "Yes, I asked to see you."

Downes remained standing.

The Mayor's aide thought a moment, then said, "Monsignor, neither the Mayor nor myself nor anyone wants to do anything that will harm this church or endanger the lives of the hostages. However—"

The Monsignor's body stiffened.

"However, if the police and my office and the people in Washington decide that negotiation is no longer possible and that there is a clear and immediate danger to the hostages...will you and the diocese stand behind our decision to send in the Emergency Services Division?"

Monsignor Downes stood motionless without answering.

Spiegel said to Bellini, "Give the Monsignor a copy of that message."

Downes took the paper and read it, then looked at Roberta Spiegel. "I'll have to check with the Vicar General. I cannot take the responsibility for this on my own." He turned and left the room.

Roberta Spiegel said, "Every time we uncover another layer of this problem I see how much we've underestimated Flynn. We're sandbagged pretty badly all around, and as the time slips by it's obvious that the easiest course of action is surrender—ours, not Flynn's."

Langley said, "Even surrender is not so easy. We may give in, but that doesn't mean Washington, London, or Dublin will."

Commissioner Rourke said to Bellini, "Captain, the only thing we can do unilaterally, without anyone's permission except the Mayor's, is to attack."

Bellini answered, "That's always the easiest decision, sir—it's the execution that gets a little sticky."

Schroeder spoke up. "I get the feeling you've given up on the negotiations."

Everyone looked at him. Burke said, "Captain, you're still the best hope we've got. If there's any middle ground between our capitulation and an attack, I'm sure you'll find it. Brian Flynn said, however, that there was no middle ground, and I think he was telling us the truth. Dawn or dead."

Maureen watched Hickey as he spoke to the Cardinal and Father Murphy at the confessional. She said to Baxter, "He's questioning them about the buzzer and about the first message."

Baxter nodded, then stood. "Let's pace a bit and stretch our legs. We'll talk."

They began walking across the altar sanctuary toward the throne, a distance of forty feet, then turned and walked back. As they walked, Baxter inclined his head. "Look over there—at the brass plate."

Maureen glanced to the right of the altar. Beyond the sacristy staircase was the large brass plate through which Hickey and Megan Fitzgerald had descended with the suitcases.

Baxter looked over the length of the Cathedral. "I've been analyzing this building. When Hickey and Fitzgerald came up from that plate, they had earth on their hands and knees. So it must be mostly crawl space. There must be large areas that are unlit or badly lit. We have an area of almost a city block in which to disappear. If we can lift that plate quickly and drop into that space, they could never flush us out."

As they paced back toward the right side of the altar the plate came into view again. She said, "Even if we could raise the plate and drop below before we were shot, we wouldn't be free, and no one on the outside would know we were down there."

"We would know we weren't up *here*."

She nodded. "Yes, that's the point, isn't it?" They walked in silence for a few minutes, then Maureen said, "How do you plan to do it?"

Baxter outlined his plan.

Father Murphy and the Cardinal entered the sanctuary, and both Maureen and Baxter noticed that the two priests looked very pale. Father Murphy looked from Maureen to Baxter. "Hickey knows, of course."

The Cardinal spoke. "I would have had no objection to trying to signal the rectory." He looked at Murphy sharply, then at Baxter and Maureen. "You must keep me informed—beforehand—of your plans."

Baxter nodded. "We're about to do that, Your Eminence. We're considering an escape plan. We want you both to come with us."

The Cardinal shook his head and said emphatically,

"My place is here." He seemed lost in thought for a moment, then said, "But I'm ready to give you my blessing." He turned to Father Murphy. "You may go if you choose."

Murphy shook his head and addressed Maureen and Baxter. "I can't leave without His Eminence. But I'll help you if I can."

Maureen looked at the three men. "Good. Let's work out the details and the timing." She looked at her watch. "At nine o'clock, we go."

CHAPTER 33

Captain Bellini said to Monsignor Downes as the Rector walked into the office, "Have you found the plans to the Cathedral yet?"

The Monsignor shook his head. "The staff is looking here and at the diocese building. But I don't believe we ever had a set on file."

Commissioner Rourke said to Langley, "What are you doing about finding the architect, Gordon Stillway?"

Langley lit a cigarette and took his time answering. He said finally, "Detectives went to his office on East Fifty-third. It was closed, of course—"

Rourke interrupted. "Are you getting a court order to go in?"

Langley noticed that the Deputy Commissioner was becoming more assertive. By midnight he'd probably try to give an order. Langley said, "Actually, someone already got in—without the benefit of a court order. No Cathedral blueprints. The detectives are trying to find a roster of employees. That's apparently missing also."

Monsignor Downes cleared his throat and said, "I

don't approve of an assault...but it must be planned for, I suppose..." He looked at the bookcase and said, "Among those books you'll find about five that are pictorial studies of the Cathedral. Some have plans in them, very sketchy plans—for tourists to follow when they walk on the main floor. The interior pictures are very good, though, and may be helpful."

Bellini went to the bookcase and began scanning the shelves.

Burke stood. "There may be a set of blueprints in Stillway's apartment. No one's answering the phone, and the detective we have stationed there says no one's answering the door. I'm going over there now."

Schroeder stood also. "You can't leave here. Flynn said—"

Burke turned on him. "The hell with Flynn."

Roberta Spiegel said, "Go ahead, Lieutenant."

Langley ripped a page from his notebook. "Here's the address. Don't gain entry by illegal means."

Monsignor Downes said, "If you should find Gordon Stillway, remember he's a very old man. Don't excite him."

"I don't do anything illegal. I don't excite people." Burke turned and walked out into the adjoining office. A heavy cloud of blue smoke hung at face level over the crowded outer office. Burke pushed his way into the hall and went down the stairs. The rectory offices on the ground floor were filled with uniformed police commanders directing the field operations. Burke approached a captain sitting at a desk and showed his badge case. "I need a squad car and a maniac to drive it."

The captain looked up from a map of midtown.

"Do you? Well, the area on the other side of the cordon is jammed solid with people and vehicles. Where is it you'd like to go in such a hurry, Lieutenant?"

"Gramercy Park. Pronto-like."

"Well, make your way to the IRT station on Lex."

"Bullshit." He grabbed a phone and went through the switchboard to the Monsignor's office. "Langley, is the helicopter still in the Palace courtyard? Good. Call and get it revved up."

Burke walked out of the rectory into Fifty-first Street and breathed in the cold, bracing air that made him feel better. The sleet was tapering off, but the wind was still strong. He walked into the deserted intersection of Fifty-first and Madison.

An eerie silence hung over the lamplit streets around the Cathedral, and in the distance he could see the barricades of squad cars, buses, and sanitation trucks that made up the cordon. Strands of communication wire ran over the sleet-covered streets and sidewalks. Sentries stood silhouetted against half-lit buildings, and National Guardsmen cruised by in jeeps, rifles pointed upward. Bullhorns barked in the wintry air, and policemen patrolled the sanitized area with shotguns. Burke heard their footsteps crunching in the unshoveled ice and heard his own quickening pace. As he walked, he thought of Belfast and, though he'd never been there, felt he knew the place. He turned up his collar and walked faster.

Across Madison Avenue a solitary figure on horseback rode slowly into the north wind. He stared at the rider, Betty Foster, as she passed beneath a streetlight. She didn't seem to notice him, and he walked on.

The wind dropped, and he heard in the distance, past the perimeter of the cordon, the sounds of music and singing. New York would not be denied its party. Burke passed the rear of the Lady Chapel, then approached the Cardinal's residence, and through the lace curtains on a groundfloor window he saw ESD men standing in a room. A lieutenant was briefing them, and Burke could see a chalkboard. *Win this one for the Gipper, lads.* Through another window on the corner Burke saw well-dressed men and women, the Governor and Mayor among them, crowded around what was probably a buffet. They didn't exactly look like they were enjoying themselves, but they didn't look as grim as the men around the chalkboard either.

In the intersection Burke turned and looked back at the Cathedral illuminated by its garden floodlights. A soft luminescence passed through the stained-glass windows and cast a colored shadow over the white street. It was a serene picture, postcard pretty: ice-covered branches of bare lindens and glistening expanses of undisturbed sleet. Perhaps more serene than it had ever been in this century—the surrounding area cleared of cars and people, and the buildings darkened....

Something out of place caught his eye, and he looked up at the two towers where light shone through the ripped louvers. In the north tower—the bell tower—he saw a shadow moving, a solitary figure circling from louver to louver, cold, probably edgy, watchful. In the south tower there was also a figure, standing motionless. Two people, one in each tower— the only eyes that stared out of the besieged Cathedral.

So much depended on them, thought Burke. He hoped they weren't the panicky type.

The police command helicopter followed Lexington Avenue south. Below, Burke could see that traffic was beginning to move again, or at least what passed for moving traffic in Manhattan. Rotating beacons at every intersection indicated the scope of the police action below. The towering buildings of midtown gave way to the lower buildings in the old section of Gramercy Park, and the helicopter dropped altitude.

Burke could see the lamps of the small private park encircled by elegant town houses. He pointed, and the pilot swung the craft toward the open area and turned on the landing lights. The helicopter settled into a small patch of grass, and Burke jumped out and walked quickly toward the high wrought-iron fence. He rattled the bars of a tall gate but found it was locked. On the sidewalk a crowd of people stared back at him curiously. Burke said, "Is anyone there a keyholder?"

No one answered.

Burke peered between the bars, his hands wrapped around the cold iron. He thought of the zoo gate that morning, the ape house, the sacristy gate, and all the prisons he'd ever seen. He thought of Long Kesh and Crumlin Road, Lubianka and Dachau. He thought that there were too many iron bars and too many people staring at each other through them. He shouted with a sudden and unexpected anger, "Come on, damn it! Who's got a key?"

An elderly, well-dressed woman came forward and produced an ornate key. Without a word she unlocked the gate, and Burke slipped out quickly and pushed roughly through the crowd.

He approached a stately old town house across the street and knocked sharply on the door. A patrolman opened the door, and Burke held up his badge, brushing by him into the small lobby. A single plainclothesman sat in the only chair, and Burke introduced himself perfunctorily.

The man answered through a wide yawn, "Detective Lewis." He stood as though with some effort.

Burke said, "Any word on Stillway?"

The detective shook his head.

"Get a court order yet?"

"Nope."

Burke began climbing the stairs. When he was a rookie, an old cop once said to him, "Everybody lives on the top floor. Everybody gets robbed on the top floor. Everybody goes nuts on the top floor. Everybody dies on the top floor." Burke reached the top floor, the fourth. Two apartments had been made out of what was once probably the servants' quarters. He found Stillway's door and pressed the buzzer.

The detective climbed the stairs behind him. "No one home."

"No shit, Sherlock." Burke looked at the three lock-cylinders in a vertical row, ranging in age from very old to very new, showing the progression of panic with each passing decade. He turned to the detective. "Want to put your shoulder to that?"

"Nope."

"Me neither." Burke moved to a narrow staircase behind a small door. "Stay here." He went up the stairs and came out onto the roof, then went down the rear fire escape and stopped at Stillway's window.

The apartment was dark except for the yellow glow of a clock radio. There was no grate on the window, and Burke drew his gun and brought it through the old brittle glass above the sash lock. He reached in, un-latched the catch, and threw the sash up, then dropped into the room and moved away from the window in a crouch, his gun held out in front of him with both hands.

He steadied his breathing and listened. His eyes became accustomed to the dark, and he began to make out shadows and shapes. Nothing moved, nothing breathed, nothing smelled; there was noth-ing that wanted to kill him, and, he sensed, nothing that had been killed there. He rose, found a lamp, and turned it on.

The large studio apartment was in stark modern contrast to the world around it. Bone-white walls, track lighting, chromium furniture. The secret modern world of an old architect who specialized in Gothic restorations. *Shame, shame, Gordon Stillway.*

He walked toward the hall door, gun still drawn, looking into the dark corners as he moved. Everything was perfectly ordinary; nothing was out of place— no crimson on the white rug, no gore on the shiny chromium. Burke holstered his revolver and opened the door. He motioned to the detective. "Back win-dow broken. Cause to suspect a crime in progress. Fill out a report."

The detective winked and moved toward the stairs.

Burke closed the door and looked around. He

found a file cabinet beside a drafting table and opened the middle drawer alphabetized J to S. He was not too surprised to find that between St.-Mark's-in-the-Bouwerie and St. Paul the Apostle there was nothing but a slightly larger space than there should have been.

Burke saw a telephone on the counter of the kitchenette and dialed the rectory, got a fast busy-signal on the trunk line, dialed the operator, got a recording telling him to dial again, and slammed down the receiver. He found Gordon Stillway's bar in a shelf unit and chose a good bourbon.

The phone rang and Burke answered, "Hello."

Langley's voice came through the earpiece. "Figured you couldn't get an open line. What's the story? Body in the library?"

"No body. No Stillway. The Saint Patrick's file is missing, too."

Langley said, "Interesting..." He paused, then said, "We're having no luck in our other inquiries either."

Burke heard someone talking loudly in the background. "Is that Bellini?"

Langley said quietly, "Yeah. He's going into his act. Pay no attention."

Burke lit a cigarette. "I'm not having a good Saint Patrick's Day, Inspector."

"March eighteenth doesn't look real promising either." He drew a long breath. "There are blueprints in this city somewhere, and there are other architects, maybe engineers, who know this place. We could have them all by midmorning tomorrow—but we don't have that long. Flynn has thought this all out. Right down to snatching Stillway and the blueprints."

Burke said, "I wonder."

"Wonder *what*?"

"Hasn't it occurred to you that if Flynn had Stillway, then Stillway would be in the Cathedral where he'd do the most good?"

"Maybe he *is* in there."

Burke thought a moment. "I don't know. Flynn would tell us if he had the architect. He'd tell us he knows ways to blow the place by mining the hidden passages—if any. He's an intelligent man who knows how to get maximum mileage from everything he does. Think about it." Burke looked around the tidy room. A copy of the *New York Post* lay on the couch, and he pulled the telephone cord as he walked to it. A front-page picture showed a good fist-flying scene of the disturbance in front of the Cathedral at noon. The headline ran: DEMONSTRATION MARS PARADE. A subline said: BUT THE IRISH MARCH. The special evening editions would have better stuff than that.

Langley's voice came into the earpiece. "Burke, you still there?"

Burke looked up. "Yeah. Look, Stillway was here. Brought home the evening paper and..."

"And?"

Burke walked around the room holding the phone and receiver. He opened a closet near the front door and spoke into the phone. "Wet topcoat. Wet hat. No raincoat. No umbrella. No briefcase. He came home in the sleet, changed, and went out again carrying his briefcase, which contained, I guess, the Saint Patrick's file."

"What color are his eyes? Okay, I'll buy it. Where'd he go?"

"Probably went with somebody who had a good set of credentials and a plausible story. Somebody who talked his way into the apartment..."

Langley said, "A Fenian who got to him too late to get him into the Cathedral—"

"Maybe. But maybe somebody else doesn't want us to have the blueprints or Stillway...."

"Strange business."

"Think about it, Inspector. Meanwhile, get a Crime Scene Unit over here, then get me an open line so I can call Ferguson."

"Okay. But hurry back. Schroeder's getting nervous."

Burke hung up and took his glass of bourbon on a tour around the apartment. Nothing else yielded any hard clues, but he was getting a sense of the old architect. Not the type of man to go out into the cold sleet, he thought, unless duty called. The phone rang. Burke picked it up and gave the operator Ferguson's number, then said, "Call back in ten minutes. I'll need to make another call."

After six rings the phone was answered, and Jack Ferguson came on the line, his voice sounding hesitant. "Hello?"

"Burke. Thought I'd get the coroner."

"You may well have. Where the hell have you been?"

"Busy. Well, it looks like you get the good-spy award this year."

"Keep it. Why haven't you called? I've been waiting for your call—"

"Didn't my office call you?"

"Yes. Very decent of them. Said I was a marked man. Who's on to me, then?"

"Well, Flynn for one. Probably the New York Irish Republican Army, Provisional Wing, for another. And I think you've outlived your usefulness to Major Martin—it *was* Martin you were playing around with, wasn't it?"

Ferguson stayed silent for a few seconds, then said, "He told me he could head off the Fenians with my help."

"Did he, now? Well, the only people he wanted to head off were the New York police."

Again, Ferguson didn't speak for a few seconds, then said, "Bastards. They're all such bloody bastards. Why is everyone so committed to this senseless violence?"

"Makes good press. What is your status, Jack?"

"Status? My status is I'm scared. I'm packed and ready to leave town. My wife's sister came and took her to her place. God, I wouldn't have waited around for anyone else, Burke. I should have left an hour ago."

"Well, why did you wait around? Got something for me?"

"Does the name Terri O'Neal mean anything to you?"

"Man or woman?"

"Woman."

Burke thought a moment. "No."

"She's been kidnapped."

"Lot of that going around today."

"I think she has something to do with what's happening."

"In what way?"

Ferguson said, "Hold on a moment. I hear someone in the hall. Hold on."

Burke said quickly, "Wait. Just tell me—Jack—Shit." Burke held the line. He heard Ferguson's footsteps retreating. He waited for the crash, the shot, the scream, but there was nothing.

Ferguson's voice came back on the line, his breathing loud in the earpiece. "Damned Rivero brothers. Got some señoritas pinned in the alcove, squeezing their tits. God, this used to be a nice Irish building. Boys would go in the basement and get blind drunk. Never looked at a pair of tits until they were thirty. Where was I?"

"Terri O'Neal."

"Right. I got this from a Boston Provo. He and some other lads were supposed to snatch this O'Neal woman last night if a man named Morgan couldn't pick her up in a disco. I assume Morgan picked her up—it's easy today, like going out for a pack of cigarettes. You know? Anyway, now these Boston lads think it was part of what happened today, and they're not happy about what the Fenians did."

"Neither are we."

"Of course," added Ferguson, "it could all be coincidence."

"Yeah." Burke thought. *Terri O'Neal.* It was a familiar name, but he couldn't place it. He was sure it wasn't in the files, because women in the files were still rare enough to remember every one of them. "Terri O'Neal."

"That's what the gentleman said. Now get me the hell out of here."

"Okay. Stay put. Don't open the door to strangers."

"How long will it take to get a car here?"

"I'm not sure. Hang on. You're covered."

"That's what Langley told Timmy O'Day last summer."

"Mistakes happen. Listen, we'll have a drink next week...lunch—"

"Fuck lunch—"

Burke hung up. He stared at the telephone for several minutes. He had a bad taste in his mouth, and he stubbed out his cigarette, then sipped on the bourbon. The telephone rang, and he picked it up. "Operator, get me Midtown North Precinct."

After a short wait the phone rang, and a deep voice said, "Sergeant Gonzalez, Midtown North."

"This is Lieutenant Burke, Intelligence." He gave his badge number. "Do you have clear radio commo with your cars?"

The harried desk sergeant answered, "Yeah, the jamming isn't affecting us here."

Burke heard the recorder go on and heard the beep at foursecond intervals. "You check me out after you hang up. Okay?"

"Right."

"Can you get a car over to 560 West Fifty-fifth Street? Apartment 5D. Pick up and place in protective custody—name of Jack Ferguson."

"What for?"

"His life is in danger."

"So is every citizen's life in this city. Comes with the

territory. West Fifty-fifth? I'm surprised he's not dead yet."

"He's an informant. Real important."

"I don't have many cars available. Things are a mess—"

"Yeah, I heard. Listen, he'll want to go to the Port Authority building, but keep him in the station house."

"Sounds fucked up."

"He's involved with this Cathedral thing. Just do it, okay? I'll take care of you. *Erin go bragh, Gonzalez.*"

"Yeah, *hasta la vista.*"

Burke hung up and left the apartment. He went out into the street and walked back toward the park, where a crowd had gathered outside the fence. As he walked he thought about Ferguson. He knew he owed Ferguson a better shot at staying alive. He knew he should pick him up in the helicopter. But the priorities were shifting again. Gordon Stillway was important. Brian Flynn was important, and Major Martin was important. Jack Ferguson was not so important any longer. Unless... *Terri O'Neal.* What in the name of God was that all about? Why was that name so familiar?

CHAPTER 34

John Hickey sat alone at the chancel organ. He raised his field glasses to the southeast triforium. Frank Gallagher sat precariously on the parapet, reading a Bible; his back was to a supporting column, his sniper rifle was across his knees, and he looked very serene. Hickey marveled at a man who could hold two opposing philosophies in his head at the same time. He shouted to Gallagher, "Look lively."

Hickey focused the glasses on George Sullivan in the long southwest triforium, who was also sitting on the parapet. He was playing a small mouth organ too softly to be heard, except by Abby Boland across the nave. Hickey focused on her as she leaned out across the parapet, looking at Sullivan like a moonstruck girl hanging from a balcony in some cheap melodrama.

Hickey shifted the glasses to the choir loft. Megan was talking to Leary again, and Leary appeared to be actually listening this time. Hickey sensed that they were discovering a common inhumanity. He thought of two vampires on a castle wall in the moonlight, bloodless and lifeless, not able to consummate their meeting in a normal way but agreeing to hunt together.

He raised the glasses and focused on Flynn, who was sitting alone in the choir benches that rose up toward the towering brass organ pipes. Beyond the pipes the great rose window sat above his head like an alien moon, suffused with the night-lights of the Avenue. The effect was dramatic, striking, thought Hickey, and unintentionally so, like most of the memorable tableaux he had seen in his life. Flynn seemed uninterested in Megan or Leary, or in the blueprints spread across his knees. He was staring out into space, and Hickey saw that he was toying with his ring.

Hickey put down the glasses. He had the impression that the troops were getting bored, even claustrophobic, if that were possible in this space. Cabin fever— Cathedral fever, whatever; it was taking its toll, and the night was yet young. Why was it, he thought, that the old, with so little time left, had the most patience? Well, he smiled, age was not so important in here. Everyone had almost the same lifespan left . . . give or take a few heartbeats.

Hickey looked at the hostages on the sanctuary. The four of them were speaking intently. No boredom there. Hickey cranked the field phone beside him. "Attic? Status report."

Jean Kearney's voice came back with a breathy stutter. "Cold as hell up here."

Hickey smiled. "You and Arthur should do what we used to do when I was a lad to keep warm in winter." He waited for a response, but there was none, so he said, "We used to chop wood." He laughed, then cranked the phone again. "South tower. See anything interesting?"

Rory Devane answered, "Snipers with flak jackets on every roof. The area as far south as Forty-eighth Street is cleared. Across the way there are hundreds of people at the windows." He added, "I feel as though I'm in a goldfish bowl."

Hickey lit his pipe, and it bobbed in his mouth as he spoke. "Hold your head up, lad—they're watching your face through their glasses." He thought, *And through their sniper scopes.* "Stare back at them. You're the reason they're all there."

"Yes, sir."

Hickey rang the bell tower. "Status report."

Donald Mullins answered, "Status unchanged...except that more soldiers are arriving."

Hickey drew on his pipe. "Did you get your corned beef, lad? Want more tea?"

"Yes, more tea, please. I'm cold. It's very cold here."

Hickey's voice was low. "It was cold on Easter Monday, 1916, on the roof of the General Post Office. It was cold when the British soldiers marched us to Kilmainham Jail. It was cold in Stonebreaker's Yard where they shot my father and Padraic Pearse and fifteen of our leaders. It's cold in the grave."

Hickey picked up the Cathedral telephone and spoke to the police switchboard operator in the rectory. "Get me Schroeder." He waited through a series of clicks, then said, "Did you find Gordon Stillway yet?"

Schroeder's voice sounded startled. "What?"

"We cleaned out his office after quitting time— couldn't do it before, you understand. That might have tipped someone as dense as even Langley or Burke.

But we had trouble getting to Stillway in the crowd. Then the riot broke."

Schroeder's voice faltered, then he said, "Why are you telling us this—?"

"We should have killed him, but we didn't. He's either in a hospital or drunk somewhere, or your good friend Martin has murdered him. Stillway is the key man for a successful assault, of course. The blueprints by themselves are not enough. Did you find a copy in the rectory? Well, don't tell me, then. Are you still there, Schroeder?"

"Yes."

"I thought you nodded off." Hickey saw Flynn moving toward the organ keyboard in the choir loft. "Listen, Schroeder, we're going to play some hymns on the bells later. I want a list of eight requests from the NYPD when I call again. All right?"

"All right."

"Nothing tricky now. Just good solid Christian hymns that sound nice on the bells. Some Irish folk songs, too. Give the city a lift. *Beannacht*." He hung up. After uncovering the keyboard and turning on the chancel organ, he put his thin hands over the keys and began playing a few random notes. He nodded with exaggerated graciousness toward the hostages who were watching and began singing as he played. "In Dublin's fair city, where the girls are so pretty..." His voice came out in a well-controlled bass, rich and full, very unlike his speaking voice. "'Twas where I first met my sweet Molly Malone..."

Brian Flynn sat at the choir organ and turned the key to start it. He placed his hands over the long curved keyboard and played a chord. On the organ was a large convex mirror set at an angle that allowed Flynn to see most of the Cathedral below—used, he knew, by the organist to time the triumphal entry of a procession or to set the pace for an overly eager bride, or a reluctant one. He smiled as he joined with the smaller organ below and looked at Megan, who had just come from the south tower. "Give us the pleasure of your sweet voice, Megan. Come here and turn on this microphone."

Megan looked at him but made no move toward the microphone. Leary's eyes darted between Flynn and Megan.

Flynn said, "Ah, Megan, you've no idea how important song is to revolution." He turned on the microphone. Hickey was going through the song again, and Flynn joined in with a soft tenor.

> "As she wheeled her wheelbarrow
> Through streets wide and narrow
> Crying cockles, and mussels,
> Alive, alive-o . . ."

John Hickey smiled, and his eyes misted as the music carried him back across the spans of time and distance to the country he had not seen in over forty years.

> "She was a fishmonger,
> And sure 'twas no wonder,
> For her father and mother were
> Fishmongers, too,
> And they each wheel'd their barrow . . ."

Hickey saw his father's face again on the night before the soldiers took him out to be shot. He remembered being dragged out of their cell to what he thought was his own place of execution, but they had beaten him and dumped him on the road outside Kilmainham Jail. He remembered clearly the green sod laid carefully over his father's grave the next day, his mother's face at the graveside....

> "And she died of a fever
> And no one could save her,
> And that was the end of sweet
> Molly Malone,
> But her ghost wheels her barrow..."

He had wanted to die then, and had tried to die a soldier's death every day since, but it wasn't in his stars. And when at last he thought death had come in that mean little tenement across the river, he found he was required to go on...to complete one last mission. But it would be over soon...and he would be home again.

CHAPTER 35

Bert Schroeder looked at the memo given him by the Hostage Unit's psychologist, Dr. Korman, who had been monitoring each conversation from the adjoining office. Korman had written: *Flynn is a megalomaniac and probably a paranoid schizophrenic. Hickey is paranoid also and has an unfulfilled death wish.* Schroeder almost laughed. What the hell other kind of death wish could you have if you were still alive?

How, wondered Schroeder, could a New York psychologist diagnose a man like Flynn, from a culture so different from his own? Or Hickey, from a different era? How could he diagnose *anybody* based on telephone conversations? Yet he did it at least fifty times a year for Schroeder. Sometimes his diagnoses turned out to be fairly accurate; other times they did not. He always wondered if Korman was diagnosing *him* as well.

He looked up at Langley, who had taken off his jacket in the stuffy room. His exposed revolver lent, thought Schroeder, a nice menacing touch for the civilians. Schroeder said to him, "Do you have much faith in these things?"

Langley looked up from his copy of the report. "I'm reminded of my horoscope—the language is such that it fits anybody...nobody's playing with a full deck. You know?"

Schroeder nodded and turned a page of the report and stared at it without reading. He hadn't given Korman the psy-profiles on either man yet and might never give them to the psychologist. The more varying opinions he had, the more he would be able to cover himself if things went bad. He said to Langley, "Regarding Korman's theory of Hickey's unfulfilled death wish, how are we making out on that court order for exhumation?"

Langley said, "A judge in Jersey City was located. We'll be able to dig up Hickey...the grave, by midnight."

Schroeder nodded. *Midnight—grave digging.* He gave a small shudder and looked down at the psychologist's report again. It went on for three typewritten pages, and as he read Schroeder had the feeling that Dr. Korman wasn't all there either. As to the real state of mind of these two men, Schroeder believed only God knew that—not Korman or anyone in the room, and probably not the two men themselves.

Schroeder looked at the three other people remaining in the room—Langley, Spiegel, and Bellini. He was aware that they were waiting for him to say something. He cleared his throat. "Well...I've dealt with crazier people.... In fact, all the people I've dealt with have been crazy. The funny thing is that the proximity to death seems to snap them out of it, temporarily. They act very rational when they realize what they're up against—when they see the forces massed against them."

Langley said, "Only the two people in the towers have that visual stimulation, Bert. The rest are in a sort of cocoon. You know?"

Schroeder shot Langley an annoyed look.

Joe Bellini said suddenly, "Fuck this psycho-crap. *Where is Stillway?*" He looked at Langley.

Langley shrugged.

Bellini said, "If Flynn has him in there, we've got a real problem."

Langley blew a smoke ring. "We're looking into it."

Schroeder said, "Hickey is a liar. He knows where Stillway is."

Spiegel shook her head. "I don't think he does."

Langley added, "Hickey was very indiscreet to mention Major Martin over the phone like that. Flynn wouldn't have wanted Martin's name involved publicly. He doesn't want to make trouble between Washington and London at this stage."

Schroeder nodded absently. He was certain the governments wouldn't reach an accord anyway—or, if they did, it wouldn't include releasing prisoners in Northern Ireland. He had nothing to offer the Fenians but their lives and a fair trial, and they didn't seem much interested in either.

Captain Bellini paced in front of the fireplace. "I won't expose my men to a fight unless I know every column, pew, balcony, and altar in that place."

Langley looked down at the six large picture books on the coffee table. "Those should give you a fair idea of the layout. Some good interior shots.

Passable floor plans. Have your men start studying them. Now."

Bellini looked at him. "Is that the best intelligence you can come up with?" He picked up the books in one of his big hands and walked toward the door. "Damn it, if there's a secret way into that place, I've got to know." He began pacing in tight circles. "They've had it all their way up to now...but I'll get them." He looked at the silent people in the room. "Just keep them talking, Schroeder. When they call on me to move, I'll be ready. I'll get those potato-eating Mick sons of bitches—I'll bring Flynn's balls to you in a teacup." He walked out and slammed the door behind him.

Roberta Spiegel looked at Schroeder. "Is he nuts?"

Schroeder shrugged. "He goes through this act every time a situation goes down. He's getting himself psyched. He gets crazier as the thing drags on."

Roberta Spiegel stood and reached into Langley's shirt pocket and took a cigarette.

Langley watched her as she lit the cigarette. There was something masculine and at the same time sensuously feminine about all her movements. A woman who had an obvious power over the Mayor—although exactly what type of power no one knew for sure. And, thought Langley, she was much sharper than His Honor. When it came down to the final decision on which so many lives hung, *she* would be the one to make it. Roberta Spiegel, whose name was known to nobody outside of New York. Roberta Spiegel, who had no ambitions of elected office, no civil service career to worry about, no one to answer to.

Spiegel sat on the edge of Schroeder's desk and leaned toward him, then glanced back at Langley. She said, "Let me be frank while we three are alone—" She bit her lip thoughtfully, then continued. "The British are not going to give in, as you know. Bellini doesn't have much of a chance of saving those people or this Cathedral. Washington is playing games, and the Governor is—well, between us, an asshole. His Honor is—how shall I put it?— not up to the task. And the Church is going to become a problem if we give them enough time." She leaned very close to Schroeder. "So...it's up to you, Captain. More than any time in your distinguished career it's all up to *you*—and, if you don't mind my saying so, Captain, you don't seem to be handling this with your usual aplomb."

Schroeder's face reddened. He cleared his throat. "If you...if the Mayor would like me to step aside—"

She came down from the desk. "There comes a time when every man knows he's met his match. I think we've *all* met our match here at this Cathedral. We can't even seem to win a point. Why?"

Schroeder again cleared his throat. "Well...it always seems that way in the beginning. They're the aggressors, you understand, and they've had months to think everything out. In time the situation will begin to reverse—"

Spiegel slammed her hand on the desk. "They know that, damn it! That's why they've given us no time. *Blitzkrieg*, Schroeder, *blitzkrieg*. Lightning war. You know the word. They're not hanging around while we get our act together. Dawn or dead. That's the truest thing anyone's said all night."

Schroeder tried to control his voice. "Miss

Spiegel...you see, I've had many years...let me explain. We are at a psychological disadvantage because of the hostages.... But put yourself in the *Cathedral*. Think of the disadvantages *they* must overcome. They don't want to die—no matter what they pretend to the contrary. That and that alone is the bottom line of their thinking. And the hostages are keeping them alive—therefore, they won't kill the hostages. Therefore, at dawn *nothing* will happen. *Nothing*. It never does. *Never*."

Spiegel let out a long breath. She turned toward Langley and reached out not for another cigarette but for his pistol. She pulled it from his shoulder holster and turned to Schroeder. "See this? Men used to settle their arguments with this." She looked closely at the blue-black metal and continued. "We're supposed to be beyond that now, but I'll tell you something. There's more of this in the world than there are hostage negotiators. I'll tell you something else—I'd rather send Bellini in with his guns than wait around with my finger up my ass to see what happens at dawn." She dropped the pistol to her side and leaned over the desk. "If you can't get a firm extension of the dawn deadline, then we go in while we still have the cover of darkness—before that self-destruct response levels this block."

Schroeder sat motionless. "There is no self-destruct response."

Spiegel said, "God, I wish I had your nerves—it *is* nerves, isn't it?" She tossed the revolver back to Langley.

Langley holstered the gun. He looked at Spiegel.

She got away with a great deal—the cigarettes, then the gun. She relieved him of his possessions with a very cavalier attitude. But maybe, he thought, it was just as well she didn't observe the cautious etiquette that men did in these situations.

Roberta Spiegel moved away and looked at the two police officers. "If you want to know what's really happening around you, don't listen to those politicians out there. Listen to Brian Flynn and John Hickey." She looked at a large wooden crucifix over Schroeder's head and then out through the window at the Cathedral. "If Flynn or Hickey say dawn or dead, they *mean* dawn or dead. Understand who you're dealing with."

Schroeder nodded, almost imperceptibly. For a split second he had seen the face of the enemy, but it disappeared again just as quickly.

There was a long silence in the room, then Spiegel continued softly, "They can sense our fear...smell it. They also sense that we're not going to give them what they want." She looked at Schroeder. "I wish the people out there could give you the kind of direction you should have. But they've confused your job with theirs. They expect miracles from you, and you're starting to believe you can deliver them. You can't. Only Joe Bellini can deliver them a miracle—a military miracle—none killed, no wounded, no damage. Bellini is looking better to the people out there. They're losing faith in the long hard road that you represent. They're fantasizing about a glorious successful military solution. So while you're stalling the Fenians, don't forget to stall the people in the other rooms, too."

CHAPTER 36

Flynn and Hickey played the organs, and George Sullivan played the pipes. Eamon Farrell, Frank Gallagher, and Abby Boland sang "My Wild Irish Rose." In the attic Jean Kearney and Arthur Nulty lay huddled together on a catwalk above the choir loft. The pipes of the great organ reverberated through the board on which they lay. Pedar Fitzgerald sat with his back against the crypt door. He half closed his tired eyes and hummed.

Flynn felt the lessening of the tensions as people lost themselves in reveries. He could sense a dozen minds escaping the cold stone fortress. He glanced at Megan and Leary. Even they seemed subdued as they sat on the choir parapet, their backs to the Cathedral, drinking tea and sharing a cigarette. Flynn turned away from them and lost himself in the thunderous organ.

Father Murphy knelt motionless before the high altar. He glanced at his watch.

Harold Baxter paced across the sanctuary floor, trying to appear restless while his eyes darted around the Cathedral. He looked at his watch. No reason, he thought, to wait the remaining minutes. They might never get an opportunity as good as this. As he passed by Father Murphy, he said, "Thirty seconds."

Maureen lay curled up on a pew, her face buried in her arms. One eye peered out, and she saw Baxter nod to her.

Baxter turned and walked back toward the throne. He passed close to the Cardinal and said, "Now."

The Cardinal stood, came down from the throne, and walked to the communion rail. He opened the gate and strode swiftly down the center aisle.

Father Murphy heard Baxter say, "Go." Murphy made the sign of the cross, rose quickly, and moved toward the side of the altar.

Flynn watched the movements on the sanctuary in the organ mirror as he played. He continued to play the lilting melody as he called out to Leary. "Turn around."

Leary and Megan both jumped down from the parapet and spun around. Leary raised his rifle.

Hickey's organ stopped, and Flynn's organ died away on a long, lingering note. The singing stopped, and the Cathedral fell silent, all eyes on the Cardinal. Flynn spoke into the microphone as he looked in the mirror. "Stop where you are, Cardinal."

Father Murphy opened the circuit-breaker box recessed into the side of the altar, pulled the switch, and the sanctuary area went dark. Baxter took three long strides, passed the sacristy staircase, and hit the floor, sliding across the marble toward the brass floorplate. Maureen rolled off the pew and crawled swiftly toward the rear of the sanctuary. Baxter's fingers found the grip on the brass plate and lifted the heavy metal until its hinges locked in place. Maureen pivoted, and her legs found the opening in the floor.

The four people in the triforia were shouting wildly. A shot rang out from the choir loft, and the shouting stopped. Four shots exploded in quick succession from the triforia.

Maureen dropped through the hole and fell to the earth floor below.

Baxter felt something—a spent bullet, a piece of marble—slam into his chest, and he rocked backward on his haunches.

The Cardinal kept walking straight ahead, but no one looked at him any longer.

Father Murphy crawled to the sacristy staircase and collided with Pedar Fitzgerald running up the steps. Both men swung wildly at each other in the partial darkness.

Baxter caught his breath and lunged forward. His arms and shoulders hung into the opening, and his feet slid over the marble trying to find traction.

Maureen was shouting, "Jump! Jump!" She reached up and grabbed his dangling arm.

Five more shots rang out, splintering marble and ringing sharply from the brass plate. Baxter felt a sharp pain shoot across his back, and his body jerked convulsively. Five more shots whistled through the dark over his head. He was aware that Maureen was pulling on his right hand. He tried to drop headfirst into the hole, but someone was pulling on his legs. He heard a shout very close to his ear, and the firing stopped.

Maureen was hanging from his arm, yelling up to him, "Jump! For God's sake, jump!"

Baxter heard his own voice, low and breathless. "Can't. Got me. Run. Run." Someone was pulling on his ankles, pulling him back from the hole. He felt Maureen's grip on his arm loosen, then break away. A pair of strong hands rolled him over on his back, and he looked into the face of Pedar Fitzgerald, who was kneeling above him, holding the submachine gun to his throat. In the half-light Baxter saw that there was blood spreading over Fitzgerald's neck and across his white shirt.

Fitzgerald looked down at him and spoke between labored breaths. "You stupid son of a bitch! I'll kill you—you goddamned bastard." He pounded his fist into Baxter's face, then crawled over him to the hole and pointed the barrel of the gun down into the opening. He steadied himself and fired two long, deafening bursts into the darkness.

Baxter was dimly aware of a warm wetness seeping over the cold floor beneath him. His eyes tried to focus on the vaulted ceiling ten stories above his face, but all he saw were the blurry red spots of the Cardinals' hanging hats. He heard footsteps running toward the altar, coming up the stairs, then saw faces hovering over him—Hickey, then a few seconds later Flynn and Megan Fitzgerald.

Baxter turned his head and saw Father Murphy lying near the stairs, his hands pressed to his face and blood running between his fingers. He heard Megan's voice. "Pedar! Are you hit? Pedar?"

Baxter tried to raise his head to look for the Cardinal. Suddenly he saw Megan's shoe flying into his face, and a red flash passed in front of his eyes, followed by blackness.

Flynn knelt beside Pedar Fitzgerald and pulled the barrel of the gun out of the hole. He touched Fitzgerald's bloody neck wound. "Just grazed you, lad." He called to Megan. "Take him back to his post. Quickly."

Flynn lay prone at the edge of the opening and called down. "Maureen! Are you all right? Are you hit?"

Maureen knelt a few yards from the opening. Her body was trembling, and she took long breaths to steady herself. Her hands ran over her body, feeling for a wound.

Flynn called down again. "Are you hit?" His voice became anxious. "For God's sake, answer me."

She drew a deep breath and surprised herself by answering, "No."

Flynn's voice sounded more controlled. "Come back."

"Go to hell."

"Come back, Maureen, or we'll shoot Baxter. We'll shoot him and throw him down there where you can see him."

"They're all dead anyway."

"No, they're not."

"Let Baxter speak to me."

There was a pause, then Flynn said, "He's unconscious."

"Bloody murdering bastards. Let me speak to Father Murphy."

"He's . . . hurt. Wait. I'll get the Cardinal—"

"Go to hell." She knew she didn't want to hear any of their voices; she just wanted to run. She called back, "Give it up, Brian. Before more people are killed, give it up." Hesitantly she called, "Good-bye."

She drew away from the opening until her back came into contact with the base of a column. She stared at the ladder that descended from the opening. She heard someone speaking in half-whispered tones, and she had a feeling someone was ready to come down.

Flynn's voice called out again, "Maureen—you're not the kind who would run out on your friends. Their lives depend on you."

She felt a cold sweat break out over her body. She thought to herself, *Brian, you make everything so damned hard.* She stepped toward the opening but then hesitated. A new thought came into her mind. *What would Brian do?* He'd run. He always ran. And not out of cowardice but because he and all of them had long ago agreed that escape was the morally correct response to tight situations. Yet...he'd stayed with her when she was wounded. She vacillated between the column and the opening.

Flynn's voice cut into the dark basement. "You're a damned coward, Maureen. All right, then, Baxter's gone."

A shot rang out on the sacristy.

After the report died away he called out again. "Murphy is next."

Maureen instinctively moved back against the column. She put her face in her hands. "Bastards!"

Flynn yelled, "The priest is next!"

She picked up her head and wiped the tears from her eyes. She peered into the darkness. Her eyes adjusted to the half-light, and she forced herself to evaulate the situation calmly. To her right was the outer wall of the sacristy staircase. If she followed it she'd find the foundation wall, beyond which was freedom. That was the way she had to go.

She looked quickly back and saw a pair of legs dropping from the opening. More of the body was revealed as it descended the ladder—Hickey. Above Hickey's head another pair of legs appeared. Megan. Both of them held flashlights and pistols by their sides. Hickey turned his head and squinted into the blackness as he climbed down. Maureen crouched down beside the column.

Hickey's voice rolled through the black, damp air. He spoke as to a child. "Coming for you, darlin'. Coming to get you. Come to old John, now. Don't let the wicked Megan find you. Run to Mr. Hickey. Come on, then." He laughed and jumped down the last few steps, switched on the flashlight, and turned toward her.

Megan was right behind him, her fiery red features looking sinister in the overhead light.

Maureen drew a long breath and held it.

CHAPTER 37

Schroeder stood tensed with the phone to his ear. He looked up at Langley, the only person left in the office. "Goddamn it—they're not answering."

Langley stood at the window, staring intently at the Cathedral. On the other side of the double doors phones were ringing and people were shouting.

One of the doors burst open, and Bellini ran in looking more agitated than when he had last left. He shouted, "I have orders from fucking Kline to go in if you can't raise them!"

Schroeder looked up at him. "Get in here and close the door!" He yelled at the police operator, "Of course I want you to keep trying, you stupid ass!"

Bellini closed the door, walked to a chair, and fell into it. Sweat streamed down his pale face. "I ... I'm not ready to go in. . . ."

Schroeder said to Bellini impatiently, "How fucking long does it take to kill four hostages, Bellini? If they're dead already, Kline can damned well wait until you have at least a half-assed idea of how to hit the place."

Suddenly Flynn's voice came over the speaker. "Schroeder?"

Schroeder answered quickly, "Yes—" He controlled his voice. "Yes, sir. Is everything all right?"

"Yes."

Schroeder cleared his throat and spoke into the phone. "What is happening in there?"

Flynn's voice sounded composed. "An ill-advised attempt to escape."

Schroeder sounded incredulous. "*Escape?*"

"That's what I said."

"No one is hurt?"

There was a long pause, then Flynn said, "Baxter and Murphy are wounded. Not badly."

Schroeder looked at Langley and Bellini. He steadied his voice. "We're sending in a doctor."

"If they needed one, I'd tell you."

"I'm sending in a doctor."

"All right, but tell him before you send him that I'll blow his brains out."

Schroeder's voice became angry, but it was a controlled anger, contrived almost, designed to show that shooting was the one thing he wouldn't tolerate. "Damn you, Flynn, you said there'd be no shooting. You said—"

"It couldn't be helped, really."

Schroeder made his tone ominous. "Flynn, if you kill anyone—so help me God, if you hurt anyone, then we're beyond the let's-make-a-deal stage."

"I understand the rules. Calm down, Schroeder."

"Let me speak to each of the hostages. Now."

"Hold on." There was silence, then the Cardinal's voice filled the room. "Captain, do you recognize my voice?"

Schroeder looked at the other two men, and they nodded. He said, "Yes, Your Eminence."

The Cardinal spoke in a tone that suggested he was being coached and closely watched. "I'm all right. Mr. Baxter has received what they tell me is a grazing wound across his back and a ricochet wound in his chest. He's resting and seems all right. Father Murphy was also hit by a ricocheting bullet—in the face—the jaw. He's stunned but otherwise appears all right. . . . It was a miracle no one was killed."

The three men in the room seemed to relax. There were murmurs from the adjoining office. Schroeder said, "Miss Malone?"

The Cardinal answered hesitantly, "She is alive. Not wounded. She is—"

Schroeder heard the phone being covered at the other end. He heard muffled voices, an angry exchange. He spoke into the receiver, "Hello? Hello?"

The Cardinal's voice came back, "That's all I can say."

Schroeder spoke quickly, "Your Eminence, please don't provoke these people. You must not endanger your own lives, because you're also endangering other lives—"

The Cardinal replied in a neutral tone, "I'll pass that on to the others." He added, "Miss Malone is—"

Flynn's voice suddenly came on the line. "Good advice from Captain Courageous. All right, you see no one is dead. Everyone calm down."

"Let me speak to Miss Malone."

"She stepped out for a moment. Later." Flynn said abruptly, "Is everything set for my press conference?"

Schroeder's voice turned calm. "We may need more time. The networks—"

"I have a message for America and the world, and I mean to deliver it."

"Yes, you will. Be patient."

"That's not one of the Irish virtues, Schroeder."

"Oh, I don't know if that's true." He felt it was time for a more personal approach. "I'm half Irish myself, and—"

"Really?"

"Yes, my mother's people were from County Tyrone. Listen, I understand your frustrations and your anger—I had a greatuncle in the IRA. Family hero. Jailed by the English."

"For what? Being a bore like his nephew?"

Schroeder ignored the remark. "I grew up with many of the same hates and prejudices that you—"

"You weren't there, Schroeder. You weren't *there*. You were *here*."

"This won't accomplish anything," said Schroeder firmly. "You might make more enemies than friends by—"

"The people in here don't need any more friends. Our friends are dead or in prison. Tell them to let our people go, Captain."

"We're trying very hard. The negotiations between London and Washington are progressing. I see a light at the end of the tunnel—"

"Are you sure that light isn't a speeding train coming at you?"

Someone in the next room laughed.

Schroeder sat down and bit the tip off a cigar.

"Listen, why don't you show us some good faith and release one of the wounded hostages?"

"Which one?"

Schroeder sat up quickly. "Well... well..."

"Come on, then. Play God. Don't ask anyone there. You tell me which one."

"The one that's the most badly wounded."

Flynn laughed. "Very good. Here's a counterproposal. Would you like the Cardinal instead? Think now. A wounded priest, a wounded Englishman, or a healthy Cardinal?"

Schroeder felt an anger rising in him and was disturbed that Flynn could produce that response. "Who's the more seriously hurt?"

"Baxter."

Schroeder hesitated. He looked around the room. His words faltered.

Flynn said, "Quickly!"

"Baxter."

Flynn put a sad tone in his voice. "Sorry. The correct response was to ask for a Prince of the Church, of course. But you knew that, Bert. Had you said the Cardinal, I would have released him."

Schroeder stared down at the unlit cigar. His voice was shaky. "I doubt that."

"Don't doubt me on things like that. I'd rather lose a hostage and make a point."

Schroeder took out a handkerchief and wiped his neck. "We're not trying to make this a contest to see who's got more nerve, who's got more... more..."

"Balls."

"Yes. We're not trying to do that. That's the

old police image. We're rolling over for you." He glanced at Bellini, who looked very annoyed. He continued, "No one here is going to risk the lives of innocent people—"

"*Innocent?* There are no innocent civilians in war any more. We're all soldiers—soldiers by choice, by conscription, by implication, and by birth." Flynn drew a breath, then said, "The good thing about a long guerrilla war is that everyone gets a chance for revenge at least once." He paused. "Let's drop this topic. I want that television now. Send Burke."

Schroeder finally lit his cigar. "I'm sorry, he's temporarily out of the building."

"I told you I wanted him around. You see, Schroeder, you're not so accommodating after all."

"It was unavoidable. He'll call you soon." He paused, then changed the tone of his voice. "Listen, along the same lines—I mean, we're building a rapport, as you said—can I ask you again to try to keep Mr. Hickey off the phone?"

Flynn didn't answer.

Schroeder went on, "I'm not trying to start any trouble there, but he's saying one thing and you're saying another. I mean, he's very negative and very . . . pessimistic. I just wanted to make you aware of that in case you didn't—"

The phone went dead.

Schroeder rocked back in his chair and drew on his cigar. He thought of how much easier it was dealing with Flynn and how difficult Hickey was. Then it hit him, and he dropped his cigar into an ashtray. *Good guy—bad guy.* The oldest con trick in the game. Now

Flynn and Hickey were pulling that on *him*. "Sons of bitches."

Langley looked at Schroeder, then glanced at the note pad he'd been keeping. After each dialogue Langley felt a sense of frustration and futility. This negotiating business was not his game, and he didn't understand how Schroeder did it. Langley's instincts screamed at him to grab the phone and tell Flynn he was a dead motherfucker. Langley lit a cigarette and was surprised to see his hands shaking. "Bastards."

Roberta Spiegel took her place in the rocker and stared up at the ceiling. "Is anybody keeping score?"

Bellini stared out the window. "Can they fight as good as they bullshit?"

Schroeder answered, "The Irish are one of the few people who can."

Bellini turned back to the window, Spiegel rocked in her chair, Langley watched the smoke curl up from his cigarette, and Schroeder stared at the papers scattered on the desk. Phones rang in the other room; a bullhorn cut into the night air, and its echo drifted through the window. The mantel clock ticked loudly, and Schroeder focused on it. 9:17 p.m. At 4:30 he'd been marching in the parade, enjoying himself, enjoying life. Now he had a knot in his stomach, and life didn't look so good anymore. Why was someone always spoiling the parade?

CHAPTER 38

Maureen slid behind the thick column and watched Hickey as he stood squinting in the half-light. Megan came up behind him, swinging her big pistol easily by her side, the way other women swung a handbag—the way she herself had swung a pistol once.

Maureen watched them whispering to each other. She knew what they were saying without hearing a word: Which way has she gone? Should they split up? Fire a shot? Call out? Turn on the flashlights? She waited close-by, not fifteen feet away, because they'd never suspect she'd be this close, watching. To them she was a civilian, but they ought to have known her better. She was angry at their low regard of her.

Suddenly the flashlights came on, and their beams poked into the dark, distant places. Maureen pressed closer to the column.

Hickey called out, "Last chance, Maureen. Give up and you won't be hurt. But if we have to flush you out..." He let his voice trail off, the implied meaning more unnerving than if he had said it.

She watched them as they conferred again. She

knew they expected her to go east toward the sacristy foundation. Flynn may even have heard the four of them discussing it. And that was the way she wanted to go but knew now she couldn't.

She prayed they wouldn't split up—wouldn't cut her off in both directions. She admitted, too, that she didn't want Megan to be away from Hickey...though perhaps if she *were* away from Hickey...Maureen slipped off her shoes, reached under her skirt, and slid off her panty hose. She twisted the nylon into a rope, wrapped the ends around her arms, and pulled it taut. She draped the nylon garrote over her shoulders and knelt, taking handfuls of earth and rubbing them across her damp face, her legs and hands. She looked down at her tweed jacket and skirt—dark but not dark enough. Silently she took them off, reversed them so the darker lining showed, and put them back on again. She buttoned the jacket over her white blouse and turned up the collar. All the while her eyes were fixed on Hickey and Megan.

Suddenly another pair of legs dropped into the hole, and a figure descended the ladder. Maureen recognized Frank Gallagher by the striped pants of his parade marshal's morning dress.

Hickey pointed toward the front of the Cathedral, and Gallagher drew a pistol and walked slowly west along the staircase wall toward the outer wall of the partially buried crypt. Hickey and Megan headed east toward the sacristy.

Maureen saw she had no way to go but south toward the crawl space beneath the ambulatory—the least likely place to find an exit, according to what

Father Murphy knew of the layout. But as she watched Gallagher's flashlight moving slowly, she realized she could beat him to the end of the crypt, and from there she had more options. She moved laterally, to her left, parallel to Gallagher's course. Fifteen feet from the first column she came to another and stopped. She watched Gallagher's light almost directly opposite her. The shaft of light from the brass-plate opening was dimmer now, and the next column was somewhere in the darkness to her left.

She moved laterally again, running silently, barefoot, over the damp earth, hands feeling for pipes and ducts. The next column was irregularly spaced at about twenty-five feet, and she thought she'd missed it, then collided with it, feeling a sudden blow against her chest that knocked the wind out of her and made her give an involuntary gasp.

Gallagher's light swung out at her, and she stood frozen behind the column. The beam swung away, and she proceeded in a parallel course. She dashed toward the next column, counting her paces as she ran. At eight strides she stopped and felt in front of her, touching the stone column, and pressed against it.

She saw she was far ahead of Gallagher now, but his beam reached out and probed the place opposite her. The sanctuary floor above her ended a few feet beyond where she stood, and the steps that led to the communion rail sloped down to the crawl space below the main floor. She also saw, by the beam of light, the corner of the crypt where the wall turned away from her. She was no more than fifteen feet from it. She stooped down and passed her hands over the earth, finding a small piece of building rubble. She threw it back toward the last column she'd come from.

Gallagher's light swung away from her intended path toward the sound. She dashed forward, trying to judge the distance. Her hand hit the brick outer wall of the crypt, and she moved left toward the corner. Gallagher's light swung back. She ducked below the beam, then slid around the corner, bracing her back against the cold crypt. She sidestepped with her back against the wall, watching the beam of Gallagher's light as it passed off to her left. She felt for the nylon around her neck and swung it from her shoulders. She conjured up a picture of Frank Gallagher: pleasant looking, sort of vacuous expression. Big, too. She wrapped the nylon tightly around her hands and looped it.

The beam of light was growing in thickness and intensity, bobbing closer to the corner of the crypt. She could actually hear Gallagher's footsteps around the corner, could hear the tight-lipped nose-breathing she knew so well. *God*, she thought, *God, I never wanted to kill so badly.*

Discretion. When to run, when to fight. When in doubt, said Brian Flynn, run. Watch the wolves, he had said to her. They run from danger without self-recrimination. Even hunger wouldn't cloud their judgment. There'd be other kills. She steadied her hands and took a long breath, then swung the nylon around her shoulders and moved along the wall, to her right, away from Gallagher's approaching footsteps. *Next time.*

Something brushed across her face, and she stifled a yell as she swatted it away. Carefully she reached out and touched a hanging object. A pull chain. She reached up and found the light bulb, unscrewed it, and tossed it gently underhand into the crawl space in front of her. She pulled the chain, switching on the electricity. She thought, *I hope he sticks his fucking finger into it and burns.*

Gallagher came to the corner and knelt. He swung his light in a wide arc under the crawl space that began a few feet from the wall.

Maureen saw in the light in front of her the bottom of the steps that led down from the raised sanctuary above her. Farther back, in the crawl space, she saw the glowing red eyes of rats. She moved down the length of the crypt wall. It seemed to go on for a long way. Gallagher's light swung up from the crawl space and began probing the length of the wall.

She moved more quickly, stumbling over building rubble. After what she judged was about twenty-five feet her right hand felt the corner where the wall turned back toward the sacristy. The beam of light fell on her shoulder, and she froze. The light played off her jacket, then swung away. She slid around the corner just as the light came back to reexplore the suspicious thing it had picked out.

Maureen turned and kept her right shoulder to the wall as she moved toward the sacristy foundation. She found another light bulb and unscrewed it, then pulled the chain. Rats squealed around her, and something ran across her bare feet.

The crypt wall turned in to meet the outer wall of the sacristy staircase, and she judged that she was on the exact opposite side of the staircase from where she'd come down through the brass plate.

So far she had eluded them, gotten the better of them in a game that was the ultimate hide-and-seek. Every Belfast alley and factory park flashed through her mind. Every heart-thumping, dry-throated crawl through the rubble came back to her, and she felt alive, confident, almost exhilarated at the dangerous game.

The ground rose, and she had to stoop lower until finally she had to crawl on all fours. She felt to her front as she moved. A rat scurried across her hand, another across her legs. Sweat ran from her face and washed the dirt camouflage into her eyes and mouth. Her breathing was so loud she thought Gallagher must hear it clearly.

Behind her the beam of Gallagher's light probed in all directions. He could have no idea that he had actually been following her...unless he had heard her or had seen her footprints, or had found one of the empty light-sockets and guessed.... *Stick your goddamned finger in one of them and fry.* She hoped he was as frightened as she was.

She kept crawling until her hand came into contact with cold, moist stone. She ran her fingers over the jagged surface, then higher up, and she felt the rounded contour of a massive column. Her hand slid down again, and she felt something soft and damp and drew away quickly. Cautiously she reached out again and touched the yielding, putty-like substance. She pulled a piece of it and brought it to her nose. "Oh, my God," she spoke under her breath. "Oh, you bastards. You really would do it."

Her knee bumped into something, and her hands reached down and felt the suitcase that they had carried down into the hole—a suitcase big enough to hold at least twenty kilos of plastic. Somewhere, probably on the other side of the staircase, was the other charge.

She wedged into the space between the stairway wall and the column's footing and took the nylon from around her shoulders. She found a half brick and held it in her right hand.

Gallagher came closer, his flashlight focused on the ground in front of him. She could see in the light the marks she had made when she had to crawl through the earth.

Gallagher's light swung up and focused on the column footing, then probed the space where she was hiding. He crawled closer and poked the light between the column and the wall.

For a long second the light rested directly on her face, and they stared at each other from less than a yard away. Gallagher's face registered complete surprise, she noticed. A stupid man.

She brought her hand down with the half brick in it and drove it between his eyes. The light fell to the floor, and she sprang out of her niche and wrapped the nylon garrote around his neck.

Gallagher thrashed over the earth floor like a wounded animal. Maureen hooked her legs around his torso and rode his back, holding the garrote like a set of reins, drawing it tightly around his neck with all the strength she could summon.

Gallagher weakened and fell forward on his chest, pinning her legs beneath him. She pulled harder on the nylon, but there was too much give in it. She knew she was strangling him too slowly, causing him unnecessary suffering. She heard the gurgling coming from deep in his throat.

Gallagher's head twisted around at an unbelievable angle, and his face stared up at her. The fallen flashlight cast a yellow beam over his face, and she saw his bulging eyes and thick protruding tongue. His skin was split where she had hit him with the brick, and his nose was broken and bleeding. Their eyes met for a brief second.

Gallagher's body went limp and lay motionless. Maureen sat on his back trying to catch her breath. She still felt life in his body, the shallow breathing, the twitching muscles and flesh against her buttocks. She began tightening the garrote, then suddenly pulled it from his neck and buried her face in her hands.

She heard voices coming around the crypt, then saw two lights not forty feet away. She quickly shut off the flashlight and threw it aside. Maureen felt her heart beating wildly again as she groped for the fallen pistol.

The beam rose and searched the ceiling. A voice—Megan's—said, "Here's another missing bulb. Clever little bitch."

The other flashlight examined the ground. Hickey said, "Here are their tracks."

Maureen's hands touched Gallagher's body, and she felt him moving. She backed off.

Hickey called out, "Frank? Are you there?" His approaching light found Gallagher's body and rested on it.

Maureen crawled backward until she made contact with the base of the column. She turned and clawed at the plastic explosive, trying to pull it loose from the footing, feeling for the detonator that she knew was embedded somewhere.

The two beams of light came closer. Hickey shouted, "Maureen! You've done well, lass. But as you see, the hounds are onto the scent. We're going to begin probing fire if you don't give yourself up."

Maureen kept pulling at the plastic. She knew there would be no probing fire with plastic so close.

The sound of the two crawling people got closer. She looked back and saw two pools of light converging on Gallagher's body. Hickey and Megan were hovering over Gallagher now. Gallagher was trying to raise himself on all fours.

Megan said, "Here, I've found his light."

Hickey said, "Look for his gun."

Maureen gave one last pull at the plastic, then moved around the column until she ran into the foundation wall that separated her from the sacristy.

She put her right shoulder against the wall and crawled along it, feeling for an opening. Pipes and ducts penetrated the wall, but there was no space for her to pass through.

Hickey's voice called out again. "Maureen, my love, Frank is feeling a bit better. All is forgiven, darlin'. We owe you, lass. You've a good heart. Come on, now. Let's all go back upstairs and have a nice wash and a cup of tea."

Maureen watched as one, then two, then three flashlights started to reach out toward her.

Hickey said, "Maureen, we've found Frank's gun, so we know you're not armed. The game is over. You've done well. You've nothing to be ashamed of. Frank owes you his life, and there'll be no retributions, Maureen. Just call out to us and we'll come take you back. You've our word you won't be harmed."

Maureen huddled against the foundation wall. She knew Hickey was speaking the truth. Gallagher owed her. They wouldn't harm her while Gallagher was still alive; that was one of the rules. The old rules, Hickey's rules, her rules. She wondered about someone like Megan, though.

Her instincts told her that it was over—that she should give up while the offered amnesty was still in effect. She was tired, cold, aching. The flashlights came closer. She opened her mouth to speak.

CHAPTER 39

Inspector Langley was reading Monsignor Downes's appointment book. "I think the good Rector entertained the Fenians on more than one occasion.... Unwittingly, of course."

Schroeder looked at Langley. It would never have occurred to him to snoop through another man's papers. That's why he had been such a bad detective. Langley, on the other hand, would pick the Mayor's pocket out of idle curiosity. Schroeder said acidly, "You mean you don't suspect Monsignor Downes?"

Langley smiled. "I didn't say that."

Bellini turned from the window and looked at Schroeder. "You didn't have to eat so much shit, did you? I mean that business about rolling over and all that other stuff."

Schroeder felt his fright turning to anger. "For Christ's sake, it's only a ploy. You've heard me use it a dozen times."

"Yeah, but this time you *meant* it."

"Go to hell."

Bellini seemed to be struggling with something. He leaned forward with his hands on Schroeder's desk and spoke softly. "I'm scared, too. Do you think I *want* to send my men in there? Christ Almighty, Bert, I'm going in, too. I have a wife and kids. But Jesus, man, every hour that you bullshit with them is another hour for them to get their defenses tightened. Every hour shortens the time until dawn, when I *have* to attack. And I won't hit them at dawn in a last desperate move to save the hostages and the Cathedral, because they *know* I have to move at dawn if they don't have what they want."

Schroeder kept his eyes fixed on Bellini's but didn't reply.

Bellini went on, his voice becoming more strident. "As long as you keep telling the big shots you can do it, they're going to jerk me around. Admit you're not going to pull it off and let me...let me know in my own mind...that I *have* to go in." He said almost in a whisper, "I don't like sweating it out like this, Bert.... My men don't like this.... I have to *know*."

Schroeder spoke mechanically. "I'm taking it a step at a time. Standard procedures. Stabilize the situation, keep them talking, calm them down, get an extension of the deadline—"

Bellini slammed his hand on the desk, and everyone sat up quickly. "Even if you *could* get an extension of the deadline, how long would it be for? An hour? Two hours? Then I have to move in the daylight—while you stand here at the window smoking a cigar, watching us get massacred!"

Schroeder stood and his face twitched. He tried to stop himself from speaking, but the words came out. "If you have to go in, I'll be right next to you, Bellini."

A twisted smile passed over Bellini's face. He turned to Langley and Spiegel, then looked back at Schroeder. "You're on, Captain." He turned and walked out of the room.

Langley watched the door close, then said, "That was stupid, Bert."

Schroeder found his hands and legs were shaking, and he sat down, then rose abruptly. He spoke in a husky voice. "Watch the phone. I have to go out for a minute—men's room." He walked quickly to the door.

Spiegel said, "I took some cheap shots at him, too."

Langley looked away.

She said, "Tell me what a bitch I am."

He walked to the sideboard and poured a glass of sherry.

He had no intention of telling the Mayor's aide she was a bitch.

She walked toward him, reached out, and took the glass from his hand. She drank, then handed it back.

Langley thought, *She did it again!* There was something uncomfortably intimate and at the same time unnervingly aggressive about the proprietary attitude she had taken with him.

Roberta Spiegel walked toward the door. "Don't do anything stupid like Schroeder did."

He looked up at her with some surprise.

She said suddenly, "You married? Divorced...separated...single?"

"Yes."

She laughed. "Watch the store. See you later." She left.

Langley looked at the lipstick mark on his glass and put it down. "Bitch." He walked to the window.

Bellini had placed a set of field glasses on the sill. Langley picked them up and saw clearly the man standing in the belfry. If Bellini attacked, this young man would be one of the first to die. He wondered if the man knew that. Of course he did.

The man saw him and raised a pair of field glasses. They stared at each other for a few seconds. The young man held up his hand, a sort of greeting. The faces of all the IRA men Langley had ever known suddenly coalesced in this face—the young romantics, the old-guard IRA like Hickey, the dying Officials like Ferguson, the cold-blooded young Provos like most of them, and now the Fenians—crazier than the Provos—the worst of the worst.... All of them had started life, he was sure, as polite young men and women, dressed in little suits and dresses for Sunday Mass. Somewhere something went wrong. But maybe they would get most of the worst crazies in one sweep tonight. Nip it in the bud here. He damn well didn't want to deal with them later.

Langley put down the glasses and turned from the window. He looked at his watch. Where the hell was Burke?

He had a sour feeling in his stomach. *Transference.* Somehow he felt he was in there with them.

Maureen watched the circle of light closing in on her and almost welcomed the light and Hickey's cajoling voice after the sensory deprivation she had experienced.

Hickey called out again. "I know you're frightened, Maureen. Just take a deep breath and call to us."

She almost did, but something held her back. A series of confused thoughts ran through her mind—Brian, Harold Baxter, Whitehorn Abbey, Frank Gallagher's ghostly face. She felt she was adrift in some foggy sea—with no anchor, misleading beacons, false harbors. She tried to shake off the lethargy and think clearly, tried to resolve her purpose, which was freedom. Freedom from Brian Flynn, freedom from all the people and things that had kept her feeling guilty and obligated all her life. *Once you're a hostage, you're a hostage the rest of your life.* She had been Brian's hostage long before he put a gun to her head. She had been a hostage to her own insecurities and circumstances all her life. But now for the first time she felt less like a hostage and less like a traitor. She felt like a refugee from an insane world, a fugitive from a state of mind that was a prison far worse than Long Kesh. *Once in, never out.* Bullshit. She began crawling again, along the foundation wall.

Hickey called out, "Maureen, we see you moving. Don't make us shoot."

She called back, "I know you don't have Gallagher's gun, because I have it. Careful I don't shoot *you.*" She heard them talking among themselves, then the flashlights went out. She smiled at how the simplest bluffs worked when people were frightened. She kept crawling.

The foundation curved, and she knew she was under the ambulatory now. Somewhere on the other side of the foundation were the fully excavated basements beneath the terraces outside that led back to the rectory.

Beneath the thin layer of soil the Manhattan bedrock rose and fell as she crawled. The ceiling was only about four feet high now, and she kept hitting her head on pipes and ducts. The ducts made a noise when she hit them and boomed like a drum in the cold, stagnant air.

Suddenly the flashlights came on again, some distance off. Megan's voice called, "We found the gun, Maureen. Come toward the light or we shoot. Last chance."

Maureen watched the beams of light searching for her. She didn't know if they had Gallagher's gun or not, but she knew she didn't have it. She crawled on her stomach, commando style, pressing her face to the ground.

The lights began tightening around her. Hickey said, "I'm counting to ten. Then the armistice is over." He counted.

Maureen stopped crawling and remained motionless, pressed against the wall. Blood and sweat ran over her face; her legs and arms were studded with pieces of embedded stone. She steadied her breathing and listened for a sound from the basement that was only feet away. She looked for a crack of light, felt for a draft that might be coming from the other side, then ran her hands over the stone foundation. Nothing. She began moving again.

Hickey's voice called out, "Maureen, you're a heartless girl, making an old man crawl in the damp like this. I'll catch my death—let's go back up and have some tea."

The light beams were actually passing over her intermittently, and she froze when they did. They didn't seem to be able to pick out her blackened features in the darkness. She noticed that the stone wall turned again, then ended. Brick wall ran from the stone at right angles, and she suspected the brick wall was not a stress-bearing foundation but a partition behind which the foundation had disappeared. She rose to a kneeling position, reached for the top of the wall, and discovered a small space near the concrete ceiling. She pressed her face to the space but saw no light, heard no noise, and felt no air. Yet she was certain she was close to finding a way out.

A voice called out. Gallagher's. "Maureen, please don't make us shoot you. I know you spared my life—come on, then, be a good woman and let's all go back."

Again she knew they wouldn't shoot, if not because of the explosives then for fear of a ricochet among all this stone. She was suddenly angry at their small lies. What kind of idiot did they think she was? Hickey might be an old soldier, but Maureen knew more about war than Megan or Gallagher would live to learn. She wanted to scream an obscenity at them for their patronizing attitude. She moved along the wall and felt it curve farther inward. She judged from the configuration of the horseshoe-shaped ambulatory that she was now below the bride's room or confessional. Suddenly her hand came into contact with dry wood. Her heart gave a small leap. She faced the wall and knelt in front of it. Her hands explored the wood, set flush into the brick. She felt a rusty latch and pulled on it. A pair of hinges squeaked sharply in the still air. The flashlight beams came toward her.

Hickey called to her. "You're leading us a merry chase, young lady. I hope you don't give your suitors as much trouble."

Maureen said under her breath, "Go to hell, you old bag of bones." She pulled slowly on the door. Cracks of light appeared around the edges, showing it to be about three feet square. She closed the door quickly, found a broken shard of brick, and threw it farther along the wall.

The light beams swung toward the noise. She pulled the door open a few inches and pushed her face to the small aperture. She blinked her eyes several times and focused on a fluorescent-lit hallway.

The hallway floor was about four feet below her— a beautiful floor, she thought, of white polished vinyl. The walls of the corridor were painted plasterboard; the ceiling a few feet above her head was white acoustical tile. A beautiful hallway, really. Tears ran down her face.

She swung the door fully open and rubbed her eyes, then pushed her hair away from her face. Something was wrong.... She put her hand out, and her fingers passed through a wire grill. A rat screen covered the opening.

CHAPTER 40

Burke walked into the Monsignor's inner office and looked at Langley, the sole person present, staring out the window. Burke said, "Everybody quit?"

Langley turned.

Burke said, "Where's Schroeder?"

"Relieving himself...or throwing up, or something. Did you hear what happened—?"

"I was briefed. Damned fools in there are going to blow it. Everyone's all right?"

"Cardinal said so. Also, you missed two good showdowns—Schroeder versus Spiegel and Schroeder versus Bellini. Poor Bert. He's usually the fair-haired boy, too." Langley paused. "I think he's losing it."

Burke nodded. "Do you think it's him, or is it us...or is it that Flynn is that good?"

Langley shrugged. "All of the above."

Burke went to the sideboard and noticed there was very little left in the decanters. He said, "Why did God let the Irish invent whiskey, Langley?"

Langley knew the drill. "To keep them from ruling the world."

Burke laughed. "Right." His voice became

contemplative. "I'll bet no Fenian has had a drink in forty-eight hours. Do you know a woman named Terri O'Neal?"

Langley concentrated on the name, then said, "No. I don't make it at all." He immediately regretted the common cop jargon and said, "I can't identify the name. Call the office."

"I called from downstairs. Negative. But they're rechecking. How about Dan Morgan?"

"No. Irish?"

"Probably Northern Irish. Louise is going to call back."

"Who are these people?"

"That's what I asked you." He poured the remainder of the brandy and thought a moment. "Terri O'Neal... I think I have a face and a voice, but I just can't remember...?"

Langley said, "Flynn's asked for a television in there. In fact, you're supposed to deliver it to him." Langley looked at Burke out of the corner of his eye. "You two get along real well."

Burke considered the statement for a few seconds. In spite of the circumstances of their meeting, he admitted that Flynn was the type of man he could have liked— if Flynn were a cop, or if he, Burke, were IRA.

Langley said, "Call Flynn now."

Burke went to the phone. "Flynn can wait." He made certain the speakers in the other rooms were not on, then turned on the voice box on the desk so that Langley could monitor. He dialed the Midtown North Precinct. "Gonzalez? Lieutenant Burke here. Do you have my man?" There was a long silence during which Burke found he was holding his breath.

"He's a prick," said Gonzalez. "Keeps screaming about police-state tactics and all that crap. Says he's going to sue us for false arrest. I thought you said he needed protection."

"Is he still there?"

"Yeah. He wants a ride to the Port Authority Terminal. I can't hold him a minute longer. If I get hit with a false arrest rap, I'm dragging you in with me—"

"Put him on."

"My pleasure. Wait."

Burke turned to Langley while he waited. "Ferguson. He's onto something. Terri O'Neal—Dan Morgan. Now he wants to run."

Langley moved beside Burke. "Well, offer him some money to stick around."

"You haven't paid him for today yet. Anyway, there's not enough money around to keep him from running."

Burke spoke into the telephone. "Jack—"

Ferguson's voice came into the room, high-pitched and agitated. "What the hell are you *doing* to me, Pat? Is this the way you treat a friend? For God's sake, man—"

"Cut it. Listen, put me on to the people you spoke to about O'Neal and Morgan."

"Not a chance. My sources are confidential. I don't treat friends the way you do. The intelligence establishment in this country—"

"Save it for your May Day speech. Listen, Martin has double-crossed all of us. He was the force behind the Fenians. This whole thing is a ploy to make the Irish look bad—to turn American public opinion against the Irish struggle."

Ferguson didn't speak for a while, then said, "I figured that out."

Burke pressed on. "Look, I don't know how much information Martin fed you, or how much information about the police and the Fenians you had to give him in return, but I'm telling you now he's at the stage where he's covering his tracks. Understand?"

"I understand that I'm on three hitlists—the Fenians', the Provos', and Martin's. That's why I'm leaving town."

"You have to stick. Who is Terri O'Neal? Why was she kidnapped by a man named Morgan? Whose show was it? Where is she being held?"

"That's your problem."

"We're working on it, Jack, but you're closer to it. And we don't have much time. If you told us your sources—"

"No."

Burke went on. "Also, while you're at it, see if you can get a line on Gordon Stillway, the resident architect of Saint Pat's. He's missing, too."

"Lot of that going around. I'm missing, too. Goodbye."

"No! Stick with it."

"Why? Why should I risk my life any further?"

"For the same reasons you risked it all along—peace."

Ferguson sighed but said nothing.

Langley whispered, "Offer him a thousand dollars—no, make it fifteen hundred. We'll hold a benefit dance."

Burke said into the phone, "We'd like to exonerate

all the Irish who had nothing to do with this, including your Officials and even the Provos. We'll work with you after this mess is over and see that the government and the press don't crucify all of you." Burke paused, then said, "You and I as Irishmen"—he remembered Flynn's attempt to claim kinship—"you mad I want to be able to hold our heads up after this?" Burke glanced at Langley, who nodded appreciatively. Burke turned away.

Ferguson said, "Hold on." There was a long silence, then Ferguson spoke. "How can I reach you later?"

Burke let out a breath. "Try to call the rectory. The lines should be clear later. Give the password...leprechaun.... They'll put you through."

"Leper is more like it, Burke. Make it leper. All right. If I can't get through on the phone, I won't come to the rectory—the cordon is being watched by all sorts of people. If you don't hear from me, let's have a standing rendezvous. Let's say the zoo at one."

Burke said, "Closer to the Cathedral."

"All right. But no bars or public places." He thought. "Okay, that small park on Fifty-first—it's not far from you."

"It's closed after dark."

"Climb the gate!"

Burke smiled. "Someday I'm going to get a key for every park in this town."

Ferguson said, "Join the Parks Department. They'll issue one with your broom."

"Luck." Burke spoke to Gonzalez. "Let him go." He hung up and took a deep breath.

Langley said, "Do you think this O'Neal thing is important enough to risk his life?"

Burke drained off the glass of brandy and grimaced. "How do people drink this stuff?"

"Pat?"

Burke walked to the window and looked out.

Langley said, "I'm not making any moral judgments. I only want to know if it's *worth* getting Jack Ferguson killed."

Burke spoke as if to himself. "A kidnapping is a subtle sort of thing, more complicated than a hit, more sinister in many ways—like hostage taking." He considered. "Hostage taking— that's a form of kidnapping. Terri O'Neal is a *hostage*...."

"Whose hostage?"

Burke turned and faced Langley. "I don't know."

"Who has to do what for whom to secure her release? No one has made any demands yet."

"Strange," agreed Burke.

"Really," said Langley.

Burke looked at Schroeder's empty chair. Schroeder's presence, in spite of everything, had been reassuring. He said half-jokingly, "Are you sure he's coming back?"

Langley shrugged. "His backup man is in another room with a phone, waiting like an understudy for the break of a lifetime...." Langley said, "Call Flynn."

"Later." He sat in Schroeder's chair, leaned back, and looked at the lofty ceiling. A long crack ran from wall to wall, replastered but not yet painted. He had a mental image of the Cathedral in ruins, then pictured the Statue of Liberty lying on its side half submerged in the harbor. He thought of the Roman Coliseum, the ruined Acropolis, the flooded temples of the Nile.

He said, "You know, the Cathedral itself is not that important. Neither are the lives of any of us. What's important is how we act, what people say and write about us afterward."

Langley looked at him appraisingly. Burke sometimes surprised him. "Yes, that's true, but you won't tell that to anybody today."

"Or tomorrow, if we're pulling bodies out of the rubble."

John Hickey's voice came to Maureen from not very far off. "So, what have we here? What light through yonder window breaks, Maureen?" He laughed, then said sharply, "Move back from there or we'll shoot you."

Maureen cocked her elbow and drove it into the rat screen. The wire bent, but the edges stayed fixed to the wall. She pressed her face to the grill. To her left the hallway ended about ten feet away. On the opposite wall toward the end of the passage were gray sliding doors—elevator doors—the elevator that opened near the bride's room above. She drove her elbow into the grill again, and one side of the frame ripped loose from the plasterboard. "Yes, yes . . . please . . ."

She could hear them behind her, scurrying over the rubble-strewn ground like the rats they were, faster, coming at the light source. Then John Hickey came out of the dark. "Hands on your head, darlin'."

She turned and stared at him, holding back the tears forming in her eyes.

Hickey said, "Look at you. Your pretty knees are all

scratched. And what's that dirt all over your face, Maureen? *Camouflage?* You'll be needing a good wash."

He ran his flashlight over her. "And your smart tweeds are turned inside out. Clever girl. Clever. And what is *that* around your neck?" He grabbed the nylon garrote and twisted it. "My, what a naughty girl you are." He gave the garrote another twist and held it until she began to choke. "Once again, Maureen, you've shown me a small chink in our armor. What would we do without you?" He loosened the tension on the nylon and knocked her to the ground. His eyes narrowed into malignant slits. "I think I'll shoot you through the head and throw you into the corridor. That'll help the police make the decision they're wrestling with." He seemed to consider, then said, "But, on the other hand, I'd like you to be around for the finale." He smiled a black, gaping smile. "I want you to see Flynn die or for him to see you die."

In a clear flash of understanding she knew the essence of this old man's evil. "Kill me."

He shook his head. "No. I like you. I like what you're becoming. You should have killed Gallagher, though. You would have been firmly planted in the ranks of the damned if you had. You're only borderline now." He cackled.

Maureen lay on the damp earth. She felt a hand grab her long hair and pull her back across the floor into the darkness. Megan Fitzgerald knelt over her and put a pistol to her heart. "Your charmed life has come to an end, bitch."

Hickey called out, "None of that, Megan!"

Megan Fitzgerald shouted back. "You'll not stop me this time." She cocked the pistol.

Hickey shouted, "No! Brian will decide if she's to die—and if she's to die, he wants to be the one to kill her."

Maureen listened to this statement without any outward emotion. She felt numb, drained.

Megan screamed back. "Fuck you! Fuck Flynn! She'll die here and now."

Hickey spoke softly. "If you shoot, I'll kill you." Everyone heard the click of the safety disengaging from his automatic.

Gallagher cleared his throat and said, "Let her alone, Megan."

No one moved or spoke. Finally Megan uncocked her pistol. She turned on her light and shone it into Maureen's face. A twisted smile formed on Megan's lips. "You're old . . . and not very pretty." She poked Maureen's breast roughly with the muzzle of her pistol.

Maureen looked up through the light at Megan's contorted face. "You're very young, and you ought to be pretty, but there's an ugliness in you, Megan, that everyone can see in your eyes."

Megan spit at her, then disappeared into the dark.

Hickey knelt over Maureen and wiped her face with a handkerchief. "Well, now, if you want my opinion, I think you're very pretty."

She turned her face away. "Go to hell."

Hickey said, "You see, Uncle John saved your life again."

She didn't respond, and he went on. "Because I really want you to see what's going to happen later.

Yes, it's going to be quite spectacular. How often can you see a cathedral collapsing around your head—?"

Gallagher made an odd gasping sound, and Hickey said to him, "Only joking, Frank."

She said to Gallagher, "He's not joking, you know—"

Hickey leaned close to her ear. "Shut up or I'll—"

"*What?*" She looked at him fiercely. "What can you do to me?" She turned toward Gallagher. "He means to see all of us dead. He means to see all your young friends follow him to the grave..."

Hickey laughed in a shrill, piercing tone.

The rats stopped their chirping.

Hickey said, "The little creatures sense the danger. They smell death. They know."

Gallagher said nothing, but his breathing filled the still, cold air.

Maureen sat up slowly. "Baxter? The others...?"

Hickey said in an offhand manner, "Baxter is dead. Father Murphy was hit in the face, and he's dying. The Cardinal is all right, though." He said in an aggrieved whisper, "Do you see what you've *done?*"

She couldn't speak, and tears ran down her face.

Hickey turned from her and played his light over the open hatchway.

Gallagher said, "We better put an alarm here."

Hickey answered, "The only alarm you'll hear from down here is from about a kilo of plastic. I'll have Sullivan come back and mine it." He glanced at Maureen. "Well, shall we go home, then?"

They began the long crawl back.

Hickey spoke as they made their way. "If I was

a younger man, Maureen, I'd be in love with you. You're so like the women I knew in the Movement in my youth. So many of the revolutionary women in other movements are ugly misfits, neurotics and psychotics. But we've always been able to attract clearheaded, pretty lasses like yourself. Why is that, do you suppose?" He said between labored breaths, "Well, don't answer me, then. Tired? Yes, me too. Slow down, Gallagher, you big ox. We've got some way to go yet before we can rest. We'll all rest together, Maureen. Soon this will be over...we'll be free of all our worries, all our bonds...before dawn...a nice rest...it won't be so bad...it won't, really....We're going home."

CHAPTER 41

Schroeder came through the double doors of the Rector's inner office. "Look who's back. Did you call Flynn?"

"Not without you here, Bert. Feeling better?"

Schroeder came around the desk. "Please get out of my chair, Lieutenant."

Burke vacated the chair.

Schroeder looked at Burke as he sat. "Can you carry a TV set?"

"Why didn't he ask for a television right away?"

Schroeder thought. Flynn *wasn't* a textbook case in many respects. Little things like not immediately asking for a television...little things that added up...

Langley said, "He's keeping the Fenians isolated. Their only reality is Brian Flynn. After the press conference he'll smash the TV or place it where only he and Hickey can use it for intelligence gathering."

Schroeder nodded. "I never know if this TV business is part of the problem or part of the solution. But if they ask, we have to give." He dialed the switchboard. "Chancel organ." He handed the receiver to Burke, turned on all the speaker switches, then sat back with his feet on the desk. "On the air, Lieutenant."

A voice came over the speakers: "Flynn here."

"Burke."

"Listen, Lieutenant, do me a great favor, won't you, and stay in the damned rectory—at least until dawn. If the Cathedral goes, you'll want to see it. Tape all the windows, though, and don't stand under any chandeliers."

Burke was aware that more than two hundred people in the Cathedral complex were listening, and that every word was being taped and transmitted to Washington and London. Flynn knew this, too, and was playing it for effect. "What can I do for you?"

"Aren't you supposed to ask first about the hostages?"

"You said they were all right."

"But that was a while ago."

"Well, how are they *now*?"

"No change. Except that Miss Malone took a jaunt through the crawl space. But she's back now. Looks a bit tired, from what I can see. Clever girl that she is she found a hatchway from the crawl space into the hallway that runs past the bride's-room elevator." He paused, then went on, "Don't touch the hatch, however, as it's being mined right now with enough plastic to give you a nasty bump."

Burke looked at Schroeder, who was already on the other phone talking to one of Bellini's lieutenants. "I understand."

"Good. And you can assume that every other entrance you find will also be mined. And you can assume the entire crawl space is seeded with mines. You can also suspect that I'm lying or bluffing, but, really, it's not smart to call my bluff. Tell that to your ESD people."

"I'll do that."

Flynn said, "Anyway, I want the television. Bring it round to the usual place. Fifteen minutes."

Burke looked at Schroeder and covered the mouthpiece.

Schroeder said, "There's one waiting downstairs in the clerk's office. But you have to get something from him in return. Ask to speak to a hostage."

Burke uncovered the mouthpiece. "I want to talk to Father Murphy first."

"Oh, your friend. You shouldn't admit to having a friend in here."

"He's not my friend, he's my confessor."

Flynn laughed loudly. "Sorry, that struck me funny, somehow. That was no lady, that was my wife. You know?"

Schroeder suppressed a smirk.

Burke looked annoyed. "Put him on!"

Flynn's voice lost its humor. "Don't make any demands on me, Burke."

"I won't bring a television unless I speak to the priest."

Schroeder was shaking his head excitedly. "Forget it," he whispered. "Don't push him."

Burke continued, "We have some talking to do, don't we, Flynn?"

Flynn didn't answer for a long time, then said, "I'll have Murphy at the gate. See you in no-man's-land.

Fifteen...no, fourteen minutes now, and don't be late." He hung up.

Schroeder looked at Burke. "What the hell kind of dialogue are you two carrying on down there?"

Burke ignored him and called through to the chancel organ again. "Flynn?"

Brian Flynn's voice came back, a bit surprised. "What is it?"

Burke found his body shaking with anger. "New rule, Flynn. You don't hang up until I'm through. Got it?" He slammed down the receiver.

Schroeder stood. "What the hell is wrong with you? Haven't you learned *anything*?"

"Oh, go fuck yourself." He wiped his brow with a handkerchief.

Schroeder pressed on. "Don't like being at the receiving end, do you? Messes up your self-image. These bastards have called me every name under the sun tonight, but you don't see me—"

"Okay. You're right. Sorry."

Schroeder said again, "What do you talk to him about down there?"

Burke shook his head. He was tired, and he was starting to lose his temper. He knew that if he was making mistakes because of fatigue, then everyone else was, too.

The phone rang. Schroeder answered it and handed it to Burke. "Your secret headquarters atop Police Plaza."

Burke shut off all the speakers and carried the phone away from the desk. "Louise."

The duty sergeant said, "Nothing on Terri O'Neal.

Daniel Morgan—age thirty-four. A naturalized American citizen. Born in Londonderry. Father Welsh Protestant, mother Irish Catholic. Fiancée arrested in Belfast for IRA activities. May still be in Armagh Prison. We'll check with British—"

"Don't check *anything* with their intelligence sections or with the CIA or FBI unless you get the go-ahead from me or Inspector Langley."

"Okay. One of those." She went on. "Morgan made our files because he was arrested once in a demonstration outside the UN, 1979. Fined and released. Address YMCA on West Twenty-third. Doubt if he's still there. Right?" She read the remainder of the arrest sheet, then said, "I've put it out to our people and to the detectives. I'll send you a copy of the sheet. Also, nothing yet on Stillway."

Burke hung up and turned to Langley. "Let's get that television."

Schroeder said, "What was that all about?"

Langley looked at Schroeder. "Trying to catch a break to make your job and Bellini's a little easier."

"Really? Well, that's the least you can do after screwing up the initial investigation."

Burke said, "If we hadn't blown it, you wouldn't have the opportunity to negotiate for the life of the Archbishop of New York or the safety of Saint Patrick's Cathedral."

"Thanks. I owe you."

Burke looked at him closely and had the impression that he wasn't being completely facetious.

Maureen came out of the lavatory of the bride's room and walked to the vanity. Her outer garments lay draped over a chair, and a first-aid kit sat in front of the vanity mirror. She sat and opened the kit.

Jean Kearney stood to the side with a pistol in her hand and watched. Kearney cleared her throat and said tentatively, "You know . . . they still speak of you in the movement."

Maureen dabbed indifferently at her legs with an iodine applicator. She didn't look up but said listlessly, "Do they?"

"Yes. People still tell stories of your exploits with Brian before you turned traitor."

Maureen glanced up at the young woman. It was an ingenuous statement, without hostility or malice, just a relating of a fact she had learned from the storytellers—like the story of Judas. The Gospel according to the Republican Army. Maureen looked at the young woman's bluish lips and fingers. "Cold up there?"

She nodded. "Awfully cold. This is a bit of a break for me, so take your time."

Maureen noticed the wood chips on Jean Kearney's clothing. "Doing some carpentry in the attic?"

Kearney turned her eyes away.

Maureen stood and took her skirt from the chair. "Don't do it, Jean. When the time comes, you and—Arthur, isn't it?—you and Arthur must not do whatever it is they've told you to do."

"Don't say such things. We're loyal—not like you."

Maureen turned and looked at herself in the mirror and looked at the image of Jean Kearney behind her. She wanted to say something to this young woman, but really there was nothing to say to someone who had willingly committed sacrilege and would probably commit murder before too long. Jean Kearney would eventually find her own way out, or she'd die young.

There was a knock on the door, and it opened a crack. Flynn put his head in, and his eyes rested on Maureen; then he looked away. "Sorry. Thought you'd be done."

Maureen pulled on her skirt, then picked up her blouse and slipped into it.

Flynn came into the room and looked around. He fixed his attention on the bandages and iodine. "History does have a way of repeating itself, doesn't it?"

Maureen buttoned her blouse. "Well, if we all keep making the same mistakes, it's bound to, isn't it, Brian?"

Flynn smiled. "One day we'll get it right."

"Not bloody likely."

Flynn motioned to Jean Kearney, and she left reluctantly, a disappointed look on her face.

Maureen sat at the vanity and ran a comb through her hair.

Flynn watched for a while, then said, "I'd like to speak to you."

"I'm listening."

"In the chapel."

"We're perfectly alone here."

"Well...yes. Too alone. People would talk. I can't compromise myself—neither can you...."

She laughed and stood. "What would people talk *about?* Really, Brian...here in the bride's room of a cathedral.... What a lot of sex-obsessed Catholics you all still are." She moved toward him. "All right. I'm ready. Let's go."

He took her arms and turned her toward him.

She shook her head. "No, Brian. Much too late." His face had a look, she thought, of desperation ... fright almost.

He said, "Why do women always say things like that? It's never too late; there are no seasons or cycles to these things."

"But there are. It's winter for us now. There'll be no spring—not in our lifetime."

He pulled her toward him and kissed her, and before she could react he turned and left the room.

She stood in the center of the bride's room, immobile for a few seconds, then her hand went to her mouth and pressed against her lips. She shook her head. "You fool. You damned fool."

Father Murphy sat in the clergy pews, a pressure bandage over the right side of his jaw. The Cardinal stood beside him. Harold Baxter lay on his side in the same pew. A winding bandage circled his bare torso, revealing a long line of dried blood across his back and a smaller spot of red on his chest. His face showed the result of Pedar Fitzgerald's blows. Megan's kick had swollen one eye nearly shut.

Maureen moved across the sanctuary and knelt beside the two men. They exchanged subdued greetings. Maureen said to Baxter, "Hickey told me you were dead and Father Murphy was dying."

Baxter shook his head. "The man's quite mad." He looked around. Flynn, Hickey, and Megan Fitzgerald were nowhere to be seen. That, for some reason, was more unnerving than having them in his sight. He felt his hold on his courage slipping and knew the others were feeling that way also. He said, "If we can't escape . . . physically escape . . . then we have to talk about a way to survive in here. We have to stand up to them, keep them from dividing us and isolating us. We have to *understand* the people who hold us captive."

Maureen thought a moment, then said, "Yes, but they're hard people to know. I never understood Brian Flynn, never understood what made him go on." She paused, then said, "After all these years . . . I thought I'd have heard one day that he was dead or had a breakdown like so many of them, or ran off to Spain like so many more of them, but he just keeps going on . . . like some immortal thing, tortured by life, unable to die, unable to lay down the sword that has become so burdensome . . . . God, I almost feel sorry for him." She had the uncomfortable feeling that her revelations about Brian Flynn were somehow disloyal.

The Cardinal knelt beside the three people. He said, "In the tower I learned that Brian Flynn is a man who holds some unusual beliefs. He's a romantic, a man who lives in the murky past. The idea of blood sacrifice—which may be the final outcome here—is consistent with Irish myth, legend, and history. There's this aura of defeat that surrounds the people here—unlike the aura of ultimate victory that is ingrained in the British and American psyche." The Cardinal seemed to consider, then went on. "He really believes he is a sort of incarnation of Finn MacCumail." He looked at Maureen. "He's still very fond of you."

Her face flushed, and she said, "That won't stop him from killing me."

The Cardinal answered, "He would only harm you if he thought you felt nothing for him any longer."

She thought back to the bride's room. "So what am I supposed to do? Play up to him?"

Father Murphy spoke. "We'll all have to do that, I think, if we're going to survive. Show him we care about him as a person...and I think at least some of us do. I care about his soul."

Baxter nodded slowly. "Actually, you know, it costs nothing to be polite...except a bit of self-respect." He smiled and said, "Then when everyone is calmed down, we'll have another go at it."

Maureen nodded quickly. "Yes, I'm willing."

The Cardinal spoke incredulously. "Haven't you two had enough?"

She answered, "No."

Baxter said, "If Flynn were our only problem, I'd take my chances with him. But when I look into the eyes of Megan Fitzgerald or John Hickey...Maureen and I spoke about this before, and I've decided that I don't want tomorrow's newspapers to speak of my execution and martyrdom, but I would want them to say, 'Died in an escape attempt.'"

The Cardinal said acidly, "It may read, 'A foolish escape attempt'...shortly before you were to be released."

Baxter looked at him. "I've stopped believing in a negotiated settlement. That reduces my options to one."

Maureen added, "I'm almost certain that Hickey means to kill us and destroy this church."

Baxter sat up with some difficulty. "There's one

more way out of here...and we can all make it.... We *must* all make it, because we won't get another chance."

Father Murphy seemed to be struggling with something, then said, "I'm with you." He glanced at the Cardinal.

The Cardinal shook his head. "It was a miracle we weren't all killed last time. I'm going to have to insist that—"

Maureen reached into the pocket of her jacket and held out a small white particle. "Do any of you know what this is? No, of course you don't. It's plastic explosive. As we suspected, that's what Hickey and Megan carried down in those suitcases. This is molded around at least one of the columns below. I don't know how many other columns are set to be blown, or where they all are, but I do know that two suitcases of plastic, properly placed, are enough to bring down the roof." She fixed her eyes on the Cardinal, who had turned pale. She continued, "And I don't see a remote detonator and wire up here. So I have to assume it's set to go on a timer. What time?" She looked at the three men. "At least one of us has to get out of here and warn the people outside."

Brian Flynn strode up to the communion rail and spoke in an ill-tempered tone. "Are you plotting again? Your Eminence, please stay on your exalted throne. The wounded gentlemen don't need your comfort. They're comforted enough knowing they're still alive. Miss Malone, may I have a word with you in the Lady Chapel? Thank you."

Maureen stood and noticed the stiffness that had spread through her body. She walked slowly to the side steps, down into the ambulatory, then passed into the Lady Chapel.

Flynn came up behind her and indicated a pew toward the rear. She sat.

He stood in the aisle beside her and looked around the quiet chapel. It was unlike the rest of the Cathedral; the architecture was more delicate and refined. The marble walls were a softer shade, and the long, narrow windows were done mostly in rich cobalt blues. He looked up at one of the windows to the right of the entrance. A face stared back at him, looking very much like Karl Marx, and in fact the figure was carrying a red flag in one hand and a sledgehammer in the other, attacking the cross atop a church steeple. "Well," he said in a neutral tone, "you know you've arrived as a lesser demon when the Church sticks your face up in a window. Like a picture in the celestial post office. Wanted for heresy." He pointed up at the window. "Karl Marx. Strange."

She glanced at the representation. "You wish it was Brian Flynn, don't you?"

He laughed. "You read my black soul, Maureen." He turned and looked at the altar nestled in the rounded end of the chapel. "God, the money that goes into these places."

"Better spent on armaments, wouldn't you say?"

He looked at her. "Don't be sharp with me, Maureen."

"Sorry."

"Are you?"

She hesitated, then said, "Yes."

He smiled. His eyes traveled upward past the statue of the Virgin on the altar, to the apsidal window above it. "The light will break through that window first. I hope we're not still here to see it."

She turned to him suddenly. "You won't burn this church, and you won't kill unarmed hostages. So stop speaking as though you were the type of man who would."

He put his hand on her shoulder, and she slid over. He sat beside her and said, "Something is very wrong if I've given the impression I'm bluffing."

"Perhaps it's because I know you. You've fooled everyone else."

"But I'm not fooling or bluffing."

"You'd shoot me?"

"Yes . . . I'd shoot myself afterward, of course."

"Very romantic, Brian."

"Sounds terrible, doesn't it?"

"You should hear yourself."

"Yes . . . well, anyway, I've been meaning to speak with you again, but with all that's been going on . . . We have some time now." He said, "Well, first you must promise me that you won't try to escape again."

"All right."

He looked at her. "I mean it. They'll kill you next time."

"So what? Better than being shot in the back of the head—by you."

"Don't be morbid. I don't think it will come to that."

"But you're not sure."

"It depends on things out of my control now."

"Then you shouldn't have gambled with my life and everyone else's—should you? Why do you think the people out there will be rational and concerned about our lives if you're not?"

"They've no choice."

"No choice but to be rational and compassionate? You've developed quite a faith in mankind, I see. If people behaved like that, none of us would be here now."

"This sounds like the argument we never finished four years ago." He stared toward the windows for a while, then turned to her. "Would you like to come with me when we leave here?"

She faced him. "When you leave here it will be for the jail or the cemetery. No, thank you."

"Damn you.... I'm walking out of here as free and alive as I walked in. Answer the question."

"What's to become of poor Megan? You'll break her dear heart, Brian."

"Stop that." He held her arm tightly. "I miss you, Maureen."

She didn't respond.

He said, "I'm ready to retire." He looked at her closely. "Really I am. As soon as this business is done with. I've learned a good deal from this."

"Such as?"

"I've learned what's important to me. Look here, you quit when you were ready, and I'm doing the same. I'm sorry I wasn't ready when you were."

"Neither you nor I believe a word of that. 'Once in, never out.' That's what you and all of them have thrown up to me all these years, so I'm throwing it right back in your face. 'Once in—'"

"No!" He pulled her closer to him. "Right now I believe I'm going to get out. Why can't you believe it with me?"

She suddenly went limp and put her hand over his. She spoke in a despondent tone. "Even if it *were* possible—there are people who have plans for your retirement, Brian, and they don't include a cottage by the sea in Kerry." She slumped against his shoulder. "And what of me? I'm hunted by the Belfast IRA still. One can't do the kinds of things we've done with our lives and expect to live happily ever after, can we? When was the last time you heard a knock on the door without having a great thump in your chest? Do you think you can announce your retirement like a respected statesman and settle down to write your memoirs? You've left a trail of blood all over Ireland, Brian Flynn, and there are people—Irish and British—who want yours in return."

"There are places we could go—"

"Not on this planet. The world is very small, as a good number of our people on the run have found out. Think how it would be if we lived together. Neither of us could ever go out to buy a packet of tea without wondering if it would be the last time we'd see each other. Every letter in the mail could explode in your face. And what if there were ... children? Think about that awhile."

He didn't reply.

She shook her head slowly. "I won't live like that. It's enough that I have to worry about myself. And it's a relief, to be honest with you, that I have no one else to worry about—not you, nor Sheila...so why should I want to go with you and worry about when they're going to kill you?...Why do you want to worry about when they're going to catch up with me?"

He stared at the floor between the pews, then looked up at the altar. "But...you would *like* to...I mean if it were possible...?"

She closed her eyes. "I wanted that once. I suppose, really, I still do. But it's not in our stars, Brian."

He stood abruptly and moved into the aisle. "Well...as long as you'd like to...that's good to know, Maureen." He said, "I'm adding Sheila's name to the list."

"Don't expect anything in return."

"I don't. Come along, then."

"Would you mind if I stayed here in the chapel?"

"I wouldn't, no. But...you're not safe here. Megan..."

"God, Brian, you speak of her as though she were a mad dog waiting to kill a sheep who's strayed from the fold."

"She's a bit...vindictive...."

"Vindictive? What have I ever done to her?"

"She...she blames you, in part, for her brother's capture.... It's not rational, I know, but she's—"

"Bloodthirsty. How in the name of God did you get mixed up with that savage? Is that what the youth of Northern Ireland's turning into?"

Flynn looked back toward the chapel opening. "Perhaps. War is all they've known—all Megan's known since she was a child. It's become commonplace, the way dances and picnics used to be. These young people don't even remember what downtown Belfast looked like before. So you can't blame them. You understand that."

She stood. "She goes a bit beyond war psychosis. You and I, Brian ... *our* souls are not dead, are they?"

"We remember some of the life before the troubles."

Maureen thought of Jean Kearney. She pictured the faces of the others. "We started this, you know."

"No. The other side started it. The other side always starts it."

"What difference does it make? Long after this is over, our country will be left with the legacy of children turned into murderers and children who tremble in dark corners. We're perpetuating it, and it will take a generation to forget it."

He shook his head. "Longer, I'm afraid. The Irish don't forget things in a generation. They write it all down and read it again, and tell it round the peat fires. And in truth you, I, and Megan are products of what came long before the recent troubles. Cromwell's massacres happened only last week, the famine happened yesterday, the uprising and civil war this morning. Ask John Hickey. He'll tell you."

She took a long breath. "I wish you weren't so damned right about these things."

"I wish you weren't so right about us. Come along."

She followed him out of the quiet chapel.

CHAPTER 42

Flynn descended the sacristy steps and saw Burke and Pedar Fitzgerald facing each other through the gate. A portable television sat on the landing beside Burke.

Flynn said to Fitzgerald, "Bring the priest here in five minutes."

Fitzgerald slung the Thompson over his shoulder and left.

Burke looked at Flynn closely. He appeared tired, perhaps even sad.

Flynn took out the microphone detector and passed it over the television. "We're both suspicious men by temperament and by profession. God, it's lonely though, isn't it?"

"Why the sudden melancholy?"

Flynn shook his head slowly. "I keep thinking this won't end well."

"I can almost guarantee you it won't."

Flynn smiled. "You're a welcome relief from that ass Schroeder. You don't bother me with sweet talk or with talk of giving up."

"Well, now, I hate to say this after that compliment, but you *should* give it up."

"I can't, even if I wanted to. This machine I've put together has no real head, no real brain. But it has many killing appendages...inside and outside the Cathedral, each spring-loaded to act or react under certain conditions. I'm no more than the creator of this thing—standing outside the organism.... I suppose I speak for it, but not *from* it. You understand?"

"Yes." Burke couldn't tell if this pessimism was contrived. Flynn was a good actor whose every line was designed to create an illusion, to produce a desired response.

Flynn nodded and leaned heavily against the bars.

Burke had the impression that Flynn was fighting some inner struggle that was taking a great deal out of him.

After a time Flynn said, "Well, anyway, here's what I wanted to speak to you about. Hickey and I have concluded that Martin's abducted the resident architect of Saint Patrick's. Why, you ask? So that you can't plan or mount a successful attack against us."

Burke considered the statement. There'd certainly be more optimism in the rectory and Cardinal's residence if Gordon Stillway was poring over the blueprints with Bellini right now. Burke tried to put it together in his mind. The Fenians had missed Stillway; that was obvious by now. Maureen Malone wouldn't have found an unsecured passage if Stillway was in there, because Stillway, no matter how brave a man he might be, would have been spilling it all out after fifteen minutes with this bunch.

And it wasn't too difficult to believe that Major Martin had anticipated Stillway's importance and snatched him before the Fenians could get to him. But to believe all that, you had to believe some very nasty and cold-blooded things about Major Martin.

Flynn broke the silence. "Are you seeing it now? Martin doesn't want the police to move too fast. He wants to drag this out—he wants the dawn deadline to approach. He's probably already suggested that you'll get an extension of the deadline, hasn't he?"

Burke said nothing.

Flynn leaned closer. "And without a firm plan of attack you're ready to believe him. But let me tell you, at 6:03 a.m. this Cathedral is no more. If you attack, your people will be ripped up very badly. The only way this can end without bloodshed is on *my* terms. *You* believe that we've beaten you. So swallow all that goddamned Normandy Beach–Iwo Jima pride and tell the stupid bastards out there that it's finished and let's all go home."

"They won't listen to that."

"*Make* them listen!"

Burke said, "To the people out there the Fenians are no more the peers of the police and government than the New York street gang that calls itself the Pagans. They *can't* deal with you, Flynn. They're bound by law to arrest you and throw you in the slammer with the muggers and rapists, because that's all terrorists are— muggers, murderers, and rapists on a somewhat larger scale—"

"Shut up!"

Neither man spoke, then Burke said in a gentler tone, "I'm telling you what their position is. I'm telling you what Schroeder won't tell you. It's true we've lost, but it's also true we won't—can't—surrender. You could surrender...honorably...negotiate the best terms possible, lay down your guns—"

"No. Not one person in here can accept anything less than we've asked for."

Burke nodded. "All right. I'll pass it on.... Maybe we can still work something out that will save you and your people and the hostages and the Cathedral.... But the people in internment..." He shook his head. "London would never..."

Flynn also shook his head. "All or nothing."

Both men lapsed into a silence, each aware that he had said more than he'd intended. Each was aware, too, that he had lost something that had been building between them.

Pedar Fitzgerald's voice came down the stairs. "Father Murphy."

Flynn turned and called back. "Send him down."

The priest walked unsteadily down the marble staircase, supporting his large frame on the brass rail. He smiled through the face bandages and spoke in a muffled voice. "Patrick, good to see you." He put his hand through the bars.

Burke took the priest's hand. "Are you all right?"

Murphy nodded. "Close call. But the Lord doesn't want me yet."

Burke released the priest's hand and withdrew his own.

Flynn put his hand to the bars. "Let me have it."

Burke opened his hand, and Flynn snatched a scrap of paper from him.

Flynn unfolded the paper and read the words written in pencil. *Hickey sent last message on confessional buzzer.* There followed a fairly accurate appraisal of the Cathedral's defenses. Flynn frowned at the first sentence: *Hickey sent last message...* What did that mean?

Flynn pocketed the paper and looked up. There was no anger in his voice. "I'm proud of these people, Burke. They've shown some spirit. Even the two holy men have kept us on our toes, I'll tell you."

Burke turned to Murphy. "Do any of you need a doctor?"

Murphy shook his head. "No. We're a bit lame, but there's nothing a doctor can do. We'll be all right."

Flynn said, "That's all, Father. Go back with the others."

Murphy hesitated and looked around. He glanced at the chain and padlock, then looked at Flynn, who stood as tall as he but was not as heavy.

Flynn sensed the danger and moved back. His right hand stayed at his side, but the position of his fingers suggested he was ready to go for his pistol. "I've been knocked about by priests before, and I owe you all a few knocks in return. Don't give me cause. Leave."

Murphy nodded, turned, and mounted the steps. He called back over his shoulder, "Pat, tell them out there we're not afraid."

Burke said, "They know that, Father."

Murphy stood at the crypt door for a few seconds, then turned and disappeared around the turn in the staircase.

Flynn put his hands in his pockets. He looked down at the floor, then lifted his head slowly until he met Burke's eyes. He spoke without a trace of ruthlessness.

"Promise me something, Lieutenant—promise me one thing tonight...."

Burke waited.

"Promise me this—that if they attack, you'll be with them."

"What—?"

Flynn went on. "Because, you see, if you know you're not involved on that level, then subconsciously you'll not see things you should see, you'll not say things you should say out there. And you'll not live so easily with yourself afterward. You know what I mean."

Burke felt his mouth becoming dry. He thought of Schroeder's foolishness. It was a bad night for rear-echelon people. The front line was moving closer. He looked up at Flynn and nodded almost imperceptibly.

Flynn acknowledged the agreement without speaking. He looked away from Burke and said, "Don't leave the rectory again."

Burke didn't reply.

"Stay close. Stay close especially as the dawn approaches."

"I will."

Flynn looked past Burke into the sacristy and focused on the priests' altar in the small chapel at the rear that was directly below the Lady Chapel altar. There were arched Gothic windows behind this altar also, but these subterranean windows with soft artificial lighting behind them, eastward-facing windows, were suffused with a perpetual false dawn. He kept staring at them and spoke softly, "I've spent a good deal of my life working in the hours of darkness, but I've never been so frightened of seeing the sunrise."

"I know how you feel."

"Good.... Are they frightened out there?"

"I think they are."

Flynn nodded slowly. "I'm glad. It's not good to be frightened alone."

"No."

Flynn said, "Someday—if there's a day after this one—I'll tell you a story about Whitehorn Abbey—and this ring." He tapped it against the bars.

Burke looked at the ring; he suspected it was some sort of talisman. There always seemed to be magic involved when he dealt with people who lived so close to death, especially the Irish.

Flynn looked down at the floor. "I may see you later."

Burke nodded and walked down the steps.

CHAPTER 43

B rian Flynn stood beside the curtain entrance to the confessional and looked at the small white button on the jamb. *Hickey sent last message...* Flynn turned toward the sound of approaching footsteps.

Hickey stopped and looked at his watch. "Time to meet the press, Brian."

He looked at Hickey. "Tell me about this buzzer."

Hickey glanced at the confessional. "Oh, that. There's nothing to tell. I caught Murphy trying to send a signal on it while he was confessing—can you imagine such a thing from a *priest*, Brian? Anyway, I think this is a call buzzer to the rectory. So I sent a few choice words, the likes of which they've never heard in the good fathers' dormitory." He laughed.

Flynn forced a smile in return, but Hickey's explanation raised more questions than it answered. *Hickey sent last message...* Who sent the previous message or messages? He said, "You should have kept me informed."

"Ah, Brian, the burdens of command are so heavy that you can't be bothered with every small detail."

"Just the same—" He looked at Hickey's chalk-white face and saw the genial twinkle in his eyes turn to a steady burning stare of unmistakable meaning. He imagined he even heard a voice: *Don't go any further.* He turned away.

Hickey smiled and tapped his watch. "Time to go give them hell, lad."

Flynn made no move toward the elevator. He knew he had reached a turning point in his relationship with John Hickey. A tremor passed down his spine, and a sense of fear came over him unlike any normal fear he had ever felt. *What have I unleashed?*

Hickey turned into the archway beside the confessional, passing into the hallway of the bride's room. He stopped in front of the oak elevator door and turned off the alarm. Slowly he began to deactivate the mine.

Flynn came up behind him.

Hickey neutralized the mine. "There we are.... I'll set it again after you've gone down." He opened the oak door, revealing the sliding doors of the elevator.

Flynn moved closer.

Hickey said, "When you come back, knock on the oak door. Three long, two short. I'll know it's you, and I'll defuse the mine again." He looked up at Flynn. "Good luck."

Flynn stepped closer and stared at the gray elevator doors, then at the mine hanging from the half-opened oak door. *I'll know it's you, and I'll defuse the mine....* He looked into Hickey's eyes and said, "I've got a better idea."

Inspector Langley and Roberta Spiegel waited in the brightly lit hallway of the subbasement. With them were Emergency Service police and three intelligence officers. Langley checked his watch. Past ten. He put his ear to the elevator doors. He heard nothing and straightened up.

Roberta Spiegel said, "This bastard has all three networks and every local station waiting for him. Mussolini complex—keep them waiting until they're delirious with anticipation."

Langley nodded, realizing that was exactly how he felt waiting for Brian Flynn to step out of the gray doors.

Suddenly the noise of the elevator motor broke into the stillness of the corridor. The elevator grew louder as it descended from the hallway of the bride's room into the subbasement. The doors began to slide open.

Langley, the three ID men, and the police unconsciously straightened their postures. Roberta Spiegel put her hand to her hair. She felt her heart in her chest.

The door opened, revealing not Brian Flynn but John Hickey. He stepped into the hall and smiled. "Finn MacCumail, Chief of the Fenians, sends his respects and regrets." Hickey looked around, then continued. "My chief is a suspicious man—which is why he's stayed alive so long. He had, I believe, a premonition about exposing himself to the dangers inherent in such a situation." He looked at Langley. "He is a thoughtful man who didn't want to place such temptation in front of you—or your British allies. So he sent me, his loyal lieutenant."

Langley found it hard to believe that Flynn was afraid of a trap—not with four hostages to guarantee his safety. Langley said, "You're John Hickey, of course."

Hickey bowed formally. "No objections, I trust."

Langley shrugged. "It's your show."

Hickey smiled. "So it is. And to whom do I have the pleasure of speaking?"

"Inspector Langley."

"Ah, yes. . . . And the lady?" He looked at Spiegel.

Spiegel said, "My name is Roberta Spiegel. I'm with the Mayor's office."

Hickey bowed again and took her hand. "Yes. I heard you on the radio once. You're much more beautiful than I pictured you from your voice." He made a gesture of apology. "Please don't take that the wrong way."

Spiegel withdrew her hand and stood silent. She had the unfamiliar experience of being at a loss for a reply.

Langley said, "Let's go."

Hickey ignored him and called down the corridor, "And these gentlemen?" He walked up to a tall ESD man and read his name tag. "Gilhooly." He took the man's hand and pumped it. "I love the melody of the Gaelic names with the softer sounds. I knew Gilhoolys in Tullamore."

The patrolman looked uncomfortable. Hickey walked up and down the hallway shaking each man's hand and calling him by name.

Langley exchanged looks with Spiegel. Langley whispered, "He makes Mussolini look like a tongue-tied schoolboy."

Hickey shook the hand of the last man, a big

flak-jacketed ESD man with a shotgun. "God be with you tonight, lad. I hope our next meeting is under happier circumstances."

Langley said impatiently, "Can we go now?"

Hickey said, "Lead on, Inspector." He fell into step with Langley and Spiegel. The three ID men followed. Hickey said, "You should have introduced those men to me. You ignored them—ignored their humanity. How can you get people to follow you if you treat them like jackstraws?"

Langley wasn't quite sure what a jackstraw was, and in any case chose not to answer.

Hickey went on. "In ancient days combatants would salute each other before battle. And a man about to be executed would shake his executioner's hand or even bless him to show mutual respect and compassion. It's time we put war and death on a personal basis again."

Langley stopped at a modern wooden door. "Right." He looked at Hickey. "This is the press room."

Hickey said, "Never been on television before. Do I need makeup?"

Langley motioned to the three ID men, then said to Hickey, "Before I take you in there, I have to ask you if you're armed."

"No. Are you?"

Langley nodded to one of the men who produced a metal detector and waved the wand over Hickey's body.

Hickey said, "You may find that British bullet I've been carrying in my hip since '21."

The metal detector didn't sound, and Langley reached out and pushed open the door. Hickey entered the room, and the sounds of conversation died abruptly. The press conference area below the sacristy was a long, light-paneled room with an acoustical tile ceiling. Several card tables were grouped around a long central conference table. Camera and light connections hung from trapdoors in the ceiling. Hickey looked slowly around the room and examined the faces of the people looking at him.

A reporter, David Roth, who had been elected the spokesman, rose and introduced himself. He indicated a chair at the head of the long table.

Hickey sat.

Roth said, "Are you Brian Flynn, the man who calls himself Finn MacCumail?"

Hickey leaned back and made himself comfortable. "No, I'm John Hickey, the man who calls himself John Hickey. You've heard of me, of course, and before I'm through you'll know me well enough." He looked around the table. "Please introduce yourselves in turn."

Roth looked a bit surprised, then introduced himself again and pointed to a reporter. Each man and woman in the press room, including, at Hickey's request, the technicians, gave his name.

Hickey nodded pleasantly to each one. He said, "I'm sorry I kept you all waiting. I hope my delay didn't cause the representatives of the governments involved to leave."

Roth said, "They won't be present."

Hickey feigned an expression of hurt and

disappointment. "Oh, I see.... Well, I suppose they don't want to be seen in public with a man like me." He smiled brightly. "Actually, I don't want to be associated with them either." He laughed, then produced his pipe and lit it. "Well, let's get on with it, then."

Roth motioned to a technician, and the lights went on. Another technician took a light reading near Hickey's face while a woman approached him with makeup. Hickey pushed her away gently, and she moved off quickly.

Roth said, "Is there any particular format you'd like us to follow?"

"Yes. I talk and you listen. If you listen without nodding off or picking your noses, I'll answer questions afterward."

A few reporters laughed.

The technicians finished the adjustments in their equipment, and one of them yelled, "Mr. Hickey, can you say something so we can get a voice reading?"

"Voice reading? All right, I'll sing you a verse from 'Men Behind the Wire,' and when I'm through, I want the cameras on. I'm a busy man tonight." He began to sing in a low, croaky voice.

> "Through the little streets of Belfast
> In the dark of early morn,
> British soldiers came marauding
> Wrecking little homes with scorn.
> Heedless of the crying children,
> Dragging fathers from their beds,
> Beating sons while helpless mothers
> Watch the blood flow from their heads—"

"Thank you, Mr. Hickey—"

Hickey sang the chorus—

> "Armored cars, and tanks and guns
> Came to take away our sons
> But every man will stand behind
> The men behind the wii-re!"

"Thank you, sir."

The camera light came on. Someone yelled, "On the air!"

Roth looked into the camera and spoke. "Good evening. This is David—" Hickey's singing came from off camera:

> "Not for them a judge or jury,
> Or indeed a crime at all.
> Being Irish means they're guilty,
> So we're guilty one and a-lll—"

Roth looked to his right. "Thank you—"

> "Round the world the truth will echo,
> Cromwell's men are here again.
> England's name again is sullied
> In the eyes of honest me-nnn—"

Roth glanced sideways at Hickey, who seemed to have finished. Roth looked back at the camera. "Good evening, I'm David Roth, and we're broadcasting live . . . as you can see . . . from the press room of Saint Patrick's Cathedral. Not too far from where we now sit, an undisclosed number of IRA gunmen—"

"Fenians!" yelled Hickey.

"Yes...Fenians...have seized the Cathedral and hold four hostages: Cardinal—"

"They know all that!" shouted Hickey.

Roth looked upset. "Yes...and with us tonight is Mr. John Hickey, one of the...Fenians...."

"Put the camera on me, Jerry," said Hickey. "Over here—that's right."

Hickey smiled into the camera and began, "Good evening and Happy Saint Patrick's Day. I am John Hickey, poet, scholar, soldier, and patriot." He settled back into his chair. "I was born in 1905 or thereabouts to Thomas and Mary Hickey in a small stone cottage outside of Clonakily in County Cork. In 1916, when I was a wee lad, I served my country as a messenger in the Irish Republican Army. Easter Monday, 1916, found me in the beseiged General Post Office in Dublin with the poet Padraic Pearse, the labor leader James Connolly, and their men, including my sainted father, Thomas. Surrounding us were the Irish Fusiliers and the Irish Rifles, lackeys of the British Army."

Hickey relit his pipe, taking his time, then went on. "Padraic Pearse read a proclamation from the steps of the Post Office, and his words ring in my ears to this day." He cleared his throat and adopted a stentorian tone as he quoted: "'Irishmen and Irishwomen—in the name of God and the dead generations from which she receives her old tradition of nationhood, Ireland, through us, summons her children to her flag and strikes for freedom.'"

Hickey went on, weaving a narrative blend of history and fancy, facts and personal prejudices, interjecting himself into some of the more famous events of the decades following the Easter Monday rebellion.

Most of the reporters leaned forward in interest; some looked impatient or puzzled.

Hickey was serenely unaware of them or of the cameras and lights. From time to time he would mention the Cathedral to keep everyone's interest piqued, then would swing into a long polemic against the British and American governments or the governments of the divided Ireland, always careful to exclude the people of these lands from his wrath.

He spoke of his sufferings, his wounds, his martyred father, his dead friends, a lost love, recalling each person by name. He beamed as he spoke of his revolutionary triumphs and frowned as he spoke darkly of the future of an Ireland divided. Finally he yawned and asked for a glass of water.

Roth took the opportunity to ask, "Can you tell us exactly how you seized the Cathedral? What are your demands? Would you kill the hostages and destroy the Cathedral if—"

Hickey held up his hand. "I'm not up to that part yet, lad. Where was I? Oh, yes. Nineteen hundred and fifty-six. In that year the IRA, operating from the south, began a campaign against the British-occupied six counties of the North. I was leading a platoon of men and women near the Doon Forest, and we were ambushed by a whole regiment of British paratroopers backed by the murderous Royal Ulster Constabulary." Hickey went on.

Langley watched him from the corner, then looked

around at the news people. They seemed unhappy, but he suspected that John Hickey was doing better with the public than with the media. Hickey had a hard-driving narrative style . . . a simplicity and almost crude-ness—sweating, smoking, and scratching—not seen on television in a long time.

John Hickey—sitting now in fifty million American living rooms—was becoming a folk hero. Langley would not have been surprised if someone told him that outside on Madison Avenue vendors were hawk-ing John Hickey T-shirts.

CHAPTER 44

Brian Flynn stood near the altar and watched the television that had been placed on the altar.

Maureen, Father Murphy, and Baxter sat in the clergy pews, watching and listening silently. The Cardinal sat nearly immobile, staring down at the television from his throne, his fingertips pressed together.

Flynn stood in silence for a long while, then spoke to no one in particular. "Long-winded old man, isn't he?"

Maureen looked at him, then asked, "Why didn't you go yourself, Brian?"

Flynn stared at her but said nothing.

She leaned toward Father Murphy and said, "Actually, Hickey seems an effective speaker." She paused thoughtfully. "I wish there were a way to get this kind of public platform without doing what they've done."

Murphy added as he watched the screen, "He's at least venting the frustrations of so many Irishmen, isn't he?"

Baxter glanced at them sharply. "He's not venting

anyone's frustrations—he's inflaming some long-cooled passions. And I think he's embellishing and distorting it a bit, don't you?" No one answered, and he went on. "For instance—if he'd been ambushed by a regiment of British paras, he wouldn't be here to talk about it—"

Maureen said, "That's not the point—"

Flynn overheard the exchange and looked at Baxter. "Harry, your chauvinism is showing. Hail Britannia! Britannia rules the Irish. Ireland—first outpost of Empire and destined to be the last."

Baxter said to Flynn, "The man's a bloody demagogue and charlatan."

Flynn laughed. "No, he's *Irish*. Among ourselves we sometimes tolerate a poetic rearrangement of facts mutually understood. But listen to the man, Harry—you might learn a thing or two."

Baxter looked at the people around him—Maureen, Murphy, Flynn, the Fenians…even the Cardinal. For the first time he understood how little he understood.

Megan Fitzgerald walked up to the sanctuary and stared at the television screen.

Hickey, in the tradition of the ancient seanachies, interrupted his narrative to break into song:

> "Then, here's to the brave men of Ireland.
> At home or in exile away;
> And, here's to the hopes of our sire land,
> That never will rust or decay.
> To every brave down-trodden nation,
> Here's liberty, glorious and bright. But,
> Oh! Let our country's salvation,
> Be toasted the warmest, to-niiight!"

Megan said, "Bloody old fool. He's making a laughing-stock of us ranting like that." She turned to Flynn. "Why the hell did you send him?"

Flynn looked at her and said softly, "Let the old man have his day, Megan. He deserves this after nearly seventy years of war. He may be the world's oldest continuously fighting soldier." He smiled in a conciliatory manner. "He's got a lot to tell."

Megan's voice was impatient. "He's supposed to tell them that the British are the only obstacle to a negotiated settlement here. I've a brother rotting in Long Kesh, and I want him free in Dublin come morning."

Maureen looked up at her. "And I thought you were here only because of Brian."

Megan wheeled around. "Shut your damned mouth!"

Maureen stood, but Father Murphy pulled her quickly into the pew.

Flynn said nothing, and Megan turned and strode off.

Hickey's voice blared from the television. The Cardinal sat motionless staring at some point in space. Baxter looked away from everyone and tried to filter out Hickey's voice, concentrating on the escape plan. Father Murphy and Maureen watched the screen intently. Flynn watched also, but his thoughts, like Baxter's, were elsewhere.

John Hickey took out a flask and poured a dark liquid into his water glass, then looked up at the camera. "Excuse me. Heart medicine." He drained off the glass and let out a sigh. "That's better. Now, where was I? Right—1973—" He waved his arms. "Oh, enough of this. Listen to me, all of you! We don't want to hurt anyone in this Cathedral. We don't want to harm a Prince of the Roman Church—a holy man—a good man—or his priest, Father Murphy...a lovely man...." He leaned forward and clasped his hands together. "We don't want to harm one single altar or statue in this beautiful house of God that New Yorkers—Americans—love so dearly. We're not barbarians or pagans, you know."

He held his hands out in an imploring gesture. "Now listen to me...." His voice became choked, and tears formed in his eyes. "All we want is another chance for the young lives being wasted in British concentration camps. We're not asking for the impossible—we're not making any irresponsible demands. No, we're only asking—begging—begging in the name of God and humanity for the release of Ireland's sons and daughters from the darkness and degradation of these unspeakable dungeons."

He took a drink of water and stared into the camera. "And who is it who have hardened their hearts against us?" He thumped the table. "Who is it who'll not let our people go?" *Thump!* "Who is it that by their unyielding policy endangers the lives of the people in this great Cathedral?" He pounded the table with both fists. "The bloody fucking British—*that's* who!"

Burke leaned against the wall in the Monsignor's office and watched the screen. Schroeder sat at his desk, and Spiegel had returned to her rocker. Bellini paced in front of the screen, blocking everyone's view, but no one objected.

Burke moved to the twin doors, opened them, and looked into the outer office. The State Department security man, Arnold Sheridan, stood by the window in deep thought. Occasionally he would eye the British and Irish representatives. Burke had the impression that Sheridan was going to give them the unpleasant news from Washington that Hickey was scoring heavily and it was time to talk. An awkward, almost embarrassed silence lay over the office as Hickey's monologue rolled on. Burke was reminded of a living room he had sat in once where the adolescents and adults had somehow gotten themselves involved in watching an explicit documentary on teenage sex. Burke turned back to the inner office and stared at the screen.

Hickey's voice was choked with emotion. "Many of you may question the propriety of our occupation of a house of God, and it was, I assure you, the hardest decision any of us has ever made in our lives. But we didn't so much *seize* the Cathedral as we took *refuge* in it—claimed the ancient privilege of *sanctuary*. And what better place to stand and ask for God's help?"

He paused as though wrestling with a decision, then said softly, "This afternoon, many Americans for the first time saw the obscene face of religious bigotry as practiced by the Orangemen of Ulster. Right here in the streets of the most ecumenical city in the world, the ugliness of religious intolerance and persecution was made unmistakably clear. The songs you heard those bigots sing were the songs the little children are taught in homes, schools, and churches...." He straightened his posture; on his face was a distasteful look that melted into an old man's sadness. He shook his head slowly.

Schroeder turned away from the screen and said to Burke, "What's the latest with those Orangemen?"

Burke kept staring at the screen as he spoke. "They still say they're Protestant loyalists from Ulster, and they'll probably keep saying that until at least dawn. But according to our interrogators they all sound like Boston Irish. Probably IRA Provos recruited for the occasion." Given all the externals of this affair, Burke thought, psychological timing, media coverage, tactical preparations, political maneuverings, and last-ditch intelligence gathering—it was clear that Flynn would not extend the deadline and risk the tide turning against him.

Spiegel said, "It was a tactical blunder to let Hickey on television."

Schroeder said defensively, "What else could I do?"

Bellini interjected, "Why don't I grab him—then we'll use him to negotiate for the hostages."

Schroeder said, "Good idea. Why don't you go cold-cock him right now before they break for a commercial?"

Burke looked at his watch. 10:25 p.m. The night was slipping away so fast that it would be dawn before anyone realized it was too late.

Hickey looked around the press room. He noticed that Langley had disappeared. Hickey leaned forward and spoke to the cameraman. "Zoom in, Jerry." He watched the monitor. "Closer. That's it. Hold it." He stared at the camera and spoke in low tones that had the suggestion of finality and doom. "Ladies and gentlemen of America—and all the unborn generations who will one day hear my words—we are outnumbered two thousand to one by police and soldiers, besieged and isolated by our enemies, betrayed by politicians and diplomats, compromised and undermined by secret agents, and censured by the world press...." He placed his hand over his chest. "But we are not afraid, because we know that out there are friends who wish us success and Godspeed in our mission. And there are the men and women, old and young, in Long Kesh, Armagh, Crumlin Road—all the hellholes of England and Northern Ireland—who are on their knees tonight, praying for their freedom. Tomorrow, God willing, the gates of Long Kesh will be thrown open, and wives will embrace husbands, children will weep with parents, brothers and sisters will meet once more...."

The tears were running freely again, and he took out a big bandanna and blew his nose, then continued, "If we accomplish nothing else this night, we'll have made the world aware of their existence. And if we die, and others die with us, and if this great Cathedral where I sit right now is a smoldering ruin by morning, then it will only be because men and women of goodwill could not prevail against the repressive forces of darkness and inhumanity." He took a long breath and cleared his throat. "Till we meet again in a happier place...God bless you all. God bless America and

Ireland and, yes, God bless our enemies, and may He show them the light. *Erin go bragh.*"

David Roth cleared his throat and said, "Mr. Hickey, we'd like you to answer a few specific questions...."

Hickey stood abruptly, blew his nose into the bandanna, and walked off camera.

Inspector Langley had returned; he opened the door, and Hickey moved quickly into the hall, followed by Langley and the three ID men. Langley came up beside Hickey and said, "I see you know when to quit."

Hickey put away his bandanna. "Oh, I couldn't go on any longer, lad."

"Yeah. Listen, you got your message across. You're way ahead. Now why don't you come out of there and give everyone a break?"

Hickey stopped in front of the elevator. His manner and voice suddenly became less teary. "Why the hell should we?"

Langley dismissed the three ID men. He took a notebook from his pocket and glanced at it. "Okay, Mr. Hickey, listen closely. I've just been authorized by representatives of the British and American governments to tell you that if you come out of the Cathedral now, the British will begin procedures to release—quietly and at intervals—most of the people on your list, subject to conditions of parole—"

"*Most?* What kind of *intervals?* What kind of *parole?*"

Langley looked up from the notebook. "I don't

know anything more than I'm telling you. I just got this over the phone. I'm only a cop, okay? And we're the only ones allowed to speak to you people. Right? So this is a little difficult but just listen and—"

"Pimp."

Langley looked up quickly. "What?"

"Pimp. You're pimping for the diplomats who don't want to make a direct proposition to us whores."

Langley flushed. "Look...look you—"

"Get hold of yourself, man. Steady."

Langley took a breath and continued in a controlled voice. "The British can't release all of them at once—not when you've got a gun to their heads—to everyone's heads. But it *will* be done. And also the State and U.S. Attorney General have agreed to allow all of you in there to post a low bond and go free awaiting trial—you understand what that means?"

"No, I don't."

Langley looked annoyed. "It means you can skip out on the fucking bail and get the hell out of the country."

"Oh...sounds dishonest."

Langley ignored the remark and said, "No one has been killed yet—that's the main thing. That gives us a lot of leeway in dealing with you—"

"It makes that much difference, does it? We've committed a dozen felonies already, terrified half the city, made fools of you, caused a riot, cost you millions of dollars, ruined your parade, and the Commissioner of Police has dropped dead of a heart attack. But you're willing to let bygones be bygones—give us a wink and run us off like Officer Muldoon stumbling onto a crap game in an alley—as long as no one's been killed. Interesting. That says a great deal about this society."

Langley drew another breath and said, "I won't make this offer again—for obvious reasons, no one will ever mention it over the telephone. So that's it." He slapped the notebook shut. "It's a fair compromise. Take it or leave it."

Hickey pressed the elevator button, and the doors opened. He said to Langley, "We wouldn't look very good if we compromised, would we? You'd look good, though. Schroeder would be booked solid on TV for a year. But we'd not have access to the airwaves so easily. All anyone would see or remember is us coming out the front doors of Saint Patrick's with our hands up. We'd do that gladly if the camps were emptied *first*. Then there's no way anyone could hide or steal our victory with diplomatic or journalistic babble."

"You'd be *alive*, for Christ's sake."

"Did you get my grave dug up yet?"

"Don't pull that spooky shit on me."

Hickey laughed.

Langley spoke mechanically, determined to deliver the last lines he had been instructed to say. "Use your power of persuasion with the people in there and your influence as a great Irish Republican leader. Don't tarnish with senseless death and destruction what you've already accomplished." He added his own thoughts. "You snowed about half of America tonight. Quit while you're ahead."

"I had a horse at Aqueduct this afternoon that quit while he was ahead . . . . But I'll pass your kind offer on to Mr. Flynn and the Fenians, and we'll let you know.

If we never mention it, then you can assume we are holding fast to all our demands."

Hickey stepped into the elevator. "See you later, God willing." He pushed the button, and as the doors slid closed he called out, "Hold my fan mail for me, Inspector."

CHAPTER 45

Brian Flynn stood opposite the elevator's oak door, an M-16 rifle leveled at it. George Sullivan stood to the side of the door, listening. The elevator stopped, and Sullivan heard a soft rapping, three long and two short. He signaled in return, then defused the mine and opened the door.

John Hickey stepped out. Flynn lowered the rifle a half second too slowly, but no one seemed to notice.

Sullivan extended his hand. "Damned fine, John. You had me laughing and weeping at the same time."

Hickey smiled as he took Sullivan's hand. "Ah, my boy, it was a dream come true." He turned to Flynn. "You would have done even better, lad."

Flynn turned and walked into the ambulatory. Hickey followed. Flynn said as he walked, "Did anyone approach you?"

Hickey walked ahead to the chancel organ. "One fellow, that Inspector Langley. Gave us a chance to surrender. Promised us a low bail—that sort of thing."

"Did the British relay any information—any indication they would compromise?"

"The British? Compromise? They're not even *ne-*

gotiating." He sat at the keyboard and turned on the organ.

"They didn't get word to you through anyone?"

"You'll not hear from them." He looked at Flynn. "You've got to play the bells now, Brian, while we still have everyone's attention. We'll begin with—let's see—'Danny Boy' and then do a few Irish-American favorites for our constituency. I'll lead, and you follow my tempo. Go on now."

Flynn hesitated, then moved toward the center aisle. Hickey began playing "Danny Boy" in a slow, measured meter that would set the tempo for the bells.

The four hostages watched Flynn and Hickey, then turned back to the television. The reporters in the Cathedral press room were discussing Hickey's speech. Baxter said, "I don't see that we're any closer to being let out of here."

Father Murphy replied, "I wonder...don't you think after this, the British...I mean..."

Baxter said sharply, "No, I don't." He looked at his watch. "Thirty minutes and we go."

Maureen looked at him, then at Father Murphy. She said, "What Mr. Baxter means is that he, too, thinks they were probably considering a compromise after Hickey's speech, but Mr. Baxter's decided that he doesn't want to be the cause of any compromise."

Baxter's face reddened.

Maureen continued. "It's all right, you know. I feel the same way. I'm not going to be used by them like a slab of meat to be bartered for what they want." She said in a quieter voice, "I've been used by them long enough."

Murphy looked at them. "Well...that's fine for you two, but I can't go unless my life is in actual danger. Neither can His Eminence." He inclined his head toward the Cardinal, who sat looking at them from his throne. Murphy added, "I think we all ought to wait...."

Maureen looked back at the Cardinal and saw by his face that he was struggling with the same question. She turned to Father Murphy. "Even if Hickey's speech has moved the people out there toward a compromise, that doesn't move *Hickey* toward a compromise—does it?" She leaned forward. "He's a treacherous man. If you still believe he's evil and means to destroy us, destroy himself, the Fenians, and this church, then we *must* try to get out of here." She fixed her eyes on Murphy's. "Do you believe that?"

Murphy looked at the television screen. A segment of John Hickey's speech was being replayed. The volume was turned low, and Hickey's voice wasn't audible over the organ. Murphy watched the mouth moving, the tears rolling down his face. He looked into the narrow eyes. Without the spellbinding voice the eyes gave him away.

Father Murphy looked out over the sanctuary rail at Hickey playing the organ. Hickey's head was turned toward them as he watched himself on television. He was smiling at his image, then turned and smiled, a grotesque smile, at Father Murphy. The priest turned quickly back to Maureen and nodded.

Baxter looked up at the Cardinal's throne; the Cardinal bowed his head in return. Baxter glanced at his watch. "We go in twenty-seven minutes."

Flynn rode the elevator to the choir practice room, then stepped out into the loft. He walked up behind Leary, who was leaning over the parapet watching the hostages through his scope. Flynn said, "Anything?"

Leary continued to observe the four people on the sanctuary. At some point years ago he had realized that not only could he anticipate people's movements and read their expression, but he could also read their lips. He said, "A few words. Not too clear. Hard to see their lips." The hostages had reached a point in their relationships to each other where they communicated with fewer words, but their body language was becoming clearer to him.

Flynn said, "Well, are they or aren't they?"

"Yes."

"How? When?"

"Don't know. Soon."

Flynn nodded. "Warning shots first, then go for the legs. Understand?"

"Sure."

Flynn picked up the field phone on the parapet and called Mullins in the bell tower. "Donald, get away from the bells."

Mullins slung his rifle and pulled a pair of shooters' baffles over his ears. He snatched up the field phone and quickly descended the ladder to the lower level.

Flynn moved to a small keyboard beside the organ console and turned the switch to activate the nineteen keys that played the bells. He stood before the waist-high keyboard and turned the pages of bell music on the music desk, then put his hands over the big keys and joined with the chancel organ below.

The biggest bell, the one named Patrick, chimed a thunderous B-flat, and the sound crashed through the bell tower, almost knocking Mullins off his feet.

One by one the nineteen huge bells began tolling in their carillon, beginning at the first bell room where Mullins had been and running upward to a point near the top of the spire twenty-one stories above the street.

In the attic a coffee cup fell off a catwalk rail. Arthur Nulty and Jean Kearney covered their ears and moved to the Madison Avenue end of the Cathedral. In the choir loft and triforia the bells resonated through the stonework and reverberated in the floors. In the south tower Rory Devane listened to the steady chiming coming from the opposite tower. He watched as the activity on the rooftops slowed and the movement in the streets came to a halt. In the cold winter air the slow rhythmical sounds of "Danny Boy" pealed through the dark canyons of Manhattan.

The crowds around the police barricades began cheering, raising bottles and glasses, then singing. More people began moving outdoors into the avenues and side streets.

Television coverage shifted abruptly from the press room of the Cathedral to the roofs of Rockefeller Center.

In bars and homes all over New York, and all over the country, pictures of the Cathedral as seen from Rockefeller Center flashed across the screens, bathed in stark blue lighting. A camera zoomed in on the green and gold harp flag that Mullins had draped from the torn louvers.

The sound of the bells was magnified by television audio equipment and transmitted with the picture from one end of the continent to the other. Satellite relays picked up the signal and beamed it over the world.

Rory Devane slipped a flare into a Very pistol, pointed it up through the louvers, and fired. The projectile arched upward, burst into green light, then floated on a parachute, swinging like a pendulum in the breeze, casting an unearthly green radiance across the buildings and through the streets. Devane went to the eastward-facing louvers and fired again.

Remote cameras located in the streets, bars, and restaurants began sending pictures of men and women singing, cheering, crying. A kaleidoscope of images flashed across video screens—bars, street crowds, the green-lit sky, close-ups of tight-lipped police, the bell tower, long shots of the Cathedral.

The flares suddenly changed from the illumination type to signal flares, star bursts, red, white, blue, then the green, orange, and white of the Irish tricolor. The crowd reacted appropriately. All the while the rich, lilting melody of "Danny Boy" filled the air from the bell tower and filled the airwaves from televisions and portable radios.

> "O Danny Boy, the pipes, the pipes are calling
> From glen to glen, and down the mountain side,
> The summer's gone, and all the roses falling,
> 'Tis you, 'tis you, must go and I must bide...."

Finally, on each station, reporters after an uncommonly long period of silence began adding commentary to the scenes, which needed none.

In the sanctuary the hostages watched the television in fascinated silence. Hickey played the organ with intense concentration, leading Flynn on the bells. Both men glanced at each other from time to time across the hundred yards that separated them.

Hickey swung into "Danny Boy" for the third time, not wanting to break the spell that the bittersweet song had laid over the collective psyche of the Cathedral and the city. He laughed as tears rolled down his furrowed cheeks.

In the Cardinal's residence and in the rectory the only sound was the pealing of the bells rolling across the courtyard and resonating from a dozen television sets into rooms filled with people.

Burke stood in the Monsignor's inner office, where the original Desperate Dozen had reassembled along with some additional members whom Burke had labeled the Anguished Auxiliaries.

Schroeder stood to the side with Langley and Roberta Spiegel, who, Burke noticed, was becoming Langley's constant companion.

Langley stared at the screen and said, "If they'd had television on V-J day, this is what it would have looked like."

Burke smiled in spite of himself. "Good timing. Good theater...fireworks...really hokey, but Christ, it gets them every time."

Spiegel added, "And talk about your psychological disadvantages."

Major Martin stood in the rear of the room between Kruger and Hogan. He kept his head and eyes straight ahead and said in an undertone, "We've always underestimated the willingness of the Irish to make public spectacles of themselves. Why don't they suffer in silence like civilized people?"

The two agents looked at each other behind Martin's back but said nothing.

Martin glanced to either side. He knew he was in trouble. He spoke with a light tone in his voice. "Well, I suppose I've got to undo this—or perhaps in their typical Irish fashion they'll undo themselves if—Oh, sorry, Hogan...."

Douglas Hogan moved away from Martin.

Monsignor Downes found his diary buried under Schroeder's paperwork and drew it toward him, opening it to March 17.

He wrote, *10:35 p.m. The bells tolled tonight, as they've tolled in the past to mark the celebration of the holy days, the ends of wars, and the deaths of presidents.* He paused, then added, *They tolled for perhaps the last time. And people, I think, sensed this, and they listened and they sang. In the morning, God willing, the carillon will ring out a glorious Te Deum—or if it is God's will, they will ring no more.* Monsignor Downes put aside his pen and closed the diary.

Donald Mullins swung his rifle butt and smashed a hole in the thick, opaque glass of the lower section of the tower. He knocked out a dozen observation holes, the noise of the breaking glass inaudible through his shooters' baffles and the chiming of the bells. Mullins slung his rifle and took a deep breath, then approached a broken window in the east side of the tower room and stared out into the cold night.

He saw that Devane was alternating star bursts with parachute flares, and the clearing night sky was lit with colors under a bright blue moon. The anxiety and despair he had felt all evening suddenly vanished in the clarity of the night, and he felt confident about meeting his death here.

CHAPTER 46

Harold Baxter didn't consult his watch. He knew it was time. In fact, he thought, they should have gone sooner, before the bells and the fireworks, before Hickey's speech, before the Fenians had transformed themselves from terrorists to freedom fighters.

He took a long last look around the Cathedral, then glanced at the television screen. A view from the tallest building of Rockefeller Center showed the cross-shape of the blue-lit Cathedral. In the upper left corner sat the rectory; in the right corner, the Cardinal's residence. Within five minutes he would be sitting in either place, taking tea and telling his story. He hoped Maureen, the priest, and the Cardinal would be with him. But even if one or all of them were killed, it would be a victory because that would be the end of the Fenians.

Baxter rose from the pew and stretched nonchalantly. His legs were shaking and his heart was pounding.

Father Murphy rose and walked across the sanctuary. He exchanged quiet words with the Cardinal, then moved casually behind the altar and looked down the staircase.

Pedar Fitzgerald sat with his back to the crypt door, the Thompson pointed down the stairs toward the sacristy gate. He was singing to himself.

Father Murphy raised his voice over the organ. "Mr. Fitzgerald."

Fitzgerald looked up quickly. "What is it, Father?"

Murphy felt a dryness in his throat. He looked across the stairwell for Baxter but didn't see him. He said, "I'm... I'm hearing confessions now. Someone will relieve you if you want to—"

"I've nothing to confess. Please leave."

Baxter steadied his legs, took a deep breath and moved. He covered the distance to the right side of the altar in three long strides and bounded down the steps in two leaps, unheard over the noise of the organ. Maureen was directly behind him.

Father Murphy saw them suddenly appear on the opposite stairs and made the sign of the cross over Fitzgerald.

Fitzgerald sensed the danger and spun around. He stared at Baxter flying toward him and raised his submachine gun.

Father Murphy heard a shot ring out from the choir loft and dived down the stairs; he looked over his shoulder for the Cardinal but knew he wasn't coming.

Leary got off a single shot, but his targets were gone in less time than it took him to steady his aim from the recoil. Only the Cardinal was left, sitting immobile on his throne, a splash of scarlet against the white marble and green carnations. Leary saw Hickey climb across the organ and drop to the sanctuary beside the Cardinal's throne. The Cardinal stood, placing himself in

Hickey's path. Hickey's arm shot out and knocked the Cardinal to the floor. Leary placed the cross hairs over the Cardinal's supine body.

Flynn continued the song on the bells, not wanting to alert the people outside that something was wrong. He watched the sanctuary in the mirror. He called out, "That will be all, Mr. Leary."

Leary lowered his rifle.

Baxter flew down the stairs, and his foot shot out, hitting Fitzgerald full in the face. Fitzgerald staggered back, and Father Murphy grabbed his arm from behind. Baxter seized the submachine gun and pulled violently. Fitzgerald wrenched the gun back.

The sound of the chancel organ had died away, but the bells played on, and for a second they were the only sound in the Cathedral until the air was split by a burst of fire from the submachine gun. The muzzle flashed in Baxter's face, and he was momentarily blinded. Pieces of plaster fell from the vaulted ceiling above, crashing over the sacristy stairs.

Father Murphy yanked back on Fitzgerald's arm but couldn't break Fitzgerald's grip on the gun. Maureen ducked around Baxter and jabbed her fingers into Fitzgerald's eyes. Fitzgerald screamed, and Baxter found himself holding the heavy submachine gun. He brought the butt up in a vertical stroke but missed Fitzgerald's groin and solar plexus, hitting him a glancing blow across the chest.

Baxter swore, raised the butt again, and drove it horizontally into the young man's throat. Father Murphy released Fitzgerald, and he fell to the floor. Baxter stood over the fallen man and raised the gun butt over Fitzgerald's face.

Maureen shouted, "No!" She grabbed Baxter's arm.

Fitzgerald looked up at them, tears and blood running from his unfocused eyes. Blood gushed from his open mouth.

Brian Flynn watched Hickey and Megan moving across the sanctuary. Leary stood beside him, fingering his rifle and murmuring to himself. Flynn turned his attention back to the bells.

The four people in the triforia had barely taken in what had happened in the last fifteen seconds. They stared down into the altar sanctuary and saw the Cardinal lying sprawled on the floor and Hickey and Megan approaching the two stairwells cautiously.

Maureen held the Thompson, steadied herself, and pulled back on the trigger. A deafening burst of automatic fire flamed out of the muzzle and slammed into the padlock and chain.

Murphy and Baxter crouched as bullets ricocheted back, cracking into the marble stairs and walls. Baxter heard footsteps on the sanctuary floor. "They're coming."

Maureen fired a long second burst at the gate, then swung the gun up at the right-hand staircase, placed Hickey in her sight, and fired.

Hickey's body seemed to twitch, then he dropped back out of view.

Maureen swung the gun around to the left and pointed it at Megan, who had stopped short on the first step, a pistol in her hand. Maureen hesitated, and Megan dived to the side and disappeared.

Baxter and Murphy ran down the stairs and tore at the shattered chain and padlock. Hot, jagged metal cut into their hands, but the chain began dropping away in pieces, and the padlock fell to the floor.

Maureen backed down the stairs, keeping the muzzle of the gun pointed up at the crypt door.

Police officers in the side corridors were shouting into the empty sacristy.

Baxter yelled to them. "Hold your fire! We're coming out! Hold it!" He tore the last section of chain away and kicked violently at the gates. "Open! Open!"

Father Murphy was pulling frantically on the left-hand gate, shouting, "No! They *roll*—!"

Baxter lunged at the right gate and tried to slide it along its track into the wall, but both gates held fast.

Flak-jacketed police began edging out into the sacristy.

Maureen knelt on the bottom stair, keeping the gun trained on the landing above. She shouted, "What's wrong?"

Baxter answered, "Stuck! Stuck!"

Murphy suddenly released the gate and straightened up. He grabbed at a black metal box with a large keyhole located where the gates joined and shook it. "They've locked it! The keys—they have the keys—"

Maureen looked back at them over her shoulder. She saw that the gate had its own lock, and she hadn't hit it even once. Baxter shouted a warning, and she spun around. She saw Hickey standing in front of the crypt door, his legs straddling Pedar Fitzgerald's body. Maureen raised the gun.

Hickey called down. "You can shoot me if you'd like, but that won't get you out of here."

Maureen screamed at him, "Don't move! Hands up!"

Hickey raised his hands slowly. "There's really no way out, you know."

She shouted, "Throw me the gate key!"

He made an exaggerated shrug. "I think Brian has it." He added, "Try shooting the lock out. Or would you rather use the last few rounds on me?"

She swore at him, spun around, and faced the gates. She shouted to Baxter and Murphy. "Move back!" She saw the police in the sacristy. "Get away!"

The police scattered back into the corridors. She pointed the muzzle at the boxlike lock that joined the gates and fired a short burst at point-blank range. The bullets ripped into the lock, scattering sparks and pieces of hot metal.

Baxter and Murphy yelled out in pain as they were hit. A piece of metal grazed Maureen's leg, and she cried out. She fired again, one round, and the rotating drum of .45-caliber bullets clicked empty. Murphy and Baxter seized the bars of the gates and pulled. The gates held fast.

Maureen swung back to find Hickey halfway down the steps, a pistol in his hand. Hickey said, "You don't see that kind of craftsmanship today. Hands up, please."

Megan Fitzgerald knelt at the landing beside her brother. She looked down at Maureen, and their eyes met for a brief second.

Hickey's voice was impatient. "Hands on your heads! Now!"

Father Murphy, Baxter, and Maureen stood motionless.

Hickey called out to the police. "Stay in the corridors, or I'll shoot them all!" He shouted to the three people, "Let's go!"

They remained motionless.

Hickey pointed the pistol and fired.

The bullet whistled past Murphy's head, and he fell to the floor.

Maureen reversed the Thompson, grabbing its hot barrel in her hands, and brought it down savagely on the marble steps. The gunstock splintered and the drum flew off. She threw the mangled gun to the side, then stood erect and raised her arms.

Baxter did the same. Murphy stood and put his hands on his head.

Hickey looked at Maureen appreciatively. "Come on, then. Calm down. That's right. Best-laid plans and all that." He moved aside to let them pass.

Maureen stepped up to the landing and looked down at Pedar Fitzgerald. His throat was already beginning to swell, and she knew he would die unless he reached a hospital soon. She found herself cursing Baxter for botching it and injuring Fitzgerald so seriously, cursing Father Murphy for not remembering the gate's lock, cursing herself for not killing Hickey and Megan. She looked down at Megan, who was wiping the blood from her brother's mouth, but it kept flowing up from his crushed throat. Maureen said, "Sit him up or he'll drown."

Megan turned slowly and looked up at her. Her lips drew back across her teeth, and she sprang up and dug her nails into Maureen's neck, shrieking, snarling.

Baxter and Murphy rushed up the remaining stairs

and pulled the two women apart. Hickey watched quietly as the struggle and the shouting subsided, then said, "All right. Everyone feel better? Megan, sit the lad up. He'll be all right." He poked the pistol at the three hostages. "Let's go."

They continued up to the sanctuary. Hickey chatted amiably as he followed. "Don't feel too badly. Damned bad luck, that's all. Maureen, you're a terrible shot. You didn't come within a yard of me."

She turned suddenly. "I hit you! I hit you!"

He laughed, put his finger to his chest, and drew it away with a small drop of pale, watery blood. "So you did."

The hostages moved toward the pews. The Cardinal was slumped in his throne, his face in his hands, and Maureen thought he was weeping, then saw the blood running through his fingers. Father Murphy made a move toward the Cardinal, but Hickey shoved him away.

Baxter looked up into the triforia and choir loft and saw the five rifles trained on them. He was vaguely aware that the bells were still pealing, and the phone beside the chancel organ was ringing steadily.

Hickey called up to Gallagher. "Frank, get down here quickly and take Pedar's place." He pushed Baxter into a pew and said, as though complaining to a close friend, "Damned dicey operation I've gotten myself in, Harry. Lose one man and there's no one to replace him."

Baxter looked him in the eyes. "In school I learned that IRA stood for I Ran Away. It's a wonder anyone's stayed here."

Hickey laughed. "Oh, Harry, Harry. After this place explodes and they find your pieces, I hope the morticians put your stiff upper lip where your asshole was and vice versa." Hickey shoved Maureen into the pew. "And you—breaking up that gun—like an old Celt yourself you were, Maureen, smashing your sword against a rock before dying in battle. Magnificent. But you're becoming a bit of a nuisance." He looked at Murphy. "And *you*, running out on your boss like that. Shame—"

Murphy said, "Go to hell."

Hickey feigned a look of shock. "Well, will you listen to this…?"

Murphy's hands shook, and he turned his back on Hickey.

Baxter stared at the television on the table. The scene had shifted back to the press room below. Reporters were speaking excitedly to their newsrooms. The gunfire, he knew, had undone the effects of Hickey's speech and the tolling bells. Baxter smiled and looked up at Hickey. He started to say something but suddenly felt an intense pain in his head and slumped forward out of the pew.

Hickey flexed his blackjack, turned, and grabbed Father Murphy by the lapel. He raised the black leather sap and stared into the priest's eyes.

Gallagher had come out of the triforium door and ran toward the sanctuary. "No!"

Hickey looked at him, then lowered the sap. "Cuff them." He moved to the television and ripped the plug from the outlet.

Maureen knelt over Baxter's crumpled body and

examined the wound on his forehead. "Bloody bastards—" She looked at the choir loft where Flynn played the bells. Gallagher took her wrist and locked on a handcuff, then locked the other end to Baxter's wrist. Gallagher cuffed Murphy's wrist and led him to the Cardinal. Gallagher knelt, then passed the cuff through the arm in the throne and gently placed the cuff over the Cardinal's blood-streaked wrist. Gallagher whispered, "I'll protect you." He bowed his head and walked away.

Father Murphy slumped down on the top step of the raised platform. The Cardinal came down from the throne and sat beside him. Neither man spoke.

Megan came out of the stairwell carrying her brother in her arms. She stood in the center of the sanctuary looking around blankly. A blood trail led from the stairwell to where she stood, and the trail became a small pool at her feet. Hickey took Pedar from his sister's arms and carried the limp body down to the chancel organ. He propped Pedar Fitzgerald against the organ console and covered him with his old overcoat.

Gallagher unslung his rifle and went down to the crypt landing. He shouted to the police who were cautiously examining the gate. "Get back! Go on!" They disappeared to the sides of the sacristy.

Megan remained standing in the pool of blood, staring at it. The only sounds in the Cathedral were the pealing bells and the persistently ringing telephone.

Brian Flynn watched from the choir loft as he tolled the bell. Leary glanced at Flynn curiously. Flynn turned away and concentrated on the keyboard, completing the last bar of "Danny Boy," then began "The

Dying Rebel." He spoke into the microphone. "Mr. Sullivan, the pipes, please. Ladies and gentlemen, a song." He began singing. Hesitantly, other voices joined him, and Sullivan's pipes began skirling.

> "The night was dark and the battle ended.
> The moon shone down O'Connell Street.
> I stood alone where brave men parted,
> Never more again to speak."

John Hickey picked up the ringing telephone.

Schroeder's voice came over the line, very nearly out of control. "What happened? What *happened*?"

Hickey growled, "Shut up, Schroeder! The hostages are not dead. Your men saw it all. The hostages are cuffed now, and there'll be no more escape attempts. End of conversation."

"Wait! Listen, are they injured? Can I send a doctor?"

"They're in reasonably good shape. If you're interested, though, one of my lads has been hurt. Sir Harold Baxter, knight of the realm, bashed his throat in with a rifle. Not at all sporting."

"God . . . listen, I'll send a doctor—"

"We'll let you know if we want one." He looked down at Fitzgerald. His throat was grotesquely bloated now. "I need ice. Send it through the gates. And a tracheal tube."

"Please . . . let me send—"

"No!" Hickey rubbed his eyes and slumped forward. He felt very tired and wished it would all end sooner than he had hoped.

"Mr. Hickey . . ."

"Oh, shut up, Schroeder. Just shut up."

"May I speak to the hostages? Mr. Flynn said I could speak to them after the press—"

"They've lost the right to speak with anyone, including each other."

"How badly are they hurt?"

Hickey looked at the four battered people on the sanctuary. "They're damned lucky to be alive."

Schroeder said, "Don't lose what you've gained. Mr. Hickey, let me tell you, there are a lot of people on your side now. Your speech was . . . magnificent, grand. What you said about your suffering, the suffering of the Irish—"

Hickey laughed wearily. "Yes, a traditional Irish view of history, which is at times in conflict with the facts but never inhibited by them." He smiled and yawned. "But everyone bought it, did they? TV is marvelous."

"Yes, sir, and the bells—did you see the television?"

"What happened to those song requests?"

"Oh, I've got some here—"

"Shove them."

After a short silence Schroeder said, "Well, anyway, it was really incredible, you know—I've never seen anything like that in this city. Don't lose that, don't—"

"It's already lost. Good-bye, Schroeder."

"Wait! Hold it! One last thing. Mr. Flynn said you'd turn off the radio jammer—"

"Don't blame your radio problems on us. Buy better equipment."

"I'm just afraid that without radio control the police might overreact to some perceived danger—"

"So what?"

"That almost happened. So, I was wondering when you were going to shut it off—"

"It will probably shut off when the Cathedral explodes." He laughed.

"Come on now, Mr. Hickey...you sound tired. Why don't you all try to get some sleep? I'll guarantee you an hour—two hours' truce—and send some food, and—"

"Or more likely it'll be consumed by the flames from the attic. Forty long years in the building— Poof—it'll be gone in less than two hours."

"Sir...I'm offering you a truce—" Schroeder took another breath, then spoke in a cryptic tone. "A police inspector gave you a...a status report, I believe...."

"Who? Oh, the tall fellow with the expensive suit. Watch that man, he's taking graft."

"Are you considering what he said to you?"

"As the Ulster Protestants are fond of saying, 'Not an inch!' Or would they now say centimeter? Inch. Yes, inch—"

"It's a fair solution to—"

"Unacceptable, Schroeder! Don't bother me with it again."

Schroeder said abruptly, "May I speak with Mr. Flynn?"

Hickey looked up at the loft. There was a telephone extension on the organ, but Flynn had not used it. Hickey said, "He's come to a difficult passage in the bells. Can't you hear it? Have a little consideration."

"We haven't heard from him in a long time. We expected him at the press conference. Is he...all right?"

Hickey found his pipe and lit it. "He's as well as any young man can be who is contemplating his imminent death, the sorrow of a lost love, the tragedy of a lost country, and a lost cause."

"*Nothing* is lost—"

"Schroeder, you understand Irish fatalism, don't you? When they start playing melancholy songs and weeping in their beers, it means they're on the verge of something reckless. And listening to your whimpering voice will not improve Brian Flynn's mood."

"No, listen, you're close—it's not lost—"

"Lost! Listen to the bells, Schroeder, and between their peals you'll hear the wail of the banshee in the hills, warning us all of approaching death." He hung up.

Megan was staring down at him from the sanctuary.

Hickey glanced at Pedar Fitzgerald. "He's dying, Megan."

She nodded hesitantly, and he looked at her. She seemed frightened suddenly, almost childlike. He said, "I can give him over to the police and he may live, but..."

She understood clearly that there would be no victory, no amnesty for them, or for the people in Northern Ireland, and that soon she and everyone in the Cathedral would be dead. She looked at her brother's blue-white face. "I want him here with me."

Hickey nodded. "Yes, that's the right thing, Megan."

Father Murphy shifted around on the throne platform. "He should be taken to a hospital."

Neither Megan nor Hickey answered.

Father Murphy went on, "Let me administer the sacrament—"

Hickey cut him off. "You've got a damned ritual for everything, don't you?"

"To save his soul from damnation—"

"People like you give eternal damnation a bad name." Hickey laughed. "I'll wager you carry some of that holy oil with you all the time. Never know when a good Catholic might drop dead at your feet."

"I carry holy oil, yes."

Hickey sneered. "Good. Later we'll fry an egg with it."

Father Murphy turned away. Megan walked toward Maureen and Baxter. Maureen watched her approach, keeping her eyes fixed steadily on Megan's.

Megan stood over the two cuffed people, then knelt beside Baxter's sprawled body and ripped the belt from his pants. She stood with her feet spread and brought the belt down with a whistling sound across Baxter's face.

Father Murphy and the Cardinal shouted at her.

Megan raised the belt again and brought it down on Maureen's upraised arms. She aimed the next blow at Baxter, but Maureen threw herself over his defenseless body and the belt lashed her across the neck.

Megan struck at Maureen's back, then struck again at her legs, then her buttocks.

The Cardinal looked away. Murphy was shouting at the top of his lungs.

Hickey began playing the chancel organ, joining with the bells. Frank Gallagher sat on the blood-smeared landing where Fitzgerald had lain and listened to the sounds of blows falling; then the sharp sounds were lost as the organ played "The Dying Rebel."

George Sullivan looked away from the sanctuary and played his bagpipe. Abby Boland and Eamon Farrell had stopped singing, but Flynn's voice called to them over the microphone, and they sang. Hickey sang, too, into the organ microphone.

> "The first I saw was a dying rebel.
> Kneeling low I heard him cry,
> God bless my home in Tipperary,
> God bless the cause for which I die."

In the attic Jean Kearney and Arthur Nulty lay on their sides, huddled together on the vibrating floor boards. They kissed, then moved closer. Jean Kearney rolled on her back, and Nulty covered her body with his.

Rory Devane stared out of the north tower, then fired the last flare. The crowds below were still singing, and he sang, too, because it made him feel less alone.

Donald Mullins stood in the tower below the first bell room, oblivious to everything but the pounding in his head and the cold wind passing through the smashed windows. From his pocket he took a notebook filled with scrawled poems and stared at it. He remembered what Padraic Pearse had said, referring to himself, Joseph Plunkett, and Thomas MacDonagh at the beginning of the 1916 uprising: "If we do nothing else, we shall rid Ireland of three bad poets." Mullins laughed, then wiped his eyes. He threw the notebook over his shoulder, and it sailed out into the night.

In the choir loft Leary watched Megan through his sniper scope. It came to him in a startling way that he had never once, even as a child, struck anyone. He watched Megan's face, watched her body move, and he suddenly wanted her.

Brian Flynn stared into the organ's large concave mirror, watching the scene on the altar sanctuary. He listened for the sound of Maureen's cries and the sound of the steady slap of the belt against her body, but heard only the vibrant tones of the chimes, the high, reedy wail of the bagpipes, the singing, and the full, rich organ below.

> "The next I saw was a gray-haired father,
> Searching for his only son.
> I said Old Man there's no use in searching
> Your only son to Heaven has gone."

He lowered his eyes from the mirror and shut them, listening only to the faraway chimes. He remembered that sacrifices took place on altars, and the allusion was not lost on him, and possibly some of the others understood as well. Maureen understood. He remembered the double meaning of sacrifice: an implied sanctification, an offering to the Deity, thanksgiving, purification.... But the other meaning was darker, more terrible—pain, loss, death. But in either case the understanding was that sacrifice was rewarded. The time, place, and nature of the reward was never clear, however.

> "Your only son was shot in Dublin
> Fighting for his Country bold.

He died for Ireland and Ireland only
The Irish flag green, white and gold."

A sense of overpowering melancholy filled him—
visions of Ireland, Maureen, Whitehorn Abbey, his
childhood, flashed through his mind. He suddenly felt
his own mortality, felt it as a palpable thing, a wrench-
ing in his stomach, a constriction in his throat, a
numbness that spread across his chest and arms.

A confused vision of death filled the blackness behind his eyelids, and he saw himself lying naked, white
as the cathedral marble, in the arms of a woman with
long honey-colored hair shrouding her face; and blood
streamed from his mouth, over his cold dead white-
ness—blood so red and so plentiful that the people
who had gathered around remarked on it curiously. A
young man took his hand and knelt to kiss his ring;
but the ring was gone, and the man rose and walked
away in disgust. And the woman who held him said,
Brian, we all forgive you. But that gave him more pain
than comfort, because he realized he had done nothing to earn forgiveness, done nothing to try to alter the
course of events that had been set in motion so long
before.

CHAPTER 47

Brian Flynn looked at the clock in the rear of the choir loft. He let the last notes of "An Irish Lullaby" die away, then pressed the key for the bell named Patrick. The single bell tolled, a deep low tone, then tolled again and again, twelve times, marking the midnight hour. St. Patrick's Day was over.

The shortest day of the year, he reflected, was not the winter solstice but the day you died, and March 18 would be only six hours and three minutes long, if that.

A deep silence lay over the acre of stone, and the outside cold seeped into the church, slowly numbing the people inside. The four hostages slept fitfully on the cool marble of the altar sanctuary, cuffed together in pairs.

John Hickey rubbed his eyes, yawned, and looked at the television he had moved to the organ console. The volume was turned down, and a barely audible voice was remarking on the new day and speculating on what the sunrise would bring. Hickey wondered how many people were still watching. He pictured all-night vigils around television sets. Whatever happened would happen live, in color, and few would be willing to go to sleep and see it on the replays. Hickey looked down at Pedar Fitzgerald. There were ice packs around his throat and a tube coming from his mouth that emitted a hissing sound. Slightly annoying, Hickey thought.

Flynn began playing the bells again, an Irish-American song this time, "How Are Things in Glocca Morra?"

Hickey watched the television. The street crowds approved of the selection. People were swaying arm in arm, beery tears rolling down red faces. But eventually, he knew, the magic would pass, the concern over the hostages and the Cathedral would become the key news story again. A lot of emotional strings were being pulled this night, and he was fascinated by the game of manipulation. Hickey glanced up at the empty triforium where Gallagher had stood, then turned and called back toward the sacristy stairs, "Frank?"

Gallagher called from the stairwell, "All quiet!"

Hickey looked up at Sullivan and Abby Boland, and they signaled in return. Eamon Farrell called down from the triforium overhead. "All quiet." Hickey cranked the field phone.

Arthur Nulty rolled over and reached out for the receiver. "Roger."

"Status."

Nulty cleared his throat. "Haven't we had enough bells, for God's sake? I can't hear so well with that clanging in my ears."

"Do the best you can." He cranked the phone again. "Bell tower?"

Mullins was staring through a shattered window,

and the phone rang several times before he was aware of it. He grabbed it quickly. "Bell tower."

Hickey said, "Sleeping?"

Mullins moved one earpiece of the shooters' baffles and said irritably, "Sleeping? How the hell could anyone sleep with *that*?" He paused, then said, "Has he gone mad?"

Hickey said, "How are they behaving outside?"

Mullins trailed the phone wire and walked around the tower. "They keep coming and going. Mostly coming. Soldiers bivouacked in the Channel Gardens. Damned reporters on the roofs have been drinking all night. Could use a rip myself."

"Aye, time enough for that. At this hour tomorrow you'll be—where?"

"Mexico City...I'm to fly to Mexico City...." He tried to laugh. "Long way from Tipperary."

"Warm there. Keep alert." Hickey cranked again. "South tower."

Rory Devane answered. "Situation unchanged."

"Watch for the strobe lights."

"I know."

"Are the snipers still making you nervous, lad?"

Devane laughed. "No. They're keeping me company. I'll miss them, I think."

"Where are you headed tomorrow?"

"South of France. It's spring there, they tell me."

"So it is. Remember, a year from today at Kavanagh's in fair Dublin."

"I'll be there."

Hickey smiled at the dim memory of Kavanagh's Pub, whose front wall was part of the surrounding wall of Glasnevin Cemetery. There was a pass-through in the back wall where gravediggers could obtain refreshments, and as a result, it was said, many a deceased was put into the wrong hole. Hickey laughed. "Aye, Rory, you'll be there." He hung up and turned the crank again.

Leary picked up the phone in the choir loft. Hickey said, "Tell Brian to give the bells a rest, then." He watched Leary turn and speak to Flynn. Leary came back on the line. "He says he feels like playing."

Hickey swore under his breath. "Hold on." He looked at the television set again. The scenes of New York had been replaced by an equally dramatic view of the White House, yellow light coming from the Oval Office windows. A reporter was telling the world that the President was in conference with top advisers. The scene shifted to 10 Downing Street, where it was 5:00 a.m. A bleary-eyed female reporter was assuring America that the Prime Minister was still awake. A quick scene-change showed the Apostolic Palace in the Vatican. Hickey leaned forward and listened carefully as the reporter speculated about the closed-door gathering of Vatican officials. He mumbled to himself, "Saint Peter's next."

Hickey spoke into the phone. "Tell Mr. Flynn that since we can expect an attack at any time now, I suggest he stop providing them with the noise cover they need." He hung up and listened to the bells, which still rang. Brian Flynn, he thought, was not the same man who strode so cockily through this Cathedral little more than six hours before. Flynn was a man who had learned a great deal in those six hours, but had learned

it too late and would learn nothing further of any con-
sequence in the final six hours.

Captain Bert Schroeder was startled out of a half-sleep
by the ringing telephone. He picked it up quickly.

Hickey's voice cut into the stillness of the office
and boomed out over the speakers in the surrounding
rooms, also startling some of the people there.
"Schroeder! Schroeder!"

Schroeder sat up, his chest pounding, "Yes! What's
wrong?"

Hickey's voice was urgent. "Someone's seized the
Cathedral!" He paused and said softly, "Or was I having a nightmare?" He laughed.

Schroeder waited until he knew his voice would be
steady. He looked around the office. Only Burke was
there at the moment, sleeping soundly on the couch.
Schroeder said, "What can I do for you?"

Hickey said, "Status report, Schroeder."

Schroeder cleared his throat. "Status—"

"How are things in Glocca Morra, London, Washington, Vatican City, Dublin? Anybody still working
on this?"

"Of course. You can see it on TV."

"I'm not the public, Schroeder. *You* tell me what's
happening."

"Well..." He looked at some recent memos.
"Well...the Red Cross and Amnesty are positioned at
all of the camps...waiting..."

"That was on TV."

"Was it? Well...Dublin...Dublin has not yet
agreed to accept released internees—"

"Tell them for me that they're sniveling cowards. Tell them I said the IRA will take Dublin within the year and shoot them all."

Schroeder said emphatically, "Anyway, we all haven't agreed on terms yet, have we? So finding a place of sanctuary is of secondary importance—"

"I want to speak with all the governments directly. Set up a conference call."

Schroeder's voice was firm. "You know they won't speak to you directly."

"Those pompous bastards will be on their knees begging for an audience by six o'clock."

Schroeder put a note of optimism in his voice. "Your speech is still having favorable repercussions. The Vatican is—"

"Speaking of repercussions and concussions and all that, do you think—now this is a technical question that you should consider—do you think that the glass façade of the Olympic Tower will fall into the street when—"

Schroeder said abruptly, "Is Mr. Flynn there?"

"You have a bad habit of interrupting, Schroeder."

"Is Mr. *Flynn* there?"

"Of course he's here, you ass. Where else would he be?"

"May I speak to him, please?"

"He's playing the bells, for God's sake!"

"Can you tell him to pick up the extension beside the organ?"

"I told you, you don't interrupt a man when he's playing the *bells*. Haven't you learned anything tonight? I'll bet you were a vice cop once, busting into hotel rooms, interrupting people. You're the type."

Schroeder felt his face redden. He heard Hickey's voice echoing through the rectory and heard a few people laughing. Schroeder snapped a pencil between his fingers. "We want to speak with Mr. Flynn—privately, at the sacristy gate." He looked at Burke sleeping on the couch. "Lieutenant Burke wants to speak—"

"As you said before, it's less confusing to speak to one person. If I can't speak to the Queen, you can't speak to Finn MacCumail. What's wrong with *me*? By the way, what have you given up for Lent? Your brains or your balls? *I* gave up talking to fools on the telephone, but I'll make an exception in your case."

Schroeder suddenly felt something inside him come loose. He made a strong effort to control his voice and spoke in measured tones. "Mr. Hickey...Brian Flynn has a great deal of faith in me—the efforts I'm making, the honesty I've shown—"

The sound of Hickey's laughter filled the office. "He sounds like a good lad to you, does he? Well, he's got a surprise in store for *you*, Schroeder, and you won't like it."

Schroeder said, "We'd rather not have any surprises—"

"Stop using that imperial *we*. I'm talking about *you*. *You* have a surprise coming." Schroeder sat up quickly, and his eyes became more alert. "What do you mean by that? What does that mean? Listen, everything should be aboveboard if we're going to bargain in good faith—"

"Is Bellini acting in good faith?"

Schroeder hesitated. This use of names by these

people was unsettling. These references to him personally were not in the script.

Hickey continued, "Where is Bellini now? Huddled around a chalk board with his Gestapo? Finding sneaky little ways to kill us all? Well, fuck Bellini and fuck you."

Schroeder shook his head in silent frustration, then said, "How are the hostages?" Hickey said, "Did you find Stillway yet?"

"Do you need a doctor in there?"

"Did you dig up my grave yet?"

"Can I send food, medicine—?"

"Where's Major Martin?"

Burke lay on the couch with his eyes closed and listened to the dialogue deteriorate into two monologues. As unproductive as the dialogue had been, it hadn't been as bizarre as what he was listening to now. He knew now, beyond any doubt, that it was finished.

Schroeder said, "What surprises does Flynn have planned for me?"

Hickey laughed again. "If I tell you, it won't be a surprise. I'll bet when you were a child you were an insufferable brat, Schroeder. Always trying to find out what people bought you for Christmas, sneaking around closets and all that."

Schroeder didn't respond and again heard the laughter from the next room.

Hickey said, "Don't initiate any calls to us unless it's to say we've won. I'll call you back every hour on the hour until 6:00 a.m. At 6:03 it's over."

Schroeder heard the phone go dead. He looked at

Burke's still form on the couch, then shut off all the speakers and dialed again. "Hickey?"

"What?"

Schroeder took a deep breath and said through his clenched jaw, "You're a dead motherfucker." He put the phone down and steadied his hands against the desk. There was a taste of blood in his mouth, and he realized that he was biting into his lower lip.

Burke turned his head and looked at Schroeder. Their eyes met, and Schroeder turned away.

Burke said, "It's okay."

Schroeder didn't answer, and Burke could see his shoulders shaking.

CHAPTER 48

Colonel Dennis Logan rode in the rear of a staff car up the deserted section of Fifth Avenue, toward the Cathedral. He turned to his adjutant, Major Cole. "Didn't think I'd be passing this way again today."

"Yes, sir. It's actually March eighteenth."

Colonel Logan overlooked the correction and listened to the bells play "I'll Take You Home Again, Kathleen," then said, "Do you believe in miracles?"

"No, sir."

"Well, see that green line?"

"Yes, sir, the long one in the middle of the Avenue that we followed." He yawned.

"Right. Well, some years ago, Mayor Beame was marching in the parade with the Sixty-ninth. Police Commissioner Codd and the Commissioner for Public Events, Neil Walsh, were with him. Before your time."

Major Cole wished that this parade had been before his time. "Yes, sir."

"Anyway, it rained that morning after the line machine went by, and the fresh green paint washed away—all the way from Forty-fourth to Eighty-sixth Street. But later that morning Walsh bought some paint and had his men hand-paint the line right in front of the Cathedral."

"Yes, sir."

"Well, when we marched past with the city delegation, Walsh turns to Codd and says, 'Look! It's a miracle, Commissioner! The line's still here in front of the Cathedral!'"

Colonel Logan laughed at the happier memory and went on. "So Codd says, 'You're right, Walsh!' and he winks at him, then looks at Beame. 'Oh my gosh!' said the little Mayor. 'I always wanted to see a miracle. I never saw a miracle before!'" Logan laughed but refrained from slapping his or Cole's knee. The driver laughed, too.

Major Cole smiled. He said, "Sir, I think we've mustered most of the officers and at least half the men."

Logan lit a cigar. "Right.... Do they look sober to you?"

"It's hard to say, sir."

Logan nodded, then said, "We're not really needed here, are we?"

"That's difficult to determine, Colonel."

"I think the Governor is looking for high marks in leadership and courage, don't you?"

Major Cole replied, "The regiment is well trained in crowd and riot control, sir."

"So are twenty-five thousand New York police."

"Yes, sir."

"I hope to God he doesn't get us involved in an assault on the Cathedral."

The major replied, "Sir," which conveyed no meaning.

Colonel Logan looked through the window as the car passed between a set of police barriers and moved slowly past the singing crowds. "Incredible."

Cole nodded. "Yes, it is."

The staff car drew up to the rectory and stopped.

* * *

Captain Joe Bellini advised the newspeople that the press conference room might cave in if the Cathedral was blown up, and they moved with their equipment to less vulnerable places outside the Cathedral complex as Bellini moved in. He stood in the room beside a chalkboard. Around the tables and along the walls, were sixty Emergency Service Division men, armed with shotguns, M-16 rifles, and silenced pistols. In the rear of the room sat Colonel Logan, Major Cole, and a dozen staff personnel from the 69th Regiment. A cloud of gray tobacco smoke veiled the bright lights. Bellini pointed to a crude outline of the Cathedral on the chalkboard. "So, Fifth Squad will attack through the sacristy gates. You'll be issued steel-cut chainsaws and bolt cutters. Okay?"

Colonel Logan stood. "If I may make a suggestion... Before, you said your men had to control their fire.... This is your operation, and my part is secondary, but the basic rules of warfare... Well, anyway, when you encounter concealed enemy positions that have a superior field of fire—like those triforia and choir loft—and you know you can't engage them with effective fire... then you have to lay down *suppressing* fire." Logan saw some signs of recognition. "In other words you flip the switches on your M-16s from semi-automatic to full automatic—rock and roll, as the men say—and put out such an intense volume of fire that the enemy has got to put his head down. Then you can safely lead the hostages back down the sacristy stairs."

No one spoke, but a few men were nodding.

Logan's voice became more intense. He was suddenly giving a prebattle pep talk. "Keep blasting those triforia, blast that choir loft, slap magazine after magazine into those rifles, raking, raking, raking those sniper perches, blasting away so long, so loud, so fast, and so hard that it sounds like Armageddon and the Apocalypse all at once, and no one—*no one*—in those perches is going to pick his head up if the air around him is filled with bullets and pulverized stone." He looked around the silent room and listened to his heart beating.

There was a spontaneous burst of applause from the ESD men and the military people. Captain Bellini waited until the noise died away, then said, "Yes, well, Colonel, that's sound advice, but we're *all* under the strictest orders not to blow the place apart—as you know. It's full of art treasures.... It's...well...you know..."

Logan said, "Yes, I understand." He wiped his face. "I'm not advocating air strikes. I mean, I'm only suggesting you increase your use of small-arms fire, and—"

"Such an intense degree of even small-arms fire, Colonel, would do"—Bellini remembered the Governor's words—"irreparable...irreparable damage to the Cathedral...the   ceiling...the   stonework...statues..."

One of the squad leaders stood. "Look, Captain, since when are art treasures more important than people? My mother thinks *I'm* an art treasure—"

Several people laughed nervously.

Bellini felt the sweat collecting under his collar. He looked at Logan. "Colonel, your mission..." Bellini paused and watched Logan stiffen.

Logan said, "My mission is to provide a tight cordon around the Cathedral during the assault. I know what I have to do."

Bellini almost smirked. "No, that's been changed. The Governor wants you to take a more active part in the assault." He savored each word as he said it. "The police will supply you with their armored personnel carrier. It's army surplus, and you'll be familiar with it." Bellini noticed that Major Cole had gone pale.

Bellini stepped closer to Logan. "You'll take the vehicle up the front steps with fifteen men inside—"

Logan's voice was barely under control. "This is *insane*. You can't use an armored vehicle in such a confined space. They might have armor-piercing ordnance in there. Good Lord, we couldn't maneuver, couldn't conceal the vehicle...These Fenians are guerrilla veterans, Captain. They know how to deal with tanks— they've seen more British armored cars than you've seen—"

"Taxis," said Burke as he walked into the press room. "That's what Flynn said to Schroeder. Taxis. Mind if Inspector Langley and I join you?"

Bellini looked tired and annoyed. He said to Logan, "Take it up with the Governor." Glancing at the wall clock, he said, "Everyone take ten. Clear out!" He sat down and lit a cigarette. The men filed out of the conference room and huddled in groups throughout the corridors.

Burke and Langley sat across from Bellini. Bellini said softly, "That fucking war hero is spooking my men."

Burke thought, *They should be spooked. They're going to get creamed.* "He means well."

Bellini drew on his cigarette. "Why are those parade soldiers in on this?"

Langley looked around, then said quietly, "The Governor needs a boost."

Bellini sipped on a cup of cold coffee. "You know...I discussed a lot of options for this attack with the Mayor and Governor. Ever notice how people who don't know shit about warfare all of a sudden become generals?" Bellini chain-lit another cigarette and went on in a voice that was becoming overwrought. "So Kline takes my hand and squeezes it—Christ, I should've squeezed his and broken his fucking fingers. Anyway, he says, 'Joe, you know what's expected of you.' Christ Almighty, by this time I don't even know if I'm allowed to take my gun in there. But my adrenaline is really pumping by now, and I say to him, 'Your Honor, we have to attack *now*, while the bells are ringing.' Right? And he says—check this—he says, 'Captain, we have an obligation'—a moral something or other—'to explore every possible avenue of negotiation'—blah, blah, blah—'political considerations'—blah, blah—'the Vatican'—blah, blah. So I say...no, I didn't say it, but I should have...I should have said, 'Kline, you schmuck, do you want to rescue the hostages and save the fucking Cathedral, or do you want to make time with the White House and the Vatican?'"

He paused and breathed hard. "But maybe then I would have sounded like an asshole, too, because I don't really care about a pile of stone or four people I don't even know. My responsibility is to a hundred of my men who I do know and to their families and to myself and my wife and kids. Right?"

No one spoke for some time, then the telephone rang. Bellini grabbed it, listened, then handed it to Burke. "Some guy called the Leper. You hang out with classy people."

Burke took the receiver and heard Ferguson's voice. "Burke, Leper here."

Burke said, "How are you?"

"Cold, scared shitless, tired, hungry, and broke. But otherwise, well. Is this line secure?"

"No."

"Okay, I have to speak to you face to face."

Burke thought a moment. "Do you want to come here?"

Ferguson hesitated. "No...I saw people hanging around the checkpoints who shouldn't see me. I'm very close to our rendezvous point. See you there."

Burke put down the receiver and said to Langley, "Ferguson's on to something."

Bellini looked up quickly. "Anything that can help me?"

Burke wanted to say, "Frankly, nothing can help you," but said instead, "I think so."

Bellini seemed to sense the lie and slumped lower in his chair. "Christ, we've never gone up against trained guerrillas...." He looked up suddenly. "Do I sound scared? Do I look scared?"

Burke replied, "You look and sound like a man who fully appreciates the problems."

Bellini laughed. "Yeah. I appreciate the hell out of the problems."

Langley seemed suddenly annoyed. "Look, you must have known a day like this would come. You've trained for this—"

"Trained?" Bellini turned on him. "Big fucking deal trained. In the army I was trained on how to take cover in a nuclear attack. The only instructor who made any sense was the one who told us to hold our helmets, put our heads between our legs, and kiss our asses good-bye." He laughed again. "Fuck trained." Bellini stubbed out his cigarette and breathed deeply. "Oh, well. Maybe Schroeder will pull it off." He smiled thinly. "He's got more incentive now." He pointed to a black bulletproof vest and a dark pullover sweater at the end of the table. "That's his."

Langley said, "Why don't you let him off the hook?"

Bellini shook his head, then looked at Burke. "How about you? What are *you* doing later?"

Burke said, "I'll be with you."

Bellini's eyes widened.

Langley looked at Burke quickly. "Like hell."

Burke said nothing.

Bellini said, "Let the man do what he wants."

Langley changed the subject and said to Bellini, "I have more psy-profiles for you."

Bellini lit a cigarette. "Put a light coat of oil on them and shove them up your ass."

Langley stiffened.

Bellini went on, enjoying the fact that no one could pull rank on him any longer. "Where's the architect, Langley? Where are the blueprints?"

Langley said, "Working on it."

"Terrific. Everybody is working on something— you, Schroeder, the Mayor, the President. Everybody's working. You know, when this started nobody paid much attention to Joe Bellini. Now the Mayor calls about every fifteen minutes asking how I'm making out. Calls me Joe. Terrific little guy."

Men started drifting back into the room.

Bellini leaned over the table. "They've got me cornered. When they start calling you by your first name, they've got you by the balls, and they're not going to let go until I charge up those fucking steps—holding not much more than my cock in one hand and a cross in the other—and get myself killed." He stood. "Believe me, Burke, it's all a fucking show. Everybody's got to play his part. You, me, the politicians, the Church, the bastards in the Cathedral. We *know* we're full of shit, but that's the way we learned how to play."

Burke stood and looked around at the ESD men, then looked closely at Bellini. "Remember, you're the good guys."

Bellini rubbed his temples and shook his head. "Then how come we're wearing black?"

CHAPTER 49

Patrick Burke stepped out of the rectory into the cold, gusty air. He looked at his watch. Nearly 1:00 a.m., March 18. They would still call it the St. Patrick's Day massacre or something catchy like that. He turned up his collar and walked east on Fifty-first Street.

At Park Avenue a city bus was drawn up to form a barricade. Burke walked around the bus, passed through a thin crowd, and crossed the avenue. A small group had congregated on the steps and terraces of St. Bartholomew's Episcopal Church, passing bottles and singing the songs that were being played on St. Patrick's bells. People were entering the church, and Burke recalled that many churches and synagogues had announced all-night prayer vigils. A news van was setting up cameras and lights.

Burke listened to the bells. Flynn—if it was Flynn playing—had a good touch. Burke remembered Langley's speculation about the John Hickey T-shirts. He envisioned a record jacket: St. Patrick's Cathedral—green star clusters—*Brian Flynn Plays the Bells*.

Burke passed by the church and continued east on

Fifty-first Street. Between two buildings lay a small park. A fence and gate ran between the flanking structures, and Burke peered through the bars. Café tables and upturned chairs stood on the terraces beneath bare sycamores. Nothing moved in the unlit park. Burke grasped the cold steel bars, pulled himself up to the top, and dropped into the park. As he hit the frozen stone walk below, he felt a sharp pain shoot through his numb legs and swore silently. He drew his pistol and remained crouched. A wind shook the trees, and ice-covered twigs snapped and fell to the ground with the sound of breaking crystal.

Burke straightened up slowly and moved through the scattered tables, pistol held at his side. As he moved, the ice crackled under his shoes, and he knew that if Ferguson were there he would have heard him by now.

An overturned table caught his attention, and he moved toward it. A chair lay on its back some distance away. The ice on the ground was broken and scattered, and Burke knelt to get a closer look at a large dark blotch that on closer inspection looked like a strawberry Italian ice but wasn't.

Burke rose and found that his legs had become unsteady. He walked up the shallow steps to the next level of the terrace and saw more overturned furniture. In the rear of the park was a stone wall several stories high where a waterfall usually flowed. At the base of the wall was a long, narrow trough. Burke walked to the trough and stared down at Jack Ferguson lying in the icy water, his face blue-white, very much, Burke thought, like the color of the façade of the Cathedral. The eyes were open, and his mouth yawned as if he were trying to catch his breath from the shock of the cold water.

Burke knelt on the low stone abutment of the trough, reached out, and grabbed Ferguson's old trench coat. He pulled the body closer and saw, as the folds of the trench coat drifted apart, the two bullet-shattered knees poking out of the worn trousers—bone, cartilage, and ligaments, very white against the deeper color of bluish flesh.

He slipped his pistol into his pocket and pulled the small man easily onto the coping stone of the abutment. A small bullet hole showed like black palm ash in the center of Ferguson's forehead. His pockets had been rifled, but Burke searched the body again, finding only a clean, neatly pressed handkerchief which reminded him that he would have to call Ferguson's wife.

Burke closed Ferguson's eyes and stood, wiped his hands on his overcoat and blew into them, and then walked away. He righted an ice-covered chair, drew it up to a metal table, and sat. Burke took a long, deep breath and steadied his hands enough to light a cigarette. He drew on the cigarette, then took out his flask and opened it, but set it on the table without drinking. He heard a noise at the fence and looked out across the park. He drew his pistol and rested it in his lap.

"Burke! It's Martin."

Burke didn't answer. "Can I come up?"

Burke cocked his revolver. "Sure!"

Martin walked toward Burke, stopped, and looked past him at the low stone wall at the base of the waterfall. "Who's that?"

Burke didn't reply.

Martin walked up to the body and looked down into the frozen face. "I know this man . . . Jack Ferguson."

"Is it?"

"Yes. I've dealt with him—only yesterday, as a matter of fact. Official IRA. Marxist. Nice chap, though."

Burke said with no intonation in his voice, "The only good Red is a dead Red. Kill a Commie for Christ. Move here where I can see you."

"Eh?" Martin moved behind Burke's chair. "What did you say . . . ? See here, you didn't . . . did you?"

Burke repeated. "Here in front where I can see you."

Martin moved around the table.

Burke said, "Why are you here?"

Martin lit a cigarette. "Followed you from the rectory."

Burke was certain no one had followed him. "Why?"

"Wanted to see where you were going. You've been most unhelpful. I've been sacked from my consulate job, by the way. Is that your doing? People are starting to say the most incredible things about me. Anyway, I'm at loose ends now. Don't know what to do with myself. So I thought perhaps I could . . . well . . . lend you a hand . . . clear my name in the process. . . . Is that a gun? You can put that away."

Burke held the gun. "Who do you think killed him, Major?"

"Well, assuming it wasn't you . . ." He shrugged. "Probably his own people. Or the Provos or the Fenians. Did you see his knees? God, that's a nasty business."

"Why would the IRA want to kill him?"

Martin answered quickly and distinctly. "He talked too much."

Burke uncocked his revolver and held it in his pocket. "Where's Gordon Stillway?"

"Gordon . . . Oh, the architect." Martin drew on his cigarette. "I wish I were half as devious as you think I am."

Burke took a drink from his flask and said, "Look, the Cathedral is going to be stormed in the next few hours."

"Sorry it had to come to that."

"Anyway, I'm concerned now about saving as many lives as possible."

"I am, too. Our Consul General is in there."

"So far, Major, you've had it all your way. You got your Irish terrorism in America. We've had it pushed in our face. The point is made and well taken. So we don't need a burned-out Cathedral and a stack of corpses."

"I'm not quite sure I'm following you."

"It would help Bellini if he had the blueprints and the architect."

"Undoubtedly. I'm working on that also."

Burke looked at Martin closely. "Settle for what you've already got. Don't push it further."

"I'm sorry, I'm losing you again."

Burke stared at Martin, who put his foot on a chair and puffed on his cigarette. A gust of cold wind moved through the enclosed park and swirled around. Ice fell from the glistening trees, landing on Martin and

Burke, but neither man seemed to notice. Martin seemed to reach a decision and looked at Burke. "It's not just Flynn, you see. My whole operation wasn't conceived just to kill Brian Flynn." Martin rubbed his chin with his gloved hand. "You see, I need more than Flynn's death, though I look forward to it. I also need a *lasting* symbol of Irish terrorism. I'm afraid I need the Cathedral to go down."

Burke waited a long time before he spoke. His voice was low, controlled. "It may become a symbol of Britain's unwillingness to negotiate."

"One gambles. But you see, London *did* offer a compromise, much to my surprise, and the Fenians, lunatics that they are, have not responded to it. And with the old man's speech and the bells and all that, it's the Fenians who are ahead, not me. Really, Burke, the only way I can influence public opinion, here and abroad, is if . . . well, if there's a tragedy. Sorry."

"It's going to backfire."

"When the dust clears, the blame will be squarely on the Irish. Her Majesty's government is very adept at expressing sorrow and pity for the loss of lives and property. Actually, the ruins of Saint Patrick's may have more value as a tourist attraction than the Cathedral did . . . . Not many good ruins in America . . . ."

Burke's fingers scratched at the cold, blue steel of the revolver in his pocket.

Martin went on, his eyes narrowing and long plumes of vapor exhaling from his nose and mouth. "And, of course, the funerals. Did you see Mountbatten's? Thousands of people weeping. We'll do something nice for Baxter, too. The Roman Church will do a splendid job for the Cardinal and the priest. Malone . . . well, who knows?"

Burke said, "You're not tightly wrapped, you know that?"

Martin lit another cigarette, and Burke saw the match quivering in the dark. Martin spoke in a more controlled voice. "You don't seem to understand. One has to spread the suffering, make it more universal before you get a sense of outrage." Martin looked at his glowing cigarette. "One needs a magnificent disaster— Dunkirk, Pearl Harbor, Coventry, Saint Patrick's . . ." He knocked the ash from his cigarette and stared down at the gray smudge on the ice-covered table. ". . . And from those ashes rises a new dedication." He looked up. "You may have noticed the phoenix on the bronze ceremonial door of Saint Patrick's. It inspired me to name this Operation Phoenix."

Burke said, "Flynn may accept the compromise. He hinted as much to me. He may also make a public statement about how British treachery almost got everyone killed."

"He wouldn't admit that the greatest IRA operation since Mountbatten's murder was planned by an Englishman."

"He doesn't want to die quite as badly as you want him to die. He'll take what he's already gotten and come out of there a hero." Burke took another drink to fire his imagination. "On the other hand . . . there's still the possibility that he may destroy the place at dawn. So the Mayor and Governor want to carry out a preemptive strike. Soon. But they need encouragement. They won't move unless Bellini says he can bring it off. But Bellini won't say that unless he gets the blue-prints and the architect...."

Martin smiled. "Very good. It's hereditary, I see—I mean the ability to manufacture heaps of malarkey at the drop of a hat."

"If we don't have the architect, we won't attack. At 6:03 Flynn will call a time out, wait until the city is full of people and the morning TV shows are rolling, then magnanimously spare the Cathedral and hostages. No funerals, no bangs, not even a broken stained-glass window."

"At 6:03 something more dreadful will happen."

"One gambles."

Martin shook his head. "I don't know.... Now you've got me worried, Lieutenant. It would be just like that bastard to doublecross me...." He smiled. "Well, double-cross may not be the word.... These people are so erratic...you never know, do you? I mean, historically they always opt for the most reckless—"

Burke said, "You've got these Micks pretty well fig-ured out, don't you, Major?"

"Well...no racial generalities intended, to be sure, but...I don't know..." He seemed to be weighing the possibilities. "The question is—do I gamble on an explosion at 6:03 or settle for a good battle before then...?"

Burke came closer to Martin. "Let me put it this way...." He breathed a long stream of cold fog in Martin's face. "If the Cathedral goes down"—he pulled his pistol, cocked it, and pressed it to Martin's temple—"then you're what we call a dead mother-fucker."

Martin faced Burke. "If anything happened to me, you'd be killed."

"I know the rules." He tapped Martin on the forehead with the muzzle of the revolver, then holstered it.

Martin flipped his cigarette away and spoke in a businesslike tone. "In exchange for Stillway I want your word that you'll do everything you can to see that the assault is carried out before Flynn makes any overtures toward a compromise. You have his confidence, I know, so use that in any way you can—with him or with your superiors. And no matter what happens, you'll make certain that Flynn is not captured alive. Understood?"

Burke nodded.

Martin added, "You'll have Stillway and the blueprints in ample time, and to show you what a good sport I am, I'll give all this to you personally. As I said yesterday morning, you can look good with your superiors. God knows, Lieutenant, you need the boost."

Martin moved away from Burke and looked down at Ferguson's frozen body. He lit another cigarette and dropped the match carelessly on Ferguson's face. He looked at Burke. "You're thinking, of course, that like our late friend here, you know too much. But it's all right. I'm willing—obligated—to make an exception in your case. You're one of us—a professional, not an amateur busybody like Mr. Ferguson or a dangerous insurgent like Mr. Flynn. So act like a professional, Lieutenant, and you'll be treated like one."

Burke said, "Thank you for setting me straight. I'll do my best."

Martin laughed. "You can do your worst, if you

like. I'm not counting only on you to see that things go my way. Lieutenant, there are more surprises inside and outside that Cathedral than even you suspect. And at first light, it will all unfold." He nodded his head. "Good evening." He turned and walked away at a leisurely pace.

Burke looked down at Ferguson. He bent over and picked the match from his face. "Sorry, Jack."

CHAPTER 50

The clock in the rear of the choir loft struck 3:00 a.m. Brian Flynn tolled the hour, then stood and looked at Leary sitting on the parapet, his legs swinging out into space three stories above the main floor. Flynn said, "If you nod off, you'll fall."

Leary answered without turning. "That's right."

Flynn looked around for Megan but didn't see her. He moved around the organ, picked up a rifle, and walked toward Leary.

Leary suddenly spun around and swung his legs into the choir loft. He said, "That's an old trick."

Flynn felt his body tense.

Leary continued. "Learned it in the army. You perch in a position that will get you hurt or killed if you fall asleep. Keeps you awake...usually."

"Interesting." He moved past Leary and entered the bell tower, then took the elevator down to the vestibule. He walked up the center aisle, his footsteps echoing in the quiet Cathedral. Sullivan, Boland, and Farrell were leaning out over the triforia. Hickey was asleep at the chancel organ. Flynn passed through the open gate of the communion rail and mounted the steps. The four hostages slept in pairs on opposite sides of the sanctuary. He glanced over at Baxter beside Maureen and watched the steady rise and fall of her chest, then looked up at where the Cardinal and Father Murphy lay cuffed to the throne, sleeping. Flynn knelt beside Maureen and stared down at her bruised face. He sensed that eyes were watching him from the high places, that Megan was watching from the dark, and that Leary's scope was centered on his lips. Flynn leaned over, his back to Leary, and positioned himself to block Leary's view of Maureen. He stroked her cheek.

She opened her eyes and looked up at him. "What time is it?"

"Late."

She said, "You've let it become late."

He said quietly, "I'm sorry...I couldn't help you..."

She turned her face away. Neither one spoke, then Maureen said, "This standoff with the police is like one of those games of nerve with autos racing toward each other, each driver hypnotized by the other's approach—and at one minute to dawn...is anyone going to veer off?"

"Bloody nonsense. This is war. Bloody stupid women, you think men play games of ego—"

"War?" She grabbed his shirt and her voice rose. "Let me tell *you* about *war*. It's not fought in churches with handcuffed hostages. And as long as you're talking about war, I'm still enough of a soldier to know they may not wait for dawn—they may be burrowing in here *right now*, and within the time it takes to draw your next breath this place could be filled with gunfire and you could be filled with bullets." She released his shirt. "War, indeed. You know no more about war than you do about love."

Flynn stood and looked at Baxter. "Do you like this man?"

She nodded. "He's a good man."

Flynn stared off at some point in the distance. "A good man," he repeated. "Someone meeting me for the first time might say that—as long as my history wasn't known." He stared down at her. "You don't like me much right now, but it's all right. I hope you survive, I even hope Baxter survives, and I hope you get on well together."

She lay on her back looking up at him. "Again, neither you nor I believe a word of that."

Flynn stepped away from her. "I have to go . . . ." He looked over the sanctuary rail at Hickey and said suddenly, "Tell me about him. What's the old man been saying? What about the confessional buzzer?"

Maureen cleared her throat and spoke in a businesslike voice, relating what she had discovered about John Hickey. She added her conclusions. "Even if you win, he'll somehow make certain everyone dies." She added, "All four of us believe that, or we wouldn't have risked so much to escape."

Flynn's eyes drifted back to Hickey, then he looked around the sanctuary at the hostages, the bouquets of now-wilting green carnations, and the bloodstains on the marble below the high altar. He had the feeling he had seen this all before, experienced something similar in a dream or vision, and he remembered that he *had*, in Whitehorn Abbey. He shook off the impression and looked at Maureen.

Flynn knelt suddenly and unlocked the handcuff. "Come with me." He helped her up and supported her as he walked toward the sacristy stairs.

He was aware that Hickey was watching from the chancel organ, and that Leary and Megan were watching also, from the shadows of the choir loft. He knew that they were thinking he was going to let Maureen go. And this, he understood, as everyone who was watching understood, was a critical juncture, a test of his position as leader. Would those three in any way try to restrict his movements? A few hours before they wouldn't have dared.

He reached the sacristy stairs and paused, not hesitantly but defiantly, and looked up into the loft, then back at the chancel organ. No one made a sound or a movement, and he waited purposely, staring into the Cathedral, then descended the steps. He stopped on the landing beside Gallagher. "Take a break, Frank."

Gallagher looked at him and at Maureen, and Flynn could see in Gallagher's expression a look of understanding and approval. Gallagher's eyes met Maureen's; he started to speak but then turned and hurried up the stairs.

Flynn looked down the remaining steps at the chained gate, then faced Maureen.

She realized that Brian Flynn had reasserted himself, imposed his will on the others. And she knew also that he was going to go a step further. He was going to free her, but she didn't know if he was doing it for her or for himself, or to demonstrate that he could do anything he damned well pleased—to show that he was Finn MacCumail, Chief of the Fenians. She walked down the staircase and stopped at the gate. Flynn followed and gestured toward the sacristy. "Two worlds meet here, the worlds of the sacred and the profaned, the living and the dead. Have ever such divergent worlds been separated by so little?"

She stared into the quiet sacristy and saw a votive candle flickering on the altar of the priests' chapel, the vestment tables lining the walls, covered with neatly folded white and purple vestments of the Lenten season. Easter, she thought. *The spring. The Resurrection and the life.* She looked at Flynn.

He said, "Will you choose life? Will you go without the others?"

She nodded. "Yes, I'll go."

He hesitated, then drew the keys from his pocket. With a hand that was unsteady he unlocked the gate's lock and the chain's padlock, and began unwinding the chain. He rolled back the left gate and scanned the corridor openings but saw no sign of the police. "Hurry."

She took his arm. "I'll go, but not without you."

He looked at her, then said, "You'd leave the others to go with me?"

"Yes."

"Could you do that and live with yourself?"

"Yes."

He stared at the open gate. "I'd be imprisoned for a long time. Could you wait?"

"Yes."

"You love me?"

"Yes."

He reached out for her, but she moved quickly up the stairs and stopped halfway to the landing. "You'll not push me out. We leave together."

He stood looking up at her silhouetted against the light of the crypt doors. "I can't go."

"Not even for me? I'd go with you—for you. Won't you do the same?"

"I *can't*...for God's sake, Maureen...I *can't*. Please, if you love me, go. Go!"

"Together. One way or the other, *together*."

He looked down and shook his head and, after what seemed like a long time, heard her footsteps retreating up the stairs.

He relocked the gate and followed, and when he walked up to the altar sanctuary, he found her lying beside Baxter again, the cuff locked on her wrist and her eyes closed.

Flynn came down from the sanctuary and walked to a pew in the center of the Cathedral and sat, staring at the high altar. It struck him that the things most men found trying—leadership, courage, the ability to seize their own destiny—came easily to him, a gift, he thought, of the gods. But love—so basic an emotion that even unexceptional men were blessed with loving women, children, friends—that had always eluded him. And the one time it had not eluded him it had been so difficult as to be painful, and to make the pain stop he made the love stop through the sheer force of his will. Yet it came back, again and again. *Amor vincit omnia*, as Father Michael used to preach. He shook his head. *No, I've conquered love.*

He felt very empty inside. But at the same time, to

his horror and disgust, he felt very good about being in command of himself and his world again.

He sat in the pew for a long time.

Flynn looked down at Pedar Fitzgerald, lying in a curled position at the side of the organ console, a blanket drawn up to his blood-encrusted chin. Flynn moved beside John Hickey, who lay slumped over the organ keyboard, and stared down at Hickey's pale, almost waxen face. The field phone rang, and Hickey stirred. It rang again, and Flynn grabbed it.

Mullins's voice came over the line. "I'm back in the bell room. Is that it for the bells, then?"

"Yes.... How does it look outside?"

Mullins said, "Very quiet below. But out farther...there're still people in the streets."

Flynn heard a note of wonder in the young man's voice. "They celebrate late, don't they? We've given them a Saint Patrick's Day to remember."

Mullins said, "There wasn't even a *curfew*."

Flynn smiled. America reminded him of the *Titanic*, a three-hundred-foot gash in her side, listing badly, but they were still serving drinks in the lounge. "It's not like Belfast, is it?"

"No."

"Can you sense any anxiety down there...movement...?"

Mullins considered, then said, "No, they look relaxed yet. Cold and tired for sure, but at ease. No passing of orders, none of that stiffness you see before an attack."

"How are you holding up against the cold?"

"I'm past that."

"Well, you and Rory will be the first to see the dawn break."

Mullins had given up on the dawn hours ago. "Aye, the dawn from the bell tower of Saint Patrick's in New York. That needs a poem."

"You'll tell me it later." He hung up and picked up the extension phone. "Get me Captain Schroeder, please." He looked at Hickey's face as the operator routed the call. Awake, the face was expressive, alive, but asleep it looked like a death mask.

Schroeder's voice came through sounding slurred. "Yes..."

"Flynn here. Did I wake you?"

"No, sir. We've been waiting for Mr. Hickey's hourly call. He said...but I'm glad you called. I've been wanting to speak to you."

"Thought I was dead, did you?"

"Well, no.... You were on the bells, right?"

"How did I sound out there?"

Schroeder cleared his throat. "You show promise."

Flynn laughed. "Well, can it be you're developing a sense of humor, Captain?" Schroeder laughed self-consciously.

"Or is it that you're so relieved to be talking to me instead of Hickey that you're giddy?"

Schroeder didn't answer.

Flynn said, "How are they faring in the capitals?"

Schroeder's tone was reserved. "They're wondering why you haven't responded to what Inspector Langley related to you."

"I'm afraid we aren't very clear on that."

"I can't elaborate over the phone."

"I see.... Well, why don't you come to the sacristy gate, then, and we'll talk."

There was a long pause. "I'm not at liberty to do that.... It's against regulations."

"So is burning down a cathedral, which is what will happen if we don't speak, Captain."

"You don't understand, Mr. Flynn. There are carefully worked out rules...as I think you know.... And the negotiator cannot expose himself to...to..."

"I won't kill you."

"Well...I know you won't...but...Listen, you and Lieutenant Burke have...Would you like to speak with him at the gate?"

"No, I would like to speak with *you* at the gate."

"I..."

"Aren't you even curious to see me?"

"Curiosity plays no part—"

"Doesn't it? It seems to me, Captain, that you of all people would recognize the value of eyeball-to-eyeball contact."

"There's no special value in—"

"How many wars would have been avoided if the chiefs could have just seen the other man's face, touched each other, got a whiff of the other fellow's sweaty fear?"

Schroeder said, "Hold on."

Flynn heard the phone click, then a minute later Schroeder's voice came through. "Okay."

"Five minutes." Flynn hung up and poked Hickey roughly. "Were you listening?"

Flynn took Hickey's arm in a tight grip. "Someday,

you old bastard, you'll tell me about the confessional, and the things you've been saying to Schroeder and the things you've been saying to my people and to the hostages. And you'll tell me about the compromise that was offered us."

Hickey flinched and straightened up. "Let go! These old bones snap easily."

"I may snap the ones in your neck."

Hickey looked up at Flynn, no trace of pain in his face. "Careful. Be careful."

Flynn released his arm and pushed it away. "You don't frighten me."

Hickey didn't answer but stared at Flynn with undisguised malice in his eyes.

Flynn met his stare, then looked down at Pedar Fitzgerald. "Are you looking after him?"

Hickey didn't answer.

Flynn stared closely at Fitzgerald's face and saw it was white—waxy, like Hickey's. "He's dead." He turned to Hickey.

Hickey said without emotion, "Died about an hour ago."

"Megan..."

"When Megan calls, I tell her he's all right, and she believes that because she wants to. But eventually..."

Flynn looked up at Megan in the loft. "My God, she'll..." He turned back to Hickey. "We should have gotten a doctor...."

Hickey replied, "If you weren't so wrapped up in your fucking bells, you could have done just that."

Flynn looked at him. "*You* could have—"

"*Me?* What the hell do I care if he lives or dies?"

Flynn stepped back from him, and his mind began to reel.

Hickey said, "What do you see, Brian? Is it very frightening?" He laughed and lit his pipe.

Flynn moved farther away from Hickey into the ambulatory and tried to get his thoughts under control. He reevaluated each person in the Cathedral until he was certain he knew each one's motives...potential for treachery...loyalties and weaknesses. His mind focused finally on Leary, and he asked the questions he should have asked months ago: Why was Leary here? Why would a professional killer trap himself in a perch with no way out? Leary had to be holding a card no one even knew existed. Flynn wiped the sweat from his brow and walked up to the sanctuary.

Hickey called out, "Are you going to tell Schroeder about his darling daughter? Tell him for me—use these exact words—tell him his daughter is a dead bitch!"

Flynn descended the stairs behind the altar. Gallagher stood on the crypt landing, an M-16 slung across his chest. Flynn said, "There's coffee in the bookshop." Gallagher climbed the stairs, and Flynn went down the remaining steps to the gate. Parts of the chain had been pieced together, and a new padlock was clamped to it. He examined the gate's mangled lock; another bullet or two and it would have sprung. But there were only fifty rounds in the drum of a Thompson. Not fifty-one, but fifty.... And an M-72 rocket could take a Saracen, and the Red Bus to Clady on the Shankill Road went past Whitehorn Abbey...and it was all supposed to be haphazard, random, with no meaning...

Flynn stared into the sacristy. He heard men speaking in the side corridors, and footsteps approached from the center opening in the left wall. Schroeder stepped into the sacristy, looked around, turned toward Flynn, and walked deliberately up the stairs. He stood on the steps below the gates, his eyes fixed on Flynn's. A long time passed before Flynn spoke. "Am I as you pictured me?"

Schroeder replied stiffly, "I've seen a photo of you."

"And I of you. But am I as you *pictured* me?"

Schroeder shook his head. Another long silence developed, then Flynn spoke abruptly. "I'm going to reach into my pocket." Flynn took the microphone sensor and passed it over Schroeder. "This is a very private conversation."

"I will report everything said here."

"I would bet my life you don't."

Schroeder seemed perplexed and wary.

Flynn said, "Are they any closer to meeting our demands?"

Schroeder didn't like face-to-face negotiating. He knew, because people had told him, that his face revealed too much. He cleared his throat. "You're asking the impossible. Accept the compromise."

Flynn noticed the extra firmness in Schroeder's voice, the lack of sir or mister, and the discomfort. "What *is* the compromise?"

Schroeder's eyebrows rose slightly. "Didn't Hickey—"

"Just tell it to me again."

Schroeder related the offer and added, "Take it before the British change their minds about parole. And for yourselves, low bail is as good as immunity. For

God's sake, man, no one has ever been offered more in a hostage situation."

Flynn nodded. "Yes.... Yes, it's a good offer—tempting—"

"Take it! Take it before someone is killed—"

"It's a little late for that, I'm afraid."

"What?"

"Sir Harold murdered a lad named Pedar. Luckily no one knows he's dead except Hickey and myself... and I suppose Pedar knows he's dead.... Well, when my people discover he's dead, they'll want to kill Baxter. Pedar's sister, Megan, will want to do much worse. This complicates things somewhat."

Schroeder passed his hand over his face. "God... listen, I'm sure it was unintentional."

"Harry bashed his throat in with a rifle butt. Could have been an accident, I suppose. It doesn't make the lad any less dead."

Schroeder's mind was racing. He swore to himself, *Baxter, you stupid bastard.*

"Look... it's a case of a POW trying to escape.... It's Baxter's duty to try.... You're a soldier..."

Flynn said nothing.

"Here's a chance for you to show professionalism... to show you're not a common crim—" He checked himself. "To show mercy, and—"

Flynn interrupted. "Schroeder, you are most certainly part Irish. I've rarely met a man more possessed of so much ready bullshit for every occasion."

"I'm serious—"

"Well, Baxter's fate depends mostly on what you do now."

"No. It depends on what *you* do. The next move is yours."

"And I'm about to make it." He lit a cigarette and asked, "How far are they along in their attack plans?"

Schroeder said, "That's not an option for us."

Flynn stared at him. "Caught you in a lie—your left eye is twitching. God, Schroeder, your nose is getting longer." He laughed. "I should have had you down here hours ago. Burke was too cool."

"Look—you asked me here for a private meeting, so you must have something to say—"

"I want you to help us get what we want."

Schroeder looked exasperated. "That's what I've been *doing.*"

"No, I mean *everything* we want. Your heart isn't in it. If the negotiations fail, you don't lose nearly as much as everyone in here does. Or as much as Bellini's ESD. They stand to lose fifty to a hundred men in an attack."

Schroeder thought of his imprudent offer to Bellini. "There will be no attack."

"Did you know Burke told me he'd go with Bellini? There's a man with a great deal to lose if you fail. Would you go with Bellini?"

"Burke couldn't have said that because Bellini's not going *anywhere.*" Schroeder had the uneasy impression he was being drawn into something, but he had no intention of making a mistake this late. "I'll try to get more for you only if you give me another two hours after dawn."

Flynn ignored him and went on. "I thought I'd better give you a very personal motive to push those people into capitulation."

Schroeder looked at Flynn cautiously.

"You see, there's one situation you never covered in your otherwise detailed book, Captain." Flynn came closer to the gate. "Your daughter would very much like you to try harder."

"What...?"

"Terri Schroeder O'Neal. She wants you to try harder."

Schroeder stared for a few seconds, then said loudly, "What the hell are you talking about?"

"Lower your voice. You'll excite the police."

Schroeder spoke through clenched teeth. "What the *fuck* are you saying?"

"Please, you're in church." Flynn passed a scrap of paper through the bars.

Schroeder snatched it and read his daughter's handwriting: *Dad—I'm being held hostage by members of the Fenian Army. I'm all right. They won't harm me if everything goes okay at the Cathedral. Do your very best. I love you, Terri.*

Schroeder read the note again, then again. He felt his knees buckle, and he grabbed at the gate. He looked up at Flynn and tried to speak, but no sound came out.

Flynn spoke impassively. "Welcome to the Fenian Army, Captain Schroeder."

Schroeder swallowed several times and stared at the note.

"Sorry," said Flynn. "Really I am. You don't have to speak—just listen." Flynn lit another cigarette and spoke briskly. "What you have to do is make the strongest possible case for our demands. First, tell

them I've paraded two score of well-armed men and
women past you. Machine guns, rockets, grenades,
flamethrowers. Tell them we are ready, willing, and able
to take the entire six-hundred-man ESD down with
us, to destroy the Cathedral and kill the hostages. In
other words, scare the shit out of Joe Bellini and his
heroes. Understand?" He paused, then said, "They'll
never suspect that Captain Schroeder's report of seeing
a great number of well-armed soldiers is false. Use
your imagination—better yet, look up at the landing,
Schroeder. Picture forty, fifty men and women parading past that crypt door—picture those machine guns
and rockets and flamethrowers.... Go on, look up
there."

Schroeder looked, and Flynn saw in his eyes exactly
what he wanted to see.

After a minute Schroeder lowered his head. His face
was pale, and his hands pulled at his shirt and tie.

Flynn said, "Please calm down. You can save your
daughter's life only if you pull yourself together. That's
it. Now...if this doesn't work, if they are still committed to an assault, then threaten to go public—radio,
TV, newspapers. Tell Kline, Doyle, and all the rest of
them you're going to announce that in all your years
of hostage negotiating, that you, as the court of last
resort for the lives of hostages, strongly and in no un-
certain terms believe that neither an attack nor further
negotiations can save this situation. You will declare,
publicly, that therefore for the first time in your career
you urge capitulation—for humanitarian as well as tactical reasons."

Flynn watched Schroeder's face but could see nothing revealed there except anguish. He went on, "You have a good deal of influence—moral and professional—with the media, the police force, and the politicians. Use every bit of that influence. You must create the kind of pressure and climate that will force the British and American governments to surrender."

Schroeder's voice was barely audible. "Time...I need time.... Why didn't you give me more time...?"

"If I'd told you sooner, you wouldn't have made it through the night, or you may have told someone. The only time left is that which remains until the dawn—less if you can't stop the attack. But if you can get them to throw open the prison gates...Work on it."

Schroeder pushed his face to the bars. "Flynn...please...listen to me...."

Flynn went on. "Yes, I know that if you succeed and we walk out of here free, they'll certainly count us, and they'll wonder where all the flamethrowers are.... Well, you'll be embarrassed, but all's fair in love and war, and *c'est la guerre*, and all that rot. Don't even think that far ahead and don't be selfish."

Schroeder's head shook, and his words were incoherent. All that Flynn could make out was "Jail." Flynn said, "Your daughter can visit you on weekends." He added, "I'll even visit you."

Schroeder stared at him, and a choked-off sound rose in his throat.

Flynn said, "Sorry, that was low." He paused. "Look, if it means anything to you, I feel bad that I had to resort to this. But it wasn't going well, and I knew you'd want to help us, help Terri, if you understood the trouble she was in." Flynn's voice became stern. "She really ought to be more selective about her bunkmates. Children can be such an embarrassment to parents, especially parents in public life—sex, drugs, wild politics . . ."

Schroeder was shaking his head. "No . . . you don't have her. You're bluffing . . . ."

Flynn continued. "But she's safe enough for the moment. Dan—that's her friend's name—is kind, considerate, probably a passable lover. It's the lot of some soldiers to draw easy duty—others to fight and die. Throw of the dice and all that. Then again, I wouldn't want to be in Dan's place if he gets the order to put a bullet in the back of Terri's head. No kneecapping or any of that. She's innocent, and she'll get a quick bullet without knowing it's about to come. So, are we clear about what you have to do?"

Schroeder said, "I won't do it."

"As you wish." He turned and began walking up the stairs. He called back. "In about a minute a light will flash from the bell tower, and my men on the outside will telephone Dan, and . . . and that, I'm afraid, will be the end of Terri Schroeder." He continued up the stairs.

"Wait! Listen, maybe we can work this out. Hold on! Stop walking away!"

Flynn turned slowly. "I'm afraid this is not negotiable, Captain." He paused and said, "It's awkward when you're involved personally, isn't it? Did you ever consider that every man and woman you've negotiated with or for was involved personally? Well, I'm not going to take you to task for your past successes. You were dealing with criminals, and they probably deserved the shoddy deals you got for them. You and I deserve a better deal. Our fates are intertwined, our goals are the same—aren't they? Yes or no, Captain? Quickly!"

Schroeder nodded.

Flynn moved down the stairs. "Good decision." He came close to the gate and put his hand out. Schroeder looked at it but shook his head. "Never."

Flynn withdrew his hand. "All right, then...all right...."

Schroeder said, "Can I go now?"

"Yes.... Oh, one more thing. It's quite possible you'll fail even if you dwell on the flamethrowers and threaten public statements and all that...so we should plan for failure."

Schroeder's face showed that he understood what was coming.

Flynn's voice was firm and businesslike. "If Bellini is to attack, in spite of everything you can do to stop it, then I'll give you another way to save Terri's life."

"No."

"Yes, I'm afraid you'll have to get down here and tell me when, where, how, that sort of thing—"

"No! No, I would never—never get police officers killed—"

"They'll get killed anyway. And so will the hostages and the Fenians and Terri. So if you want to at least save her, you'll give me the operational plans."

"They won't tell me—"

"Make it your business to know. The easier solution is to scare Bellini out of his fucking mind and get *him* to refuse. You've a great many options. I wish I had as many."

Schroeder wiped his brow. His breathing was erratic, and his voice was shaky. "Flynn ... please ... I'll move heaven and earth to get them to surrender—I swear to God I will—but if they don't listen—" He drew up his body. "Then I won't betray them. Never. Even if it means Terri—"

Flynn reached out and grabbed Schroeder by the arm. "Use your head, man. If they're repulsed once, they aren't likely to try again. They're not marines or royal commandos. If I beat them back, then Washington, the Vatican, and other concerned countries will pressure London. I can almost guarantee there'll be *fewer* police killed if I stop them in their tracks ... stop them before the battle gets too far along.... You *must* tell me if they've got the architect and the blueprints ... tell me if they will use gas, if they're going to cut off the lights.... You know what I need. And I'll put the hostages in the crypt for protection. I'll send a signal, and Terri will be freed within five minutes. I won't ask any more of you."

Schroeder's head shook.

Flynn reached out his other hand and laid it on Schroeder's shoulder. He spoke almost gently. "Long after we're dead, after what's happened here is only a dim memory to an uncaring world, Theresa will be alive, perhaps remarried—children, grandchildren. Step outside of what you feel now, Captain, and look into the future. Think of her and think also of your wife—Mary lives for that girl, Bert. She—"

Schroeder suddenly pulled away. "Shut up! For God's sake, shut up ...." He slumped forward, and his head rested against the bars.

Flynn patted him on the shoulder. "You're a decent man, Captain. An honest man. And you're a good father.... I hope you're still a father at dawn. Well...will you be?"

Schroeder nodded.

"Good. Go on, then, go back, have a drink. Get yourself together. It'll be all right. No, don't go thinking about your gun. Killing me or killing yourself won't solve anyone's problem but your own. Think about Terri and Mary. They need you and love you. See you later, Captain, God willing."

CHAPTER 51

Governor Doyle stood in a back room of the Cardinal's residence, a telephone in his hand. He listened to a succession of state officials: policemen, public relations people, legislators, the Attorney General, the commander of the state's National Guard. They spoke to him from Albany, from the state offices in Rockefeller Center, from their homes, and from their vacation hotels in warmer climates. All of these people, who normally couldn't decide on chicken or roast beef at a banquet, had decided that the time had come to storm the Cathedral. The Lieutenant Governor told him, frankly, if not tactfully, that his ratings in the polls were so low he had nothing to lose and could only gain by backing an assault on the Cathedral regardless of its success or failure. Doyle put the receiver into its cradle and regarded the people who were entering the room.

Kline, he noticed, had brought Spiegel, which meant a decision could be reached. Monsignor Downes took a seat beside Arnold Sheridan of the State Department. On the couch sat the Irish Consul General, Donahue, and the British Foreign

Office representative, Eric Palmer. Police Commissioner Rourke stood by the door until Kline pointed to a chair.

Doyle looked at Bartholomew Martin, who had no official status any longer but whom he had asked to be present. Martin, no matter what people were saying about him, could be counted on to supply the right information.

The Governor cleared his throat and said, "Gentlemen, Miss—Ms.—Spiegel, I've asked you here because I feel that *we* are the ones most immediately affected by this situation." He looked around the room. "And before we leave here, we're going to cut this Gordian knot." He made a slicing movement with his hand. "Cut through every tactical and strategic problem, political consideration, and moral dilemma that has paralyzed our will and our ability to *act*!" He paused, then turned to Monsignor Downes. "Father, would you repeat for everyone the latest news from Rome?"

Monsignor Downes said, "Yes. His Holiness is going to make a personal appeal to the Fenians, as Christians, to spare the Cathedral and the lives of the hostages. He will also appeal to the governments involved to show restraint and will place at their disposal the facilities of the Vatican where they and the Fenians can continue their negotiations."

Major Martin broke the silence. "The heads of state of the three governments involved are making a point of *not* speaking directly to these terrorists—"

The Monsignor waved his hand in a gesture of dismissal. "His Holiness would not be speaking as head of the Vatican State but as a world spiritual leader."

The British representative, Palmer, said, "Such an appeal would place the American President and the Prime Ministers of Ireland and Britain in a difficult—"

Monsignor Downes was becoming agitated by the negative response. "His Holiness feels the Church must do what it can for these outcasts because that has been our mission for two thousand years—these are the people who need us." He handed a sheet of paper to the Governor. "This is the text of His Holiness's appeal."

Governor Doyle read the short message and passed it to Mayor Kline.

Monsignor Downes said, "We would like that delivered to the people inside the Cathedral at the same time it's read on radio and television. Within the next hour—before dawn."

After everyone in the room had seen the text of the Pope's appeal, Eric Palmer said, "Some years ago, we actually did meet secretly with the IRA, and they made it public. The repercussions rocked the government. I don't think we're going to speak with them again—certainly not at the Vatican."

Donahue spoke with a tone of sadness in his voice. "Monsignor, the Dublin government outlawed the IRA in the 1920s, and I don't think Dublin will back the Vatican on this...."

Martin said, "As you know we've actually passed on a compromise to them, and they've not responded. The Pope can save himself and all of us a great deal of embarrassment if he withholds this plea."

Mayor Kline added, "The only way the Fenians can

go to the Vatican is if I *let* them go. And I can't do that. I have to enforce the law."

Arnold Sheridan spoke for the first time, and the tone of his voice suggested a final policy position. "The government of the United States has reason to believe that federal firearm and passport laws have been violated, but otherwise it's purely a local affair. We're not going anywhere to discuss the release of Irish prisoners in the United Kingdom or immunity from prosecution for the people in the Cathedral."

Spiegel looked at Downes. "The only place negotiations can be held is right here—on the phone or at the sacristy gate. It is the policy of the police in this city to contain a hostage situation—not let it become mobile. And it is the law to arrest criminals at the first possible opportunity. In other words, the trenches are dug, and no one is leaving them under a truce flag."

The Monsignor pursed his lips and nodded. "I understand your positions, but the Church, which many of you consider so ironbound, is willing to try *anything*. I think you should know that personal appeals to all parties involved will be forthcoming from the Archbishop of Canterbury, the Primate of Ireland, and from hundreds of other religious leaders of every faith and denomination. And in almost every church and synagogue in this city and in other cities, all-night prayer vigils have been called. And at 5:00 a.m., if it's not over by then, every church bell in this city, and probably in the country, will begin ringing—ringing for sanity, for mercy, and for all of us."

Roberta Spiegel stood and lit a cigarette. "The mood of the people, notwithstanding bells and singing in the streets, is very hard line. If we take a soft approach and it explodes in our faces at 6:03, all of us will be out on our asses, and there'll be no all-night prayer vigils for us." She paused, then said, "So let's cut through the bullshit—or the Gordian knot—and decide how and when we're going to attack, and get our stories straight for afterward."

Cigarettes were being lit, and Major Martin was helping himself to the Cardinal's sherry.

The Governor nodded appreciatively. "I admire your honesty and perception, Ms. Spiegel, and—"

She looked at him. "This is why you asked us here, so let's get on with it, Governor."

Governor Doyle flushed but controlled his anger and said, "Good idea." He looked around. "Then we all agree that a compromise is not an option, that the Fenians won't surrender, and that they'll carry out their threats at dawn?"

There were some tentative nods.

The Governor looked at Arnold Sheridan and said, "I'm on my own?"

Sheridan nodded.

Doyle said, "But—off the record—the administration would like to see a hard-line approach?"

Sheridan said, "The message the government wants to convey is that this sort of thing will always be met by force—local force." Sheridan walked to the door. "Thank you, Governor, for the opportunity to contribute to the discussion. I'm sure you'll reach the right decision." He left.

Mayor Kline watched the door close and said, "We've been cut adrift." He turned to Donahue and Palmer. "You see, the federal system works marvelously—they collect taxes and pass laws, Mayor Kline fights terrorists."

Kline stood and began pacing. He stopped in front of Donahue and Palmer. "Do you understand that it is in my power, as the duly elected Mayor of this city, to order an assault on that Cathedral?"

Neither man responded.

Kline's voice rose. "It is my *duty*. And I don't have to answer to *anyone*."

Eric Palmer stood and moved toward the door. "We've offered all the compromises we can.... And if this is, as you indicate, a local matter, then there's no reason for Her Majesty's government to involve itself any further." He looked at Martin, who made no move to follow, then nodded to the others. "Good morning." He walked out.

Tomas Donahue stood. "I feel bad about all of this.... I've lived in this city for five years.... Saint Patrick's is my parish church.... I know the Cardinal and Father Murphy...." He looked at Monsignor Downes. "But there's *nothing* I can do." He walked to the door and turned back. "If you need me, I'll be in the consulate. God bless...." He left quickly.

Spiegel said, "Nice clean exits."

Governor Doyle hooked his thumbs on his vest pockets. "Well...there it is." He turned to Martin. "Major...won't you give us your thoughts.... As a man who is familiar with the IRA...what would be your course of action?"

Martin said without preamble, "It's time you discussed a rescue operation."

The Governor nodded slowly, aware that the phrase "rescue operation," as opposed to attack or assault, was a subtle turning point. The phraseology for the coming action was being introduced and refined. He turned abruptly to Monsignor Downes. "Are you willing to give your blessing to a rescue operation?"

The Monsignor looked up quickly. "Am I...? Well..."

Governor Doyle moved close to Downes. "Monsignor, in times of crisis it's often people like ourselves, at the middle levels, who get stuck holding the bag. And *we* have to act. Not to act is more immoral than to act with force." He added. "Rescue, we have to *rescue*—"

Monsignor Downes said, "But...the Papal plea..."

Mayor Kline spoke from across the room. "I don't want to see the Pope or the other religious leaders make fools of themselves. If God himself pleaded with these Fenians, it would make no difference."

The Monsignor ran his hands across his cheeks. "But why *me*...? What difference does it make what *I* say?"

Kline cleared his throat. "To be perfectly honest with you, Monsignor, I won't do a damned thing to rescue those people or save that Cathedral unless I have the blessing of a ranking member of the Catholic clergy. A Monsignor will do, preferably Irish like yourself. I'm no fool, and neither are you."

Monsignor Downes slumped into his chair. "Oh God..."

Rourke rose from his chair and walked to Downes.

He knelt beside the Monsignor's chair and spoke with anguish in his voice. "My boys are mostly Catholic, Father. If they have to go in here...they'll want to see you first...to make their confessions...to know that someone from the Church is blessing their mission. Otherwise, they'll...I don't know...."

Monsignor Downes put his face in his hands. After a full minute he looked up and nodded slowly. "God help me, but if you think it's the only way to save them..." He stood suddenly and almost ran from the room.

For a few seconds no one spoke, then Spiegel said, "Let's move before things start coming apart."

Mayor Kline was rubbing his chin thoughtfully. He looked up. "Schroeder will have to state that he's failed absolutely."

Governor Doyle said, "That should be no problem. He has." He added, "It would help also if we put out a news release—concurrent with the rescue—that the Fenians have made *new* demands in addition to the ones we were willing to discuss—" He stopped abruptly. "Damn it, there are *tapes* of every phone conversation.... Maybe Burke can—"

Kline interrupted. "Forget Burke. Schroeder is speaking in person to Flynn right now. That will give Schroeder the opportunity to state that Flynn has made a set of new demands."

The Governor nodded. "Yes, very good."

Kline said, "I'll have Bellini report in writing that he believes that there's a good chance of carrying out a rescue with a minimum loss of life and property."

Doyle said, "But Bellini's like a yo-yo. He keeps changing his mind—" He looked sharply at Rourke. "Will he write such a statement?"

Rourke's tone was anxious. "He'll carry out any orders to attack…but as for signing any statement…he's a difficult man. I know his position is that he needs more solid intelligence before he says he *approves*—"

Major Martin said, "Lieutenant Burke tells me he's very close to an intelligence breakthrough."

Everyone looked at Martin.

Martin continued. "He'll have at least the blueprints, perhaps the architect himself, within the next hour. I can almost guarantee it." Martin's tone suggested that he didn't want to be pressed further.

Kline said, "What we need from Inspector Langley are psy-profiles showing that half the terrorists in there are psychotic."

Governor Doyle said, "Will these police officers cooperate?"

Spiegel answered. "I'll take care of Langley. As for Schroeder, he's very savvy and politically attuned. No problem there. Regarding Bellini, we'll offer a promotion and transfer to wherever he wants." Spiegel walked toward the telephone. "I'll get the media right now and tell them that the negotiations are reaching a critical stage and it's absolutely essential they delay on those Church appeals."

Doyle said almost smugly, "At least I know *my* man, Logan, will do what he is told." He turned to Kline. "Don't forget, I want a piece of this, Murray. At least one squad has to be from the Sixty-ninth."

Mayor Kline looked out the window. "Are we doing the right thing? Or have we all gone crazy?"

Martin said, "You'd be crazy to wait for dawn." He added, "It's odd, isn't it, that the others didn't want to share this with us?"

Roberta Spiegel looked up as she dialed. "Some rats have perceived a sinking ship and jumped off. Other rats have perceived a bandwagon and jumped on. Before the sun rises, we'll know which rats saw things more clearly."

* * *

Bert Schroeder sat at his desk in the Monsignor's office. Langley, Bellini, and Colonel Logan stood, listening to Mayor Kline and Governor Doyle tell them what was expected of them. Schroeder's eyes darted from Kline to Doyle as his thoughts raced wildly.

Roberta Spiegel sat in her rocker staring into the disused fireplace, absently twirling a brandy snifter in her hands. The room had grown cold, and she had Langley's jacket draped over her shoulders.

Major Martin stood at the fireplace, occupied with the curios on the mantel.

Police Commissioner Rourke stood beside the Mayor, nodding agreement at everything Kline and Doyle said, trying to elicit similar nodding from his three officers.

The Governor stopped speaking and looked at Schroeder a moment. Something about the man suggested a dormant volcano. He tried to gauge his reaction. "Bert?"

Schroeder's eyes focused on the Governor.

Doyle said, "Bert, this is no reflection on you, but if dawn comes and there's no compromise, no extension of the deadline—and there won't be—and the hostages are *executed* and the Cathedral *demolished*...well, it will be *you*, Bert, who'll get most of the public abuse. Won't it?"

Schroeder said nothing.

Mayor Kline turned to Langley. "And it will be *you*, Inspector, who will get a great deal of the official censure."

"Be that as it may—"

Bellini said heatedly, "We can handle criminals, Your Honor, but these are guerrillas armed with military ordnance—intrusion alarms, submachine guns, rockets, and...and God knows what else. What if they have flamethrowers? Huh? And they're holed up in a national shrine. Christ, I still don't understand why the army can't—" The Mayor put a restraining hand on Bellini with a look of disappointment. "Joe...Joe, this is not like you."

Bellini said, "It sure as hell is."

Governor Doyle looked at Logan, who appeared uncomfortable. "Colonel? What's *your* feel?"

Colonel Logan came to a modified position of attention. "Oh...well...I am convinced that we should act without delay to mount an att—a rescue operation."

The Governor beamed.

"However," continued Logan, "the tactical plan is not sound. What you're asking us to do is like...like shooting rats in a china cabinet without breaking the china...or the cabinet...."

The Governor stared at Logan, his bushy eyebrows rising in an arc like squirrel tails. "Soldiers are often asked to do the impossible—and to do it well. National Guard duty is not all parades and happy hours."

"No, sir...yes, sir."

"Can the Fighting Irish hold up their end of the operation?"

"Of course!"

The Governor slapped Logan's shoulder soundly. "Good man."

The Mayor turned to Langley. "Inspector, you will have to come up with the dossiers we need on the Fenians."

Langley hesitated.

Roberta Spiegel fixed her eyes on him. "By no later than noon, Inspector." Langley looked at her. "Sure. Why not? I'll do some creative writing with the help of a discreet police psychologist— Dr. Korman—and come up with psy-profiles of the Fenians that would scare the hell out of John Hickey himself."

Major Martin said, "May I suggest, Inspector, that you also show a link between the death of that informer—Ferguson, I think his name was—and the Fenians? That will tidy up that business as well."

Langley looked at Martin and understood. He nodded.

Kline looked at Bellini. "Well, Joe...are you on our team?"

Bellini looked troubled. "I am...but..."

"Joe, can you honestly say that you're absolutely

convinced these terrorists will not shoot the Cardinal and the others at dawn and then blow up Saint Patrick's Cathedral?"

"No . . . but—"

"Are you convinced your men cannot conduct a successful rescue operation?"

"I never said anything like that, Your Honor. I just won't sign anything . . . . Since when are people required to sign something like that?"

The Mayor patted his shoulder gently. "Should I get someone *else* to lead your men against the terrorists in a rescue operation, Joe? Or should I just let Colonel Logan handle the whole operation?"

Bellini's mind was filled with conflicting thoughts, all of them unhappy.

Spiegel snapped, "Yes or no, Captain? It's getting late, and the fucking sun is due at 6:03."

Bellini looked at her and straightened his posture. "I'll lead the attack. If I get the blueprints, then I'll decide if I'm going to sign anything."

Mayor Kline let out a deep breath. "Well, that's about it." He looked at Langley. "You'll of course reconsider your resignation."

Langley said, "Actually, I was thinking about chief inspector."

Kline nodded quickly. "Certainly. There'll be promotions for everyone after this."

Langley lit a cigarette and noticed his hands were unsteady. Kline and Doyle, he was convinced, were doing the right thing in attacking the Cathedral. But with the sure instincts of the politician, they were doing it for the wrong reasons, in the wrong way, and going about it in a slimy manner. But so what? That was how half the right things got done.

Mayor Kline was smiling now. He turned to Schroeder. "Bert, all we need from you is some more time. Keep talking to them. You're doing a hell of a job, Bert, and we appreciate it.... Captain?" He smiled at Schroeder the way he always smiled at someone he had caught not paying attention. "Bert?"

Schroeder's eyes focused on Kline, but he said nothing.

Mayor Kline regarded him with growing apprehension. "Now...now, Bert, I need a signed statement from you saying that it is your professional opinion, based on years of hostage negotiating, that you recommend a cessation of negotiations. Right?"

Schroeder looked around the room and made an unintelligible noise.

The Mayor seemed anxious but went on. "You should indicate that when you saw Flynn he made *more* demands...crazy demands. Okay? Write that up as soon as possible." He turned to the others. "All of you—"

"I won't do that."

Everyone in the room looked at Schroeder. Kline said incredulously, "What—what did you say?"

Roberta Spiegel stood quickly, sending the rocker sliding into Governor Doyle.

Doyle moved the rocker aside and approached Schroeder. "Those are true statements! And you haven't accomplished shit so far!"

Schroeder stood and steadied himself against the desk. "I've listened to all of you, and you're all crazy."

Spiegel said to Langley, "Get the backup negotiator."

Schroeder shouted, "No! No one can speak with Flynn but me.... He won't speak to anyone else.... You'll see he won't speak.... I'll call him now...." He reached for the telephone, but Langley pulled it away. Schroeder fell back in his chair.

Mayor Kline looked stunned. He tried to speak but couldn't get a word out.

Spiegel moved around the desk and looked down at Schroeder. Her voice was soft and dispassionate. "Captain, sometime between now and the time Bellini is ready to move, you will prepare a statement justifying our decision. If you don't, I'll see to it that you are brought up on departmental charges, dismissed from the force, and lose your pension. You'll end up as a bank guard in Dubuque—if you're lucky enough ever to get a gun permit. Now, let's discuss this intelligently."

Schroeder stood and took a deep breath. His voice had the control and tone of the professional negotiator again. "Yes, let's do that. I'm sorry, I became overwrought for a moment. Let's discuss what Brian Flynn really said to me, not what you'd have liked him to say." Schroeder looked at Bellini and Logan. "It seems those forty-five corned beef dinners were not a ruse—there were people to eat those dinners. I saw them. And flamethrowers...let me tell you about the flamethrowers...." He lit a cigar with shaking hands, then continued.

Schroeder went on in cool, measured tones, but everyone could hear an undercurrent of anxiety in his voice. He concluded, "Flynn has assembled what amounts to the largest, best-equipped armed force of trained insurgents this country has seen since the Civil War. It's too late to do anything except call Washington and tell them we've surrendered what is in our power to surrender...."

CHAPTER 52

Langley found Burke lying on a bed in a priest's room. "They've decided to hit the Cathedral!"

Burke sat up quickly.

Langley's voice was agitated. "Soon. Before the Pope's appeal—before the church bells ring and Monsignor Downes comes to his senses—"

"Slow down."

"Schroeder spoke to Flynn at the gate—said he saw forty or fifty armed Fenians—"

"Fifty?"

"But he didn't. I *know* he didn't."

"Hold on. Back up."

Langley paced around the small room. "Washington perceived a sinking ship. Kline and Doyle perceived a bandwagon. See? Tomorrow they'll both be heroes, or they'll be in Mexico wearing dark glasses and phony noses—"

Burke found some loose aspirin in the night table and chewed three of them.

Langley sat down on a chair. "Listen, Spiegel wants to see you." He briefed Burke quickly, then added, "You're the negotiator until they decide about Schroeder."

Burke looked up. "Negotiator?" He laughed. "Poor Bert. This was going to be his perfect game.... He really wanted this one." He lit a cigarette stub. "So"— he exhaled a stream of acrid smoke—"we attack—"

"No! We *rescue*! You have to call it a rescue operation now. You have to choose your words very carefully, because it's getting very grim and none of them is saying what they mean anymore—they never did anyway—and they lie better than we do. Go on, they're waiting for you."

Burke made no move to leave. "And Martin told them I would produce Stillway!"

"Yes, complete with blueprints. That was news to me—how about you?"

"And he never mentioned Terri O'Neal?"

"No—should he?" Langley looked at his watch. "Does it matter anymore?" Burke stared out the window into Madison Avenue. "Martin killed Jack Ferguson, you know."

Langley came up behind him. "No. The Fenians killed Jack Ferguson."

Burke turned. "Lots of phony deals going down tonight."

Langley shook his head. "Damned right. And Kline is passing out promotions like they were campaign buttons. Go get one. But you have to pay."

Langley began pacing again. "You have to sign a statement saying you think everything Kline and Doyle do is terrific. Okay? Make them give you a captain's pay. I'm going to be a chief inspector. And get out of ID. Ask for the Art Forgery Squad—Paris, London, Rome. Promise me you'll visit Schroeder in Dubuque—"

"Get hold of yourself."

Langley waved his arms. "Remember, Martin is in, Schroeder is out. Logan is in with Kline and Doyle but out with Bellini—are you following me? Watch out for Spiegel. She's in rare form—what a magnificent bitch. The Fenians are lunatics, we're sane.... Monsignor Downes blesses us all.... What else?" He looked around with wild darting eyes. "Is there a shower in this place? I feel slimy. You still here? Beat it!" Langley fell back on the bed. "Go away."

Burke had never seen Langley become unglued, and it was frightening. He started to say something, then thought better of it and left.

Burke walked beside Roberta Spiegel up the stairs. He listened to her brisk voice as they moved. Martin was climbing silently behind him.

Burke opened the stairshed door and walked onto the flat rooftop of the rectory. A wind blew from the north, and frozen pools of water reflected the lights of the tall buildings around them. Spiegel dismissed a team of ESD snipers, turned up her coat collar, and moved to the west side of the roof. She put her hands on the low wrought-iron fence that ran around the roof's perimeter and stared at the towering Cathedral rising across the narrow courtyard.

The streets below were deserted, but in the distance, beyond the barricades, horns blared, people sang and shouted, bagpipes and other instruments played intermittently. Burke realized it was after 4:00 a.m., and the bars had closed. The party was on the streets now, probably still a hundred thousand strong, maybe more, tenaciously clinging to the night that had turned magic for them.

Spiegel was speaking, and Burke tried to concentrate on her words; but he had no topcoat, and he was cold, and her words were blowing away in the strong wind. She concluded, "We've gotten our act together, Lieutenant, but before it comes apart, we're going to move. And we don't want any more surprises. Understand?"

Burke said, "Art Forgery Squad."

Spiegel looked at him, momentarily puzzled, then said, "Oh...all right. Either that or shower orderly at the academy gym." She turned her back to the wind and lit a cigarette.

Burke said, "Where's Schroeder?"

Spiegel replied, "He understands we don't want him out of our sight and talking to the press, so rather than suffer the indignity of a guard, he volunteered to stick with Bellini."

Burke felt a vague uneasiness pass through him. He said, "And I'm the negotiator?"

Spiegel said, "In fact, yes. But for the sake of appearances, Schroeder is still on the job. He's not without his political connections. He'll continue his duties, with some modifications, of course, and later...he'll go on camera."

Martin spoke for the first time. "Captain Schroeder should actually go back to the sacristy and speak with Flynn again. We have to keep up appearances at this critical moment. Neither Flynn nor the press should sense any problem."

Burke cupped his hands and lit a cigarette, looking at Martin as he did. Martin's strategy was becoming clear. He thought about Schroeder hanging around Bellini, about Schroeder meeting Flynn again at the gate. He thought, also, that Flynn did not have fifty well-armed people, and therefore Schroeder was mistaken, stupid, or gullible, which seemed to be the consensus. But he knew Schroeder was none of these things. *When you have excluded the impossible,* said Sherlock Holmes, *whatever remains, however improbable, must be the truth.* Schroeder was lying, and Burke was beginning to understand why. He pictured the face of a young woman, heard her voice again, and placed her at a promotion party five or six years before. Almost hesitantly he made the final connection he should have made hours ago. Burke said to Spiegel, "And Bellini's working on a new plan of attack?"

Spiegel looked at him in the diffused light and said, "Right now Bellini and Logan are formulating plan B—escalating the response, as they say—based on the outside possibility that there is a powerful force in that Cathedral. They won't go in any other way. But we're counting on *you* to give us the intelligence we need to formulate a plan C, an infiltration of the Cathedral and surprise attack, using the hidden passages that many of us seem to believe exist. That may enable us to actually save some lives and save Saint Patrick's."

She looked out at the looming structure. Even from the outside it looked labyrinthine with its towers, spires, buttresses, and intricate stonework. She turned to Burke. "So, do you feel, Lieutenant Burke, that you've put your neck on a chopping block?"

"There's no reason why my neck shouldn't be where yours is."

"True," she said. "True. And yours is actually a little more exposed, since I understand you're going in with Bellini."

"That's right. How about you?"

She smiled unpleasantly, then said, "You don't *have* to go.... But it wouldn't be a bad idea...if you don't produce Stillway."

Burke glanced at Martin, who nodded slightly, and said, "I'll have him within...half an hour."

No one spoke, then Martin said, "If I may make another suggestion...let's not make too much of this architect business in front of Captain Schroeder. He's overwrought and may inadvertently let something slip the next time he speaks with Flynn."

There was a long silence on the rooftop, broken by the sounds of shoes shuffling against the frozen gravel and the wind rushing through the streets. Burke looked at Spiegel and guessed that she sensed Bert Schroeder had a real problem, was a real problem.

Spiegel put her hands in the pockets of her long coat and walked a few paces from Burke and Martin. For a few brief seconds she wondered why she was so committed to this, and it came to her that in those seven miserable years of teaching history what she had really wanted to do was make history; and she would.

Captain Joe Bellini rubbed his eyes and looked at the clock in the press conference room. 4:26 a.m. *The fucking sun is due at 6:03.* In his half-sleep he had pictured a wall of brilliant sunlight moving toward him, coming to rescue him as it had done so many times in

Korea. *God*, he thought, *how I hate the sound of rifles in the night.*

He looked around the room. Men slept on cots or on the floor, using flak jackets for pillows. Others were awake, smoking, talking in low tones. Occasionally someone laughed at something that, Bellini guessed, was not funny. Fear had a special stink of its own, and he smelled it strongly now, a mixture of sweat, tobacco, gun oil, and the breath from labored lungs and sticky mouths.

The blackboard was covered with colored chalk marks superimposed on a white outline of St. Patrick's. On the long conference table lay copies of the revised attack plan. Bert Schroeder sat at the far end of the table, flipping casually through a copy.

The phone rang, and Bellini grabbed it. "ESD operations, Bellini."

The Mayor's distinctive nasal voice came over the line. "How are you holding up, Joe? Anxious to get rolling?"

"Can't wait."

"Good.... Listen, I've just seen your new attack plan.... It's a little excessive, isn't it?"

"It was mostly Colonel Logan's, sir," Bellini said.

"Oh...well, see that you tone it down."

Bellini picked up a full soft-drink can in his big hand and squeezed it, watching the top pop off and the brown liquid run over his fingers. "Approved or disapproved?"

The Mayor let a long time go by, and Bellini knew he was conferring, looking at his watch. Kline came back on the line. "The Governor and I approve ... in principle."

"I thank you in principle."

Kline switched to another subject. "Is he still there?"

Bellini glanced at Schroeder. "Like dog turd on a jogger's sneakers."

Kline forced a weak laugh. "Okay, I'm in the state offices in Rockefeller Center with the Governor and our staffs—"

"Good view."

"Now, don't be sarcastic. Listen, I've just spoken to the President of the United States."

Bellini detected a note of self-importance in Kline's tone.

"The President says he's making definite progress with the British Prime Minister. He's also making noises like he might federalize the guard and send in marshals ...." Kline lowered his voice in a conspiratorial tone. "Between you and me, Joe, I think he's putting out a smokescreen ... covering himself for later."

Bellini lit a cigarette. "Who isn't?"

Kline's voice was urgent. "He's under pressure. The church bells in Washington are already ringing, and there are thousands of people marching with candles in front of the White House. The British Embassy is being picketed—"

Bellini watched Schroeder stand and then walk toward the door. He said into the phone, "Hold on." Bellini called to Schroeder, "Where you headed, Chief?"

Schroeder looked back at him. "Sacristy." He walked out the door.

Bellini watched him go, then said into the phone, "Schroeder just went to make a final pitch to Flynn. Okay?"

Kline let out a long breath. "All right...can't hurt. By the time he gets back you'll be ready to move—unless he has something very solid, which he won't."

Bellini remembered that Schroeder had never had a failure. "You never know."

There was a long silence on the line, then the Mayor said, "Do you believe in miracles?"

"Never actually saw one." He thought, *Except the time you got reelected.* "Nope, never saw one."

"Me neither."

Bellini heard a click on the line, followed by a dial tone. He looked across the quiet room. "Get up! Off your asses! Battle stations. Move out!"

Bert Schroeder stood opposite Brian Flynn at the sacristy gate. Schroeder's voice was low and halting as he spoke, and he kept looking back nervously into the sacristy. "The plan is a fairly simple and classical attack.... Colonel Logan drew it up.... Logan himself will hit the front doors with an armored carrier, and the ESD will hit all the other doors simultaneously with rams.... They'll use scaling ladders and break through the windows.... It's all done under cover of gas and darkness...everyone has masks and night scopes. The electricity will be cut off at the moment the doors are hit...."

Flynn felt the blood race through his veins as he listened. "Gas..."

Schroeder nodded. "The same stuff you used at the reviewing stands. It will be pumped in through the air ducts." He detailed the coordination of helicopters, snipers on the roofs, firemen, and bomb disposal men. He added, "The sacristy steps"—he looked down as though realizing he was standing in the very spot— "they'll be hit with steel-cut chain saws. Bellini and I will be with that squad.... We'll go for the hostages...if they're on the sanctuary..." He shook his head, trying to comprehend the fact that he was saying this.

"The hostages," said Flynn, "will be dead." He paused and said, "Where will Burke be?"

Schroeder shook his head, tried to go on, but heard his voice faltering. After some hesitation he slipped a sheaf of papers from his jacket and through the bars.

Flynn slid them under his shirt, his eyes darting between the corridor openings. "So there's nothing that the famous Captain Schroeder can do to stop this?"

Schroeder looked down. "There never was.... Why didn't you see that...?"

Flynn's voice was hostile. "Because I listened to you all night, Schroeder, and I think I half believed your damned lies!"

Schroeder was determined to salvage something of himself from the defeat and humiliation he had felt at the last confrontation. "Don't put this on *me*. You *knew* I was lying. You knew it!"

Flynn glared at him, then nodded slightly. "Yes, I knew it." He thought a moment, then said, "And I know you're finally speaking the truth. It must be a great strain. Well, I can stop them at the doors...if, as you say, they haven't discovered any hidden passages and they don't have the architect—" He looked suddenly at Schroeder. "They *don't* have him, do they?"

Schroeder shook his head. He drew himself up and spoke rapidly. "Give it up. I'll get you a police escort to the airport. I know I can do that. That's all they really want—they want you out of here!"

Flynn seemed to consider for a brief moment, then shook his head.

Schroeder pressed on. "Flynn—listen, they're going to hit you hard. You're going to *die*. Can't you grasp that? You can't delude yourself any longer. But all you have to do is say you're willing to take less—"

"If I wanted less, I would have asked for less. No more hostage negotiating, please. God, how you go on. Talk about self-delusion."

Schroeder drew close to the gate. "All right, I've done all I could. Now you release—"

Flynn cut him off. "If the details you've given me are accurate, I'll send a signal to release your daughter."

Schroeder grabbed at the bars. "What *kind* of signal? When? The phones will be cut off.... The towers will be under sniper fire—What if you're ... dead? Damn it, I've given you the plans—"

Flynn went on. "But if you've lied to me about any part of this, or if there should be a change in plans and you don't tell me—"

Schroeder was shaking his head spasmodically. "No. No. That's not acceptable. You're not living up to your end."

Flynn turned and walked up the stairs.

Schroeder drew his pistol and held it close against

his chest. It wavered in his hand, the muzzle pointing toward Flynn's back, but his hand shook so badly he almost dropped the gun. Flynn turned the corner and disappeared.

After a full minute Schroeder holstered the pistol, faced around, and walked back to the side corridor. He passed grim-faced men standing against the walls with slung rifles. He found a lavatory, entered it, and vomited.

CHAPTER 53

Burke stood alone in the small counting room close by the press room. He adjusted his flak jacket over his pullover and, after putting a green carnation in a cartridge loop, started for the door.

The door suddenly swung open, and Major Martin stood before him. "Hello, Burke. Is that what everyone in New York is wearing now?" He called back into the corridor, and two patrolmen appeared with a civilian between them. Martin smiled. "May I present Gordon Stillway, American Institute of Architects? Mr. Stillway, this is Patrick Burke, world-famous secret policeman."

A tall, erect, elderly man stepped into the room, looking confused but otherwise dignified. In his left hand he held a briefcase from which protruded four tubes of rolled paper.

Burke dismissed the two officers and turned to Martin. "It's late."

"Is it?" Martin looked at his watch. "You have fifteen full minutes to head off Bellini. Time, as you know, is relative. If you're eating Galway Bay oysters, fifteen minutes pass rather quickly, but if you're hanging by your left testicle, it drags a bit." He laughed at his own joke. "Bellini is hanging by his testicle. You'll cut him down—then hang him up there again after he's spoken to Mr. Stillway."

Martin moved farther into the small room and drew closer to Burke. "Mr. Stillway was kidnapped from his apartment by persons unknown and held in an empty loft not far from here. Acting on anonymous information, I went to the detectives in the Seventh Precinct and, *voilà*, Gordon Stillway. Mr. Stillway, won't you have a seat?"

Gordon Stillway remained standing and looked from one man to the other, then said, "This is a terrible tragedy...but I'm not quite certain what I'm supposed to—"

Martin said, "You, sir, will give the police the information they must have to infiltrate the Cathedral and catch the villains unawares."

Stillway looked at him. "What are you talking about? Do you mean they're going to attack? I won't have that."

Martin put his hand on Stillway's shoulder. "I'm afraid you've arrived a bit late, sir. That's not negotiable any longer. Either you help the police, or they go in there through the doors and windows and cause a great deal of death and destruction, after which the terrorists will burn it down and blow it up—or vice versa."

Stillway's eyes widened, and he let Martin maneuver him into a chair. Martin said to Burke, "You'd better hurry."

Burke came toward Martin. "Why did you cut it this close?"

Martin took a step back and replied, "I'm sorry. I had to wait for Captain Schroeder to deliver the attack plans to Flynn, which is what he's doing right now."

Burke nodded. Bellini's attack had to be canceled no matter what else happened. A new plan based on Stillway's information, if he had any, would jump off so close to 6:03 that it would probably end in disaster anyway. But Martin had delivered Stillway and therefore would be owed a great favor by Washington. He looked at Martin. "Major, I'd like to be the first to thank you for your help in this affair."

Martin smiled. "Now you're getting into the right spirit. You've been so glum all night, but you'll see— stick with me, Burke, and as I promised, you'll come out of this looking fine."

Burke addressed Stillway. "Are there any hidden passages into that Cathedral that will give the police a clear tactical advantage?"

Stillway sat motionless, contemplating the events that had begun with a sunny day and a parade, proceeded to his kidnapping and rescue, and ended with him in a subterranean room with two men who were obviously unbalanced. He said, "I have no idea what you mean by a clear tactical advantage." His voice became irritable. "I'm an architect."

Martin looked at his watch again. "Well, I've done my bit...." He opened the door. "Hurry now. You promised Bellini you'd be at his side, and a promise is sacred and beautiful. And oh, yes, later—if you're still alive—you'll see at least one more mystery unfold in that Cathedral. A rather good one." He walked out and slammed the door.

Stillway regarded Burke warily. "Who was he? Who are *you*?"

"Who are *you*? Are you Gordon Stillway—or are you just another of the Major's little jokes?"

Stillway didn't answer.

Burke extracted a rolled blueprint from the briefcase, unfurled it, and stared at it. He threw the blueprint on the table and looked at his watch. "Come with me, Mr. Stillway, and we'll see if you were worth the wait."

Schroeder walked into the press conference room and hurried toward a phone. "This is Schroeder. Get me Kline."

The Mayor's voice was neutral. "Yes, Captain, any luck?"

Schroeder looked around the nearly empty room. Rifles and flak jackets had disappeared, and empty boxes of ammunition and concussion grenades lay in the corner. Someone had scrawled on the chalkboard:

FINAL SCORE:
   CHRISTIANS AND JEWS———
   PAGANS AND ATHEISTS———

Kline's voice was impatient. "Well?"

Schroeder leaned against the table and fought down a wave of nausea. "No...no extension...no compromise. Listen..."

Kline sounded annoyed. "That's what eveyone's been telling you all night."

Schroeder drew a long breath and pressed his hand to his stomach. Kline was speaking, but Schroeder wasn't listening. Slowly he began to take in more of his surroundings. Bellini stood across the table with his arms folded, Burke stood at the opposite end of the room, two ESD men with black ski masks stood very near him, and an old man, a civilian, sat at the conference table.

The Mayor went on. "Captain, right now you are still very much a hero, and within the hour you will be the police department's chief spokesman." Schroeder examined Bellini's blackened face and thought Bellini was glaring at him with unconcealed hatred, as though he *knew*, but he decided it must be the grotesque makeup.

Kline was still speaking. "And you will not speak to a newsperson until the last shot is fired. And what's this I hear about you volunteering to go in with Bellini?"

Schroeder said, "I ... I have to. That's the least I can do...."

"Have you lost your mind? What's wrong with you, anyway? You sound—have you been drinking?"

Schroeder found himself staring at the old man who, he now noticed, was studying a large unrolled length of paper. His eyes passed over the silent men in the room again and focused on Burke, who seemed ... almost sad. Everyone looked as though someone had just died. Something was wrong here—

"Are you drunk?"

"No . . . ."

"Pull yourself together, Schroeder. You'll be on television soon."

"What . . . ?"

"*Television!* You remember, the red light, the big camera. . . . Now you get clear of that Cathedral—get over here as soon as possible."

Schroeder heard the phone go dead and looked at the receiver, then dropped it on the table. He extended his arm and pointed at Gordon Stillway. "Who is *that*?"

The room remained silent. Then Burke said, "You know who that is, Bert. We're going to redraw the attack plans."

Schroeder looked quickly at Bellini and blurted, "No! No! You—"

Bellini glanced at Burke and nodded. He turned to Schroeder. "I can't believe you did that." He came toward Schroeder, who was edging toward the door. "Where're you going, ace? You going to tip your pal, cocksucker?"

Schroeder's head was shaking spasmodically.

Bellini drew closer. "I can't hear you, you shit! Your golden voice sounds like a toilet flushing."

Burke called out. "Joe—no hard stuff—just take his gun." Burke moved closer to the two men. The two ESD officers held their rifles at their hips, not understanding exactly what was going on but ready to fire if Schroeder made a move for his gun. Gordon Stillway looked up from his blueprints.

Schroeder found his voice. "No . . . listen . . . I have

to talk to Flynn . . . because . . . you see . . . I've got to try one more time—"

Bellini held out his hand. "Give me your gun—left hand—pinky in the trigger guard—nice and easy, and no one's going to get hurt."

Schroeder hesitated, then slowly reached into his jacket and carefully extracted the pistol with a hooked finger. "Bellini—listen—what's going on? Why—"

Bellini reached for the pistol with his left hand and swung with his right, hitting Schroeder a vicious blow to the jaw. Schroeder fell back against the door and slid down to the floor.

Burke said, "You didn't have to do that."

Bellini flexed his hand and turned to Burke. "You're right—I should've yanked his nuts out and shoved them up his nose." He looked back at Schroeder. "Tried to kill me, did you, scumbag?"

Burke saw that Bellini was contemplating further violence. "It had nothing to do with you, Bellini. Just cool out." He came up beside Bellini and put his hand on his shoulder. "Come on. You've got lots to do."

Bellini motioned to the ESD men. "Cuff this cocksucker and dump him in a closet somewhere." He turned to Burke. "You think I'm stupid, don't you? You think I don't know that you're all going to cover for that motherfucker, and as soon as the shit storm is over at dawn he's going to be the Mayor's golden boy again." He watched the ESD men carry Schroeder out and called after them, "Find some place with rats and cockroaches." He sat down and tried to steady his hands as he lit a cigarette.

Burke stood beside him. "Life is unfair, right? But

someone handed us a break this time. Flynn thinks you're doing one thing, and you're going to do something else. So it didn't turn out so bad, right?"

Bellini nodded sulkily and looked at Stillway. "Yeah...maybe..." He rubbed his knuckles and flexed his fingers again. "That hurt...but it felt so good." He laughed suddenly. "Burke, come here. Want to know a secret? I've been looking for an excuse to do that for five years." He looked at the ceiling. "Thank you, God." He laughed again.

The room began filling with squad leaders hastily recalled from their jump-off points, and Bellini watched them file into the room. The absolutely worst feeling in the whole world, Bellini thought, was to get yourself psyched out of your mind for a fight and have it postponed. The squad leaders, he saw, were in a bad mood. Bellini looked at Burke. "You better call His fucking Honor and explain. You can cover Schroeder's ass if you want, but even if you don't, it won't matter to Kline, because they'll still promote him and make him a national hero."

Burke took off his flak jacket and pullover. "I have to see Flynn and come up with a good reason why Schroeder isn't staying in touch with him."

Bellini moved to the head of the conference table and took a long breath. He looked at each of the twelve squad leaders and said, "Men, I've got some good news and some bad news. Thing is, I don't know which is which."

No one laughed, and Bellini went on. "Before I tell you why the attack is postponed, I want to say something.... The people in the Cathedral are desperate men and women...guerrillas.... This is combat...war...and the goal is not to apprehend these people at the risk of your own lives—"

A squad leader called out, "You mean shoot first and ask questions later, right?"

Bellini remembered the military euphemism for it. "Make a clean sweep."

CHAPTER 54

Father Murphy stood on the crypt landing, a purple stole around his neck. Frank Gallagher knelt before him, making a hasty confession in a low, trembling voice. Flynn waited just inside the large crypt door, then called out to Gallagher, "That's fine, Frank."

Gallagher nodded to the priest, rose, and moved into the crypt. Flynn handed him a sheet of paper and said, "Here's the part of the attack plan which deals with the sacristy gate." He briefed Gallagher, then added, "You can take cover here in the crypt while you keep the gates under fire." As Flynn spoke, Gallagher focused on the brownish blood that had flowed so abundantly from Pedar Fitzgerald's mouth. Father Murphy was standing in the center of the bloodstain, apparently without realizing it, and Gallagher wanted to tell the priest to move—but Flynn was clasping his hand. "Good luck to you, Frank. Remember, Dublin, seventeenth of March next."

Gallagher made an unintelligible noise, but he nodded with a desperate determination.

Flynn came out of the crypt and took Murphy's arm. He led the priest up the stairs, across the sanctuary, and down the side steps into the ambulatory. Father Murphy disengaged himself from Flynn and turned toward the chancel organ. John Hickey sat talking on the field phone, Pedar Fitzgerald's covered body at his feet. The priest knelt and pulled the coat back from Pedar's head. He anointed his forehead, stood, and looked at Hickey, who had hung up the receiver.

Hickey said, "Sneaked that in, did you? Well, where now is Pedar Fitzgerald's soul?"

Father Murphy kept staring at Hickey.

Hickey said, "Now, like a good priest, you'll ask me to confess, and you assume I'll refuse. But what if I do confess? Would my entire past life, including every sin, sacrilege, and blasphemy that you can imagine, be forgiven? Would I gain the kingdom of heaven?"

Murphy said, "You know you must repent."

Hickey slapped the top of the organ. "I *knew* there was a catch!"

Flynn took Murphy's arm and pulled him away. They passed beside the confessional, and Flynn paused to look at the small white buzzer. "That was clever, Padre. I'll give you that." Flynn looked back across the ambulatory at Hickey. "I don't know what messages you, Maureen, or Hickey sent, but you can be sure none of you accomplished anything beyond adding to the confusion out there."

Father Murphy replied, "I still *feel* better about it."

Flynn laughed and began walking. Murphy followed, and Flynn spoke as they walked. "You feel better, do you? My, what a big ego you have, Father." Flynn stopped in the transept aisle between the two south triforia. He turned and looked up at the triforium they'd just passed beneath and called up to Eamon Farrell. "I know you're devout, Eamon, but Father Murphy can't fly, so you'll have to miss this confession."

Farrell looked as though this were the one confession he didn't want to miss.

Father Murphy called up, "Are you sorry for all your sins?"

Farrell nodded. "I am, Father."

Murphy said, "Make a good act of contrition—you'll be in a state of grace, Mr. Farrell. Don't do anything to alter that."

Flynn was annoyed. "If you try any of that again, you'll not hear another confession."

Murphy walked away, and Flynn outlined the coming attack to Farrell. He added, "If we stop them, your son will be free at dawn. Good luck."

Flynn walked to the wide transept doors. The priest was staring at the two khaki-colored mines attached to the doors and four more can-shaped mines placed at intervals on the floor. Trip wires ran from them in all directions. "You see," said Flynn conversationally, "when the doors are smashed in, these two mines explode instantly, followed at fifteen-second intervals by the other four, producing, so to speak, a curtain of shrapnel of a minute's duration. Every doorway in here will be clogged with writhing bodies. The screams...wait until you hear the screams.... You wouldn't believe that men can make such noises. My God, it makes the blood run cold, Father, and turns the bowels to ice water."

Murphy continued to stare at the mines.

Flynn motioned overhead. "Look at these commanding views.... How in the world do they expect to succeed?" He led the priest to the small door in the corner of the transept and motioned Murphy to go first. They walked wordlessly up the spiral stairs and came out in the long triforium five stories above the main floor.

Abby Boland stood by the door, an M-16 rifle cradled in her arms. She had found a pair of overalls in a maintenance closet, and she wore them over her cheerleader's uniform. Flynn put his arm around her and walked her away from the priest as he explained the coming attack and went through her assignments. Flynn looked across the nave at George Sullivan, who was watching them. He took his arm from her shoulder and said, "If we don't stop them...and if you determine in your own mind that killing more of them won't help anything, then get into the bell tower.... Don't try to cross the choir loft to get to George.... Stay away from Leary and Megan. Understand?"

Her eyes darted to the choir loft, and she nodded.

Flynn continued. "The attic will take a while to fall in, and the bombs won't damage the towers—they'll be the only things left standing. George will be all right in the south tower."

"George and I understood we'd not see each other again after this." She looked at Sullivan, who was still watching them.

"Good luck to you." Flynn moved toward the tower passage and left her with Father Murphy.

After a few minutes Murphy rejoined Flynn, and

Flynn looked at his watch. "We don't have a great deal of time, so keep these things short."

"How do you know how much time you've got? Am I to understand that you know the details of this attack?" He looked at the sheaf of rolled papers in Flynn's hand.

Flynn tapped Murphy on the shoulder with the paper tube. "Each man has a price, as you know, and it often seems pitifully low, but did anyone ever consider that Judas Iscariot may have *needed* that silver?" He laughed and indicated the spiral stairs. They climbed three stories up into the tower, until they reached the level that passed beside the attic. Flynn opened a large wooden door, and they stepped onto a catwalk. Murphy peered into the dimly lit expanse, then walked to a pile of chopped wood and votive candles. He turned back and stared at Flynn, who met his stare, and Murphy knew there was nothing to be said.

Jean Kearney and Arthur Nulty moved out of the shadows and approached along a catwalk, their arms around each other. The expressions on their faces showed that they found the sight of Flynn and the priest to be ominous. They stopped some distance from the two men and looked at them, long plumes of breath coming from their mouths. Father Murphy was reminded of two lost souls who were not allowed to cross a threshold unless invited.

Flynn said, "The good Father wants to hear your sins."

Jean Kearney's face flushed. Nulty looked both embarrassed and frightened.

Flynn's eyebrows rose, and he let out a short laugh.

He turned to the priest. "Self-control is difficult in times like these."

Murphy's face betrayed no anger or shock, but he let out a long, familiar sigh that Flynn thought must be part of the seminary training. Flynn motioned Murphy to stay where he was and strode across the catwalk. He handed Jean Kearney three sheets of paper and began briefing the two people. He concluded, "They'll come with the helicopters anytime after 5:15." He paused, then said, "Don't be afraid."

Jean Kearney answered, "The only thing we're afraid of is being separated." Nulty nodded.

Flynn put his arms around their shoulders and moved with them toward the priest. "Make Father Murphy a happy man and let him save your souls from the fires of hell at least." Flynn moved toward the door, then called back to Murphy. "Don't undermine the troops' morale, and no lengthy penances."

Flynn reentered the tower and waited in the darkness of a large, opaque-windowed room. He looked at his watch. According to Schroeder there were twenty minutes left until the earliest time the attack might begin.

He sat down on the cold, dusty floor, suddenly filled with a sense of awe at what he had done. One of the largest civil disturbances in American history was about to end in the most massive police action ever seen on this continent—and a landmark was going to be deleted from the guidebooks. The name of Brian Flynn would enter history. Yet, he felt, all that was trivial compared to the fact that these men and women were willingly following him into death.

Abruptly he pivoted around, drew his pistol, and

knocked out a pane of thick glass, then looked out at the night. A cold wind blew feathery clouds across a brilliant blue, moonlit sky. Up the Avenue dozens of flags hung from protruding staffs, swaying stiff and frozen in the wind. The sidewalks were covered with ice and broken glass, sparkling in the light. *Spring*, he thought. "Dear God, I'll not see the spring."

Father Murphy cleared his throat, and Flynn spun around. Their eyes met, and Flynn rose quickly. "That was fast."

Flynn began the climb up the winding stairs that gave way to a series of ladders. Murphy followed cautiously. He'd never been this high in either tower, and despite the circumstances he was eager in a boyish sort of way to see the bells.

They climbed into the lowest bell room, where Donald Mullins crouched behind the stonework that separated two louvers. He wore a flak jacket, and his face and hands were blackened with soot from a burned cork whose odor still hung in the cold room.

Father Murphy looked at the ripped louvers with obvious displeasure and then stared up at the bells hanging from their cross-beams. Flynn said nothing but looked out into the Avenue. Everything appeared as before, but in some vague, undefined way it was not. He said to Mullins, "Can you tell?"

Mullins nodded. "When?"

"Soon." Flynn gave him two sheets of paper. "They've got to blind the eyes that watch them before the rest of the attack can proceed. It's all there in the order of battle."

Mullins ran a flashlight over the neatly typed pages,

only vaguely interested in how Flynn came to have them. "My name here is Towerman North. Sounds like a bloody English lord or something." He laughed, then read, "If Towerman North cannot be put out with sniper fire, then high explosive and/or gas grenades will be fired into bell room with launchers. Helicopter machine gunners will be called in if Towerman North is still not neutralized...." He looked up. "Neutralized...God, how they've butchered the language here...."

Flynn saw that Mullins's smile was strained. Flynn said, "Try to keep us informed on the field phone.... Keep the receiver off the cradle so we can hear what's happening...."

Mullins pictured himself thrashing around on the floor, small animal noises coming from his mouth into the open receiver.

Flynn went on, "If you survive the snipers, you'll survive the explosion and the fire."

"That barely compensates me for freezing half to death."

Flynn moved to the west opening and stared down at the green and gold harp flag, glazed with ice, and ran his hand over it. He looked out at Rockefeller Center. Hundreds of windows were still lit with bright fluorescent light, and figures passed back and forth. He took Mullins's field glasses and watched. A man was eating a sandwich. A young woman laughed on the telephone. Two uniformed policemen drank from cups. Someone with field glasses waved to him. He handed the glasses back. "I never hated them before..."

Mullins nodded. "It's so maddeningly common-place...but I've gotten used to it." Mullins turned to Father Murphy. "So, it's that time, is it?"

"Apparently it is."

Mullins came close to Murphy. "Priests, doctors, and undertakers give me worse chills than ever a north wind did."

Father Murphy said nothing.

Mullins's eyes stared off at some indeterminate place and time. He spoke in a barely audible voice. "You're from the north, and you've heard the caoine—the funeral cry of the peasants. It's meant to imitate the wail of a chorus of banshees. The priests know this but never seem to object." He glanced at Murphy. "Irish priests are very tolerant of these things. Well, I've heard the actual banshees' wail, Father, whistling through the louvers all night...even when the wind was still."

"You've heard nothing of the sort."

Mullins laughed. "But I have. I *have*. And I've seen the coach-a-bower. Immense it was and black-polished, riding over these rooftops, a red coffin mounted atop it, and a headless Dullahan madly whipping a team of headless horses...and the coach drew past this window, Father, and the coachman threw in my face a basin of cold blood."

Murphy shook his head.

Mullins smiled. "Well...I fancy myself a poet, you see...and I've license to hear things...."

Murphy looked at him with some interest. "A poet..."

"Aye." A faint smile played over his blue lips, but

his voice was melancholy. "And some time ago I fell in love with Leanhaun Shee, the Gaelic muse who gives us inspiration. She lives on mortal life, as you may know, in return for her favor. That's why Gaelic poets die young, Father. Do you believe that?"

Murphy said, "They die young because they eat badly, drink too much, and don't dress well in winter. They die young because unlike most civilized poets they run off to fight in ill-conceived wars. Do you want to make your confession?"

Mullins knelt and took the priest's hands.

Flynn climbed down to the room below. A strong gust of wind came through the shattered windows and picked up clouds of ancient dust that had been undisturbed for a century.

Father Murphy came down the ladder. "This"—he motioned toward the broken windows—"this was the only thing that bothered him .... I suppose I shouldn't tell you that...."

Flynn almost laughed. "Well, one man's prank may be another's most tormenting sin, and vice versa." He jumped onto the ladder and descended to the spiral stairs, Father Murphy following. They came out of the tower into the subdued lighting and warmer air of the choir loft.

As Father Murphy moved along the rail he felt that someone was watching him. He looked into the choir pews that rose upward from the keyboard, and let out a startled gasp.

A figure stood above them, motionless in the shadows, dressed in a hooded monk's robe. A hideous, inhuman face peered out from the recesses of the cowl, and it was several seconds before Father Murphy recognized it as the face of a leopard. Leary's voice came out of the immobile face. "Scare you, priest?"

Murphy regained his composure.

Flynn said, "A bit of greasepaint would have done, Mr. Leary."

Leary laughed, an odd shrill laugh for a man with so deep a voice.

Megan rose from between the pews, dressed in a black cassock, her face covered with swirls of dull-colored camouflage paint, expertly applied, thought Flynn, by another hand.

She moved into the center aisle, and Flynn saw that it was an altar boy's robe and that it revealed her bare forearms. He saw also that her legs and feet were bare. He studied Megan's face and found that the paint did not make her features so impenetrable that he could not see the same signs he had seen in Jean Kearney. He said, "With death so near, Megan, I can hardly blame you."

She thrust her chin out in a defiant gesture.

"Well, if nothing else good comes of this, you've at least found your perfect mate."

Father Murphy listened without understanding at first, then drew in a sharp breath.

Megan said to Flynn, "Is my brother dead?"

Flynn nodded.

Her face remained strangely impassive. She motioned toward Leary as she fixed her deep green eyes on Flynn. "We won't let you surrender. There will be no compromises."

Flynn's voice was sharp. "I don't need either of you to explain my duty or my destiny."

Leary spoke. "When are they coming? How are they coming?"

Flynn told them. He said to Leary, "This may be your richest harvest."

"Long after you're all dead," said Leary, "I'll still be shooting."

Flynn stared up into the dark eyes that were as fixed as the mask around them. "Then what?"

Leary said nothing.

"I find it difficult, Mr. Leary, to believe you're prepared to die with us."

Megan answered, "He's as dedicated as you are. If we have to die, we'll die here together."

Flynn thought not. He had an impulse to warn Megan, but he didn't know what to warn her about, and it didn't seem to matter any longer. He said to her, "Good-bye, Megan. Good luck."

She moved back into the pews, beside Leary.

Murphy looked at the two robed figures. They stared back at him. He suspected they would snuff out his life from their dark perch with no more hesitation than a man swatting an insect. Yet... "I have to ask."

Flynn said, "Go ahead—make a fool of yourself again."

Murphy turned to him. "You're the fool who brought them here."

Megan and Leary seemed to sense what the discussion was about. Megan called out in a mocking voice, "Come up here, Father. Let us tell you our sins." Leary laughed, and Megan went on, "Keep you up nights, Father, and turn your face as scarlet as a cardinal's hat. You've never heard sins like ours." She laughed, and

Flynn realized he had never heard the sound of her laugh.

Flynn took the priest's arm again and moved him into the south tower without resistance. They climbed the stairs and passed through a door into the long southwest triforium.

George Sullivan stood at the parapet staring down at the north transept door. Sullivan's kilts and tunic, thought Flynn, were incongruous with his black automatic rifle and ammunition pouches. Flynn called to him, "Confessions are being heard, George."

Sullivan shook his head without looking up and lit a cigarette. His mind seemed to be elsewhere. Flynn nudged him and indicated the empty triforium across the transept. "You'll have to cover Gallagher's sectors."

Sullivan looked up. "Why doesn't Megan go up there?"

Flynn didn't answer the question, and Sullivan didn't press him. Flynn looked out at Abby Boland. These personal bonds had always been the Fenian strength—but also the weakness.

Sullivan also glanced across the nave. He spoke almost self-consciously. "I saw she made a confession to the priest.... These damned women of ours are so guilty and ashamed.... I feel somehow betrayed..."

Flynn said lightly, "You should have told him your version."

Sullivan started to reply but thought better of it. Flynn extended his hand, and Sullivan took it firmly.

Flynn and Father Murphy walked together back into the south tower and climbed the ten stories into the louvered room where Rory Devane stood in the dark, his face blackened and a large flak jacket hanging from his thin shoulders. Devane greeted them affably, but the sight of the priest wearing the purple stole was clearly not a welcome one.

Flynn said, "Sometime after 5:15 snipers will begin pouring bullets through all eight sides of this room."

"The room will be crowded, won't it?"

Flynn went on. "Yet you have to stay here and engage the helicopters. You have to put a rocket into the armored carrier."

Devane moved to a west-facing opening and looked down. Flynn briefed Devane, then said, "Father Murphy is interested in your soul."

Devane looked back at the priest. "I made my confession this morning—right here in Saint Pat's, as a matter of fact. Father Bertero, it was. I've done nothing in the meanwhile I need to confess."

Murphy said, "If you say an act of contrition, you can regain a state of grace." He turned and dropped into the ladder opening.

Flynn took Devane's hand. "Good luck to you. See you in Dublin."

"Aye, Brian, Kavanagh's Pub, or a place close by the back wall."

Flynn turned and dropped down the ladder, joining Murphy on the next level. The two men left the south tower and made their way across the choir loft. They entered the bell tower, and Flynn indicated the spiral staircase. "I have to speak with Mullins again."

Murphy was about to suggest that Flynn use the field phone, but something in Flynn's manner compelled him not to speak. They climbed until they reached a level where the stairs gave way to ladders somewhere below the first bell room where Mullins was.

Flynn looked at the large room they were in. The tower here was four-sided, with small milky-glass windows separated by thick stone. Mullins had knocked holes in some of the panes in the event he had to change his location, and Flynn pulled off a thick triangle of glass and looked at it, then looked at Murphy. "A great many people watching this on television are morbidly fascinated with the question of how this place will look afterward."

Murphy said, "I don't need any more revelations from you tonight. As a priest nothing shocks me any longer, and I still cling to my faith in humanity."

"That is truly a wonder. I'm in awe of that . . . ."

Murphy saw that he was sincere. "I observed how your people cared for each other, and for you . . . . I've heard some of their confessions . . . . There are hopeful signs amid all this."

Flynn nodded. "And Hickey? Megan? Leary? And me?"

"May God have mercy on all your souls."

Flynn didn't respond.

Murphy said evenly, "If you're going to kill me, do it quickly."

Flynn's face looked puzzled, then almost hurt. "No . . . why would you think that?"

Murphy automatically mumbled an apology but immediately felt it was unnecessary under the circumstances.

Flynn reached out and grabbed his arm. "Listen,

I've kept my promise to you and let you run around doing your duty. Now I want a promise from you."

Father Murphy looked at him cautiously.

Flynn said, "Promise me that after this is finished, you'll see that all my people are buried together in Glasnevin with Ireland's patriots. You can have a Catholic ceremony, if that'll make you feel better.... I know it won't be easy.... It may take you years to convince those swine in Dublin.... They never know who their heroes are until fifty years after they're dead."

The priest looked at him without comprehension, then said, "I...won't be alive to..."

Flynn took the priest's big hand firmly as though to shake it, but slapped the end of a handcuff on his wrist and locked the other end around the ladder's rail.

Father Murphy stared at his tethered wrist, then looked at Flynn. "Let me loose."

Flynn smiled weakly. "You weren't even supposed to be here. Now just keep your wits about you when the bullets start to fly. This tower should survive the explosion."

Murphy's face went red, and he shouted again. "You've no right to do this! Let me go!"

Flynn ignored him. He pulled a pistol from his belt and jumped down into the ladder opening. "It may happen that Megan, Hickey...someone may come for you...." He laid the pistol on the floor. "Kill them." He dropped down the ladder. "Good luck, Padre."

Murphy bent down and grabbed the pistol with his free hand. He pointed it at the top of Flynn's head. "Stop!"

Flynn smiled as he continued his climb down. "*Erin

go bragh, Timothy Murphy." He laughed, and the sound echoed through the stone tower.

Murphy shouted after him. "Stop! Listen...you must save the others too.... Maureen...For God's sake, man, she loves you...." He stared down into the dark hole and watched Flynn disappear.

Father Murphy threw the pistol to the floor and tugged at the cuffs, then sank to his knees beside the ladder opening. Somewhere in the city a church bell tolled, then another joined in, and soon he could hear the sounds of a dozen different carillons playing the hymn "Be Not Afraid." He thought that every bell in the city must be ringing, perhaps every bell in the country, and he hoped the others could hear them, too, and know they were not alone. For the first time since it had all begun, Father Murphy felt tears forming in his eyes.

CHAPTER 55

Brian Flynn came down from the tower and walked up the nave aisle, his footsteps echoing from the polished marble. He turned into the ambulatory and approached John Hickey, who stood on the raised platform of the chancel organ and watched him approach. Flynn walked deliberately up the steps and stood facing Hickey. After a short silence Hickey said, "It's 4:59. You let Murphy waste valuable time trying to save already damned souls. Does everyone know their orders at least?"

"Has Schroeder called?"

"No—that means either nothing is new or something is wrong." Hickey took out his pipe and filled it. "All night I've worried that my tobacco would run out before my life. It really bothered me.... A man shouldn't have to scrimp on his tobacco before he dies." He struck a match, and it sounded inordinately loud in the stillness. He drew deeply on his pipe and said, "Well, where's the priest?"

Flynn motioned vaguely toward the towers. "We've no grudge against him.... He shouldn't pay the price for being in the wrong place at the wrong time."

"Why not? That's why the rest of us are going to die." He flashed a look of feigned enlightenment. "Ah, I suppose playing God means you have to save a life for every ten score you take."

Flynn said, "Who *are* you?"

Hickey smiled with unrestrained glee. "Have I frightened you, lad? Don't be frightened, then. I'm just an old man who amuses himself by playing on people's fears and superstitions." Hickey stepped over the body of Pedar Fitzgerald and came closer to Flynn. He sucked noisily on his pipe, a pensive look on his face. "You know, lad, I've had more fun since I had myself buried than ever I did before I was interred. You get a lot of mileage out of resurrection—someone made a whole religion out of it once." He jerked a thumb toward the crucifix atop the altar and laughed again.

Flynn felt the old man's breath against his face. He put his right hand on the organ console. "Do you know anything about this ring?"

Hickey didn't look at it. "I know what you believe it is."

"And what is it *really*?"

"A ring, made of bronze."

Flynn slipped it from his finger and held it in his open palm. "Then I've held it too long. Take it."

Hickey shrugged and reached for it.

Flynn closed his hand and stared at Hickey.

Hickey's eyes narrowed into dark slits. "So, you want to know who I am and how I got here?" Hickey looked into the glowing bowl of his pipe with exaggerated interest. "I can tell you I'm a ghost, a thevshi, come from the grave to retrieve the ring and bring about your destruction and the destruction of the new Fenians—to perpetuate this strife into the next generation. There's the proper Celtic explanation you're looking for to make you feel better about your fears." He looked directly into Flynn's eyes. "But I can also tell you the truth, which is far more frightening. I'm *alive*. Your own dark soul imagined the thevshi, as it imagines the banshee, and the pooka, and the Far Darrig, and all the nightmarish creatures that walk the dark landscape of your mind and make you huddle around flickering peat fires. Aye, Brian, that's a fright, because you can't find sanctuary from those monsters you carry within you."

Flynn stared at him, examining the furrowed white face. Suddenly Hickey's eyes became benign, sparkling, and his mouth curled up in a good-natured smile. Hickey said, "You see?"

Flynn said, "Yes, I see. I see that you're a creature who draws strength from other men's weaknesses. It's my fault you're here, and it's my responsibility to see that you do no further harm."

"The harm is done. Had you stood up to me instead of wallowing in self-pity, you could have fulfilled your responsibility to your people, not to mention your own destiny."

Flynn stared at Hickey. "No matter what happens, I'll see you don't leave here alive." Flynn turned and walked to the sanctuary. He stood before the high throne. "Cardinal, the police will attack anytime after 5:15. Father Murphy is in a relatively safe place—we are not, and we will most probably die."

Flynn watched the Cardinal's face for a show of

emotion, but there was none. He went on, "I want you to know that the people out there share in the responsibility for this. Like me they are vain, egotistical, and flawed. A rather sorry lot for products of so many thousands of years of Judeo-Christian love and charity, wouldn't you say?"

The Cardinal leaned forward in the throne. "That's a question for people who are looking for a path to take them through life. Your life is over, and you'll have all your answers very soon. Use the minutes left to you to speak to her." He nodded toward Maureen.

Flynn was momentarily taken aback. It was perhaps the last reply he expected from a priest. He stepped away from the throne, turned, and crossed the sanctuary.

Maureen and Baxter remained seated, cuffed together in the first pew. Without a word Flynn unlocked the handcuffs, then spoke in a distant voice. "I'd like to put you both in a less exposed place, but that isn't acceptable to some of the others. However, when the shooting starts, you won't be executed, because we may repel them and we'll need you again." He looked at his watch and continued in a dispassionate voice. "Sometime after 5:15 you'll see all the doors explode, followed by police rushing in. I know you are both capable of keeping a cool head. Dive between the pews behind you. As 6:03 approaches . . . if you're still alive . . . get out of this area no matter what's happening around you. That's all I can do for you."

Maureen stood and looked at him closely. "No one asked you to do anything for us. If you want to do something for everyone, get down those stairs right now and open the gates to them. Then go into the pulpit and tell your people it's finished. No one will stop you, Brian. I think they're waiting to hear from you."

"When they open the gates of Long Kesh, I'll open the gates here."

Her voice became angry. "The keys to the jails of Ulster are *not* in America, or in London or Dublin. They are in Ulster. Give me a year in Belfast and Londonderry, and I'll get more people out of jail than you've ever had released with your kidnappings, raids, assassinations—"

Flynn laughed. "A *year*? You wouldn't last a year. If the Catholics didn't get you, Maureen, the Prods would."

She drew a shallow breath and brought her voice under control. "Very well . . . it's not worth going into that again. But you've no right to con these people into dying. Your voice can break the spell of death that hangs over this place. Go on! Do it! Now!" She swung and slapped him on the face.

Baxter moved off to one side and looked away.

Flynn pulled Maureen to him and said, "All night everyone's been very good about giving me advice. It's odd, isn't it, how people don't pay much attention to you until you've set a time bomb ticking under them?" He released her arms. "You, for instance, walked out on me four years ago without much advice for my future. All the things you've said to me tonight could have been said then."

She glanced at Baxter and felt curiously uncomfortable that he was hearing all of this. She spoke in a low voice. "I said all I had to say then. You weren't listening."

"You weren't speaking so loudly, either."

Flynn turned to Baxter. "And you, Harry." He moved closer to Baxter. "Major Bartholomew Martin needed a dead Englishman in here, and you're it."

Baxter considered this and accepted it in a very short time. "Yes...he's a sick man...an obsessed man. I suppose I always suspected..."

Flynn looked at his watch. "Excuse me, I have to speak to my people." He turned and walked toward the pulpit.

Maureen came up behind him and put her hand on his shoulder, turning him toward her. "Damn it, aren't you at least going to say good-bye?"

Flynn's face reddened, and he seemed to lose his composure, then cleared his throat. "I'm sorry...I didn't think you...Well—good-bye, then.... We won't speak again, will we? Good luck..." He hesitated, then leaned toward her but suddenly straightened up again.

She started to say something, but Gallagher's deep voice called out from the sacristy stairs, "Brian! Burke's here to see you!"

Flynn looked at his watch with some surprise.

Hickey called out from the organ, "It's a trap!"

Flynn hesitated, then looked at Maureen. She nodded slightly. He held her eyes for a moment and said, "Still trusting." He smiled and walked quickly around the altar and descended the stairs.

Burke stood at the gate in his shirt-sleeves, his shoulder holster empty and his hands in his pants pockets.

Flynn approached without caution and stood

close to the gate. "Well?" Burke didn't answer, and Flynn spoke curtly. "You're not going to ask me to give up or—"

"No."

Flynn called up to Gallagher, "Take a break." He turned to Burke. "Are you here to kill me?"

Burke took his hands out of his pockets and rested them on the bars. "There's an implied white flag here, isn't there? Do you think I'd kill you like that?"

"You should. You should always kill the other side's commander when you have a chance. If you were Bellini, I'd kill you."

"There're still rules."

"Yes, I just gave you one."

A few seconds passed in silence, then Flynn said, "What do you want?"

"I just wanted to say I have no personal animosity toward you."

Flynn smiled. "Well, I knew that. I could see that. And I've none toward you, Burke. That's the hell of it, isn't it? I've no personal hatred of your people, and most of them have none toward me."

"Then why are we here?"

"We're here because in 1154 Adrian the Fourth gave Henry the Second of England permission to bring his army to Ireland. We're here because the Red Bus to Clady passes Whitehorn Abbey. That's why I'm here. Why are you here?"

"I was on duty at five o'clock."

Flynn smiled, then said, "Well, that's damned little reason to die. I'm releasing you from your promise to join the attack. Perhaps in exchange you'll decide to kill Martin. Martin set up poor Harry to be here—did you figure that out?"

Burke's face was impassive.

Flynn glanced at his watch. 5:04. Something was wrong. "Hadn't you better go?"

"If you like. Also, if you'd like, I'll stay on the phone with you until 6:03."

Flynn looked at Burke closely. "I want to speak to Schroeder. Send him down here."

"That's not possible."

"I want to speak to him! Now!"

Burke answered, "No one is intimidated by your threats anymore. Least of all Bert Schroeder." He exhaled a deep sigh. "Captain Schroeder put the muzzle of his gun in his mouth . . ."

Flynn grabbed Burke's arm. "You're lying! I want to see his body."

Burke pulled away and walked down into the sacristy, then looked back toward Flynn. "I don't know what pushed him off the edge, but I know that somehow you're to blame." Burke stood at the corridor opening. Barely three feet away stood a masked ESD man with a Browning automatic shotgun. Burke edged toward the opening and looked back at Flynn. He seemed to vacillate, then said, "Good-bye."

Flynn nodded. "I'm glad we met."

CHAPTER 56

Bellini stood close to the conference table in the press room, his eyes focused on four long, unrolled sheets of blueprints, their corners weighted with coffee cups, ashtrays, and grenade canisters. Huddled around him were his squad leaders. The first three blueprints showed the basement, the main floor, and the upper levels. The fourth was a cutaway drawing of a side view of the Cathedral. Now that they were all in front of him, Bellini was unimpressed.

Gordon Stillway was seated in front of the blueprints, rapidly explaining the preliminary details. Bellini's brow was creased. He looked around to see if anyone was showing signs of enlightenment. All he could read in the blackened, sweaty faces was impatience, fatigue, and annoyance at the postponement.

Burke opened the door and came into the room. Bellini glanced up and gave him a look that didn't convey much gratitude or optimism. Burke saw Langley standing by the rear wall and joined him. They stood side by side and watched the scene at the table for a few seconds, then Burke spoke without looking away from the conference table. "Feeling better?"

Langley's tone was cool. "I've never felt better in my life."

"Me too." He looked at the spot on the floor where Schroeder had fallen. "How's Bert?"

Langley said, "A police doctor is treating him for physical exhaustion." Burke nodded.

Langley let a few seconds go by. "Did Flynn buy it?"

Burke said, "His next move may be to threaten to kill a hostage if we don't show him Schroeder's body . . . with the back of his head blown away."

Langley tapped the pocket that held Schroeder's service revolver. "Well . . . it's important that Flynn believes the plans he has are the plans Bellini will use . . . ." He inclined his head toward the squad leaders. "Lots of lives depend on that . . . ."

Burke changed the subject. "What are you doing about arresting Martin?"

Langley shook his head. "First of all, he's disappeared again. He's good at that. Secondly, I checked with the State Department joker, Sheridan, and Martin has diplomatic immunity, but they'll consider expelling—"

"I don't want him expelled."

Langley glanced at him. "Well, it doesn't matter because I also spoke with our FBI buddy, Hogan, and he says Martin has happily expelled himself—"

"He's gone?"

"Not yet, of course. Not before the show ends. He's booked on a Bermuda flight out of Kennedy—"

"What time?"

Langley gave him a sidelong glance. "Departs at 7:35. Breakfast at the Southampton Princess—forget it, Burke."

"Okay."

Langley watched the people at the conference table for a minute, then said, "Also, our CIA colleague, Kruger, says it's their show. Nobody wants you poking around. Okay?"

"Fine with me. Art Forgery Squad, you say?"

Langley nodded. "Yeah, I know a guy in it. It's the biggest fuck-off job anyone ever invented."

Burke made appropriate signs of attentiveness as Langley painted an idyllic picture of life in the Art Forgery Squad, but his mind was on something else.

Gordon Stillway concluded his preliminary description and said, "Now, tell me again what precisely it is you want to know?"

Bellini glanced at the wall clock: 5:09. He drew a deep breath. "I want to know how to get into Saint Patrick's Cathedral without using the front door."

Gordon Stillway spoke and answered questions, and the mood of the ESD squad leaders went from pessimism to wary optimism.

Bellini glanced at the bomb disposal people. Their lieutenant, Wendy Peterson, the only woman present in the room, leaned closer to the blueprint of the basement and pulled her long blond hair away from her face. Bellini watched the woman's cold blue eyes scanning the diagram. There were seventeen men, one woman, and two dogs, Brandy and Sally, in the Bomb Squad, and Bellini knew beyond a doubt that they were all certifiable lunatics, including the dogs.

Lieutenant Peterson turned to Stillway. Her voice was low, almost a whisper, which was a sort of trademark of this unit, thought Bellini. Peterson said, "If you wanted to plant bombs—let's assume you didn't have a great deal of explosives with you but you were looking for maximum effect—"

Stillway marked two *X*'s on the blueprints. "Here and here. The two big columns flanking the sacristy stairs." He paused reflectively and said, "About the time I was six years old they blasted the stairs through the foundation here and weakened the bedrock on which these columns sit. This is recorded information for anyone who cares to look it up, including the IRA."

Wendy Peterson nodded.

Stillway looked at her curiously. "Are you a bomb disposal person? What kind of job is that for a woman?"

She said, "I do a lot of needlepoint."

Stillway considered the statement for a second, then continued. "These columns are big, but with the type of explosives they have today, as you know, a demolition expert could bring them down, and half the Cathedral goes down with them...and God help you all if you're in there." He stared at Lieutenant Peterson.

Wendy Peterson said, "I'm not interested in the explosion."

Stillway again considered this obscure response and saw her meaning. He said, "But *I* am. There are not many like me around to rebuild the place...." He let his voice trail off.

Someone asked the question that had been on many people's minds all night. "*Can* it be rebuilt?"

Stillway nodded. "Yes, but it would probably look like the First Supernatural Bank."

A few men laughed, but the laughter died away quickly.

Stillway turned his attention back to the basement plans and detailed a few other idiosyncracies on the blueprints.

Bellini rubbed the stubble on his chin as he listened. He interrupted: "Mr. Stillway, if we were to bring an armored personnel carrier—weighing about ten tons...give or take a ton—up the front steps, through the main doors—"

Stillway sat up. "*What?* Those doors are invaluable—"

"Could the floor hold the weight?"

Stillway tried to calm himself and thought a moment, then said reluctantly, "If you have to do something so insane...destructive...Ten tons? Yes, according to the specs the floor will hold the weight...but there's always some question, isn't there?"

Bellini nodded. "Yeah.... One other thing...they said—these Fenians said—they were going to set fire to the Cathedral. We have reason to believe it may be the attic.... Is that possible...?"

"Why not?"

"Well...it looks pretty solid to me—"

"Solid *wood*." He shook his head. "What bastards..." Stillway suddenly stood. "Gentlemen—Miss—" He moved through the circle of people. "Excuse me if I don't stay to listen to you work out the details—I'm not feeling so well—but I'll be in the next room if you need me." He turned and left.

The ESD squad leaders began talking among themselves. The Bomb Squad people moved to the far end of the room, and Bellini watched them huddled around Peterson. Their faces, he noted, were always expressionless, their eyes vacant. He looked at his watch. 5:15. He would need fifteen to twenty minutes to modify the attack plan. It was going to be close, but the plan that was forming in his mind was much cleaner, less likely to become a massacre. He stepped away from the squad leaders and walked up to Burke and Langley. He hesitated a second, then said, "Thanks for Stillway. Good work."

Langley answered, "Anytime, Joe—excuse me—*Inspector*. You call, we deliver—architects, lawyers, hit men, pizza—"

Burke interrupted. "Do you feel better about this?"

Bellini nodded. "I'll take fewer casualties, the Cathedral has a fifty-fifty chance, but the hostages are still dead." He paused, then said, "Do you think there's any way to call off Logan's armored cavalry charge up Fifth Avenue?"

Langley shook his head. "Governor Doyle really has his heart set on that. Think of the armored car as one of those sound trucks they use in an election campaign."

Bellini found a cigar stub in his pocket and lit it, then looked at his watch again. "Flynn expected to be hit soon after 5:15, and he's probably sweating it out right now. Picture that scene—good, *good*. I hope the motherfucker is having the worst time of his fucking life."

Langley said, "If he's not now, I expect he will be shortly."

"Yeah. Cocksucker." Bellini's mouth turned up in a

vicious grin, and his eyes narrowed like little pig slits. "I hope he gets gut-shot and dies slow. I hope he pukes blood and acid and bile, until he—"

Langley held up his hand. "Please."

Bellini spun around and looked at Burke. "I can't believe Schroeder *told him*—"

Burke cut him off. "I never said that. I said I found the architect, and you should revise your attack. Captain Schroeder suffered a physical collapse. Right?"

Bellini laughed. "Of course he collapsed. I hit him in the face. What did you expect him to do—dance?" Bellini's expression became hard, and he made a contemptuous noise. "That cocksucker sold me out. He could have gotten a hundred men killed."

Burke said, "You forget about Schroeder, and I'll forget I heard you plant the idea in your squad leaders' heads about making a clean sweep in the Cathedral."

Bellini stayed quiet a minute, then said, "The attack is not going to be the way Schroeder told Flynn.... What's going to happen to his daughter?"

Langley took a file photo of Dan Morgan out of his pocket and laid it on a bridge table beside a snapshot of Terri O'Neal that he'd taken from Schroeder's wallet. "This man will murder her." He pointed to Terri O'Neal's smiling face.

The telephone rang, and Bellini looked at it. He said to the two men, "That's my buddy, Murray Kline. His Honor to you." He picked up the extension on the bridge table. "Gestapo Headquarters, Joe speaking."

There was a stammer on the other end, then the Mayor's voice came on, agitated. "Joe, what time are you moving out?"

Bellini felt a familiar heart-flutter at the sound of the military expression. Never again after today did he want to hear those words.

"Joe?"

"Yeah ... well, the architect was worth the wait—"

"Good. Very good. What *time* are you jumping off?"

Jumping off. His heart gave another leap, and he felt like there was ice water in his stomach. "About 5:35—give or take."

"Can't you move it up?"

Bellini's voice had an insolent tone. "No!"

"I told you there are people trying to stop this rescue—"

"I don't get involved in politics."

Roberta Spiegel's voice came on the line. "Okay, forget the fucking politicians. The bombs, Bellini—"

"Call me Joe."

"You're leaving the Bomb Squad damned little time to find and defuse the goddamned *bombs*, Captain."

"Inspector!"

"Listen, you—"

"*You* listen, Spiegel—why don't you crawl around with the fucking dogs and help them sniff out the bombs? Brandy, Sally, and Robbie." He turned to Burke and Langley and smiled, a look of triumph on his face.

Langley winced.

Bellini continued before she could recover, knowing there was no reason to stop now. "They're short on dogs since your last fucking budget cuts, and they could use the help. You have your big nose into everything else."

There was a long silence on the line, then Spiegel laughed. "All right, you bastard, you can say what you want now, but later—"

"Yeah, later. I'd give my left arm for a guaranteed later. We move at 5:35. That's not negotiable—"

"Is Inspector Langley there?"

"Hold on." He covered the mouthpiece. "You want to talk to the Dragon Lady?" Langley's face flushed, and he hesitated before taking the phone from Bellini, who moved back to the conference table. "Langley here."

Spiegel said, "Do you know where Schroeder is? His backup negotiator can't locate him."

Langley said, "He's collapsed."

"Collapsed?"

"Yeah, you know, like fell down, passed out."

"Oh . . . well, get him inflated again and get him here to the state offices in Rockefeller Center. He has to do his hero act later."

"I thought he was supposed to be the fall guy."

She said, "No, you're a little behind on this. . . . We've rethought that. He's the hero now no matter what happens. He's got lots of good press contacts."

"Who's the fall guy?"

She went on, "You see, there are no such things as victory or defeat anymore—there are only public relations problems—"

"Who's the fall guy?"

Spiegel said, "That's you. You won't be alone, though . . . and you'll come out of it all right. I'll see to that."

Langley didn't answer.

She said, "Listen, Philip, I think you should be here during the assault."

Langley's eyebrows went up at the use of his first name. He noted that her voice was pleasant, almost demure. "Rescue. You have to call it a rescue, Roberta." He winked at Burke.

Spiegel's voice was a little sharper. "Whatever. We—*I* want you up here."

"I think I'll stay down here."

"You get your ass up here in five minutes."

He glanced at Burke. "All right." He hung up and stared down at the phone. "This has been a screwy night."

"Full moon," said Burke. There was a lengthy silence, then Langley said, "Are you going in with Bellini?"

Burke lit a cigarette. "I think I should . . . to tidy up those loose ends . . . get hold of any notes the Fenians might have kept. There are secrets in that place . . . mysteries, as the Major said. And before Bellini starts blowing heads off . . . or the place goes up in smoke . . ."

Langley said, "Do what you have to do . . . ." He forced a smile. "Do you want to change places with me and go hold Spiegel's hand?"

"No thanks."

Langley glanced nervously at his watch. "Okay . . . listen, tell Bellini to keep Schroeder locked in that room. At dawn we'll come for Schroeder and parade him past the cameras like an Olympic hero. Schroeder's in, Langley's out."

Burke nodded, then said, "That mounted cop . . . Betty Foster . . . God, it seems so long ago . . . .

Anyway, make sure she gets something out of this...and if I don't get a chance to thank her later...you can..."

"I'll take care of it." He shook his head. "Screwy night." He moved toward the door, then turned back. "Here's another one for you to work out when you get in there. We lifted the fingerprints off the glass that Hickey used." He nodded toward the chair Hickey had sat in. "The prints were smudged, but Albany and the FBI say it's ninety percent certain it was Hickey, and we've got a few visual identifications from people who saw him on TV—"

Burke nodded. "That clears that up—"

"Not quite. The Jersey City medical examiner did a dental check on the remains they exhumed and..." He looked at Burke. "Spooky...really spooky..."

Burke said quickly, "Come off it, Langley."

Langley laughed. "Just kidding. The coffin was filled with dirt, and there was a note in there in Hickey's handwriting. I'll tell you what it said later." He smiled and opened the door. "Betty Foster, right? See you later, Patrick." He closed the door behind him.

Burke looked across the room. More than a dozen ESD leaders, completely clad in black, grouped in a semicircle around the table. Above them a wall clock ticked off the minutes. As he watched they all straightened up, almost in unison, like a football team out of a huddle, and began filing out the door. Bellini stayed behind, occupied with some detail. Burke stared at his black, hulking figure in the brightly lit room and was reminded of a dark rain cloud in a sunny sky.

Burke walked over to the conference table and

pulled on a black turtleneck sweater, then slipped back into his flak jacket. He adjusted the green carnation he'd gotten from an ESD man who had passed out a basketful of them. Burke looked down at the blueprints and read the notations of squad assignments hastily scrawled across them. He said to Bellini, "Where's the safest place I can be during the attack?"

Bellini thought a moment, then said, "Los Angeles."

CHAPTER 57

Brian Flynn stood in the high pulpit, a full story above the main floor. He looked out at the Cathedral spread before him, then spoke into the microphone. "Lights."

The lights began to go out in sections: the sanctuary, ambulatory, and Lady Chapel lights first, the switches pulled by Hickey; then the lights in the four triforia controlled by Sullivan, followed by the choirloft lights, and finally the huge hanging chandeliers over the nave, extinguished from the electrical panels in the loft. The vestibules, side altars, and bookstore darkened last as Hickey moved through the Cathedral pulling the remaining switches.

A few small lights still burned, Flynn noticed. Lights whose switches were probably located outside the Cathedral. Hickey and the others smashed the ones that were accessible, the sound of breaking glass filling the quiet spaces.

Flynn nodded. The beginning of the attack would be signaled when the last lights suddenly went out, a result of the police pulling the main switch in the rectory basement. The police would expect a dark

Cathedral where their infrared scopes would give them an overwhelming advantage. But Flynn had no intention of letting them have such an advantage, so every votive candle, hundreds and hundreds of them, had been lit, and they shimmered in the surrounding blackness, an offering of sorts, he reflected, an ancient comfort against the terrors of the dark and a source of light the police could not extinguish. Also, at intervals throughout the Cathedral, large phosphorus flares were placed to provide additional illumination and to cause the police infrared scopes to white out. Captain Joe Bellini, Flynn thought, had a surprise in store for him.

Flynn placed his hands on the cool Carrara marble of the pulpit balustrade and blinked to adjust his eyes to the dim light as he examined the vast interior. Flickering shadows played off the walls and columns, but the ceiling was obscure. It was easy to imagine there was no roof, that the towering columns had been relieved of their burden and that overhead was only the night sky—an illusion that would be reality on the following evening.

The long black galleries of the triforia above, dark and impenetrable in the best of light, were nearly invisible now, and the only sense he had of anything being up there was the sound of rifles scraping against stone.

The choir loft was a vast expanse of blackness, totally shrouded from the murky light below as if a curtain had been drawn across the rail; but Flynn could feel the two dark presences up there more strongly than when he had seen them, as though they basked in blackness and flourished in the dark.

Flynn drew a long breath through his nostrils. The burning phosphorus exuded an overpowering, pungent smell that seemed to alter the very nature of the Cathedral. Gone was that strange musky odor, that mixture of stale incense, tallow, and something else that was indefinable, which he had labeled the Roman Catholic smell, the smell that never changed from church to church and that evoked mixed memories of childhood. *Gone, finally gone*, he thought. *Driven out.* And he was inordinately pleased with this, as though he'd won a theological argument with a bishop.

He lowered his eyes and looked over the flares and the dozens of racks of votive candles. The light seemed less comforting now, the candles burning in their red or blue glass like brimstone around the altars, and the brilliant white phosphorus like the leaping flames of hell. And the saints on their altars, he noticed, were moving, gyrating in obscene little dances, the beatific expressions on their white faces suddenly revealing a lewdness that he had always suspected was there.

But the most remarkable metamorphosis was in the windows, which seemed to hang in black space, making them appear twice their actual size, rising to dizzying heights so that if you looked up at them you actually experienced some vertigo. And above the soaring choir loft, atop the thousands of unseen brass pipes of the organ, sat the round rose window, which had become a dark blue swirling vortex that would suck you out of this netherworld of shadows and spirits— which was only, after all, the anteroom of hell—suck you, finally and irretrievably, into hell itself.

Flynn adjusted the microphone and spoke. He doubted his voice would break the spell of death, as she had said, and in any case he had the opposite purpose. "Ladies and gentlemen...brothers and sisters..." He looked at his watch. 5:14. "The time, as you know, has come. Stay alert...it won't be much longer now." He drew a short breath, which carried out through the speakers. "It's been my great honor to have been your leader.... I want to assure you we'll meet again, if not in Dublin, then in a place of light, the land beyond the Western Sea, whatever name it goes by...because whatever God controls our ultimate destiny cannot deny our earthly bond to one another, our dedication to our people...." He felt his voice wavering. "Don't be afraid." He turned off the microphone.

All eyes went from him to the doors. Rockets and rifles were at the ready, and gas masks hung loosely over chests where hearts beat wildly.

John Hickey stood below the pulpit and threw a rocket tube, rifle, and gas mask to Flynn. Hickey called out in a voice with no trace of fear, "Brian, I'm afraid this is good-bye, lad. It's been a pleasure, and I'm sure we'll meet again in a place of incredible light, not to mention heat." He laughed and moved off into the half-shadows of the sanctuary.

Flynn slung the rifle across his chest, then broke the seal on the rocket and extended the tube, aiming it at the center vestibule.

His eyes became misty, from the phosphorus, he thought, and they went out of focus, the clear plastic aiming sight of the rocket acting as a prism in the dim candlelight. Colors leaped all around the deathly still spaces before him like fireworks seen at a great distance, or like those phantom battles fought in his worst silent nightmares. And there was no sound here either but the steady ticking of his watch near his ear, the rushing of blood in his head, and the faraway pounding of his chest.

He tried to conjure up faces, people he had known from the past, parents, relatives, friends, and enemies, but no images seemed to last more than a second. Instead, an unexpected scene flashed into his consciousness and stayed there: Whitehorn Abbey's subbasement, Father Donnelly talking expansively, Maureen pouring tea, himself examining the ring. They were all speaking, but he could not hear the voices, and the movements were slow, as if they had all the time in the world. He recognized the imagery, understood that this scene represented the last time he was even moderately happy and at peace.

John Hickey stood before the Cardinal's throne and bowed. "Your Eminence, I have an overwhelming desire," he said matter-of-factly, "to slit your shriveled white throat from ear to ear, then step back and watch your blood run onto your scarlet robe and over that obscene thing hanging around your neck."

The Cardinal suddenly reached out and touched Hickey's cheek.

Hickey drew back quickly and made a noise that sounded like a startled yelp. He recovered and jumped back onto the step, pulled the Cardinal down from his throne, and pushed him roughly toward the sacristy stairs.

They descended the steps, and Hickey paused at the landing where Gallagher knelt just inside the doors of the crypt. "Here's company for you, Frank." Hickey prodded the Cardinal down the remaining stairs, pushing him against the gates so that he faced into the sacristy. He extended the Cardinal's right arm and handcuffed his wrist to the bars.

Hickey said, "Here's a new logo for your church, Your Eminence. Been a good while since they've come up with a new one." He spoke as he cuffed the other extended arm to a bar. "We've had Christ on the cross, Saint Peter crucified upside down, Andrew crucified on an X cross, and now we've got you hanging on the sacristy gates of Saint Patrick's. Lord, that's a natural. Sell a million icons."

The Cardinal turned his head toward Hickey. "The Church has survived ten thousand like you," he said impassively, "and will survive you, and grow stronger precisely because there are people like you among us."

"Is that a fact?" Hickey balled his hand into a fist but was aware that Gallagher had come up behind him. He turned and led Gallagher by the arm back to the open crypt doors. "Stay here. Don't speak to him and don't listen to him."

Gallagher stared down the steps. The Cardinal's outstretched arms and red robes covered half the grillwork. Gallagher felt a constriction in his stomach; he looked back at Hickey but was not able to hold his stare. Gallagher turned away and nodded.

Hickey took the staircase that brought him up to the right of the altar and approached Maureen and Baxter. They rose as he drew near.

Hickey indicated two gas masks that lay on the length of the pew that separated the two people. "Put those on at the first sign of gas. If there's one thing I can't stand, it's the sight of a woman vomiting— reminds me of my first trip to Dublin—drunken whores ducking into alleys and getting sick. Never forgot that."

Maureen and Baxter stayed silent. Hickey went on, "It may interest you to know that the plan of this attack was sold to us at a low price, and the plan doesn't provide much for your rescue or the saving of this Cathedral."

Baxter said, "As long as it provides for your death, it's a fine plan."

Hickey turned to Baxter. "You're a vindictive bastard. I'll bet you'd like to bash in another young Irishman's throat, now you've got the hang of it and the taste for it."

"You're the most evil, twisted man I've ever met." Baxter's voice was barely under control.

Hickey winked at him. "Now you're talking." He turned his attention to Maureen. "Don't let Megan or Leary shoot you, lass. Take cover between these pews and lie still in the dark. Very still. Here's your watch back, my love. Look at it as the bullets are whistling over your head. Keep checking it as you stare up at the ceiling. Sometime between 6:03 and 6:04 you'll hear a noise, and the floor will bounce ever so slightly beneath your lovely rump, and the columns will start to tremble. Out of the darkness, way up there, you will see great sections of ceiling falling toward you, end over end, as in slow motion, right onto your pretty face. And remember, lass, your last thoughts while you're being crushed to death should be of Brian—or Harry…any man will do, I suppose." He laughed as he turned away and walked toward the bronze plate on the floor. He bent over and lifted the plate.

Maureen called after him: "My last thought will be that God should have mercy on all our souls…and that your soul, John Hickey, should finally rest in peace."

Hickey threw her a kiss, then dropped down the ladder, drawing the bronze plate closed over him.

Maureen sat back on the pew. Baxter stood a moment, then moved toward her. She looked up at him and put out her hand. Baxter took it and sat close beside her so that their bodies touched. He looked around at the flickering shadows. "I tried to picture how this would end…but *this*…"

"Nothing is ever as you expect it to be…. I never expected you to be…"

Baxter held her more tightly. "I'm frightened."

"Me too." She thought a moment, then smiled. "But we made it, you know. We never gave them an inch."

He smiled in return. "No, we never did, did we?"

Flynn peered into the darkness to his right and stared at the empty throne, then looked out through the carved wooden screen to where the chancel organ keyboard stood on its platform beside the sanctuary. A candle was lit on the organ console, and for a moment he thought John Hickey was sitting at the keys. He blinked, and an involuntary noise rose in his throat. Pedar Fitzgerald sat at the organ, his hands poised over the keys, his body upright but tilted slightly back. His face was raised toward the ceiling as if he were about to burst into song. Flynn could make out the tracheal tube still protruding from his mouth, the white dead skin, and the open eyes that looked alive as the flame of the candle danced in them. "Hickey," he said softly to himself, "Hickey, you unspeakable, filthy, obscene..." He glanced up into the choir loft but could not see Megan, and he concentrated again on the front doors.

5:20 came, then 5:25—

Flynn looked around the column to his rear and saw Maureen and Baxter huddled together. He watched them briefly, then turned back to the vestibule.

5:30.

A tension hung in the still, cold air of the Cathedral, a tension so palpable it could be heard in the steady beating chests, felt on the sweaty brows, tasted in the mouth as bile, seen in the dancing lights, and smelled in the stench of burning phosphorous.

5:35 came, and the thought began to take hold in the minds of the people in the Cathedral that it was already too late to mount an attack that would serve any purpose.

In the long southwest triforium George Sullivan put down his rifle and picked up his bagpipes. He tucked the bag under his arm, adjusted the three drone pipes over his shoulder, and put his fingers on the eight-holed chanter, and then put his mouth to the blowpipe. Against all orders and against all reason he began to play. The slow, haunting melody of "Amazing Grace" floated from the chanter and hummed from the drone pipes into the candlelit silence.

There was a very slight, almost imperceptible lessening of tension, a relaxing of vigilance, coupled with the most primitive of beliefs that if you anticipated something terrible, imagined it in the most minute detail, it would not happen.

BOOK V

Assault

For the great Gaels of Ireland
Are the men that God made mad,
For all their wars are merry,
And all their songs are sad.

G. K. Chesterton

CHAPTER 58

Bellini stood at the open door of the small elevator in the basement below the Archbishop's sacristy. An ESD man stood on the elevator roof and shone a handheld spotlight up the long shaft. The shaft began as brick, but at a level above the main floor it was wood-walled and seemed to continue up, as Stillway had pointed out, to a level that would bring it through the triforium's attic.

Bellini called softly, "How's it look?"

The ESD man replied, "We'll see." He took a tension clamp from a utility pouch, screwed it tightly to the elevator cable at hip level, and then stepped onto it and tested its holding strength. He screwed on another and stepped up to it. Step by step, very quickly now, he began working his way up the shaft to the triforium level eight stories above.

Bellini looked back into the curving corridor behind him. The First ESD Assault Squad stood silently, laden with equipment and armed with silenced pistols and rifles that were fitted with infrared scopes.

On the floor just outside the elevator a communications man sat in front of a small field-phone switchboard that was connected by wire to the remaining ESD Assault Squads and to the state office in Rockefeller Center. Bellini said to the man, "When the shit hits the fan, intersquad communication takes priority over His Honor and the Commissioner.... In fact, I don't want to hear from them unless it's to tell us to pull out."

The commo man nodded.

Burke came down the corridor. His face was smeared with greasepaint, and he was screwing a big silencer onto the barrel of an automatic pistol.

Bellini watched him. "This don't look like Los Angeles, does it, Burke?"

Burke stuck the automatic in his belt. "Let's go, Bellini."

Bellini shrugged. He climbed the stepladder and stood on the roof of the elevator, and Burke came up beside him in the narrow shaft. Bellini shone his light up the wall until it rested on the oak door that opened on the Archbishop's sacristy twenty feet above. He said to Burke in a quiet voice, "If there's a Fenian standing there with a submachine gun and he hears us climbing, there'll be a waterfall of blood and bodies dropping back on this elevator."

Burke shifted Bellini's light farther up and picked out the dim outline of the climbing man, now about one hundred feet up the shaft. "Or there may be an ambush waiting up there at the top."

Bellini nodded. "Looked good on paper." He shut off his light. "You got about one minute to stop being all asshole and get out of here."

"Okay."

Bellini glanced up at the dark shaft. "I wonder...I wonder if that door or any door in this place is mined?" Bellini was speaking nervously now. "Remember in the army...all the phony minefield signs? All the other bullshit psy-warfare...?" He shook his head. "After the first shot everything is okay...it's all the shit before.... Flynn's got me psyched out.... He understands...I'm sure he's crazier than me...."

Burke said, "Maybe Schroeder told him how crazy you really are...maybe Flynn's scared of *you*."

Bellini nodded. "Yeah..." He laughed, then his face hardened. "You know something? I *feel* like killing someone.... I have an *urge*...like when I need a cigarette...you know?"

Burke looked at his watch. "At least this one can't go into overtime. At 6:03 it's finished."

Bellini also checked his watch. "Yeah...no overtime. Just a two-minute warning, then a big bang, and the stadium falls down and the game is over." He laughed again, and Burke glanced at him.

The ESD climber reached the top of the shaft. He tied a nylon rope ladder to the pulley crossbeam and let the ladder fall. Bellini caught it before it hit the metal roof of the elevator. The communications man threw up a field-phone receiver, and Bellini clipped it to the shoulder of his flak jacket. "Well, Burke...here goes. Once you get *on* the ladder, you're not getting *off* the ladder so easy." He began climbing. Burke followed, and one by one the ten ESD men climbed behind them.

Bellini paused at the oak door of the Archbishop's sacristy and put his ear to it. He heard footsteps and froze. Suddenly the crack of light at the bottom of the door disappeared. He waited several more seconds, his rifle pointed at the door and his heart pounding in his chest. The footsteps moved away. His phone clicked, and he answered it quietly. "Yeah."

The operator said, "Our people outside report all the lights are going out in there—but there's…like candlelight…maybe flares lighting up the windows."

Bellini swore. The flares, he knew, would be white phosphorus. *Bastards.* Right from the beginning…right from the fucking beginning…He continued up the swaying ladder.

At the top of the shaft the climber sat on the crossbeam, pointing his light farther up, and Bellini saw a small opening where the shaft wall ended a few feet from the sloping ceiling of the triforium attic. Bellini mumbled, "Caught a fucking break at least." He stood precariously on the crossbeam, eight stories above the basement, and stretched toward the opening, grabbing at the top of the wooden wall. He pulled himself up, squeezing his head and broad shoulders into the space, a silenced pistol in his hand. He blinked in the darkness of the half attic, fully expecting to be shot between the eyes. He waited, then turned on his light, cocking his pistol at the same time. Nothing moved but his pounding chest against the top edge of the wall. He slid down headfirst five feet to a beam that ran over the plaster lathing, breaking his fall with his outstretched arms and righting himself silently.

Burke's head and shoulders appeared in the opening, and Bellini pulled him through. One by one the First Assault Squad dropped into the small side attic behind the triforium.

Bellini crawled over the beams, sidled up to the wooden knee-wall and moved along it until he felt a small door Stillway had described. On the other side of the door was the southeast triforium, and in the triforium, he was certain, were one or more gunmen. He put a small audio amplifier to the door and listened. He heard no footsteps, no sound of life in the triforium, but somewhere in the Cathedral a bagpipe was playing "Amazing Grace." He mumbled to himself, "Assholes."

He backed carefully away from the wall and led his squad to the low, narrow space where the sloping roof met the stone of the outside wall. He unclipped the field phone from his jacket and spoke quietly to his switchboard below. "Report to all stations—First Squad in place. No contact."

* * *

The Second Assault Squad of ESD men climbed the rungs of the wide chimney, fire axes slung to their backs. They passed the steel door in the brick and continued up to the chimney pot.

The squad leader attached a khaki nylon rappelling line to the top rung and held the gathered rope in his hands. The cold night air blew into the chimney, making a deep, hollow, whistling sound. The squad leader stuck a periscope out of the chimney pot and scanned the towers, but the Fenians were not visible from this angle, and he pointed the scope at the cross-shaped roof. Two dormers faced him, and he saw that the hatches on them were open. "Shit." He reached back, and the squad commo man cranked the field phone slung to his chest and handed him the receiver. The squad leader reported, "Captain, Second Squad in position. The damned hatches are open now, and it's going to be tough crossing this roof if there're people leaning out those dormers shooting at us."

Bellini answered in a barely audible voice. "Just hold there until the towers are knocked out. Then move."

The Third Assault Squad climbed the chimney behind the Second Squad but stopped their ascent below the steel door. The squad leader maneuvered to a position beside the door, directing a flashlight on the latch. Slowly he reached out with a mechanical pincher and tentatively touched the latch, then drew it away. He called Bellini on the field phone. "Captain. Third in position. Can't tell if there are alarms or mines on the door."

Bellini answered, "Okay. When Second Squad clears the chimney, you open the door and find out."

"Right." He handed the phone back to the commo man hanging beside him, who said, "How come we never rehearsed anything like this?"

The squad leader said, "I don't think the situation ever came up before."

At 5:35 the ESD sniper-squad leader in Rockefeller Center picked up the ringing field phone on the desk in a tenth-floor office. Joe Bellini's voice came over the line, subdued but with no hesitation. He gave the code word. "Bull Run. Sixty seconds."

The sniper-squad leader acknowledged, hung up, drew a long breath, and pushed the office intercom buzzer in an alerting signal.

Fourteen snipers moved quickly to the seven windows that faced the louvered sections of the towers across Fifth Avenue and crouched below the sills. The intercom sounded again, and the snipers rose and threw open the sashes, then steadied their rifles on the cold stone ledges. The squad leader watched the second hand of his watch, then gave the final short signal.

Fourteen silenced rifles coughed, and the metallic sound of sliding operating rods clattered in the offices, followed by whistling sounds, then the coughs of another volley, breaking up into random firing as the snipers fired at will. Spent brass cartridge casings dropped silently on the plush carpets.

Brian Flynn looked down at the television sitting on the floor of the pulpit. The screen showed a close-up shot of the bell tower, the blue-lit shadow of Mullins staring out through the torn louvers. Mullins raised a mug to his lips. The scene shifted to another telescopic close-up of Devane in the south tower, a bored look on his face. The audio was tuned down, but Flynn could hear the droning voice of a reporter. The reporter gave the time. Everything seemed very ordinary until the camera panned back, and Flynn caught a glimpse of light from the rose window, which should have been dark. He realized he was seeing a video replay from early in the evening. Flynn reached for the field phone.

A dozen Fenian spotters in the surrounding buildings watched the Cathedral through field glasses.

One spotter saw movement at the mouth of the chimney. A second spotter saw the line of windows in Rockefeller Center open.

Strobe lights began signaling to the Cathedral towers.

Rory Devane knelt behind a stone mullion, blowing into his cold hands, his rifle cradled in the bend of his arms. His eye caught the flashing strobes, and then he saw a line of muzzle flashes in the building across the Avenue. He grabbed for the field phone, and it rang simultaneously, but before he could pick it up, shards of disintegrating stone flew into his face. The dark tower room was filled with sharp pinging sounds and echoed with the metallic clatter of tearing copper louvers.

A bullet slammed into Devane's flak jacket, sending him reeling back. He felt another round pass through his throat, but didn't feel the one that ricocheted into his forehead and fractured his skull.

Donald Mullins stood in the east end of the bell room staring out across the East River trying to see the predawn light coming over Long Island. He had half convinced himself that there would be no attack, and when the field phone rang he knew it was Flynn telling him the Fenians had won.

A strobe light flashed from a window in the Waldorf-Astoria, and his heart missed a beat. He heard one of the bells behind him ring sharply, and he spun around. Muzzle flashes, in rapid succession like popping flashbulbs, ran the width of the building across the Avenue, and more strobe lights flashed in the distance; but these warnings, which he had been watching for all night, made no impression on his mind. A series of bullets slammed into his flak jacket, knocked the breath out of him, and picked him up off his feet.

Mullins regained his footing and lunged for the field phone, which was still ringing. A bullet shattered his elbow, and another passed through his hand. His rifle fell to the floor, and everything went black. Still another round entered behind his ear and disintegrated a long swath of his skull.

Mullins staggered in blind pain and grabbed at the bell straps hanging through the open stairwell. He felt himself falling, sliding down the swinging straps.

Father Murphy huddled against the cold iron ladder in the bell tower, half unconscious from fatigue. A faint peal of the bell overhead made him look up, and he saw Mullins falling toward him. Instinctively he grabbed at the man before he passed through the opening in the landing.

Mullins veered from the gaping hole and landed on the floor, shrieking in pain. He lurched around the room, his hands to his face and his sense of balance gone along with his inner ear, blood running between his fingers. He ran headlong toward the east wall of the tower and crashed through the splintered glass, tumbling three stories to the roof of the northwest triforium.

Father Murphy tried to comprehend the surrealistic scene that had just passed before his cloudy eyes. He blinked several times and stared at the shattered window.

Abby Boland thought she heard a sound on the roof of the triforium's attic behind her and froze, listening.

* * *

Leary thought he heard the pealing of a bell from the tower and strained to listen for another.

Flynn was calling into the field phone, "South tower, north tower, answer."

In the chimney the commo men with the two squads answered their phones simultaneously and heard Bellini's voice. "Both towers clear. Move!"

The Second Squad leader threw the gathered rope up and out of the chimney and scrambled over the top into the cold air. They had gambled that by leaving on the blue floodlights that bathed the lower walls of the Cathedral, they wouldn't alert the Fenian spotters in the surrounding buildings or in the attic. But the squad leader felt very visible as he rappelled down the side of the chimney. He landed on the dark roof of the northeast triforium, followed by his ten-man Assault Squad. They moved quickly over the lower roof to a slender pinnacle that rose between two great windows of the ambulatory. The squad found the iron rungs in the stone that Stillway said would be there and climbed up to a higher roof, partially visible in the diffused lighting. Dropping onto the roof, they lay in the wide rain gutter where the wall met the sloping expanse of gray slate shingles, then began crawling in the gutter toward the closest dormer. The squad leader kept his eyes on the dormer as he moved toward it. He saw something poke out of the open hatchway, something long and slender like a rifle barrel.

The Third Assault Squad leader at the steel door watched the last dark form disappear from the chimney pot overhead and hooked his pinchers on the door latch, muttered a prayer, and lifted the latch, then slowly pushed in on the door, wondering if he was going to be blown up the chimney like soot.

Jean Kearney and Arthur Nulty stood in dormered hatchways, which were on opposite sides of the pitched roof, scanning the night sky for helicopters. Nulty, on the north slope of the roof, thought he heard a sound below. He looked straight down at the triforium roof but saw nothing in the dark. He heard a sound to his immediate right and turned. A long line of black shapes, like beetles, he thought, was crawling through the rain gutter toward him. He couldn't imagine how they got there without helicopters or without the spotters in the surrounding buildings seeing them climb the walls. Instinctively he raised his rifle and drew a bead on the first man, who was no more than twenty feet away.

One of the men shouted, and they all rose to one

knee. Nulty saw rifles coming into firing position, and he squeezed off a single round. One of the black-clad men slapped his hand over his flak jacket, lost his balance and fell out of the rain gutter; he dropped three stories to the triforium roof below, making a loud thump in the quiet night.

Jean Kearney turned at the sound of Nulty's shot. "Arthur! What—?"

The dormer where Nulty stood erupted in flying splinters of wood, and Nulty fell back into the attic. He rose very quickly to his feet, took two steps toward Jean Kearney, his arms waving, then toppled over the catwalk and crashed to the plaster lathing below.

Kearney stared down at his body, then looked up at the dormer hatch and saw a man hunched in the opening. She raised her rifle and fired, but the man jumped out of view.

Kearney ran along the catwalk and dived across the wooden boards, reaching a glowing oil lamp. She flung it up in an arc, and it crashed into a pile of chopped wood. She rolled a few feet farther and reached for the field phone, which was ringing.

Men were dropping into the attic from the open hatches, scrambling over the catwalks and firing blindly with silenced rifles into the half-lighted spaces. Bullets hit the rafters and floor around her with a thud.

Kearney fired back, and the noise of her rifle attracted a dozen muzzle flashes. She felt a sharp pain in her thigh and cried out, dropping her rifle. Blood gushed through her fingers as she held a hand under her skirt against the wound. With her other hand she felt on the floor for the ringing phone.

The woodpile was beginning to blaze now, and the light silhouetted the dark shapes moving toward her. They were throwing canisters of fire-extinguishing gas into the blazing wood, but the fire was growing larger.

She picked up her rifle again and shot into the blinding light of the fire. A man cried out, and then answering shots whistled past her head. She dragged herself toward the bell tower passage, leaving a trail of blood on the dusty floor. She reached another oil lamp and flung it into the pile of wood that lay between her and the tower, blocking her escape route.

She lay in a prone position, firing wildly into the flame-lit attic around her. Another man moaned in pain. Bullets ripped up the wood around her, and the windows in the peak behind her began shattering. The fires were reaching toward the roof now, curling around the rafters. The smell of burning wax candles mixed with the aroma of old, seasoned oak, and the heat from the fires began to warm her chilled body.

In the northeast triforium Eamon Farrell heard a distinct noise on the roof in the attic behind him. His already raw nerves had had enough. He held his breath as he looked down into the Cathedral at Flynn in the pulpit cranking the field phone. Sullivan and Abby Boland across from him were leaning anxiously out over the balustrades. Something was about to happen, and Eamon Farrell saw no reason to wait around to see what it was.

Farrell turned slowly from the balustrade, lay down his rifle, and opened the door in the knee wall behind him. He entered the dark attic and turned his flashlight on the steel door in the chimney. God, he was certain, had given him an escape route, and he had been right to keep it from Flynn and right to use it.

Carefully he approached the door, put the flashlight in his pocket, then lowered himself through the opening until his feet found an iron rung. He closed the door and stepped down to the next rung in the total darkness. His shoulder brushed something, and he gave a startled yelp, then reached out and touched a very taut rope.

He looked upward and saw a piece of the starlit sky at the mouth of the chimney, which was partly obscured by a moving shape. His stomach heaved as he became aware that he was not alone.

He heard someone breathe, smelled the presence of other bodies in the sooty space around him, pictured in his mind dangling shapes swinging on ropes in the darkness like bats, inches from him. He cleared his throat. "Wha—who . . . ?"

A voice said, "It ain't Santa Claus, pal."

Farrell felt cold steel pressed against his cheekbone, and he shouted, "I surrender!" But his shout panicked the ESD man, and darkness erupted in a silent flash of blinding light. Farrell fell feet-first and then somersaulted into the black shaft, blood splattering over his flailing arms.

The Third Squad leader said, "I wonder where *he* was going?" The squad moved silently through the chimney door and assembled in the dark attic over the bride's room.

Flynn turned off the television. He spoke into the pulpit microphone. "It's begun. Keep alert. Steady now. Watch the doors and windows. Rockets ready."

Bellini squatted at the door in the knee wall and listened to Flynn's voice through the public address system. "Yeah, motherfuckers, you watch the doors and windows." The First Squad knelt to the sides with rifles raised. Bellini put his hand to the latch, raised it, and pushed. The ESD men behind him converged on the door, and Bellini threw it open, rolling onto the floor into the dark triforium. The men poured through after him, diving and rolling over the cold floor, weapons pointing up and down the long gallery.

The triforium was empty, but on the floor lay a black morning coat, top hat, and a tricolored sash with the words Parade Marshal.

Half the squad crawled along the parapet, spacing themselves at intervals. The other half ran in a crouch to where the triforium turned at a right angle overlooking the south transept.

Bellini made his way to the corner of the right angle and raised an infrared periscope. The entire Cathedral was lit with candles and phosphorus flares and, even as he watched, the burning phosphorus caused the image to white out and disappear. He swore and lowered the periscope. Someone handed him a daylight periscope, and he focused on the long triforium across the transept. In the flickering light from below he could see a tall man in a bagpiper's tunic leaning over the balustrade and aiming a rifle at the transept doors across the nave. He shifted the periscope and looked down toward the dark choir loft but saw nothing, then scanned right to the long triforium across the nave and caught a glimpse of what looked like a woman in overalls. He focused on her and saw that her young face looked frightened. He smiled and traversed farther right to the short triforium across the sanctuary where the chimney was. It appeared empty, and he began to wonder just how many people Flynn had used to take the Cathedral and fuck up everyone's day.

Burke came up behind him, and Bellini whispered in his ear, "This is not going so bad." Bellini's field phone clicked, and he put it to his ear. The Third Squad reported to all points. "In position. One Fenian in chimney—KIA."

A voice cut in, and Bellini heard the excited shouts of the Second Squad leader. "Attic ablaze! Fighting fire! Three ESD casualties—one Fenian dead—one still shooting. Fire helicopters in position, but they won't come in until attic is secure. May have to abandon attic!"

Bellini looked up to the vaulted ceiling. He cupped his hand around the mouthpiece and spoke quickly. "You stay there and fight that fucking fire, you kill the fucking Fenian, and you bring those fire choppers in. You piss on that fire, you spit on that fire, but you do not leave that fire. Acknowledge."

The squad leader seemed calmer. "Roger, Roger, okay...."

Bellini put down the field phone and looked at Burke. "The attic is burning."

Burke peered up into the darkness. Somewhere above the dimly outlined ceiling, about four stories up, there was light and heat, but here it was dark and cold. Somewhere below there were explosives that could level the entire east end of the Cathedral. He looked at his watch and said, "The bombs will put the fire out."

Bellini looked at him. "Your sense of humor sucks, you know?"

* * *

Flynn stood in the pulpit, a feeling of impotence growing in him. It was ending too quietly, no bangs, not even whimpers, at least none that he could hear. He was becoming certain that the police had finally found Gordon Stillway, compliments of Bartholomew Martin, and they weren't going to come in through the doors and windows—Schroeder had lied or had been used by them. They were burrowing in right now, like rot in the timbers of a house, and the whole thing would fall with hardly a shot fired. He looked at his watch. 5:37. He hoped Hickey was still alive down there, waiting for the Bomb Squad in the darkness. He thought a moment, and the overwhelming conviction came over him that Hickey at least would complete his mission.

Flynn spoke in the microphone. "They've taken out the towers. George, Eamon, Frank, Abby, Leary, Megan—keep alert. They may have found another way in. Gallagher, watch the crypt behind you. Everyone, remember the movable blocks on the floor; watch the bronze plate on the sanctuary: scan the bride's room, the Archbishop's sacristy, the bookstore and the altars; keep an ear to the walls of the triforium attics—" Something made him look up to his right at the northeast triforium. "Farrell!"

No one answered.

Flynn peered into the darkness above. "Farrell!" He slammed his fist on the marble balustrade. "Damn it!" He cranked the field phone and tried again to raise the attic.

Bellini listened to the echoes of Flynn's voice die away from the speakers. The squad leader beside him said, "We have to move—now!"

Bellini's voice was cool. "No. Timing. It's like trying to get laid—it's all timing." The phone clicked, and Bellini listened to the Third Squad leader in the attic of the opposite triforium. "Captain, do you see anyone else in this triforium?"

Bellini answered, "I guess the guy called Farrell was the only one. Move into the triforium." He spoke to the operator. "Get me the Fourth Squad."

The Fourth Squad leader answered, and his voice resonated from the duct he was crawling through. "We jumped off late, Captain—got lost in the duct work. I think we're through the foundation—"

"*Think!* What the hell is wrong with you?"

"Sorry—"

Bellini rubbed his throbbing temples and brought his voice under control. "Okay . . . okay, we make up the time you lost by moving your time of last possible withdrawal from 5:55 to 6:00. That's fair, right?"

There was a pause before the squad leader replied, "Right."

"Good. Now you just see if you can find the block-square crawl space. Okay? Then I'll send the Bomb

Squad in." He hung up and looked at Burke. "Glad you came?"

"Absolutely."

Flynn cranked the field phone. "Attic! Attic!"

Jean Kearney's voice finally came on the line, and Flynn spoke hurriedly. "They've taken out the towers, and they'll be coming through the roof hatches next— I can hear helicopters overhead. There's no use waiting for it, Jean—light all the fires and get into the bell tower."

Jean Kearney answered, "All right." She stood propped against a catwalk rail, supported by two ESD men, one of whom had the big silencer of a pistol pressed to her head. She shouted into the phone, "Brian—!" One of the men pulled the phone out of her hand.

She steadied herself on the rail, feeling light-headed and nauseous from the loss of blood. She bent over and vomited on the floor, then picked her head up and tried to stand erect, shaking off the two men beside her. Hoses hung from hovering helicopters and snaked their way through the roof hatches, discharging billows of white foam over the flickering flames. She felt defeated but relieved that it was over. She tried to think about Arthur Nulty, but her thigh was causing her such pain that all she could think about was that the pain should go away and the nausea should stop. She looked at the squad leader. "Give me a pressure bandage, damn it."

The squad leader ignored her and watched the firemen coming through the hatches, taking over the hoses from his Assault Squad. He shouted to his men. "Move out! Into the bell tower!"

He turned back to Jean Kearney, noticing the tattered green Aer Lingus uniform; he looked at her freckled features in the subdued light and pointed at a smoldering pile of wood. "Are you *crazy*?"

She looked him in the eye. "We're loyal."

The squad leader listened to the sound of his men double-timing over the catwalks toward the tower passage. As he reached for the aid kit on his belt his eyes darted around at the firemen who were occupied with the large chemical hoses.

Jean Kearney's hand flew out and expertly snatched his pistol, put it to her heart, and fired. She back-pedaled, her arms swinging in wide circular motions until she toppled over to the dusty catwalk.

The squad leader looked at her, stunned, and then bent over and retrieved his pistol. "Crazy...crazy."

A thick mass of foam moved across the catwalk and slid over Jean Kearney's body; the white billowing bubbles tinged with red.

Flynn used the field phone to call the choir loft. He spoke quickly to Megan. "I think they've taken the attic. They'll be coming through the side doors into the choir loft. Keep the doors covered so Leary can shoot."

Megan's voice was angry, nearly hysterical. "How the hell did they take the attic? What the bloody hell is going on, Brian? What the *fuck* is going wrong here?"

He drew a long breath. "Megan, when you've been on fifty missions, you'll know not to ask those questions. You just fight, and you die or you don't die, but

you never ask—listen, tell Leary to scan Farrell's post—
I think they're also up there—"

"Who the hell ever said you were a military genius?"

"The British—it made them feel more important."

She hesitated, then said, "Why did you let Hickey
do that to my brother?"

Flynn glanced at Pedar Fitzgerald's body propped
up on the organ bench. "Hickey—like Mr. Leary—is a
friend of yours, not mine. Ask Hickey when next you
meet. Also, tell Leary to scan Gallagher's triforium—"

Megan cut in. "Brian...listen...listen..."

He recognized the tone of her voice, that childlike
lilt she used when she became repentant about something. He didn't want to hear what she had to say and
hung up.

Bellini scanned with the periscope as he reported
to all points on the field phone. "Yeah...they're starting to look over their shoulders now. Man at the
chancel organ...but he looks...dead...Still don't see
Hickey.... Might be in the crawl space. Two
hostages...Malone and Baxter...Murphy still missing...shit...Cardinal still missing—"

The Fifth Squad leader in the octagon room to the
side of the sacristy gates cut in. "Captain, I'm looking at the gates with a periscope...bad angle...but
someone—looks like the Cardinal—is cuffed to them.
Advise."

Bellini swore softly. "Make sure it's him, and stand
by for orders." He turned to Burke. "These Mick bastards still have some tricky shit up their shillelaghs—
Cardinal's cuffed to the gates." He focused the
periscope on Flynn in the pulpit directly below. "Smart

guy.... Well, this potato-eating bastard is mine...but it's a tough shot.... Canopy overhead and a marble wall around him. He knows it's going down the tube, but he can't do shit about it. Cocksucker."

Burke said, "If the attic is secure and you get the bombs...you ought to try negotiating. Flynn will talk with twenty rifles pointing down at him. He's a lot of things, but stupid isn't one of them."

"Nobody told me nothing about asking him to surrender." Bellini put his face close to Burke's. "Don't get carried away with yourself and start giving orders, or I swear to God I'll grease you. I'm doing okay, Burke—I'm doing fine—I'm golden tonight—fuck you and fuck Flynn—let him squirm—then let him die."

The Fifth Assault Squad dropped one at a time from the duct opening and lay on the damp floor of the crawl space, forming a defensive perimeter. The squad leader cranked his field phone and reported, "Okay, Captain, we're in the crawl space. No movement here—"

Bellini answered, "You sure you're not in the fucking attic now? Okay, I'm sending the dogs and their handlers through the ducts with Peterson's Bomb Squad. When you rendezvous, move out. Be advised that Hickey may be down there—maybe others. Keep your head out of your ass."

Bellini signaled to Wendy Peterson. "Perimeter secure. Move through the ducts. Follow the commo wire and don't get lost."

She answered in a laconic voice that echoed in the ducts, "We're already moving, Captain."

Bellini looked at his watch. "Okay...it's 5:45 now. At 6:00—at 5:55 my people are getting the hell out of there, whether or not you think you got all the bombs. I suggest you do the same."

Peterson answered, "We'll play it by ear."

"Yeah, you do that." He hung up and looked at Burke. "I think it's time—before our luck turns."

Burke said nothing.

Bellini rubbed his chin, hesitated, then reached for the phone and called the garage under Rockefeller Center. "Okay, Colonel, the word is Bull—fucking—Run. Ready?"

Logan answered, "Been ready a while. You're cutting it close."

Bellini's voice was caustic. "It's past close—it's probably too damned late, but that doesn't mean you can't earn a medal."

Colonel Logan threw the field phone down from the commander's hatch of the armored carrier and called to the driver, "Go!"

The twenty thousand pounds of armor began rumbling up the ramp of the underground garage. The big overhead door rose, and the carrier slid into Forty-ninth Street, turned right, and approached Fifth Avenue at twenty-five miles per hour, then veered north up the Avenue gathering speed.

Logan stood in the hatch with an M-16 rifle, the wind billowing his fatigue jacket. He stared at the Cathedral coming up on his right front, then glanced up at the towers and roof. Smoke billowed over the Cathedral, and helicopters hovered, beating the smoke downward, thick hoses dropping into the attic hatches. "Good Lord..."

Logan looked into the silent predawn streets, empty except for the police posted in recessed doorways. One of them gave him a thumbs up, another saluted. Logan stood taller in the hatch; his mind raced faster than the carrier's engines, and his blood pounded through his veins.

The armored carrier raced up to the Cathedral. The driver locked the right-hand treads, and the carrier pivoted around, ripping up large slabs of the blacktop. The driver released the treads as the carrier pointed toward the front doors, and he gunned the engines. The vehicle fishtailed and raced across the wide sidewalk, bounced, and hit the granite steps, tearing away the stone as the treads climbed upward. The brass handrails disappeared beneath the treads, and the ten tons of armor headed straight for the ten tons of bronze ceremonial doors.

Logan made the sign of the cross, ducked into the hatch, and pulled the lid shut. The truck tires attached to the front of the carrier hit the doors, and the bolts snapped, sending the massive doors flying inward. The alarms sounded with a piercing ring. The carrier was nearly into the vestibule when the delayed mines on the doors began to explode, scattering shrapnel across the sides of the vehicle. The carrier kept moving through the vestibule and skidded across the marble floor to a stop beneath the choir loft overhang.

Harold Baxter grabbed Maureen and pulled her down beneath the clergy pews.

Brian Flynn raised a rocket launcher and took aim from the pulpit.

The rear door of the carrier dropped, and fifteen

men of the 69th Regiment, led by Major Cole, scrambled over the door and began fanning out under the choir loft.

Frank Gallagher was speaking to the Cardinal when the sound of the exploding doors rolled through the Cathedral. For a moment he thought the bombs beneath him had gone off, then he recognized the sound for what it was. His chest heaved, and his body shook so badly that his rifle fell from his hands. He lost control of his nerves as he heard the reports of rifle fire in the Cathedral behind him. He let out a high-pitched wail and ran down the sacristy steps, falling to his knees beside the Cardinal. He grabbed at the hem of the red robe, tears streaming from his eyes and snatches of prayer forming on his lips. "God...O God...Father...Eminence...dear God..."

The Cardinal looked down at him. "It's all right, now. There...there..."

Colonel Logan rose quickly through the carrier hatch and rested his automatic rifle on the machine gun mount in front of him. He peered into the darkness as he scanned to his front, then saw a movement in the pulpit and zeroed in.

The First Squad, including Bellini and Burke, had risen up in unison from behind the balustrade, rifles raised to their shoulders.

Abby Boland saw the shadows appear along the ledge, black forms, eerie and spectral in the subdued light. She saw the tiny pinpoint flashes and heard the silencers cough like a roomful of old people clearing their throats. She screamed, "George!" Sullivan was intent on the transept doors opposite him but looked up when she screamed.

The Third Squad had burst out of the attic and occupied Farrell's triforium. They lined up along the parapet and searched the darkness for targets.

Brian Flynn steadied the M-72 rocket as a burst of red tracers streaked out of the commander's hatch of the carrier and cracked into the granite column behind him. He squeezed the detonator. The rocket roared out of the tube, sailed over the pews with a fiery red trail, and exploded on the sloping front of the armored carrier.

The carrier belched smoke and flame through ruptured seams, and the driver was killed instantly. Logan shot up from the hatch, flames licking at his clothing, and nearly hit the overhang of the loft. His smoking body fell back toward the blazing carrier, spread-eagled like a sky diver, and disappeared in clouds of black smoke and orange flame.

The First and Third ESD squads in the triforia were firing into the candlelit Cathedral, the operating mechanisms of their rifles slapping back and forth as the silencers wheezed, and spent brass piled up on the stone floors.

Abby Boland stood rigid for a split second as the scream died in her throat. She got off a single shot, then felt something rip the rifle from her hands, and the butt rammed her face. She fell to the floor, picked up a rocket, and stood again.

Sullivan fired a long automatic burst into Farrell's triforium and heard a scream. He shifted his fire to the triforium where Gallagher had been, but a single bullet hit him squarely in the chest. He tumbled to the floor, landing on his bagpipes, which emitted a sad wail that pierced the noises in the Cathedral.

Abby Boland saw him go down as she fired the rocket across the Cathedral.

Bellini watched the trail of red fire illuminating the darkness. It came toward him with a noise that sounded like a rushing freight train. "Duck!"

The rocket went high and exploded on the stonework above the triforium. The triforium shook, and the window above blew out of its stone mullions, sending thousands of pieces of colored glass raining down in sheets past the triforium to the sanctuary and pulpit below.

Bellini's squad rose quickly and poured automatic fire onto the source of the rocket.

Abby Boland held a pistol extended in both hands and fired at the orange flashes as the stonework around her began to shatter. The loud pop of a grenade launcher rolled across the Cathedral, and the top of the balustrade in front of her exploded. Her arms flew up and splattered blood and pistol fragments across her face. She fell forward, half blinded, and her mangled hands clutched at the protruding staff of the Papal flag. In her disorientation she found herself hanging out over the floor below. A burst of fire tore into her arms, and she released her grip. Her body tumbled head over heels and crashed into the pews below with a sharp splintering sound.

Pedar Fitzgerald's dead body took a half-dozen hits and lurched to and fro, then fell against the keyboard and produced a thundering dissonant chord that continued uninterrupted amid the shouting and gunfire.

Flynn crouched in the pulpit, fired long bursts at Farrell's triforium, then shifted his fire toward the vestibules where the men of the 69th Regiment had retreated from the burning carrier. Suddenly the carrier's gasoline exploded. Flames shot up to the choir loft, and huge clouds of black smoke rose and curled around the loft. The National Guardsmen retreated back farther through the mangled doors onto the steps.

Bellini leaned out of the triforium and sighted his rifle almost straight down and fired three shots in quick succession through the bronze pulpit canopy.

Flynn's body lurched, and he fell to his knees, then rolled over the pulpit floor. Bellini could see his body dangling across the spiral stairs. He took aim at the twitching form. Burke hit Bellini's shoulder and deflected his shot. "No! Leave him."

Bellini glared at Burke for a second, then turned his attention to the choir loft. He saw a barely perceptible flash of light, the kind of muzzle fire that came from a combination silencer/flash suppressor and that could only be seen from head on. The light flashed again, but this time in a different place several yards away. Bellini sensed that whoever was in there was very good, and he had a very good perch, a vast sloping area completely darkened and obscured by rising smoke. Even as he watched he heard a scream from the end of the triforium, and one of his men fell back. He heard another moan coming from the opposite triforium.

In a short time everyone was on the floor as bullets skimmed across the ledge of the balustrade a few feet above their heads. Burke sat with his back against the wall and lit a cigarette as the wood above him splintered. "That guy is good."

Bellini crouched across from him and nodded. "And he's got the best seat in the house. This is going to be a bitch." He looked at his watch. The whole thing, from the time Logan had hit the doors to this moment, had taken just under two minutes. But Logan was dead now, the National Guardsmen were nowhere to be seen, and he had lost some good people. The hostages might be dead, the people in the crawl space weren't reporting, and someone in the choir loft was having a good day.

Bellini picked up the field phone and called Fifth Squad in the corridor off the sacristy. "All the bastards are dead except one or two in the choir loft. You have to go for the Cardinal and the two hostages under the pews."

The squad leader answered, "How the hell do we rush that gate with the Cardinal hanging there?"

"Very carefully. Move out!" He hung up and said to Burke, "The sniper in the choir loft isn't going to be easy."

* * *

The ESD men from the Fifth Assault Squad moved out of the octagon rooms on both sides of the sacristy gate and slid quickly along the walls, converging on the Cardinal.

The squad leader kept his back to the wall and peered carefully around the opening. His eyes met the Cardinal's, and both men gave a start; then the squad leader saw a man kneeling at the Cardinal's feet. Gallagher let out a surprised yell, and the squad leader did the same as he fired twice from the hip.

Gallagher rocked back on his haunches and then fell forward. His smashed face struck the bars, and he rolled sideways, sliding down the Cardinal's legs.

The Cardinal stared down at Gallagher lying in a heap at his feet, blood rushing from his head over the steps. He looked at the squad leader, who was staring at Gallagher. The squad leader turned and looked up at the top landing, saw no one, and gave a signal. ESD men with bolt cutters swarmed around the gates and severed the chain that tied them together. One of the men snapped the Cardinal's handcuffs while another one opened the gate lock with a key. So far no one had spoken a word.

The assault squad slid open the gates, and ten men ran up the stairs toward the crypt door.

The Cardinal knelt beside Gallagher's body, and a medic rushed out of a side corridor and took the Cardinal's arm. "Are you okay?" The Cardinal nodded. The medic stared down at Gallagher's face. "This guy don't look so good, though. Come on, Your Eminence." He tugged at the Cardinal's arm as two uniformed policemen lifted the Cardinal, steering him toward the corridor that led back to his residence.

One of the ESD men stood to the side of the crypt door and lobbed a gas canister down into the crypt. The canister popped, and two men wearing gas masks rushed in through the smoke. After a few seconds one of them yelled back, "No one here."

The squad leader took the field phone and reported, "Captain, sacristy gate and crypt secured. No ESD casualties, one Fenian KIA, Cardinal rescued." He added impulsively, "Piece of cake."

Bellini replied, "Tell me that after you get up those stairs. There's a motherfucker in the choir loft that can circumcise you with two shots and never touch your nuts."

The squad leader heard the phone click off. "Okay. Hostages under the pews—let's move." The squad split into two fire teams and began crawling up the opposite staircases toward the sanctuary.

Maureen and Baxter stayed motionless beneath the clergy pews. Maureen listened to the sounds of striking bullets echoing through the Cathedral. She pressed her face close to Baxter's and said, "Leary—maybe Megan—is still in the loft. I can't tell who else is still firing."

Baxter held her arm tightly. "It doesn't matter as long as Leary is still there." He took her wrist and looked at her watch. "It's 5:36. At 6:00 we run for it."

She smiled weakly. "Harry, John Hickey is a man who literally would not give you the right time of day. For all we know it's 6:03 right now. Then again, my watch may be correct, but the bombs may be set for right now. Hickey does not play fair—not with us nor with Brian Flynn."

"Why am I so bloody naïve?"

She pressed his arm. "That's all right. People like

Hickey, Flynn...me...we're treacherous.... It's as natural as breathing...."

Baxter peered under the pews, then said, "Let's run for it."

"Where? This whole end of the Cathedral will collapse. The doors are mined. Leary's in the loft, and Gallagher is at the gate."

He thought a moment. "Gallagher owes you...."

"I wouldn't put myself at the mercy of any of them. We couldn't reach those stairs anyway. I won't be shot down by scum like Leary or Megan. I'm staying here."

"Then you'll be blown up by John Hickey."

She buried her face in her hands, then looked up. "Over the back of the sanctuary, keeping the altar between us and the choir loft. Into the Lady Chapel—the windows are about fifteen feet from the floor. Climb the chapel altar—one of us boosts the other up. We won't get that far, of course, but—"

"But we'll be heading in the right direction."

She nodded and began moving under the pews.

The Fifth Assault Squad crouched on the two flights of steps behind the high altar. The squad leader peered around the south side of the altar and looked to his left at the bronze floor-plate. He turned to the right, put his face to the floor, and tried to locate the hostages under the clergy pews, but in the bad light and at the angle he was looking he saw no one. He raised his rifle and called softly, "Baxter? Malone?"

They were both about to spring out toward the rear of the sanctuary but dropped to a prone position. Baxter called back, "Yes!"

The squad leader said, "Steps are clear. Cardinal's safe. Where is Father Murphy?"

Maureen peered across the sanctuary floor to the stairwell thirty feet away. "Somewhere in the towers, I think." She paused, then said, "Gallagher? The man who—"

The squad leader cut her off. "The bomb under us hasn't been found yet. You have to get out of there."

"What time is it?" Baxter asked.

The squad leader looked at his digital watch. "It's 5:46 and twenty seconds."

Maureen stared at the face of her watch. Ten minutes slow. "Bastard." She reset it and called back. "Someone's got to get the snipers in the loft before we can move."

The squad leader poked his head around the altar, looked up at the choir loft illuminated by candles and flares, and tried to peer into the blackness beyond. "He's too far away for us to get him or for him to get you."

Baxter shouted with anger in his voice, "If that were so, we wouldn't be here. That man is very good."

The squad leader said, "We're sitting on a *bomb*, and so far as I'm concerned it could go off *anytime*."

Maureen called out to the squad leader, "Listen, two people planted the bombs, and they were down in the crawl space less than twenty minutes. They carried two suitcases."

The squad leader called back, "Okay—I'll pass that on. But you have to understand, lady, that the Bomb Squad could blow it—you know? So you have to make a break."

Maureen called back, "We'll wait."

"Well, we won't." The squad leader looked up at the triforium directly overhead where Bellini was, but saw no one at the openings. He called on the field phone. "Captain, Malone and Baxter are under the pews below you—alive." He passed on the information about the bombs and added, "They won't try to cross the sanctuary." Bellini's voice came over the line. "I don't blame them. Okay, in thirty seconds everyone fires into the loft. Tell them to run for it then."

"Right." He hung up and relayed the message to Maureen and Baxter.

Maureen called back, "We'll see—be careful—"

The squad leader turned and shouted to his men on the opposite stairs. "Heavy fire into the loft!" The men moved up the steps and knelt on the floor, firing down the length of the Cathedral. The squad leader moved the remainder of his squad around the altar and opened fire as the two triforia began shooting. The sound of bullets crashing into stone and brass in the loft rolled back through the Cathedral. The squad leader shouted to Malone and Baxter. "Run!"

Suddenly two rifles started firing rapidly from the choir loft with extreme accuracy. The ESD men on both sides of the altar began writhing on the cold sanctuary floor. Both teams pulled back to the staircases, dragging their wounded and leaving a trail of blood on the white marble.

The squad leader swore loudly and peered around the altar. "Okay, okay, stay there!" He glanced quickly up at the choir loft and saw a muzzle flash. The marble in front of him disintegrated and hit him full in the face. He screamed, and someone grabbed his ankles, dragging him back down the stairs.

Medics rushed up from the sacristy and began carrying away the wounded. The commo man cranked his field phone and reportd to Bellini in a shaky voice. "Hostages pinned down. This altar is the wrong end of a shooting gallery. We can't help them."

The Fourth Assault Squad moved slowly through the dark crawl space, the squad leader scanning his front with an infrared scope. The two dogs and their handlers moved with him. Behind the advancing line of men moved Wendy Peterson and four men of the Bomb Squad.

Every few yards the dogs strained at their leashes, and the Bomb Squad would uncover another small particle of plastic explosive without timers or detonators. The entire earth floor seemed to be seeded with plastic, and every column had a scrap of plastic stuck to it. A dog handler whispered to the impatient squad leader, "I can't stop them from following these red herrings."

Wendy Peterson came up beside the squad leader and said, "My men will follow up on these dogs. Your squad and I have to move on—faster—to the other side."

He stopped crawling, lay down an infrared scope, and turned his head toward her. "I'm moving like there were ten armed men in front of me, and that's the only way I know how to move when I'm crawling in a black fucking hole . . . Lieutenant."

The Bomb Squad men hurried up from the rear. One of them called, "Lieutenant?"

"Over here."

He came up beside her. "Okay, the mine on the corridor hatchway is disarmed, and we can get out of here real quick if we have to. The mine had a detcord running from it, and we followed it to the explosives around the main column on this side." He paused and caught his breath. "We defused that big mother— about twenty kilos of plastic—colored and shaped to look like stone—simple clock mechanism—set to go at 6:03—no bullshit about that." He held out a canvas bag and pressed it into Peterson's hands. "The guts."

She hunched over and lit a red-filtered flashlight, emptying the contents of the bag on the floor. Alarm clock, battery pack, wires, and four detached electric detonators. She turned on the clock, and it ticked loudly in the still air. She shut it off again. "No tricks?"

"No. We cut away all the plastic—no booby traps, no anti-intrusion devices. Very old techniques but very reliable, and top-grade plastic—smells and feels like that new C-5."

She picked off a clinging piece of plastic, kneading it between her thumb and forefinger, then smelled it.

The squad leader watched her in the filtered light and was reminded of his mother making cookie dough, but it was all wrong. "Really good stuff, huh?"

She switched off the light and said to the squad leader, "If the mechanism on the other one is the same, I'd need less than five minutes to defuse that bomb."

He said, "Good—now all you need is the other bomb. And *I* need about eight minutes to get the hell out of here and into the rectory basement. So at 5:55, no matter what's coming down, I say adios."

"Fair enough. Let's move."

He made no move but said, "I have to report the good news." He picked up the field phone. "Captain, the north side of the crawl space is clear of bombs."

Bellini answered, "Okay, very good." He related Maureen's information. "Move cautiously to the other side of the crypt. Hickey—"

"Yeah, but we can't engage him. We can move back to the hatchway, though, so you can have somebody drop concussion grenades through that bronze plate in the sanctuary. Then we'll move in and—"

Bellini cut him off. "Fifth Squad is still on the sacristy stairs. Took some casualties.... They're going to have trouble crossing the sanctuary floor—sniper up in the loft—"

"Well, blow him the fuck away and let's get it moving."

"Yeah...I'll let you know when we do that."

The squad leader hesitated, then said, "Well...we'll stay put...."

Bellini let a few seconds pass, then said, "This sniper is going to take awhile.... I'm not *positive* Hickey or anyone is down there.... You've got to get to the other column."

The squad leader hung up and turned to the dog handlers. "Okay, drag those stupid mutts along, and don't stop until we get to the other side." He called to his men. "Let's go."

The three teams—ESD Assault Squad, Bomb Squad, and the dog handlers, twenty people in all—began moving. They passed the rear wall of the crypt and turned left, following the line of columns that would lead them to the main column flanking the sacristy stairs and what they hoped would be the last bomb.

They dropped from their hands and knees to a low-crawl position, rifles held out in front of them, the squad leader scanning with the infrared scope.

Peterson looked at her wristwatch as they moved. 5:47. If the mechanism on this side wasn't tricky, if there were no mines, if there were no other bombs, and if no one fired at them, then she had a very good chance of keeping St. Patrick's Cathedral from blowing up.

As she moved, though, she thought about triggers—all the ways a bomb could be detonated besides an electric clock. She thought about a concussion grenade that would set off an audio trigger, a flashlight that would set off a photo trigger, movement that would set off an inertial trigger, trip wires, false clocks, double or triple mechanisms, spring-loaded percussion mechanisms, remote mechanisms—so many nasty ways to make a bomb go off that you didn't want to go off. Yet, nothing so elaborate was needed to safeguard a time bomb until its time had come if it had a watchdog guarding it.

John Hickey knelt beside the main column, wedged between the footing and the sacristy stairwell, contemplating the mass of explosives packed around the footing and bedrock. His impulse was to dig out the clock and advance it to eternity. But to probe into the plastic in the dark might disconnect a detonator or battery connection. He looked at his watch. 5:47. Sixteen minutes to go. He could keep them away that long—long enough for the dawn to give the cameras good light. He grinned.

Hickey pushed himself farther back into the small space and peered up through the darkness toward the spot where the bronze plate sat in the ceiling. No one had tried to come through there yet, and as he listened to the shooting overhead, he suspected that Leary and Megan were still alive and would see to it that no one did. A bullet struck the bronze plate, and a deep resonant sound echoed through the dark. Four more bullets struck the plate in quick succession, and Hickey smiled. "Ah, Leary, you're showing off now, lad."

Just then his ears picked up the sound of whimpering. He cupped his ear and listened. Dogs. Then men breathing. He flipped the selector switch on his rifle to full automatic and leaned forward as the sound of crawling came nearer. The dogs had the scent of the massed explosives and probably of him. Hickey pursed his lips and made a sound. "Pssst!"

There was a sudden and complete silence.

Hickey did it again. "Pssst!" He picked up a piece of rubble and threw it.

The squad leader scanned the area to his front, but there was not even the faintest glimmer of light for the infrared scope to pick up and magnify.

Hickey said, "It's me. Don't shoot."

No one answered for several seconds, then the squad leader called out in a voice that was fighting to maintain control. "Put your hands up and move closer."

Hickey placed his rifle a few inches from the ground and held it horizontally. "Don't shoot, lads—please don't shoot. If you shoot... you'll blow us all to hell." He laughed, then said, "I, however, can shoot." He squeezed the trigger and emptied a twenty-round magazine across the ground in front of him. He slapped another magazine into the well as the reports died away, and he heard screaming and moaning. He emptied another full magazine in three long bursts of grazing fire. He heard a dog howling, or, he thought, perhaps a man. He mimicked the howling as he reloaded and fired again.

The ESD snipers in both triforia were shooting down the length of the Cathedral into the choir loft, but the targets there—at least two of them—were moving quickly through the darkness as they fired. ESD men began to fall, dead and wounded, onto the triforium floors. An ESD man rose up beside Bellini and leaned out over the balustrade, putting a long stream of automatic fire into the loft. The red tracer rounds arched into the loft and disappeared as they embedded themselves into the woodwork. The organ keyboard was hit, and electrical sparks crackled in the darkness. The man fired again, and another stream of tracers struck the towering brass pipes, producing a sound like pealing bells. The tracer rounds ricocheted back, spinning and dancing like fiery pinwheels in the black space.

Bellini shouted to the ESD man and pulled at his flak jacket. "Too long! Down!"

All of a sudden the man released his rifle and slapped his hands to his face, then leaned farther out and rolled over the balustrade, crashing to the clergy pews below.

An ESD man with a M-79 grenade launcher fired. The small grenade burst against a wooden locker with a flash, and robes began to burn. Bellini picked up his bullhorn and shouted, "No grenades." The fire blazed for a few seconds, then began to burn itself out. Bellini crouched and held the bullhorn up. "Okay—First and Third squads—all together—two full magazines—automatic—on my command." He grabbed the rifle beside him and shouted into the bullhorn as he rose, "Fire!"

The remaining men in both triforia rose in unison and fired, producing a deafening roar as streams of red tracers poured into the black loft. They emptied their magazines, reloaded, fired again, then ducked.

There was a silence from the choir loft, and Bellini rose carefully with the bullhorn, keeping himself behind a column. He called out to the loft. "Turn the lights on and put your hands up, or we'll shoot again." He looked down at Burke sitting cross-legged beside him. "That's negotiating!" He raised the bullhorn again.

Leary knelt at the front of the loft in the north corner and watched through his scope as the bullhorn came up behind the column, diagonally across the Cathedral. He lay flat on top of the rail and leaned out precariously like a pool player trying to make a hard shot, putting the cross hairs of his scope over a small visible piece of Bellini's forehead. He fired and rolled back to the choir loft floor.

The bullhorn emitted an oddly amplified moan as Bellini's forehead erupted in a splatter of bone and blood. He dropped straight down, landing on Burke's crossed legs. Burke stared at the heavy body sprawled across him. Bellini's blackened temple gushed a small fountain of red...like a red rosebud, Burke thought abstractedly.... He pushed the body away and steadied himself against the parapet, drawing on his cigarette.

There was very little noise in the Cathedral now, he noted, and no sound at all from the survivors of the First Squad around him. Medics had arrived and were treating the wounded where they lay; they carried them back into the attic for the descent down the elevator shaft. Burke looked at his watch. 5:48.

Father Murphy listened to the sounds of footsteps approaching from below. His first thought was that the police had arrived; then he remembered Flynn's words, and he realized it might be Leary or Megan coming for him. He picked up the pistol and held it in his shaking hand. "Who is it? Who's there?"

An ESD team leader from the Second Assault Squad two levels below motioned his fire team away from the open well. He raised his rifle and muffled his voice with his hand. "It's me.... Come on down...attic burning."

Father Murphy put his hand to his face and whispered, "The attic...oh...God..." He called down. "Nulty! Is that you?"

"Yes."

Murphy hesitated. "Is...is Leary with you? Where's Megan?"

The team leader looked around at his men, who appeared tense and impatient. He called up the ladder well, "They're here. Come down!"

The priest tried to collect his thoughts, but his mind was so dulled with fatigue he just stared down into the black hole.

The team leader shouted, "Come down, or we're coming up for you!"

Father Murphy drew back from the opening as far as his cuffed wrist permitted. "I've got a gun!"

The team leader motioned to one of his men to fire a gas canister into the opening. The projectile sailed upward through the intervening level and burst on the ladder near Father Murphy's head. A piece of the canister struck him in the face, and his lungs filled with gas. He lurched back, then stumbled forward, falling through the opening. He hung suspended from his handcuffs, swinging against the ladder, his stomach and chest heaving as choked noises rose from his throat.

An ESD man with a submachine gun saw the figure dropping out of the darkness and fired from the hip. The body jerked, then lay still against the ladder. The ESD team moved carefully up to the higher level.

City lights filtered through the broken glass and cast a weak, shadowy illumination into the tower room. A cold wind blew away the smell of gas. An ESD man drew closer to the ladder, then shouted, "Hey! It's a priest."

The team leader dimly recalled some telephone traffic regarding the missing hostage, the priest. He cleared his throat. "Some of them were dressed as priests . . . right?"

The man with the submachine gun added, "He said

he had a gun.... I heard it fall.... Something fell on the floor here...." He looked around and found the pistol. "See...and he called them by name...."

The man with the grenade launcher said, "But he's *cuffed*!"

The team leader put his hands to his temples. "This is fucked up.... We might have fucked up...." He put his hand on the ladder rail and steadied himself. Blood ran down the rail and collected in a small pool around his fingers. "Oh...oh, no...no, no, *no*—"

The other half of the Second Squad from the attic made its way carefully down through the dark bell tower, then rushed into the long triforium where Abby Boland had been. They hit the floor and low-crawled down the length of the dark gallery, passing over the blood-wet floor near the flagstaff and turning the corner overlooking the north transept. Two men searched the triforium attic as the team leader reported on the field phone, "Captain, northwest triforium secured. Anything you see moving up here is us."

A voice came over the wire. "This is Burke. Bellini is dead. Listen...send some men down to the choir loft level.... The rest of you stay there and bring fire down on that loft. There're about two snipers there—at least one of them is very accurate."

The team leader acknowledged and hung up. He looked back at his four remaining men. "Captain got greased. Okay, you two stay here and fire down into the loft. You two come with me." He reentered the tower and ran down the spiral stairs toward the loft level.

One of the remaining two men in the triforium leaned out over the balustrade, steadying his rifle on the protruding flagstaff, which he noticed was splintered and covered with blood. He looked down and saw in the light of a flare a young woman's body lying in a collapsed pew.

"Jesus . . ." He looked into the dark loft and fired a short burst at random. "Flush those suckers out . . . ."

A single shot whistled up out of the loft, passed through the wooden staff and punched into his flak jacket. He rose up off his feet, and his rifle flew into the air. The man lay stretched out on the floor for a few seconds, then rolled over on his hands and knees and tried to catch his breath. "Good God . . . Jesus H. Christ . . ."

The other man, who hadn't moved from his kneeling position, said, "Lucky shot, Tony. Bet he couldn't do it again."

The injured man put his hand under his flak jacket and felt a lump the size of an egg where his breast bones met. "Wow . . . fucking wow . . . ." He looked at the other man. "Your turn."

The man pulled off his black stocking cap and pushed it above the balustrade on the tip of his rifle. A faint coughing sound rolled out of the choir loft, followed by a whistle and crack, then another, but the hat didn't move. The ESD man lowered the hat. "He stinks." He moved to a position several yards down the triforium and peered over the edge of the balustrade. The huge yellow and white Papal flag was no longer hanging from the staff but was stretched across the pews below, covering the body of the dead woman. The ESD man stared back at the staff and saw the two severed flag-ropes swaying. He ducked quickly and looked at the other man. "You're not going to believe this..."

Someone in the choir loft laughed.

An ESD man beside Burke picked up Bellini's bullhorn and began to raise it above the balustrade, then thought better of it. He pointed it upward from his kneeling position and called out, "Hey! You in the loft! Show's over. Nobody left but you. Come to the choir rail with your hands up. You won't be harmed." He shut off the bullhorn and said, "You'll be blasted into hamburger, motherfucker."

There was a long silence, then a man's voice called out from the loft. "You'll never take us." There were two sharp pistol shots, followed by silence.

The ESD man turned to Burke. "They blew their brains out."

Burke said, "Sure."

The man considered for a moment. "How do we know?" he finally asked. Burke nodded toward Bellini's body.

The ESD man hesitated, then wiped Bellini's face and forehead with a handkerchief, and Burke helped him heft Bellini's body over the parapet.

Immediately there was a sound like a bee buzzing, followed by a loud slap, and Bellini's body was pulled out of their hands and crashed to the triforium floor behind them. An odd shrillish voice screamed from the loft, "Live ones! I want *live* ones!"

For the first time since the attack began Burke felt sweat forming on his brow.

The ESD man looked pale. "My God...."

The Second Squad leader led his remaining two men down the dark bell tower until they found the choir practice room. They searched it carefully in the dark and located the door that led out to the loft. The squad leader listened quietly at the door, then stood to the side and put his hand on the knob and turned it, but there was no alarm. The three men hugged the walls for a second before the squad leader pushed the door open, and they rushed the opening in a low crouch.

A shotgun exploded five times in the dark in quick succession, and the three men were knocked back into the room, their faces, arms, and legs ripped with buckshot.

Megan Fitzgerald stepped quickly into the room and shone a light on the three contorted bodies. One of the men looked up at the black-robed figure through the light and stared at her grotesquely made-up face, distorted with a repulsive snarl. Megan raised a pistol, deliberately shot each of the writhing figures in the head, then closed the door, reset the silent light alarm, and walked back into the loft. She called to Leary, who was moving and firing from positions all over the loft. "Don't let Malone or Baxter get away. Keep them pinned there until the bombs explode!"

Leary shouted as he fired, "Yeah, yeah. Just watch the fucking side doors."

A long stream of red tracers streaked out of the long

northwest triforium and began ripping into the choir pews. Leary got off an answering shot before the last tracer left the muzzle of the ESD man's rifle, and the firing abruptly stopped.

Leary moved far back to the towering organ pipes and looked out at the black horizon line formed by the loft rail across the candle- and flare-lit Cathedral. It was strictly a matter of probability, he knew. There were thirteen hundred square feet of completely unlit loft and less than twenty police in a position to bring fire into the loft. And because of their overhead angle they couldn't bring grazing fire across the sloping expanse, but only direct fire at a specific point of impact, and that reduced the killing zone of their striking rounds. In addition, he and Megan had flak jackets under their robes, his rifle was silenced and the flash was suppressed, and they were both moving constantly. The ESD night scopes would be whited out as long as the phosphorus below kept burning, but he was firing into a lit area, and he could see their shapes when they came to the edge of the triforia. Probability. Odds. Skill. Vantage point. All in his favor. Always were. Luck did not exist. God did not exist. He called to Megan, "Time?"

She looked at her watch and saw the luminous minute hand tick another minute. "Fourteen minutes until 6:03."

He nodded to himself. There were times when he felt immortal and times when immortality only meant staying alive for just long enough to get the next shot off. Fourteen minutes. No problem.

Burke heard the field phone click and picked up the receiver from the floor. "Burke."

Mayor Kline's voice came through the earpiece. "Lieutenant, I didn't want to cut in on your command network—I've been monitoring all transmissions, of course, and not being there to see the situation, I felt it was better to let Captain Bellini handle it—but now that he's—"

"We appreciate that, sir." Burke noticed Kline's voice had that cool preciseness that was just a hair away from whining panic. "Actually, I have to get through to the crawl space, Mr. Mayor, so—"

"Yes—just a second—I was wondering if you could fill us in—"

"I just did."

"What? Oh, yes. Just one second. We need a situation report from you as the ranking man in there—you're in charge, by the way."

"Thanks. Let me call you right back—"

"Fine."

He heard a click and spoke to the police operator. "Don't put that asshole through again." He dropped the receiver on the floor.

The Sixth Assault Squad of ESD rappelled from police helicopters into the open attic hatches. They ran across the foam-covered catwalks to the south tower and split up, one team going up toward Devane's position, the other down toward the triforium and choir loft levels.

The team climbing into the tower fired grenades ahead of them, moving up level by level until they reached the copper-louvered room where Devane had been posted. They looked for the body of the Fenian sniper in the dark, smoke-filled room but found only bloodstains on the floor and a gas mask lying in the corner.

The squad leader touched a bloodstain on the ascending ladder and looked up. "We'll go with gas from here."

The men pulled on gas masks and fired CS canisters to the next level. They moved up the ladder, floor by floor, the gas rising with them, into the narrowing spire. Above them they heard the echoing sounds of a man coughing, then the deep, full bellow of vomiting. They followed the blood trail on the rusty ladder, cautiously moving through the dark levels until they reached a narrow, tapering, octagonal room about fifteen stories above the street. The room had clover-shaped openings, without glass, cut into the eight sides of the stonework. The blood trail ended on the ladder, and the floor near one of the openings was smeared with vomit. The squad leader pulled off his gas mask and stuck his head and shoulders out of the opening and looked up.

A series of iron rungs ran up the last hundred feet of the tapering spire toward the copper cross on top. The squad leader saw a man climbing halfway up. The man lost his footing, then recovered and pulled himself up to the next rung. The squad leader dropped back into the small, cold room. He unslung his rifle and chambered a round. "These fucks blew away a lot of our people—understand?"

One of his men said, "It's not too cool to blow him away with all those people watching from Rockefeller Center."

The squad leader looked out the opening at the buildings across the Avenue. Despite orders and all the police could do, hundreds of people were at the windows and on the rooftops watching the climber make his way up the granite spire. A few people were shouting, making encouraging motions with their hands and bodies. The squad leader heard cheering and applauding and thought he heard gasps when the man slipped. He said, "Assholes. The wrong people are *always* getting the applause." He released the safety switch, moved toward the opening, and looked up. He shouted, "Hey, King Kong! Get your ass back here!"

The climber glanced down but continued up the spire.

The squad leader pulled his head back into the room. "Give me the rappelling line." He took the nylon rope and began hooking himself up. "Well, as the homicide detectives say, 'Did he fall or was he pushed?' That is the question."

The other half of the Sixth Assault Squad descended through the south tower and, following a rough sketch supplied by Gordon Stillway, located the door to the long southwest triforium. One of the men kicked the door in, and the other four rushed down the length of the long gallery in a crouch. An ESD man spotted a man dressed in kilts lying crumpled at the corner of the balustrade, a bagpipe sticking out from under his body.

Suddenly a periscope rose from the triforium across the transept, and a bullhorn blared. "Get down! The loft! Watch the loft!"

The men turned in unison and stared down at the choir loft projecting out at a right angle about thirty feet below them. A muzzle flashed twice, and two of the five men went down. The other three dove for the floor. "What the hell ... ?" The team leader looked wildly around the long dark gallery as though it were full of gunmen. "Where did that come from ... the loft?" He looked at the two dead men, each shot between the eyes. "I never saw it .... I never heard anything ...."

One of the men said, "Neither did they."

The fifteen men of the 69th Regiment had moved back into the Cathedral after the carrier had stopped burning, and they lay on the floor under the choir loft, sighting their rifles down the five wide aisles toward the raised sanctuary. Major Cole rose to one knee and looked over the pews with a pair of binoculars, then scanned the four triforia. Nothing seemed to be moving in the Cathedral, and the loudest sound was the striking of bullets from the Fenian sniper overhead. Cole looked at the smoking armored carrier beside him. The smell of burnt gasoline and flesh made his stomach heave.

A sergeant came up beside him. "Major, we have to do something."

The major felt his stomach heave again. "We are not supposed to interfere with the police in any way. There could be a misunderstanding ... an accident ..."

A runner came up the steps, moved through the battered doors, and crossed the vestibule, finding Major Cole contemplating his watch. The runner crouched beside him. "From the Governor, sir."

Cole took the handwritten report without enthusiasm and read from the last paragraph. "Father Murphy still missing. Locate and rescue him and rescue the other two hostages beneath the sanctuary pews...." Cole looked up at the sergeant.

The sergeant regarded Cole's pale face. "If I found a way into that loft and zapped the sniper, you could dash up the aisle and grab the two hostages—" He smiled. "But you got to move quick because you'll be racing the cops for them."

Major Cole said stiffly, "All right. Take ten men into the loft." He turned to the runner. "Acknowledge message. Have the police command call their men in the triforia and tell them to hold fire on the loft for... five minutes." The runner saluted and moved off. Cole said to the sergeant, "Don't get anyone hurt."

The sergeant turned and led ten Guardsmen back into the south vestibule and opened the door to the spiral staircase. The soldiers double-timed up into the tower until they saw a large wooden door in the wall. The sergeant approached it cautiously and listened, but heard nothing. He put his hand on the knob and turned it slowly, then drew open the door a crack. There was complete blackness in front of him. At first he thought he wasn't in the loft, but then he saw in the distance candlelight playing off the wall of the long northern triforium above, and he recognized the empty flagstaff. He drew open the door, crouched with his rifle held out, and began walking in one of the cross aisles. The ten soldiers began following at intervals.

The sergeant slid his shoulder along the pew enclosure on his left as he moved, blinking into the darkness, listening for a sound somewhere in the cavernous loft. His shoulder slipped into an opening, and he turned, facing the wide aisle that ran up the center of the sloping loft. The entire expanse was pitch black, but he had a sense of its size from the massive rose window looming in the blackness, larger than a two-story house, glowing with the lights of Rockefeller Center across the Avenue. The sergeant took a step up the rising aisle, and he heard a sound like rustling silk in the pews above him.

A woman stood a few feet in front of him on the next higher step. The sergeant stared up at two points of burning green light that reflected the candlelight rising from the Cathedral behind him. The piercing eyes held him for a fraction of a second before he raised his rifle.

Megan screamed wildly and discharged a shotgun blast into his face. She jumped up on a pew and began firing down into the aisle below. The soldiers scrambled back along the aisle, buckshot pelting their helmets, flak jackets, and limbs as they retreated into the tower.

Leary shouted, "Keep them away, Megan! Keep me covered. I'm shooting like I never shot before. Give me time." He fired and moved, fired again and moved again.

Megan picked up her automatic rifle and fired quick bursts at the tower doors. Leary saw a periscope poking over the parapet in the southeast triforium and blew it away with a single shot. "I'm hot! God, I'm hot today!"

Burke heard the shotgun blasts from the loft, followed by the short, quick bursts of the M-16 and then the whistling of the sniper's rifle as rounds chipped away at the balustrade over his head.

The ESD man beside him said, "Sounds like the weekend commandos didn't capture the choir loft."

Burke picked up the field phone and spoke to the other three triforia. "At my command we throw everything we've got into the loft." He called the sacristy stairs. "Tell Malone and Baxter we're putting down suppressing fire again, and if they want to give it a try, this is the time to do it—there won't be another time."

Burke waited the remainder of the five minutes he had given the 69th, to be sure they were not going to try again to get into the loft, then put the field phone to his mouth. "Fire!"

Twenty-five ESD men rose in the four triforia and began firing with automatic rifles and grenade launchers. The rifles raked the loft with long traversing streams, while the launchers alternated their loads, firing beehive canisters of long needles, buckshot, high explosives, gas grenades, illumination rounds, and fire-extinguishing gas.

The choir loft reverberated with the din of exploding grenades, and thick black smoke mingled with the yellowish gas. The smoke and gas rose over the splintering pews, then moved along the ceiling of the Cathedral like an eerie cloud, iridescent in the light of the burning flares below.

Megan and Leary, wearing gas masks, knelt in the bottom aisle below the thick, protruding parapet that ran the width of the loft. Leary fired into the triforia, moved laterally, fired, and moved again. Megan sent streams of automatic fire into the sanctuary as she raced back and forth along the parapet.

Burke heard the sounds of the grenade launchers tapering off as the canisters were used up, and he heard an occasional exclamation when someone was hit. He stood and looked over the balustrade, through the smoke, and saw small flames flickering in the loft. From the field phone in his hand came excited voices as the other triforia called for medics. And still the firing from the loft went on. Burke grabbed an M-16 from one of the EDS men. "Goddamned sons of bitches—" He fired a full magazine without pause, reloaded and fired again until the gun overheated and jammed. He threw the rifle down savagely and shouted into the field phone, "Shoot the remaining fire-extinguishing canisters and get down."

The last of the canisters arched into the loft, and Burke saw the fires begin to subside. Impulsively he grabbed the bullhorn and shouted toward the loft, "I'm coming for you, cocksuckers. I'm—" He felt someone knock his legs out from under him, and he toppled to the floor as a bullet passed through the space where he had stood.

An ESD man sat cross-legged looking down at him. "You got to be cool, Lieutenant. There's nothing personal between them and us. You understand?"

Another man lit a cigarette and added, "They're giving it their best shot, and we're giving it our best shot. Today they got the force with them—see? And we don't. Makes you wonder, though.... I mean in a cathedral and all that..."

Burke took the man's cigarette and got control of himself. "Okay.... okay.... Any ideas?"

A man dabbing at a grazing wound across his jaw answered, "Yeah, offer them a job—my job."

Another man added, "Somebody's got to get *into* the loft through the towers. That's the truth."

Burke saw the dial of the other man's watch. He picked up the phone and called the sacristy stairs. "Did the hostages make it?"

The commo man answered, "Whoever's behind that M-16 up there wasn't shooting at you guys— it was raining bullets on the floor between the pews and the stairs—Christ, somebody up there has it in for these two."

"I'm sure it's not personal." Burke threw the phone down. "Still, I'm getting a little pissed off."

"What the hell is driving those two Micks on?" an ESD man asked. "Politics? I mean, I'm a registered Democrat, but I don't get *that* excited about it. You know?"

Burke stubbed out a cigarette and thought about Bellini. He looked down at the coagulated gore on his trousers that had been part of Bellini, those great stupid brains that had held a lot more knowledge than he had realized. Bellini would know what to do, and if he didn't, he would know how to inspire confidence in these semi-psychotics around him. Burke felt very much out of his element, unwilling to give an order that would get one more man killed; and he appreciated—really and fully appreciated—the reason for Bellini's erratic behavior all night. Unconsciously he rubbed at the stains on his trousers until someone said, "It doesn't come off."

Burke nodded. He realized now that he had to go to the loft, himself, and finish it one way or the other.

Maureen listened to the intense volume of fire dying away. The arm of the policeman who had fallen from the triforium above dangled between the pews, dripping blood into a large puddle of red. Through the gunfire she had thought she heard a sound coming from the pulpit.

Baxter said, "I think that was our last chance, Maureen."

She heard it again, a low, choked-off moan. She said, "We may have one more chance." She slid away from Baxter, avoiding his grasp, and rolled beneath the pews, coming out where they ended near the spiral pulpit staircase a few feet across a patch of open floor. She dove across the opening and flattened herself on the marble-walled steps, hugging the big column around which the steps circled. As she reached the top she noticed the red bloodstains on the top stairs. She looked into the pulpit and saw that he had dragged himself up to a sitting position, his back to the marble wall. His eyes were shut, and she stared at him for several seconds, watching the irregular rising and falling of his chest. Then she slid into the pulpit. "Brian."

He opened his eyes and focused on her.

She leaned over him and said quietly, "Do you see what you've done? They're all dead, Brian. All your trusting young friends are dead—only Leary, Megan, and Hickey are left—the bastards."

He took her hand and pressed it weakly. "Well...you're all right, then...and Baxter?"

She nodded, then ripped open his shirt and saw the bullet wound that had entered from the top of his shoulder. She moved her hands over his body and found the exit wound on his opposite hip, big and jagged, filled with bone splinters and marrow. "Oh, God..." She breathed deeply several times, trying to bring her voice under control. "Was it *worth* it?"

His eyes seemed clear and alert. "Stop scolding, Maureen."

She touched his cheek. "Father Murphy...Why did you...?"

He closed his eyes and shook his head. "We never escape what we were as children.... Priests awe me...." He drew a shallow breath. "Priests...cathedrals...you attack what you fear...primitive...self-protecting."

She glanced at her watch, then took him by his shoulders and shook him gently. "Can you call off Leary and Megan? Can you make them stop?" She looked up at the pulpit microphone. "Let me help you stand."

He didn't respond.

She shook him again. "Brian—it's over—it's finished—stop this killing—"

He shook his head. "I can't stop them.... You know that...."

"The bombs, then. Brian, how many bombs? Where are they? What time—?"

"I don't know...and if I did...I don't know...6:03...sooner...later...two bombs...eight...a hundred....Ask Hickey...."

She shook him more roughly. "You're a damned fool." She said more softly, "You're dying."

"Let me go in peace, can't you?" He suddenly leaned forward and took her hands in a surprisingly tight grip, and a spasm shook his body. He felt blood rising from his lungs and felt it streaming through his parted lips. "Oh...God...God, this is slow...."

She looked at a pistol lying on the floor and picked it up.

He watched her as she held the pistol in both hands. He shook his head. "No.... You've got enough regrets...don't carry that with you.... Not for me...." She cocked the pistol. "Not for you—for *me*."

He held out his hand and pushed her arm away. "I *want* it to be slow...."

She uncocked the pistol and flung it down the steps. "All right...as you wish." She looked around the floor of the pulpit, and from among a pile of ammunition boxes she took an aid kit and unwrapped two pressure bandages.

Flynn said, "Go away.... Don't prolong this.... You're not helping...."

"You want it to be slow." She dressed both wounds, then extracted a Syrette of morphine from the kit.

He pushed her hand away weakly. "For God's sake, Maureen, let me die my way.... I want to stay clearheaded...to think...."

She tapped the spring-loaded Syrette against his arm, and the morphine shot into his muscle. "Clearheaded," she repeated, "clearheaded, indeed."

He slumped back against the pulpit wall. "Cold...cold...this is bad...."

"Yes...let the morphine work. Close your eyes."

"Maureen...how many people have I done this

to...? My God...what *have* I done all these years...?"

Tears formed in her eyes. "Oh, Brian...always so late...always so late...."

Rory Devane felt blood collecting in his torn throat and tried to spit, but the blood gushed from his open wound again, carrying flecks of vomit with it. He blinked the running tears from his eyes as he moved upward. His hands had lost all sensation, and he had to look at them to see if they were grabbing the cold iron rungs.

The higher he climbed, the more his head throbbed where the ricochet had hit him, and the throbbing spread into his skull, causing a pain he wouldn't have believed possible. Several times he wanted to let go, but the image of the cross on the top drew him upward.

He reached the end of the stone spire and looked up at the protruding ornamental copper finial from which rose the cross. Iron spikes, like steps, had been driven into the bulging finial. He climbed them slowly, then threw his arms around the base of the cross and put his head down on the cold metal and wept. After a while he picked up his head and completed his climb. He draped his numb arms over the cross and stood, twenty-eight stories above the city.

Slowly Devane looked to his front. Across the Avenue, Rockefeller Center soared above him, half the windows lit and open, people waving at him. He turned to his left and saw the Empire State Building towering over the Avenue. He shifted his body around and looked behind him. Between two tall buildings he saw the flatland of Long Island stretching back to the horizon. A soft golden glow illuminated the place where the earth met the dark, starlit sky. "Dawn."

* * *

Burke knelt on the blood-covered floor of the triforium. The wounded had been lowered down the elevator shaft, and the dead, including Bellini, were laid out in the attic. Four ESD men of the First Assault Squad remained, huddled against the parapet. The sniper in the choir loft was skimming bullets across the top of the balustrades, but from what Burke could hear, few of the ESD men in the three other triforia were picking their heads up to return the fire. Burke took the field phone and called the opposite triforium. "Situation."

The voice answered, "Squad leader got it. Wounded evacuated down the chimney, and replacements moving up but—listen, what's the word from Rockefeller Center? It's late."

Burke had a vivid image of Commissioner Rourke throwing up in a men's room, Murray Kline telling everyone to be calm, and Martin, looking very cool, giving advice that was designed to finish off the Cathedral and everyone in it. Burke glanced at his watch. It would be slow going down that chimney. He spoke into the phone. "Clear out."

"I hear you."

Burke signaled the switchboard. "Did you get through to the towers or attic yet?"

The operator answered, "Attic under control. Upper parts of both towers are secure, except for some clown climbing the south tower. But down at the loft level everything's a fucking mess. Some weird bitch dressed like a witch or something is blasting away at the tower doors. Some ESD guys got wasted in the choir room. Army guys got creamed coming into the loft from the other tower. Very unclear. You want to speak to them? Tell them to try again?"

"No. Tell them to stand by. Put me through to the crawl space."

The operator's voice was hesitant. "We can't raise them. They were reporting fine until a few minutes ago—then I lost them." The man paused, then added, "Check the time."

"I know the fucking time. Everybody knows the fucking time. Keep trying the crawl space. Connect me with Fifth Squad."

An ESD man on the sacristy stairs answered, and Burke said, "Situation."

The man reported, "Sacristy behind me is filled with fresh Assault Squads, but only two guys at a time can shoot from behind the altar. We definitely cannot reach that bronze plate. We cannot reach the hostages, and they can't reach us. Christ, those two bastards up there can *shoot*." He drew a deep breath. "What the hell is happening?"

"What's happening," Burke answered, "is that this end of the Cathedral will probably collapse in ten minutes, so send everyone back to the rectory basement except two or three men to keep contact with the hostages."

"Right."

Langley's voice came on the line. "Burke—get the hell out of there. Now." Burke answered, "Have the ESD and Bomb Squad send more people into the crawl space—Hickey must've nailed the others. There's at least one bomb left, and he's probably guarding it like a dog with a meaty bone. Get on it."

Langley said, "The bomb could blow *any* time. We can't send any more—"

Mayor Kline cut in, and his voice had the tone of a man speaking for the tape recorders. "Lieutenant, *on your advice*, I'll put one more Assault Squad and bomb team in there, but you understand that their chances—"

Burke ripped the wire out of the phone and turned to the man beside him. "Get everyone down the elevator shaft, and don't stop until you reach the basement of the Cardinal's residence."

The man slung his rifle. "You coming?"

Burke turned and moved around the bend in the triforium that overlooked the south transept. He stood and looked over the balustrade. The line of sight of the choir loft was blocked by the angle of the crossed-shaped building, and the ESD men had shot a line across the transept to the long triforium. Burke slipped into a rope harness and began pulling himself, hand over hand, across the hundred-foot-wide transept arm.

An ESD man on the far side reached out and pulled him over the balustrade. The two men walked quickly to the corner where Sullivan lay sprawled across his bagpipes, his kilts and bare legs splattered with blood. Both men crouched before they turned the corner, and Burke moved down the length of the triforium, passing six kneeling ESD snipers and two dead ones. He took a periscope and looked over the balustrade.

The choir loft was about three stories below, and from here he could see how huge and obscure it was, while the police perches were more defined by the candlelight playing off the window-like openings. Still, he thought, it was incredible that anyone in the loft had survived the volleys of fire, and he wondered why those two were so blessed.

He lowered the scope and moved farther to his right, then stood higher and focused the periscope on the floor below. The shattered front of the armored vehicle stuck out from under the loft, and he saw part of a body sprawled over it—Logan. Two blackened arms stuck straight out of what had been the driver's compartment. Major Cole and a few men knelt to the side of the carrier, looking grim but, he thought, also relieved that the day's National Guard exercises were nearly over.

A shot whistled out of the loft, and the periscope slapped Burke in the eye and flew out of his hands. Burke toppled and fell to the floor.

The ESD man beside him said, "You held it up too long, Lieutenant. And that was our last scope."

Burke rubbed his eye and brought his hand away covered with watery blood. He rose to one knee and looked at the man, who appeared blurry. "Any word from the towers?"

Before the man answered, a short staccato burst of fire rolled out of the loft, followed by another, and the man said, "That's the word from the towers—the witch wants nobody near her doors." He looked at his watch and said, "What a fucking mess.... We almost had it. Right?"

Burke looked at the ESD man across from him, who was a sergeant. "Any ideas?"

"The thing hinges on knocking out the loft so that Malone and Baxter can make it to the stairs and so the ESD people there can drop concussion grenades through the plate and turn that guy Hickey's brains to mashed potatoes. Then the bomb guys can get the bombs. Right?"

Burke nodded. This seemed to be the inescapable solution to the problem. The choir loft dominated the entire Cathedral, as it was meant to do for a different purpose. And Flynn had placed two very weird people up there. "What are our options for knocking out the loft?"

The ESD sergeant rubbed his jaw. "Well, we could bring new spotlights into the triforia, have helicopters machinegun through the rose window, break through the plaster lathing in the attic over the loft.... Lots of options... but all that ordnance isn't handy... and it takes time...."

Burke nodded again. "Yeah..."

"But the best way," said the sergeant, "is for somebody to sneak into that loft from one of the towers. Once you're past the door, you've got space to maneuver, just like them, and you're as invisible as they are."

Burke nodded. The alternate answer was to get to the explosives through the crawl space and worry about the sniper and the hostages later. Then 6:03 wouldn't matter anymore. Burke picked up the field phone and spoke to the switchboard. "What's the situation in the crawl space?"

The operator answered, "The new ESD squad is in—found some survivors dragging wounded back. Dogs and handlers dead. Bomb Squad people all out of it except Peterson, who's wounded but still functioning. There's a crazy guy down there with an automatic weapon. The survivors say there's no way to get to any remaining bombs except through the bronze plate." The operator hesitated, then said, "Listen . . . Peterson said this guy could probably set off the bombs anytime he wants . . . so I'm signing off because I'm a little close to where the bombs are supposed to be. Commo is going to be broken until I get this switchboard set up someplace else. Sorry, Lieutenant." He added, "They're searching both towers and the attic for the radio jammer, and if they find it, you'll have radio commo. Okay? Sorry."

The phone went dead. Burke turned on a radio lying near his feet, and a rush of static filled the air. He shut it off.

The ESD commo man beside him said, "That's it. Nobody is talking to nobody now. We can't coordinate an attack on that loft if we wanted to—or coordinate a withdrawal . . . ."

Burke nodded. "Looks like getting in was the easy part." He looked around the dark gallery. "Well, it's a big place. Looks pretty solid to me. The architect seemed to think this end would stand if the main columns over there went . . . ."

One of the men asked, "Anybody guaranteeing that? Is anybody sure there aren't bombs under these columns?" He tapped one of the columns.

Burke responded, "Logically, they wouldn't have

bothered with fires in the attic if the whole place was rigged to explode. Right?" He looked at the men huddled around him, but no one seemed relieved by his deductions.

The sergeant said, "I don't think logic has anything to do with how these cocksuckers operate."

Burke looked at his watch. 5:54. He said, "I'm staying...you're staying." He entered the south tower and began to climb down to the loft level.

Maureen looked at her watch, then said to Flynn, "I'm going back."

"Yes...no...don't leave...." His voice was much weaker now.

She wiped his brow with her hand. "I'm sorry...I can't stay here."

He nodded.

"Do you have much pain, Brian?"

He shook his head, but as he did his body stiffened.

She took another Syrette of morphine and removed the cap. With the blood he had lost, she knew this would probably kill him, but there would be no pain. She bent over and put her arm around his neck, kissing him on the lips as she brought the Syrette to his chest, near his heart.

Flynn's lips moved against hers, and she turned her head to hear. "No...no...take it away...."

She drew the Syrette back and looked at him. He had not opened his eyes once in the last several minutes, and she did not understand how he knew...unless it was that he just knew her too well. She held his hand tightly and felt the large ring pressing into her palm. She said, "Brian...can I take this...? If I leave here...I want to return it...to bring it home...."

He pulled his hand away and clenched his fingers. "No."

"Keep it, then—the police will have it."

"No.... Someone must come for it."

She shook her head and then kissed him again. Without a word she slid back toward the winding stairs.

He called to her, "Maureen...listen...Leary...I told him...not to shoot at you.... He follows orders.... You can tell when Megan is covering the tower door...then you can run...."

She lay still on the stairs, then said, "Baxter...?"

"Baxter is as good as dead.... You can go...go..."

She shook her head. "Brian...you shouldn't have told me that...."

He opened his eyes and looked at her, then nodded. "No, I shouldn't have...stupid.... Always doing the wrong thing...." He tried to sit up, and his face went white with pain. "Please...run...live..." His chest began to rise and fall slowly.

Maureen watched him, then slid slowly down the stairs and rolled quickly over the few feet of exposed floor and crawled between the pews, coming up beside Baxter.

Baxter said, "I wanted to follow you...but I thought perhaps..."

She took his hand and pressed it.

"He's dead?"

"No."

They lay side by side in silence. At 5:55 Baxter

asked, "Do you think he could—or would—call off Leary and Megan?"

She said, "I didn't ask."

Baxter nodded. "I see . . . . Well, are you ready to run for it?"

"I'm not certain that's what I want to do."

"Then why did you come back here?"

She didn't answer.

He drew a short breath and said, "I'm going . . . ."

She held his arm tightly and peered under the pew at the long expanse of blood-streaked white marble that seemed to radiate an incandescence of its own in the candlelight. She heard the staccato bursts of Megan's fire hitting the tower doors but no longer heard the sound of Leary's bullets striking in the Cathedral. "Leary is waiting for us."

"Then let's not keep him waiting." He began moving toward the end of the pew.

She kept a grip on his arm. "No!"

A policeman's voice called out from the sacristy stairwell behind the altar. "Listen, you're keeping two men here—I don't like to put it this way, but we'd rather be gone—you know?—so are you coming or not?" He thought he spoke just loud enough for them to hear, but the acoustics carried the sound through the Cathedral.

Two shots whistled out of the loft and cracked into the marble midway between the pews and the altar. Maureen slid beside Baxter and turned her face to him. "Stay with me."

He put his arm around her shoulders and called out to the stairwell. "Go on—there's no point in waiting for us."

There was no answer, and Maureen and Baxter edged closer to each other, waiting out the final minutes.

Wendy Peterson knelt behind the back wall of the crypt as a medic wound a bandage around her right forearm. She flexed her fingers and noticed that they were becoming stiff. "*Damn*."

The medic said, "You better go back." Another medic was tying a pressure bandage around her right heel.

She looked around the red-lit area. Most of the original group had been left behind, dead from head wounds as a result of the ground-skimming fire. The rest were being evacuated, suffering from wounds in the limbs or buttocks or from broken clavicles where the flak jackets had stopped the head-on bullets. In the red light, pale faces seemed rosy, red blood looked black, and, somehow, the wounds seemed especially ugly. She turned away and concentrated on moving her fingers. "Damn it."

The new ESD squad leader assembled his men at the corner of the crypt and looked at his watch. "Eight minutes." He knelt down beside Peterson. "Listen, I don't know what the hell I'm supposed to be doing down here except collecting bodies because, let me tell you, there's no way to get that joker out of there, Lieutenant."

She moved away from the medics and limped to the edge of the vault. "You sure?"

He nodded. "I can't fire—right? He's got a gas mask, and concussion grenades are out. But even if we got him, there's not much time to defuse even one bomb, and we don't know how many there are. The damned dogs are dead, and there aren't any more dogs—"

"Okay . . . okay . . . . Damn it . . . we're so close."

"No," said the squad leader, "we are not close at all." Some of the men around him coughed nervously and pointedly. The squad leader addressed Peterson. "They said this was your decision . . . and Burke's decision." He picked up the field phone beside him, but it was still dead. "Your decision."

A voice called out from the dark, an old man's voice with a mocking tone. "Fuck you! Fuck all of you!"

A nervous young policeman shouted back, "Fuck you!"

The squad leader stuck his head around the crypt corner and shouted, "If you come out with your hands—"

"Oh, baloney!" Hickey laughed, then fired a burst of bullets at the red glow coming around the corner of the crypt. The gunfire caused a deafening roar in the closed space and echoed far into the quarteracre of crawl space. Hickey shouted, "Is there a bomb squad lad there? Answer me!"

Peterson edged toward the corner. "Right here, Pop."

"*Pop*? Who are you calling Pop? Well, never mind—listen, these bombs have more sensitive triggers to make them blow than . . . than Linda Lovelace." He laughed, then said, "Terrible metaphor. Anyway, lass, to give you an example you'll appreciate professionally—I mean demolitions, not blowing—where was I? Oh, yes, I've lots of triggers—photosensitive, audio—all kinds of triggers. Do you believe that, little girl?"

"I think you're full of shit."

Hickey laughed. "Well, then send everyone away, darlin', and toss a concussion grenade at me. If that doesn't blow the bombs, then a demo man can come back and defuse them. *You* won't be able to with your brains scrambled, and I won't be able to stop him with *my* brains scrambled. Go on, lassie. Let's see what you're made of."

Wendy Peterson turned to the squad leader. "Give me a concussion grenade and clear out."

"Like hell. Anyway, you know we don't carry those things in spaces like this."

She unsheathed the long stiletto that she used to cut plastic and moved around the corner of the crypt.

The squad leader reached out and pulled her back. "Where the hell are you going? Listen, I thought of that—it's over sixty feet to where that guy is. *Nobody* can cover that distance without making some noise, and he'll nail you the second he hears you."

"Then cover me with noise."

"Forget it."

Hickey called out, "What's next, folks? One man belly-crawling? I can hear breathing at thirty–forty feet. I can smell a copper at sixty feet. Listen, gentlemen—and lady—the time has come for you to leave. You're annoying me, and I have things to think about in the next few minutes. I feel like singing—" He began singing a bawdy version of the British army song:

"Fuck you aaa-lll, fuck you aaa-lll,
The long and the short and the taa-lll.
Fuck all the coppers, and fuck all their guns,

Fuck all the priests and their bastard sons.
S-o-oo, I'm saying good-bye to you all,
The ones that appeal and appall.
I stall and tarry,
While you want to save Harry,
But nevertheless fuck you aaa-lll."

Wendy Peterson put the stiletto back in its sheath and let out a long breath. "Let's go."

The procession began making its way back toward the open hatch to the corridor, moving with an affected casualness that disguised the fact that they were retreating at top speed. No one looked back except Wendy Peterson, who glanced over her shoulder once or twice. Suddenly she began running in a crouch, past the moving line of men, toward the open hatch.

John Hickey squeezed out of the tight space and sat down against the column footing, the mass of plastic explosive conforming to his back. "Oh...well..." He filled his pipe, lit it, and looked at his watch. 5:56. "My, it's late...." He hummed a few bars of "An Irish Lullaby," then sang softly to himself, "...toora-loo-ra-loo-ra, hush now don't you cry...."

* * *

The Sixth Squad leader climbed the iron rungs of the south spire alone, a nylon line attached to his belt. He moved quietly through the cold dark night to a point five feet below Rory Devane, who still clung to the arms of the cross. The ESD man drew his pistol. "Hey! Jesus! Don't move, or I'll blow your ass off."

Devane opened his eyes and looked down behind him.

The squad leader raised his pistol. "You armed?"

Devane shook his head.

The squad leader got a clear look at Devane's
bloodied face in the city lights. "You're really fucked
up—you know that?"

Devane nodded.

"Come on down. Nice and easy."

Devane shook his head. "I can't."

"Can't? You got up there, you bastard. Now get down.
I'm not hanging here all fucking day waiting for you."

"I can't move."

The squad leader thought that about half the world
was watching him on television, and he put a concerned expression on his face, then smiled at Devane
good-naturedly. "You asshole. For two cents I'd jam
this gun between your legs and blow your balls into
orbit." He glanced at the towering buildings of Rockefeller Center and flashed a resolute look for the telescopic cameras and field glasses. He took a step
upward. "Listen, sonny boy, I'm coming up with a
line, and if you pull any shit, I swear to God, motherfucker, you're going to be treading air."

Devane stared down at the black-clad figure approaching. "You people talk funny."

The squad leader laughed and climbed up over the
curve of the finial and wrapped his arms around the
base of the cross. "You're okay, kid. You're an asshole,
but you're okay. Don't move." He circled around to
the side and pulled himself up until his head was level
with Devane's shoulder, then reached out and looped

a line around Devane's torso. "You the guy who fired the flares?"

Devane nodded.

"Real performer, aren't you, Junior? What else do you do? You juggle?" He tied the end of the long line to the top of the cross and spoke in a more solemn voice. "You're going to have to climb a little. I'll help you."

Devane's mind was nearly numb, but something didn't seem right. There was something incongruous about hanging twenty-eight stories above the most technologically advanced city in the world and being asked to climb, wounded, down a rope to safety. "Get a helicopter."

The squad leader glanced at him quickly.

Devane stared down into the man's eyes and said, "You're going to kill me."

"What the hell are you talking about? I'm risking my goddamned life to save you—shithead." He flashed a smile toward Rockefeller Center. "Come on. Down."

"No."

The squad leader heard a sound and looked up. A Fire Rescue helicopter appeared overhead and began dropping toward the spire. The helicopter dropped closer, beating the cold air downward. The squad leader saw a man in a harness edging out of the side door, a carrying chair in his hands. The squad leader hooked his arms over Devane's on the cross and pulled himself up so that they were face to face, and he studied the young man's frozen blue features. The blood had actually crystallized in his red hair and glistened in the light. The squad leader examined his throat wound and the large discolored mass on his forehead.

"Caught some shit, did you? You should be dead—you know?"

"I'm going to live."

"They're stuffing some of my friends in body bags down there—"

"I never fired a shot."

"Yeah.... Come on, I'll help you into the sling."

"How can you commit murder—*here*?"

The squad leader drew a long breath and exhaled a plume of fog.

The Fire Rescue man was dangling about twenty feet above them now, and he released the carrying chair, which dropped on a line to within a few feet of the two men. The squad leader put his hands on Devane's shoulders. "Okay, Red, trust me." He reached up and guided the chair under Devane, strapped him in, then untied the looped rope. "Don't look down." He waved off the helicopter.

The helicopter rose, and Devane flew away from the spire, swinging in a wide arc through the brightening sky. The squad leader watched as the line was reeled in and Devane disappeared into the helicopter. The squad leader turned and looked back at Rockefeller Center. People were leaning from the windows, civilians and police, and he heard cheering. Bits of paper began sailing from the windows and floated in the updrafts. He wiped his runny eyes and waved toward the buildings as he began the climb down from the cross. "Hello, assholes—spell my name right. Hi, Mom—fuck you, Kline—I'm a hero."

Burke ran down the spiral stairs of the south tower until he reached a group of Guardsmen and police on the darkened choir loft level. Burke said, "What's the situation?"

No one answered immediately, then an ESD man said, "We sort of ran into each other in the dark." He motioned toward a neat stack of about six bodies against the wall.

"Christ...." Burke looked across the tower room and saw a splintered door hanging loosely from its hinges.

An ESD man said, "Stay out of the line of fire of that door."

"Yeah, I guessed that right away."

A short burst of rifle fire hit the door, and everyone ducked as the bullets ricocheted around the large room, shattering thick panes of glass. A National Guardsman fired a full magazine back through the door.

The steady coughing of the sniper's silencer echoed into the room, but Burke could not imagine what was left to fire at. He circled around the room and slid along the wall toward the door.

Wendy Peterson ran to the top step of the sacristy stairs behind the altar. Her breathing came hard, and the wound on her heel was bleeding. She called back to the crypt landing where the two remaining ESD men stood. "Concussion grenade."

One of the men shrugged and threw up a large black canister.

She edged out and glanced to her right. About thirty feet separated the hostages under the pews from the stairs. To her left, toward the rear of the sanctuary, five feet of floor separated her from the bullet-scarred bronze plate. How heavy, she wondered, was that plate? Which way did it hinge? Where was the handle? She turned back to the crypt landing. "The hostages?"

One of the men answered, "We can't help them. They have to make a break when they think they're ready. We're here in case they make it and are wounded... but they're not going to make it. Neither are we if we hang around much longer." He cleared his throat. "Hey, it's 5:57—can those bombs go before 6:03?"

She motioned toward the bronze plate. "What are my chances?"

The man looked down at the blood-streaked stairs and unconsciously touched his ear, which had been nicked by a shot from the loft—a shot fired from over a hundred yards away through the dim lighting. "Your chances of getting to the plate are good—fifty-fifty. Your chances of opening it, dropping that grenade, waiting for it to go, then dropping in yourself, are a little worse than zero."

"Then we let the place go down?"

He said, "No one can say we didn't try." He ran his foot across the sticky blood on the landing. "Cut out."

She shook her head. "I'll hang around—you never know what might happen."

"I *know* what's going to happen, Lieutenant, and this is not the place to be when it happens."

Two shots struck the bronze plate and ricocheted back toward the Lady Chapel. Another shot struck the plaster ceiling ten stories above. Peterson and the two ESD men looked up at the black expanse and dodged pieces of falling plaster. A second later one of the Cardinal's hats that had been suspended over the crypt dropped to the landing beside one of the ESD men. The man picked it up and examined the tasseled red hat.

Leary's voice bellowed from the loft. "Got a cardinal—on the wing—in the dark. God, I can't miss! I can't *miss!*"

The ESD man threw the hat aside. "He's right, you know."

Peterson said, "I'll talk to the hostages. You might as well go."

One of the men bounded down the stairs toward the sacristy gates. The other climbed up toward Peterson. "Lieutenant"—he looked down at the bloody, soiled bandages wrapped around her bare foot—"it takes about sixty seconds to make it to the rectory basement...."

"Okay."

The man hesitated, then turned and headed for the sacristy gates.

Peterson sat down on the top step and called out to Baxter and Malone, "How are you doing?"

Maureen called back, "Go away."

Peterson lit a cigarette. "It's okay...we have time yet.... Anytime you're ready...think it out." She spoke to them softly as the seconds ticked away.

Leary grazed a round over each of the four triforium balustrades, changed positions, fired at the statue of St. Patrick, moved laterally, picked out a flickering votive candle, fired, and watched it explode. He moved diagonally over the pews, then stopped and put two bullets through the cobalt blue window rising above the east end of the ambulatory. The approaching dawn showed a lighter blue through the broken glass.

Leary settled back into a bullet-pocked pew near the organ pipes and concentrated on the sanctuary—the stairwell, the bronze plate, and the clergy pews. He flexed his arm, which had been hit by shrapnel, and rubbed his cheek where buckshot had raked the side of his face. At least two ribs had been broken by bullets where they had hit his flak jacket.

Megan was firing at each of the tower doors, alternating the sequence and duration of each burst of automatic fire. She stood in the aisle a few feet below Leary and watched the two doors to her right and left farther down the loft. Her arms and legs were crusted with blood from shrapnel and buckshot, and her right shoulder was numb from a direct bullet hit. She suddenly felt shaky and nauseous and leaned against a pew. She straightened up and called back to Leary, "They're not even trying."

Leary said, "I'm bored."

She laughed weakly, then replied, "I'm going to blast those pews and flush those two out. You nail them."

Leary said, "In about six minutes half the Cathedral will fall in on them ... or I'll get them if they make a break. Don't spoil the game. Be patient."

She knelt in the aisle and raised her rifle. "What if the police get the bombs?"

Leary looked at the sanctuary as he spoke. "I doubt they got Hickey.... Anyway, I'm doing what I was told—covering that plate and keeping those two from running."

She shouted as she took aim at the clergy pews. "I want to *see* her die—before I die. I'm going to flush them. You nail them. Ready?"

Leary stared down at Megan, her silhouette visible against the candlelight and flares below. He spoke in a low, contemplative voice. "Everyone's dead, Megan, except Hickey and, I guess, Malone and Baxter. They'll all die in the explosion. That leaves only you and me."

She spun around and peered up into the blackness toward the place from which his voice had come.

He said, "You understand, I'm a professional. It's like I said, I only do what I'm told—never more, never less—and Flynn told me to make especially sure of you and Hickey."

She shook her head. "Jack . . . you can't . . . . Not after we . . ." She laughed. "Yes, of course . . . . I don't want to be taken . . . . Brian knew that . . . . He did it for me. Go on, then. Quickly!"

He raised a pistol, aimed at the dark outline, and put two bullets in rapid succession through her head. Megan's body toppled back, and she rolled down the aisle, coming to rest beside the Guard sergeant she had killed.

Burke stood in his stocking feet with his back to the wall just inside the tower door, a short, fat grenade launcher nestled in the bend of his elbow. He closed his eyes against the glare of the lights coming through the broken windows and steadied his breathing. The men in the tower room were completely still, watching him. Burke listened to the distant sound of a man and woman talking, followed by two pistol shots. He spun rapidly into the doorway and raced up the side aisle along the wall, then flattened himself in the sloping aisle about halfway up the loft. From farther back near the organ pipes came the sound of breathing. The breathing stopped abruptly, and a man's voice said, "I *know* you're there."

Burke remained motionless.

The man said, "I see in the dark, I smell what you can't smell, I hear *everything*. You're dead."

Burke knew that the man was trying to draw him into a panic shot, and he was not doing a bad job of it. The man was good. Even in a close-in-situation like this he was very cool.

Burke rolled onto his back, lifted his head, and looked out over the rail into the Cathedral. The cable that held the chandelier nearest the choir loft swayed slightly as it was being drawn up by the winch in the attic. The chandelier rose level with the loft, and Burke saw the Guardsman sitting on it, his rifle pointed into the loft. He looked, Burke thought, like live bait. *Live ones*, he wanted live ones. Burke's muscles tensed.

Leary fired, and the body on the chandelier jerked.

Burke jumped to his feet, pointed the grenade launcher at the direction of the sound, and fired its single beehive round. The dozens of needle darts buzzed across the quiet loft, spreading as they traveled. There was a sharp cry, followed immediately by the flash of a rifle that Burke saw out of the corner of his eyes as he turned and dove for the floor. A powerful blow on the back of his flak jacket propelled him headfirst into the wall, and he staggered, then collapsed into the aisle. Another shot ripped through the pews and passed inches over his head.

Burke lay still, aware of a pain in the center of his spine that began to spread to his arms and legs. Several more shots struck around him. The firing shifted to the doors, and Burke tried to crawl to another position but found that he couldn't move. He tried to reach the pistol in his belt, but his arm responded in short, spastic motions.

The firing shifted back toward him, and a round grazed his hand. His forehead was bleeding where he had crashed into the wall, and throbbing pains ran from his eyes to the back of his skull. He felt himself losing consciousness, but he could hear distinctly the sound of the man reloading his rifle. Then the voice said, "Are you dead, or do you just wish you were?"

Leary raised his rifle, but the persistent stabbing pain in his right leg made him lower it. He sat down in the center aisle, rolled back his trouser leg, and ran his fingers over his shin, feeling the tiny entry hole where the dart had hit him. He brought his hand around to his calf and touched the exit wound, slightly larger, with a splinter of bone protruding from the flesh. "Ah...shit...shit..."

He rose to his knee and emptied his rifle toward the doors and the side aisle, then ripped off his rubber mask and pulled the gas mask from around his neck. He tore off the long robe, using it to wipe his sniper rifle from end to end as he crawled down the center aisle. Leary placed the rifle in Megan's warm hands, reached into the front pew, and retrieved another rifle. He rose and steadied himself on the edge of the pew and slid onto the bench. Leary called out, "Martin! You out there?"

There was a silence, then a voice called back from the choir practice room. "Right here, Jack. Are you alone?"

"Yeah."

"Tell the police you're surrendering."

"Right. Come out here—alone."

Martin walked briskly into the choir loft, turned on a flashlight, and made his way through the dark into the center aisle. He stepped over Megan's body. "Hello, Jack." He approached Leary and edged into the pew. "Here, let's have that. That's a good lad." He took Leary's rifle and pistol, then called out, "He's disarmed."

ESD men began to move cautiously from both towers into the choir loft. Martin called to them. "It's all right—this man is an agent of mine." Martin turned to Leary and gave him a look of annoyance. "A bit early, aren't you, Jack?"

Leary spoke through clenched teeth. "I'm hit."

"Really? You look fine."

Leary swore. "Fitzgerald was starting to become a problem, and I had to do her when I had the chance. Then someone got into the loft, and I took a needle dart in the shin. Okay?"

"That's dreadful...but I don't see anyone in here.... You really should have waited."

"Fuck you."

Martin shone his light on Leary's shin. Like so many killers, he thought, Leary couldn't stand much pain. "Yes, that looks like it might hurt." He reached out and touched Leary's wound.

Leary let out a cry of pain. "Hey! God . . . that feels like there's still a needle in there."

"Might well be." Martin looked down at the sanctuary. "Malone and Baxter . . . ?"

A policeman shouted from the side of the loft. "Stand up!"

Leary placed his hands on the pew in front of him and stood. He said to Martin, "They're both under the sanctuary pews there—"

The lights in the loft went on, illuminating the sloping expanse of ripped pews, bullet-pocked walls, burnt lockers, and scarred aisles. The towering organ pipes shone brightly where they had been hit, but above the pipes the rose window was intact. Leary looked around and made a whistling sound. "Like walking in the rain without getting wet." He smiled.

Martin waved his hand impatiently. "I don't understand about Baxter and Malone. They're dead, aren't they?"

The police stepped over the bodies in the aisle and moved up carefully into the pews, rifles and pistols raised.

Leary automatically put his hands on his head as he spoke to Martin. "Flynn told me not to kill her—and I couldn't shoot into the pews at Baxter without taking the chance of hitting her—"

"*Flynn*? You're working for *me*, Jack."

Leary pushed past Martin and hobbled into the aisle. "You give orders, he gives orders . . . . I do only what I'm told—and what I'm paid for—"

"But Flynn's money came from *me*, Jack."

Leary stared at Martin. "Flynn never bullshitted me.

He told me this loft would be hell, and I knew it. You said it would be—how'd that go?—relatively without risk?"

Martin's voice was peevish. "Well, as far as I'm concerned you didn't fulfill your contract, I'll have to reconsider the nature of the final payment."

"Look, you little fuck—" Two ESD men covered the remaining distance up the aisle and grabbed Leary's upraised arms, pulling them roughly behind his back, then cuffing him. They pushed him to the floor, and he yelled out in pain, then turned his head back toward Martin as the police searched him. "If they got Hickey from below, they got the bombs anyway. If they didn't get him, you'll still get your explosion."

Martin noticed Burke moving toward him, supported by two ESD men. Martin cleared his throat. "All right, Jack—that's enough."

But Leary was obviously offended. "I lived up to my end. I mean, Christ, Martin, it's after six—and look around you—enough is enough—"

"Shut up."

Two ESD men pulled Leary to his feet. Leary said, "This leg...it feels funny...burns..."

Martin said nothing.

Leary stared at him. "What did you...? Oh...no..."

Martin winked at him, turned, and walked away.

An ESD man raised a bullhorn and called out into the Cathedral. "Police in the choir loft! All clear! Mr. Baxter—Miss Malone—run! Run this way!"

Baxter picked up his head and looked at Maureen. "Was that Leary?"

She forced a smile. "You're learning." She listened to the bullhorn call their names again. "I don't know..." She pressed her face against Baxter's, and they held each other tightly.

Wendy Peterson looked around the altar and stared up into the choir loft. It was completely lit, and she saw the police moving through the pews. Without looking at her watch she knew there were probably not more than three minutes left—less, if the bomb were set earlier, and she didn't remember one that was set for later than the threatened time.

She ran to the bronze plate, pulling the pin on the concussion grenade as she moved and calling back to the pews. "Run! Run!" She bent over and pulled up the heavy bronze plate with one hand.

Maureen stood, looking first at Wendy Peterson and then toward the illuminated expanse at the upper end of the Cathedral as Baxter came up beside her.

A bullhorn was blaring. "Run! Run this way!"

They began to run, but Maureen suddenly veered and dashed up the pulpit stairs, grabbing Flynn's arm and dragging him back down the steps. Baxter ran up behind her and pulled at her arm. She turned to him. "He's alive. *Please...*" He hesitated, then put Flynn over his shoulders, and they ran toward the communion rail.

Wendy Peterson watched silently until they reached a point in the center aisle where she thought they would be safe if the grenade detonated the bomb. She released the safety handle and flung the grenade into the hole with a motion that suggested *What the hell....* She dropped the plate back and stood off several feet, holding her hands over her ears.

The grenade exploded, ripping the bronze plate from its hinges and sending it high into the air. A shock wave rolled through the Cathedral, and the sanctuary trembled beneath her feet. Everything seemed to hang in suspension as she waited for a secondary explosion, but there was nothing except the ringing in her ears. She dropped through the smoke down the ladder.

Burke moved slowly toward Martin as the echoes of the shock wave passed through the loft.

Martin said, "Well, Lieutenant Burke, this is a surprise. I thought you'd be . . . well, somewhere else. You look terrible. You're walking strangely. Where are your *shoes*?" Martin checked his watch. "Two minutes . . . less, I think. Good view from here. Do you have cameras recording this? You won't see this again." He peered over Burke's shoulder at the sanctuary. "Look at all that metalwork, that marble. Magnificent. It's going to look exactly like Coventry in about three minutes." He patted the lapel of his topcoat as he turned back to Burke. "See? I've kept my carnation. Where's yours?" He looked anxiously into the sanctuary again. "What *is* that crazy woman up to? Turn around, Burke. Don't miss this."

Martin brushed past Burke and drew closer to the rail. He watched Baxter and Maureen approaching, accompanied by Major Cole and four Guardsmen. Brian Flynn's limp body was being carried on a stretcher by two of the Guardsmen. Martin said to Burke, "Governor Doyle will be pleased with his boys—Mayor Kline will be *furious* with you, Burke." Martin called down.

"Harry, old man? Up here!" He waved. "Nicely done, you two."

Martin turned and looked back as Leary, almost unconscious, was being carried into the choir practice room. He said to Burke, "Ballistics will show that the rifle I took from him never fired a shot that killed anyone. He did kill that young woman sniper, though, the very moment he had—what do you call it?—the drop on her. Well, at least that's the way he's made it appear. He'll go free if he is tried." Martin looked back over his shoulder. "Good-bye, Jack. I'll see you later in the hospital." He called to an ESD squad leader. "Easy with that man—he works for me." Martin turned back to Burke as Leary disappeared into the choir room. "Your people are in an ugly mood. Well...the mysteries are unfolding now...Burke? Are you listening to me? Burke—" Martin looked at his watch, then at the sanctuary, and continued in a new vein. "The problem with you people is no fire discipline. Shoot first and ask questions later—great tradition. That's why Father Murphy is hanging dead from a ladder in the bell tower here—oh, you didn't know that, Burke?"

Martin walked to the edge of the loft and rested his hands on the parapet, looking straight down. Baxter and Malone were standing with their backs to him now. Flynn was lying near them on the floor, a National Guard medic crouched over him. Baxter, Martin noticed, had his arm around Maureen Malone's shoulder, and she was slumped against him. Martin said to Burke, "Come closer—look at this, Burke. They've made friends." He called down, "Harry, you old devil. Miss Malone. Get down, you two—there'll be a bit of falling debris." He turned to Burke behind him. "I feel rather bad about being the one who pushed for Baxter being on the steps.... If I had had *any* idea it would be so risky..."

Burke moved beside Martin and leaned on the rail. The feeling began to return to his legs and arms, and the numbness was replaced by a tingling sensation. He looked out into the Cathedral, focusing on the sanctuary. A dead ESD man lay in the clergy pews, and black smoke drifted out of the hole. Green carnations were strewn across the black-and-white marble floor, and hundreds of fragments of stained glass glittered where they'd fallen from above. Even from this distance he could see the blood splattered across the raised altar, the bullet marks everywhere. The police in the choir pews behind him fell silent and began to edge closer to the rail. The towers and attic had emptied, most of the police leaving the Cathedral through the only unmined exit—the damaged ceremonial doors. Some congregated in the two long west triforia, away from the expected area of destruction. They stared at the sanctuary, a block away, with a mesmerized fascination. Burke looked at his watch: 6:02, give or take thirty seconds.

Wendy Peterson shone her light into Hickey's face and poked his throat with her stiletto, but he was dead— yet there was no blood running from his nose, mouth, or ears, no protruding tongue or ruptured capillaries to indicate he had been killed by concussion. In fact, she thought, his face was serene, almost smiling, and he had probably died peacefully in his sleep and with no help from her or anyone else.

She set the light down pointing at the base of the column and switched on the lamp of her miner's helmet. "Photosensitive, my ass," she said aloud. "Bullshitting old bastard." She began speaking to herself, as she always did when she was alone with a bomb.

"Okay, Wendy, you silly bitch, one step at a time...." She drew a deep breath, and the oily smell of the plastic rose in her flaring nostrils. "All the time in the world..." She passed her hands gently over the dusty surface of the plastic, feeling for a place where the mechanism might be embedded. "Looks like stone.... Clever...all smoothed over...okay..." She slipped her wristwatch off and stuck it into the plastic. "Ninety seconds, Wendy, give or take.... Too late to clear out...stupid..." She was cutting with the stiletto, making a random incision into the plastic. "You get only two or three cuts now...." She thrust her right hand into the opening but felt nothing. The wound on her arm had badly stiffened her fingers. "Sixty seconds...time flies when you're..." She put her ear to the plastic and listened, but heard nothing except the blood pounding in her head. "...when you're having a good time.... Okay...cut here.... *Okay*, God? Careful...nothing here.... Where'd you put it, old man? Where's that ticking heart? Cut here, Wendy.... When you wish upon a star, makes no difference... *There*... *there*, that's it." She pushed back the plastic, enlarging the incision and revealing the face of a loudly ticking alarm clock. "Okay, clock time, 6:02. My time, 6:02—alarm time, 6:03.... You play fair, old man.... All right...." She wanted to yank the clock out, rip away the wires, or squash the crystal and advance the alarm dial, but that, more often than not, set the damned thing off. "Easy, baby...you've come so far now...." She thrust her hand into the plastic and worked her long, stiff fingers carefully through the thick, damp substance, feeling for anti-intrusion detonators as she dug toward the rear of the clock. "Go gently into this crap, Peterson.... Hand behind the clock...there...simple mechanism.... Where's the off switch? Come on...damn it...6:03—shit—*shit*—no alarm yet...few more seconds...steady, Wendy. Dear God, steady, *steady*..." The alarm rang loudly, and Wendy Peterson listened to it carefully, knowing it was the last sound she would ever hear.

* * *

A deep silence came over the Cathedral. Martin rested his folded arms on the rail as he stared into the sanctuary. He tapped his fingers on the watch crystal. "What time do you have, Burke? Isn't it late? What seems to be the problem?"

In the rectory and in the Cardinal's residence people had moved back from the taped windows. On all the rooftops around the Cathedral police and newspeople stood motionless. In front of televisions in homes and in the bars that had never closed, people watched the countdown numbers superimposed on the silent screen showing an aerial view of the Cathedral brightening slowly in the dawn light. In churches and synagogues that had maintained all-night vigils, people looked at their watches. 6:04.

Wendy Peterson rose slowly from the hole and walked to the middle of the sanctuary, blinking in the brighter lighting. She held something in both hands and stared at it, then looked slowly up at the triforia and loft. Her face was very pale, and her voice was slightly hesitant, but her words rolled through the silent Cathedral. "The detonating device..." She held up a clock connected by four wires to a large battery pack, from which ran four more wires. She raised it higher, as though it were a chalice, and in her other hand she held four long cylindrical detonators that she had clipped from the wires. White plastic still clung to the mechanism, and in the stillness of the Cathedral the ticking clock sounded very loud. She ran her tongue over her dry lips and said, "All clear."

No one applauded, no one cheered, but in the silence there was an audible collective sigh, then the sound of someone weeping.

The quiet was suddenly broken by the shrill noise of a long scream as a man fell headfirst from the choir loft. The body hit the floor in front of the armored carrier with a loud crack.

Maureen and Baxter turned and looked down at the awkwardly sprawled body, a splatter of blood radiating over the floor around the head. Baxter spoke in a whisper. "Martin."

Burke walked haltingly across the floor beneath the choir loft. The tingling in his back had become a dull pain. A stretcher was carried past him, and he caught a glimpse of Brian Flynn's face but couldn't tell if he was dead or alive. Burke kept walking until he came to Martin's body. Martin's neck was broken, his eyes were wide open, and his protruding tongue was half bitten off. Burke lit a cigarette and dropped the match on Martin's face.

He turned and looked absently at the huge, charred carrier and the blackened bodies on it, then watched the people around him moving, speaking quickly, going about their duties; but it all seemed remote, as though he were watching through an unfocused telescope. He looked around for Baxter and Malone but saw they were gone. He realized he had nothing to do at the moment and felt good about it.

Burke moved aimlessly up the center aisle and saw Wendy Peterson standing alone in the aisle and looking, like himself, somewhat at loose ends. Weak sunlight came through the broken window above the east end of the ambulatory, and she seemed, he thought, to be deliberately standing in the dust-moted shaft. As he walked past her he said, "Very nice."

She looked up at him. "Burke..."

He turned and saw she held the detonating mechanism. She spoke, but not really, he thought, to him. "The clock is working...see? And the batteries can't all have failed.... The connections were tight.... There're four separate detonators...but they never..." She looked almost appalled, he thought, as though all the physical laws of the universe that she had believed in had been revoked.

He said, "But you—you were—"

She shook her head. "*No*. That's what I'm telling you." She looked into his eyes. "I was about two seconds late.... It *rang*...I *heard* it ring, Burke.... I *did*.

Then there was a strange sort of a feeling...like a presence. I figured, you know, I'm dead and it's not so bad. They talk about—in this business they talk about having an Angel on your shoulder while you work—you know? God Almighty, I had a regiment of them."

BOOK VI

Morning, March 18

And the Green Carnation withered,
as in forest fires that pass.

G. K. Chesterton

Patrick Burke blinked as he walked out through the ceremonial doors, down the center of the crushed steps between the flattened handrails, and into the thin winter sunlight.

The night's accumulation of ice was running from rooftops and sidewalks and melting over the steps of St. Patrick's into the littered streets. Burke saw on the bottom step the hand-lettered sign that the Fenians had stuck to the front doors, half torn, the words blurring over the soggy cardboard. The splatter of green paint from the thrown bottle bled out across the granite, and a long, barely visible trail of blood from the dead horse led into the Avenue. You wouldn't know what it all was, thought Burke, if you hadn't been there.

A soft south wind shook the ice from the bare trees along Fifth Avenue, and church bells tolled in the distance. Ambulances, police vehicles, and limousines splashed through the sunlit pools of water, and platoons of Tactical Police and National Guardsmen marched in the streets, while mounted police, half-asleep on their horses, moved in apparently random directions. Many of the police, Burke noticed, had black ribbons on their badges, most of the city officials wore black armbands, and many of the flags along the Avenue were at half-mast, as though this had all been thought out for some time, anticipated, foreseen.

Burke heard a sound on the north terrace and saw the procession of clergy and lay people who were completing their circle of the Cathedral walls, led by the Cardinal wearing a white stole. They drew abreast of the main doors and faced them, the Cardinal intoning, "Purify me with hyssop, Lord, and I shall be clean of sin. Wash me, and I shall be whiter than snow."

Burke stood a few yards off, listening as the assembly continued the rite of reconciliation for the profaned church, oblivious to the people swarming around them. He watched the Cardinal sprinkle holy water against the walls as the others prayed, and he wondered how so obscure a ritual could be carried out so soon and with such Roman precision. Then he realized that the Cardinal and the others must have been thinking about it all night, just as the city officials had rehearsed their parts in their minds during the long black hours. He, Burke, had never let his thoughts get much beyond 6:03, which was one reason why he would never be either the Mayor or the Archbishop of New York.

The procession moved through the portal two by two and past the smashed ceremonial doors into the Cathedral. Burke took off his flak jacket and dropped it at his feet, then walked slowly to the corner of the steps near Fiftieth Street and sat down in a patch of pale sunlight. He folded his arms over his knees and rested his head, falling into a half-sleep.

The Cardinal moved at the head of the line of priests who made up the Cathedral staff. A cross-bearer held a tall gold cross above the sea of moving heads, and the Litany of the Saints was chanted as the line went forward through the gate of the communion rail.

The group assembled in the center of the sanctuary where Monsignor Downes awaited them. The altar was entirely bare of religious objects in preparation for the conclusion of the cleansing rite, and police photographers and crime lab personnel were hurrying through their work. The assembly fell silent, and people began looking around at the blood-splattered sanctuary and altar. Then heads began to turn out toward the ravaged Cathedral, and several people wept openly.

The Cardinal's voice cut off the display of emotion. "There will be time enough for that later." He spoke to two of the priests. "Go into the side vestibules where the casualties have been taken and assist the police and army chaplains." He added, "Have Father Murphy's body taken to the rectory."

The two priests moved off. The Cardinal looked at the sacristans and motioned around the sanctuary. "As soon as the police have finished here, make it presentable for the Mass that will be offered at the conclusion of the purification." He added, "Leave the carnations."

He turned to Monsignor Downes and spoke to him for the first time. "Thank you for your prayers, and for your efforts during this ordeal."

Monsignor Downes lowered his head and said softly, "I...they asked me to sanction your rescue...this attack..."

"I know all of that." He smiled. "More than once during the night I thanked God it wasn't I who had to deal with those...questions." The Cardinal turned and faced the long, wide expanse of empty pews. "God arises, His enemies are scattered, and those who hate Him flee before Him."

Captain Bert Schroeder walked unsteadily up the steps of St. Patrick's, a bandage covering the left side of his chalk-white jaw. A police medic and several Tactical Police officers escorted him.

Mayor Kline raced up to Schroeder, hand extended. "Bert! Over here! Bring him here, men."

A number of reporters had been let through the cordon, and they converged on Schroeder. Cameras clicked and newsreel microphones were thrust in his face. Mayor Kline pumped Schroeder's hand and embraced him, taking the opportunity to say through clenched teeth, "Smile, damn it, and look like a hero."

Schroeder looked distraught and disoriented. His eyes moved over the throng around him to the Cathedral, and he stared at it, then looked around at the people talking excitedly and realized that he was being interviewed.

A reporter called out, "Captain, is it true you recommended an assault on the Cathedral?"

Schroeder didn't answer, and Kline spoke up. "Yes, a rescue operation. The recommendation was approved by an emergency committee consisting of myself, the Governor, Monsignor Downes, Inspector Langley of Intelligence, and the late Captain Bellini. Intelligence indicated the terrorists were going to massacre the hostages and then destroy the Cathedral. Many of them were mentally unbalanced, as our police files show." He looked at each of the reporters. "There were no options."

Another reporter asked, "Who exactly was Major Martin? How did he die?" Kline's smile dropped. "That's under investigation."

There was a barrage of questions that Kline ignored. He put his arm around Schroeder and said, "Captain Schroeder played a vital role in keeping the terrorists psychologically unprepared while Captain Bellini formulated a rescue operation with the help of Gordon Stillway, resident architect of Saint Patrick's." He nodded toward Stillway, who stood by himself examining the front doors and making notes in a small book.

Kline added in a somber tone, "The tragedy here could have been much greater—" A loud Te Deum began ringing out from the bell tower, and Kline motioned toward the Cathedral. "The Cathedral stands! The Cardinal, Sir Harold Baxter, and Maureen Malone are alive. For this we should thank God." He bowed his head and after an appropriate interval looked up and spoke emphatically. "This rescue *will* be favorably compared to similar humanitarian operations against terrorists throughout the world."

A reporter addressed Schroeder directly. "Captain, did you find this man, Flynn—and the other one, Hickey—very tough people to negotiate with?"

Schroeder looked up. "Tough . . . ?"

Mayor Kline hooked his arm through Schroeder's and shook him. "Bert?"

Schroeder's eyes darted around. "Oh...yes, yes I did—no, no, not...not any tougher than—Excuse me, I'm not feeling well.... I'm sorry...excuse me." He pulled loose from the Mayor's grip and hurried across the length of the steps, avoiding reporters. The newspeople watched him go, then turned back to Kline and began asking him about the large number of casualties on both sides, but Kline evaded the questions. Instead, he smiled and pointed over the heads of the people around him.

"There's the Governor crossing the street." He waved. "Governor Doyle! Up here!"

Dan Morgan stood near the window, his eyes focused on the television screen that showed the Cathedral steps, the milling reporters, police and city officials. Terri O'Neal sat on the bed, fully dressed, her legs tucked under her body. Neither person spoke nor moved.

The camera focused on Mayor Kline and Captain Schroeder, and a reporter was speaking from off camera commenting on Schroeder's bandaged jaw.

Morgan finally spoke. "It appears he didn't do what he was asked."

Terri O'Neal said, "Good."

Morgan let out a deep sigh and walked to the side of the bed. "My friends are all dead, and there's nothing good about that."

She kept looking at the television as she spoke in a hoarse whisper. "Are you going to kill...?"

Morgan drew his pistol from his belt. "No. You're free." He placed his hand on her shoulder as he pointed the silencer at the center of her head.

She put her face in her hands and began weeping.

He squeezed back on the trigger. "I'll get your coat...."

She suddenly took her face out of her hands and turned. She realized she was looking into the barrel of the pistol "Oh...no..."

Morgan's hand was shaking. He looked at her and their eyes met. The end of the silencer brushed her cheek, and he jerked the pistol away and shoved it in his belt. "There's been enough death today," he said. He turned and walked out of the bedroom. Terri O'Neal heard the front door open, then slam shut.

She found the cigarettes Morgan left behind, lit one, and stared at the television. "Poor Daddy."

Burke shifted restlessly, brought out of his short sleep by the noise around him and the pounding pain in his back. He rubbed his eyes and noticed that the injured eye was blurry again, and every inch of his body felt blurry; numb, he supposed, was a better word, numb except the parts that hurt. And his mind seemed numb *and* blurry, free-floating in the sunny light around him. He stood unsteadily, looked over the crowded steps, and blinked. Bert Schroeder and Murray Kline were holding court—and it was, he realized, just as he would have pictured it if he had allowed himself to think of the dawn. Schroeder surrounded by the press, Schroeder looking very self-possessed, handling questions like a pro—but as he watched he saw that the Hostage Negotiator was not doing well. He saw Schroeder suddenly break loose and make his way across the steps, through the knots of people like a broken-field runner, and Burke called out as he passed, "Schroeder!"

Schroeder seemed not to hear and continued toward the arched portal of the south vestibule. Burke came up behind him and grabbed his arm. "Hold on." Schroeder tried to pull away, but Burke slammed him against the stone buttress. "Listen!" He lowered his voice. "I know—about Terri—"

Schroeder looked at him, his eyes widening. Burke went on. "Martin is dead, and the Fenians are all dead or dying. I had to tell Bellini . . . but he's dead, too. Langley knows, but Langley doesn't give away secrets—he just makes you buy them back someday. Okay? So just shut your mouth and be very cool." He released Schroeder's arm.

Tears formed in Schroeder's eyes. "Burke . . . God Almighty . . . do you *understand* what I did . . . ?"

"Yeah . . . yeah, I understand, and I'd really like to see you in the fucking slammer for twenty, but that won't help anything. . . . It won't help the department, and it won't help me or Langley. And it damn sure won't help your wife or daughter." He moved closer to Schroeder. "And don't blow your brains out, either. . . . It's a sin—you know? Hang around long enough in this job and someone will blow them out for you."

Schroeder caught his breath and spoke. "No . . . I'm going to retire—resign—confess . . . make a public—"

"You're going to keep your goddamned mouth shut. No one—not me or Kline or Rourke or the DA or anyone—wants to hear your fucking confession, Schroeder. You've caused enough problems—just cool out."

Schroeder hung his head, then nodded. "Burke ... Pat ... thanks ...."

"Fuck you." He looked at the door beside him. "You know what's in this vestibule?"

Schroeder shook his head.

"Bodies. Lots of bodies. The field morgue. You go in there and you talk to those bodies—and say something to Bellini—and you go into the Cathedral and you make a confession, or you pray or you do anything you have to do to help you get through the next twenty-four hours." He reached out and opened the door, took Schroeder's arm, and pushed him into the vestibule, then shut the door. He stared down at the pavement for a long time, then turned at the sound of his name and saw Langley hurrying up the steps toward him.

Langley started to extend his hand, then glanced around quickly and withdrew it. He said coolly, "You're in a little trouble, Lieutenant."

Burke lit a cigarette. "Why?"

"*Why?*" He lowered his voice and leaned forward. "You pushed a British consulate official—a *diplomat*—out of the choir loft of Saint Patrick's Cathedral to his *death*. That's *why*."

"He fell."

"Of course he fell—you pushed him. What could he do but fall? He couldn't *fly*." Langley ran his hand over his mouth, and Burke thought he was hiding a smile. Langley regained his composure and said caustically, "That was very stupid—don't you agree?"

Burke shrugged.

Roberta Spiegel walked unnoticed through the crowd on the steps and came under the portal, stopping beside Langley. She looked at the two men, then said to Burke, "Christ Almighty, right in front of about forty policemen and National Guardsmen. Are you crazy?"

Langley said, "I just asked him if he was stupid, but that's a good question, too." He turned to Burke. "Well, are you stupid or crazy?"

Burke sat down with his back to the stone wall and watched the smoke rise from his cigarette. He yawned twice.

Spiegel's voice was ominous. "They're going to arrest you for *murder*. I'm surprised they haven't grabbed you yet."

Burke raised his eyes toward Spiegel. "They haven't grabbed me because you told them not to. Because you want to see if Pat Burke is going to go peacefully or if he's going to kick and scream."

Spiegel didn't answer.

Burke glared at her, then at Langley. "Okay, let me see if I know how to play this game. A file on Bartholomew Martin—right? He suffered from vertigo and fear of heights. Or how about this?—twenty police witnesses in the loft sign sworn affidavits saying Martin took a swat at a fly and toppled—No, no, I've got it—"

Spiegel cut him off. "The man was a *consulate official*—"

"Bullshit."

Spiegel shook her head. "No one can fix this one, Lieutenant."

Burke leaned back and yawned again. "You're Ms. Fixit in this town, lady, so you fix it. And fix me up with a commendation and captain's pay while you're about it. By tomorrow."

Spiegel's face reddened. "Are you *threatening* me?" Their eyes met, and neither turned away. She said, "And who's going to believe *your* version of anything that was discussed tonight?"

Burke stubbed out his cigarette. "Schroeder, who is a hero, will corroborate *anything* I say."

Spiegel laughed. "That's absurd."

Langley cleared his throat and said to Spiegel. "Actually, that's true. It's a long story . . . . I think Lieutenant Burke deserves . . . well, whatever he says he deserves."

Spiegel looked at Langley closely, then turned back to Burke. "You've got something on Schroeder— right? Okay, I don't have to know what it is. I'm not looking to hang you, Burke. I'll do what I can—"

Burke interrupted. "Art Forgery Squad. It would be a really good idea if I was in Paris by this time tomorrow."

Spiegel laughed. "Art Forgery? What the hell do you know about art?"

"I know what I like."

"That's true," said Langley. "He does." He stuck his hand out toward Burke, "You did an outstanding job tonight, Lieutenant. The Division is very proud of you."

Burke took his hand and used it to pull himself up. "Thank you, Chief Inspector. I shall be clean of sin. Wash me, and I shall be whiter than snow."

Langley said, "Well...we'll just get you a commendation or something...."

Spiegel lit a cigarette. "How the hell did I ever get involved with cops and politicians? God, I'd rather be on the stroll in Times Square."

Burke said, "I thought you looked familiar."

She ignored him and surveyed the steps and the Avenue. "Where's Schroeder, anyway? I see lots of news cameras, but smiling Bert isn't in front of any of them. Or is he at a television studio already?"

Burke said, "He's in the Cathedral. Praying."

Spiegel seemed taken aback, then nodded. "That's *damned* good press. Yes, yes. Everyone's out here sucking up on the coverage, and he's in there praying. They'll eat it up. Wow...I could run that bastard for councilman in Bensonhurst..."

Stretcher-bearers began bringing the bodies out of the Cathedral, a long, silent procession, through the doors of the south vestibule, down the steps. The litters carrying the police and Guardsmen passed through a hastily assembled honor guard; the stretchers of the Fenians passed behind the guard. Everyone on the steps fell silent, police and army chaplains walked beside the stretchers, and a uniformed police inspector in gold braid directed the bearers to designated ambulances. The litters holding the Fenians were placed on the sidewalk.

Burke moved among the stretchers and found the tag marked Bellini. He drew the cover back and looked into the face, wiped of greasepaint—a very white face with that hard jaw and black stubble. He dropped the cover back and quickly walked a few steps off, his hands on his hips, staring down at his feet.

The bells had ended the Te Deum and began to play a slow dirge. Governor Doyle stood with his retinue, his hat in his hand. Major Cole stood beside him holding a salute. The Governor leaned toward Cole and spoke as he lowered his head in respect. "How many did the Sixty-ninth lose, Major?"

Cole looked at him out of the corner of his eye, certain that he had detected an expectant tone in the Governor's voice. "Five killed, sir, including Colonel Logan, of course. Three wounded."

"Out of how many?"

Cole lowered his salute and stared at the Governor. "Out of a total of eighteen men who directly participated in the attack."

"The *rescue*...yes..." The Governor nodded thoughtfully. "Terrible. Fifty percent casualties."

"Well, not quite fif—"

"But you rescued two hostages."

"Actually, they saved themselves—"

"The Sixty-ninth Regiment will be needing a new commander, Cole."

"Yes...that's true."

The last of the police and Guardsmen were placed in ambulances, and the line of vehicles began moving away, escorted by motorcycle police. A black police van pulled up to the curb, and a group of stretcher-bearers on the sidewalk picked up the litters holding the dead Fenians and headed toward the van.

An Intelligence officer standing beside the van saluted Langley as he approached and handed him a small stack of folded papers. The man said, "Almost every one of them had an identifying personal note on him, Inspector. And here's a preliminary report on each one." The man added, "We also found pages of the ESD attack plan in there. How the hell—?"

Langley took the loose pages and shoved them in his pocket. "That doesn't go in your report."

"Yes, sir."

Langley came up beside Burke sitting under the portal again, with Spiegel standing in front of him.

Burke said, "Where are Malone and Baxter?"

Spiegel answered, "Malone and Baxter are still in the Cathedral for their own protection—there may still be snipers out there. Baxter's in the Archbishop's sacristy until we release him to his people. Malone's in the bride's room. The FBI will take charge of her."

Burke said, "Where's Flynn's body?"

No one answered, then Spiegel knelt on the step beside Burke. "He's not dead yet. He's in the bookstore."

Burke said, "Is that the Bellevue annex?"

Spiegel hesitated, then spoke. "The doctor said he was within minutes of death...so we didn't...have him moved."

Burke said, "You're murdering him—so don't give me this shit about not being able to move him."

Spiegel looked him in the eye. "Everybody on both sides of the Atlantic wants him dead, Burke. Just like everyone wanted Martin dead. Don't start moralizing to me...."

Burke said, "Get him to Bellevue."

Langley looked at him sharply. "You know we can't do that now...and he knows too much, Pat...."

Schroeder...other things.... And he's dangerous. Let's make things easy on ourselves for once. Okay?"

Burke said, "Let's have a look."

Spiegel hesitated, then stood. "Come on."

They entered the Cathedral and passed through the south vestibule littered with the remains of the field morgue that smelled faintly of something disagreeable—a mixture of odors, which each finally identified as death.

The Mass was beginning, and the organ overhead was playing an entrance song. Burke looked at the shafts of sunlight coming through the broken windows. He had thought that the light would somehow diminish the mystery, but it hadn't, and in fact the effect was more haunting even than the candlelight.

They turned right toward the bookstore. Two ESD men blocked the entrance but moved quickly aside. Spiegel entered the small store, followed by Burke and Langley. She leaned over the counter and looked down at the floor.

Brian Flynn lay in the narrow space, his eyes closed and his chest rising and falling very slowly. She said, "He's not letting go so easily." She watched him for a few seconds, then added, "He's a good-looking man...must have had a great deal of charisma, too. Very few are born into this sorry world like that.... In another time and place, perhaps, he would have been...something else.... Incredible waste..."

Burke came around the counter and knelt beside Flynn. He pushed back his eyelids, then listened to his

chest and felt for his pulse. Burke looked up. "Fluid in
the chest...heart is going...but it may take a while."

No one spoke. Then Spiegel said, "I can't do
this...I'll get the stretcher-bearers...."

Flynn's lips began to move, and Burke put his ear
close to Flynn's face. Burke said, "Yes, all right." He
turned to Spiegel. "Forget the stretcher...he wants to
speak to her."

Maureen Malone sat quietly in the bride's room while
four policewomen tried to make conversation with her.

Roberta Spiegel opened the door and regarded her
for a second, then said abruptly, "Come with me."

She seemed not to have heard and sat motionless.

Spiegel said, "He wants to see you."

Maureen looked up and met the eyes of the other
woman. She rose and followed Spiegel. They hurried
down the side aisle and crossed in front of the
vestibules. As they entered the bookstore Langley
looked at Maureen appraisingly, and Burke nodded to
her. Both men walked out of the room. Spiegel said,
"There." She pointed. "Take your time." She turned
and left.

Maureen moved around the counter and knelt beside Brian Flynn. She took his hands in hers but said
nothing. She looked through the glass counter and realized there was no one else there, and she understood.
She pressed Flynn's hands, an overwhelming feeling of
pity and sorrow coming over her such as she had never
felt for him before. "Oh, Brian...so alone...always
alone..."

Flynn opened his eyes.

She leaned forward so that their faces were close and said, "I'm here."

His eyes showed recognition.

"Do you want a priest?"

He shook his head.

She felt a small pressure on her hands and returned it. "You're dying, Brian. You know that, don't you? And they've left you here to die. Why won't you see a priest?"

He tried to speak, but no sound came out. Yet she thought she knew what he wanted to say and to ask her. She told him of the deaths of the Fenians, including Hickey and Megan, and with no hesitancy she told him of the death of Father Murphy, of the survival of the Cardinal, Harold Baxter, Rory Devane, and of the Cathedral itself, and about the bomb that didn't explode. His face registered emotion as she spoke. She added, "Martin is dead, also. Lieutenant Burke, they say, pushed him from the choir loft, and they also say that Leary was Martin's man.... Can you hear me?"

Flynn nodded.

She went on. "I know you don't mind dying...but I mind...mind terribly.... I love you, still.... Won't you, for me, let a priest see you? Brian?"

He opened his mouth, and she bent closer. He said, "...the priest..."

"Yes...I'll call for one."

He shook his head and clutched at her hands. She bent forward again. Flynn's voice was almost inaudible. "The priest...Father Donnelly...here..."

"What...?"

"Came here...." He held up his right hand. "Took back the ring...."

She stared at his hand and saw that the ring was gone. She looked at his face and noticed for the first time that it had a peaceful quality to it, with no trace of the things that had so marked him over the years.

He opened his eyes wide and looked intently at her. "You see...?" He reached for her hands again and held them tightly.

She nodded. "Yes...no...no, I don't see, but I never did, and you always seemed so sure, Brian—" She felt the pressure on her hand relax, and she looked at him and saw that he was dead. She closed his eyes and kissed him, then took a long breath and stood.

Burke, Langley, and Spiegel stood at the curb on the corner of Fifth Avenue and Fiftieth Street. The Sanitation Department had mobilized its huge squadrons, and the men in gray mingled with the men in blue. Great heaps of trash, mostly Kelly-green in color, grew at the curbsides. The police cordon that had enclosed two dozen square blocks pulled in tighter, and the early rush hour began building up in the surrounding streets.

None of the three spoke for some time. Spiegel turned and faced the sun coming over the tall buildings to the east. She studied the façade of the Cathedral, then said, "In class I used to teach that every holiday will one day have two connotations. I think of Yom Kippur, Tet. And after the Easter Monday Rising in 1916, that day was never the same again in Ireland. It became a different sort of holiday, with different connotations—different associations—like Saint Valentine's Day in Chicago. I have the feeling that Saint Patrick's Day in New York may never be the same again."

Burke looked at Langley. "I don't even *like* art—what the hell do I care if someone forges it?"

Langley smiled, then said, "You never asked me about the note in Hickey's coffin." Langley handed him the note, and Burke read: *If you're reading this note, you've found me out. I wanted to spend my last days alone and in peace, to lay down the sword and give up the fight. Then again, if something good comes along—In any case, don't put me here. Bury me beneath the sod of Clonakily beside my mother and father.*

There was a silence, and they looked around for something to occupy their attention. Langley saw a PBA canteen truck that had parked beside the wrecked mobile headquarters. He cleared his throat and said to Roberta Spiegel, "Can I get you a cup of coffee?"

"Sure." She smiled and put her arm through his. "Give me a cigarette."

Burke watched them walk off, then stood by himself. He thought he might make the end of the Mass, but then decided to report to the new mobile headquarters across the street. He began walking but turned at the sound of an odd noise behind him.

A horse was snorting, thick plumes of fog coming from its nostrils. Betty Foster said, "Hi! Thought you'd be okay."

Burke moved away from the spirited horse. "Did you?"

"Sure." She reined the horse beside him. "Mayor make you nervous?"

Burke said, "That idiot.... Oh, the horse. Where do you *get* these names?"

She laughed. "Give you a lift?"

"No...I have to hang around...."

She leaned down from the saddle. "Why? It's over. *Over*, Lieutenant. You *don't* have to hang around."

He looked at her. Her eyes were bloodshot and puffy, but there was a determined sort of recklessness in them, brought on, he supposed, by the insanity of the long night, and he saw that she wasn't going to be put off so easily. "Yeah, give me a lift."

She took her foot from the stirrup, reached down, and helped him up behind her. "Where to?"

He put his arms around her waist. "Where do you usually go?"

She laughed again and reined the horse in a circle. "Come on, Lieutenant—give me an order."

"Paris," said Burke. "Let's go to Paris."

"You got it." She kicked the horse's flanks. "Gi-yap, Mayor!"

Maureen Malone rubbed her eyes in the sunlight as she came through the doors of the north vestibule flanked by FBI men, including Douglas Hogan. Hogan indicated a waiting Cadillac limousine on the corner.

Harold Baxter came out of the south vestibule surrounded by consulate security men. A silver-gray Bentley drew up to the curb.

Maureen moved down the steps toward the Cadillac and saw Baxter through the crowd. Reporters began converging first on Baxter and then around her, and her escort elbowed through the throng. She pulled away from Hogan and stood on her toes, looking for Baxter, but the Bentley drove off with a motorcycle escort.

She slid into the back of the limousine and sat quietly as men piled in around her and the doors slammed shut. Hogan said, "We're taking you to a private hospital."

She didn't answer, and the car drew away from the curb. She looked down at her hands, still covered with Flynn's blood where he had held them.

The limousine edged into the middle of the crowded Avenue, and Maureen looked out the window at the Cathedral, certain she would never see it again.

A man suddenly ran up beside the slow-moving vehicle and held an identification to the window, and Hogan lowered the glass a few inches. The man spoke with a British accent. "Miss Malone..." He held a single wilted green carnation through the window. "Compliments of Sir Harold, miss." She took the carnation, and the man saluted as the car moved off.

The limousine turned east on Fiftieth Street and passed beside the Cathedral, then headed north on Madison Avenue and passed the Cardinal's residence, Lady Chapel, and rectory, picking up speed as it moved over the wet pavement. Ahead she saw the gray Bentley, then lost it in the heavy traffic. She said, "Lower the window."

Someone lowered the window closest to her, and she heard the bells of distant churches, recognizing the distinctive bells of St. Patrick's playing "Danny Boy," and she sat back and listened to them. She thought briefly of the journey home, of Sheila and Brian, and she recalled a time in her life, not so long ago, when everyone she knew was alive—parents, girl friends and boyfriends, relatives and neighbors—but now her life was filled with the dead, the missing, and the wounded, and she thought that most likely she would join those ranks. She tried to imagine a future for herself and her country but couldn't. Yet she wasn't afraid and looked forward to working, in her own way, to accomplish the Fenian goal of emptying the jails of Ulster.

The bells died in the distance, and she looked down at the carnation in her lap. She picked it up and twirled the stem in her fingers, then put it in the lapel of her tweed jacket.

John Corey is back and in the middle of a
new Cold War with a clock-ticking plot that
has Manhattan in its crosshairs.

Please turn the page
for an excerpt from Nelson DeMille's
forthcoming novel

Radiant Angel

If I wanted to see assholes all day, I would have become a proctologist. Instead, I watch assholes for my country.

I was parked in a black Chevy Blazer down the street from the Russian Federation mission to the United Nations on East Sixty-Seventh Street in Manhattan, waiting for an asshole named Vasily Petrov to appear. Petrov is a colonel in the Russian Foreign Intelligence Service—the SVR in Russian—which is the equivalent to our CIA, and the successors to the Soviet KGB. Vasily—who we have affectionately code-named Vaseline—has diplomatic status as Deputy Representative to the UN for Human Rights Issues—which is a joke—but his real job is SVR Legal Resident in New York—the equivalent of a CIA station chief. I have had Colonel Petrov under the eye on previous occasions; and though I've never met him, he's reported to be a very dangerous man, and thus an asshole.

I'm John Corey, by the way, former NYPD homicide detective, now working for the federal government as a contract agent. My NYPD career was cut short by three bullets that left me seventy-five percent disabled (twenty-five percent per bullet?) for retirement pay purposes. In fact, there's nothing wrong with me physically, though the mental health exam for this job was a bit of a challenge.

Anyway, sitting next to me behind the wheel was a young lady who I'd worked with before, Tess Faraday. Tess was maybe early thirties, auburn hair, tall, trim, and attractive. Also in the SUV, looking over my shoulder was my wife, Kate Mayfield, who was actually in Washington, but I could feel her presence. If you know what I mean.

Tess asked me, "Do I have time to go to the john, John?"

She thought that was funny. "You have a bladder problem?"

"I shouldn't have had that coffee."

"You had two." Guys on surveillance pee in the container and throw it out the window. I said, "Okay, but be quick."

She exited the vehicle and double-timed it to a Starbucks around the corner on Third Avenue.

Meanwhile, Vasily Petrov could come out of the mission at any time, get into his chauffeur-driven Mercedes S550, and be off.

But I've got three other mobile units plus four agents on legs, so Vasily is covered while I, the team leader, am sitting here while Ms. Faraday is sitting on the potty.

And what do we think Colonel Petrov is up to? We have no idea. But he's up to something. That's why he's here. And that's why I'm here.

In fact, Petrov arrived only about four months ago, and it's the recent arrivals who are sometimes sent on the field with a new game play, and these guys need more watching than the SVR agents who've been stationed here awhile and who are engaged in routine espionage. Watch the new guys.

The Russian UN mission occupies a thirteen-story brick building with a wrought-iron fence in front of it, conveniently located across the street from the Nineteenth Precinct whose surveillance cameras keep an eye on the Russians 24/7. The Russians don't mind being watched by the NYPD because they're also protected from pissed-off demonstrators and people who'd like to plant a bomb outside their front door. FYI, I live five blocks north of here on East Seventy-Second, so I don't have far to walk when I get off duty at four. I could almost taste the Buds in my fridge.

So I sat there, waiting for Vasily Petrov and Tess Faraday. It was a nice day in early September; one of those beautiful, dry, and sunny days you get after the dog days of August. It was a Sunday, a little after 10 A.M., so the streets and sidewalks of New York were relatively quiet. I volunteered for Sunday duty because Mrs. Corey (my wife, not my mother) had taken the Delta shuttle to DC this morning, and I'd rather be working than trying to find something to do on a Sunday. My mother would suggest church, though considering the weather, I should have called in sick and gone to the beach.

Kate was in DC because she's an FBI special agent with the Anti-Terrorist Task Force, headquartered downtown at 26 Federal Plaza. Special Agent Mayfield was recently promoted to Supervisory Special Agent, and her new duties take her to Washington a lot. She sometimes goes with her boss, Special Agent-in-Charge Tom Walsh, who used to be my ATTF boss, too, but I don't work for him or the ATTF any longer. And that's a good thing for both of us. We were not compatible. Walsh, however, likes Kate, and I think the feeling is mutual. I wasn't sure if Walsh was with Kate on this trip because I never ask, and she rarely volunteers the information.

On a less annoying subject, I now work for the Diplomatic Surveillance Group—the DSG. The group is also headquartered at 26 Fed, but with this new job I don't need to be at headquarters much, if at all.

My years in the Mideast section of the Anti-Terrorist Task Force were interesting, but stressful. And according to Kate, I was the cause of much of that stress. Wives see things husbands don't see. Bottom line: I had some issues and run-ins with the Muslim community (and my FBI bosses), which led directly or indirectly to my being asked by my superiors if I'd like to find other employment. Walsh suggested the Diplomatic Surveillance Group, which would keep me (A) out of his sight, (B) out of his office, and (C) out of trouble.

Sounded good. Kate thought so, too. In fact, she got the promotion after I left.

Coincidence?

My Nextel phone is also a two-way radio, and it blinged. Tess's voice said, "John, do you want a doughnut or something?"

"Did you wash your hands?"

Tess laughed. She thinks I'm funny. "What do you want?"

"A chocolate chip cookie."

"Coffee?"

"No." I signed off.

Tess's career goal is to become an FBI special agent, and to do that she has to qualify for appointment under one of five entry programs—accounting, computer science, language, law, or what's called diversified experience. Tess is an attorney and thus qualifies. Most failed lawyers become judges or politicians, but Tess tells me she wants to do something meaningful, whatever that means. Meanwhile, she's working with the Diplomatic Surveillance Group.

Most of the DSG men and women are twenty-year retirees from various law enforcement agencies, so we have mostly experienced people, ex-cops mixed with inexperienced young attorneys like Tess Faraday who see the Diplomatic Surveillance Group as a stepping-stone where they can get some street creds that look good on their FBI app.

Tess got back in the SUV and handed me an oversized cookie. "My treat."

She had another cup of coffee. Some people never learn.

She was wearing khaki cargo pants, a blue polo shirt, and running shoes, which are necessary if the target goes off on foot. Her pants and shirt were loose enough to hide a gun, but Tess is not authorized to carry a gun.

In fact, all of the Diplomatic Surveillance Group agents are theoretically not authorized to carry guns. But we're not as stupid as the people who make the rules, so almost all the ex-cops carry. In situations like this where I bend the rules, my personal motto is *Better to face twelve jurors than to be carried by six pallbearers.* Therefore, I had my 9mm Glock in a pancake holster in the small of my back, beneath my loose-fitting polo shirt.

So we waited for Vasily to show.

Colonel Petrov lives in a big high-rise in the upscale Riverdale section of the Bronx. This building, which we call the 'plex—short for complex—is owned and wholly occupied by the Russians who work at the UN, and it is a nest of spies. The building itself, located on a high hill, sprouts more antennas than a garbage can full of cockroaches.

The National Security Agency, of course, has a facility nearby and they listen to the Russians who are listening to us, and we all have fun trying to block each other's signals. And round it goes. The only things that have changed since the days of the Cold War are the encryption codes.

On a less technological level, the game is still played on the ground as it has been forever: Follow that spy. The Diplomatic Surveillance Group also has a confidential off-site facility—what we call the Bat Cave—near the Russian apartment complex; and the DSG team that was watching the 'plex this morning reported that Vasily Petrov had left, and they followed him here to the mission, where my team picked up the surveillance.

The Russians don't usually work in the office on Sundays, so my guess was that Vasily was in transit to someplace else—or that he was going back to the 'plex—and that he'd be coming out shortly and getting into his chauffeur-driven Benz.

Colonel Petrov, according to the intel, is married, but his wife and children have remained in Moscow. This in itself is suspicious because the families of the Russian UN delegation love to live in New York on the government ruble. Or maybe there's an innocent explanation for the husband-wife separation. Like they hate each other.

Tess informed me, "I have two tickets to the Mets doubleheader today." She further informed me, "I'd like to catch at least the last game."

"You can listen to them lose both games on the radio."

"I'll pretend you didn't say that." She reminded me, "We're supposed to be relieved at four."

"You can relieve yourself any time you want."

She didn't reply.

A word about Tess Faraday. Did I say she was tall, slim, and attractive? She also swims and plays paddleball, whatever that is. She's fairly sharp, and intermittently enthusiastic, and I guess she's idealistic, which is why she left her Wall Street law firm to apply to the FBI where the money is not as good.

But money is probably not an issue for Ms. Faraday. She mentioned to me that she was born and raised in Lattingtown, an upscale community on the North Shore of Long Island, also known as the Gold Coast. And by her accent and mannerisms I can deduce that she came from some money and good social standing. People like that who want to serve their country usually go to the State Department or into intelligence work, not the FBI. But I give her credit for what she's doing and I wish her luck.

Also, needless to say, Tess Faraday and John Corey have little in common, though we get along during these days and hours of forced intimacy.

One thing we do have in common is that we're both married. Her husband's name is Grant, and he's some kind of international finance guy, and he travels a lot for his work. I've never met Grant, and I probably never will, but he likes to text and call his wife a lot. I deduce, by Tess's end of the conversation, that Grant is the jealous type, and Tess seems a bit impatient with him. At least when I'm in earshot of the conversation.

Tess inquired, "If Petrov goes mobile, do we stay with him, or do we hand him over to another team?"

"Depends."

"On what?"

"No, I mean you should wear Depends."

One of us thought that was funny.

But to answer Tess's question, if Vasily went mobile, most probably my team would stay with him. He wasn't supposed to travel farther than a twenty-five-mile radius from Columbus Circle without State Department permission, and according to my briefing, he hadn't applied for a weekend travel permit. The Russians rarely did, and when they did, they would apply on a Friday afternoon so that no one at State had time to approve or disapprove their travel plans. And off they'd go, in their cars or by train or bus to someplace outside their allowed radius. Usually the women were just going shopping at some discount mall in Jersey, and the men were screwing around in Atlantic City. But sometimes the SVR or the military intelligence guys—the GRU—were meeting people or looking at things like nuclear reactors that they shouldn't be looking at. That's why we follow them. But we almost never bust them. The FBI, of which the DSG is a part, is famous—or infamous—for watching people and collecting evidence for years. Cops act on evidence. The FBI waits until the suspect dies of old age.

I said to Tess, "Let me know now if you can't stay past four. I'll call for a replacement."

She replied, "I'm yours."

"Wonderful."

"But if we get off at four, I have an extra ticket."

I considered my reply, then said, perhaps unwisely, "I take it Mr. Faraday is out of town."

"He is."

"Why have we not heard from Grant this morning?"

"I told him I was on a very discreet—and quiet—surveillance."

"You're learning."

"I don't need to learn what I already know."

"Right." Escape and evasion. Perhaps Grant had reason to be jealous. You think?

Regarding the nature of our surveillance of Colonel Vasily Petrov, this was actually a nondiscreet surveillance—what we call a bumper lock, meaning we were going to be up Vasily's ass all day. They always spotted a bumper lock surveillance, and sometimes they acknowledged the DSG agents with a hard stare, or if they were pricks, they gave you the Italian arm salute.

Vasily was particularly unfriendly, probably because he was an intel officer, a big wheel in the Motherland, and he found it galling to be on the receiving end of a surveillance. Well, fuck him. Everybody's got a job to do.

Vasily sometimes plays games with the surveillance team, and he's actually given us the slip twice in the last four months or so, which has earned him the name Vaseline. He's never given me the slip, but some other DSG teams lost him. And there's hell to pay when you lose the SVR Resident. And that wasn't going to happen on my watch. I don't lose anyone. Well, I lost my wife once in Bloomingdale's. I can't figure out the logic of a woman's shopping habits. They don't think like us.

Surveillances can be boring, which is why some people try to make it not boring. Two guys together talk about women, and two women together probably talk about guys. A guy and a woman together either have nothing to talk about, or the long hours lead to whatever.

In the last six months, Tess Faraday has been assigned to me about a dozen times, which, with one hundred fifty DSG agents in New York, defies the odds. As the team leader, I could reassign her to another vehicle or to leg surveillance. But I haven't. Why? Because I think she's asking to work with me; and, being a very sensitive man, I don't want to hurt her feelings. And why does she want to work with me? Because she wants to learn from a master. Or something else is going on.

And by the way, I haven't mentioned Tess Faraday to Kate. Kate is not the jealous type, and there's nothing to be jealous about. Also, like Kate, I keep my work problems and associations to myself. Kate doesn't talk about Tom Walsh, and I don't talk about Tess Faraday. Marital ignorance is bliss. Dumb is happy.

Meanwhile, Vasily has been inside the mission for over an hour, but his Mercedes is still outside, so he's going someplace. Probably back to the Bronx. He sometimes runs in Central Park, which is a pain in the ass. Everyone on the team wears running shoes, of course, and I think we're all in good shape, but Vasily is in excellent shape. Older FBI agents have told me that the Soviet KGB guys were mostly lard asses who smoked and drank too much. But these guys from the new Russia were into granola and health clubs. Their boss, bare-chested Putin, sort of set the new standard.

Vasily, being who he is, also has a girlfriend in town, a Russian lady named Svetlana who sings at a few of the Russian nightclubs in Brighton Beach. I caught a glimpse of her once and she looks like she has good lungs.

I did a radio check with my team and everyone was awake.

A soft breeze fluttered the white, blue, and red Russian flag in front of the mission. I remember when the Soviet hammer and sickle flew there. I kind of miss the Cold War. But I think it's back.

My team today consists of four leg agents and four vehicles—my Chevy Blazer, a Ford Explorer, and two Dodge minivans. We usually have one agent in each vehicle, but today we had two. Why? Because the Russians are particularly tricky, and sometimes they travel in groups and scatter like cockroaches, so recently we've been beefing up the surveillance teams. Today I had two DSG agents in the other three vehicles, all former NYPD. I had the only trainee, an FBI wannabe who probably thinks the DSG job sucks. Sometimes I think the same thing.

In the parlance of the FBI, the DSG is called a "quiet end," which really means a dead end.

But I'm okay with that. No office, no adult supervision, and no bullshit. Just follow that asshole. And do not lose that asshole.

A quiet end. But in this business, there is no such thing.